# SOMETIMES A GREAT NOTION

ALSO BY KEN KESEY

*One Flew over the Cuckoo's Nest*

Sometimes I live in the country,
Sometimes I live in the town;
Sometimes I get a great notion
To jump into the river . . . an' drown.
—From the song "Good Night, Irene,"
by Huddie Ledbetter and John Lomax

# Sometimes a Great Notion

## a novel by Ken Kesey

NEW YORK: THE VIKING PRESS

First published in 1964 by The Viking Press, Inc.

Published simultaneously in Canada by
The Macmillan Company of Canada Limited

Library of Congress catalog card number: 64-12227

M B G · Set in Electra and Perpetua types and

A portion of this book first appeared, in somewhat different form, in *Genesis West 5*.
Acknowledgment is made to the following publishers for permission to quote from song lyrics:
Adams, Vee & Abbott, Inc., for (p. 26) "Smoke on the Water" by Earl Nunn and Zeke Clements. Copyright 1943 and 1951 Adams, Vee & Abbott, Inc., Chicago, Ill. Reprinted by permission.
Hill and Range Songs, Inc., for (pp. 54, 55, 57, 192) "I'm Movin' On" by Hank Snow. Copyright 1950 by Hill and Range Songs, Inc., New York, N.Y., and for (p. 339) "Candy Kisses" by George Morgan. Copyright 1948 by Hill and Range Songs, Inc., New York, N.Y. Used by permission.
Hollis Music, Inc., for the two lines quoted on p. 19, suggested by the song "Going Down the Road" by Woody Guthrie and Lee Hays. © Copyright 1960 Hollis Music, Inc., New York, N.Y.
Joy Music, Inc., for (pp. 500, 501, 502, 505) "The Doughnut Song." Words and music by Bob Merrill. © 1950 by Joy Music, Inc., New York, N.Y.
Ludlow Music, Inc., for (4 lines on title page) "Good Night, Irene." Words and music by Huddie Ledbetter and John Lomax. © Copyright 1936, Ludlow Music, Inc., © Copyright Renewed 1964 Ludlow Music, Inc., New York, N.Y. Used by permission.

To my mother and father—

Who told me songs were for the birds,

Then taught me all the tunes I know

And a good deal of the words.

SOMETIMES A GREAT NOTION

*A*long the western slopes of the Oregon Coastal Range . . . come look: the hysterical crashing of tributaries as they merge into the Wakonda Auga River . . .

The first little washes flashing like thick rushing winds through sheep sorrel and clover, ghost fern and nettle, sheering, cutting . . . forming branches. Then, through bearberry and salmonberry, blueberry and blackberry, the branches crashing into creeks, into streams. Finally, in the foothills, through tamarack and sugar pine, shittim bark and silver spruce—and the green and blue mosaic of Douglas fir—the actual river falls five hundred feet . . . and look: opens out upon the fields.

Metallic at first, seen from the highway down through the trees, like an aluminum rainbow, like a slice of alloy moon. Closer, becoming organic, a vast smile of water with broken and rotting pilings jagged along both gums, foam clinging to the lips. Closer still, it flattens into a river, flat as a street, cement-gray with a texture of rain. Flat as a rain-textured street even during flood season because of a channel so deep and a bed so smooth: no shallows to set up buckwater rapids, no rocks to rile the surface . . . nothing to indicate movement except the swirling clots of yellow foam skimming seaward with the wind, and the thrusting groves of flooded bam, bent taut and trembling by the pull of silent, dark momentum.

A river smooth and seeming calm, hiding the cruel file-edge of its current beneath a smooth and calm-seeming surface.

The highway follows its northern bank, the ridges follow its southern. No bridges span its first ten miles. And yet, across, on that southern shore, an ancient two-story wood-frame house rests on a structure of tangled steel, of wood and earth and sacks of sand, like a two-story bird with split-shake feathers, sitting fierce in its tangled nest. Look . . .

Rain drifts about the windows. Rain filters through a haze of yellow smoke issuing from a mossy-stoned chimney into slanting sky. The sky runs gray, the smoke wet-

1

yellow. Behind the house, up in the shaggy hem of mountainside, these colors mix in windy distance, making the hillside itself run a muddy green.

On the naked bank between the yard and humming river's edge, a pack of hounds pads back and forth, whimpering with cold and brute frustration, whimpering and barking at an object that dangles out of their reach, over the water, twisting and untwisting, swaying stiffly at the end of a line tied to the tip of a large fir pole . . . jutting out of a top-story window.

Twisting and stopping and slowly untwisting in the gusting rain, eight or ten feet above the flood's current, a human arm, tied at the wrist, (just the arm; look) disappearing downward at the frayed shoulder where an invisible dancer performs twisting pirouettes for an enthralled audience (just the arm, turning there, above the water) . . . for the dogs on the bank, for the blinking rain, for the smoke, the house, the trees, and the crowd calling angrily from across the river, "Stammmper! Hey, goddam you anyhow, Hank Stammmmmmper!"

And for anyone else who might care to look.

East, back up the highway still in the mountain pass where the branches and creeks still crash and roar, the union president, Jonathan Bailey Draeger, drives from Eugene toward the coast. He is in a strange mood—owing, largely, he knows, to a fever picked up with his touch of influenza—and feels at once oddly deranged and still quite clear-headed. Also, he looks forward to the day both with pleasure and dismay—pleasure because he will soon be leaving this waterlogged mud wallow, dismay because he has promised to have Thanksgiving dinner in Wakonda with the local representative, Floyd Evenwrite. Draeger does not anticipate a very enjoyable afternoon at the Evenwrite household—the few times he had occasion to meet with Evenwrite at his home during this Stamper business, those times were certainly no joy—but he is in a good humor nevertheless: this will be the last of the Stamper business, the last of this whole Northwest business for a good long time, knock wood. After today he can get back down south and let some of that good old California Vitamin D dry up this blasted skin rash. Always get skin rash up here. And athlete's foot all the way to the ankle. The moisture. It's certainly no wonder that this area has two or three natives a month take that one-way dip—it's either drown your blasted self or rot.

Yet, actually—he watches the scenery swim past his windshield—it doesn't seem such an unpleasant land, for all the rainfall. It seems rather nice and peaceful, rather easy. Not as nice as California, God knows, but the weather is certainly far nicer than weather back East or in the Middle West. It's a bountiful land, too, so it's easy as far as survival goes. Even that slow, musical Indian name is easy: Wakonda Auga. Wah-kon-dah-ah-gah-h-h. And those homes built along the shoreline, some next to the highway and some across—those are very nice homes and not at all the sort one would imagine housing a terrible depression. (*Homes of retired pharmacists and hardwaremen, Mr. Draeger.*) All this complaining about the terrible hardship brought on by the strike . . . these homes seem a far cry from terrible hardship. (*Homes of weekend tourists and summertime residents who winter over in the Valley and make enough to take it comfy near the up-river salmon run in the fall.*) And quite modern, too, to find in a country one might think of as somewhat primitive. Nice little places. Modern, but tastefully so. In the ranch-style motif. With enough yard between the house and the river to allow for additions. (*With enough yard, Mr. Draeger, between the house and the river to allow for the yearly six inches the Wakonda Auga takes as its yearly toll.*) It has always seemed odd, though: no houses at all on the bank—or no houses at all on the bank if one excludes the blasted Stamper home. One would think that some houses would be built on the bank for convenience's sake. That has always seemed peculiar about this area. . . .

Draeger bends his big Pontiac around the riverside curves, feeling feverish and mellow and well fed, with a sense of recent accomplishments, listlessly musing about a peculiarity that the very house he muses about would find not the least bit peculiar. The houses know about riverside living. Even the modern weekend summertime places have learned. The old houses, the very old houses that were built of cedar shake and lodgepole by the first settlers at the turn of the eighteen-hundreds, were long ago jacked up and dragged back from the bank by borrowed teams of horses and logging oxen. Or, if they were too big to move, were abandoned to tip headlong into the water as the river sucked away the foundations.

Many of the settlers' houses were lost this way. They had all wanted to build along the river's edge in those first years, for con-

venience's sake, to be close to their transportation, their "Highway
of Water," as the river is referred to frequently in yellowed news-
papers in the Wakonda Library. The settlers had hurried to claim
banksite lots, not knowing at first that their highway had a habit of
eating away its banks and all that those banks might hold. It took
these settlers a while to learn about the river and its habits. Listen:

"She's a brute, she is. She got my house last winter an' my barn
this, by gum. Swallered 'em up."

"So you wouldn't recommend my building here waterside?"

"Wouldn't recommend or wouldn't not recommend, neither one.
Do what you please. I just tell you what I seen. That's all."

"But if what you say is so, if it *is* widenin' out at that rate, then
figure it: a hundred years ago there wouldn't have been no river at
all."

"It's all in the way you look at it. She runs both directions, don't
she? So maybe the river ain't carryin' the land out to sea like the
government is tellin' us; maybe it's the sea carryin' the water in to
the land."

"Dang. You think so? How would *that* be . . . ?"

A while to learn about the river and to realize that they must plan
their homesites with an acknowledged zone of respect for its steady
appetite, surrender a hundred or so yards to its hungry future. No
laws were ever passed enforcing this zone. None were needed. Along
the whole twenty miles, from Breakback Gully, where the river
crashes out of the flowering dogwood, all the way to the eel-grassed
shores at Wakonda Bay, where it fans into the sea, no houses at all
stand on the bank. Or no houses at all on the bank if one excludes
that blasted home, if one excludes this single house that acknowledged no zone of respect for *nobody* and surrendered seldom a scant
inch, let alone a hundred or so yards. This house stands where it
stood; it has not been jacked up and dragged back, nor has it been
abandoned to become a sunken hotel for muskrats and otters. It is
known through most of the western part of the state as the Old
Stamper Place, to people who have never even seen it, because it
stands as a monument to a piece of extinct geography, marking the
place where the river's bank once held . . . Look:

It, the house, protrudes out into the river on a peninsula of its
own making, on an unsightly jetty of land shored up on all sides
with logs, ropes, cables, burlap bags filled with cement and rocks,
welded irrigation pipe, old trestle girders, and bent train rails. White

timbers less than a year old cross ancient worm-rutted pilings. Bright silvery nailheads blink alongside oldtime squarehead spikes rusted blind. Pieces of corrugated aluminum roofing jut from frameworks of iron vehicle frames. Barrel staves reinforce sheets of fraying plywood. And all this haphazard collection is laced together and drawn back firm against the land by webs of wire rope and log chain. These webs join four main two-inch heavy-duty wire-core construction cables that are lashed to four big anchoring firs behind the house. The trees are protected from the sawing bite of the cables by a wrapping of two-by-fours and have supporting guy lines of their own running to wooden deadmen buried deep in the mountainside.

Under normal circumstances the house presents an impressive sight: a two-story monument of wood and obstinacy that has neither retreated from the creep of erosion nor surrendered to the terrible pull of the river. But today, during flood time, with a crowd of half-drunk loggers on the bank across, with parked press cars, a state patrol car, pick-ups, jeeps, mud-daubed yellow crew carriers, and more vehicles arriving every minute to line the embankment between the highway and river, the house is a downright spectacle.

Draeger's foot lifts from the accelerator the instant he turns the bend that brings the scene into view. "Oh dear God," he moans, his feeling of accomplishment and well-being giving way to that feverish melancholy. And to something more: to a kind of sick foreboding.

"What have the fools done now?" he wonders. And can see that good old California Vitamin D suddenly receding out of sight down another three or four weeks of rain-soaked negotiations. "Oh damn, what can have happened!"

As his car coasts closer he recognizes some of the men through the slashing windshield wipers—Gibbons, Sorensen, Henderson, Owens, and the lump in the sportscoat probably Evenwrite—all loggers, union members he has come to know in the last few weeks. A crowd of forty or fifty in all, some squatting on their haunches in the three-walled garage next to the highway; some sitting in the collection of steamy cars and pick-ups lining the embankment; others sitting on crates beneath a small makeshift lean-to made of a Pepsi-Cola sign ripped from its mooring: BE SOCIABLE—with a bottle lifted to wet red lips four feet across . . .

But most of the fools standing out in the rain, he sees, in spite of the ample room in the dry garage or beneath the sign, standing out there as though they have lived and worked and logged in wet so long that they are no longer capable of distinguishing it from the dry. "But *what?*"

He swings across the road toward the crowd, rolling down his window. On the bank a stubble-faced logger in stagged pants and a webbed aluminum hat has cupped his mouth with gloved hands and is shouting drunkenly across the water— "Hank STAMMMM-Perrrr . . . Hank STAMMMMPerrr"—with such dedicated concentration that he doesn't turn even when Draeger's lurching car sloshes mud from the ruts onto the back of his coat. Draeger starts to speak to the man but can't recall his name and drives on toward the thicker part of the crowd where the lump in the sports coat stands. The lump turns and squints at the approach of the automobile, rubbing vigorously at wet latex features with a freckled red rubber hand. Yes, it's Evenwrite. All five and a half boozy feet of him. He comes slogging his way toward Draeger's car.

"Why now, look here, boys. Why, just lookee here. Look who come back to teach me some more lessons about how to rise to power in the labor world. Why, ain't that nice."

"Floyd." Draeger greets the man pleasantly. "Boys . . ."

"Very pleasant surprise, Mr. Draeger," Evenwrite says, grinning down at the open window, "seeing you up and about on such a miserable day."

"Surprise? But Floyd, I was under the impression that I was expected."

"Daw-gone!" Evenwrite bongs the roof of the car. "That is the truth. For Thanksgivin' supper. But, see, Mr. Draeger, they's been a *little* change of plans."

"Oh?" Draeger says. Then looks about at the crowd. "Accident? Somebody drive off into the drink?"

Evenwrite turns to inform his buddies, "Mr. Draeger wants to know, boys, if somebody drove off into the drink." He turns back and shakes his head. "Naw, Mr. Draeger, nothing so fortunate as all that."

"I see"—slowly, calmly, not yet knowing what to make of the man's tone. "So? what exactly did happen?"

"Happen? Why nothing *happened,* Mr. Draeger. Nothing yet. You might say we—us boys—are here to see nothing does. You might say that us boys are here to take up where your methods left off."

"What do you mean 'left off,' Floyd?"—voice still calm, still quite pleasant, but . . . *that sick foreboding is spreading from stomach up through lungs and heart like an icy flame.* "Why not just tell me what has happened?"

"Why, by jumping Jesus—" Evenwrite realizes with dawning incredulity—"he *don't know!* Why, boys, Johnny B. Draeger he don't even the fuck *know!* How do you account for *that?* Our own leader and he ain't even *heard!*"

"I heard that the contracts were drawn and ready, Floyd. I heard that the committee met last night and all were in complete accord." His mouth feels quite dry *the flame reaching up to the throat—oh damn; Stamper couldn't have—* But he swallows and asks imperturbably, "Has Hank changed his plans?"

Evenwrite bongs the car top again, angry now. "I'll by godfrey say he changed his plans. He just chucked 'em out the *window* is how he changed his plans!"

"The whole agreement?"

"The *whole* motherkilling agreement. That's right. The *whole* deal we were so certain of"—*bong!*—"just like that. Looks to me like you called a wrong shot this *one time,* Draeger. Oh me . . ." Evenwrite shakes his head, anger giving way to profound gloom, as though he had just announced the end of the world. "We are right where we started before you came."

In spite of the doomsday tone in Evenwrite's dramatics, Draeger can easily perceive the triumph behind the words. *Of course the fat fool must crow a bit,* Draeger realizes, *even though my defeat is his own. But how could Stamper have changed his mind?* "You are certain?" he asks.

Evenwrite shuts his eyes and nods. "You must of made a slight miscalculation."

"How peculiar," Draeger mutters, trying to keep any sound of alarm from his voice. *Never show alarm,* he always maintained. Jotted in a notebook in his breast pocket: "Alarm, when used for anything less than a fire or an air attack, is certain to muddle the mind, unsettle the senses, and, in most cases, more than double the danger." *But where is that slight miscalculation?* He looks back at Evenwrite. "What were his reasons? What did he give as his reasons?"

Evenwrite's features snap back to anger. "I'm the bastard's brother? His bunkmate maybe? How do you expect me—how do you expect *any-motherkilling-one* to know Hank Stamper's reasons? Shit. I figure myself doing damned good keeping track of his *actions,* let alone his reasons!"

"But you had to find out about those actions in some manner, Floyd; did he float a message into town in a bottle?"

"The same as, practically. Les called me from the Snag to say he heard Hank's wife come in and tell it to Lee, that smartass brother of Hank's, tell that Hank was planning to rent a tug and make the run after all."

Draeger looks toward Gibbons. "Did you overhear any reason for this sudden change?"

"Well, the boy seemed to know why, the way he ranted around. . . ."

"All right, then, did you ask him?"

"Why no, I never; I just put in a call to Floyd. You reckon I shoulda?"

Draeger runs his gloved hands over the steering wheel, admonishing himself for getting so stupidly upset by the fool's mocking innocence. Must be this fever. "All right. If I went in to talk with this boy do you think he might explain Stamper's change of mind? I mean if I asked him?"

"I doubt it, Mr. Draeger. Because he's gone." Evenwrite waits a moment, grinning. "Hank's wife's still in there, though. Now you, with all your methods, you might get something out of her. . . ."

The men laugh, but Draeger appears lost in thought. He moves his hands over the plastic of the steering wheel. A lone mallard whistles past low overhead, tilting a purple eye at the crowd. Under the canneries, the tomcats are crying. Draeger feels the smooth plastic through the glove's leather for a moment, then looks back up. "But didn't you try to call Hank? To ask him personally? I mean—"

"Call? Call? Hellsfire, what do you think we been doin' ever since we got out here? Listen to Gibbons hollering yonder."

"I mean the phone. Didn't you try to phone?"

"Of course we tried to phone."

"Well . . . ? What was his answer? I mean—"

"His answer?" Evenwrite rubs his face again. "Why, I'll show you what his answer was—is. Howie! Come over here'th them glasses. Mr. Draeger here wants to know what Hank's answer is."

The man on the bank turns slowly. "Answer . . . ?"

"Answer! Answer! What he told us when we ast him to reconsider, so to speak. Bring here them glasses and let Mr. Draeger have a look."

The binoculars are drawn from the belly pouch of a rain-gray sweat shirt. They are cold in Draeger's hands, even through the heavy elkhide. The men crowd forth. "There." Evenwrite points triumphantly. "There's Hank Stamper's answer!"

He follows the point and notices something through the fog there, the swing of some object hanging like fish bait from a big stick in front of that ancient and ridiculous house across the river there. . . . "But what does this—" He lifts the glasses and leans into the eye-pieces, forefinger twiddling the focus knob. Hears the men waiting. "I still don't—" The object blurs, fuzzes over, blurs, twisting, then clicks solid into focus so close he momentarily experiences the reek-ing stench of it high in his burning throat—"It looks like a man's arm, but I still don't—" then feels that growing foreboding blossom full. "I'll—what?" Hears the rising of wet laughter from around his car. Curses and thrusts the glasses back at a face unrecognizable in mirth. Rolls up his window but he can still hear it. Leans over the wheel toward the beating wipers—"I'll talk to that girl, his wife—Viv?—in town and find—" and spins out the ruts onto the highway, away from the laughing.

He clamps his jaw and follows the lip of that grinning river. Con-fused and furious; he has never been laughed at before, not by such a pack of fools—not by *anyone!* Confused, and bleakly, crazily furious, and haunted by the suspicion that he is not only being laughed at by that pack of fools back there on the riverbank—as if their fools' response concerned him one dime's worth!—but that there is *also* some other fool laughing at him unseen from the upstairs window of that damned house. . . .

"What could have *happened?*"

Where whoever had hanged the arm from its pole had made certain that it was as much a gesture of grim and humorous defiance as the old house; where whoever had taken the trouble to swing the arm out into sight of the road had also taken trouble to tie down all the fingers but the middle finger, leaving that rigid and universal sentiment lifted with unmistakable scorn to all that came past.

And somehow lifted especially, Draeger could not help feeling, to him. "To *me!* Disparaging me personally for . . . being so mistaken. For . . ." Lifted as a deliberate refutation of all he believed to be true, *knew* to be true about Man; as a blasphemous affrontery to a faith forged over an anvil of thirty years, a precise and predictable faith hammered out of a quarter-century of experience dealing with labor and management—a religion almost, a neatly noted-down, red-ribboned package of truths about men, and Man. *Proven!* that the fool Man will oppose everything except a Hand Extended; that he will stand up in the face of every hazard except Lonely Time; that for the sake of his poorest and shakiest and screwiest principles he will lay down his life, endure pain, ridicule, and even, sometimes, that most demeaning of American hardships, discomfort, but will relinquish his firmest stand for Love. Draeger had seen this proven. He had watched oak-hard mill bosses come to ridiculous terms rather than have their pimply daughters pilloried at the local junior high, seen die-hard right-wing labor-hating owners grant another two bits an hour and hospital benefits rather than risk losing the dubious affection of a senile aunt who happened to play canasta with the wife of the brother of a striking employee that the owner didn't even know by sight or name. Love—and all its complicated ramifications, Draeger believed—actually does conquer all; Love—or the Fear of Not Having It, or the Worry about Not Having Enough of It, or the Terror of Losing It—certainly does conquer all. To Draeger this knowledge was a weapon; he had learned it young and for a quarter-century of mild-mannered wheeling and easy-going dealing he had used that weapon with enormous success, conquering a world rendered simple, precise, and predictable by his iron-hammered faith in that weapon's power. And now some illiterate logger with a little gyppo show and not an ally in the world was trying to claim that he was invulnerable to that weapon! Christ, this blasted fever . . .

Draeger hunches over the wheel, a man who enjoys thinking of himself as mild-mannered and under control, and watches the speed mount on the speedometer in spite of all he can do to restrain it. The big car has taken command. It has speeded up beneath him of its own accord. It rushes toward the town with an anxious, sucking hiss of wet tires. The white lines flicker by. The willows fluttering beyond the windows vibrate toward motionlessness, like spokes standing still on a careening Hollywood wagon wheel. He runs his gloved fingers nervously over his stiff gray crew-cut, sighing, giving in to his foreboding: if what Evenwrite says is true—and why would he lie?—it means weeks more of the same enforced patience that has left him exhausted and sleepless two nights out of three for the last month. More forced smiling, more forced talking. More feigned listening. And more Desenex for a case of athlete's foot capable of making medical history. He sighs again, resigning himself, oh what the devil, anybody is liable to call it wrong once in a while. But the car does not slow, and far down in his precise and predictable heart, where the foreboding first sprouted and where the resignation lies now like a brooding moss, another bloom is budding.

"But if I *didn't* call a wrong shot . . . if I *didn't* make a miscalculation . . ."

A different bloom. Petaled with wonder.

"Then there may be more to this particular fool than I imagined."

And perhaps, therefore, more to all fools.

He stops the car, skidding the whitewalls against the curb in front of the Sea Breeze Cafe. Through the rushing windshield he can see the whole length of Main Street. Deserted? Just rain and tomcats. He flips up his collar and steps out without taking time to put on his overcoat, hurries across to the neon-filled front of the Snag. Inside, the bar also looks deserted; the jukebox is lighted, playing softly, *but there is no one in sight. Odd . . . Has the whole town driven out to stand about in the mud to be laughed at? That seems terribly*—Then sees the fat and pallid stereotype of a bartender standing near the window, watching him from beneath long curling lashes.

"Really coming down out there, isn't it, Teddy?" *There's more to this than*—

"I suppose so, Mr. Draeger."

"Teddy?" *Look: even this little effeminate frog of a bartender— even he knows more than I do.* "Floyd Evenwrite told me I could find Hank Stamper's wife here."

"Yes sir," Draeger hears the little man tell him. "Way at the back, Mr. Draeger. In the depot section."

"Thank you. Oh say, Teddy; why do you think that—" *That . . . what?* He stands a moment, unaware that he is staring until the bartender blushes beneath the blank gaze and drops his long lashes down over his eyes. "Never mind." Draeger turns and walks away: *I can't ask him. I mean he couldn't tell me—even if he knew, wouldn't tell me . . .* past the juke as it clicks, whirs, introduces another tune:

> Why don't you cuddle up . . . an' console me,
> Snuggle up . . . an' comfort me,
> Pacify my heart jes' one more time?

Down the long bar past the gently throbbing glow of the jukebox, the shuffleboard, through the partitioned gloom of empty booths, finally finding the girl at the very back. By herself. With a beer glass. The upturned collar of a heavy pea jacket frames her slim, moist face. The moisture—he can't tell—is it rain or tears or just *too damned hot in here* sweat? Her pale hands resting on a large maroon album . . . she watches him approach, the slightest smile turning her lips. *And so does she,* Draeger realizes, greeting her; *more than I do. Odd . . . that I could have thought I understood so much.*

"Mr. Draeger . . ." The girl indicates a chair. "You look like a man after information."

"I want to know what happened," he says, sitting. "And why."

She looks down at her hands, shaking her head. "More information than I can give, too, I'm afraid." She raises her head and smiles at him again. "Honest; I'm afraid I really can't explain 'and why' "—her smile wry but not all derisive as the grins of those other fools had been, wry, but sincerely sorry and somehow quite sweet. Draeger is surprised by the anger generated in him by her reply—*this damned flu!*—surprised by the rapid beating of his heart and the uncontrolled rising of his voice.

"Doesn't that imbecile husband of yours *realize?* I mean the *danger* of making such a run down the river without help?"

The girl continues smiling at him. "You mean doesn't Hank realize what the town will *think* of him if he goes through with it . . . isn't that what you started to say, Mr. Draeger?"

"All right. Yes. Yes, that's right. Isn't he *aware* that he is risking complete—*total*—alienation?"

"He's risking more than that. He may lose his little wife if he goes through with it. For one thing. And he may lose his life, for another."

"Then *what?*"

The girl studies Draeger a moment, then takes a sip of her beer. "You could never understand it all. You just want a reason, two or three reasons. When there are reasons going back two or three hundred years . . ."

"Rubbish. All I want to know is what changed his mind."

"You would have to know what made it up in the first place, wouldn't you?"

"Made what?"

"His mind, Mr. Draeger."

"All *right.* I mean all right. I have plenty of time."

The girl takes another sip of beer. She closes her eyes and wipes a lock of wet hair back from her forehead. Draeger suddenly realizes that she is completely exhausted—dazed, almost. He waits for her to open her eyes again. The smell of disinfectant floats from a nearby toilet. The jukebox beats against the smoke-varnished knotty pine walls:

> *To try an' ferget I turn to the wine . . .*
> *A empty bottle a broken heart*
> *An' still you're on my mind.*

The girl opens her eyes and pulls up a sleeve to look at her watch. Then folds her hands on the maroon album again. "I guess, Mr. Draeger, things used to be different around this area." *Rubbish; the world is always the same.* "No. Don't scowl, Mr. Draeger. Really. I didn't quite believe it myself . . ." *She knows what I'm thinking!* ". . . but I gradually came around. Here. Let me show you something." She opens the book; the smell reminds her of the attic. (Oh, the attic. He kissed me good-by and my sore lip . . .) "This is the family history, sort of. I've finally got around to reading up on it." (I've got around to admitting . . . my lips blister, every winter.)

She pushes the book across the table toward Draeger; it is a large photograph album, awkward with old prints. Draeger opens it slowly, hesitant since his experience with those binoculars. "There isn't anything written here. Just dates and pictures . . ."

"Use your imagination, Mr. Draeger; that's what I've been doing. Come on, it's fun. Look."

The girl turns the book facing him, lightly touching the corner of her mouth with the tip of her tongue. (Every winter, since I been in this country . . .) Draeger leans close to the dimly lit album. *Rubbish; she doesn't know any more than . . .* The juke bubbles as he turns a couple of pages of faces:

> *Ah cast a lone-some shadow*
> *An' Ah play a lone-some game.*

The rain hums against the roof overhead. Draeger pushes the book away, then pulls it back. *Rubbish; she doesn't—*He tries to situate himself more comfortably in the wooden chair, hoping to overcome the unruly feeling of disorientation that has been building ever since he twisted that focus knob. "Nonsense." *But that's the trouble, that is the trouble . . .* "This is senseless." He pushes the book away again. *It is nonsense.*

"Not at all, Mr. Draeger. Look." (Every danged winter . . .) "Let me leaf through a bit of the Stamper family past . . ." *Giddy bitch, the past has nothing to do*—"For instance, here, 1909, let me read you"—*with the ways of men today.* " 'During the summer the red tide came in and turned the clams bad; killed a dozen injuns and three of us Christians.' Fancy that, Mr. Draeger." *The days are the same, though, damn it* (days that you feel like pages of soft wet sandpaper in your fingers, the silent pliant teeth of time eating away); *the summers are the same.* "Or . . . let's see . . . here: the winter of 1914 when the river froze solid." *The winters are the same too.* (Every winter there is mildew, see it licking its sleepy gray tongue along the baseboards?) *Or not essentially any different* (every winter mildew, and skin rash, and fever blisters on your lip). "And you must go through one of these winters to have some notion. Are you listening, Mr. Draeger?"

Draeger starts. "Certainly." The girl smiles. "Certainly, go on. It's just . . . that jukebox." Burbling: "*Ah cast a lonesome shadow/An' Ah play a lonesome game . . .*" Not really loud but—"But, yes; I am listening."

"And using your imagination?"

"Yes, yes! Now what" *difference should these bygone years make?* (every winter a new tube of Blistex) "were you saying?" "*Though you're gone, Ah still dance on . . .*" The girl assumes the air of one in a trance, closing her eyes. "As I see it, Mr. Draeger, the 'whys' go a long way back . . ." *Nonsense! Rubbish!* (Yet every winter, feel the hole already forming? Lower lip?) "As I recall, Hank's granddad— Henry's father—now let me think . . ." *But. Perhaps.* (Relentlessly.) "*Shadows lone-some.*" "Of course there are—" *Nevertheless.* (Still.) "On the other—" *Stop . . . stop.*

*STOP! DON'T SWEAT IT. SIMPLY MOVE A FEW INCHES LEFT OR RIGHT TO GET A NEW VIEW-POINT. Look . . . Reality is greater than the sum of its parts, also a damn sight holier. And the lives of such stuff as dreams are made of may be rounded with a sleep but they are not tied neatly with a red bow. Truth doesn't run on time like a commuter train, though time may run on truth. And the Scenes Gone By and the Scenes to Come flow blending together in the sea-green deep while Now spreads in circles on the surface. So don't sweat it. For focus simply move a few inches back or forward. And once more . . . look:*

As the barroom explodes gently outward into the rain, in spreading spherical waves:

Dusty Kansas train depot in 1898. The sun lip-reading the bright gilt scrawl on the Pullman door. There stands Jonas Armand Stamper, with a furl of steam wafting past his thin waist, like a half-mast flag from an iron-black flagpole. He stands near the gilted door, a little apart, with a black flat-brimmed hat clamped in one iron hand, a black leatherbound book clamped in the other, and silently watches the farewells of his wife and three boys and the rest of his gathered kin. A sturdy-enough-looking brood, he decides, in their stiff-starched muslin. A very impressive-looking flock. And knows also that, to the eyes of the noontime depot crowd, he appears more sturdy-looking, stiff-starched, and impressive than all the others put together. His hair is long and glossy, showing Indian blood; his eyebrows and mustache exactly horizontal, as though rulered parallel onto his wide-boned face with a heavy graphite pencil. Hard jaw, tendoned neck, deep chest. And though he is inches under six feet he stands in such a way as to appear much taller. Yes, impressive. The stiff-starched, leatherbound, iron-cored patriarch, fearlessly moving his family west to Oregon. The sturdy pioneer striking out for new and primitive frontiers. Impressive.

"Be careful, Jonas."

"God will provide, Nate. It's the Lord's work we are doing."

"You're a good man, Jonas."

"God will see to His own, Louise."

"Amen, amen."

"It's the Lord's will that you should go."

He nods stiffly and, turning to step onto the train, catches sight of his three boys . . . Look: they are all grinning. He frowns to remind them that, while they may have been the ones that argued for this move from Kansas to the wilds of the Northwest, it is still *his* decision and no other that allows it, *his* decision and *his* permission and they hadn't, praise God, better forget it! "It is the good Lord's will," he repeats and the two younger boys drop their eyes. The oldest boy, Henry, continues to meet his father's stare. Jonas starts to speak again but there is something about the boy's expression, something so blatantly triumphant and blasphemous that the fearless patriarch's words stop in his throat, though it is much later before he really understands the look. *No, you knew the moment you saw it. Branded there like the leer of Satan. You knew the look and your blood ran cold when you saw what you had unknowingly been party to.*

The conductor calls. The two youngest boys move past the father into the train, muttering thanks, thank ya kindly for the wrapped lunches offered by the queue of relatives who have come to see them off. Their nervous, wet-eyed mother follows, kissing cheeks, pressing hands. The oldest boy next, with his fists knotted in his trousers pockets. The train bucks suddenly and the father grasps the bar and swings on board, lifting his hand to the waving relatives.

"So long."

"You write, Jonas, hear?"

"We'll write. We look to see you folks following before long."

"So long . . . so long."

He turns to mount the hot iron steps and sees again that look as Henry passes from the landing into the car. Lord have mercy, he whispers, without knowing why. *No, admit it; you did know. You knew it was the family sin come back from the pit, and you knew your part in it; you knew your part just as surely as your knew the sin.* "A born sinner," he mutters, "born cursed."

For, to Jonas and his generation, the family history was black with the stain of that selfsame sin: *You know the sin. Curse of the Wanderer; curse of the Tramp; bitter curse of the Faithless; always turning their backs on the lot God had granted. . . .*

"Always troubled with itchy feet," contended the more easygoing.

"Idiocy!" thundered those advocating stability. "Blasphemers!"

"Just roamers."

"Fools! *Fools!*"

Migrants, is what the family's history shows. A stringy-muscled brood of restless and stubborn west-walkers, their scattered history shows. With too much bone and not enough meat, and on the move ever since that first day the first skinny immigrant Stamper took his first step off the boat onto the eastern shore of the continent. On the move with a kind of trancelike dedication. Generation after generation leapfrogging west across wild young America; not as pioneers doing the Lord's work in a heathen land, not as visionaries blazing trail for a growing nation (though they quite often bought the farms of discouraged pioneers or teams of horses from disillusioned visionaries making tracks back to well-blazed Missouri), but simply as a clan of skinny men inclined always toward itchy feet and idiocy, toward foolish roaming, toward believing in greener grass over the hill and straighter hemlocks down the trail.

"You bet. We get to that place down the trail, *then* we sit back and take 'er easy."

"Right. We got plenty time then. . . ."

But, always, just as soon as the old man finally got all the trees cut and the stumps cleared and the old lady finally got the linseed coating she'd been so long griping about for her hemlock floor, some gangly, frog-voiced seventeen-year-old would stand looking out the window, scratching a stringy-muscled belly, and allow, "You know . . . we can do *better* than this yere sticker patch we got now."

"Do better? Just when we finally got a toehold on 'er?"

"I believe we can, yes."

"*You* can do better, may-be—though I truly do have my misgivin's about it—but your father an' me, we ain't leaving!"

"Suit yourself."

"No sir, Mister Antsy Pants! Your father an' me, we come to the end of it."

"Then Father an' you suit yourselfs, 'cause I'm movin' on. You an' the old man do what you please."

"*Wait* a minute now, bud—"

"Ed!"

"Just hold your horses now, makin' up *my* mind for *me* what *I* do, woman. Okay, bud, what egzackly was it you had in mind, just outta curiosity?"

"Ed!"

"Woman, the boy an' me is talkin'."

"Oh, *Ed* . . ."

And the only ones that ever stayed behind were either too old or too sick to continue west. Too old or too sick, or, as far as the family was concerned, too dead. For when one moved, they all moved. Tobacco-scented letters found in heart-shaped candy boxes in attics are filled with excited news of this moving.

". . . the air out here is real good."

". . . the kids do fine tho the school as you can well imagine this far from civilization is nothing to holler about."

". . . we look to see you folks out thisaway very soon now hear?"

Or with the dejected news of restlessness:

". . . Lu tells me I should not pay any attention to you that you and Ollen and the rest always put a burr in my blanket but I don't know I tell her I don't know. I tell her for one thing I am not as of yet ready to settle that what we got here is the whole shebang and give up that we can not improve our situation some. So I'll think on it . . ."

So they moved. And if, as the years passed, some parts of the family went slower than others, moving only ten or fifteen miles during their lifetime, still the movement was always west. Some had to be dragged from tumbledown homes by insistent grandchildren. Gradually some even managed to be born and to die in the same town. Then, eventually, there came Stampers of a more sensibly practical nature; Stampers clearheaded enough to stop and stand still and look around; deep-thinking, broodful Stampers able to recognize that trait they began calling "the flaw in the family character" and to set about correcting it.

These clearheaded men made a real effort to overcome this flaw, made a truly practical effort to put once and for all an end to this senseless fiddlefooting west, to stop, to settle down, to take root and be content with whatever portion the good Lord had allotted them. These sensible men.

"All right now . . ." Stopping on a flat Midwestern land where they could see in all directions: "All right, I do feel we have come about far enough." Stopping and saying, "It's high time we put an end to this foolishness that has been prodding at our ancestors; when a man can stand here—and see in every direction and left's no better'n right and forward's got just as much sage and buffalo weed as backward, and over that rise yonder is just more flat, more of the same we been walkin' over for two hundred years, then why, praise Jesus, why go further?"

And when no one could come up with a good reason the practical men gave a stiff nod and thumped a worn boot against the flatiron land: "All right. Then this is the whole shebang, boys, right here underfoot. Give up and admit it."

To begin devoting their restless energies to pursuits more tangible than wandering, more practical than walking, pursuits like business and community and church. They acquired bank accounts, positions in local government, and even, sometimes, these stringy-muscled men, potbellies. Pictures of these men found in boxes in attics: black suits poised with rigid determination before a photographer's mural, mouths grim and resolute. Letters: " . . . we have come far enough."

And they folded up in leather chairs like jackknives closing and climbing into scabbards. They bought family plots in cemeteries in Lincoln and Des Moines and Kansas City, these pragmatic men, and mail-ordered huge cushiony maroon chesterfields for their living rooms.

"Ah boy. Yes sir. This is the life. It's about time."

Only to be set in motion again by the first young wildeye able to sucker the old man into listening to his dreams. *Admit; you knew that look even then; by the first frog-voiced young foot-itcher able to get Pop to believing that they could outdo this sticker patch by moving farther west. Be all set in plodding, restless motion again, you knew that look and could have saved us the heartache* . . . like animals driven by a drought, by an unquenchable thirst—*but you didn't*—driven by a dream of a place where the water tastes like wine:

> *This Springfield water tastes like turpentine,*
> *I'm goin' down . . . that long dusty road.*

Going until at last the whole family, the whole clan, reached the salty wall of the Pacific.

"Where from here?"

"Beats the piss outa me; all I know's this don't taste much like wine."

"Where from here?"

"I don't know." Then desperately: "But someplace, someplace else!" With a desperate and cornered grin. "Someplace else, I can tell ya." Not accepting God's intended lot, Jonas says under his breath, driven by a curse. *You could have saved them the trouble of looking for that someplace. You know now that all is vanity and vexation of the spirit. Could you only of mustered the courage when you first saw that devil's leer shining through Henry's grin there at the train station, you could of stopped it and saved us all the trouble.* He turns his back on his son and lifts his hand to the flock of cousins and brothers who walk alongside the slowly moving train.

"Mind, Jonas, you be thoughtful; don't be too stiff on Mary Ann or th' boys. It's a hard new country."

"I won't, Nathan."

"And mind, Jonas, them bad old Oregon bears and Indians, hee hee hee."

"Pshaw, now, Louise."

"Write, now, soon's you get settled. Old Kansas is looking gosh-awful flat."

"We'll do that." *You could of stopped it then, could you of only mustered the courage.* "We'll write and advise you all."

"Yessir; those bears and Indians, Jonas, don't let such as them get you all."

The Oregon bears, Jonas Stamper found, were well fed on clams and berries, and fat and lazy as old house cats. The Indians, nourished on the same two limitless sources of food, were even fatter and a damn sight lazier than the bears. Yes. They were peaceful enough. So were the bears. In fact the whole country was more peaceful than he had expected. But there was this odd . . . *volatile* feeling about the new country that struck him the very day he arrived, struck him and stuck, and never left him all the three years he lived in Oregon. "What's so hard about this country?" Jonas wondered when they arrived. "All it needs is somebody to whip it into shape."

No, it wasn't such as bears or Indians that got stern and stoic Jonas Stamper.

"But I wonder how come it's still as unsettled as it is?" Jonas wondered when he arrived; others wondered when he left. "Tell me, weren't they a Jonas Stamper hereabouts?"

"He was here, but he's gone."

"Gone? Just up and gone?"

"Just up and scoot."

"What come of his family?"

"They're still around, her'n' the three boys. Folks here are kinda helpin' keep their heads above water. Old Foodland Stokes sends 'em a bit of grocery every day or so, back up river. They got a sort of house—"

Jonas started the big frame house a week after they settled in Wakonda. He divided three years, three short summers and three long winters, between his feed-and-seed store in town and his building site across the river—eight acres of rich riverbank land, the best on the river. He had homesteaded his lot under the 1880 Land Act before he left Kansas—"Live on the Highway of Water!"—homesteaded it sight unseen, trusting to the pamphlets that a riverbank site would be a good site for a patriarch to do the Lord's work. It had sounded good on paper.

"Just scooted out, huh? That sure don't sound like Jonas Stamper. Didn't he leave anything?"

"Family, feed store, odds and ends, and a whole pisspot of shame."

He had sold a feed store in Kansas, a good feed store with a rolltop desk full of leatherbound ledgers to finance the move, then had sent the money ahead so it was already waiting for him when he arrived, waiting bright green and growing, like everything else in the rich new land, the rich new *promising frontier* he'd read about in all the pamphlets his boys had brought him from the post office back in Kansas. Pamphlets sparkling red and blue, ringing with wild Indian names like bird-call signals in the forest: Nakoomish, Nahailem, Chalsea, Silcoos, Necanicum, Yachats, Siuslaw, and Wakonda, at Wakonda Bay, on the Peaceful and Promising Wakonda Auga River, Where (the pamphlets had informed him) A Man Can Make His Mark. Where A Man Can Start Anew. Where (the pamphlets said) The Grass Is Green And The Sea Is Blue And The Trees And Men Grow Tall And True! Out In The Great Northwest, Where (the pamphlets made it clear) There Is Elbow Room For A Man To Be As Big And Important As He Feels It Is In Him To Be!*

Ah, it had sounded *right* good on paper, but, as soon as he saw it, there was something . . . about the river and the forest, about the clouds grinding against the mountains and the trees sticking out of the ground . . . something. Not that it was a hard country, but something you must go through a winter of to understand.

*But that's what you did not know. You knew the cursed look of wanderlust but you did not know the hell that lust was leading you into. You must go through a winter first. . . .*

"I'll be switched. Just gone. It sure don't sound like old Jonas."

"I wouldn't be too tough on him; for one thing, you got to go through a rainy season or so to get some idee."

*You must go through a winter to understand.*

For one thing, Jonas couldn't see all that elbow room that the pamphlets had talked about. Oh, it was there, he knew. But not the way he'd imagined it would be. And for *another* thing, there was nothing, *not a thing!* about the country that made a man feel Big And Important. If anything it made a man feel dwarfed, and about as important as one of the fish-Indians living down on the clamflats. Important? Why, there was something about the whole blessed country that made a soul feel whipped before he got started. Back home in Kansas a man had a *hand* in things, the way the Lord *aimed* for His servants to have: if you didn't water, the crops died. If you didn't feed the stock, the stock died. As it was ordained to be. But there, in that land, it looked like our labors were for naught. The flora and fauna grew or died, flourished or failed, in *complete* disregard for man and his aims. A Man Can Make His Mark, did they tell me? Lies, lies. Before God I tell you: a man might struggle and labor his livelong life and make *no* mark! None! No permanent mark at all! I say it is true.

*You must go through at least a year of it to have some notion.*

---

* Courtesy of Ken Babbs

I say there was no permanence. Even that town was temporary. I say it. All vanity and vexation of the spirit. One generation passeth away, and another cometh: but the earth abideth forever, or as forever as the rain lets it.

You must rise from your quilts early that morning, without waking the wife or boys, and walk from the tent into a low, green fog. You have not stepped out onto the bank of the Wakonda Auga but into some misty other-world dream . . .

And even as I pass away, that blamed town, that piteous little patch of mud wrested briefly away from the trees and brush, it shall pass also. I knew so the moment I saw it. I knew all the time I lived there and I knew when death took me back. And I know now.

Fog is draped over the low branches of vine maple like torn remnants of a gossamer bunting. Fog ravels down from the pine needles. Above, up through the branches, the sky is blue and still and very clear, but fog is on the land. It creeps down the river and winds around the base of the house, eating at the new yellow-grained planks with a soft white mouth. There is a quiet hiss, not unpleasant, as of something pensively sucking . . .

For what profit hath a man of all his labor which he taketh under the sun if the trees and the brush and the moss strive everlastingly to take it back? Strive everlastingly until a soul felt that the town was only a sort of prison cell with green prison walls of brush and vine and he had to labor everlastingly, day in day out, just to hang onto whatever pitiful little profit he might have made, labor everlastingly day in day out just to hang onto a floor of mud and a ceiling of clouds so low sometimes he felt he must stoop. . . . Floor and ceiling and a green prison wall of trees. I say it. The town? It may grow, but abide? It may grow and spread and proliferate, but abide? No. The old forest and land and river will prevail, for these things are of the earth. But the town is of man. I say it. Things cannot abide which are new and wrought by man. Is there anything whereof it may be said, See, this is new? It hath already of old time, which was before us. I say it.

. . . Yawning, walking thigh-deep through the ground-mist toward the house, you wonder vaguely if you are still asleep and at the same time not asleep, still dreaming and at the same time not dreaming. Couldn't it be? This swathed and muffled ground is like a sleep; this furry silence is like dream silence. The air is so still. The foxes aren't barking in the woods. The crows aren't calling. You can see no ducks flying the river. You cannot hear the usual morning breeze fingering *the buckthorn leaves. It is very still. Except for that soft, delicious, wet hissing . . .*

And space? Didn't the pamphlets claim there was elbow room? Perhaps, but with all that hellish greenery on every side could a soul tell it? Could he see more'n a couple hundred yards in any direction? Back on the plains, there is space. I will admit that a man back on the plains might feel a freezing emptiness in his bowels when he looked in all directions and saw nothing but what has gone before and what will come, nothing but far-stretching flat land and sage. But I say a man can get *accustomed*, get comfortable and *accustomed* to emptiness, just the way he can get accustomed to the cold or accustomed to the dark. That place, however, that . . . place, when I cast my eyes about, at fallen trees decaying under the vines, at the rain chewing away the countryside, at the river which runs into the sea yet the sea is not full . . . at all . . . at things such as . . . a soul cannot find the words . . . such as plants and flowers, the beasts and the birds, the fishes and the insects! I do not mean that. At all the things going *on* and *on* and *on*. Don't you see? It just all came at me so downright thick and fast that I knew I could never get accustomed to it! But I do not mean that. I mean I had no choice but do as I did; God as my witness . . . I had no choice!

*. . . In a reverie of movement you dip your hand into the nail keg and remove a few nails. You place the nails between your teeth and take up your hammer and go along the wall you were working on, half wondering if the blow of the hammer will be able to penetrate this cushioning silence or be stolen away by the fog and drowned in the river. You notice you are walking on tiptoe . . .*

After the second year Jonas was sick with longing to leave Oregon and return to Kansas. After the third year his longing had turned to a constant burn. But he dared not mention it to his family, especially not to his eldest. For the three years of rain and wilderness that had weakened the stiff, practical plainsman's starch in Jonas had nurtured a berry-vine toughness in his sons. Like the beasts and plants, the three boys grew on and on. Not larger by size; they were, like most of the family, small and wiry, but larger by look, harder. They watched the look in their father's trapped eyes get more frantic after each flood, while their own eyes turned to green glass and their faces to leather.

"Sir," Henry would ask, smiling, "You don't look so perky. Is something grievin' you?"

"Grieving?" Jonas fingered the Bible. " 'For in much wisdom is much grief: and he that increaseth knowledge increaseth sorrow.' "

"Yeah?" Henry shrugged and walked away before his father could go on. "Now what do you think of that."

In the dark attic above the feed store the boys whispered jokes about the tremble in their father's hands and about the squeak creeping into his onetime leatherbound meeting-house voice. "He gettin' so he look more glare-eyed and twitch-lipped and skittish ever' day, like a dog comin' into heat." They laughed in their corn-shuck pillows. "He gettin' so he look itchy an' uncomfortable: you reckon he's been slippin' off to Siskaloo for some of that red meat? That'll give you the itch, I hear tell."

Joked and laughed, but behind their grins were already despising old Jonas for what they could sense old Jonas was already bound to do.

. . . *You move along the wall, your shoulder brushing the fresh budded beads of pitch which have sprung like jewels from the green wood. You move along slowly . . .*

The family was living in the feed store in town when it was very cold, and the rest of the time in the big tent across the river where they were working on the house, which, like everything else in the land, grew on and on with slow, mute obstinacy over the months, seemingly in spite of all Jonas could do to delay it. The house itself had begun to haunt Jonas; the larger it became the more frantic and trapped he felt. There the blamed thing stood on the bank, huge, paintless, Godless. Without its windows it resembled a wooden skull, watching the river flow past with black sockets. More like a mausoleum than a house; more like a place to end life, Jonas thought, than a place to start fresh anew. For this land was permeated with dying; this bounteous land, where plants grew overnight, where Jonas had watched a mushroom push from the carcass of a drowned beaver and in a few gliding hours swell to the size of a hat—this bounteous land was *saturated* with moist and terrible dying.

"By gosh, sir, you sure are lookin' peaked, an' that's a fack. You want I should bring you back some salts from Grissom's while I'm in town?"

Saturated and *overflowing!* The feeling haunted Jonas's days and tortured his sleep. O, Jesus, light of life, fill the darkness. He was being smothered. He was being drowned. He felt he might awake some foggy morn with moss across his eyes and one of those hellish toadstools sprouting in the mist from his own carcass. "No!"

"What did you say, sir?"

"I said no salts, no. Something to let me sleep! Or to wake me up! One way or other, something to clear the *mist!" hangs from the limbs like gray bunting. In a dream you slide along the plank wall, eyes drifting about at the draped morning.* . . . *Snails in the night write glistening scripture on the planks; this wild-rose vine signals something to you with his many slow fingers . . . what? what?* His lean face is bent in an attitude of broken sleep as he moves along, one hand reaching to take a nail from the cluster jutting like quills from his now gray mustache. Then he stops, with the hand still raised, face still bent, unchanged. And leans forward, thrusts his head forward, straining to make out something a few yards ahead of him. The fog hiding the river has opened a small round hole in itself, lifting its corner for him to see. Through this opening he sees there has been another tiny cave-in at the bank since last night. A few more inches of soil have crumbled into the river. That cave-in is the source of that soft hissing sound, there, where the river sucks with rapt innocence at the new cut in its bank. Watching, it occurs to Jonas that it isn't the bank that is giving way, as one might naturally assume. No. It is the river that is getting wider. How many winters before that seesaw current will reach the foundation where he is now standing? Ten years? Twenty? Forty? Even so, what difference?

(A car pulled up and parked out on the wharf near the fishhouse, exactly forty years later. The car radio sent twanging strains of hill-billy-western across the gull-strewn bay. Two sailors home on leave from the Pacific told fabulous lies of Jap atrocities to a pair of wide-eyed sweethearts. The sailor in front paused to point to a yellow pick-up stopping down the ramp below them at the water's edge. "Look there: isn't that old Henry Stamper and his boy Hank? What the hell they got there in back?")

Dreamily, still staring down at the cave-in, Jonas runs his tongue over the nails in his mouth. He starts to turn back to the house, then stops again, his face running gradually into a puzzled frown. He takes one of the square nails out and holds it in front of his eyes. The nail is rusted. He looks at another nail and finds more rust. One at a time he removes each nail from his mouth and looks at it, studying for a long time the way a slight powder of rust is already splotching the iron like a fungus. And it didn't rain last night. In fact, it hasn't rained now in almost two incredible days, that was why he hadn't bothered tacking the lid back on the nail keg when he

finished work the day before. Yet, rain or no, the nails have rusted.
Overnight. The whole keg, come all the way from Pittsburgh, four
weeks on the road, bright and shiny as silver dimes . . . rusted overnight . . .

"By golly, you know, it looks like a coffin!" the sailor said.

. . . So, nodding to himself, he replaces the nails in the keg and
lays the hammer on the dewy grass, then walks thigh-deep through
fog to the river and gets in the boat and rows across to the dirt road
where a lean-to stables the mare. And saddles the mare and goes back
to Kansas, to the dry, flatiron prairies where sage struggles for a grip
in the meager soil, and jackrabbits nibble barrel cactus for the moisture, and decay goes on slow and unseen under the baked brick sky.

"It is a coffin! In a shipping box like on trains."

"Oh, look what they're doing!"

The other sailor and his girl untangled swiftly, and the four of
them watched the old man and the boy on the launching dock unload
the pick-up's cargo and drag it across the planks and tip it into the
bay—then get back in the pick-up and drive away. The sailors and
the two girls sat in the car and watched the box up-end and slowly
sink over many minutes. Eddy Arnold sang:

> There'll be smoke on the water, on the land
> an' the sea,
> When our Army and our Navy overtake the
> en-ah-mee . . .

as the box gave a stiff lurch and finally slid under, leaving a spreading
circle, trailing bubbles down through winding kelp and algae into the
green-brown purple-brown avenues of rubbery sea grass where crabs
with eyes on stalks patrol a dreary collection of bottles, old plumbing,
blown-out tires, iceboxes, lost outboard motors, broken porcelain, and
all the other debris that decorates the bottom of the bay.

In the pick-up, home from the docks, the tight-knit little man with
the bottle-green eyes and the hair already turning white tried to ease
his sixteen-year-old son's curiosity by reaching over to knuckle the
boy's head. "Watcha say, Hankas? How'd ya like to drift down to
Coos Bay tonight an' watch the old man tie one on. I'm gonna need
a level head to look after me."

"What was in it, Papa?" the boy asked (didn't even know then
that the thing was a coffin . . .).

"Was what?"

"In the big box."

Henry laughed. "Meat. Old meat I didn't want stinkin' up the place." The boy glanced swiftly at his father—(Old meat, he says . . . Pa said. . . . And I didn't know any better for lord, it's hard to say, for a couple of months anyhow when Boney Stokes—who's been the local doom-teller around town as far as I can remember—took me aside when he was out to the house visiting and we sit there for a good half-hour, me squirming around and him all the goddam time laying that goddam spit-dripping hand on my leg or my arm or my head or any other place he could get to me with it like he just won't rest a wink till everybody else is saddled with whatever germ it is he's vending. "Ah, Hank, Hank," he says, wagging his head back and forth on a neck about the size of his skinny wrist, "I hate to do it but I feel it my Christian duty to tell you some of the hard facts of life." Hate to, bull: He'd rather play the ghoul with other people's dead than ride a speedboat. "About who was in that box. Yes, I feel some-one should tell you about your grandfather, and his early years in this land . . .")—but said nothing. They drove on in silence. (" . . . in his early years, Hank, child"—old man Stokes leaned back and let his eyes get misty—"things wasn't just the way they are now. Your family didn't always have a big logging business. Yes . . . yes; your family, one might say, suffered some terrible misfortunes . . . back then . . .")

That foggy morning the eldest boy, Henry, was the first to wake and discover his father missing. He took up the hammer and, work-ing along side his two brothers Ben and Aaron, completed more work on the house that day than had been accomplished in the last week.

Boasting: "We got 'er by the tail, men. Yessir. Goddam right."

"What's that, Henry? What we got?"

"The tail, you dumb bunny! We'll show these boogers in town who been sniggerin' in their beards. That Stokes bunch. We'll show 'em. We'll whup this swamp from hell to breakfast."

"What about him?"

"About who? About old All-Is-Vanity? Old No-Profit-under-the-Boogin'-Sun? Shit. Ain't he already made hisself crystal clear where he stands? Ain't it apparent he's run out? Give up?"

"Yeah, but what about he comes back, Henry?"

"He comes back, he comes back crawlin' on his belly an' even then—"

"But Henry, what about he *don't* come back?" Aaron, the youngest, asked. "How'll we make it?"

Hammering: "We'll make it. We'll *whup* it! We'll *whup* it!" Slamming the hammer head into the springy white planks.

(So I first heard from Boney Stokes about how old Henry's daddy, Jonas Stamper, disgraced Henry and the rest of us. Then heard from Uncle Ben about how Boney had spent so many years trying to rub it in on Pa. But it was from Pa himself that I found out what it all come to, how the disgrace and the rubbing-in had built an iron-clad commandment. Not that Pa come out and told me. No. Maybe some fathers and sons talk with each other like that, but me and old Henry was never able to hack it. But he did something else. He wrote it down for me, and hung it up on my wall. On the very day I was born, they tell me. I didn't catch on to the whole of it till a good spell later. Sixteen years. And then it still wasn't the old man that told me; it was his wife, my stepmother, the girl he brought from back East . . . But I'll get to that directly . . .)

They found Jonas had taken the money from the feed store and left them with little more than the building and what meager stock was on hand and the house across the river. The stock was mostly seed, nothing that would bring in cash until spring, and they made it through that first winter largely on charity from the most well-to-do family in the county, the Stokes family. Jeremy Stokes was unofficial governor, mayor, justice of the peace, and moneylender of the county, having been granted the positions by that old unwritten decree: First Come, First Served. What he had first served himself to was an enormous warehouse left empty by Hudson's Bay. He moved in; when no one ever came around to move him out, he turned the warehouse into the town's first general store and worked out a nice deal with the shipping line that steamed every two or three months into the bay, a sweet little deal whereby they received a little something extra for the privilege of selling to no one but him. "It's on account of I'm a member," he explained, but never made it clear of exactly what. He talked vaguely of some obscure union in the East between the steamboat men and the merchants, "And I propose, friends and fellow pioneers, to make all of us around here members: I'm a generous man."

Generous was hardly the word. Hadn't he fed that tragic Mrs. Stamper and her brood after their old man left? The goods had been delivered for seven months by his oldest boy, a thin, pale drink of water—Bobby Stokes, who not only enjoyed the distinction of being one of the few white natives of the county but was as well the only member of the town ever to take a cruise all the way to Europe; "None of the doctors around here," Aaron once remarked, "could really *appreciate* the *quality* of Boney's cough." Delivered daily, for seven charitable months, "And the only thing father asks," the boy said after the term of generosity was up, "is that you become a member of the Wakonda Co-op." He handed a sharpened pencil and a paper to the mother. She took glasses from a black coin purse and studied the document for a long time.

"But . . . doesn't this mean our *feed* store?"

"Just a formality."

"Sign it, Mama."

"But . . ."

"Sign it."

It was Henry, the eldest. He stepped forward and took the paper from his mother and put it on a plank. He put the pencil in her hand. "Just sign it."

The thin boy smiled, watching the paper warily. "Thank you, Henry. You're very wise. Now, as shareholding members this entitles you folks to certain deductions and privileges—"

Henry laughed, an odd, tight laugh he had recently developed, able to cut off conversation like a knife. "Oh, I reckon we'll whup 'er without certain privileges." He picked up the signed paper and held it just out of the other boy's reach. "Probably without being members of anything, too."

"Henry . . . old man—" The other boy blinked solemnly, following the paper's teasing movements, then began reciting in unconscious parody of his father, "We are founders of a new frontier, workers in a new world; we must all strive together. A unified effort will—"

Henry laughed and pushed the paper into the boy's hand; then stooped to select some choice rocks from the river bank. He skipped one out across the wide gray-green water, flashing. "Oh, I reckon we'll whup 'er."

His failure to be duly impressed by the offer made the other boy uneasy and a little irritated. "Henry," he said again softly and touched Henry's arm with two fingers thin as icicles, "I was born in this land. I spent my youth here amongst the wilderness and savages. I *know* the way a pioneer needs his fellow man. To survive. Now; I truly like you, old fellow; I wouldn't want to see you forced to leave by the untamed elements. Like . . . some others."

Henry threw his handful of pebbles all together into the river. "Nobody's leaving, Bobby Stokes, Boney Stokes—nobody else is leaving." Laughing that old man's ferocious laugh at the other's somber and fatalistic expression. As the pebbles slowly melt beneath the current.

And years later, after he had used this same ferocity to build a small fortune and a logging operation the size of which was limited only by the number of relatives that migrated to the area to work for him, Henry rowed across one morning to find Boney waiting at the garage in the delivery truck.

"Morning, Henry. How's Henry Stamper, Junior?"

"Noisy," Henry answered, squinting a little as he looked sideways at his old friend standing like a post near the door of the truck. Boney was holding a ragged brown package against his thigh. "Yep. Noisy and hungry." He waited, squinting.

"Oh." Boney suddenly remembered the package. "This came for you this morning. I guess they must of got word about the birth back in Kansas."

"I guess they must of done that."

Boney looked forlornly at the package. "It appears to be from Kansas City. A relative, perhaps?"

Henry grinned into his hand, a gesture so like the one used by Boney to cover his barking cough that people of the town sometimes wondered if Henry had copied the move to further plague his morose companion. "Well—" He laughed at Boney's fidgeting. "What the hell, let's see what he sent."

Boney already had his pocketknife open to cut the string. The package contained a wall plaque, one of those sentimental souvenirs picked up at county fairs: a frame of wooden cherubs around a copper bas-relief of Jesus carrying a lamb through a field of daisies, and raised copper letters declaring, "Blessed Are the Meek, for They Shall Inherit the Earth. Matt. 6"—and a note saying, "This here is for my Grandchild; may he grow up to have more Christian Love and Sympathy and Charity than the rest of my family who have never understood nor communicated with me. J. A. Stamper."

Boney was shocked. "You mean to tell me you've never even written to that poor old fellow? Never?" Boney was more than shocked, he was horrified. "You've done him a terrible wrong!"

"You reckon? Well, I'll see ifn I can't make it up some way. Come take a little ride to the house with me." And in the mother's room Boney's horror turned to petrified disbelief as he stood watching Henry paint the plaque with dull yellow machine paint. Henry dried the paint with the heat of the burning note, and with one of the heavy red pencils used for marking the footage on the end of logs, finally put into words, into writing, what to Henry was nothing more than a good rule for his son to grow up under, but what essentially was the core of that family sin Jonas had seen in the eyes of his son in the Kansas sunlight: sitting on the edge of the bed that contained the forty-five-year-old woman he had married upon his mother's death, with Boney looking on incredulous as a totem pole, and the newborn child crying his lungs out, Henry had laboriously lettered his own personal gospel over the raised copper words of Jesus; bent tensely over the plaque, grinning his fierce, irreverent grin at his wife's protests and Boney's stare, and at the thought of what pious old Jonas would say if he could just see his gift now. "That ought to do 'er." He stood up, right pleased with his work, and walked across the room and nailed the plaque into the wall over the enormous crib he and the boys at the mill built for Henry Junior. (Where the goddamned ugly outfit hangs, all the time I'm growing up. NEVER GIVE A INCH! In Pa's broad, awkward hand. The dirtiest, crummiest, cruddiest yellow under the sun and that awkward school-kid lettering in red. NEVER GIVE A INCH! Just like one of them mottos you might see in a Marine sergeant's orderly office, or like something Coach Lewellyn might of drawn up to hang alongside his other hardnose signs all over the locker room. NEVER GIVE A INCH! Just like the corny, gung-ho, guts-ball posters that I seen a good thousand of, just exactly like, except for that raised picture of Jesus and his lamb under the gobby machine paint and them curlicue words you could read with your fingers at night when the lights went out, "Blessed are the meek" and so forth and so on. . . . It hung there and I never had no more idea than a duck what all was behind it till I was sixteen and she told me what she knew about it and I connected what Boney told me with what the old man told me, then hooked all this up with the women. Funny, how things sometimes take so long to click together, and how something like that sign can hang unnoticed right next to your head for so many years; yet you have to be beat across the knob with it before it starts to dawn just how much it was noticed, whether you knew it or not . . .)

When the boy Hank was ten, his mother, always grim and gray and distant—an almost identical remake of the nondescript grandmother he never knew—took to her bed in one of the dark rooms of the old house and devoted two months to some fervent ailing, then got up one morning, did a washing, and died. She looked so natural and unchanged in her coffin that the boy found himself striving to re-create conversations he had had with her—sentences she might have used, expressions—in an attempt to convince himself that she had once been more than that carved, peaceful form nestled there in ruffles of satin.

Henry didn't expend half as much thought. The dead's dead, was the way he looked at it; get 'em in the ground and look to the live ones. So, as soon as he had paid Lilienthal, the mortician, he picked a carnation from one of the wreaths, stabbed it into the lapel of his funeral suit, and caught a train to New York and was gone for three months. Three precious months, right out of the middle of cutting season. Henry's youngest brother, Aaron, and his family, stayed at the house to take care of the boy. Aaron's wife began to fret for her brother-in-law after the first weeks of his mysterious absence lengthened into months.

"Two months now. That poor man, grieving so. He's more heart-broke than any of us would have ever believed."

"Heartbroke the dickens," Aaron said. "He's back East somewhere looking for some girl to take the old lady's place."

"Now how in the world do you know *that*? Who does Henry know back East?"

"Nobody that I ever heard tell of. But that's how Henry thinks: women come from back East, that's how it is. You need a woman, go back East and get you one."

"Why, that is out*landish!* That poor man is fifty-some years old. What reasonable woman would—"

"Reasonable woman the dickens. Henry's back yonder looking for some woman he considers fit to be little Hank's mother. And when he finds her, her being reasonable won't have *beans* to do with whether she comes or not." Aaron lit his pipe and smiled pleasantly, accustomed after many years to sit back and enjoy watching the world follow along whenever Henry took it by the nose. "An' would you care to make a little bet about whether that *poor* old man comes back with her or not?"

Henry was fifty-one at the time, and to those who saw him pacing the New York streets, with a boyish grin beneath a black derby and wrinkles at the side of his face looking like fresh cracks in old wood, he looked possibly twice his age, as easily half. To the casual observer he was more archetype than human: the country rube come to the city, the illiterate hick with a young man's wiry and vigorous stride and an old man's face, with too much stringy wrist showing from the cuff of a coat that looked right out of an undertaker's parlor, and too much neck stuck out of the collar. With his uncut mane going white as that of an old wolf and his green eyes excited and glittering, he looked like a comic-strip character of a prospector struck it rich. He looked like he might curse in the best dining room and spit on the finest rug. He looked like anything but a man capable of acquiring a young bride.

That summer Henry became quite the current topic, he and his derby and his funeral-parlor suit, and toward the end of his stay was being invited to the best occasions to be laughed at. This laughter reached its peak when he announced one evening at a party that he'd picked the woman he aimed to marry! The partyers were over-joyed. Why, this was absolutely precious, better than a drawing-room farce. Not that it was his choice that the fellows were laughing at—secretly they were impressed that this skinny fool had had the per-ception to pick the most comely, the most witty and charming of all the eligibles, a young co-ed home for the summer from her studies at Stanford—it was the gall, the audacious, swaggering *gall* of this leering old lumberjack to even *consider* such a girl: *that* was what the fellows laughed at. Old, leering Henry, always good for a chuckle or two, whacked his thin flank and snapped his broad canvas galluses and paraded around like a burlesque clown, laughing right along with them. But noticed that the fellows' laughter got pretty watered down when he walked across the room and led the co-ed blushing and giggling from the parlor. Imagined the laughter got even weaker when, after weeks of persistent courting, he headed back West, taking the girl along as his fiancée.

(Even after Boney'd told me about the plaque I never really paid it any more mind than a fly on the wall—till that year I was sixteen; when Myra comes into my bedroom for the first time. In fact, I'd just turned sixteen. It was my birthday. I'd got presents—baseball gear—from everybody at the house but her. I hadn't expected a gift; she'd never given me much more than the time of day. I didn't think she'd even noticed how old I was. But it was like she'd been waiting till I was old enough to appreciate my present. She just came in and stood there. . . .)

Possibly the only one more astonished than the fellows was the girl herself. She was twenty-one and had one year to go for a degree at Stanford. She was dark-haired and slight, with delicate bones (like some kind of funny bird, stood there, like some kind of weird, rare bird always looking at the sky . . .). She had three horses of her own stabled at Menlo Park, two lovers—one a full professor—and a parrot that had cost her father two hundred dollars in Mexico City; all these things she left behind.

(Just stood there.)

She had perhaps a dozen Bay Area organizations she was active in, and as many in New York, where she had been active during the summer. Her family life had been moving along smooth as that of any of her friends. Wherever she was, East Coast or Stanford, when she composed a guest list for a party, it always ran into three figures. But all this had been thrown aside. And for what? For some gangly old logger in some muddy logging town clear up north of nowhere. What had she been *thinking* when she'd let herself be pressured into such a ridiculous change? (She had a funny way of looking, too, that was like a bird looked: you know, with the head turned, never dead at something, but kind of past it, past it like she could see something nobody else could see; and whatever it was she saw sometimes scared her like a ghost. "I'm lonely," she says.)

She spent her first year in Wakonda wondering whatever on God's green earth had possessed her. ("I've always been lonely. It's always been in me, like a hollow . . .") By the end of her second year she had given up wondering and had definitely made up her mind to leave. She was already making secret plans for departure when she discovered that somehow, in some dark dream, something had slipped up and got to her and she would have to postpone her trip a few months . . . just a few more months . . . then she would be gone, gone, gone, and would at least have some little something to show for her sojourn in the north woods. ("I thought Henry would be able to fill that hollow. Then I thought the child would . . .")

So Hank got himself a little brother and Henry got a second son. The old man, busy with expanding his logging operations, took no special notice of the blessed event other than christening the boy Leland Stanford Stamper in what he considered a favor to his young wife; he stomped into her room in Wakonda, calk boots and all, trailing sawdust, mud, and the stink of machine oil, and announced, "Little honey, I intend to let you call that boy there after that school you're forever mooning about quittin'. How does that strike you?"

With impact enough, apparently, to stun any objection she might have had to the name, because her only reaction was a feeble nod. Henry nodded back and stomped proudly from the room.

That was his only gesture of acknowledgment. The twelve-year-old Hank, busy riffling through the magazines in the waiting room, seemed determined to dismiss the birth completely.

"You want to run in to take a quick look at your little brother?"

"He ain't my little brother."

"Well, don't you imagine you ought to leastways say something to the new mother?"

"She ain't never said nothing to me." (Which was about the truth. Because she hadn't said more than hello and good-by until that day when she comes in on my birthday. It's late spring; I'm racked up in bed with a broken tooth I got from trying to field a bad hop with my mush, and my head's about to blow to pieces from the pain of it. She looks quick at me, then away, walks across the room and flutters there against the window like a bird. She's wearing yellow and her hair's long and blue-black. She's got in her hand a story book she's been reading to the kid. He's three or four at the time. I hear him fussing next door. She stands there at the window, fluttering around like, waiting for me to say something about her being lonely, I guess. But I don't say anything. Then her eyes light on that plaque nailed up there beside the bed. . . .)

In the years that followed Henry paid little attention to this second son. Where he had insisted on raising his firstborn to be as strong and self-sufficient as himself, he was content to let this second child—a large-eyed kid with his mother's pale skin and a look like his veins ran skim milk—spend his youth alone in a room next to his mother's, doing what-the-hell-ever it was that that sort of kid does alone in his room all day. (She looks at the plaque for a long time, twisting that book in her hands, then looks down at me. I see she's commencing to cry. . . .)

The two boys were twelve years apart and Henry saw no reason to try to bring them together. What was the sense? When the boy Lee was five and had his drippy nose in a book of nursery rhymes, Hank was seventeen and he and Ben's boy, Joe, were busy running that second-hand Henderson motorcycle into every ditch between the Snag in Wakonda and the Melody Ranch Dance Hall over in Eugene.

"Brothers? I mean, what's the sense? Why push it? Hank's got Joe Ben ifn he needs a brother; they always been like ham an' eggs and Joe's at the house most of the time anyhow, what with his daddy always hellin' around the country. An' little Leland Stanford, he's got his mama. . . ."

"But who," the loafers matching pennies in the Snag wondered, "has little Leland Stanford's mama got?" The sweet little spooky thing, living the best years of her life over there in that bear den across the river with an old fart twice her age, living there after she's sworn, time and again to everybody who'd stop and listen, that she was leaving for the East just as soon as little Leland was school age, and that was how long ago? ". . . so who does she have?" Boney Stokes shook his head slowly at Henry, the woes of all mankind marking his face. "I just am thinkin' of the girl, Henry; because able as you still are, you can't be the stud you once was—ain't you concerned for her, day in and day out alone over yonder?"

Henry leered, winked, grinned into his hand. "Why shoot, Boney. Who's to say whether I'm the stud of old or not?" Modest as a turkey gobbler. "Besides, some men are so wonderfully blest by nature that they don't need to prove theirselfs night after night; they're so fine-lookin' and so special, they can keep a woman pantin' with the pure mem'ry an' the wild hope that what has happened once is liable to happen again!"

And no other explanation for his young wife's fidelity ever penetrated the old man's cock-certainty. In spite of all the hints and innuendos he remained doggedly certain of her devotion to pure memory and wild hope for the fourteen years she lived in his wooden world. And even after. His veneer of vanity was not even scratched when she announced that she was leaving Oregon for a while to take Leland to one of the Eastern schools.

"It's for the kid she's doin' it," Henry told them. "For the little feller. He gets these sick spells the doctors here'bouts can't put their finger on the reason; maybe asthma. Doc reckons he'd feel better someplace drier so we'll give it a go. But her, no, don't fool yourself, it's tearing' the poor soul to pieces to leave her old man: cryin', carryin' on for days now. . . ." He dipped a dark brown thumb and finger into his snuff can and regarded the pinch with narrow eyes. "Carryin' on so about leavin' it makes my heart sore."

He situated the wad between his lower lip and gums, then glanced quickly up with a grin. "Yessir boys, some of us got it, and some don't."

(Still crying, reaches down and touches my puffed lip with a finger, then all of a sudden her head jerks back up to that plaque. Like something finally dawned on her. It was weird. She stopped crying just like that and shivered like a north wind hit her. She puts down the book, slow, reaches out and gets hold of the plaque; I know she can't pull it off on account of it's got two sixpenny nails in it. She quits trying. Then she gives a little high, quick laugh, tilting her head at the plaque like a bird: "If you were to come into my room—I'll put Leland in his playroom—do you think you would *still* be under its influence?" I look away from her and mumble something about not getting her drift. She gives me this kind of trapped, desperate grin and takes me by the little finger, like I was so light she could pick me right up by it. "I mean, if you came next door into the sanctuary of my world, where you can't look at it or it can't look at you—do you suppose you could?" I still give her this dumb look and ask suppose I could what? She just tilts her head toward the plaque and keeps smiling at me, then says, "Haven't you ever wondered about this monstrosity you've had hanging over your bed for sixteen years?" All the while pulling my finger. "Haven't you ever wondered about the *loneliness* it can cause?" I shake my head. "Well, you just come on into the next room with me and I'll explain it to you." And I remember thinking, why, by God, look here: she can lift me up by one finger after all. . . .)

"You don't reckon," Boney called haltingly as Henry walked toward the saloon door, "Henry, ah, you don't reckon, do you . . ." reluctantly, with an apologetic tone as though hating it that he'd been driven to asking—for his old friend's good, of course—to asking this painful question ". . . that her leavin' . . . could have anything to do with Hank joinin' the U. S. Armed Services when he did? I mean, her decidin' to *leave* when he decided to *join?*"

Henry paused, scratching at his nose. "Might be, Boney. Never can tell . . ." He pulled on his jacket, then jerked the zipper to his chin and flipped the collar. "Except she announced she was *leavin'* days before Hank had any notion a-tall about *joinin'*." His eyes flicked to Boney and the scurrilous grin snapped triumphant, like a rope jerked taut. "See you niggers around."

(And next door I remember thinking, She's right about that

plaque, too. It is nice to be out of sight of the godawful outfit. But I found that just being next door didn't make any difference about getting away from it. In fact, over in the next room, after she told me what she felt it was doing to me, was when I really began to see that plaque. With a pine wall in the way, I saw it—the yellow paint, the red lettering, and all the stuff underneath the red and yellow—clearer than ever before in my life. But by the time I noticed it, I guess it was too late not to. Just like by the time I noticed what that little trip next door had started—and if I was forced to mark a place where this whole business commenced, that's where I'd have to put it—it was way too late to stop it.)

It is a later spring, years now since chasing tricky grounders. The air is chilled and tasting of wild mint. The river runs dappled from the mountains, catching the fragrant blizzard blown from the blossoming blackberry vines that line its banks. The sun throbs off and on. Unruly mobs of young clouds gather in the bright blue sky, riotous and surging, full of threat that convinces no one. On the dock in front of the old house Henry helps Hank and Joe Ben load clothes, bundles, birdcages, hatboxes . . . "Crap enough to have a purty fair auction, wouldn't you say, Hank?"—cantankerous and jovial, becoming boyish with age as he had been once prematurely aged and grim.

"Sure, Henry."

"Son of a gun, look at the boogerin' stuff!"

The big, cumbersome, low-slung hauling boat rocks and heaves as it is loaded. The woman stands watching, thin bird hand resting on the shoulder of her twelve-year-old son, who leans against her hip, polishing his eyeglasses with the hem of her canary-yellow skirt. The three men work, carrying boxes from the house. The boat heaves, sinking deeper. The colors strike with stinging clarity, cutting the scene deep: blue sky, white clouds, blue water, white petals floating, and that sparkling patch of yellow . . .

"Crap an' corruption enough to stay a lifetime, let 'lone a few months." He turns to the woman. "What you takin' so much of your own stuff for, as well as the boy's? Travel fast and travel light, I allus say."

"It may take longer than I anticipated, getting him settled." Then adds quickly, "But I'll be back as soon as possible. I'll be back just as soon as possible."

"Oho." The old man winks at Joe Ben and Hank as they carry

a trunk along the dock. "See there, boys? See there. Can't go too long on san'wiches an' salad when she's used to steak an' potatoes."

Blue and white and yellow, and from that pole jutting out of the second-story window hangs the flag that signals the grocery truck what supplies to leave; a sewn black number on a tailgate banner, red. Blue and white and yellow and red.

The old man stalks back and forth alongside the boat, studying the packing job. "I guess it'll ride. Okay. Now then. Hank, whilst I'm driving them to the station you an' Joe Ben see to gettin' those parts we need for the donkey engine. You might have to take your cycle up to Newport and look around there, try Nyro Machine, they generally stock all the Skagit gear. I'll be back from the depot by dark; leave me a boat other side. Where's my hat at?"

Hank doesn't answer. He bends instead to check the river's level on the marker nailed to one of the pilings. The sun splashes silver on his pale metal hat. He straightens and pokes his fists in the pockets of his Levis and looks down river. "Just a minute . . ." The woman doesn't move; she is a yellow patch sewn against the blue river; old Henry is absorbed whittling a sliver to stick in a leak he has discovered in the sideboards of the boat; the gnomish Joe Ben has gone into the boathouse for a tarp to cover the boat's cargo in case those jostling clouds decide to take action.

"Just a minute . . ."

Only the boy's head comes around with a jerk, swinging the pale brown cowlick. Only the boy seems to hear Hank speak. He leans toward his big brother, glasses flashing the spring sun.

"Just a minute . . ."

"What?" the boy whispers.

". . . I guess I'll ride along, if it's no skin offn nobody."

"You?" the boy says. "You guess you'll—"

"Yeah, bub, I just guess I'll ride on along to town with you instead of comin' in later. My bike ain't runnin' to form anyhow—that sound all right, Henry?"

The hounds, suddenly aware of the activity on the dock, come pouring from beneath the house and charge barking down the plank walk. "Fine with me," the old man says and steps into the boat. The woman follows, her face lowered. Hank pushes the hounds away and steps in, almost overloading the boat. The boy still stands, with a look of disbelief, surrounded by dogs.

"Well, sonny?" Henry looks up, squinting against the sun behind the boy. "You comin' along or not? Dang that glare. Where the hell's that hat?"

The boy gets in and sits on a trunk near his mother.

"Yonder I see it, under that box. D'ya mind, Myra?"

The woman proffers the hat. Joe Ben brings out the folded gray square of canvas, and Hank takes it from him.

"What you say, Henry?" Hank asks, reaching for the oars. "You want me to take it across?"

The old man shakes his head and takes up the oars himself. Joe Ben unties the rope and, bracing himself against a piling, shoves the boat away from him into the current. "See you people later. G'by, Myra. G'by, Lee, hang tough." Henry cranes his head around for a sight on the landing at the garage across and commences to pull with a steady, measured strength, green eyes shaded beneath the brim of the tin hat.

The blossom-covered surface of the river is smooth, stretched taut from bank to bank like a polka-dotted fabric. The prow of the boat rips a passage through with a sizzling hiss. The woman keeps her eyes closed, withdrawn into some vague half-sleep, as though fighting the pain of a headache. Henry rows steadily. Hank looks off down river where fishducks are slapping the water with beaded wings. Little Lee squirms nervously atop his perch on the trunk at the back of the boat.

"Well now,"—old Henry spaces his words between oar strokes. "Well now, Leland"—in a detached, remote, inviolable voice—"I'm sorry you think you need"—cords snapping in his neck as he leans backward with the pull—"need a back East schooling . . . but that's the long and short of it, I reckon . . . this ain't no easy row to hoe out here . . . specially if you ain't allus feeling up to snuff . . . and some just ain't equal to it. . . . But it's okeedoke . . . I want you to do proud back there . . ." *A litany spoken over me, Lee thinks later, listened to only for the rhythm, a chant in a primitive dialect, an incantation perpetrating a spell; anesthetized time; nothing moves and everything is at once. He thinks one time, years later.* ". . . yes, do yourself and all of us proud . . ." (Now it's done, Hank thought. Then. Taking them across to the train. Now it's finished, and I won't ever see no more of her again.) ". . . an', well, when you get stronger . . ." (I was right about not seeing her no more . . .) *A litany, chanted over me . . .* (I was right about that much—) They row through the glittering water. And reflections swirling gently among the flower petals. Jonas rows alongside, muffled from the neck down in green fog: *You have to know.* Lee meets himself coming back across twelve years after with twelve years of decay penciled on his pale face, and translucent hands cupping a vial of poison for Brother Hank. . . . *or, more aptly, like a spell.* . . . (But I was wrong about it being finished. Dead wrong.) *You have to know there is no profit and all our labor avoideth naught.* Jonas pulls, straining at the fog. Joe Ben goes into a state park with a brush knife and an angel's face, seeking freedom. Hank crawls through a tunnel of blackberry vines, seeking thorny imprisonment. The arm twists and slowly untwists. The logger sitting in the mud calls curses across the water. "I'm hollowed out with loneliness," the woman cries. The water moves. The boat moves with measured heaves. Rain begins to fall suddenly; the wink of a million white eyes on the water. Hank looks up, intending to offer the woman his hat to protect her, but she has drawn a quilt over her dark hair against the rain. The red and yellow and blue patchwork shape heaves softly up and down, tossed by waves the boat does not feel. Hank shrugs and closes his mouth. He spreads out the tarp and turns to look down river again, but his eyes connect with the boy's, locking there finally.

For long seconds the two stare at each other.

Hank is the first to break the painful current of the stare. Dropping his eyes, he grins warmly and attempts to pass off the tension by reaching out to playfully squeeze the boy's kneebone. "What ya say, bub? You going to like New York for a home? All them . . . museums and galleries and that sort of thing? All them cute little college mice after you, you being such a big stud logger from the north woods?"

"Mmm, wait, I—"

Henry laughs. "That's right, Leland"—pulling steadily—"that's how I got your mama . . . them Eastern girls just go all to pieces . . . at the sight of one of us big good-lookin' lumberjacks . . . just you ask her if that ain't so."

"Mm. Oh, I—" (*Just you ask her. Just you ask her . . .*)

The boy's head goes back, mouth opening.

"What's the trouble, son?"

"Oh . . . I . . . Mmm—" (*The taunt was wordlessly repeated to every ear but the old man's: "Just you ask her"—an echoing litany that became a spell.*)

"I ask ya, what's the trouble?" Henry stops rowing. "You feeling sick again? The sinus trouble?"

The boy's hand clutches his lips, to try to control his voice, mangling the words with his fingers. He shakes his head, making a humming sound through his fingers.

"No? Maybe—maybe, then, it's the boat rockin'. You get hold of something to make you sick this morning?"

He doesn't see the tears until the boy's face comes forward again. The boy appears not to have heard the old man. Henry shakes his head. "Must of been somethin' godawful rich to make you so sick."

The boy isn't looking at Henry. He is glaring at his brother. He thinks the words have come from Hank. "You . . . just . . . wait," he says, squeezing out the threat. "Mmm. Mm boy, Hank, someday you'll get it for what you—"

"Me? *Me?*" Hank erupts, twisting in his seat. "You're lucky I don't bust your scrawny little *neck!* Because let me tell you, bub—"

"You just wait till—"

"—if you wasn't a kid and I found out what you'd been—"

"—till I'm a big guy!"

"—found about what a *low*down, crummy—in fact, I might even of gone back like she—"

"—just wait till I'm big enough to—"

"—but you'd just pull the same crummy—"

"*What!*" Old Henry silences the outburst. "In God's *creation!* Are you two *talking* about!"

The brothers look at the bottom of the boat. The hump of colored quilt is very still. Finally Hank laughs. "Ah, some little business me an' the kid had. No big deal, right, bub?"

Silence forces the boy to nod weakly. Old Henry takes up the oars again, apparently satisfied, and rows on; Hank mumbles that them prone to gettin' seasick ought to know better'n eat rich foods before getting into a boat. The boy controls his tears. He clamps his jaw and turns pompously to look off into the water, after whispering, "You, . . . " one more time, indicating with crossed arms that he has said all he intends to say on the subject. "Yeah . . . just . . . you . . . wait."

And remains so silent all the rest of the boat ride and car trip on in to the Wakonda station—even while Hank is offering comical good-bys and good wishes to him and his mother at the train—remains so silent, so dramatically grim and brooding and vengeful, that it would seem he, not his older brother, were the one waiting.

And whether Lee consciously thought about it or not, he waited twelve years—before a postcard arrived from Joe Ben Stamper in Wakonda, Oregon, saying that old Henry was out of commission with a bad arm and leg and plenty old anyhow and the logging operation was in a kind of tight and they needed another man up in the woods to help them meet a contract deadline—another Stamper, natch, to keep them clear of the union—so since you're the only footloose relative left not already working for us, what you say, Lee? If you think you're equal to it, we could sure use another jack . . .

And penciled at the bottom, in a thicker, stronger hand: *You should be a big enough guy now, bub.*

*I* often feel it would be nice to have a pitchman handy to push the product. A winking, grinning, vegetable-slicing salesman, a scrawny State Fair con artist with a throat mike hung over his beckoning Adam's apple, to lean from his booth, white cuffs rolled from hypnotic long-fingered hands, to con the attention and ballyhoo the passing eyes: "Lookee lookee look! At this little Wonder of the Everyday World, fellas and gals. A viz-yoo-al rarity, I'm certain you'll agree. Tilt it, tip it, peer through it from any position . . . and your gaze you'll notice comes out someplace else. Seenow: the spheres lie concentrically one inside the other like diminishing glass balls becoming so minute! . . . you cannot perceive the smallest without the aid of scientific devices. Yessir, a real rarity, buddies, a ab-so-lute-ly unique article I'm positive you'll agree. . . ."

Yet, all up and down the West Coast, there are little towns much like Wakonda. Up as far as Victoria and down as far as Eureka. Towns dependent on what they are able to wrest from the sea in front of them and from the mountains behind, trapped between both. Towns all hamstrung by geographic economies, by rubber-stamp mayors and chambers of commerce, by quagmire time . . . canneries all peeling dollar-a-quart Army surplus paint, mills all sprouting moss between curling shingles . . . all so nearly alike that they might be nested one inside the other like hollow toys. Wiring all corroding, machinery all decaying. People all forever complaining about tough times and trouble, about bad work and worse pay, about cold winds blowing and colder winters coming . . .

There will be a small scatter of boxlike dwellings somewhere near a mill, usually on a river, and a cannery on the docks, needing a new floor. The main street is a stripe of wet asphalt smeared with barroom neon. If there is a stoplight, it is more a status symbol than a safety precaution . . . *Traffic Commissioner at the City Council:* "Those boys up there't Nahalem got *two* stoplights! I can't see no reason we don't even have one. The trouble with this town, by Gawd, is not enough Civic Pride."

That's the trouble as he sees it.

44

There is a movie-show house, open Thurs., Fri. & Sat. Nites, located next door to a laundry, both establishments owned by the same sallow and somber businessman. The theater marquee reads: THE GUNS OF NAVARONE G PECK & THREE SHIRTS 99¢ THIS WEAK ONLY."

According to this bleached citizen the trouble is not enough E's.

Across the street, behind windows filled with curl-cornered photographs of retouched homes and farmhouses, the Real Estate Man sits with a lapful of white pine shavings . . . The bald brother-in-law of the sad-eyed movie-laundry magnate, this Real Estate Man is known as a shrewd cooky with a mortgage and a hotwire speaker at the Tuesday Jaycee luncheons: "She's a comin' area, boys, she's a sleepin' giant. We had some trouble, sure. Still have, because of eight hard years under the administration of that tight-fisted Army bastard in the White House, but now we're out of the woods, we're roundin' the turn!"

And on his desk his collection of free-to-the-customer statues, little white pine replicas of Johnny Redfeather whittled by the Real Estate Man's own skilled fingers, stand like a stalwart Community Chest army and turn their wooden eyes out the window down a long row of empty storefronts. Where FOR RENT signs on the doors make forlorn appeals for someone to come back and take the whitewash from the windows and put it back on the walls, come back and fill the shelves with bright tin rows of deviled meat and spiced beans, fill the glass-topped candy counter with cartons of Day's Work, Copenhagen, Skol, Climax; fill the benches around the woodstove with the booming throng of bearded, steaming, calk-booted men who used to—a while back, three or four decades back—pay three or four times the city price for a dozen eggs; men who dealt only in paper money because pants pockets weren't mended to hold anything as measly as a two-bit piece. FOR RENT, FOR SALE, FOR LEASE say the signs on the doors, "Prosperity and New Frontiers," says the Real Estate Hotwire over a glass of beer. The shrewd cooky whose only deal since Founder's Day involved his sister's flour-faced husband and a little rundown bankrupt movie-show house next to the laundry. "You damn betcha. Smooth slidin' from here on. Our only trouble is we have just suffered a minor recession under the regime of that general!"

But the citizens in Wakonda begin to disagree—toward agreement. The union members at first contend: "The trouble ain't administration, it's automation. Homelite saws, one-man yarders, mobile donkeys—why *half* the men can cut *twice* the trees. The solution is simple: the wood-worker's got to have the six-hour day, just like the shingle-weavers've got. Boys, give us the Six-Hour Day with Eight-Hour Pay, and I tell you we'll put *all* our members to cuttin' twice the trees!"

And all the members holler and whistle and stamp their agreement, even though they know that later, in the bar after the meeting, some wet blanket will always recall that "the trouble is we ain't got twice the trees any more; some snake in the grass chopped *down* a big bunch over the last fifty or so years."

"No! No!" says the Real Estate Man. "What's wrong isn't the lack of timber—it is a lack of *Goals!*"

"Perhaps," says the Reverend Brother Walker of the Church of God and Metaphysical Science, "it is a lack of God." He takes a calculated sip of his beer before he goes on. "Our present spiritual trouble is certainly greater than our economic trouble."

"Certainly! Far be it from me to de-emphasize *that*, but—"

"But what Mr. Loop means, Brother Walker, is a man needs a little meat and taters to keep his morale up."

"Man's got to live, Brother."

"Yes, but 'not by bread alone,' remember?"

"Certainly! But not, by God, just by God alone neither."

"And I say if we ain't got the timber to cut—"

"There's wood and aplenty! Ain't Hank Stamper cuttin' full time with *his* show? Ain't he? Huh?"

They all take a thoughtful drink.

"So the trouble ain't lack of timber . . ."

"Nope. No siree . . ."

They had been drinking and discussing since early afternoon at the huge oval table traditionally reserved for such caucuses, and, while they formed no official organization, this casual group of eight or ten citizens, they were nevertheless recognized as the ruling body of the town's opinion and their decisions were as sanctified as the hall where they met.

"Innerestin' point, you know—about Hank Stamper?"

This hall, the Snag Saloon, is a few doors down from the movie-show house and across the street from the grange hall. Its interior is no more out of the ordinary than its patrons—the booths and stools are replicas of similar settings in similar logging-town bars—but its streetfront is spectacular in the extreme. The wide front window contains an assortment of neon signs that have been collected from the fronts of numerous competing bars that Teddy has forced out of business over the years, and when the dusk falls and Teddy throws the switch under his bar, the sudden effect on the unsuspecting drinker is sometimes so terrifying that the crash of a dropped glass accompanies the crash of light. The neons fill the front of the bar with a shifting dance of color. The colors flicker and twist, crowding for window space, overlapping and intertwining and hissing like electronic snakes. Twisting and untwisting. So bright and so clashing are the many signs that on a dark night their effect is almost audible. On a dark, wet night they create an earsplitting din. Listen: Next to the door a fire-crimson signs shrills out, *Red Dragon*; a green and yellow blinker just below this one insists on *The Nite Cap* and flashes a martini glass with a cherry in it; beside this is a huge orange creation bellowing COME AN' GIT IT!; and beside this *The Bullskinner* shoots a darting red arrow to the barbershop next door. *The Gull* and the *Black Kat* scream back and forth at each other in discordant reds greens. *The Alibi* and the *Crab Pot* and the *Wakonda House* clash together. All the beer companies shout competing slogans: *It's the water* . . . and *Where there's life* . . . and *Mabel, Black Label* . . .

Yet, The Snag, which boasts a score of banners, has no sign of its own. Years ago the words *Snag Saloon & Grill* had been painted onto the greened glass of the windows, but as Teddy began buying other bars and closing them, he scraped off more and more of the green to make room for the captured neons which he flaunted like enemy scalps. On a clear day, when the neons are off, a man standing close might make out the dim edges of a few letters on the glass, but nothing you could really call a name. And on a dark night, when the neons are on, they overlap too much for any one to stand out.

There is one sign, however, that is afforded individual distinction; this is not an electric display but an elaborately scrolled shingle hanging alone by two eyescrews above the door. Acquired not by his usual financial onslaught on competition but by a past marriage that lasted only four months, this practically unnoticed sign is Teddy's favorite above all the blarers and blinkers; in a calm and tasteful blue this obscure little sign reminds all the others to "*Remember . . . One Drink Is Too Many. WCTU.*"

A short, plump polyp of man in a land of rangy loggers, Teddy is appeased by his collection of signs. Napoleon needed no elevator

shoes to make him as big as the next man: he had a chestful of
medals. It was these symbols of success that proved his size. Yes,
wearing his medals he could remain silent while the brutes whined
about their troubles . . .

"Teddybear—another round."

. . . and slobbered in their glasses . . .

"Teddy?"

. . . and died of slow, brute fear . . .

"Teddy! Damn it, boy, let's come to life."

"Yes, sir." He was jarred from his thoughts. "Oh, yes, sir, beer?"
"Christ yes, beer." "Coming right up, sir. . . ." Standing at the end
of the bar, hearing the barroom chatter through the haze of light,
he could become completely removed from their crude, bellowing
world. Now, in a great fluster, he rushed back and forth behind the
bar, his aplomb shattered. His fat fingers shook as he gathered a
supply of glasses. "Be right with you." He hustled their order to the
table with a great show of haste to make up for the delay. But they
had already returned to their discussion of the local trouble, ignoring
him. Sure. Already the big idiots had to ignore him. They were afraid
to look too close. It is threatening to perceive superiority in someone
so much—

"Teddy!"

"Yes sir. I forgot; you said light? I'll change it just as soon as we
get the rest of these glasses . . ."

But the man was already drinking his beer. Teddy moved back
behind his bar, crepe-soled and spectral and ignored.

The electrified screen door at the front of the bar opened, and
through the sunny arch of glass came another figure—larger, older,
clumping loudly past in calked boots—yet a figure somehow as spectral as Teddy. This was the hermit of the area, a heavy-bearded gray
man known only as "that old wino boltcutter from someplace out
the South Fork." Once a topnotch rigger, he was now so old and
crippled he was reduced to making a living driving a broken-springed
pick-up into the logged-over slopes around the area, where he cut
down cedar snags one or two days a week and split them into shinglebolts. These he sold to the shingle mill on the other side of town
at ten cents a bolt. A great comedown, rigger to boltcutter. And the
ignominy of this comedown had apparently rotted away most of
that apparatus which projects a man's presence; he moved past the
eye like something shrouded in fog, and after he had passed, no one

could agree for certain on his description or even, for certain, on his existence. Yet, because he was so seldom seen at the Snag (even though he drove right past it at least once a week) his presence could not be ignored as could Teddy's. He was too much a rarity, and Teddy was only a fixture. He paused for a moment to listen to the men's talk before going to the bar. Under his scrutiny the conversation faltered, faded, and died out completely. Then he snuffed loudly in his beard and moved away without speaking.

He had his own ideas about what the trouble was.

The discussion didn't resume until the old man had purchased a large glass of red wine from Teddy and gimped his way on back to the gloomy rear of the bar.

"Poor old duffer," the Real Estate Man managed, the first to overcome the momentary feeling of nervousness that had descended on the table.

"Yeah," said the logger in the beaten gray hat.

"That stuff you hear about him is the real McCoy, you know."

"Wine?"

"Cheap port. I hear tell he gets it from Stokes by the case, a case a week."

"Too bad," said the movie-laundry owner.

"Tsk, tsk," said Brother Walker. And, as he had learned the comment from *Joe Palooka*, it came out 'tisk tisk," the way he assumed it was pronounced.

"Yeah. Too damn bad."

"Too damn many years in the woods for an old fellow; it's a shame."

"Shame?" said the logger. "It's a fuckin' *crime*, is what it is, pardon me, Brother Walker, but I feel strongly about it." Then, moved to even greater passion and recalling his interrupted argument, he slammed his black-fuzzed fist down on the table. "But it *is* a fuckin' crime! And a *sin!* That a poor old jack like him should hafta—Listen now: pensions and guaranteed annual wage, ain't that what Floyd Evenwrite been preachin' about for nearly two years?"

"That's right, that is the truth."

They were getting back in gear again.

"The *trouble* with this town is we can't get behind the very organization that is built to help us: the *union!*"

"My God; ain't Floyd been *sayin'* so? He says Jonathan Bailey

Draeger says that Wakonda is *years* behind the other woods towns. And that has become my thinking exactly."

"And that sort of thinkin' brings us right back to you-know-who and his whole hardnosed brood!"

"Right! Exactly!"

The man in the hat slammed the table again. "A shame!"

"And as much as I personally like an' admire Hank and his folks —Christ, didn't we grow up together?—I for one am of the opinion that right there is where our issue is, ifn you got to aim a gun some-place—right out there at that house, in my opinion."

"Amen, brother."

"Goddam right amen! Now you all *look*." Startled again by the violence of this order, Teddy raises his eyes. "Ifn you got to point a finger, then right *that* way is the way you point it!"

Looking through the glass he is polishing, Teddy sees the finger spring thrusting from the greasy, black-fuzzed fist.

"Right out at that goddamned house!"

. . . the jukebox whirs, bubbles, pulsing color. The electric screen buzzes. The men breathe softly together. The finger, a knuckled iron rod there in the slanting late-afternoon sun, swings slowly to fix like a compass needle. The house. Brute, monolithic structure, thick now with the light of coming dawn and noisy already with the prepara-tions for breakfast . . .

"Yeah, you may be right, Henderson."

"Damn right I'm right! If you want my considered opinion, there's where your trouble is!"

Lights and shouts pouring from the kitchen window; laughter, curses. "Wake it an' shake it, boys. The ol' man's already out ahead of ya, old an' crippled as he is." And the ringing smell of frying sausages. This is Hank's bell. This is the way he likes it. This is Hank's bell ringing.

And from behind his bar, standing out of the sun, Teddy watches the men and listens to their logic and is secretly certain that the trouble is not financial—just now, during that idiotic discussion on the lack of working capital, he'd brought in close to twelve dollars, and in *broad daylight*—and also seriously doubts that it could all be laid at the doorstep of that Stamper house. No, it is another trouble. In his considered opinion . . .

"Say, by the way, Henderson, your mentioning Floyd brings to mind: I haven't seen him in a good day or so."

West of the house, in her shack on the mudflats, Indian Jenny rises from her cot and dons a rose-red dress turned mudflat brown, and begins to wonder whom to blame for the sorry state of her life and why can't she ever find her goddam Saint Christopher medal? South, Jonathan Bailey Draeger watches the road ahead for a place to spend the night before continuing on to Oregon. East, a postman tries to interpret the penciled scrawl of a threepenny postcard's address and almost gives up . . .

"Yeah, where is Evenwrite?"

"Up north, in Portland. Tryin' to get the goods once an' for all on this *very subject* we been discussing, by God . . ."

The fist closes, but the finger still points. The old house hunches over breakfast, still noisy and bustly, and ignorant of the fingers beginning to swing from all around the country in a polarization of blame, beginning to converge like points on a constricting circle. . . .

Up North, in Portland, Floyd Evenwrite sat like a rubber toy in a forty-dollar suit, stiff and inscrutable and gas-filled. He had just finished plowing laboriously through a pile of yellow paper. The papers, once neat and crisp, lay on the table in front of him like a pile of limp fallen leaves. You could see the sweat on the papers. His hands always sweated a lot when he used them for anything besides manual labor. Matter of fact, he couldn't remember for sure that they used to sweat at all. And now, as he rubbed his forehead and smallish red nose, they barely felt like his own. They felt naked, and nervous, and like somebody else's hands. No calluses was how come. Funny. You wouldn't think a man could get so attached to something like calluses, would you? Maybe they're like cork boots; with corks it don't make no matter *how long* since you quit wearing 'em because once you been used to going around *with* 'em, then the ground underfoot is always gonna seem slippery and strange *without*—though you maybe been wearing oxfords for years and years.

Finished with his facial rub, he sat for a moment without moving and let his eyes remain closed. His eyes were tired. And his back was tired. In fact all the hell over he was tired. But it had been worth it. He knew he'd made a good impression on the flunky. And he was pleased by the report; it proved conclusively that the Stamper mills were in absolute *fact*, by Jesus, contracted to supply Wakonda Pacific with lumber. No damn wonder old man Jerome or the rest of the WP bunch hadn't been sweating the month-long walkout. The boys could strike till hell froze shut and it wouldn't be hurting profits. Not as long as Stamper and his scabby kind were cutting for them! It was even worse than he'd figured. He'd figured Jerome had contacted Stamper and maybe made a deal to buy some logs later on to make up for the setback suffered during the strike. He'd suspicioned this when he saw how hot and heavy the Stampers were hitting it. And it had griped his ass anyhow, them working while the rest of the town laid off. So he'd written Jonathan Draeger, and Draeger had put this union detective to researching the suspicion. And Christ, what that research had turned up: since back as far as August, Stamper'd been contracted to WP, cutting and storing the booms at his place so nobody'd know. So them sonsabitches across the river there were not only *working*, business as *usual* while the rest of the town sweated a strike, they'd been doing twice, maybe *three goddam times* as much business as usual!

His eyes opened with a snap. He scooped up the untidy bundle of papers and clapped them in a manila folder. "This oughta do it," he said, nodding at the thin flunky who had sat across the table from him, drumming his fingers nervously, all the while Floyd had studied the report. The man seemed reluctant for Floyd to leave. "Ah—you used to go to school with Hank Stamper, I heard," he said, in a voice too friendly for Floyd's taste.

"You heard wrong," Floyd replied coldly, refusing to look at the man. He picked up a can of beer in his other hand and took a drink from it. He knew the man had been watching him. He knew his every twitch and belch were being recorded by this little, thin-shouldered information flunky and would eventually get back to Mr. Draeger himself; this report, different as it was, showed that. It was thorough to a gnat's eyelash. His report to Draeger would likely be just as thorough. Floyd didn't like the man's little bootlicking grin and he ached to bring his fist hammering down on that nervous handful of fingers. He hated it that this sort of man had to be associated with the union at all. And when he'd made an impression on the boys at the *top*, Floyd promised himself he'd see to getting shut of this sniveling little snake. But if you aim to impress the ones on top, you damn sure have to impress the ones on the bottom. So he kept his face impassive and his spine stiff and forced himself to take another sip of the flat beer.

"Least that's what I been told about you," the man went on.

Evenwrite lifted the veined bumps of his eyes to the wheedling voice and tried to gauge the success of his visit. He had personally driven all the way from Wakonda to get this report. He'd wanted to test himself on this man before dealing directly with Draeger. It had taken him nearly an hour to find the flunky's home in Portland's confusing street system. He'd been in the city only once before, and he'd been so furious and outraged then that he could remember it only as a red blur. That was the time his teammates at Florence had taken a collection to pay his bus fare to the Shrine All-State Game, giving him the ticket and consoling him, "You shoulda been picked, Floyd. You was a better fullback. You was screwed."

That screwing—and the resulting charity—had been brought back by the sight of the river and the lights of Portland, and the red blur as well. He'd become lost time and again, trying to follow the written directions through this blur. And he'd had no time to stop for supper. And the stale beer burned his guts. And his eyes stung; it had been a struggle camouflaging his shamefully slow reading speed by making it seem instead to be shrewd caution. And his back hurt from sitting so straight to keep his belly in. But looking now at the man's face, he decided he'd handled it. He could tell the man was impressed by this first encounter with the District Coordinator from Wakonda. Impressed and cowed just enough. Deliberately Floyd put his beer can back on the table and wiped his hand on his thigh.

"No," he said. "That ain't—isn't exactly correct." He spoke with distinguished resonance; someday he would speak to a press conference this way. "No, I went to high school at Florence, a town about ten miles south of Wakonda. I didn't move to Wakonda till *after* high school. What you probably heard"—he paused, furrowing his brow to remember—"is we both played offensive fullback and defensive ends on our . . . respective teams, and all four years played right across from each other. Even at the Shrine All-State game."

That was a little risky, but he doubted if the flunky was acquainted enough with sports to realize that he could not possibly have made All-State if Hank had, both being from the same district. He took a quick look at his watch, then stood up. "Well, I got a long drive." The union fink came off his stool by the sink and extended his hand. Evenwrite, who had once been compelled to run fifty yards down a hill to wash his paw in a creek before a visiting union dignitary would deign to touch it, now looked at the flunky's hand as though he saw bugs between the fingers. "You done real good," he said, then left the

house. Outside he buttoned the top button of his trousers and complimented himself: pretty slick, that maneuver, pretty bygod smooth—
leaving the little runt standing there with his paw stuck out and his
eyes batting. Yep, he'd handled the whole business pretty smooth.
Impression is the ticket. Teach 'em respect; impress 'em; show 'em
you're just as good, just as big as they are. Bigger!

But when he paused to rub his eyes again before getting into his
car, his hand felt very small and limp. And stranger than ever. The
fingers not his own. Somebody else's. They fumble after the car keys,
nervously. The chain snaps, spraying keys into the streetlight. Jenny
searches the shelves for her Saint Christopher. Gives up and instead
mixes herself a drink, then goes to sit and look out through the spider-
web that laces her little shack's lone window. Squinting, she studies
the sky. A full moon leans desperately against the landward rush of
small clouds. She watches, sighing. The screen buzzes in the afternoon. Someone offers a dime to the bubbling jukebox. Hank Snow
comes highballing out:

> Mr. Engineer, take that throttle in hand
> 'Cause this rattler's the fastest in the
>     southern land.
> Keep movin' on. . . .

The old boltcutter props the rim of his glass of port against his lower
lip and tips in the wine, watching grayly from the dusty gloom. The
postman crosses a bright green lawn in New Haven, holding the
card. The old house, shimmering and tiny under the dawn sky, like
a pebble beneath an abalone shell, opens to emit two figures in
logging garb.

"He can raise one hell of a fuss for an invalid," Hank said, shaking
his head.

"Invalid? Why, you'd have to cut off both legs to invalid *him!*"
Joe Ben laughed, delighted by the stamina the old man had shown in
his breakfast antics. "Oh yeah, Henry ain't one to let a bad hand
make him turn in his chips. A bad hand! Hey, how 'bout that? Two
levels. I mean, a hand of cards an' then, too, him with his arm in
a cast?"

"You got a great future in TV comedy," Hank said halfheartedly.
"But, you know, Joby? I truly am surprised at the hole it's left in
the show, his being laid up. Damned if it doesn't look like we're

gonna have to find somebody to come in to help us make that quota. I sure don't know who, though."

"Don't you?" Joe asked.

"No . . ." Hank said.

"Don't you, now?"

Hank knew Joe was grinning at him, but he continued on down toward the dock, not looking at his little banty-legged cousin. "I'm havin' Viv call everybody together for a meeting—to bring 'em up to date, I told her. I guess I'll have to, too. Some, anyhow. But even if they knew the whole score I still don't know of one who'd come to work that ain't already workin'."

"You don't?" Joe asked. Joe had known from the beginning where the conversation was leading, and enjoyed teasing Hank about the roundabout route he was taking getting there. "You can't think of a solitary soul, huh? Sonofagun."

Hank still pretended to miss the taunt. "Oh, I suppose I'll come up with some shirttail kin," he said finally, as though the subject were closed for the time. "It'll just take some time and thought."

"Yeah," Joe said, "I suppose it will." Then added, with as much innocence as he could muster, "Considerin' how much time an' thought it took comin' up with a legitimate reason to need this particular shirttail."

He danced nimbly away from Hank down the dock, waving his metal hat in the early-morning light and hooting his amusement.

In the Snag the jukebox continues barrel-assing across the country-side:

> *I'm movin' on,*
> *Just hear my song. . . .*

Floyd gets his car started and begins trying to retrace his path back out of Portland. The postman mounts the steps. Draeger finds a motel and in the office, under a softly fluttering fluorescent lamp, shakes his head and politely refuses the motel manager's offer to buy him a drink.

"I used to do some log work myself, y'know," the manager had mentioned as soon as he found out who Draeger was.

"I'm sorry, but no go on the drink," Draeger said again. "I've a meeting tomorrow to prepare for. But thanks all the same. It's been pleasant talking with you. Good night."

Outside in the buzzing glare of the neon—FREE TV POOL HEATED

ELECTRIC BLANKET—he searched through his pockets sluggishly. Like Floyd, he was tired. He'd met with the owners of Wakonda Pacific Lumber at Sacramento that morning, then got right on the road; he planned to spend a few days in Red Bluff sitting in on negotiations with a grievance committee over from Susanville, then, unless matters improved, continue on up north to look into this Wakonda tie-up. And some logger-turned-farmer-turned-motelman wanted to buy him a drink. Jesus Christ!

He finally found what he was searching for, a small notebook with an automatic pencil clipped to his inside coat pocket. He took it out, flipped through the pages, and in the heartbeat red of the neon wrote, "Men are forever eager to press drink upon those they consider their superiors, hoping thereby to eliminate that distinction between them."

The note-taking habit was a carry-over from his college days, when he had A'd all tests by being the most ready. He read the phrase over and smiled approvingly. He had been collecting such aphorisms for years now, and dreamed of some day compiling them into a book of essays. But even if the dream failed to come off, the little phrases came in quite handy in his work, little notes taken daily in the lesson of life.

Should a test ever present itself, he would be ready. . . .

The old house falls quiet now, with breakfast over. The kids still aren't up. Old Henry has labored, exhausted but satisfied, back up the stairs to bed. The dogs have eaten and are asleep. Viv throws the coffee grounds out the back door into the rhododendron bed, as the sun is just chalking the tops of the firs back up in the hills. . . .

The postman reaches to drop his card in the mail slot. Floyd Evenwrite finally finds the highway out and begins looking for a bar. Draeger sits on the motel bed and notes the first sign of athlete's foot between the third and fourth toes of his right foot; already, and not even out of California. At the window of her one-room shack Indian Jenny sips her bourbon and snuff and becomes more interested in the moonlit march of clouds. They come trooping in from the sea in mighty masculine columns, and, squinting, she leans bulkily forward to try to make out the half-remembered faces of this army—handsome, handsome and tall they were, an army handsome and tall and white as snow, stretching back over the horizon of her memory. "Was a goddam span of 'em," she recalled with wistful pride and mixed herself another spoonful of snuff in a glass of warm whisky, the better to review the army's passing. Which one was the tallest, among these soldiers of mist? Which one was the handsomest? the wildest? the fastest? Which soldier of them all had she liked the best? Of course, all, one-an-everyone-all they was good men, and she'd refund the two dollars *doublemoneyback* to any man jack of that throng just to be able to host him again this minute—but, just for fun, which one of all that army had she liked the *very* best?

. . . and, with this just-for-fun contest, begins springing on herself an old, old trap.

While Jonathan Bailey Draeger, comfortable under his electric blanket watching an old Bette Davis movie on his free TV, takes from the nightstand beside his bed the little notebook and adds to his last note: "And women, when confronted by superiors, substitute for drink the crippling liquor of their sex."

While Floyd Evenwrite jumps from his car and rubber-balls his grumpy way across the parking apron toward the door of a roadside bar on the outskirts of Portland, mad at everything in sight. While the old wino boltcutter listens to the citizens in the Snag talk about tough times and trouble. And the electric screen pops and snaps at hapless flies. And Hank Snow presses loudly onward:

> *Fireman, shovel that coal,*
> *Let this rattler roll,*
> *'Cause I'm movin' on.*

And, East, the mailman drops the card and is answered by a blast that lifts him like a cork before a wave and tosses him all the way back to the middle of the lawn.

"Hoo-*what!*"

After a timeless period of severed consciousness—while his head cleared, while the lawn bucked and tossed, rippled and glittered like a square of rolling emerald sea—the mailman perceived a far-off ringing. This ringing gradually filled the fissure torn in his senses. Numbly he rose to his hands and knees and watched time ticking red off the end of his bloodied nose. He remained all-foured in this bemused state, aware only of his bleeding nose and the shatters of demolished windows that lay about him, until a crackling of walked-on glass from the cottage porch brought him scrambling to his feet in a wide-eyed fury.

"What!" he demanded. "What the everloving devil"—swinging

about, holding his bag clutched tight over his fly in the event of a recurrence of the eruption—"is going on here, you!" Thin, lint-filled smoke parted momentarily to emit a tall young man with a face covered with soot and flecks of tobacco clinging like pockmarks. The mailman watched the scorched apparition swing its head to meet its interrogator's eyes and lick blackened lips through the singed remnants of a beard. The face was at first blank, stunned, then the features clicked abruptly into positions intended to convey the pretentious insolence of a fop; this affected expression of amused arrogance and disdain was made even more phony by the comically blackened face, so obviously phony that it appeared to be more a caricature of contempt than an affectation—like a mime's expression. Yet there was something about the very falseness of the attitude—perhaps the acknowledged falseness—that vastly increased its stinging effect. The mailman began again to protest—"I mean just what do you think you're *doing*, you . . ."—but was so enraged by the taunting expression that his anger sputtered away to frustration. They stood facing each other another few moments, then the scorched mask closed its lashless eyelids, as though it had seen enough of irate federal employees, and informed the mailman haughtily, "I *think*—I'm attempting to kill myself, thank you; but I'm not quite sure I've found exactly the right method. Now, if you will excuse me a moment, I'll have another go."

Then pompously—and still making the sharpness of his contempt somehow explicit in his mockery of himself—the young man turned and walked back across the porch, into the smoking house. Leaving the mailman standing in front of the steps, feeling strangely puzzled and more disoriented than he had been since rising from the lawn. Which reels and rolls, and glitters in the sun . . .

The jukebox bubbles and throbs. The clouds troop past. Draeger slips off to dream of a labeled world. Teddy studies fear through a polished shot glass. Evenwrite pushes through the door of the Bigtime Bar and Aristocratic Cuisine, planning to have a drink or two to unkink the kinks he picked up sitting in that goddam straightback chair reading that goddam meticulous report that little spy had compiled—hard to fit the sort of citified finks like him, or the sort of red tape that made this sort of report necessary, in with the picture of honest-to-god men who had started the whole labor game, the good old Wobs, the Wobblies, but it looked like that's what it'd come to so that's how you gotta play it—anyhow . . . aiming to drink, unkink, unwind and unlimber over a couple beers, and to once more prove to any one of these big-city bigasses in here who might doubt it, that Floyd Evenwrite, ex-bushler and chokersetter from the little pissant town of Florence, was just as goddam good as anybody else whateverthefuck size of the city they come from! "Barkeep!" He thumps the bartop with both balled fists for service. "Bring 'em on an' keep 'em comin'!"

And to prove to himself that these balled and sweating hands are still the fists they always were.

At the house the relatives begin to arrive for the meeting, and Hank slips away for a drink—not to unlimber, but to fortify himself for another round. At the mudflats clouds line up grandly between moon and sea, and Indian Jenny's contest to pick from her populous past the man she had liked very best is cut off in mid-reverie by the appearance of an intruder memory in the ranks: old Henry Stamper, his hands in his mackinaw pockets and his stubborn green eyes mocking her from the face he wore thirty years ago—"Bastid!"—stubborn, mocking and disdainful of Jenny's wares since that day she set up shop on the clamflats so long back. She saw his wink again, and heard his snicker, and that haunting whisper, "Y'know what I think?" Out of the half-dozen men who had stood at her front stoop making mumbled wisecracks thirty years ago her obsidian eyes had been on Henry Stamper's handsome features, so his had been the only remark she heard:

"I think anybody'd hump a injun," she heard him say, "would hump a she-bear."

"Would what?" she asked slowly.

Surprised at being overheard, Henry didn't have time to think up a tactful substitute so he repeated it with bravado. "Would hump a she-bear . . ."

"Bastid!" she squeaked; his intended compliment to masculine courage became an unforgivable insult to both her race and her sex. "You—you bastid, you get gone from here! This is one injun, one Indian you won' hump. I won' hump you till, till—" she drew herself up, recalling her heritage, filled her lungs and threw back her shoulders—"till all the moons in the Great Moon is gone an' all the tides in the Great Tide is come."

And watched him shrug unconcernedly and disappear, still green-eyed and still handsome, back over the muddy horizon of her memory —"who cares for you anyway, you old donkey?"—with her heart still tagging behind, wondering, Just how many moons and tides is that exactly?

And Lee, having located his glasses and cleaned the soot from their one unbroken lens, studied the singed ruin of his face and beard in the toothpaste-spattered bathroom mirror and asked himself two questions: one springing from a dim and faraway childhood memory— "What is it like to wake up dead?"—and the other from an event much less distant: "I thought I saw that hand drop a postcard . . . from where on this world might I receive a postcard?"

The face in the mirror didn't seem to know what or where, or even care very much, but only looked back at him with thirsty eyes. He drew a glass of water and opened the medicine cabinet on a large array of pill bottles; chemicals waiting like tickets for whatever ride the heart desired. But he was undecided as to the direction he wanted the ticket to take him: he felt a definite need for something to bring him down after that blast, but he also felt that he needed to be lifted to a state of hustle and bustle, especially if he were to go somewhere before that federal employee returned with some hard-headed New England fuzz who might ask a lot of fuzzy questions. Like: "Why should one wish to wake up dead anyway?" Which direction was most necessary, up or down? He compromised and took two phenobarbs and two Dexedrines, washed them down, then began hurriedly hacking away at the remains of his demolished beard.

By the time he had finished shaving he had resolved to leave town. If there was one thing he had no inclination toward right now it was a big scene with the police and the landlord and the postal authorities and Christ knows who else decides to make it his business. Neither did he want to face his roommate, whose dissertation papers were spread like confetti about all three small rooms of the cottage. Anyway, why not? As far as school went he'd long ago concluded that it would be a waste of both his time and the department's to take the tests over again; he hadn't opened a textbook in months, or any other book except the collection of old comics kept locked beside his bed in a battered Navy surplus footlocker. So why not? Why not just split, just take the VW and cut out to . . . the City, probably, borrow some on the car, see if he could move in again with Belemy and Jimmy Little—except . . . Jimmy, the last time, after he had moved out of Mother's apartment that summer, had come on so funny like . . . but that might have been imagination. Or projection. Anyway, until things blow over, as they say . . . it would be best probably if—

The sight of his washed and shaved face in the mirror startled him from his reverie. There were tears flowing from both eyes. It seemed that he was crying. He felt no grief, no remorse, none of the emotions he traditionally associated with the memory of tears—but the tears were there. The sight at once disgusted him and frightened him—that red stranger's face there, with one cracked lens and an expression of vacuous peace, spewing tears like a damned faucet.

He turned and rushed from the bathroom into the clutter of books and papers about his bed. He hunted about the rooms until he found his pair of prescription dark glasses in among the stacks of dirty dishes on the table. He polished the glasses hurriedly with a napkin and switched them for the pair he wore.

He returned to the bathroom for another look. The glasses were indeed an improvement; his face didn't look half so bad with a sea-green tint.

He smiled and assumed a look of jaunty insolence, tipping his head back slightly. A devil-may-care look. He let his eyes droop. A look of a rootless roamer, a vagabond. He put a cigarette between his lips. A look of a man who could pull up stakes at any time and flee the melee . . .

Finally satisfied, he left the bathroom to begin packing.

He took only his clothes and a few books, throwing them into his roommate's suitcase. Haphazardly, he stuck notes and bits of paper in his pockets.

He returned to the bathroom and carefully emptied half the contents of each pill bottle into an old Marlboro pack and put the rolled-up pack in the pocket of a pair of slacks in his suitcase. The bottles he put in the toe of a battered tennis shoe; then stuffed a dirty sweat sock after them and placed the shoe under Peters' bed.

He started to put his portable typewriter in its case, then became suddenly frantic with haste and left it overturned on the table.

"Addresses!" He tore through the drawers of his desk until he found a small leather-covered book, but after leafing through it tore out one page and threw the rest to the floor.

Finally, holding the big suitcase with both hands and breathing rapidly, he took a quick look around—"Okay"—and dashed out to the car. He pushed the suitcase into the back seat and jumped in and slammed the door. The thump hurt his ears. "No windows open." And hot, oven-grill dashboard . . .

He tried twice for the reverse gear, gave up and put it in forward, turning across the lawn and back on the driveway until he was facing the street. But he didn't pull onto the street. He sat, racing the motor, looking out at the clean sweep of pavement passing in front of him. "Come on, man . . ." His ears were ringing from the door slam, as they had after the blast. He raced the motor, urging the car to decide which way to turn onto the street. "Come on, man . . . be serious." Gearshift hot as a poker, and ears ringing . . . finally, palm to face to somehow press away the ringing—I seemed to feel a tendoned hand playfully squeezing my knee, and a bagpipe's whirling skirl wheezing in my throat—and discovers that he is weeping again; squeezing, wheezing and rattling the scene . . . and it is then—"Or if you can't be serious," I scolded, "at least be *rational*; who could *possibly* in this wasted world . . . ?"—that he remembers the postcard lying on the porch.

(. . . the clouds file past. The bartender brings 'em on. The jukebox bubbles. And at the house Hank shouts hoarsely into a roomful of resistance: ". . . but goddammit what we're talking about *ain't* whether we're gonna be the most *popular* folks in town if we sell to WP . . . but about *where* we gonna get us some more labor?" He stops, looking about at the faces. "So . . . has anybody got any suggestions? Or want to volunteer for extra work?" After a short silence Joe Ben pops a handful of sunflower seeds into his mouth and holds up his hand. "I definitely ain't volunteering for more labor," he says, chewing, then bends his mouth back to his hand and begins spitting out the seeded hulls, "but I *might* have a little suggestion . . .")

The card was on the bottom step—a threepenny postcard in heavy black pencil with one line showing black and blacker, larger and larger than all the rest of the message.

*"You should be a big enough guy now, bub."*

At first, I refused to believe it; but that hand kept squeezing my knee and those pipes kept wheezing in my chest, until a mirthless laughter began to spew out, as uncontrollable and uncalled-for as had been my attack of griefless tears—"From home . . . oh Christ, a card from the *kinfo'k!*"—and I was finally forced to face up to its existence.

I walked back to sit in the idling car to read it, trying to control my spasms of laughter enough to make out the print. It was signed Uncle Joe Ben, and even through my mirth I could make out that the message was penciled in a rambling grade-school hand that could be none but Joe's. "Sure. Uncle Joe's hand. Absolutely." But it was the heavier, surer addition at the bottom that commanded my eye, and as I read it it wasn't Uncle Joe's hand but Brother Hank's voice that recited the words inside my head.

"Leeland. Old Henry stove up bad in accident—the show is in a bad tight for help—we need somebody but has to be a Stamper to keep unyon off our necks—good pay if you think your equal to it—" Then *stab* in a different pen hand: "You should be a big enough, etc." And after that, after this outrageous and outsized signature—a signature written in capitals, "Something so *fitting* about big brother printing his signature in capitals . . ."—there was added an ungainly attempt at cordiality.

"P & S you ain't even met my wife Vivian bub. You sort of got a sister now too."

This last line was perhaps what broke the spell. The thought of my brother mated was so ludicrous that I found some actual humor in the idea, enough to give me a real laugh and the courage of contempt besides. "Bah!" I exclaimed contemptuously, tossing the card to the back seat and in the teeth of the ghost of the past grinning at me there from beneath his logger's hat. "I know what you are: naught but a product of my indigestion. A touch of cole slaw perhaps become spoiled in my refrigerator. A bit of underdone potato eaten last night. Humbug! There's more of gravy than of the grave to you!"

But, like his Dickensian counterpart, the specter of my older brother rose forth with a terrible clamor, rattling his log chain, and cried out in a dreadful voice, "You're a big guy now!" and sent me careening from the driveway out into the street, laughing still but now with some reason: the irony in this pat, nick-of-time arrival of this quote Unexpected Letter unquote had given me my first bit of fun in months. "The idea! asking me to come back and help the business . . . as if I had nothing else in the world to do but jump to the aid of a logging outfit."

And had given me as well someplace to go.

By noon I had sold the VW—or what I owned of it—taking five hundred dollars less than I knew it was worth, and by one o'clock I was dragging Peters' suitcase and the paper sack full of junk cleaned from the glove compartment to the bus depot, ready for the trip. Which, according to the ticket-pusher, would take a solid three days of driving.

I had close to an hour before my bus left, and, after I had spent fifteen minutes at the paperback counter putting it off, I finally succumbed to my conscience and placed a call to Peters at the department. When I told him I was at the depot waiting for a bus to take me home he at first misunderstood. "A bus? What happened to the car? Just hang there, why don't you, and I'll cut my seminar and pick you up."

"I appreciate your offer, but I shouldn't think you would want to lose the three days; six days, actually, there and back . . ."

"Six days *where* and back? Lee damn you, what's hapening? Where are you?"

"Just a minute . . ."

"You at the bus depot no shit?"

"Just a moment . . ." I opened the door of the booth and held the phone out into the raucous comings and goings of the depot. "What do you think?" I asked, shouting at the receiver. I felt strangely giddy and lightheaded; the combination of barbiturate and amphetamine was making me feel both feverish and drunk, as though one was putting me to sleep and the other was turning that sleep into a freewheeling, highly charged dream. "And when I speak of *home*, Peters, my man"—I closed the door of the booth again, and sat down on the upended suitcase—"I do not mean that scholar's squalor we've been living in these last eight months—which is now, by the way, in the process of being aerated as you'll see—but I mean home! The West Coast! Oregon!"

After a moment he asked, "Why?" becoming a little suspicious.

"To seek out my lost roots," I answered gaily, trying to ease his suspicion. "To stir up old fires, to eat fatted calves."

"Lee, what's happened?" Peters asked, now more patient than suspicious. "You out of your gourd? I mean, what's wrong?"

"Well, I shaved my beard, for one thing—"

"Lee! Don't give me this other shit . . ." In spite of my attempt at gaiety I could hear both suspicion and patience giving away to concerned anger, the very thing I wanted to avoid. "Just tell me goddammit *why!*"

It wasn't the reaction I had been hoping for from Peters. Far from it.

I was disappointed and put out with him for getting so wrought up while I was being so cool. At the time I thought it unlike him to be so demanding (not realizing until later how fucked-up I must have sounded) and damned unfair of him to disregard so flagrantly the rules of our relationship. We had ideas about relationship. We both agreed that each pair of people must have a mutually compatible system all their own within which they can communicate, or communication falls like the Tower of Babel. A man should be able to expect his wife to play the role of Wife—be she bitchy or dutiful—when she relates to him. For her lover she may have a completely different role, but at home, on the Husband-Wife set, she must stay within the confines of that part. Or we would all wander around never knowing our friends from our strangers. And in our eight months of rooming together and years-long friendship, this homely, lantern-jawed Negro and I had established a clear set of limits within which we knew we could comfortably communicate, a sort of dramatic tradition wherein he always played the sagacious and slow-talking Uncle Remus to my intellectual dandy. Within this framework, behind our shammed masks, we had been able to approach the most extreme personal truths in our conversations without suffering the embarrassment of such intimacies. I preferred it that way, even under the new conditions, and I tried again.

"The apple orchards will be in fruit; the air thick with the smell of warm mint and blackberry—ah, I hear my native land a-beckoning to me. Besides, I have a score there to settle."

"Oh man—" he started to protest from the other end of the line, but I went on unheeding, unable to stop.

"No, listen: I received a postcard. Let me recreate the scene for you—condensed somewhat, because my bus will soon be loading. But listen, it was a superbly styled vignette of some kind or other: I had just returned from walking on the beach—down toward Mona's place; I didn't go in; her damned sister was there—anyway I had just come in after what I always like to think of as one of my 'TB or not TB' walks, and, after a few decisive coughs, I finally decided to take arms against a sea of troubles . . . and flick it all in for good."

"Lee, come on please; what is it you're—"

"Just listen. Hear me out." I drew nervously from my cigarette. "Interruptions only mar the meter." I heard the rattle of machinery nearby. A plump Tom Sawyer had just activated the pinball machine next to my glass booth; the lights spun in a hysterical tallying of astronomical scoring, numbers mounting with a rapid-fire banging. I hurried on.

"I walk in through our careful clutter. It's about noon, a bit before. The apartment is cold; you've left that damned garage door open again—"

"Shit; if somebody didn't let a little cold air in on you you'd never

get out of bed. Decided what? What do you mean you finally decided—"

"Hush. Watch closely. I close the door and lock it. Dishtowel, wet,
across the bottom. Check all windows, moving cryptically about my
task. Then open all the jets on all the wall heaters—no, hush, just
listen—turn on all the burners on that godawful grimy stove you
left . . . I remember the pilot light on the water heater . . . go
back, kneel piously at the little door to blow it out (the flame spewed
symbolically from three jets, describing a fiery cross. You would have
applauded my cool: I draw a breath . . . 'There's a divinity that
shapes our'—*pfft*—'ends.') Then, satisfied with the arrangement, having removed my shoes, you will notice—a gentleman to the last—I
climb onto the bed to await sleep. Who knows what dreams? Then. I
decide—even the Mad Dane of Denmark would have allotted himself
a last cigarette, I mean, if that wishy-washy coward had ever had my
courage, or my cigarettes—and *just then*, beautifully timed, just as
this ghostly hand appeared, fixed, in that little window you know
above the mail slot, to drop its message calling me home . . . *just as*
the card fluttered to the floor . . . I flicked my cigarette lighter and
blew out all the windows in the place."

I waited. Peters was silent while I had another drag on my cigarette.

"So. It was my usual way—a rotten failure. But with a rather nice
turn this time, don't you think? I wasn't hurt. Singed a little, my
beard and eyebrows gone, no loss, and my watch stopped—let's see:
it's going again now. But it knocked the poor postman all the way
down the steps into the hydrangeas. I suspect you'll find his carcass
there when you get home from class, plucked by the gulls, nothing remaining but his mailbag and cap. No, listen: there's a pinball machine going insane right next to the booth and I can't hear you anyway. So just listen. After a rather sticky moment or two spent trying
to understand why I wasn't dead, I got up and walked to the door—
oh hey! I remember thinking, the first thing after the blast: 'Well,
Leland, you blew it.' Isn't that nice?—and find that card. With growing incredulity I decipher the tight little penciled scrawl. What? A
card from home? Asking me to come back and help out? How very
*timely*, considering that I've been living the last three months off the
earnings of my spade roommate. . . . Then, listen: standing there,
I heard this voice. 'WATCH OUT!' the voice booms, with the brutal
authority of panic. 'WATCH OUT! LOOK OUT FROM BE-
HIND!' I've told you about this voice. An old and familiar friend,

perhaps the oldest of all my mental Board of Directors; the true arbiter of all my interior negotiations and easily distinguished from all other members of the board—you remember me telling you?—by his loud upper-case mandates. 'WATCH OUT!' he booms. 'LOOK OUT FROM BEHIND!' So I spin quickly to face my attacker. 'BEHIND!' he screams again. 'LOOK OUT FROM BEHIND!' I spin again, to no avail. And again, faster, and again, getting dizzy as hell—all to no avail. And you know why, Peters? Because one can *never*, no matter how fast he is on the spin, face an attack from behind."

I paused a moment and closed my eyes. The booth racketed about me in a sort of anarchy. I placed my hand over the mouthpiece and drew a deep breath, hoping to calm myself. I could hear the loudspeaker outside, pealing unintelligible instructions, and the pinball's machine-gunning. But as soon as I heard Peters start, "Lee, why don't you just wait for me to—" I was off again.

"So, after this little ritual . . . I stand there in our demolished doorway with that terrible card dancing in my hand. Completely forgetting that I wanted to be gone before the postman could fetch the fuzz in to ask about my health—by the way: the cops didn't come but while I was shaving the gas company arrived to shut off the gas. No reason given; I don't know whether they just happened to pick that moment to take action because we haven't paid our bill or whether the public utilities are taking it upon themselves to punish anyone using their product for nefarious ends by subjecting them to cold canned soup and chilly nights. Anyway, standing there with that little slip of penciled paper in my poor fricasseed fingers and a ringing in my ears ten decibels louder than the ringing the explosion had caused, I had a great insight into myself: while it was certainly humiliating to discover myself so affected by that postcard, it was even more surprising. Because . . . well, hell, I thought I was beyond being bugged by my past, you know, I thought I had cemented myself forever from the years of my youth; I was certain that Doctor Maynard and I had succeeded in dismantling the past, second by ticking second, like a time-bomb team; I thought we'd left the treacherous device deactivated and dead, powerless to affect me. And see: since I had considered myself cut loose from my past I had seen no reason to guard that direction. Right? Thus it was all for naught, the 'Watch outs,' the spinning. Because all my beautiful fortifications, built so cunningly and carefully on Maynard's couch, had been designed in accord with information indicating that the only dangers lay in front, ahead of me—and were fortifications, alas, quite powerless against even the meagerest offensive from the rear. Dig? So that postcard, sneaking up as it had from behind, had caught me more unawares than my aborted suicide; the explosion, though certainly a bit of a shocker, was nevertheless *immediately* comprehensible, you see? A here-and-now holocaust. But this postcard was a kidney kick out of the past, coming by the *most* devious route. It had jumped all *customary* postal tracks, of course, to travel through dark time zones and bleak wastelands of yore, accompanied by the eerie wailing note of an oscilloscope and other science-fiction movie background music . . . speeding through nimbus shadows and along the undulating mist of bubbling dry ice . . . then we cut to close-up: ah. A solitary crystal hand appearing at my mail slot . . . floating there for an instant, like chemical statuary designed to immediately dissolve as soon as it deposits the invitation that requests my humble presence at a gathering being held twelve (twelve? that long ago? Jesus . . .) *twelve* years previous to the day of its delivery! Whew! Any wonder it left me a little ringy?"

I didn't wait for an answer, or pause when the voice at the other end attempted to interrupt my manic monologue. As the loudspeaker announced departures and the pinball scoreboard outside the booth clattered and clashed and ran its meaningless numbers upwards in maddened acceleration, I kept talking, compulsively filling the phone with words in order not to leave an opening of silence for Peters to speak into. Or, more accurately, to question into. I think I must have phoned Peters, not so much out of thoughtfulness for an old friend as out of a need to verbalize my reasons, and a desperate wish to logically *explain* my actions—but I wanted to explain without anyone questioning my explanations. I must have suspected that any extensive probing would surely reveal—to Peters, to myself—that I really had no logical explanation, either for my abortive attempt at suicide or for my impulsive decision to return home.

". . . so the card convinced me, among other things, that I am still much more at the mercy of my past than I ever imagined. You wait; the same thing will happen to you: you'll get a call from Georgia one of these days and realize that you've many a score to settle back home before you can get on with your business."

"I doubt that I could settle that many scores," Peters said.

"True; your scene is different. But with me it's just one score. And one man. It was amazing the number of pictures of him that card conjured up: booted feet, with spikes no less. Muddy sweatshirt. Gloved hands forever scratching scratching scratching at a navel or an ear. Raspberry-red lips draped in a drunken grin. A lot of other equally ridiculous pictures to choose from, but the picture that came on the clearest was of his long, sinewy body diving into the river, naked and white and hard as a peeled tree . . . this was the predominant image. You see, Brother Hank used to spend hours swimming steadily into the river's current as he trained for a swimming meet. Hours and hours, swimming steadily, doggedly, and remaining in exactly the same place a few feet from the dock. Like a man swimming a liquid treadmill. The training must have paid off because by the time I was ten he had a shelf simply *gleaming* with trophies and cups; I think even held for a time a national swimming record in one of the events. Lord God! All this brought back by that one tiny postcard; and with such astonishing clarity. Lord. Just a card. I dread to imagine what a complete letter might have produced."

"Okay. But just what in the shit do you hope to accomplish going home? Even, say, you do settle some funny score—"

"Don't you see? It's even in the card: 'You think you're big enough now?' It was that way all my time at home—Brother Hank always held up to me as the man to measure up to—and it's been that way ever since. In a psychologically symbolic way, of course."

"Oh, of course."

"So I'm going home."

"To measure up to this psychological symbol?"

"Or pull him down. No, don't laugh; it's become ridiculously clear: until I have settled my score with this shadow from my past—"

"Crap."

"—I'll go on feeling inferior and inadequate."

"Crap, Lee. Everybody has a shadow like that, their old man or somebody—"

"Not even able to get on with the business of gassing myself."

"—but they don't go running home to even things, for shitsakes—"

"No, I'm serious, Peters. I've thought it all out. Now listen, I hate to leave you with the hassle of the place and all, but I've—thought it all out and I've no choice. And could you tell them at the department?"

"What? That you blew yourself up? That you've gone home to settle a score with the naked ghost of your brother?"

"Half-brother. No. Just tell them . . . I was forced because of financial and emotional difficulties to—"

"Oh man, come on, you can't be serious."

"And try to explain to Mona, will you?"

"Lee, wait; you're out of your head. Let me come over—"

"They're calling my bus number. I've got to rush. I'll send what I owe you as soon as I can. Good-by, Peters; I'm off to prove Thomas Wolfe was wrong."

I placed Peters, still protesting, back on the hook, and once more drew that long breath. I complimented myself on my control. I had pulled it off nicely. I had managed to remain religiously within the boundaries in spite of Peters' attempts to subvert our system and in spite of a mixture of Dexedrine and phenobarb which was bound to make a fellow a little giddy. Yes, Leland old man, no one can say that you didn't present a concise and completely rational explanation *regardless* of all the rude distractions . . .

And the distractions were getting more rude by the second; I noticed this as I pushed out of the booth into the rush of the depot. The fat boy was humping the pinball machine toward a frenzied orgasm of noise, neon, and numbers. The crowd was pushing. The suitcase was pulling. The loudspeaker was advising me in a roar that if I didn't get on my bus I would be *left!*

"Too much up," I decided and at the water fountain washed down another two phenobarbitals. Just in time to be swept up in a maelstrom of motion that landed me, marvelously and just in time, on the loading platform in front of my bus.

"Leave the suitcase and find yourself a seat," the driver told me impatiently, as though he'd been waiting for me alone. Which proved to be exactly right: the bus was completely empty. "Not many going West these days?" I asked, but he didn't answer.

I walked unsteadily down the aisle to a seat at the back (where I am to remain almost unmoving for almost four days, getting off at stops to go to the can and buy Coke). As I stood, removing my jacket, the door thumped closed at the other end of the bus with a loud hish of compressed air. I jumped and looked toward the noise, but it was so dark in the unlit bus in the garage I couldn't see the driver. I thought he had gone out and the door closed behind him. Left me locked in here *alone!* Then the motor beneath me thundered and began straining in pitch. The bus started out of the murky cement grotto toward the bright New England afternoon, lurching over the sidewalk and throwing me finally into my seat. Just in time.

I still hadn't seen the driver return.

The weird, billowing anarchy of motion and sound that had started in the phone booth was now surging around me in earnest. As though the debris had finally begun to settle back after hanging suspended overhead all the hours since the blast. Scenes, memories, faces . . . like pictures embroidered on curtains billowing in the wind. The pinball machine clattered and clung to my eyes. The postcard rang in my ears. My stomach rolled, voices tolled in my head—that interior monitor of mine bellowing for me to WATCH OUT! HANG ON! THIS IS IT! YOU'RE FINALLY COMPLETELY FLIPPING! I clutched the armrests of the bus seat desperately, terrified.

Looking back (I mean now, here, from this particular juncture in time, able to be objective and courageous thanks to the miracle of modern narrative technique), I see the terror clearly, but I find it a little difficult to believe that I was sincerely able to blame much of this burgeoning terror on the rather hackneyed fear of going mad. While it was quite fashionable at the time for one to claim to be constantly threatened by the fear of finally flipping out, I don't think I had been able to honestly convince myself of my right to the claim for a good while. In fact, I remember that one of the scenes swirling past me as I clutched my seat was a scene with Dr. Maynard, a session at his office where I had told him in dramatic desperation, "Doctor . . . I'm going mad; the final complete flip, it's swooping down out of the hills at me!"

He had only smiled, condescendingly and therapeutically. "No, Leland, not you. You, and in fact quite a lot of your generation, have in some way been exiled from that particular sanctuary. It's become almost impossible for you to 'go mad' in the classical sense. At one time people conveniently 'went mad' and were never heard from again. Like a character in a romantic novel. But now"—And I think he even went so far as to yawn—"you are too hip to yourself on a psychological level. You all are too intimate with too many of the symptoms of insanity to be caught completely off your guard. Another thing: all of you have a talent for releasing frustration through clever fantasy. And you, you are the worst of the lot on that score. So . . . you may be neurotic as hell for the rest of your life, and miserable, maybe even do a short hitch at Bellevue and certainly good for another five years as a paying patient—but I'm afraid never completely out." He leaned back in his elegant Lounge-o-Chair. "Sorry to disappoint you but the best I can offer is plain old schizophrenia with delusional tendencies."

Recalling this, and the wise doctor's words, I relaxed my grip on the armrests and pulled the lever to recline the seat. Hell, I sighed, exiled even from the sanctuary of insanity. What a drag. Madness might have been a good way to explain terror and excuse anarchy, I mooned, a good whipping boy to blame in the event of mental discomfort, an interesting avocation to while away the long afternoon of life. What a crashing drag . . .

But then . . . on the other hand, I decided, as the bus thundered slowly through town, you never can tell: it might have constituted as bad a drag as sanity. You would probably have to work too hard at it. And at times, almost certainly, a little sneak of memory would slip past your whipping boy and you would be whacked just as hard as ever by that joker's bladder of reality, of pain and heartache and hassle and death. You might hide in some Freudian jungle most of your miserable life, baying at the moon and shouting curses at God, but at the end, right down there at the damned end when it counts . . . you would sure as anything clear up *just* enough to realize the moon you have spent so many years baying at is nothing but the light globe up there on the ceiling, and God is just something placed in your bureau drawer by the Gideon Society. Yes, I sighed again, in the long run insanity would be the same old coldhearted drag of too solid flesh, too many slings and arrows, and too much outrageous fortune.

I reclined my seat another notch and closed my eyes, trying to resign myself that there was nothing I could do about this runaway anarchy I had hold of but wait for the pharmaceutical pilot to come on and take over the controls and let me sleep. But the pills seemed uncommonly slow in coming on. And in this ten- or fifteen-minute wait—the billowing; the ringing; the bus, empty but for its solitary passenger in the back, huffing and whooshing through the town—before the barbiturates took effect . . . I was forced at last to consider those questions I had been skirting so skillfully.

Like: "What in the shit you hope to accomplish running back *home*?" I knew that all that obscure Oedipal pap I had fed Peters about measuring up or pulling down might be approaching some kind of truth . . . but even if I were able to bring off one of these coups, what did I hope to *accomplish?*

And like: "Why should one want to wake up dead anyway?" If the

glorious birth-to-death hassle is the only hassle we are ever to have
. . . if our grand and exhilarating Fight of Life is such a tragically
short little scrap anyway, compared to the eons of rounds before and
after—then why should one want to relinquish even a few precious
seconds of it?

And—thirdly—like: "If it's such a goddamned hassle—why fight
it?"

The three questions lined up in front of me, just like that: three
insistent bullies, hands on their hips and sneers on their faces, challenging me to meet them face to face, once and for all. The first one I
made a little headway with, owing to its more pressing nature and the
help I had during the trip. The second didn't receive satisfaction until
weeks later when circumstances following that trip happened to occasion another challenge. And the third still waits right now. While
I take another trip. Back into the memory of what happened.

And the third one is the toughest bully of them all.

But that first question I set to work on straightaway. What do I
hope to accomplish going home? Well, myself, for one thing . . . my
little old self!"

"Man," Peters says over the phone, "you don't do that by running
off someplace. That's like running from the beach to go swimming."

"There are beaches East and beaches West," I let him know.

"Crap," he says.

Looking back on that trip (and forward on this one), I can calcu-
late and know it took four days (the thing about being removed,
thanks to modern technique, is, while it may afford objectivity and
perspective—with all events tunneling back from this point like
images in opposing mirrors, yet each image changed—it presents a
tricky problem of tense) . . . but looking back I remember the
depot, the gas, the bus trip, the blast, the disjointed narrative to
Peters on the phone—all these scenes as one scene, composed of
dozens of simultaneously occurring events . . .

"Something's wrong," Peters says. "No, wait . . . something's happened, dammit Lee; what? You're in New York to identify what? But
man, that's more than a year ago."

I could now (possibly) go back and restretch those shrunken hours,
flake the images separate, arrange them in accurate chronological
order, (possibly; with will-power, patience, and the proper chemicals)
but being accurate is not necessarily being honest.

"Lee!" This time it's Mother. "Where are you going? Are you ever *going* anywhere?"

Nor is chronological reporting by any means always the most truthful (each camera has its own veracity) especially when, in all good faith, one cannot truthfully claim to remember what happened accurately. . . .

The fat boy turns to leer at me from the pinball machine. "You can win 'em all but that last one, hot shot." He grins. Stenciled on his T-shirt is TILT in large orange letters outlined in green.

Or accurately claim to remember what happened *truthfully* . . .

And Mother plummets past my bedroom window, forever and ever.

Besides, there are some things that can't be the truth even if they *did* happen.

The bus stops (I hang up the phone and hurry out to the car and drive to the Campus Diner) and starts again, jerkily. The diner is crowded but subdued. The people remote. A film of tobacco smoke drawn over the faces makes them look like displays behind glass. I peer through this film and see Peters sitting at his table back near the cigarette machine, sharing a beer with Mona and someone who leaves. Peters sees me coming and licks the foam from his mustache, the surprising pink of the Negro tongue darting out at me. "Enter Leland Stanford, stage left," he says. He picks the candle from the table and lifts it toward me in a theatrical gesture. "Rage, rage and remember Dylan Thomas," he says, and Mona says, "When you get home, Lee, look around and see if you dropped it back there somewhere." Sweetly.

I tell them I have just failed my tests again. Peters says, "Crap. Is *that* all?" And Mona says, "I saw your mother fall past."

"Oh," says Peters. "And guess who was with us? He left when you came in, still naked."

The pinball machine goes rigid with light and I hear Peters breathing into the receiver, sympathetic and waiting for my fits to finally cease. "Nobody, man," he says sadly, "can go home again."

I want to say something about my family. I tell them, "My father is a filthy capitalist and my brother is a motherfucker." Peters says, "Some people have all the luck," and we laugh. I want to say more but at that moment I hear Mother enter the café. I recognize the loud stab of her heels against the tile. Everyone turns and looks, then goes on drinking coffee. I can't find a dime and Mother stands at the door, looking back and forth through the people at the walls. She touches the black hair with her hand, and it is painful for me to look because then she turns into chromium and cosmetics. She walks briskly to the counter, puts her purse on one stool and her car coat on another, and seats herself between them.

"Anyway, man . . . what to accomplish?"

I watch Mother pick up a cup of coffee . . . her elbow resting on the countertop, fingers dropping to close over the cup . . . now she crosses her legs beneath the gray skirt and swings the fulcrum of her elbow to her knee and is revolving slowly around on the stool. I wait for the arm to lower and the hand to empty its load into the waiting truckbed. But she sees something that startles her so she drops the cup. I turn, but he's already gone again.

I ask for a glass of water. The postman brings it and the loud-speaker calls for all aboard. The postman says, "Well, one thing you'll accomplish when you get back there: you'll find out if it's true or not." "What's that?" I ask, but he goes somersaulting away. I guess that's a postman's system.

The phone rings and it's that horrible greened-over preacher friend of Mother's calling me from New York to tell me what happened. And how upset Mother has been by the news that I failed my exams. And how sorry she has been for failing me. And how sorry he is. And how desperately griefstricken he knows I must be and then offers the consolation that we are all of us, dear boy . . . trapped by our existence. I tell him that this is neither very profound nor very consoling but when I lie on the bed with the moon jigsawing my body I keep seeing this picture of a tiny birdcage inlaid with rhinestones chugging along a little track, mother trapped inside performing the feeble repertory of her movements as the cage moves along the track round and around up the concrete to the forty-first floor where the rails stop out in space.

"Who trapped her?" I scream and the postman rushes in to hand me the card again. "Message out of the past, sir," he says, giggling. "A pastcard." "Crap," says Peters.

It occurs to me . . . that . . . if I am as vulnerable to this world of the past as she has been . . . then perhaps I am being screwed out of everything I was ever to have—Peters, listen!—because I have always felt compelled to measure up to a memory."

"The same crap," Peters says at the other end of the line.

"No, listen. This card came just in time. Perhaps he is right. Perhaps I am a Big Enough guy now, don't you see? a Strong Enough guy to demand the return of the sun I've been cheated of . . . a Desperate Enough guy to see that my demands are met even if it means eradicating this specter casting this shadow!"

Excited by this possibility—and by the incessant honking as the bus tried to goad a cautious milk truck away from the stop sign ahead of us out into the heavy traffic of the highway—I jerked momentarily awake. I was drowsy and dopey as hell, but the strange billowing sensation had ceased. And the feeling of terror had given way to a kind of capricious optimism. Because, by George, what if Little Leland were a Big Enough guy now? Wasn't it possible? Ah? Just on the basis of years? Hank was no young buck any more. A lot of water had flowed past since those days of stud prizes and swimming trophies. Here I am, just approaching my prime; Hank is past his—*bound* to be! Can I possibly go back and wrest from my past some remnant of a better beginning? Some start toward a better scene? *That* would be worth running back to accomplish, Lord knows . . .

The milk truck finally dived into the stream of traffic and the bus moved into position. I let my eyes close and my head sink back again, euphoria tingling with a taste of confidence. "How about it, fellas?" I inquired of those standing in the nearby shadows. "Does Little Leland have any sort of chance against this illiterate spook who has charged out of the past to once more goad me with his grin? Do I actually have a *chance* to wrest from him the life that I have been cheated out of, the life that we both knew was mine? Rightfully mine? *Justly* mine?"

Before any of my friends present can answer, the ghost himself slips out of the melting shadows and raps me over the head with a bladder, knocking loose a hailstorm of silver barbiturate burrs. Still drunk with confidence, I half rose from my seat to demand of the grinning giant looming above me in a sweat shirt, number 88, "Whither wilt thou lead me?" fixing him with the most withering Shakespearean gaze my goof-balled eyes could muster. "Speak, I'll go no further."

"Oh?" A sneer played at his lip. "You'll go no further, is it? The *hell* if you won't! Now you get your tail on over here an' sit it down; didn't you hear me callin' you?"

"You've no hold on me"—in a quavering voice—"no hold at all."

"Why, willya listen at this: he says I ain't got no hold on him. Boys, you hear that: I got no *hold* on smart-ass here. Bub, you look: I aim t' ast you purty-please just one more time, then lose my

patience. So *move*, blast you! An' quit that fidgetin' around! Stan'
still! *Move*, I tell ye!"

Our young hero, cowed and bullied and in a furor of frustration,
plops to the ground quivering with protoplasmic confusion. The giant
prods the glob with the toe of his spiked logging boot. "Gaa. Look
what a mess he went an' made. Well, jeez . . . *boys!*" He raises his
head and calls, "Dip him up an' get him on in the house fertheshit-
sakes so's we can get on with this business. Jeez, *look* at him . . ."

A horde of kinsmen rush forth from the wings; their plaid shirts,
spike boots, and manly physiques bespeak the logging trade; a uni-
formity of features indicates they are all members of the same family,
for they all boast noble Roman noses, sandy-brown hair wafted free
by the fragrant northern breezes, and iron-green eyes. They are
ruggedly handsome. All save the Smallest Fellow, whose face has been
horribly mutilated by constant use as the family dartboard; the darts
are barbed and the flesh hangs in shreds where the barbs have torn it.
This poor wretch trips in his haste and falls in a heap. The giant leans
down and picks him up between a great thumb and forefinger and
regards him with the kindly scorn one might reserve for a cricket.

"Joe Ben," the giant says patiently, "ain't I *tole* you 'bout thisyere
fumble-fart-an'-fallin' *down* all the time? Don't you know that it's
call to get you drummed right out o' the clan if you keep on? What'd
folks think, a Stamper ploppin' on his butt all the time? Now hop it
up an' get on over yonder an' help your cousins sop my kid brother
up before he drains away down the gopher holes. Now git!"

He places the Smallest Fellow on the ground and fondly watches
him scuttle to the sopping. "Good ol' Joby." Hank smiles after the
lovable little gnome in a manner to betray the tender heart that beats
beneath his rough exterior. "I'm might glad old Henry didn't have
him drownt like he did the rest of the runts; Joe's good fer a lotta
laughs."

By this time the kinsmen have managed to contain our melted
hero and are bearing him toward the house in a polyethylene bag;
during the passage across the spacious and tastefully landscaped front
bog the plucky lad overcomes his fright enough to gradually pull
himself back to some semblance of human form.

The house is disguised as a pile of discarded scrap lumber stacked
precariously into the clouds; the door, which can be opened only by
the insertion of a log in an enormous keyhole, swings inward, and for
an instant young Leland can make out through his transparent con-

fines the dim trappings of a spacious hall—mastiffs stalking among great fir-tree pillars wherein double-edged axes are stuck, sheepskin mackinaws hanging carelessly on their handles—then the door swings shut with a booming echo that reverberates off distant walls, and all is dark once again.

This is mighty Stamper Hall. It was built sometime during the reign of Henry (Stamper) the Eighth and for centuries has been condemned by every public-safety agency in the land. Water can be heard dripping even in the severest drought, and the long maze of decaying corridors is filled with constant dark scurryings and a continual drumming of blind frogs. At intervals these sounds are broken by the thundering collapse of an obscure wing of the house, and entire branches of the family have disappeared into its passageways never to be heard from again.

The domain is an absolute monarchy in which no one dares make a move, not even the crown prince himself, without first consulting the Great Ruler. Hank steps to the head of the band of kinsmen and cups his hands about his mouth to summon this exalted potentate.

"Oh . . . PAW!"

The roar rolls rumbling through the inky blackness, crashing into wooden walls. He yells again and this time a candle comes on in the distance, illuminating first the craggy profile, then the whole grisly visage of old Henry Stamper. He is sitting in a rocking chair waiting to be a hundred. His hawklike beak turns slowly in the direction of his son's voice. His hawklike eyes pierce the gloom. He coughs loudly and spits a blazing ember hissing through the damp air. He coughs again and speaks, looking at the plastic sack.

"Wellsir now . . . aye doggies . . . heeheehee . . . lookee yonder . . . how's 'bout *that*. What in tarnation you youngsters found floatin' in the river *this* time? I swan, *allus* draggin' in some crap or other . . ."

"Didn't rightly find it, Pa; sorter *conjured* it up."

"You don't tell me!" He leans forward, displaying more interest. "Nasty-lookin' outfit . . . what you reckon it be? Somethin' come in on the tide?"

"I'm afeared, Pa"— Hank hangs his head and scuffs his toe at the floor, shredding white pine in all directions with his spikes—"that it be"—scratches his belly, swallows— "be yer youngest son, Leland Stanford."

"*Damnation!* I told you once I told you a friggin' *hunnert* times, I don't *never!* want the name o' that *quitter!* spoke in thisyere house again! Phoo. Cain't stand the sound of him, lit-lone the *sight!* Jesus, son, what got into you to pull such a boner?"

Hank steps closer to the throne. "Paw, I knowed how ya felt. I cain't help but feel the same way myself—worst, mebbe, comes down to it; I'd as leave never heard his name again the rest o' my nachrul life—but I didn't see no way gettin' around it, considerin' the situation we is in."

"What situation!"

"The labor situation."

"You mean—" The old man gasps; his hand lifts in a gesture of involuntary horror.

"I'm afeared so. We come to the end of the bench, old fellow, to the last of the beans. You knowed when we saved out Joe Ben that we was scrapin' the bottom of the barrel. So it was like we didn't have a choice, Pa . . ." He crosses his arms, waiting. . . .

(*In the low mountains the crows sleep fitfully. Jenny works with need and loneliness and the magic of her ignorance. At the old house the discussion of Joe Ben's idea for writing other relatives in other states is halted suddenly by Orland's demand to see the books. "I'll bring them right down," Hank volunteers and heads for the steps . . . welcoming the opportunity to leave the noise and hubbub for a moment . . .*)

Henry stares forlornly at young Leland, who is feebly waving at his venerable father from inside the plastic bag. Henry wags his old head.

"So. This is how it is, eh? It's finally come to *this.*" Then, fired by a sudden fury, he lurches standing from the chair and shakes his cane at the cringing kinsmen. "Ain't I been *tellin'* you boys this was a-comin'? Ain't I been sayin' till I'm blue in the face, 'Leave off this diddlin' of your cousins and sisters an' the like an' get out an' knock us up some *other* women fer a change!' I'm sick 'n tired of all these freaks an' halfwits you been turnin' out. We cain't be inbreedin' all the time like a buncha damn *hawgs!* The family got to be *healthy* an' *strong* t' keep up the standards. I don't aim to tolerate weaklings! No, b' gawd, I don't. We need examples by gawd, like my own boy, Hank there, like the stock *I* turn out—"

His face freezes for an instant as his eyes light once more on the plastic sack, then his stoic features shatter with humiliation. He collapses backward into his rocker, gasping and clutching at his tormented heart. When the fit has passed, Hank goes on in a subdued voice:

"I know how it galls ya, Pa. I know how he took away your young an' faithful wife with his weakness an' his whining. But here's how it looked to me when I realized we had to bring up the un-pleasant subject." He rolls a log up close and seats himself, becoming confidential. "I figured . . . that we're a *family* first, and that's the most important. We got to keep ourselfs free of racial pollution. We ain't some bunch o' niggers or Jews or *ordinary* people; we're *Stampers*."

A flourish of trumpets; Hank, tin hat in hand, waits for the ranks to finish the Family Anthem.

"An' that the most *important* thing was to keep them ordinary people *from* by God ever fergittin' *it!*"

Shouts and whistles. "You tell 'em, Hank!" "Thatsa boy!" "Yeh!"

"An' the only way we gonna do that . . . is keep *our empire* goin', come hell or high water; no matter what degree of family scum it takes—that's how to prove what a superior race we are."

More applause. Jaws become grim and nod in terse, manly affirmative. Old Henry dries his eyes and swallows. Hank is standing. He jerks one of his handy axes from a pillar and waves it about dramatically.

"An' didn't we all sign in blood that we'd by god fight to our last by god man? Okay then . . . let's *fight.*"

More trumpets. The men join Hank in a closed-rank march about a flag mounted in the center of the hall. They march each with right hand clapped firmly on the shoulder of the man ahead, singing snatches of World War One battle songs. There is an air of relief and good fellowship among the kinsmen now that the crisis has past, and they call back and forth to one another in raucous voices: "Yea bo! You betcha! Damn right!" As they march past the plastic sack they conceal their shame beneath a veneer of humor: "Lookee there." "When we said last man, we never thought anything like *this.*"

"You right certain he qualifies as last man? Mebbe we oughta run a check . . ."

"Naw. Let 'im be. I don't want the ol' man havin' us paw around on him again; it 'uz nasty enough gettin' 'im in that sack," he warns them.

*(Hank mounts the steps, feeling a little shaky. He turns down the corridor toward the room used as an office. He hears Viv call from the*

kitchen, where she and the other wives are doing dishes, "Boots, honey." He stops and supports himself with one hand against the wall while he removes his dusty boots. He takes off the wool socks and puts them inside the boots and continues on barefooted, sighing deeply . . .)

The clansmen have all squatted on their haunches before the ornate old woodstove into which they periodically spit tobacco; each of these oral projectiles provokes a lovely bloom of flame which lights the robust faces of the revelers a merry red. They all open pocketknives and begin whittling. Some clearing of throats . . .

"Men . . . ?" Hank goes on. "Now to the problem at hand: who's gonna teach thisyere boy to ride a motorcycle an' doodle a cousin an' all that sorta thing?"

(Once inside the office Hank stands for a while with his eyes closed before going to the desk for the figures Orland demanded. He finds the papers, in a folio labeled, in Viv's graceful hand, "P & L statements, January to June, 1961." He closes the desk drawer and walks across the room. He opens the door a few inches but doesn't go back out into the corridor. He stands, looking at the yellowed wallpaper, his ear turned slightly toward the buzz of talk from downstairs; but he can distinguish nothing except the ceaseless barking laugh of that little bitch Orland married . . .)

"Who's gonna learn him to shave with a ax blade? To nut a nigger? We got to tend to these details. Who's gonna see to him gettin' a tattoo on his hand?"

(From the kitchen Orland's wife laughs, like sticks breaking. The pinball banging light bursts into a steel guitar run, "Shovel that coal, let this rattler roll . . . 'cause I'm movin' on." Evenwrite stumbles out to his car to sleep, his fists bloodied but his pride still unpacified: who'd ever of thought that that galoot in the bar there would know the name of the All-State high-school fullback from twenty years back? Jonathan Draeger makes a neat unruffled ridge of bedspread, and a face handsome and impassive in the calculated center of his pillow. Lee slumps against the window as the bus idles at the stop sign. Hank draws a deep breath, opens the office door, and strides into the hall. His face assumes a look of belligerent amusement and he begins whistling and smacking his thigh with the folio of profit-and-loss statements. Joe Ben comes out of the bathroom and waits at the head of the stairs, buttoning the fly of his ill-fitting slacks while he watches his cousin approach . . .)

"Look at him." Joe contorted his features into a derisive grin. "Look at him with that whistling, leg-slapping, nothing-bothers-me baloney," he whispered as Hank approached.

"Appearances, Joby. You know what the old man says about appearances . . ."

"In *town*, maybe, but who's gonna care about appearances in *that* ratpack?"

"Joe! Now boy, that there is your *family* you're calling a ratpack."

"Not that Orland. Not him." Joe dug into the pocket of his slacks for more sunflower seeds. "Hank, you should of smacked him in the mouth for what he said down there."

"Hush. And give me some of those seeds. Besides, what would I want to smack good old cousin Orly for? He didn't say anything—"

"Okay, maybe not in so many words, but with what they all think about Leland and his mother and all—"

"Hell, do I give a shit what they think? What people think about a man, Joby, now that doesn't even bark the hide on his shins."

"Just the same—"

"Okay, drop it. And give me some of those."

Hank held out his hand. Joe Ben gave him a few seeds. Sunflower seeds were Joe's latest obsession and in the month he and his family had been staying with Hank at the old house while they completed his new home in town, the halls had become littered with the shells. The two men leaned against the hand-polished two-by-four that served as a banister, and ate the little seeds in silence for a few minutes. Hank felt himself growing calmer. A little bit more and he'd be ready to get back down and lock horns again. If only Orland —who as a member of the school board was naturally worried about his social position—had kept his mouth shut about the past . . . But he knew better than to expect such, from Orland anyhow. "Well, Joe"—he threw aside the rest of the seeds—"let's get with it."

Abruptly Hank stooped to pick up his boots, spat away a sunflower-seed shell, and started thumping down the steps toward the waiting furor of relatives, telling himself, Hell; what people think don't even leave a blue spot.

While to the west, almost a week away, Indian Jenny is just getting around to telling herself that Henry Stamper *musta* had reason to avoid her other'n her being Indian; didn't he fool with them Yachats squaws up north? And them squaws at Coos Bay? No, it isn't her being Indian that's kept him from her. So it must be that somebody *close* to him objects to Henry partying with Indians . . . somebody *elset* that's kept them apart all these years . . .

Downstairs Hank finished up the meeting as quickly as he could, telling the relatives, "Let's leave it hang till we get some answers back from our letters. But, say we do decide to log for WP, just remember: if we was running this outfit to the town's liking we'd of been shut down years ago." Telling himself, Besides, even if they *do* leave a blue spot or two . . . they don't really mean any harm by it.

To the north Floyd Evenwrite is awakened by a state highway patrolman. He mumbles a thanks and climbs out of the back seat and seeks a nearby gas station restroom. Where he vows to his red-nosed and red-eyed image in the mirror that he'll make Hank Stamper rue the day he used his family influence to get picked on that All-State team over him, by jumping Jesus!

Ten minutes after he had finished up the meeting Hank was outside in the barn, leaning his cheek against the warm, drumtight and pulsing stomach of the Jersey milk cow, grinning to himself over the way he had consented to do the milking while Viv helped clear up the kitchen. "Just this once, woman," he had let her know. "Just this once. So don't go gettin' any notions." She had smiled and looked away; he knew she hadn't been fooled by his hardass tone any more than Joe had been fooled by his whistling upstairs. Viv knew what Old Henry said about appearances. He wondered if she also knew just how much he enjoyed coming out and doing the milking.

He moved his ear to the animal's sleek bulk and could hear her guts working. He liked the sound. He liked the cow. He liked feeling her warmth and squeezing the rhythm of milk into the pail. It was a dumb-ass thing keeping a milk-cow these days when you could buy milk cheaper'n alfalfa, but dammit a cow's tit was a nice change from an ax-handle, and the soft working of a cow's gut was a relief after the old man's snortin' and fartin' and John's bullshitting and Orland's wife's screeching. Oh, well; they didn't really means anything by it.

The milk rang into the pail, then muffled its ringing in folds of white froth, a measured bell sounding through thick, creamy warmth.

This is Hank's bell.

On the river the motorboat gnashed at the leaf-dappled water as Joe Ben ferried the loads of people across. Cars started, spinning gravel to get back onto the highway. Henry's plaster cast thundered and rolled on the docks.

A dumb-ass thing, keeping a cow.

In the deepening sky where the spearpoint firs scratch the clouds, already a moon—like a cast-off paring from the setting sun. This is Hank's bell, too.

But god oh mighty ain't they warm to lean against?

On the docks the noisy woodpecker of a man parades up and down, shaking his plume of hair that is yellow and coarse as a bundle of broken toothpicks when seen close up; fifty yards away it is white as a thunderhead; fifty yards away at the wrong end of a telescope the drink-whipped cheeks of John glow with ruddy health, and Orland's wife steps into the waiting boat with a foot as demure and dainty as that of a thoroughbred colt. Joe Ben's poor hacked gridiron of a face shines out across the green water as pure as a cameo, and his potato-shaped wife is a swan in polka-dotted taffeta. Fifty yards away.

This is Hank's bell—secret between peaks of foam, muffled in warm white valleys—this is Hank's bell ringing.

In her cluttered kitchen amid an architectural marvel of dirty dishes, Viv wipes with her wrist that lock of hair that always touches her brow when she hurries, and hums "Mine eyes have seen the glory of the coming umming umm." The dogs bulge the back screen as they watch the venison bones and bread scraps and gravy leavings pile up in the chipped porcelain pan. Past the barn up in the orchard the little iron trees with the dusty gray-green leaves beginning to curl at the edges hang out their tributes to the sun: brass apples, and the summer sun sliding away into the ocean, old and mellow, takes the offering graciously. The gulls rock above a red surf; the long, strung-out flocks of black long-necks that like to play that they are part of the sea and fly always a foot above the water, matching every swell, every trough, make one last black thrust before finally settling to roost on the water like a speckled blanket against the night.

When it rings it's like ripples in a pool, spreading in all directions.

In town Grissom reads the comic books from his bookracks, his eyes glittering with Batman and Robin and paregoric. Boney Stokes comes from his house and moves along the sidewalk like a comical black stork, step-hop-stepping the distance to his store to check his son's bookkeeping and counting the steps to make sure no one has stolen a piece of the sidewalk. Coach Lewellyn blows his whistle and sends the team into one last clattering, sweating, dull runthrough of a play they have already practiced a dozen times; Hank sets himself for the blow of the defensive end's knee, fakes a quick sidestep, cuts back neatly, catching the boy's charge on his thighpad. The end goes down with a tired grunt and they roll together in the crushed smells of grass and sand as the halfback gallops past through the opening; the coach blows his whistle to call an end to practice; the sound stringing out on the dusk like a piece of tinsel . . .

"Hay-ank . . ."

Be nice if it could ring like this all the time . . .

"Hank?"

But it's hard to stop out other noises.

"In here, Joe; the milkhouse."

"Hankus?" Joe Ben poked his face through the milkhouse window, spitting away a sunflower seed. "I done that postal card to Leland. You want to come in and put something on it? From you personal?"

"I'll be in in just a shake. I'm just stripping out the last of her."

Joe's head withdrew. Hank put the milking stool back on top of the big box that housed the emergency generator and carried the pail of milk to the side door. He put his shoulder against the door and slid it wide, then returned to unlatch the stanchion from the cow's drowsing head and hurry her back into the pasture with a slap on the flank.

By the time he had walked back to the house with the pail of milk knocking against his leg, Viv had finished the dishes and Jan was upstairs getting her kids ready for bed. Joe was bent intently over the postcard on the breakfast table, rereading it.

Hank put the pail down on the drainboard and wiped his hands on his thighs. "Let me have a look at it . . . I suppose I should add something."

. . . and the postman, sneezing blood over a tableful of third class, advises his superior: "I don't think it was any accident; I think it was too perfect to be coincidental. I think that boy out there is a dangerous psycho and I think the blast was planned!"

And the pinball machine flashes. And the clouds file past. The bus huffs and hisses its blunt nose out into the traffic finally, where it swings hugely, ceremoniously west through the bright, picture-postcard countryside. The hand appears. The postcard flutters, dips, explodes, splintering wood and window. The lawn bucks and glitters. Evenwrite spreads his rear end on another gas station toilet seat and opens another package of Tums. Jonathan Draeger leaves a meeting in Red Bluff before it is half over, with the excuse that he has to drive on north to Eugene, but goes instead to a café where he sits and writes in his notebook: *"Man is certain or nothing but his ability to fail.* It is the deepest faith we have, and the unbeliever—the blasphemer, the dissenter—will stimulate in us the most righteous of furies. A schoolboy hates the cocky-acting kid who says he can walk the fence and never fall. A woman despises the girl who is confident that her beauty will get her man. A worker is never so angered as by an owner who *believes* in the predominance of management. And this anger can be tapped and used."

And inside the bus, reclined in his seat near the window, Lee dozed and woke, and dozed again, seldom opening more than one eye at a time to watch America flash past behind his tinted glasses: SLOW . . . STOP . . . RESUME SPEED . . . STEP UP TO QUALITY . . . with elegant young sociables entertaining each other at a cookout . . . IT'S WHAT'S UP FRONT with the same young sociables elegantly relaxing indoors after the ordeal outside . . . CAUTION . . . SLOW . . . STOP . . . RESUME SPEED . . .

Lee dozed and woke, moving west over the bus's big strumming engine; (*Evenwrite leapfrogs down the Southbound 99, from restroom to restroom*) dozing and waking indifferently, and watching the roadsigns explode past; (*Draeger cruises up from Red Bluff, stopping frequently for coffee and writing in his book*) and was rather glad that he hadn't bought that paperback novel (*Jenny watches the clouds marshaling out to sea, and begins a low singsong deepdown chant, "Oh clouds . . . oh rain . . ."*). From New Haven to Newark, to Pittsburgh WHERE THERE'S LIFE with lots of even teeth, lots of spaghetti and garlic bread THERE'S BUD and beercans turned label-to-camera (*Dyin' of the drizzlin' shits, goddammitall! Evenwrite chalked another mark up against his Nemesis as he swung to stop at another station*). Cleveland and Chicago "Get your kicks . . . on Route 66! (*"Café owners are more frustrated than the common laborer," Draeger writes. "The common laborer answers only to the foreman; the café owner answers to every patron who stops in"*) St. Louis . . . Columbia . . . Kansas City for a MAN SIZE way to stop perspiration odor MENNEN SPEED STICK with the scent that's all man! (*Who does that hardnose think he is, dammit, actin' like God Almighty?*) Denver . . . Cheyenne . . . Laramie . . . Rock Springs THE SOFT COAL CAPITAL OF THE WORLD. (*"The hardest man," Draeger writes, "is but a shell."*) Pocatello . . . Boise . . . WELCOME TO OREGON SPEED LIMIT STRICTLY ENFORCED. (*Just wait*

*till I shove this report under that damned hardnose!)* . . . Burns
. . . Bend . . . 88 MILES TO EUGENE OREGON'S SECOND MARKET
(*"Man,"* Draeger writes, *"is . . . does . . . will . . . can't . . ."*)
. . . Sisters . . . Rainbow . . . Blue River (*"Oh clouds,"* Jenny
chants, *"Oh rain . . . come against the man I say . . ."*) . . . Finn
Rock . . . Vida . . . Leaburg . . . Springfield . . . and only in Eugene seemed to come awake. He had made his trip without quite
realizing it. During stops he had bought candy bars and Coke and
gone to the bathroom, then returned to his seat, though there might
have been twenty minutes left before departure. But as he neared
Eugene the scenery began to brush long-shut doors and rattle rusty
locks, and as the bus—a different bus, rickety and uncomfortable—
began the climb from Eugene into the long range of mountains that
separates the coast from the Willamette Valley and the rest of the
continent, he found himself becoming more alert and excited. He
watched the green stand of mountains build before him, the densen-
ing of ditch growth, the clear, silver-shrouded clouds moored to the
earth by straight and thin strands of autumn smoke, like dirigibles.
And those great growling, gear-grinding log-trucks, charging out of
the wilderness with grilled grins . . . they were like (like Grendel's
dam, I would probably throw in at this time or rather, then, at that
time to keep the alliterative rolling, but as a child they were like
terrible dragons that nightly came bawling down out of the bewitched
mountains to make a shambles of my little-boy dreams. Airships of
silver mist, GMC fiends . . . these resurrections, and by no means
the last of the fancies of flight and fiend that would follow that
postcard from Oregon. Airships of silver mist, GMC fiends . . .
these resurrected childhood similes, these fancies of flight and ferocity
were the first awakening sights in my days of riding. And the first
indication that I had perhaps made a hasty choice.)

"I could still turn around and go back," I reminded myself. "I
could do that."

"What's that?" asked the man sitting across the aisle from me,
an unshaven sack of odors that I had not noticed before. "What's
that you say?"

"Nothing. Excuse me; I was just thinking out loud."

"I dream out loud, you know that? I do for a fact. Runs the old
lady nuts."

"Keeps her awake?" I asked cordially, a little embarrassed by my
slip.

"Yeah. No, not the talkin'. She keeps awake all the time waitin', see, for me to dream. She's scared, see, she'll miss me sayin' somethin' . . . I don't mean just ketch me at somethin'—she knows I'm past gallavantin', or she sure as hell should know—but just, she says, because it's like a fortune-teller the way I carry on. I dream like the dickens, predictions an' everything."

To prove his point he let his head drop back to the pillow on the seat and closed his eyes. He grinned broadly—"You'll see"—his lips slackened, parted, and in another minute he was snoring and muttering away. "Ya must not buy that place from Elkins. Mark this well . . ." Great God, I thought, looking at the yellow grillwork of this new dragon, what have you come back to?

I turned away from the stubble-cheeked sight beside me to stare out the bus window at the receding geometry of the Willamette Valley farmland—rectangle walnut groves, parallelograms of bean-fields, green trapezoid pastures dotted with red cattle; the abstract splash of autumn—and tried to assure myself, You have just come back to quaint old Oregon is all. That's all, quaint, beautiful, blooming Oregon . . .

But the dreamer beside me hiccupped and added, ". . . place is jus' overrun with Canada thistle an' nigger-heads." And my reassuring picture of assurance faded like the wind.

( . . . only a few miles ahead of Lee's bus, on the same road, Evenwrite decides to stop at the Stamper house before going on into Wakonda. He wants to confront Hank with the evidence, to see the look on the bastard's face when he sees we got the goods on him! )

We crested the summit and started down. I caught sight of a sign on a narrow white bridge that stood like a guidepost in my memory. WILDMAN CREEK, the sign instructed me. Meaning the little stream we had just crossed. Fancy that, man, ol' Wildman Creek; how my little imagination used to seize upon that name when I accompanied Mother on one of her frequent trips to Eugene and back. I leaned close to the window to see if any of the creatures I had fashioned still inhabited the prehistoric banks. Down a familiar stretch of high-way Wildman Creek ran, snorting and squalling, foam whipping about the mossy teeth of rock, shaggy green hair of pine and cedar slashings, a beard matted with fern and berry vine . . . Through the fogging window I watched him as he crouched snarling in a little glade, catching his breath in a blue pool before he went leaping off again down a grade, tearing away bank and bottom in a frenzy of impatience, and I recalled that he was the first of the tributaries that would eventually merge down these slopes into big Wakonda Auga—the Shortest Big river (or Biggest Short, pick your own) in the world.

(*Joe Ben answered Evenwrite's honking and took the boat across to get him. Inside the house they found Hank reading the Sunday funnies. Evenwrite shoved the report under his nose and demanded, "How does this smell, Stamper?" Hank took a long sniff, looking about. "Smells like somebody in here dirtied his britches, Floyd. . . .")*

And watching, seeing half-remembered farmhouses and landmarks stroking past, I couldn't quite shake the sensation that the road I traveled moved not so much through miles and mountains, as back, through time. Just as the postcard had come forward. This uneasy sensation provoked a glance at my wrist, and I thereupon discovered that my days of inactivity had allowed my self-winder to unwind.

"Say, excuse me." I turned again to the sack across from me. "Could you tell me the time?"

"*The time?*" His stubble split in a grin. "Golly, fella, we don't have such a thing as *the* time. You from outa state, ain't that so?"

I admitted it and he thrust hands in his pockets and laughed as through they were tickling him in there. "Time, eh? Time? They got the time so fouled up that I guess there doesn't nobody really know it. You take me," he offered, leaning the whole prize toward me. "Now you take me. I'm a millworker an' I work switch shifts, sometimes weekends off, sometimes a day here, a night someplace else, so you'd think that'd be *enough* of a mess, wouldn't you? But *then* they got this *time* thing and I sometimes work one day standard, the next day daylight. Sometimes even come to work on daylight and go home on standard. Oh boy, time? I tell you, you name it. We got fast time, slow time, daylight time, night time, Pacific time, good time, bad time . . . Yeah, if we Oregonians was hawking time we'd be able to offer some variety! Awfullest mix-up they ever had."

He laughed and shook his head, looking as though he could not have enjoyed the confusion more. The trouble started, he explained, when the Portland district was legislated daylight time, and the rest of the state standard. "All them dang farmers got together is why daylight got beat for the rest of the state. Danged if I see why a cow can't learn to get up at a different time just as easy as a man, do you?" During the ride I managed to find out that the chambers of commerce of other large cities—Salem, Eugene—had decided to follow Portland's lead because it was better for their business, but the danged mudballs in the country would have no part of such high-handed dealing with their polled wishes and they continued to do business on standard. So some towns didn't officially change to daylight but adopted what they called fast time, to be used only during the week. Other towns used daylight only during store hours. "Anyway, what it comes down to is nobody in the whole danged all-fired state knowin' what time it is. Don't that take all?" I joined him in his laughter, then settled back to my window, pleased that the whole danged all-fired state was as ignorant of the time of day as I was; like brother Hank signing his name in capitals, it fit.

(*At the house Hank finished glancing through the report, then asked of Evenwrite, "How come such a big strike tryin' to get a little free time, anyhow? What are you boys gonna do with a few extra hours a day if you get it?" "Never mind, that. In this day and age a fellow needs more free time." "Might be, but I'm damned if I'm gonna foot the bill for that fellow's free time."*)

Down through the druid wood I saw Wildman join with Cleaver Creek, put on weight, exchange his lean and hungry look for one of more well-fed fanaticism. Then came Chichamoonga, the Indian Influence, whooping along with its banks war-painted with lupine and columbine. Then Dog Creek, then Olson Creek, then Weed Creek. Across a glacier-raked gorge I saw Lynx Falls spring hissing and spitting from her lair of fire-bright vine maple, claw the air with silver talons, then crash screeching into the tangle below. Darling Ida Creek slipped demurely from beneath a covered bridge to add her virginal presence, only to have the family name blackened immediately after by the bawdy rollicking of her brash sister, Jumping Nellie. There followed scores of relatives of various nationalities: White Man Creek, Dutchman Creek, Chinaman Creek, Deadman Creek, and even a Lost Creek, claiming with a vehement roar that, in spite of hundreds of other creeks in Oregon bearing the same name, she was the one and only original. . . . Then Leaper Creek . . . Hideout Creek . . . Bossman Creek . . . I watched them one after another pass beneath their bridges to join in the gorge running alongside the highway, like members of a great clan marshaling into an army, rallying, swelling, marching to battle as the war chant became deeper and richer.

(*At the peak of the argument Old Henry came crashing in, making so much noise neither Hank nor Evenwrite could hear. Joe Ben took*) *the old man aside. "Henry, you bein' in here is gonna make things worse. How about you waiting over in the pantry—" "The boogerin' pantry!" "Sure; that way you can sneak a listen without them being onto you, you see?")*

Stamper Creek was the last of the small tributaries to join. Family history had it that this was the creek up which my Uncle Ben had disappeared in a frenzy of drink and despair to masturbate himself to death. This creek crossed under the highway, fell into the gorge with all the others, and these waters enlisted the South Fork, which had been rallying its own band from the mountains to my left, then, with a catching of breath and a racing of pulse, I saw what had a few miles back been wild streams and rivulets turn from charging green and white into the wide, composed, blueback surface of the Wakonda Auga, moving across the green valley like liquid steel.

There should have been background music.

*(Through the crack in the pantry door old Henry could hear Hank and Evenwrite speaking. The voices were angry, he could tell that much. He concentrated, trying to make out what they were saying, but his own breath was too loud; it roared about the little closet like a gale. Cain't hear so red-hot no more. Breath pretty good, though, jest listen. He grinned at himself in the dark, smelling the apples in their boxes, the Clorox smell of rat droppings, the banana oil of the old shotgun he held . . . Yeah, and smell good, too. Keen nose still on the old dog. He grinned, fumbling with the shotgun in the dark, wishing he could hear clear enough to know what to do.)*

When the bus dropped on down out of the foothills and rounded a curve and I got my first look at the house across that cold blue surface, I received something of a pleasant shock; the old house was ten times more striking than I remembered. In fact, it did not seem possible that I could have forgotten its looking so magnificent. They must have rebuilt it completely, I thought. But as the bus drew closer I was forced to concede that I could discern no actual change, no repairs or renovations. If anything, it looked older. But, yes, that was it. Someone had removed the cracked coat of cheap white paint from all the sides. The window sills, the shutters, and all the other trimmings had been kept up in dark green, almost blue-green, but the rest of the house had been relieved of all paint; the crazy porch with its rough-hewn posts, the broad handsplit shaking that covered roof and sides, the huge front door—all had been stripped to allow the salt wind and bleaching rain to polish the wood to a rich pewter-gray shine.

The bushes along the bank were trimmed, but instead of being attacked with that mathematical dedication one so often finds in suburban landscaping, they had been trimmed for a purpose, to let in light, or to afford a better view of the river and make the dock walk more accessible. The flowers that bloomed at random around the porch and along the sides of the embankment had obviously required great care and attention, but again there was nothing forced or unnatural: they were not flowers bred in Holland and raised in California and flown in to be pampered in local nurseries; they were the flowers common to the area, rhododendron and wild rose, trillium and ghost fern, and even some of the cursed Himalaya berry that the denizens of the coast battle the year round.

I was thunderstruck because, difficult as it was for me to imagine either old Henry or brother Hank or even Joe Ben accidentally achieving the subtle, spare beauty that I saw across the river there, it was a hundred times more ridiculous imagining that any of them had done it on purpose.

(*It useta be so simple when I could hear better. Things was easy to figure. You come up to a rock you either jumped it or heaved it outten the path. Now I don't know. Twenty or thirty years ago I'd of made sure there were a shell in this barrel instead of make sure there ain't. Now I don't know. The old nigger don't hear so clear no more is one trouble.*)

With my last dollar I purchased from the bus driver the privilege of alighting in front of the garage instead of having to ride eight miles on into town and walk back. As I stood in the dust the driver advised me that my measly buck paid for nothing more than his stopping and letting me off; he couldn't foul up his schedule by opening the baggage compartment—"Sonny this ain't the Wells Fargo Stage Coach!" And left me protesting in his exhaust.

So there stands our hero, with nothing but the wind in his hair, the clothes on his back, and the carbon monoxide in his nostrils. Quite a contrast, I mused, crossing the road, from that boatload of essentials I left with twelve years ago. I hope the calf is well fatted.

On the gravel apron near the garage a new pea-green Bonneville gleamed in the sun. I walked past it and on into the three-sided affair that served as shelter, machine shop, dockhouse, and garage. Grease and dust upholstered the floor and walls in a rich mauve velvet; mud hornets whizzed through dusty sunbeams near the roof; a yellow jeep heaped with equipment rested boxlike and resigned to its load near one wall, and beyond its cracked headlights I saw that Hank had purchased a bigger and brighter motorcycle; it was tethered on a chain against the back wall and bedecked with black leather and polished brass like a show horse in parade trappings. I looked about the garage for a phone; I had taken for granted that they must have installed some kind of device for signaling when a boat was desired, but I saw nothing, and when I glanced through the cobwebbed window toward the house across the river I caught sight of something that made me forsake all hope of such modern convenience; swung from a pole was a tattered cloth with numbers on it, the signal used for ordering wares from the Stokes grocery truck that came by every other day, the same primitive method of communication that had been going on years before my birth.

(*But by god the old hound don't need good ears for some things goddammit. He don't need good ears to know where to draw the boogin' line! And all this goddam telling me it's best old man you keep outta sight and outta trouble that don't set so good. I get tired! I get tired of!*)

I left the garage and was wondering how my modulated tenor, tuned for polite classroom intercourse back in a civilized world, could be expected to carry across the expanse of water, when I saw a disturbance at the massive front door across the way. (*By god I maybe can't hear so good but I know what's right and what ain't by god if I don't!*) I saw a stocky man in a brown suit come running across the lawn in thick-legged haste, holding his hat to his head with one hand and an attaché case in the other, shouting back at the house. Stirred by the shouts, a battalion of hounds charged from beneath the house and the man cut short his tirade, paused a moment to flail at the pack with the case, which burst open in a bright yellow blizzard of paper, turned to run again, dogs and paper flapping at his heels. (*By god one thing I just ain't about to tolerate is!*) The front door banged again and another figure came charging out (*goddammit is is is;*) brandishing an ugly black shotgun and making a clamor that put to shame the barking and shouting that had gone before. The man in the suit dropped his case, turned to recover it, saw the terrifying approach of this new menace, and ran on without it down the incline to the dock, leaped into the fire-engine-red launch at the mooring, and began wildly jerking at the motor rope.

He paused once to look back up the plank walkway at the awesome creature storming through the dogs and bearing vengefully down on him, then redoubled his frantic efforts to start the motor (Get back! Henry Stamper, you gone crazy with age there's laws in this country [is IS is] oh Jesus he's got a shotgun. Start! Start!) as the other man came closer and closer (*What's wrong'th this boogin' gun* [Start! Start!] *I'll by the goddam see to who unloaded one thing I won't tolerate by god is is is*) louder and louder. (Start! oh god here he comes [IS IS IS] oh god START!)

Across the river Henry had dropped his gun. No; now he had it again! Now he was down. Now he was moving toward the dock again! His hair flew out behind him in a long white mane. His arm pumped him onward. He was impressive in a plaid shirt and a pair of knee-length wool undershorts and a plaster cast that ran in one piece from the tip of one foot seemingly all the way up his side and out over his shoulder, forcing him to carry that arm bent before him as though ossified there. Why, the old trouper has grown so venerably ancient, I thought, that he is preserving his matchless idiocy for posterity by gradually having himself done over in limestone (*if anybody goddammit thinks for one minit that just because I'm I'm I'm*).

He swayed and teetered in his restricted advance and struck at the welter of hounds with the shotgun, which served alternately as firearm, crutch, and club. He reached the dock and I could hear the thundering boom of his plaster leg as it sounded on the boards, the report reaching me a second after the foot set down, so the sound appeared to issue from the lifting foot instead of the dock. He lumbered forward down the dock like a comic Frankenstein's monster, booming that foot, striking about with that gun, and cursing so fast and loud that the words were sacrificed to wholesale noise (*because I never yet rose to see the GODDAM day I weren't up to RUNNING my own SONVABITCHING affairs and if any BASTARD thinks*).

The man in the boat jerked the motor to life and threw off the mooring just as the three other characters in this drama came running from the house and down onto the dock: two men and what I ventured to think a woman in jeans and an orange-colored apron, and a long braid flopping down the back of the ubiquitous sweat shirt. She passed the two men and scampered across the dock to try to calm Old Henry's raving; the two men held back, letting him rave his damnedest and laughing so they could barely walk. Henry ignored the calming and laughing alike and continued to rail at the man in the boat, who must have concluded that the gun was empty or broken because he had pulled a safe twenty yards away from the dock and was idling the boat at a standstill into the current so he could have his turn at shouting back at the others. All up and down the river I could see startled gulls flapping airward in a frightened flight from the uproar.

(*Oh lordy what am I doing with this here scattergun? Oh lordy I don't hear so good. I truly do not . . .*)

Henry appeared to be tiring. One of the men, the taller one, who I decided must be Hank—what other Caucasian ever moved with that slack-limbed indolence?—left the others and loped into the boatshed and reappeared, bent in an odd position as he shielded something with his cupped hands. He stood at the edge of the dock in this position for a moment, then straightened up to throw whatever he held in the direction of the boat. (*Oh lordy, what's happening?*) And then there was nothing but *silence* as the whole cast—the figures on the dock, the petrified brown lump in the boat, even the pack of dogs—stood perfectly still and quiet for perhaps two and three-quarters seconds before a thundering blast right next to the boat jammed a white column of water forty feet into the hot, smoky air, ka-*whooomp!* like an Old Faithful erupting in the middle of the river.

As the water fell back into the boat the men on the dock roared with laughter. They stumbled with their laughter, they grew weak with it, they finally collapsed under it like drunks. Even Old Henry's cursing became so diluted with laughter that he was finally forced to lean weakly against a piling, no longer able to support both himself and the colossal amusement that shook him. The lump in the boat saw Hank heading back into the shed to reload and overcame his shellshock enough to gun the boat motor on full so that he was out of range of Hank's next throw by a good three feet. The explosion bucked the boat forward like a surfboard catching a fifteen-foot comber, and this set off new hysterics on the dock. (*Anyhow by god I guess I showed him he can't tell me how to run my my . . . business, hear good or no!*)

The boat pulled up to the landing where I watched, and the man grabbed for a hold on one of the bumper tires that were dangling in the water. He leaped out onto the landing without tying the boat or turning off the motor, and I was compelled to make a courageous lunge to catch the rope at the rear of the boat lest it escape pilotless down river. As I stood there with my feet braced, holding the boat while it tugged to be off again like a whale on a leash, I thanked the man pleasantly for bringing transportation across to me and congratulated him on the little welcoming-home skit he had so generously taken part in. He stopped gathering what was left of his papers and raised a reddened round face in my direction, seeming to notice me for the first time.

"And I'll just bet you're another one of the scabbin' bastards!" He thrust his Jiggs-like face in my direction. Little rivulets of water running out of his frizzy red hair kept getting in his eyes, forcing him to blink and rub at the sockets with both fists like a child crying. "Ain't I right?" he demanded, rubbing and blinking. "Huh? Ain't I now?" But before I could summon an appropriately clever answer he turned and lurched up the planks toward his new car, cursing so mournfully that I wasn't sure whether to laugh at the man or pity him.

I lashed the impatient boat to a mooring and went back to the garage for the jacket I had left lying on the jeep. When I returned I saw across the way that Hank had removed his shirt and shoes and was in the process of pulling down his trousers. He and the other man—Joe Ben, from the banty-legged way he stood—were still laughing. Old Henry was working his way back up the bank toward the house, much more laboriously than he had come down.

As Hank pulled a leg from his pants he supported himself by leaning a hand on the shoulder of the woman standing near him. This must be brother Hank's pale wildwoods flower, I decided; barefooty and fattened out round and comfortable on huckleberry and pemmican. Hank finished with his pants and made a flat, whacking dive into the river, the same racing dive I had watched him practice years ago as I peeked from behind curtains of my room. As he started stroking across I noticed that the neat, strength-conserving stroke of the racing swimmer was somehow marred. There was a hitch in the smoothness of the movement every two or three strokes, a jog in the rhythm that seemed caused by something other than a lack of practice; if one could be permitted the term in reference to a swimmer, I suppose we might say that Hank had developed a limp. As I watched I thought, I was right, he is past his prime; the old giant is weakening. Perhaps that recompense of blood will not be so difficult to claim as I feared.

Heartened by this thought I got into the boat, untied the rope, and with some experimenting managed to turn the bow about and head in Hank's direction. The boat moved only slightly faster than idling speed, but I couldn't fathom the throttle on the motor and had to proceed at the rate Jiggs had left for me; by the time I had putted out to Hank he was better than halfway across.

When I got close he stopped swimming and trod water, squinting against the water to see who was picking him up, as he waited for me to stop the boat for him. But I found I was no more able to slow the motor than I had been able to speed it up. I had to make three runs before Hank realized I couldn't stop for him; he got a hand over the side on the third time by and jerked himself on board, his long, veined arm snapping his body into the air like an arrow fired from a lemonwood bow. As he rolled into the boat I saw why he had limped in his swimming stroke and why he had used only the one hand to pull himself from the water: two fingers were missing from the other, but other than that he still seemed pretty much in prime.

He lay for a moment in the bottom of the boat, blowing water, then climbed onto a seat facing me. He dropped his face into his hand as though he were rubbing the bridge of his nose, or wiping the water from his mouth; this was his characteristic attempt to either hide the grin you already knew was there, or to draw your attention to it. Watching him, watching the way he had jerked himself into the boat with flawless physical control and now watching the composure with which he confronted me—at ease, as though he had not only known it was me coming to pick him up but had planned it that way —I felt the momentary optimism I had experienced back on the dock replaced by a surge of apprehension. . . . If the giant is weakening WATCH OUT! WATCH OUT! then he has chosen a poor way to demonstrate it.

Still he didn't speak. I fumbled out some apology for being unable to stop the motor to pick him up, and was about to explain that Yale offered no course on seamanship when he raised his wet eyebrows—without moving his face, without lifting it from his hand— raised his brown and beaded eyebrows and looked at me with eyes as bright and green and poisonous as copper sulfate crystals.

"You had three tries, bub," he observed wryly, "and missed me every time; now don't that frost you?"

. . . While Indian Jenny, having swallowed enough snuff and

whisky to make her feel confident of her race's ability to influence certain phenomena, looked out through the spider web that laced her lone window and finished her spell: "Oh clouds . . . oh rain. I call down all sorts bad weather an' bad luck on Hank Stamper, uh-huh!" Then turned her black little eyes back into the empty shack to see if the shadows were impressed.

. . . And Jonathan Draeger, in a motel in Eugene, wrote: "Man will do away with anything that threatens him with loneliness—even himself."

. . . And Lee, riding with his brother across the river toward the old house, wondered, Home again all right, but now what?

All up and down the coast there are little towns like Wakonda, logging bars like the Snag, where weary little men talk about hard times and trouble. The old wino boltcutter has seen them all, has heard all the talk. He has been listening over his shoulder all afternoon, hearing the younger men talk about the trouble nowdays as though their dissatisfaction is a recent development, a sign of unusual times. He listened for a long time while they talked and pounded the table and read bits from the *Eugene Register Guard* blaming the despondency on "these troubled times of Brinkmanship, Blamesmanship, and Bombsmanship." He listened to them accuse the federal government of turning America into a nation of softies, then listened to them condemn the same body for its hardhearted refusal to help the faltering town through the recession. He usually makes it a rule on his drinking trips into town to remain aloof from nonsense such as this, but when he hears the delegation agreeing that much of the community's woes can be laid at the feet of the Stampers and their stubborn refusal to unionize, it is too much for him to take. The man with the union button is in the middle of explaining that these times demand more sacrifice on the part of the goddamned individual, when the old boltcutter rises noisily to his feet.

"These times?" He advances on them, his bottle held dramatically aloft. "What do you think, everything used to be apple-pie 'n' ice cream?"

The citizens look up in surprised indignation; it is regarded as something of a breach in local protocol to interrupt these sessions.

"That bomb talk? All horseshit." He rears over their table, unsteady in a cloud of blue smoke. "That depression talk and that other business, that strike business? More horseshit. For twenty years, thirty years, forty years, all th' way back to the Big War, somebody been sayin' oh me, the trouble is such, oh my the trouble is so; the trouble is the ray-dio, the trouble is the Republicans, the trouble is the Democrats, the trouble is the Commy-ists . . ." He spat on the floor with a pecking motion of his head. "All horseshit."

"What, in your opinion, is the trouble?" The Real Estate Man tilts back his chair and grins up at the intruder, preparing to humor him. But the old fellow beats him to the punch; he laughs sadly, the sudden anger turning as suddenly to pity; he shakes his head and looks about at the citizens—"You boys, you boys . . ."—then places his empty bottle on the table and crooks a long, knob-knuckled forefinger around the neck of a full bottle and shuffles out of the bright sun that slants through the Snag's front window. "Don't you see it's just the same plain old horseshit as always?"

Y*ou can make a mark across the night with the tip of an embered stick, and you can actually see it fixed in its finity. You can be absolutely certain of its treacherous impermanence. And that is all. Hank knew . . .*

As well as he knew that the Wakonda has not always run this course. (Yeah . . . you want to know something about rivers, friends and neighbors?)

Along its twenty miles numerous switchbacks and oxbows, sloughs and backwaters mark its old channel. (You want me to tell you a thing or two about rivers?) Some of these sloughs are kept clean by small currents from nearby streams, making them a chain of clear, deep, greenglass pools where great chubs lie on the bottom like sunken logs; in the winter the pools in these sloughs are nightly stopovers for chevrons of brant geese flying south down the coast; in the spring the pole willows along the banks arch long graceful limbs out over the water; when an angler breeze baits the tree, the leafy tips tickle the surface and tiny fingerling salmon and steelhead dart up to strike, sometimes shooting clear into the sunshine like little silver bullets fired from the depths. (Funny thing is, I didn't learn this thing about rivers from the old man or any of the uncles, or even Boney Stokes, but from old Floyd Evenwrite, a couple years ago, that first time Floyd and us locked horns about the union.)

Some sloughs are flooded spear-fields of cattail and skunk cabbage where loons and widgeon breed; some are bogs where maple leaves and eelgrass and snakeweed skeleton with decay and silently dissolve into purple, oil-sheened mud; and some of the sloughs have silted in completely and dried enough to become rich blue-green deer pastures or two-story-high berry thickets. (The way it happened I'd come to town to meet with Floyd Evenwrite that first time this Closed Shop business came up and instead of taking the cycle I figured I'd use the boat to try out this brand-new Johnson Seahorse 25 I'd picked up in Eugene not a week before, and swinging in toward the municipal dock I whanged into something floating out of sight; probably an old deadfall washed loose, and the boat and motor went down like a rock and I had to swim it, mad as hell and sure as shooting in no frigging mood to talk Labor Organization.)

There is one such berry thicket up river from the Stamper house, a thicket so dense, so woven and tangled that even the bears avoid it: from the mossy bones of deer and elk trapped trying to trample a path rises a wall of thorns that appears totally impenetrable. (In the meeting Floyd did most of the talking, but I didn't do my share of the listening. I couldn't get my mind on him. I just sat there looking out the window where my boat and motor had sunk, feeling my Sunday slacks shrink dry on me.) But when Hank was a boy of ten he found a way to penetrate this thorny wall: he discovered that the rabbits and raccoons had tunneled an elaborate subway system next to the ground, and by pulling on a hooded oilskin poncho to protect his hide from the thorns, he was able to half crawl, half worm his way through that snarl of vines. (Floyd kept talking on and on; I knew he was expecting me and the half-dozen or so other gyppo men to be mowed right over by his logic. I don't know about them other boys, but for myself I wasn't able to follow him worth sour apples. My pants dried; it got warmer; I pulled on my motorcycle shades so's he couldn't see if I dropped off during his talk; and I leaned back and sulked about that boat and motor.)

When the spring sun was bright above the thicket, enough light filtered down through the leaves so he was able to see, and he would spend hours on his hands and knees exploring the smooth passageways. He frequently came face to face with a fellow explorer, an old boar coon, who, the first time he encountered the boy, had huffed and growled and hissed, then turned loose a musk that put a skunk to shame, but as they met again and again the old masked outlaw gradually came to regard this hooded intruder as something of a partner in crime; in a dim passageway of thorn the boy and the animal stand nose to nose and compare booty before they go on with their furtive ramblings: "What you got, old coon? A fresh wapatoo? Well, look here at my gopher skull . . ." (Floyd talked on and on and on and—what with sitting there half asleep stewing about the boat and river and all—I got to thinking about something that'd happened a long time before, something I'd clean forgot about . . .) He found countless treasures in the passageways: a foxtail caught in the thorns; a fossilized bug that still struggled against a millennium of mud; a rusted ball-and-cap pistol that reeked still of rum and romance . . . but never anything near to equaling the discovery made one chilly April afternoon. (I got to thinking about the bobcats I found in the berry vines, is what; I got to remembering them bobcats.)

There were three kittens at the end of a strange new passageway, three kittens with their blue-gray eyes but a few days open, peering up at him from a mossy, hair-lined nest. Except for the nub of a tiny tail, and the tassels of hair at the tip of each tiny ear, they looked much the same as barn kittens that Henry drowned by the sackful every summer. The boy stared wide-eyed at them playing in their nest, overcome by his remarkable good fortune. "Suck egg mule," he whispered reverently, as though such a find needed the awed respect of Uncle Aaron's expressions instead of the forceful punch of old Henry's curses. "Three little baby bobcats all by theirselves . . . suck egg mule."

He picked up the nearest kitten and began to fight and tear at the vine until he had made a space large enough to turn around in. He headed back the way he'd come, reasoning, without even consciously thinking about it, that the mother would most likely pick a route that he hadn't used, she would most likely steer clear of a tunnel with man-smell in it. He found he was being slowed by holding the hissing and snapping kitten in his hands so he took the scruff of its neck between his teeth. The kitten became immediately calm and swung placidly from the boy's mouth as Hank sped through the blackberries as fast as elbows and knees could carry him. "Beat it out; *beat it!*"

When he emerged from the thicket he was scratched and bleeding from a score of places on his hands and face, but he didn't remember any pain, he didn't remember any of the scratches; all he could recall was the soft flutter of panic beneath his chest. What would have happened had that old bitch bobcat suddenly run smack dab into a boy toting one of her offspring in his mouth? A boy pinned down and practically helpless under fifteen feet of blackberry vines? He had to sit down and breathe deeply before he could manage the ten more yards to the empty blasting-cap crate where he put the kitten.

Then, for some reason, instead of securing the box and beating it back to the house as he advised himself, he hesitated to inspect his catch. Carefully he slid back the lid and bent to look into the box.

"Hey you. Hey there you, Bobby the Cat . . ."

The little animal ceased its frantic scurrying from corner to corner and lifted its fuzzy face toward the sound of the voice. Then uttered a cry so tragic, so pleading, so frightened and forlorn, that the boy winced with sympathy.

"Hey, you lonely, ain't you? Huh, ain't you?"

The kitten's yowled answer threw the boy into an intense conflict, and after five minutes of reminding himself that nobody no-body but a snotnosed moron would go back in that hole, he gave in to that yowling.

The other two kittens had fallen asleep by the time he reached the nest. They lay curled about each other, purring softly. He paused for an instant to catch his breath, and in the silence that descended, now that the brambles were no longer scratching and resounding on his oilskin hood, heard the first kitten crying from its box at the edge of the thicket; the thin, pitiful wail penetrated the jungle like a needle. Why, a noise like that must carry for miles! He grabbed up the next kitten, clamped his teeth over the fur at the back of the neck, thrashed quickly around in the little turning space that was already beginning to take on a smooth, used appearance, and once more sprinted on elbows and knees for that opening to safety that lay an ever farther distance away through an ever smaller tube of thorns and terror. It seemed to take hours. Time got snagged on a sticker. The vines hissed past. It must have started to rain, for the tunnel had grown quite dim and the ground slick. The boy squirmed through with eyes straining, that bobcat's child swaying and swinging in his mouth, keening a shrill plea for help, the other in the box echoing and relaying the plea. The tunnel got longer as it grew dimmer, he was certain of it. Or the other way around. He gasped for breath through the fur in his teeth. He battled the mud and vine as though it were water drowning him, and when he broke into the clear at the end of the tunnel he drew a huge breath like a swimmer coming after many minutes into the glorious air.

He placed the second kitten in the box with the first. They both hushed their yowling and became quiet and drowsy against each other. They began to purr quietly along with the soft swish of rain through the pines. And the only other noise, through all the forest, was the brokenhearted wailing of that third kitten, alone and frightened and wet, back in that nest at the end of that tunnel.

"You'll be okay." He called assurance toward the thicket. "Sure. It's rainin' now; mama'll be hustlin' back from huntin', now it's rainin'."

And this time even went so far as to pick up the box and walk a few yards toward home.

But something was strange; safe as he knew himself to be—he had picked up the .22 from the hollow log where he always stashed it during his forays into the thicket—his heart still pounded and his stomach still heaved with fear, and the image of that mother cat's wrath still burned in his head.

He stopped walking and stood very still with his eyes closed. "No. No sir, by gosh, I ain't." Shaking his head back and forth: "No. I ain't such a dummy as *that*, I don't care what!"

But the fear continued to shake against his ribs, and it occurred to him that it had been shaking that way constantly from the moment he'd found the three kittens playing peacefully in their nest. Because it had known—it, the fear, *the being-awful-scared-of-something*—had known the boy better than he knew himself, had known all along from that first glance that he wasn't going to be satisfied until he had all three kittens. It didn't make any difference if they were baby dragons and mama dragon was breathing fire on him every step of the way.

So it wasn't until he emerged the third time with the third kitten between his teeth that he was able to sigh and relax and peacefully start toward the house, triumphantly shouldering the explosives box as if it were spoils of a mighty battle. And when he met the old coon waddling toward him on the muddy path he saluted the inscrutable animal and advised him, "Maybe you better leave off the thickets t'day, Mister Jig; it's fierce in yonder for a old man."

Henry was in the woods. Uncle Ben and Ben, Junior—a boy called Little Joe by everyone but his father, shorter and younger than Hank and already showing his hell-raising father's heavenly good looks— were staying at the house while Uncle Ben's present woman cooled off enough to take them back into her home in town. They saw the kittens and Hank's scratched and bleeding condition and both arrived at the same conclusion.

"Did you really?" asked the boy. "Did you really, Hank, fight a wildcat for 'em?"

"No, not really," Hank replied modestly.

Ben looked at his nephew's scratched and muddy face and triumphant eyes. "Oh, you did. Oh yeah you did, kid. Maybe not head on. Maybe not a wildcat. But you fought something." Then surprised both Hank and his own boy by spending the rest of the afternoon helping build a cage out near the river's edge.

"I don't care much for cages," he told them. "I'm not keen on cages of any kind. But if these cats are ever to get big enough to hold their own against those hounds, it's gonna have to be in protected confinement. So we'll make it a good cage, a comfortable cage; we'll make the world's *best* cage."

And that short, beautifully featured black sheep of the family, who prided himself on never working with more than his wink and his smile, slaved away all afternoon helping two boys build a true paragon among cages. It was made from an old pick-up-truck box that had once been on Aaron's pick-up but had sucked too much dust to suit him. When finished, this box was painted, calked, reinforced, and stood majestically a few feet from the ground on sawn four-by-four legs. Half of it, including the floor, was of wire mesh to make it easy to keep clean, and the door was large enough that Hank or Joe Ben could get right in with the regular tenants. There were boxes for hiding, straw for burrowing, and a burlap-covered post for climbing to the peaked top of the cage, where a wicker basket was lined with an old pair of woolens. There were a little tree to climb and rubber balls hung from the mesh ceiling with string, and a dishpan full of fresh river sand in case bobcats, like other cats, were inclined that way. It was a beautiful cage, a strong cage, and, as comfort in cages went, the goddamned cat cage—as Henry came to call it whenever smell indicated it was past time for cleaning—was as comfortable as a cage could be.

"The *best* of all possible cages." Ben stepped back to regard the job with a sad smile. "What more can one ask?"

Hank spent a large part of that summer in the cage with the three kittens, and by fall they were all so accustomed to his morning visit that if it was delayed by so much as five minutes there was such a howl raised that old Henry would pardon his son from whatever chore he was doing and send him running to attend to that damned menagerie in the goddam boogering cat cage. By Halloween the cats were tame enough to bring into the house to play; by Thanksgiving Hank had promised his classmates that on Playday, the day before Christmas vacation, he would bring all three to school.

The night before this event the river had risen four feet in response to three hard days of rain; Hank was worried that the boats might be swept loose from their moorings, as they had been last year, and prevent him from making it across to the school bus. Or, worse, that the river might even rise clear up to the cage. Before going up to bed he put on rubber boots over his pajamas and pulled on a poncho and went out with a lantern to check. The rain had slowed to a thin, cold spitting that came with occasional gusts of wind; the worst of the storm was over; the white blur above the mountains showed the moon trying to clear a way through the clouds. In the buttery yellow light of the lantern he could see the rowboat and the motorboat covered with green tarpaulins, bobbing in the dark water. They tugged at their ropes, pulling to be away up river, but they were safe. The tides at the river's mouth were flooding, and the river was flowing inland instead of toward the sea. The current usually flowed four hours toward the sea, then stood an hour, then turned and flowed two or three hours in the other direction. During this backward up-river flow, as the salt water from the sea rushed to embrace the mud-filled rainwater from the mountains, the river would be at its highest. Hank noted the water's height on the marker at the dock—black water swirling at the number five; five feet, then, above the normal high-tide mark—then he went on to the end of the dock and followed the rickety plank walk around the edge of the jetty to the place where his father was clinging with a crooked elbow to a cable, seemingly glued to the side of the foundation by the sticky light of his lantern while he hammered spikes into a two-by-six he was adding to the tangle of wood and cable and pipe. Henry held his hammer and squinted against the blowing gusts of rain.

"Is that you, boy? What do you want out here this time of night?" he demanded fiercely, then as an afterthought asked, "You come out to give the old man a hand at floodtime, is that it?"

The last thing in the boy's mind was freezing for an hour in this wind, hammering aimlessly on that crazy business of his father's, but he said, "I don't know. I might, then I might not." He hung, swinging outward by the cable, and looked past old Henry's streaking features; by the light coming from his mother's upstairs window he could see the outline of the cat cage against black clouds. "No sir, I just don't know. . . . How much higher you reckon she'll raise to-night?"

Henry leaned out to spit his exhausted wad of snuff down into the water. "The tides'll shift in an hour. At the rate she's risin' now she'll come up two more feet, three at the darnedest, then start easin' back. Especial now that the rain's quittin'."

"Yeah," Hank agreed, "I reckon that's about the way I see it." Looking at the cage he realized that the river would have to rise a good fifteen feet to reach even the legs, and by that time the house, the barn, probably the whole town of Wakonda would be washed away. "So I guess I'll go on in an' hit the sack. She's all yours," Hank called over his shoulder.

Henry looked after his son. The moon had finally made it through, and the boy moving away down the planks in his shapeless poncho, black outlined in glistening silver, was as much a mystery to the old man as the clouds he resembled. "Feisty little outfit." Henry dipped out another charge of snuff, jammed it into the breech, and resumed his hammering.

By the time Hank was in bed the rain had stopped completely and patches of stars were showing. The big moon meant good clamming at the flats as well as colder, drier weather. Before he fell asleep he could tell by the absence of sound from the river that it had crested and from here on would drain back to the sea.

When he woke in the morning he looked out and saw the boats were fine and the river wasn't much higher than usual. He hurried through breakfast, then took the box he had prepared and ran out toward the cage. He went first to the barn to pick up some burlap sacks to put in the bottom of the box. The morning was cold; a light frost was sifted into all the shadows and the cow breath was like skim milk in the air. Hank pulled some sacks from the pile in the feed room, scattering mice, and ran on out through the back door. The chill air in his lungs made him feel light and silly. He turned the corner and stopped: *the bank!* (About the time I went to nodding into my dream about the cats, Floyd and old man Syverson who used to run the little mill at Myrtleville had really got into it about something; they snapped me out of it, hollering back and forth at each other to beat hell.) . . . *The whole bank where the cage stood is gone; the new bank shines bright and clean, as though a quick slice had been made into the earth last night with the edge of a huge moonstropped razor.* ("Syverson," Evenwrite yells, "don't be so dunderheaded; I'm talkin' sense!" And Syverson says, "Bull. What you mean, sense!" "Sense! I'm talking *sense!*" "Bull. You talkin' sign over t' you all the say-so I got of my business is what you talkin'!") *At the bottom of this slice, in the mud and roots, the corner of the cage protrudes above the turgid surface of the river. Floating in the corner behind the wire mesh are the contents of the cage—the rubber balls, the torn cloth Teddy bear, the wicker basket and sodden bedding, and the shrunken bodies of the three cats.* ("How much's it want," Syverson yells, "how much, this organization you tell us about?" "Dang it, Syve, all it wants is what's fair—" "Fair! It wants advantage is what.") *Looking so very small with their wet fur plastered against their bodies, so small and wet and ugly.* ("Okay! okay!" Floyd hollered, getting rattled, "but all it wants is its fair advantage!")

*He doesn't want to cry; he hasn't allowed himself to cry in years. And to stop that old scalding memory mounting in his nose and throat he forces himself to imagine exactly what it must have been like—the crumbling, the cage rocking, then falling with the slice of earth into the water, the three cats thrown from their warm bed and submerged in struggling icy death, caged and unable to swim to the surface. He visualizes every detail with painful care and then runs the scene over and over through his mind until it is grooved into him, until a call from the house puts a stop to his torture. . . .* (Everybody laughed when Floyd made that slip, even old Floyd himself. And for some time after folks kidded him about it. "All it wants is its fair advantage." But me, not paying attention, nodding on and off, thinking about my drowned cats and my new Johnson outboard at the bottom of the drink, I kind of switched what he said to something else.) *Until the pain and guilt and loss are replaced by something different, something larger . . .*

After putting the box and gunny sacks down I went back into the house and got my lunch along with that bony little peck the old lady laid on my cheek every morning. Then I went out to where old Henry was readying the boat to ferry me and Joe Ben across to wait for the school bus. I kept still, hoping neither of them'd notice me not having the box of cats like I'd planned. (*. . . replaced for good by something far stronger than guilt or loss.*) And they might not of, because the motorboat wouldn't start, it being so cold, and after Henry had jerked and kicked and cussed and raved at it for about ten minutes he finally barked the hide off his knuckles and then he wasn't in any shape to notice anything. We all got into the row boat and I thought I was gonna make it, but on the way across old bright-eyed Joe Ben gave a yell and pointed at the bank. "The cat cage! Hank, the cat cage!"

I didn't say anything. The old man stopped rowing and looked, then turned to me. I frigged around, acting like I was all wrapped up tying my shoe or something. But pretty quick I saw they weren't gonna let me off the hook without I said something or other. So I just shrugged and told them, cool and matter-of-fact, "It's a dirty deal, is all. Nothing but just a crappy deal."

"Sure," the old man said. "The way the football bounces."

"Sure," Joe Ben said.

"Just a tough break," I said.

"Sure," they said.

"But boy, I'll tell ya I'll tell—you . . ." I could feel that cool, matter-of-fact tone slipping away, but couldn't do diddle about it. "If I ever—ever, I don't care when—get me any more of them bobcats—oh, Christ, Henry, that crappy river, I should, I should of—"

And when I couldn't go on I went to beating at the side of the boat until the old man took me by the fist and stopped me.

And after that the whole thing was done and shut and forgot. None of the family ever mentioned it. For a while kids at school asked me how about them *bobcats* I was always blowing about, how come I hadn't brought them *bobcats* to school? . . . but I just told them to fuck off, and after I told them enough times and showed them I meant what I said a time or two, *nobody* mentioned it any more. So I forgot it. Leastways the part of a man that remembers out loud forgot it. But years later it used to wonder me just how come I'd sometimes get all of a sudden so itchy to cut out from basketball practice, or from a date. It would really wonder me. To other people—Coach Lewellyn or a drinking buddy, or whatever honey I might have been necking with—I would say that if I waited too long the river would be up too high to cross. "Report of high water," I'd say. "If she gets up too big there's a chance the boat might be pulled loose and there I'd be, you know, up that ol' creek without that ol' canoe." I'd tell buddies and coaches that I had to beat it home "on account of that ol' Wakonda is risin' like a wall between me and the supper table." I'd tell dates just ready to tip over that "sorry kid, I got to up and hustle or the boat might be swamped." But myself, I'd tell myself, Stamper, you got deals going with it, with that river. Face it. You might've put all kinds of stories on the little girlies from Reedsport, but when it comes right down to it you know them stories are so much crap and you got deals going with that snake of a river.

It was like me and that river had drawn ourselves a little contract, a little grudge match, and without me knowing exactly why. "It's like this, sweetie-britches," I might say to some little high-school honey we was parked someplace, steaming up the windows of the old man's pick-up in some Saturday-night battle of the bra. "It's like if I don't go *now*, then it might be shiver all night long waitin' to get across; it's rainin', look out there at it come down like a cow wettin' on a flat rock!" Feed her any dumb tale but know what you meant was you *had to*—for some reason I didn't know then—*had* to get home and get into a slicker and corks and get a hammer and nails and lay on the timbers like a crazy man, maybe even give up a sure *hump* just to freeze a half an hour out on that goddamned jetty!

And I never understood why until that afternoon in Wakonda at the union meeting, sitting there remembering how I'd lost my bob-cats, looking out the window of the grange hall at the spot where my boat had sung in the bay, and hearing Floyd Evenwrite say to old man Syverson: "All it wants is its fair advantage."

So as close as I can come to explaining it, friends and neighbors, that is why that river is no buddy of mine. It's maybe the buddy of the brant geese and the steelhead. It is mighty likely a buddy of old lady Pringle and her Pioneer Club in Wakonda—they hold oldtime get-togethers on the docks every Fourth of July in honor of the first time some old moccasined hobo come paddling across in his dugout a hundred years ago, the Highway of Pioneers they call it . . . and who the hell knows, maybe it *was*, just like now it is the railroad we use to float our log booms down—but it still is no personal friend of *mine*. Not just the thing about the bobcats; I could tell you a hundred stories, probably, give you a hundred reasons showing why I got to fight that river. Oh, *fine* reasons; because you can spend a good deal of time thinking during those thinking times, when you're taking timber cruises walking all day long with nothing to do but check the pedometer on your foot, or sitting for hours in a stand blowing a game call, or milking in the morning when Viv is laid up with cramps—a *lot* of time, and I got a lot of things about myself straight in my mind: I know, for an instance, that, if you want to play this way, you can make the river stand for all *sorts* of other things. But doing that it seems to me is taking your eye off the ball; making it more than what it is lessens it. Just to see it clear is plenty. Just to feel it cold against you or watch it flood or smell it when the damn thing backs up from Wakonda with all the town's garbage and sewage and dead crud floating around in it stinking up a breeze, that is plenty. And the best way to see it is not looking behind it—or beneath it or beyond it—but dead at it.

And to remember that all it wants is its fair advantage.

So by keeping my eye on the ball I found it just came down to this: that that river was after some things I figured belonged to me. It'd already got some and was all the time working to get some more. And in as how I was well known as one of the Ten Toughest

Hombres this side of the Rockies, I aimed to do my best to *hinder* it.

And as far as I was concerned, hindering something meant—had always meant—going after it with everything you *got*, fighting and kicking, stomping and gouging, and cussing it when everything else went sour. And being just as strong in the hassle as you got it in you to be. Now that's real logical, don't you think? That's real simple. If You Wants to Win, You Does Your Best. Why, a body could paint that on a plaque and hang it up over his bedstead. He could live by it. It could be like one of the Ten Commandments for success. "If You Wants to Win You Does Your Best." Solid and certain as a rock; one rule I was gut-sure I could bank on.

Yet it took nothing more than my kid brother coming to spend a month with us to show me that there are *other* ways of winning—like winning by giving in, by being soft, by not gritting your goddam teeth and getting your best hold . . . winning by not, for *damned* sure, being one of the Ten Toughest Hombres west of the Rockies. And show me as well that there's times when the only way you can win is by being weak, by losing, by doing your worst instead of your best.

And learning that come near to doing me in.

When I climbed out of that cold water into the boat and saw that the skinny boy in specs was none other than little Leland Stamper— fumbling and mumbling and flustered with the running of the boat and no more capable than he ever was when it came to handling any machinery bigger than a wristwatch—I was plenty tickled. Truth. And plenty pleased and surprised too, though I didn't let on. I said some dumb thing or other, then just went on sitting there, cool and matter-of-fact, like him being out here in the middle of the Wakonda Auga where nobody'd seen him for a good dozen years was just the most ordinary old thing that had happened all day to me—like, if anything, I was a little *disappointed*, maybe, that he hadn't been there yesterday or the day before. I don't know why. Not for any real meanness. But I never been one to carry on about things like homecomings, and I guess I said what I did because I was uneasy and wanted to devil him some, the way I devil Viv when she starts getting soapy and makes me uneasy. But I see from his face that it hits him wrong, and that I'd got to him a lot more than I'd intended.

I'd done a lot of thinking about Lee in the last year, remembering him the way he was at four and five and six. Partly, I imagine, because the news of his mom got me thinking about the old days, but

some because he was the only little kid I've ever been around and
there'd be lots of times when I'd think, That's what our kid'd been
like now. That's what our kid'd be saying now. And in some ways he
was good to compare to, in some ways not. He always had a lot of
savvy but never much sense; by the time he started school he knew
his multiplication tables all the way to the sevens, but never was able
to figure why three touchdowns come to twenty-one points if a team
kicked all their conversions, though I took him to ball games till the
world looked level. I remember—let's see, I guess when he was nine
or ten or so—I tried to teach him to throw jump passes. I'd run out
and he'd pass. He wasn't none too bad an arm, either, and I figured
he should make somebody a good little quarterback someday if he
would get his butt in gear to match his brains; but after ten or fifteen
minutes he'd get disgusted and say, "It's a stupid game anyway; I
don't care if I ever learn to pass."

And I'd say, "Okay, look here: you're quarterbacking the Green
Bay Packers. It's fourth down and third in the third quarter, fourth,
and third, and you're behind, nineteen to ten, a quarter to go. You're
on their thirty. Okay . . . what do you do?"

He'd shuffle around, looking around, looking at the ball. "I don't
know. I don't care."

"You'd go for the three-point field goal, nutty, and why don't you
care?"

"I just don't is all."

"Don't you want your team to get the league championship? You
need that field goal three points. Then, see, after the field goal you
got a chance to pick up the six and one and put you out ahead nineteen to twenty."

"No, I don't."

"Don't?"

"Care if they win the league championship. None at all."

And I'd finally get pissed. "Okay then, why are you playing if you
don't care?" And he'd walk off from the ball.

"I'm not. I never will."

Like that. And it was the same in a lot of other ways. He couldn't
seem to get his teeth into anything. Except books. The things in
books was darn near more real to him than the things breathing and
eating. That's why he was so easy to shuck, I guess, because he was
just content as you please to accept whatever demon I might happen
to trot in—especially if I made it kinda vague. Like . . . well, another

thing comes to mind: When he was a little kid he'd always be out on the dock in a life jacket waiting when we come in from work; bright orange life jacket, like an orange popsicle. He'd stand there, hugging a piling and watching us through his glasses, and like as not the first thing I'd say would be some kind of bull. "Lee, bub," I'd say, "you got any idea what I found up on them hills today?"

"No." He'd look away from me with a frown on his face, *telling* himself he wasn't gonna get took *this* time. Not after I'd shucked him so bad the day before. No sirree bob! Not little bright-eyed, bushy-tailed, book-reading Leland Stanford who already knew the multiplication tables up to the sevens and could add a dozen figures in his head. So he'd stand, and fiddle, and flip rocks into the river while we packed away the gear. But you could bet he was interested, for all his ignoring.

I'd act like I'd dismissed the subject, keep on working.

Finally he'd say, "No . . . I don't think you found *anything.*"

I'd shrug and keep on packing the gear in the boathouse.

"Maybe you *saw* something is all, but you never *found* anything."

I'd give him a long look like I was oh, trying to *dee-*cide whether to tell him or not, him being just a kid and all; he'd start getting fidgety.

"Come *on,* Hank; what was it you saw?"

And I'd say, "It was a Hide-behind, Lee." Then I'd look around to see if anybody might be overhearing such a god-awful news; nobody but the dogs. I'd lower my voice. "Yessir, a honest-to-goodness Hide-behind. Shoot. I been *hopin'* we wouldn't have any more trouble with those fellows. Had enough of 'em in the thirties. But now, oh gracious me . . ."

Then I'd maybe click my tongue and shake my head, make to look over the boat or something, like what'd been said was aplenty. Or like it didn't look to me he was even interested. But all the time knowing I'd sunk the hook clean to the shank. He'd follow me to the house, keeping still long as he could, scared to ask because I'd fooled him so last week with that whopper about the one-winged pinnacle grouse that flew in circles, or the sidehill dodger that had its uphill leg inches shorter than its downhill leg so's it could maneuver easy on the slopes. He'd be still. He knew better. But always, finally, if I waited long enough, he'd have to break down and ask.

"Okay, then, what's a *Hide-*behind supposed to be?"

"A Hide-*behind?*" I'd give him what Joe Ben called my ten-count squint, then say, "You never heard tell of the Hide-behind? I'll be a sonofabitch. Hey, Henry, goddammit . . . listen to this: Leland Stanford here never heard tell of the Hide-behind. What do you think of *that?*"

The old man would turn at the door, his tight little hairy gut pooching out where he'd already unbuttoned his pants and long johns to get comfortable, and give the kid a look like there was just no more hope for such a ninny. "It figures." Then go on in the house.

"Lee, bub," I would tell him, toting him on in the house on my hip, "the Hide-behind is one of the worst cree-churs a logging man can be plagued with. One of the very worst. He's *little*, not big at all, actually, but *fast*, oh Christ, fast as quicksilver. And he stays *behind* a man's back all the time so no matter how quick you turn he's run the other way, out of your seeing. You can hear one of 'em sometimes when it's real still in the swamp, and when the wind ain't blowing. Or sometimes you can catch just the *least* glimpse of him outa the corner of your eye. You ever notice, when you're alone out in the woods, seein' just a *speck* of something outa the corner of your eye? Then when you turn, *whooshee*, nothing?"

He'd nod yes, eyes big as saucers.

"And the Hide-behind will hang right in there behind a fellow and wait; he makes *sure* they're all alone, the two of them—because the Hide-behind is scared to glom onto a man if somebody else might be around who could get him before he can wrench his fangs loose and make a getaway, he's wide open then—stay *right behind* a fellow till he's deep in the woods and *bam!* Lay it to him."

And he'd look from me to the old man reading the paper, half believing and half suspicious, and think it over awhile. Then he'd ask, "Okay, if he's always behind you how'd you know he was there?"

I'd sit and pull him in closer. Pull him right to where I could whisper to him. "There's one thing about a Hide-behind: they don't show in a mirror. Just like vampires don't, you know? So this afternoon when I think I heard something slipping along behind me I reached in my pocket for my compass—this compass right here, see how it reflects good as a mirror?—and I held it up and looked behind me. And goddammit, Lee, you know? I couldn't see *nothing!*"

He stood there with his mouth open, and I knew I still had him and might of really poured it on if the old man hadn't went to sputtering and choking and got me to where I couldn't keep a straight face. Then it would be just like all the other times when he'd find himself hooked. "Ah, Hank," the kid would holler, "ah, *Hank*," then go storming off to his mother, who would give us a hard look and take him away from such lying lowbrows as us.

So during the ride across the river, when I see how skittish he gets from my deviling him, I half expect him to holler, "Ah, Hank!" and go storming off. But things are different. As high-mettled and spooky and skittish as he still looks, I know he's not a six-year-old any more. Behind those tight-honed features I can still see some of the old Lee, the little boy Lee I used to carry on my hip up from the dock, sitting there wondering how much of his crazy half-brother's bullshit should he swallow, but things are different now. For one thing he's a college graduate—the first that a family of illiterates can point to—and all that education has whetted him pretty keen.

For another, there's nobody for him to go storming off to any more.

Watching him there across the boat from me, I see something in his eyes that lets me know he's in no condition for any of my prime stupidity. He looks like this time it's *him* that suspects a Hide-behind after him, like the ground is pretty shaky underfoot and things like what I said to him aren't making it any steadier. So I mark myself down for a good butt-kicking when I get myself alone later, and try to make things a little easier the rest of the boat ride by asking him about school. He snaps at the chance, goes to running on about classes and seminars and the pressure of academic politics and keeps it up a blue streak all the way on toward the dock, idling that boat along slow as Christmas. All the time keeping a keen weather eye ahead for sunken snags, or checking up at the clouds, or watching a kingfisher dive, anything to keep from having to look at me. He doesn't want to look at me. He doesn't want to meet my eyes. So I quit looking at him, except sideways now and then while he talks.

He's made a good-sized gink, bigger than any of us would ever of expected. He must be an easy six foot, an inch or two taller than me and probably outweighs me a good twenty pounds, for all his lankiness He's all knobby shoulders and elbows and knees through the white shirt and slacks he's wearing, hair long at the ears, glasses with rims that look like they'd peter a man's neck out holding them up, a tweed jacket laid across his knees with a bulge in the pocket I'd give eight-to-five was a pipe . . . ball-point pen in his shirt pocket, dirty low-cut tennis shoes, dirty state-property gym socks. And I swear he looks like death warmed over. For one thing his face is all burned,

like he fell asleep under a sunlamp; and there's big inky pools under
the eyes; and where he used to be deadpan as an owl, he's took on a
kind of beaten and fretful grin, like his mother had. Except there's
just the barest crook to his version, showing he knows just a skosh
more than she did. And probably wishes he didn't. When he talks,
that crook comes into his grin for just a flicker, just a wink, making
him look sadder than ever because the crook turns it into one of those
grins you see on a man across the card table when you lay your full
house on his ace-high straight and it's been happening like that all
day and he's got inside information it's going on happening like that
all night. The way Boney Stokes grinned when he'd take the rag
away from his cough and look down in it and see that his condition was just as bad as he feared . . . grinning because—well, look: . . .
Boney Stokes was this oldtime acquaintance of Henry's and figured
the best way to pass the time of day was by gradually dying. Every
so often Joe Ben—who figured the best way to pass the time of day
was *never* gradually, but full steam ahead—would come across Boney
at the Snag or when Boney and the old man were playing dominoes
for the Centennial bucks Boney'd taken in at the store during Oregon
Centennial and had hung on to past time to redeem, and Joe would
rush over and pump Boney's hand and tell him how good he looked.

"Mr. Stokes, you're lookin' sicker'n I seen you in months."

"I know, Joe, I know."

"You seeing a doctor? Oh yeah, I'm sure you are, I tell ya you
come on over to services this Saturday night and we'll see if Brother
Walker can do you some good. I've seen him bring round some men
with one foot in the grave and scuffin' up dirt with the other."

Boney'd shake his head. "I don't know, Joe. I'm afraid we've let
my condition get too advanced."

Joe Ben'd reach up and take the old ghoul by the chin and turn
his head first to one side, then the other, squinting close at the
wrinkled craters where the eyes were sunk. "Might be. Oh yeah,
it *might* be. Too far gone for even the help of Divine Power." And
leave Boney sitting there, blooming with bad health.

For Joe Ben, see, was *that* way; probably one of the most accommodating guys in the world. That is, he came to be one of the most
accommodating. He didn't use to be when he was little. As kids
we was together about as much as later, but then he didn't have a
lot going. Sometimes he wouldn't say more'n a word or so a week.
This was because he was afraid what he might say would be some-

thing he'd picked up hearing his old man say. He looked so much like old Ben Stamper that he was scared to death he would grow up to be the same person. He even looked a lot like him, they tell me, clear back on the day he was born, with the shiny black hair and the pretty face, and he got to looking more like him every year. In high school he would stand in front of the locker-room mirror and screw up his mouth all sorts of ways and try to hold the face he made, but it didn't work; girls were already panting after him like women were always panting after Uncle Ben. As Joe got more handsome he got more scared, until the summer before our senior year he was about to give in to it and admit he didn't have any say-so about what he was going to be—he'd even got him a slick-looking Mercury like his dad used to have, all primered and chopped with zebra seats —when just in the nick of time he got into some kind of hassle off there in the state park with the homeliest girl in school, and she shredded his pretty face with a brush-cutting knife. He never said much about what brought on the hassle, but it sure changed him. With a new face he figured he was able to open up and become himself.

"Hank, I tell you, if I'd waited another year look where I'd be now."

At the time he said this, Joe's old man had just disappeared into the mountains never to be seen alive again; Joe claimed he'd just barely escaped the same fate.

"Maybe so; but I want to know what *happened* out there in the state park with you and that little owl, Joby."

"Ain't she a corker? I'm gonna marry that girl, Hank; you see if I don't. Just as quick as they get all these stitches out. Oh yeah, things're due to be *fine!*"

He married Jan while I was overseas and by the time I got back he already had a boy and a girl. And both of them pretty as any doll, pretty as he had even been. I wondered if he was worried about that.

"No. That's fine." He grinned, jumping around, tickling one, then the other, and laughing enough for all three. "Because the *prettier* they are the less likely they are to look like their old man, you see? Oh yeah. You see, they got their own row to hoe right from the start."

He had three more kids, each one more a doll than the last. By the time Jan was pregnant with the last one Joe Ben had got in pretty deep in the Church of God and Metaphysical Science and was beginning to pay attention to omens. So when that last child was born he declared that it was to be the clincher, on account of the various omens that took place on the day it was born. And there was some doozers. There was a big hurricane in Texas; and a whale swam into Wakonda Bay at high tide and grounded himself on the flats and made the whole town sick for a month before a demolition crew from Seattle got shut of him; and the remains of Ben Stamper was found in a lonely mountain cabin full of girlie books; and that night old Henry got the telegram from New York saying his wife had jumped forty stories to her death.

That news got to me a hell of a lot more than it did to the old man. I studied about it a good long while. And riding across in the boat I come awful near to just blurting out and asking Lee about the circumstances of that jump and what he figured brought it on; but I decided against it for the same reason I decided against asking him why he'd give up the big-time Yale University life he was coming on so strong about, to come back and help us out logging. I just kept still. I figured I already said plenty and that he will talk about such things in his own good time.

We get to the dock and I tie up the boat and throw a little tarp over the motor after I shut it off. I think for just a second about asking Lee to shut off the motor while I tie up—figuring he'd grab that live plug like old Henry does at least once a week and shock the shit out of himself—but I decide against that too. I'm deciding against things right and left, it looks like. Because for one thing I'm thinking more and more that there is some kind of truly big strain on the kid. He's quit talking and is looking around at the place. His eyes are kind of glassy. And there's a silence stretched between us like barbed wire. But for all of that I feel pretty good. He did come back; by god he did come back. I cough and spit in the water and look out to where the sun's tumbling toward the bay like a big dusty red rose. In the fall when they burn the stubble off the fields the sun gets this dusty hazy color, and the mare's-tail clouds whipping along near Wakonda Head look like goldenrod bent over by the wind. It's always real pretty. You can almost hear it ring in the sky.

"Look yonder," I say, pointing at the sunset.

He turns slow, batting his eyes like he's in a daze. "What?" he says.

"There. Look there. There where the sun is."

"There *what?*" WATCH OUT. "Where?"

I start to tell him but I see he just can't see it, it's clear he can't. No more than a color-blind man can see color. Something is really haywire with him. So I say, "Nothing, nothing. A salmon jumped is all. You missed it."

"Oh yeah?" *Lee keeps his gaze turned from his brother, but is alert to his every move: WATCH OUT NOW . . .*

I keep telling myself to go shake his hand and tell him how glad I am that he's come, but I know it's something I can't pull off. I couldn't do that no more than I could kiss the old man's whiskery chin and tell him how bad I feel about him getting busted up. Or no more than the old man could pat my back and tell me what a goddam good job I been doing since he got busted up and I been handling the work of two. It just ain't our style. So the kid and me just kind of stand there sucking on our teeth until the whole crew of hounds wakes up to the fact that there's folks about and all come loping out to see if maybe we can't use their wonderful assistance in some way or other. They grin and grovel and wag their worthless tails and put on just about the finest display of whining and yowling and carrying on that I've see since the last time somebody got out of a boat a whole hour ago.

"Christ, look at 'em. One of these days I'll drown the whole smelly lot of 'em. Ain't they a mess?"

A couple jump up on my bare leg while I'm trying to pull my pants back on and they're just so unbearable happy to see me that nothing'll do but to rake my leg clean to the bone. I go to whipping at them with my pants. "Get back, you sonsabitches! Get the hell down from me! You got to jump on somebody, jump up on Leland Stanford here; he's got pants on. Go welcome him, you got to welcome somebody."

*Lee reaches out his hand: But watch it; be careful . . .*

And for the first time in his brainless life one of the fools minds what somebody tells him. One old deaf, half-blind redbone with mange on his rump, he gets down from me and limps over and licks at Lee's hand. Lee stands there a second . . . *the colors about Lee and his half-brother strike against the ringing air; sky-blue, cloud-white, ringing, and that sparkling patch of yellow. Lee watches. Where is this place? . . .* and then the kid puts his jacket on the boat-house and squats down, and you'd think that damned dog hadn't had anybody to scratch his ear in a century, the way he responds. I finish pulling my pants on and pick up my sweat shirt and stand and wait for Lee to finish. He stands up and the dog rears up and puts both paws on his chest. I start to holler him down but Lee says no, wait a minute: *Wait; wait, please.* . . . "Hank . . . is this Plover? Is this old Plover? I mean, Plover was old even when I was a kid . . . Could he still—"

"Why, by god, that *is* old Plover, Lee. How did you know? Is he that old? Lord, I guess he must be if he was around when you was. By god, look there; he acts like he recollects who you are!"

Lee grins at me, then pulls the dog's muzzle right up next to his face. "Plover? Hi, Plover, hi . . ." he keeps saying over and over. ". . . hi there old Plover, hi . . ." he says. . . . *blue and white and yellow, and red, where that flag swings in the breeze. The trees shimmer behind an invisible veil of lupine smoke. The old house rears soundless and gigantic against the distant mountains and leans down over the dock: What house is this?* I stand there watching the kid and that old hound, shaking my head. "Boy and his dog," I say, "And don't that beat the band: just look at the old buzzard carry on; I believe he *does* remember who you are, bub. Look at him. He's tickled to have you back, you know that?"

I shake my head again, then pick up my boots and walk on up the planks toward the house, leaving Lee back there overcome with the hello he was getting from that old deaf hound, determined to do what I could to help straighten that kid out, thinking I'm gonna have to shape him up before he comes clean apart. Poor kid. Tears in his eyes like a damned girl. Am I ever gonna have to shape him up. But not right now. Later. Leave him be right now.

So I walked on in the house, determined and diplomatic (besides I didn't want to be around in case my little brother, who had a college education and could add a dozen sums in his head by the time he was six, got to remembering that old Plover had been at the very least ten or eleven and a lame old yard dog to boot when Lee'd left. And that was twelve years ago. Which would put the dog pretty far along, pretty old. I can't come up with the exact figure right off, but, I mean, I may not be a college graduate but I know that there's times that you're better off being a little dense in things like arithmetic.)

*What land is this?* Lee continued to ask himself. *What am I doing here?* A breeze ruffled the inverted world on the gently rocking water beside the dock, shattering the clouds and sky and mountains into a bright mosaic. The breeze died. The mosaic cleared, and again the world throbbed upside down in a wobbling, eerie flux. Lee turned his eyes from the reflection, gave the dog's bony gray head a last rub, then stood up to look after his brother. Hank was walking barefoot up the dock, carrying his sweat shirt over a freckled shoulder and his boots clamped between thumb and finger of that maimed hand. Lee marveled at the scamper of small muscles across the narrow white back, at the swing of the arms and the lift of the neck. Did it take that much muscle just to walk, or was Hank showing off his manly development? Every movement constituted open aggression against the very air through which Hank passed. He doesn't just breathe, Lee decided, listening to Hank's broken-nosed puffing, he gobbles the oxygen. He doesn't just walk; he consumes distance step by carnivorous step. Open aggression is what it is all right, he concluded.

Yet couldn't help but notice the way those shoulders seemed to savor the swing of the arms, or the way those feet relished the feel of the dock. *These people . . . am I one of these people?*

The wood that led along the dock was so perforated by years of calk boots, soaked by rain, dried and perforated and soaked again, that it had attained the quality of a rich, firm silver-gray carpet of finely woven wool. The planks sprang beneath the step, slapping the river. The pilings along which the dock moved up and down with the rise and fall of the river were worn flat with rubbing next to the dock and draped with shaggy mollusks the rest of the way around; three feet above the surface of the river these barnacles and mussels sizzled and clicked in the sun, talking of tides past and tides to come.

At the end of the dock a hinged plank incline with one railing ran up the embankment to the hedge bordering the yard; in high water, when the floating dock rose, this walkway inclined to a gradual slope, in low water it slanted down so steeply that time and again in wet weather spikeless-shoed climbers would slip and zoom like otters out into the river. Hank mounted this incline at a run and when the hounds heard the hollow thudding they swung as a pack and dashed after him, whooping their confidence: anyone heading in the direction of the house was headed in the direction of the rows of coffee cans nailed along the edge of the steps, the dogs reasoned, and any time is suppertime.

The dogs left Lee standing alone. Even the old redbone, gimping and whining at the rear of the pack, forsook him for the possibility of a meal. Lee stood for a moment watching the old dog strain up the incline, then took his jacket from the tarpaper roof of the boat-house and started after him.

From the power lines swooping across the water a kingfisher dived at his shadow: *What are these creatures? Where is this land?*

At one place on the dock the backwash of the explosion had swept water across the planks; beyond this puddle the dogs had tracked a polka-dot pattern on the ruglike surface of the dock as they chased after Hank's larger tracks. "But for his heelprint," Lee observed out loud looking down at the tracks, "the whole pack of prints might be made by the same species." His voice sounded stark and strange, and not at all wry as he had hoped.

He noticed another set of prints as he walked along: dim, phan-tasmal sketches faded almost dry. Probably the tracks of the woman he'd seen, Hank's mate. He looked more closely. He had been right; brother Hank's wildwoods flower *had* been barefooty, just as he'd predicted. But as he traced the tracks up the incline he noted also how incredibly narrow and high the instep was, how precise and light the placing—as though this set of prints had been made not by slapping feet, like Hank's or the dogs', but with the touch of a curved feather. Barefooty, all right, but he decided he might not be as correct about her size and weight.

He topped the rise and paused to look about him at the house and land. Beside the riverstone chimney a great pyramid of split firewood was stacked against the sunshine like ingots of some bright metal. A single-edged ax sticking from a round chopping stump directed his eye on toward the old port-red barn. One side of the barn was covered with the yellowing leaves of an ambitious grape-vine. On the front, tacked on the huge sliding door sagging off its trolley, a display of coon and fox and muskrat hides dried and stiffened. *Who trapped the animals and stripped the hides? In this world, in this day? Who played at Dan'l Boone in a forest full of fallout?* And at the side of this door, distinguished and alone, looking more like a big, ill-cut window than an animal skin, was the massive dark patch of a bear hide. *What tribe is this so sunk in itself that it dreams in a night gone crazy?*

He stared at the dark pool of fur as at a dark window, trying to see through it, as Hank entered the house . . .

(When I got on in the kitchen I saw the old man's already up to his elbows. I tell him the kid's come home and he looks up with a chop bone sticking out of his greasy mug like the tusk out of a wild hog. "What kid?" he hollers around the bone. "What kid's come home where?"

"Your kid's come home here," I tell him. "Leland Stanford, big as life. Christ, look at you; you didn't waste any time tearing inta the groceries, did you?" Cool and matter-of-fact because I don't want him blowing a gasket. I turn to Joe Ben. "Where's Viv, Joby?"

"Upstairs powderin' her nose, I imagine. Her an' Jan here are—"

"Hold on! What's this you was talkin' about, this kid?"

"Your kid, goddammit, Leland,"

"Bullshit!" He thinks I'm shucking him again. "Ain't nobody come nowhere."

"Have it your way." I shrug and make like I'm going to sit down. "Just thought I'd tell you—"

"What—" He whangs the table with his fork—"the hell's going on behind me now, I wanta know! By god, I won't tolerate—"

"Henry, take that bone outa your mouth and listen to me. If you'll quit stuffing your face a minute maybe I can get something through to your ears. Your son, Leland, has come home—"

"Where? Let me see this bullshit!"

"Easy, dammit. This is why I got to talk to you; if you'll slack off a minute—I don't want you shoveling him in your mouth an' half gumming him to death before you catch on he ain't a pork chop. Now listen. He'll be in in a jiffy. But before he is let's get some things straight. Sit back down." I reach out and ease him back down and straddle a chair myself. "And forchrissakes take that bone outa your face. And look here."

Lee turned his head, mechanically. Beyond the yard a pen of pigs worked the ground like quarrelsome grubs. Farther still a grove of runty fruit trees offered shriveled apples to the sun. And beyond this hung the vast green curtain of forest, woven from fern and berry and pine and fir, a flat drop of forest scenery furled down from the clouds to the earth below. *These hokey sets went out with "The Girl of The Golden West"; what audience still attends such period pieces? What actors still act in them?*

That green curtain had been one edge of Lee's childhood world; that steel-plated river, the other. Two walls, running parallel. Lee's mother had striven to make him as conscious of these two imprisoning walls as she was. He was never, she intoned, to go up into that forest, and above all never to go near the edge of that river. He was to consider those mountains and that river as *walls*, did he understand? Yes, Mother. Was he sure? Yes. Was he *sure?* Yes; the mountains and the river were walls. Very well then, run on out and play . . . and watch out.

*But what of the other walls?* The east and west walls that should have been joined the southern wall of the forest and the northern wall of the river to form a completed cell? What about up river, Mother, where there were slick and mossy rocks perfect for the break-ing of clumsy bones? or down river, where the rusty guts of an abandoned sawmill threatened blood-poisoning at every turn and a herd of marauding hogs ate men whole . . . what about that?

No; only the forest and the river. Her cell had only two walls; his cell needed but two walls. She had been sentenced at conception to life imprisonment between parallel lines. Or not quite parallel. For one day they had crossed.

*But who chopped that firewood and slopped those pigs and raised those apples from the crippled earth? And what kind of freak of optics lets a man see that spare star of trillium beside a silver-gray step of fir, and not see the fly agaric growing there? How could one look at the dusty rose sun shining off the river and not see the slab-ful of gore with a tag still tied to her toe?*

"Look at the sunset my eye!"

(And dammit the thing is when I finally *do* get the old fart to get the bone out of his mouth and get him settled across the table from me with a streak of pork gravy running into his eyebrows, waiting for me to say what's on my mind, I realize I *can't* say what's on my mind. "Look here," I say, "It's just that . . . well, Christ, Henry, for one thing it's probably been a long hard old trip on him. He told me he'd come all the way on the bus. That right there's enough to make him green around the gills . . ."—can't say it on account I don't want the old man to get all fired up and go to asking all the questions I'm thinking . . .)

Over his shoulder Lee saw the stricken sun drowning in a putre-scent mire, and its icy cries sank deep into his flesh. He shivered and walked on up the path to the front door and stepped inside. Whoever had redecorated the exterior of the old house had stopped there; the inside was even more cluttered and unsightly than he remembered it: guns, paperback Westerns, beer cans, ash trays overflowing with orange peels and candy wrappers; greasy parts of invalid machinery convalescing on coffee tables . . . Coke bottles, milk bottles, wine bottles—all spread so evenly about the room that it almost looked as though an effort had been made for uniform distribution. The Northwestern trend in interior furnishing, Lee concluded, trying to smile: the junk motif. I can see it: "I think this side of the room is overbalanced by that; get some more bottles scattered around here . . ."

*Who scattered this junk?*

Not much had changed: decades of muddy boots had deepened the dark path from the front door across the still unfinished floor to the center of the room where gray-yellow socks still hung, still steaming, from crisscrossing wires strung above the great iron woodstove that still smoked where the stovepipe was still ill-fitted into the chimney.

The big door swung shut of its own weight. The junk vanished. Lee found he was alone in the lofty, soot-colored room. Just he and the old stove moaning and sighing like an obese robot as it gawked at him with its glowing quartz-glass eye. Hank's wet tracks led dimly across the floor, beneath the closed kitchen door where Lee could hear the murmured reaction to his arrival. He couldn't make out what was being said but he knew they would soon all descend on him along that stripe of light that was drawn from the edge of the door across the room. He hoped they waited. He wished they would give him a little time, just a little bit of time to reorient himself with the terrain. He stood still. WATCH OUT. Perhaps they hadn't heard him come in yet. If he kept still they might not be aware of his presence. WATCH OUT NOW . . .

Breathing as silently as possible, he began to move his head about in an attempt to see through the gloom. The three small windows of the room, composed of many panes held in place with lead stripping, afforded a rather morose and sanguine illumination. Some of the panes were colored. And even the clear panes were so old and of such a poor-quality glass that what light they allowed in had a green undersea tint. This phlegmatic luminance seemed to impair rather than aid vision. The room was filled with shifting clouds of irridescent gas. Had it not been for the stove, seeing would have been practically impossible; the firelight flickering through the quartz kept the objects of the room pinned squirming in their proper places. *Who is so square any more as to use such Gothic trappings? What collection of chain-rattlers feeds that ruminating stove and breathes these pastel gases?*

He wished for more light but didn't dare risk tiptoeing across to the lamp. He'd have to be satisfied with the fire pulsing and winking from the round eye of that stove. The light darted softly about the room, touching one object after another . . . a gaily bedecked pair of French royalty dancing a ceramic minuet in a bric-a-brac ballroom; an antler-handled hunting knife skinning buckskin wallpaper from a wall; a full battalion of *Reader's Digest Condensed Books* marching in close order across an L-braced plank; hassocks crouching; shades breathing; stools walking long-legged along a web of shadows . . . *and where are the real denizens?*

("Listen." I take a scan of the yard through the kitchen window. "I think he's out there now in the front room," I whisper to the old man. "He must've come on in the house and's just standin' out there."

"All by himself?" Old Henry whispers too, not even knowing it, like you whisper in a library or a whorehouse. "What in hell's wrong with him?"

"*Nothing's* wrong with him, I told you. I just said he looked a little fuzzy at the edges."

"Then why don't he come on here in the kitchen an' get a bite to eat if he's out there if nothin's wrong with him? I *swear* I don't know what's happening here—"

"Shush, Henry," Joe Ben says. All his kids are sitting still at their plates, eyes big as dollars, like Jan's. "It's just that Hank thinks the boy's wore out from the trip."

"I know that; we talked about *that!*"

"Shush now."

"All this shushin' . . . my god, you'd think we was hiding from him. He's my *son,* dammit. I want to know why on *earth*—"

"Pa," I say, "all I ask is give him a second before you go roaring out there asking all kinds of things."

"All kinds of things like what?"

"Christ, you know."

"Well, I like *that.* What'd you think I'd be asking? About his mom? About who pushed her or something like that? By god, I ain't a *complete* boob, I don't care what you sonsabitches think, I beg your pardon, Jan, for my language, but *these two sonsabitches* seem to think—"

"Okay, Henry, okay . . ."

"I mean what the hell? Ain't he my own flesh-and-blood son? I might *look* like it but I ain't turned to rock yet."

"All right, Henry, I just didn't want—"

"So if it is *okay* by you . . ." He pushes himself standing. I see it won't do no good talking to him. He teeters a moment with one gnarled hand on the formica top of that new chrome dinette set that is always tripping him up because the legs don't go straight down to the floor like you'd expect but sort of flare out, and I make a little jump to catch him. But he holds up his hand, wagging a finger back and forth. He stands there, balanced, in top shape, perfect control, no sweat, and looks all of us over for a good long pause, then ruffles the hair of little John, who's been kind of scared by it all, and says, "So. If it is okay . . . I just believe I'll mosey on out yonder and say hello to my *son*. I may be mistook, but I *think* I'm up to that much." And pivots on his cast and goes rocking off. "I *believe* I am up to handling *at least* that much . . .")

The stove hummed and moaned, brooding insolently on its four bowed legs. Lee stood before it with one finger lifted pensively to the corner of his lips as he gazed about him at the display of trivia collected by years of living: satin pillows from the San Francisco Exposition; a framed testimonial making Henry Stamper a charter member of the Muscle Monkeys of Wakonda County; a quiver of arrows and a bow stalking knotholes; picture postcards tacked to a two-by-four; a sprig of mistletoe lurking near the ceiling; a plastic pull-toy duck with rolling eyes for a nearby Teddy bear reclining in provocative position; photos of fish held hip high; photos of bears with dogs sniffing; photos of cousins and nephews and nieces—all inscribed with the date of capture. *Who snapped those shots and inked those dates and bought that atrocious collection of Chinatown plates?*

(I come out and watch. The old man stops at the hall door in front of the stairs. "I wish I could just hear better." He leans to look in. "Boy?" he says. "You here in the dark?" I come past him to find the light switch and flick it on for him. Lee, he's standing there in the old man's path with his hand at his mouth, looking like he don't know whether to charge or retreat.

"Leland! Boy!" the old man hollers and goes clumping toward him. "You sonofabitch you! What the hell you say? Put 'er there. God amighty, Hank, willya just look at the size of him. He's shot up like a bean pole; get a little meat on those bones and we'll work hell out of him. Put 'er there, Leland."

The kid's having a tough time answering, what with the old man roaring down on him, and he gets even more flustered when Henry sticks out his left hand to shake and Lee switches and starts to stick out *his* left hand to shake but by then the old man's decided to go to feeling Lee's arm and shoulders like he was thinking of buying him for the locker. And Lee don't know what hand to try next. I have to laugh watching them, in spite of myself.

"But, say, he's just skin and bones, Hank, skin and bones. We'll have to get some *meat* on him before he'll be worth a shit. Leland, goddam you, how've you been?")

*Is this him?* The hand on Lee's arm was hard as wood. "Oh, I've been getting by." Lee shrugged uncomfortably and dropped his face to avoid looking at his father's frightening countenance. The hand continued on down the length of the arm as the old man talked, until it twined around his fingers with the slow, inexorable constriction of tree roots, sending little sparks of pain jumping toward his shoulder. Lee looked up to protest and realized that the old man was still loudly addressing him in that irrepressible and overpowering voice. Lee managed to convert his grimace to an uncomfortable smile; it wasn't as if his father intended him any pain with the prolonged grip. Probably just tradition to crush the metacarpal. Every fraternity has a special grip, why not the Muscle Monkeys of Wakonda? They probably also had strenuous initiations and free-for-all socials. Why not a special Muscle Monkey grip? *And am I his?*

He was engaged in pondering these questions when he realized that Henry had stopped talking and they were all waiting for him to speak.

"Yes, I've been surviving. . . ." *What did I use to call him?* Looking into those green eyes that showed white all the way around the pupils: *Papa . . . ?* At the incredible landscape of face gullied by the Oregon winters and burned by coastal winds. "Not making a lot of headway"—while his hand was being jerked up and down like a whistle rope—"but I've been getting by." *Or had it been Daddy?*

And felt again that first billowing of wings against his cheek, the objects in the room fluttering about like pictures on a blown lace curtain . . .

"Good!" The old man was greatly relieved by the news. "Gettin' by is just about all a man can hope for these days the way these Soslists are bleedin' you. Here. Sit you down. Hank tells me you been on the road a pretty good piece?"

"Enough to last me a while." *Papa* . . . ? *Daddy* . . . ? This was his *father*, an incredulous voice kept trying to convince him. "Enough," he added, "to make me think I'll stand a while if you don't mind."

The old man laughed. "I don't wonder. Hard on the old him-rongs, huh?" He winked obscenely at Lee, still clutching the hapless hand. Joe moved into view, followed by his wife and children. "Ah. Here we go. Joe Ben—you remember Joe Ben, don't you, Leland? Your Uncle Ben's boy? Let's see, though . . . was he cut up like this before you and your—"

"Oh yeah!" Joe came rushing forward to rescue Lee's hand. "Sure! Lee was still around after I got my face lifted. I think he was even— no, wait a minute, I didn't get married to Jan till 'fifty-one and you was gone in what was it? 'Forty-nine? 'Fifty?"

"Something like that. I've kind of lost count."

"Then you was gone before I got married. You ain't met my woman! Jan, come here. This is Lee. A little sunburned, but him all the same. This is Jan. Ain't she a honey, Leland?"

Joe hopped aside and Jan came bashfully out of the shadowed hall-way, drying her hands on her apron. She stood stolidly beside her bandy-legged husband as he introduced her and the children. "Pleased t'meetcha," she mumbled when he had finished, then faded backward into the hall again, like a nocturnal creature back into the night.

"She's a little edgy around strangers," Joe Ben explained proudly, as if listing the qualities of a prize bird dog. "But these here outfits ain't, are you?" He dug the twins in the ribs, making them jump and squirm. "Hey, Hankus, where's your woman, long as we're showing our stock off to Leland?"

"Damned if I know." Hank looked about him. "Viv-*yun!* I haven't seen her since outside. Maybe she seen ol' Lee here coming an' run for safety."

"She's up getting out of her Levis," Jan volunteered, then added quickly, "an' inta a dress, inta a dress. Me an' her are going in to hear this fella at the church talk."

"Viv's trying to be what they called a 'Informed Female,' bub," Hank apologized. "Ever' so often a woman gets an itch to be in on the social whirl, you know. Gives 'em something to do."

"Well sir by god if we ain't gonna sit down"—the old man pivoted on the rubber tip mounted at the bottom of his cast—"then let's get

back at the grub. Let's start puttin' some meat on this boy." He
rocked away toward the kitchen.

"You want something to eat right now, bub?"

"What? I hadn't thought about it."

"Come on!" Henry called from the kitchen. "Bring that boy in
here to the table." Lee stared numbly in the direction of the voice.
"You sprouts keep out from underfoot. Joe, get your brood out from
underfoot afore they get ground to dust!" The children scattered,
laughing. Lee stood, blinking at the bald kitchen light through the
hallway:

"Hank, I think what I might like to do—"

He heard the boom of the cast returning.

"Leland! You like pork chops, don't you? Jan, could you get the
boy a plate?"

"I might like to—" Who is this brittle old creation of limestone
and wood, played by Lon Chaney? Is this my father?

"Here. Put your jacket right over here. You dang *kids!*"

"Better watch out, bub. Don't ever get between him an' the dinner
table."

"Hank"—WATCH OUT—"I think I'll—"

"Sit here, boy." Henry pulled him into the brightly lit kitchen by
the wrist. "I got you some java, that'll perk you up." Tree roots. "Here
you go, two or three of these chops an' this here sweet potato . . ."

"Maybe you'd like some peas?" Jan asked.

"Thanks, Jan, I—"

"You bet!" Henry thundered around the chair toward the stove.
"You ain't got nothin' agin black-eye peas, do you, son?"

"No, but, what I might do . . ."

"And how 'bout some of this pear preserves."

"Might be a bit too . . . a bit of time. I mean, I'm out on my feet
from the trip. Maybe I could take a little nap before—"

"Why hell!" Henry came thundering back. He shimmered before
Lee in the kitchen heat. "The boy's probably dead on his feet!
What's the matter'th us. Sure. Take a plate up to your room." At the
cupboard he pulled handfuls of cookies from a jar shaped like Santa
Claus and began piling them on Lee's plate. "Here we go, here we
go now."

"Mommy, can we have some cookies?"

"Just as soon."

"Say! I know!" Joe Ben sprang suddenly up from his chair the kitchen *is very crowded* and started to say something *why is every-body standing up?* but choked on the biscuit he had in his mouth. He began clearing his throat in rapid little explosions, thrusting his neck forward like a rooster attempting to clear his throat to crow: "I-ee, i-ee."

"Mom-mee!"

"Not *now*, sweetie."

"You sure, bub? You couldn't eat a bit first?" Hank was pounding the wheezing and gray-faced Joe Ben unconcernedly on the back. "Be chilly upstairs, for eatin' . . ."

"I'm too tired to swallow, Hank."

Joe Ben dislodged his piece of biscuit and croaked in a mangled voice, "His bags. Where's his bags? I was gonna go get his bags."

"Way ahead of you," Hank said, starting for the back door.

"Here's some fruit."

Jan brought two wizened apples from the refrigerator.

"Wait, Hank—"

"Lordymercy, Jan. Can't you see the boy's dead standing up. He wants a place to get a little rest, not no two of those little piss-ant winesaps. I swear, Leland, I can't see how people stand them sour outfits anyhow. But I tell you"—the refrigerator swung open again— "we got any of them pears left I picked the other day?"

"What is it, bub?"

"I don't have any bags, remember? not in the boat, anyway."

"*That's* right. I remember puzzling about that on the way across."

"The bus driver couldn't see his way—"

Henry's head came back out of the refrigerator. "Yeah! Try one of these for size!" The pear made a place for itself with the cookies. "Good after a long trip; a trip always gets me bound up, an' there ain't nothing like a pear." *Everybody WATCH OUT is standing up!*

"Say!" Joe Ben snapped his fingers. "Does he have a *bed* some-place?"

*Oh god. Everybody keeps jumping—*

"Hey, now." Old Henry swung the refrigerator door shut. "That's right." He lumbered half into the hallway, craning his neck as though there might have been a desk clerk. "That *is* right. He'll have to have a room, you know?"

*Please. Everybody just—*

"I got him one all picked out, Papa."

"Mommee, *now!*"

"I'll tote his bags!" Joe Ben bounded ahead of them.

"He said they was at the bus depot."

"Don't forget your plate, Lee!"

"You reckon that'll be enough grub, boy? Give him a glass of milk, Jan."

"No. Really. Please." *Please!*

"Come on, bub." *Hank* . . .

"And if they's anything else you give us a holler!"

"I'll—"

"Never mind, bub . . ."

"I'll—"

"Never mind. Just come on upstairs."

Lee wasn't aware of Hank's hand guiding him through the hall; the touch blended into the rest of the quake. . . . *Am I this? Are these mine? These people? These insane people?*

("We'll talk later, boy," the old man calls. "We'll have plenty of time to talk later." The boy starts to answer but I tell him, "Let's just get on upstairs, bub; he'll chew your leg off." And I steer him out of the hall to the stairs not a second too soon. He goes up the steps ahead of me, walking like he's stunned or something. When we get to the top I don't have to direct him which way to go. He stops at the door to his old room and waits till I open it, then goes in. You'd of thought he'd wired for reservations, he was so sure.

"You coulda been wrong, you know." I grin at him. "I *might not* of meant this particular room."

He takes a look at the room all set up with fresh linen and clean towels and the bed ready and everything, then says back to me, "You could've been wrong too, Hank," he says, quiet, looking at the way I fixed up his old room. "I might not have come." But he don't grin; it ain't a funny thing to him.

"Well, it's like Joe Ben always tells his kids, bub: better to be ready and wrong than a pound of cure."

"That's a thought to sleep on," he says. "I'll see you in the morning."

"Morning? You planning to sleep your life away? It ain't but five-thirty or six."

"I mean later. I'll see you later."

"Okay, bub. Good night."

"Good night," he says and steps back into the room and shuts the door and I can almost hear the poor bastard sigh.)

Lee stood for a second in the medicinal silence of the room, then walked quickly to the bed and placed the plate and the glass of milk on the bedside table. He sat down on the bed, gripping his knees. Through a haze of fatigue he was dimly aware of the footsteps booming off down the hall. They were the footsteps of some enormous mythical character on his way to make a meal of unwary shepherds. "Fee Fi Fo Fum," Lee whispered, then kicked off his shoes and swung his legs onto the bed. He crossed his arms behind his head and stared up at a pattern of knotholes that became gradually familiar. "It is kind of a psychological fairy tale. With a new twist. We find the hero in the ogres' den, but *why* is he there? What is his motive? Has he come, sword of truth clasped bravely in his hand, sworn to slay these giants which have so long pillaged the countryside? Or has he brought his body to sacrifice to these demons? A nice addition to the traditional Jack up the Beanstalk; the element of mystery; who gets it—Jack? Or the Giant?" *these people . . . this scene . . . how will I cut it? Oh god, how?*

As he drifted into numb sleep he thought he heard someone singing in the room next to his, an answer that he couldn't quite interpret . . . sweet . . . high . . . the succulent warbling of a rare fairyland bird:

> *". . . when you wake, you'll have cake*
> *And all the pretty little horses . . ."*

In sleep his face relaxed, the features softening. And the singing ran like cool water across his parched brain.

> *". . . dapples and grays, purple and bays,*
> *All the pretty little horses."*

The echoes of her singing spread, circling. The kingfishers quarrel outside on the phone line. In town, at the Snag, the citizens are wondering again what has become of Floyd Evenwrite. In her shack at the mudflats Indian Jenny is writing a letter to the publishers of *Classic Comics*, wondering if they put out an illustrated edition of the Tibetan *Book of the Dead*. In the mountains up the South Fork the old wino boltcutter walks to the edge of the cliff and shouts across, just to hear the sound of a human voice come back. Boney Stokes rises from the supper table and decides to mosey down and count the canned goods. Hank walks to the stairwell after leaving Lee in his room, and turns at the sound of Viv's singing and comes back to rap lightly on her door.

"You 'bout ready, hon? You wanted to be there at seven."

The door opened, Viv stepped out, buttoning up a white car coat. "Who did I hear?"

"That was the kid, hon. That was him. He did for a fact show up. . . . What do you think of that?"

"Your brother? Let me say hello—" She started for Lee's room, but Hank held her arm.

"Not right now," he whispered. "He looks in a pretty sorry state. Wait till he rests up a piece." They walked to the stairs and started down. "You can meet him when you get back from town. Or tomorrow. Right now you're runnin' late as it is. . . . What took you so long, anyhow?"

"Oh, Hank . . . I don't know. I just don't know if I want to go in or not."

"Well, hell's fire, then, don't. There's sure nobody here pushing you."

"But Elizabeth called me especially—"

"Shoot. Elizabeth Pringle; old Pucker Pringle's daughter . . ."

"She—they all acted so darned hurt, though, that first meeting; when I wouldn't play their word game. Other girls didn't play and nobody minded; what did I say that was so wrong?"

"You said no. To some people that's always wrong."

"I suppose. And I guess I really haven't made much effort to be friendly."

"Have they? Have they ever come out here to visit you? I told you before we was married not to expect to win any popularity contests. Honey, you're the cutthroat's wife, they're bound to be a little snicky to you."

"It isn't that. It isn't just that . . ." She paused for a moment to study her make-up in the mirror at the bottom of the stairs. "It seems like they want to take something out on me. Like they have a grudge or something . . ."

Hank released her arm and walked on toward the door; "No, honey," he said, looking at the grain on the big door, "it's nothin' at all but you being soft in the heart; so you're pecked at." He smiled, recalling something. "Man alive: you shoulda seen Myra, Lee's mom—you shoulda seen how she dealt with that bunch of hens."

"But Hank, I would like to be friends with them, some of them . . ."

"Yes sir," he remembered fondly, "she knew how to tell them to go piss up a rope, the bunch of heifers. C'mon, let's make it."

Viv followed him down the porch steps onto the lawn, resolving to try to be a little less soft in the heart this time, and trying to remember if she used to have to try so hard to make friends, back home only a few years ago: Have I changed so much in only a few years?

North, on the highway heading back to Portland, Floyd Evenwrite sweats in the gravel to change a tire not two months old and already blowed goddammitall *out!* And every time the lug wrench slips in the dark he peels another inch of skin from his knuckles, gets a good grip on his leaky bowels, and runs again through the string of names he'd been calling Hank Stamper ever since the fiasco at the house: ". . . *cocksuckin', asslickin', fartknockin', shiteatin'* . . ."—in a curious methodical, rhythmed chant that is becoming almost reverent.

And Jonathan Draeger, in a motel in Eugene, runs his finger down the list of people he is supposed to see, counting twelve in all, twelve meetings before he continues on over to this Wakonda to see this— he checked the list—this Hank Stamper and talk some sense into him . . . thirteen meetings, unlucky thirteen, before he can anticipate returning home. Oh well; a rolling stone and all that. Closes the little book, yawns, and begins searching for his tube of Desenex.

And Hank returns from ferrying Viv across to the jeep just in time to hear Joe Ben call from the porch, "Hustle up here an' give me a hand; the old man's got a earwig crawled into his leg cast and he's goin' at himself with a ballpeen hammer!"

"Th' least o' my worries," Hank mutters, amused, hurriedly mooring fast the motorboat.

And in Wakonda, in a bright Main Street office, acquired by foreclosure, the Real Estate Hotwire broods as he gouges pieces of white pine from the half-carved figure in his lap. He takes special pains with the face; sometimes, if he didn't take pains, these faces came to look like a wooden caricature of a recent general and President. The Hotwire had served in the European Theater in the early forties as a mess sergeant, gaining a small reputation as a real go-getter of a chef. It was there that he met the man that was to haunt the next twenty years of his life. One morning this particular general and his entire entourage of aides, assistants, and asswipers had arrived in camp for a meeting. The general had announced he would mess with the enlisted men and was pleased to discover that one particular mess-bench boasted one particular go-getter of a chef. At noon he and his entourage filed past that bench. He complimented the go-getter on the smell of the food and commended him on the appearance of his kitchen, then, minutes later, complained of something alien in his ox-tail soup. This particular something turned out to be a German officer's ring which the Hotwire had bought from an infantryman to send home to his father. He was petrified when he saw what it was. Not only did he refuse to claim the bauble and deny having ever laid eyes on it before, he went as well on to *insist*—though the point had never been questioned—that the bone which the ring had graced was *definitely* an ox-tail bone. The expression of the general's face showed him his error, but it was too late to retract it. And he spent the remainder of the war in a constant sweat waiting for an ax that never fell, and was discharged a nervous and bewildered man. What had happened? He'd been so certain of reprisal. He didn't understand what had stayed that terrible ax until years later that same general had the evil audacity to run for President and the insidious gall to be elected. Now, *now* it would come! And did. A recession fell. His budding restaurant business withered and died without blooming. In his heart he always knew that this financial drought was nothing but a diabolic tactic perpetrated on the whole innocent nation for the sole purpose of squeezing dry his root-beer stand. Not that he cared that much for his business, but the *whole nation!* All that suffering! He couldn't help feeling partly responsible. If it hadn't been for him, it would have never happened. And what other disasters lay ahead?

Even worse ones. He made it through the eight years of that general's term by nothing short of the grace of God and his wife's needlework and was just now getting so he could pick up a newspaper without fear of finding himself declared a traitor and ordered shot on sight, was just beginning to make some headway in a very tricky world. If this nasty strike didn't break his back. This strike? Could the same old . . . ? No. He decides not; it is somebody else now that has it in for him, that's all there is to it. Moodily he gouges at the little wooden figure in his lap, grinding his teeth against old memories. . . . The sonofabitch could have at least returned the ring!

And, above the town, the timbered ridges move, steadily, under the edge of the silver moon, like stacks of lath passing beneath a gleaming and silent circle saw. Behind the grange hall berry vines feel for handholds with tough, blind fingers. Wood rots quietly in the cannery house. The salt wind blowing off the ocean sucks the life from pistons, gears, wiring, transmissions. . . . On the Main Street a short, plump, plush-looking pastry of a woman leaves the Snag and stalks up the sidewalk with short, angry steps. The evening mist collects in her eyelashes and the street lights glaze her curly black hair. She passes friends in a fury, looking neither right nor left. Her round, breadloaf shoulders are stiff with indignation. Her mouth is a grim dab of raspberry jam. She holds this air of outraged morality until she turns the corner of Shahelem Street and is out of sight of Main. There she stops against the fender of her little Studebaker, and the leavening goes out of her wrath. "Oh, oh, oh." She sinks against the dew-glazed fender with a dejected sigh like a cake falling. . . .

Her name was Simone and she was French. After marrying a paratrooper in 1945 she had come to Oregon, like a character strayed from the pages of de Maupassant. She hadn't seen her husband since he'd disappeared without so much as a parting Geronimo of farewell seven years ago, leaving her a mortgaged car, a down-payment washer and dryer, and five children still owned largely by the hospital. Though slightly embittered by the treachery, she had nevertheless managed to keep her head above water by keeping her buoyant little body under the covers, sleeping from charitable bed to bed with beneficent logger after logger. Never for pay, of course—she was a professed Catholic and a devout amateur—but for love, only for love, and whatever reasonable fringe benefits might be thrown in. So amiable was this little muffin of misfortune, so reasonable were her benefactors, that after seven years the washer-dryer was hers flat out, the car was nearly paid off, and the children no longer had to report monthly to the Hospital Finance Plan. Yet, in spite of her success, it had somehow never occurred to the townspeople, any more than it had to her, to consider this style of making ends meet the slightest bit shady. Contrary to popular rumors, a small town is not always so eager to cast the first stone. Not at the risk of hitting a good thing. Expedience, in a small town, often must pre-empt morality. The women of the town said, "Simone's as nice a little soul as I ever met, I don't care if she is foreign." Because the hook shop in Coos Bay charged ten dollars a throw, twenty-five a night.

The men said, "Simone's a good, clean kid." Because Coos Bay was noted for the scratchingest men in the state.

"And maybe she's no saint," the women allowed, "but she's certainly no Indian Jenny."

So Simone kept her amateur standing. Whenever it was questioned, men and women alike rose to her defense. "She's a sweet little mother," the women said. "She's had a tough shake," the men said, "and I for one am always plenty willing to help her out in a pinch."

And helped her out in a pinch faithfully and regularly. But just helped. Her regular means of support came from the occasional cooking jobs she held. Why, everybody knew this. And until tonight the plump little woman had never thought to question what everybody else knew.

She had been drinking beer with Howie Evans, a topper from Wakonda Pacific who wore on a chain around his neck a vertebra that had been removed in the hospital after a fall. The lack of the bone in his back, or the weight of it around his neck, gave him an odd stoop that produced horror in his wife, disgust in his mother-in-law, and a flood of maternal pity in Simone. They had been talking politely all evening while bumping knees under the table, and when the proper number of beers had been drunk she had observed that it was getting late. Howie had helped her into her coat and mentioned in passing that he thought he might drop over to his brother's cabin to see if his brother would like to help him put a lid on the night. Simone knew Howie's brother was serving one-to-eight in Vacaville for passing bad checks; she waited for Howie to go on, smiling happily at the thought of trying to rub some of that crook out of poor Howie's back in the brother's cabin in the brother's absence. She gazed up at him and wet her lips, but just as she could see the question rising to the surface—"An' I was thinking, Simone, how, if you ain't got anything else going"—he had suddenly stopped.

Howie stepped away from her. "By godfrey, Simone," he said after a moment, giggling at her and shaking his head with dawning wonder. "By godfrey, I was aiming to ask you if you might like—" Again he stopped. "Huh, now. I'll be darned. How about that. I never thunk of that before."

She frowned as he giggled in head-shaking amazement at some fact he'd never thunk of before. He shrugged and held out both work-shiny hands, palms up, as though showing her they were empty. He continued to giggle nervously and shake his head.

"I'm *broke*, Simone, chicken . . . that's what. Busted. This dang strike. And the house payments and so forth, with me being out of work so long . . . I just clean ain't got the cash for it."

"The cash? The cash? The cash for what?"

"For you, chicken. I ain't got the cash for you."

She had snapped into rigid, scandalized outrage, slapped his face decorously, and stomped from the bar. She was certainly no Indian Jenny! So angry had she been with the implication, that the two quarts of beer—a mere drop ordinarily—had commenced to boil and bubble savagely inside her, and by the time she reached the car she had been forced to give them up.

And weakened by the vomiting—limp, resting her dimpled baby's hand on the fender of the car that in one more month would be hers—the realization strikes her as absolutely and irrevocably as it did Howie, and she gives in to a long-denied truth. "Never never never again!" she swears aloud as she sobs there in the street with horrible shame—"Never again, Holy Mother, I swear!"—dimly searching the doughy matter of her mind for someone to blame, someone to hate. She thinks at first of her ex-husband—"The deserter! The heartless runaway"—but he is both too weak and too inaccessible to blame satisfactorily. It must be someone else, someone closer, and stronger, and big enough to bear the burden of blame she is baking in her hot little oven of a heart . . .

The finger points. Evenwrite curses. Draeger sleeps. The Real Estate Man hacks at his white pine carving, studying the features and crooning absently as the white chips fly. Across the street his brother-in-law closes a thin ledger and walks despondently to the drinking fountain in the lobby to rinse the red ink from his bleached hands. Jenny, breathing hoar-frost at the moon, collects tiny tree frogs in a chamois bag; whenever she plucks one of the half-frozen creatures from a limb or rock she mutters the words memorized that afternoon from the *Classic Comics* she took from the drugstore while Grissom took his Coke into the storeroom for a lace of paregoric: " 'Double, double, toil an' trouble,' " The toad squirms in her fingers; she feels her pulse quicken. " 'Fire burn an' cold one bubble . . .' " (Later she steamed her catch along with a bay leaf she had picked, and ate them with butter and lemon.) Out in the dunes, under the roof of a lodge-pole pine, a fly agaric pushes up through a pine-needle floor like something sneaking out of hell. In the deer-grass meadows the long last of the summer's flowers take long last looks through the fall's first frost at the dark garden of stars and wave their windy good-bys: the spiderwort and blue verrain, the trout lily and adder's tongue, the bleeding heart and pearly everlasting, and the carrion weed with its death-scented bloom. In the Scandinavian slums at the edge of town bloodroot vines reach garroting fingers for knotholes, warpholes, and window sills. The tide grinds piling against dock, dock against piling. Batteries corrode. Cables ravel. Lee sleeps with his lips parted in an expression of childlike terror and dreams childhood dreams of falling, running, being chased, and falling, over and over until abruptly awakened by a noise so close and loud that at first he thinks it only a dream noise lingering in his ears. But the noise continues. Suddenly wide awake, he lurches to his feet beside the bed; he stands there trembling, eyes pressed against the always treacherous darkness. Strangely enough it isn't the surroundings that confound him; he knows immediately where he is. He is in his old room, in the old house, on the Wakonda Auga. But he is completely unable to recall why. Why is he here? And *when?* Something is banging inside his ear, but at *what point* in his existence *is all this black cacophony taking place?* "Huh? Huh?" His head twists back and forth in the center of a tornado of dim objects. "What?" Like a child being awakened to panic by a sudden and strange new sound.

Except . . . this sound was not exactly new; it was the mocking echo of something that had once been very familiar (wait; it'll come back in a moment) . . . of something once heard very frequently. And that was why the sound was so damned confusing: because I *recognized* it.

As my eyes became more accustomed to the room I saw it wasn't as dark as I had first thought (*a small shaft of light cuts across the room to spotlight his jacket*) nor was the sound the fifty-decibel roar it had seemed (*the jacket lies on the foot of his bed with its arms wrapped about itself in a frozen agony of fright. The small shaft of light comes through a hole from the room next door . . .*) and instead of my ear it came from somewhere outside the window. Touching the smooth bedstead, I walked around the bed, then hesitatingly across the room to that gray square of light and raised it. The sound cut sharply through the chill fall air: "Whack whack whack . . . *thonggggg* . . . whack whack whack." I bent and put my head through the open window and saw below the buttery gleam of a kerosene lantern sliding along the bank foundation. A low fog muffled the light, yet seemed to amplify the sound. The lantern would pause, suspended, shimmering like an iridescent piece of night-blooming fluff—"Whack whack whack"—then move on a few yards before pausing again: *"Thongggg."* I then remembered I used to lie humming Beethoven's Fifth, "Whack whack whack *thongggg!"* Dum dum dum *dong!* And then I remembered it was Hank out on the bank before he went to bed, working his way along a dew-slick plank walkway with a hammer and a lantern, striking at the boards and cables as he listened for the sound that might indicate a spike loosened by the constant drag of the river, or a wire frayed by rust. . . .

A nightly ritual, I remembered, this ordeal out shoring up the embankment. I was overcome with relief and nostalgia, and, for the first time since setting foot inside the racketing old house, able to appreciate some of the scene's noisy humor and relax with it. (*He looks away from the light in the wall, toward the window* . . .) The sound stirred up a gaudy whirl of musty old funny-paper fantasies—not the sort of nightmares that accompanied the sound of log-trucks, but fantasies of a much more controllable nature. At night I used to imagine I was perishing in a hellish prison, condemned for deeds I had not done. And brother Hank was the trusty old turnkey, making his nightly rounds, testing the bars with his ubiquitous nightstick as they did in all the Jimmy Cagney thrillers. Lights out! Lights out! Reverberating clash of power-operated gates; toot of the curfew. At my desk, in the forbidden light of a stashed candle, I fashion elaborate prison-break schemes involving smuggled tommy-guns, split-second timing, and cocksure cohorts with names like Johnny Wolf and Big Louie and The Arm, all of whom respond instantly to my signal tap on the plumbing: zero hour. Footsteps running across the dark yard. Searchlights! Sirens wailing! Two-dimensional figures in blue pop into sight on the walls, scattering machine-gun fire over the melee as the dead pile up. The prisoners retreat, snarling. The break is thwarted. Or so it appears to the casual eye. But this is just a ruse; Wolf and Big Louie and The Arm have been sacrificed to diversion in the yard, a mere distraction action, while I—and Mother—tunnel to freedom beneath the river.

I laughed a moment at the flickering drama and the dreamer that had written it (*he draws his head back in—"Sure, tunneling underneath the river; to freedom"—back in from the cold, pine-smoky night into the smell of mothballs and mice. . . .*), then began looking about the room to see if I could find any other remnants of this little playwright or his product. (*He can't close the window; it is jammed open. He leaves and goes back to sit on the bed . . .*) I discovered nothing more in the room except a box of ancient comic books beneath the windowbox. (*He eats the cold pork and one of the pears, looking straight ahead at the still-open window. The smell of burning pine reaches him, chill and dark. . . .*) I sat for a time on the bed, wondering what my next move would be, while I leafed through a few of the black-outlined adventures of Plastic Man, Superman, Aquaman, Hawkman, and, of course, Captain Marvel. There were more Captain Marvels in the box than all the various other assorted marvels put together. (*He puts the plate on the floor and takes his jacket from the bed and bends to lay it aside on a chair; as he straightens back up, that beam of light that he has been so carefully avoiding catches him full in the face. . . .*) My one great hero, Captain Marvel, still head and shoulders above such late starters as Hamlet or Homer (*the beam holds him—"I used to imagine the wicked Sir Mordred doing his best to ensnare that nimble marauder of his castle. Gallant Sir Leland of Stanford who knows every secret tunnel and hidden stone stairway from the highest tower to the deepest dripping dungeon"—spears his face and holds it spitted there like some stage illusion head produced by hidden mirrors . . .*) and still my favorite over all the rest of the selection of superdoers. Because Captain Marvel was not continuously Captain Marvel. No. When he wasn't flying around batting the heads of archfiends together he was a kid about ten or twelve named Billy Batson, a scrawny and ineffectual punk who could be transformed, to the accompaniment of lightning and thunder, into a cleft-chinned behemoth capable of practically anything. (*He sits for a very long time, looking at the light exploding through the hole in the wall. Outside the sound goes on in demented and insensate voodoo cadence. . . . "I used to dance to the crackle of electrodes and sing along with switches activating stiff-legged golems." And the rest of the semi-lit room sifts out of his seeing . . .*) And all this kid had to do to bring off this transformation was say his word: Shazam: S for Solomon and wisdom; H for Hercules and strength; and so on with Atlas, Zeus, Achilles, and Mercury. "Shazam." I said the word softly aloud into the chilly room, smiling at myself but thinking: maybe it wasn't really Captain Marvel that was my hero; maybe it was Billy Batson and his magic word. I always used to try to figure out what my word was, my magic phrase that would turn me instantly enormous and invulnerable . . . (*Finally* the rest of the room is gone. There is just that bright hole, like a lone star in a black sky swelling to nova proportions—"I used to weave ectoplasmic afghans from the wispy effluvium left in the wake of Invisible Men . . .") In fact, wasn't that perhaps what I was still searching for? My magic word? (The light draws at him, pulling him up from the bed. . . .)

The notion interested me; and I had leaned to examine the page more closely when I realized where the light came from that was illuminating my book: from the hole. From that forgotten hole in my wall that had once been my eyepiece to the hard and horny facts of life. From the hole that had opened into my mother's room. (He slides slowly across the floor in his stockinged feet. "I used to be shorter." The spot of light moves from his eye down his face, from his face down his neck—"When I was ten years old and awakened in my flannel pajamas by werewolves next door, I used to be much shorter" —from his neck down his chest, becoming smaller and smaller until he stands against the wall and the spot is a silver coin in his pocket. . . .)

I stared at the point of light across the room. I was amazed that Hank hadn't plugged it by now, and for a crazy moment thought he had perhaps arranged for me to see the hole again, as he had arranged my room for my arrival. And maybe! he'd even arranged the room next door as well! (He touches the lighted rim of the small opening, feeling the notches made by the meat knife, smooth now, as though the passage of light has worn away the sharp edges—"I used to know its every notch. . . .") It was an odd anxiety. For a moment it was all I could do (kneeling: "I used to—") to force myself to take the peek (kneeling and shivering with the chill: "I used to see awful—") that would prove my fears foolish (". . . see awful ah! . . . Ahhh."). But one look was all I needed. I gave a sigh, then walked back to the bed for the pear and cookies. I munched them together happily, chiding my foolish trepidation and reminding myself that, luckily, time waits for no one, not even a schizophrenic with delusional tendencies. . . .

Because the room had in no way whatsoever resembled my mother's.

I sat on the bed again for a long, indecisive moment, feeling pretty well drained—the long ride; the hectic greeting downstairs; now this room—but not quite drained enough to be bereft of a burning curiosity: I had to have another look at the room of the old house's new mistress. (*He pulls a chair to the wall to allow himself more comfort with his spying. He finds he is too low when seated and finally turns the back of the chair to the wall and is able to make himself reasonably comfortable at about the right height with his knees on the chair's cane bottom. He takes another bite from the pear and leans to the hole. . . .*)

The room had none of Mother's furniture left in it, nor any of her pictures or curtains or embroidered pillows. Missing were the rows of fragrant, faceted bottles that had lined her dresser (*enormous jewels filled with gold-and-amber potions of love*) and gone was the big bed with its curlicue brass that had risen majestically above her (*the pipes of a grotesque organ tuned to the fluting of lust*). And the chairs (*draped with musky pink rayon*), and the dressing table (*brushing long black tresses before the mirror*), and the regiment of stuffed animals (*with collegiate colors and button eyes who had watched like rooters for the other team . . .*), all gone. Even the walls had been changed, the pale, ephemeral mauve changed to brilliant white. Nothing like her room . . . (*Yet as he looks he can't help feeling that some subtle portion of her personality still lingers in the room. "Very likely some object, some object that recalls a memory of a former furnishing; as the sound of the hammering had recalled an earlier night." He scans the small room, attempting to uncover the disguised bit of nostalgia.*)

Now that I was rid of this foolish anxiety concerning this little cubicle next door, I was eager to know something of its tenant. The room was decorated simply, almost bare, almost vacant; but it was a calculated vacancy, as an Oriental print is almost vacant. Most unlike Mother's chiffon and frill. A sewing machine and a lamp sat on one table, and a tall black vase of brown and scarlet vine-maple leaves sat on a smaller table near the couch. The couch seemed to be nothing more than a covered mattress on a platform of wood made from a door and a set of wrought iron legs; you see a hundred such makeshift couches in Village apartments, but those couches always suggested to me a kind of ostentatious poverty, not the clean, purposeful simplicity of this piece.

One hardback chair was pushed up to the table under the sewing machine; a bookcase made of bricks and planks painted light gray offered a raggedy selection of hardbounds and paperbacks; the floor was partially covered with a brightly colored hooked rug. Besides this rug and the vase of leaves the only other ornaments in the room were what appeared to be a small wooden watermelon on the bookcase, and a large piece of driftwood sitting on the floor and extending along my wall out of my line of vision.

(*The room has the atmosphere of a den, he thinks; of a sanctuary where someone—someone female, certainly . . . though he is at a loss to see what makes it so positively feminine—would go to read; and sew; and be alone. That's it. That's why it reminds me of Mother's old room; her room had this same atmosphere of sanctuary, a private and personal castle keep where she might enjoy a few moments' respite from that grimy horror going on downstairs. It is the same kind of place, a sort of Over the Rainbow Land wherein the weary soul can convalesce with bluebirds and troubles melt like lemon drops away above the chimney tops . . . that's where you'll find me . . .*)

I had decided at first glance that the room must belong to brother Hank's wildwoods flower. Who else could have fashioned it? None of the men. Surely not that little potato I had met downstairs. So it had to be Hank's wife; we must give the devil his due even if his due is devilishly hard to imagine as his mate. (*He removes his eye from the hole and sits there with his forehead against the cold wood; why should it come as a surprise that Hank has an exceptional woman for a wife? Quite the contrary; it would be a surprise if he did not. Because he has found his word and it is—*)

And while I was sitting there in the dark, ruminating over my pear and my thoughts about Hank, heroes, and how-am-I-ever-going-to-find-my-magic-words . . . (*the chair's cane bottom suddenly cracks . . .*) I heard a call from across the river. (*He jackknifes through, cracking his chin on the back of the chair . . .*) It was a female voice (*the same rich bird-note from his dreams; he falls sideways, his knees trapped in the chair bottom . . .*) sliding in to me on the chill, misty air through my window. I heard it again, then heard someone start the motorboat to go across for the caller. (*On the floor he is able to push the chair from his legs . . . stands back up and hurries again to the window . . .*) After a few minutes I heard the boat return and a couple rumble up the plank incline from the dock. It was brother Hank, and he was obviously strung-out about something. They passed directly beneath my window. . . .

". . . Honey, listen, I told you we can't afford to get all tore up about what somebody like Dolly McKeever or what her pimply old man either for that matter, for what they think about the way I run my outfit. I ain't in business to line their birdhouses."

The other voice sounded close to tears. "All Dolly McKeever said was to *ask* you."

"Okay, you asked me. Next time you see her you tell her you asked me."

"There won't be a next time. I can't keep—I can't *take* that much catty stuff. From people I—I—"

"Oh, Christ now. Here. Don't get all snarled up. You'll make it through. This won't last much longer."

"Not much *longer?* They don't even *know.* What about when Floyd Evenwrite gets back. He can have that report duplicated, can't he?"

"Okay, okay."

"He's bound to let people know—"

"Okay, so he lets other people know. None of the wives out here ever got elected the queen of the May. But *they* endured it. . . . Boy, you ought to have endured some of the catty stuff aimed at, say, Henry's second wife, or—"

I barely heard the girl's muttered comment—"I feel like I maybe have"—then the front door slammed on the conversation. In a few moments I heard sobbing in the next room. I held my breath and waited. The door closed and I heard Hank's pleading whisper. "I'm sorry, kitten. Please, I was just hacked off at McKeever. Not you. C'mon to bed and we'll see about it in the morning. I'll talk to the old man about it in the morning. C'mon, Viv, kitten, please. . . . Please . . . ?"

As quietly as possible I climbed back into bed and covered up, and lay for a long time before I fell asleep, listening to Hank beg in a tired, irritated, and most unheroic whisper from next door. (*He closes his eyes, smiling slightly. "I used to think in his comic-book domain there could be no equals: There was but one Captain Marvel and little Billy was his prophet . . ."*) And I thought again of the limp I had noticed earlier that afternoon in Hank's swimming stride. A limp and a whine: these were the first of much evidence I would try to amass to convince myself that this man wasn't really so much; he wasn't really going to be so hard to measure up to or pull down when the time came. (*"I used to try. Eyes clenched prayerfully I used to exhaust every possible pronunciation of that magic Shazam before resigning myself that no one, especially me, could ever hope* to contest that mighty Orange Giant of the cleft chin and cod-piece . . .") And that it wasn't going to be really so hard finding —this time, this second try—("I used to try . . .") finding my magic word. ("But it didn't occur to me until now . . . that I might not only have been saying the wrong Shazam, but that I must also have been seeking lightning from the wrong source . . .") And fell asleep to dream of flying instead of falling . . .

Next door to Lee, alone in her room, Viv broods as she combs out her hair for bed: maybe she should have said something to Hank before letting him storm off to bed; something to let him know she doesn't really care what Dolly McKeever says—or her pimply old man either . . . but . . . why can't he see it my way just once? Then scolds herself for her self-indulgence and rises to turn out the light.

In Wakonda the Real Estate Man finishes his carving and places it alongside the others: well, the face doesn't resemble that general this time, by gosh—although, there is something kind of familiar about the features, ridiculously familiar, frighteningly familiar—and feels the carving knife go sweaty in his palm.

And in Portland, Floyd Evenwrite turns his practiced cursing on the union flunky who has not made a duplicate and won't be able to compile a report in less than two weeks because he is going to the hospital in the morning to have a hernia tucked . . . the damn little snake!

And Simone falls asleep before her candlelit Virgin, certain that the little wooden figure is convinced of her purity, but more than ever tangled in her own doubts. And Jenny rises from bed with a pain in her stomach, throws the leftovers of her boiled tree toads into the slop jar, and burns her illustrated copy of Macbeth in the stove. And the old boltcutter, having shouted so long across the river and drunk so much thunderbird, begins to forget that the voice call-ing to him is his own. And the vines and tides climb; and mildew stalks the front-room rug where Hank left wet footprints; and the river roams the fields like a glistening bird of prey.

*T*o know a thing you have to trust what you know, and all that you know, and as far as you know in whatever direction your knowing drags you. I once had a pet pine squirrel named Omar who lived in the cotton secret and springy dark of our old green davenport; Omar knew that davenport; he knew from the Inside what I only sat on from the Out, and trusted his knowledge to keep him from being squashed by my ignorance. He survived until a red plaid blanket—spread to camouflage the worn-out Outside—confused him so he lost his faith in his familiarity with the In. Instead of trying to incorporate a plaid exterior into the scheme of his world he moved to the rainspout at the back of the house and was drowned in the first fall shower, probably still blaming that blanket: damn this world that just won't hold still for us! Damn it anyway!

Of Hank's wife the loungers lounging outside the union office or sitting in the Snag know this:

"She come from outa state. She reads books but's no back-East big-city bluenose like old Henry's second woman. And she's mighty nice, to my thinking."

"Maybe so, but—"

"Oh, she's a dust-bowl girl. And skinny as second-growth pine. But I wouldn't kick her from between the sheets."

"No; neither would I but—"

"She's a very sweet kid, Viv is. Always friendly when you run into her . . ."

"Yeah, I know all that, but . . . there's something peculiar about her, you know?"

"Well, hell, remember where she's living at; the fact that any woman survives over in that snake pit is a case for Ripley. And bound to make her a little ding-y . . ."

"I don't mean that. I mean—well, say, how come Hank don't ever bring her around town?"

"Same reason *nobody* brings in his old woman, Mel, you dumb cluck: cause she'd cramp his style if he wanted to cut up a little.

Hank ain't above honky-tonking some. Remember how he used to go tearing off to the beach with Anne May Grissom or Barbara the Barmaid from Yachats or one of those carhops out at the A and W Root Beer place hanging onto him and that motorcycle for dear life?"

"Yeah, Mel; and besides . . . it probably ain't too pleasant for her in town, people feeling like they do. So he keeps her home and happy, as the saying goes . . ."

"Yeah but that's one of the things I mean: what kind of woman would stand for that noise like she has? I tell you, there's *something* funny about her . . ."

"Maybe so, but—funny something and all—I still wouldn't kick her out from between the sheets."

And refuse to speak more about that funny something.

They also know many other things about Viv that they never speak of, as though they fear that to admit noticing the girl's peculiar floating walk, or her slender, flickering hands, or her white neck, or the way she sometimes wears a small cluster of leaves on her blouse like a corsage, would be admitting more than a passing attention. Talk of Simone's billowing breasts is frequently heard in front of the union hall, as well as occasional debates arguing how many feet of number-four line some intrepid adventurer would need for an exploration of Indian Jenny's cavern. In fact, except for Viv, any local female anatomy is target for talk; but when Viv comes up in the conversation the men act as though they have noticed only the scantiest qualities: Nice kid . . . friendly . . . little on the lean side but meat's sweeter close to the bone. As though that is all she has going. As though by omission they categorically deny noticing more.

Viv came from Colorado, from a hot, flat, swart town where scorpions hid in black cracks in the clay and tumbleweeds lined the fences to watch the cattle trucks roll by. Rocky Ford was the town's name, and, across a white wooden arch that supported a green wooden watermelon and spanned the incoming railroad, was lettered the town's fame: "The Watermelon Capitol of the World." The arch has fallen now, but when Hank came wheeling across from New York—July, zigzagging west from Connecticut on the Harley he'd bought with his muster-out pay—the painted legend and the wooden watermelon both glazed bright green in the sulphur sun and a wide oilcloth banner announced the Annual Watermelon Fair, *All the Melon a Man can Eat . . . FREE!!!!*"

"Hard to beat a deal like that," Hank concluded amiably and geared the cycle down to avoid the crowd mingling through the streets in flowered shirts and billowing slacks, sullen straw hats and hazy blue bib overalls. He called to the first baked face that turned slowly in the direction of his cycle, "Hey, Dad, which way to the free melons?" The question had surprising effect. The baked face shattered in a pattern of cracks like a clay pond bed drying suddenly in the terrific sun. "Sure!" the mouth croaked. "Sure! I work myself rag-assed t' give melons away t' the first, t' the first smelly hobo who comes—" Then, as the face had shattered, the voice crumbled, becoming a rusty outraged squeak like a well sucking dust. Hank drove on, leaving the man clutching at his swollen red neck.

"I'd probably do better," he decided, "asking one of the towns-people, or the tourists . . . and leave the poor devils from the farms alone. They act a little salty about free produce."

He drove slowly, down a main street bright with red and white striped bunting and rodeo posters, feeling the sweat start on his forehead now that he'd slackened his speed. *This is Hank's bell.* He liked driving a motorcycle on a July afternoon with his shirt un-buttoned for the wind to whip his sweat chill. He even liked smart-ass boys tossing torpedoes at the wheels to make the cycle rear in fright. He liked the look of people milling about the sidewalks with bright satin ribbons pinned to their breast pockets, dangling little wooden melons. He liked cranky children, smeared with mustard, clutching long sticks to fat green balloons striped to look like watermelons; and hot women sitting shadowed in pick-ups fanning their cheeks with *Watchtower* pamphlets; and the melons stacked on gleaming straw in the backs of these pick-ups lettered across the tailgate with white shoe polish. FOUR BITS EACH THREE FOR A DOLLAR. He liked the month. His money belt held almost a thousand dollars in muster pay and he liked being free from the bone-dissolving grasp of the United States Military with a thousand dollars' muster pay sweated against his hide under his pants, a good new used cycle between his legs, and a whole country to roam across at just the speed he chose. *This is Hank's bell ringing.* . . . Yet—yet with all these myriad joys going for him, Hank had never in his life been more unhappy and less able to explain why.

Because in spite of all these things so enjoyable, there was some-thing off kilter. He couldn't say exactly what was off, but after days of denying it he was finally grudgingly admitting that he and the world just were not seeing eye to eye. And it griped him that this was so.

A band pumped at a lagging march somewhere up the street and Hank felt that lagging beat hammer at his temples in the brassy glare. Maybe he needed a straw hat, he thought, and plucked one from the head of the first passer-by who looked like he had the same head size; the hatless man stared with his mouth open, but seeing the look on Hank's face remembered he had a better hat at home on the draining-board anyway. Hank rolled the cycle against a pole where a flag hung limp in the windless heat and went into a grocery for a quart of cold beer; he held the paper sack twisted about the bottle-neck and drank the beer as he worked his way down the sidewalk in the direction of the band music. He tried to smile, but his face felt as baked as the farmers'. Besides, why bother? The hicks look like hicks and the tourists and townspeople keep glancing from left to right, looking for photographers from *Life* or watching out for ex-ploding torpedoes from the smart-ass kids. Everyone, he thought, looks like they're waiting for something to happen, or pissed because they just missed it. "Oh, just the heat," he told himself.

He'd seen these same faces fixed with these same looks in every town and city he'd driven through since he'd left New York. "The trouble," he told himself, "is nothing but the heat, and the World Situation." Still, the people he met, why were they all either hurrying nervously to some deal, some big shady deal that they didn't really believe would ever materialize? or all bitching halfheartedly because that deal had just fallen through? Their alert preoccupation annoyed him. Dammit, he'd just returned from a police action that had taken more lives than the First World War, to find the Dodgers in a slump, frozen apple pie just like Mom useta make in all the super-markets, and a sour stench in the sweet land of liberty he'd risked his life defending. Plus an unusual foreign worry on the Average Ameri-can Guy he'd just saved from the insidious peril of Communism. What the hell was wrong? There was a kind of bland despair and the sky was filled with tinfoil. What was wrong with people? He didn't remember people around Wakonda being so damned watered down, or so revved up either. "Those boys out West, they got style . . . grit." But as he pushed his face into the arid American wind and moved through Missouri, Kansas, Colorado without observing any evidence of that style or grit, he had grown more and more uneasy. "The heat, and that muddle overseas"—he tried to diagnose a national malady. "That's really all it is." (But how come it's every place I look? from the littlest kid to the oldest rummy?) "And of course the humidity," he added lamely. (But how come I felt like I was going wild with a sort of bloated exasperation and I had to hold in for all I was worth to keep from popping one of those sunstruck faces and yelling wake up, blast your ass, wake up and look around you! Here I am just back from risking my hide in Korea making America safe from the Commies . . . Wake up an' take advantage.

I bring this up, this occasional urge to pop somebody and wake them up, because it was one urge I knew I was going to have trouble with now that the kid was back. The urge generally follows that feeling of bloat and exasperation. Like it wasn't long after I got that bloaty feeling cycling across country that me and some gleef in a bar got into it pretty good. In that town where I met Viv. A big guy, about three sheets gone and me about the same. He made some crack about the military when he saw a drunk soldier on the street outside the bar and I told him if it wasn't for that soldier out there he'd maybe be over in Siberia right now working off that spongy gut instead of sitting with his ugly nose in a beer. . . . He came back with something about me being a typical product of Pentagon propaganda and I said something about his looking like the product of somebody's bullshit himself and before we knew it we were in a devil of an argument. Now I knew better. I knew even before we got it rolling that this here was the type asshole that subscribed to magazines like the *Nation* and *Atlantic* and probably even read them, and that I didn't stand a *snowball's* chance against him in an argument; but I was too oiled to keep my mouth shut. And it was like it usually is when I get in an argument with somebody who knows more asleep than I do wide awake: I talked myself out on one of these little crickety limbs to no place and ended up hanging out there like a damned fool; with the adrenalin pumping and my mouth flapping its wings to try to fly farther ferchrissakes *out* instead of retreating *back* along that same illogical limb I got my dumb ass out on in the first place. So after I'd talked myself out far enough with this guy I got down to doing what I'd been working up to all along.)

As he walked down the sidewalk of the small Colorado truck-farming town during fair time, feeling the brass band beat at his ears, his anger mounted with the mercury in the thermometer. His kidneys throbbed from the long jarring on the cycle. The quart of beer had given him a dull headache. The slow, stumbling, worn-out beat of "The Stars and Stripes Forever" was a stinging insult to a man just out of uniform. And when a suntanned stroller in a bar with his flowered shirt unbuttoned to his hairy navel decided to calmly discuss some of the faults of the current foreign policy it was the last straw; (and just like *I* should of known better than to get into it with a guy who I could tell was bound to beat my ears down with facts and figures, *this* gleef should of known better than to kept on arguing with some guy who *he* could tell was eventually going to have to kick the living shit out of him . . .) after ten minutes of discussion Hank found himself cursing that ragged red and white and gold high-school band with the lagging beat through the bars of his cell window. (And I ended up the day cooling my heels in the local jug.)

He hollered at the band until he became hoarse and self-conscious under the gaze of a crowd of large boys who gathered under his window to watch him; then he retired to his cot and plopped down in a cloud of dust that drifted through the beams of sun streaming between the bars. He smiled to himself. Apparently he'd made quite a spectacle out there, been the big event of the day. Through the window he could still hear the awed story of his fight being told and retold by the fortunate witnesses. Within an hour he had grown six inches and had a terrible scar running across his face, and it had taken ten men to subdue his drunken frenzy. (Of course, this feeling doesn't last long—in fact, my cross-country exasperation was gone as soon as I'd busted that guy in Rocky Ford, so I didn't even much mind the little rest with the law; and that's where Viv and me met for the first time, too, in that jail—but that's getting off the track . . .)

Hank was wakened by a rapping on the bars. The cell was stifling and he lay soaked in sweat. The bars undulated grotesquely before his eyes for a second, then snapped straight; there stood a cop in khaki sweated dark under both arms; at his side was the tourist Hank had swatted, his face swollen and blue under the tan. A girl drifted past behind the two, half-transparent in the heat like some creature glimpsed uncertainly out of the corner of the eye.

"Accordin' to your things," the cop said, "you just got back from overseas."

Hank nodded, trying to smile, trying to catch another glimpse of that girl. In the limbs of the chinaberry tree beyond the bars a bug creaked in the heat.

"You were in the Marines," the tourist informed him, a little nostalgically. "I served in the Pacific during the war . . . did you see any combat?"

It took Hank perhaps a second to size up what was happening, probably less. He dropped his head. He nodded woefully. He caught the bridge of his nose between thumb and finger and massaged it with his eyes closed. How was it? the tourist wanted to know, the Korean fighting? Hank told him he couldn't talk about it yet. Why me? the tourist asked, as though he might cry, why did you come after me? Hank shrugged and brushed his dusty hair back from his eyes. "I guess," he murmured softly, "it was because you were the biggest one I could find."

He said it for effect, but speaking it—I'm sorry, mister, but you were just right—he realized that the reason wasn't far from the truth.

The cop and the tourist retired to the other side of the room and, after some whispering, returned to announce that charges were being dropped provided Hank apologized and got his danged machine outa town by sundown. As Hank was proclaiming his sorrow he was once again aware of the moving apparition that slid across the background. Outside, against the white-hot firing-squad wall of the stucco jail, he blinked at the sun and waited. He knew the girl had been intensely aware of him in there. Just like a woman who doesn't turn at your whistle is aware. That's a woman you can hustle. After a few moments the girl slipped out from the back of the jail and stood beside him, shimmering against the heat of the stucco wall. She asked if he'd like a place where he could wash up and relax. He asked if she had such a place handy.

They made love that night outside town in the straw-filled bed of a pick-up. Their clothes lay nearby on the bank of a muddy pond where an irrigation ditch had been dammed by the town boys for swimming. They could hear the water trickling over the top of the dam and the frogs serenading one another across the water. A cottonwood stood nearby, sifting lint onto their naked bodies like warm snow. *This is Hank's bell; clear now, clear . . .*

The pick-up belonged to the girl's uncle. She had borrowed it to drive to Pueblo to a movie and had driven to the bar where Hank waited. He had followed her into the fields on his cycle. And as he lay in the sweet-smelling straw beside her, feeling the stars on his bare stomach, had asked for the girl's story: where was she from? what did she do? what did she like? From experience he knew that women felt entitled to this type of talk as a kind of payment; he always complied dutifully with halfhearted interest:

"What I mean is," he said, yawning, "is *tell* me about yourself."

"There's no need for that," the girl replied in a contented voice.

Hank waited a while in silence. The girl began humming a simple little tune while he lay perplexed, wondering if she understood as much as her statement seemed to imply; he decided not.

"No. Listen, sweetheart; I'm serious. Tell me, oh . . . what you *want* out of life."

"What I want" She sounded amused. "Now, do you really care? I mean come on, there isn't any need, really; it's fine just being a man and a woman; it's fine." She thought a moment. "Well, look: my aunt took me to Mesa Verde Indian dwellings one summer when I was sixteen. And at the Indian dances a boy and I kept looking at each other. All during the first part of the dance. The Indians were fat and old and I didn't truly care who was the bird god or who was the sun god and the boy didn't either. I think we were both much more beautiful than the dances. I remember I wore Levis and a plaid blouse; and oh, my hair was braided. The boy had very dark skin, foreign I think . . . dark, dark as one of the Indians even. And he had on leather shorts like you see mountain-climbers wear. And the moon was shining. I told my aunt I had to go to the john and I went out on the edge of the cliff and waited till he came. We made love right there on the sandstone. He could have been foreign, you know? . . . Neither of us ever spoke a word."

She rolled her face toward him, pulling her hair back so he could see her dim smile.

"So, anyway . . . do you really want to know what I *want* out of life?"

"Yeah," Hank said slowly, beginning to mean it. "Yes, I think I do."

She rolled again to her back and crossed her hands behind her head. "Well . . . of course I want a home and some kids and like that, all the usual things. . . ."

"And the unusual things?"

This time she waited a while before she spoke. "I guess . . ." she said slowly, "I want somebody. All I mean to my uncle and aunt is help at the jail and the fruit stand. I want a lot of other unusual things too, like a page-boy cut, and a good sewing machine and a German roller singing canary like I remember my mother had—but mostly, I guess, I want to really mean something to somebody, be something to somebody more'n just a jail cook and a watermelon weigher."

"Like what? What do you want to be?"

"Whatever this Somebody wants, I guess." Not sounding at all like she was guessing.

"Dang, now; that don't sound like much of a ambition to me. What if this Somebody just happens to *want* a cook an' a melon tender, then where'd you be?"

"He won't," she answered.

"Who?" Hank asked, with more concern in his voice than he intended. "Who won't?"

"Oh, I don't know." She laughed, and again answered his unspoken question. "Just the Somebody. Whoever he someday turns out to be."

Hank was relieved. "Boy, if you ain't a case: waiting someday to be a something to a Somebody you don't even know, yet. And, yeah, how about that? How will you *know* this Somebody when you come across him?"

"I won't know . . ." she said, and sat up to slide over the side of the pick-up, with the quiet and lazy speed of a cat; she stood in the wet sand of the ditch bank, coiling her hair into a loose knot at the back of her head, ". . . he will." And turned her back to him.

"Hey. Where you going?"

"It's all right," she answered in a whisper, "just in the ditch," then stepped into the water so delicately that the frogs across the ditch continued singing undisturbed. *This is Hank's bell ringing . . .*

There was no moon, but the night was bright and clear and the girl's naked body seemed almost to glow she was so pale. How in the world could she keep so white, Hank wondered, in a country where even the bartenders are baked brown?

The girl began humming again. She turned facing the pick-up and stood for a moment facing him, ankle-deep in the pond full of stars and cottonwood fluff, then, still humming, began walking slowly backward. Hank watched her pale body dissolve from the feet upwards into the dark as the water grew gradually deeper—her knees, her trim hips made feminine only by a trimmer waist, her stomach, her dots of nipple—until only her face flickered bodiless there under the cottonwood. The sight was incredible. "Suck egg mule," he whispered to himself, "if she ain't something."

"I like the water," the girl remarked matter-of-factly, and disappeared altogether without a ripple and with an effect so eerie that Hank had to argue with his impulses by reminding himself that the ditch was only four feet or so at the deepest. He stared transfixed at the circling water. He'd never felt himself so hooked by a girl; and while she remained under water he wondered, half amused and half frightened, just which of them had been doing the hustling.

And the sky, he noticed, no longer seemed made of tinfoil.

He stayed over the next day, meeting the girl's aunt, who was married to the cop. He read detective magazines while he waited for her to return from her cleaning chores at the jail. He still wasn't able to pin her down about her age or background or anything, though he found out from the wire-haired aunt that her parents were dead and she lived most of the time at a fruit stand out on the highway. They spent another night in the pick-up, but Hank was becoming uneasy. He told the girl he had to leave at dawn, be back later, okay? She smiled and told him that it had been very fine, and when he kicked his motorcycle to noisy life in the gray plains dawn she stood on the hood of the pick-up and waved as he pulled a great plume of white dust down the road out of sight.

Up through Denver, over the Rabbit Ears into Wyoming, where an icy wind cut his face so raw that he had to have a doctor in Rock Springs prescribe an ointment . . . down to Utah and another fight, this time in the City of the Saints . . . along the Snake River caddis flies hatched and died against his goggles . . . into Oregon.

As he came down out of the twisting Santiam Pass into the green explosion of the Willamette Valley he realized that he had almost completed a circle. West, west, sailing out of San Francisco west and after two years landing on the Eastern Seaboard, where his ancestors had first set foot. He'd traveled in a straight line and completed a circle.

He roared down out of the Coast Range and passed the old house across the river without even slowing. He was eager to see some of the good old woodsmen around town. Men with style and grit. He entered the Snag triumphantly, bringing his boots down hard.

"Sonofabitch if this place isn't got as much riffraff in it as the day I left. Hey there, Teddy."

"Why hello, Mr. Stamper," Teddy said politely. The other men smiled and waved casually.

"Let's have us a bottle, Teddyboy. A whole bottle . . . let's see. Make her Jim Beam, by God!" He leaned his elbows on the bar and beamed at the patrons sitting with lunch pails on the tables beside their beers.

"Mr. Stamper . . ." Teddy began timidly.

"How you been, Floyd? Gettin' fat? Mel . . . Les. Come on over here an' let's section up this bottle we—Teddy, you snake."

"Mr. Stamper, it's against the law to sell a bottle over the counter in Oregon. You must've forgot."

"I didn't forget, Teddy, but I'm home from the wars! I want to bust loose a little. What d'ya say, boys?"

The jukebox whirred. Evenwrite glanced at his watch, stood up, and stretched. "What do you say we raincheck that bottle till Saturday night, Hank. It's goin' on suppertime."

"Mr. Stamper, I can't sell . . ."

"Same with me, Hank," Les said. "Good to see you though."

"And the rest of you niggers?" Hank addressed the others good-naturedly. "You got other irons in the fire, too, I suppose. Okay, it's more for me. Teddy . . . ?"

"Mr. Stamper, I can't sell . . ."

"Okay, okay. We'll all raincheck it. See you birds later. I think I'll drive around for a look at the town."

They called farewells, his old friends with style and grit and other irons in the fire, and he left, wondering what had come over them. They acted tired, scared, asleep. Outside he noticed how dull the mountains looked and wondered if the whole world had gone to seed while he was off fighting to save it.

He drove on past the bay, past the commercial docks where blunt gray motors squatted in boats saying "buddha buddha buddha" while the fishermen tossed gleaming salmon into community coffins, past the clam flats and the gull-infested dump out the road through the dunes to the beach. He passed the heaps of driftwood and finally stopped at the foam's edge to wait, stopped with the cycle propped between his legs in the hard wet sand to actually wait for something to happen, for some mystic revelation to explode in his mind making all things clear forever, holding his breath like a sorcerer just finished with all the steps necessary to some world-shaking spell. He was the first of the Stampers to complete the full circle west. He waited.

And the gulls cried, and the sand fleas swarmed over drowned surf birds, and the waves cracked against the earth with the methodic regularity of a clock ticking.

Hank laughed out loud and stomped the starter bar with his

instep. "Okeedoke," he said, laughing and stomping again. "Okee-doke, okeedoke, okeedoke . . ."

He returned then, with sand still in his pants cuffs and zinc oint-ment still on his nose, to the old wooden warren across that waiting river. And found the old man still on the levee, with hammer and nail and number nine cable, working still to make the river wait a little longer.

"I come home," he let the old man know, and walked on up the path.

To the rattling woods for a few months with the smoke and wind and rain, to the mill for a few more, thinking that indoor work might settle an immigrant heart, that the zinc ointment of indoor air might salve his windburned hide—for a while even managed to convince himself that he liked the quarterbacking task of sitting that sawyer's seat and handling all those controlling levers and buttons that made the big machines hump and run—then back again to the woods at the first crack of spring. But that sky . . . ! How could a sky so full of blue feel so empty?

He worked those summer woods the hardest he had worked since training for the state wrestling championship his senior year at Wakonda High, but at the end of this season, when he was rock-hard and trained to a razor's edge, there were no tournaments to enter, no opponents to pin, no medals to win.

"I'm going off again," he let the old man know in the fall. "There's somebody I got to see."

"What the bleedin' hell you talkin' about, right here at the peak of cuttin'? What the boogin' devil you talkin', somebody you got to see why?"

He grinned at the puffing red face. "Why? Well, I got to see this somebody, Henry, to see if I'm that Somebody. I won't be gone more'n a couple weeks. I'll straighten things around good before I take off."

He left the old man fuming and cursing on the levee and walked to the house, and after two days going over the books with Janice and through the woods with Joe Ben packed a small bag and caught a train East, wearing tight new shoes and a stiff new flannel one-button roll.

There was no watermelon fair waiting for him that fall, but the oilcloth banner announcing last year's event still hung from the wooden arch. It snapped and fluttered in a dusty red wind and the faded letters peeled and fell like strange leaves beneath the train's wheels. He went first to the jail, where the uncle gave him directions and sold him a repossessed Chevy pick-up. He left the jail and the uncle and found Viv behind a tarpaper fruit stand on the highway, scratching estimated weights into the waxy green rind of a pile of melons with a sharp stick: look at a melon, think a few seconds, then scratch a number.

"You just guess?" he asked, coming up behind. "How do you knew you're right?"

She straightened up and shaded her eyes to look at him. A lock of the sorrel hair was sweated to her brow. "I'm generally pretty close," she said.

She asked that he wait on the other side of the muslin curtain that separated her tiny room from the rest of the fruit stand. Hank thought that she would be ashamed for him to see the squalor of her dwelling, and complied in silence while she ducked through the curtain to pack. But what he mistook for shame was closer to reverence; in the little cluttered room that had been her home since her parents' death, Viv was shriving herself like a nun before communion. She let her eyes roam over the room's shabby walls—the travel pictures, the clippings, the arrangements of dried straw flowers, all the childhood adornments that she knew she must leave as sure as the walls themselves, until she finally let her eyes meet with those looking out at her from a wood-framed oval mirror. The face that looked out at her was cramped into the lower part of the mirror to avoid a crack in the glass, but it didn't seem to mind the inconvenience; it smiled brightly back, wishing her luck. She glanced about once more and made a silent excited vow of allegiance to all the holy old dreams and hopes and ideals that these walls had held, then, chiding herself for being such a silly, kissed the face in the glass good-by.

And when she came out, with a small wicker bag in one hand, and in a sunflower-yellow cotton dress and a wide-brimmed straw hat that all but had a price tag hanging from it, she had two requests to make before they left. "When we get to where we're going, to Oregon . . . you know what I'd like? You remember me talking about wanting a canary—"

"Sweetpants," Hank interrupted, "I'll get you a whole damn flock of birds if you want. I'll get you doves and sparrows and cockatoos and canaries till the world looks level. Oh me, but you look pretty, you know that? About as pretty a thing as I think I ever saw. But . . .

how come you tucked your hair all up in your hat like that? I like you better with it all hanging and swinging—"

"But it gets in the way so, all long, and gets so dirty—"

"Well then, maybe we'll just have to dye it black." He laughed, taking the bag and sweeping her along to the pick-up. "But we'll leave it long."

So she never made the second request.

She loved the lush greenery of her new home, and the old man, and Joe Ben and his family. She learned quickly how to fit in with the Stamper life. When old Henry accused Hank of picking a limp little Miss Mousie, Viv was compelled to change the old man's mind the first time they went raccoon-hunting together by outwalking, outyelling, and outdrinking every man on the hunt and having to be dragged giggling and singing back out of the woods on a makeshift travois like an Indian wounded in battle. After that the old man stopped teasing her, and she went on a number of hunts. She didn't care for the killing part, where the dogs tore up a screaming coon or fox, but she liked the walking part, and she liked to be with all of them, and she could let them think she didn't mind the other if that's what they wanted to think. She could be like that if they wanted.

As much as she took part in the Stamper activities, she still was obviously without a world truly her own. It bothered Hank at first and he thought he could help this by giving her her own room— "Not to sleep in, of course, just a place where you can go and sew and stuff, and it's yours, do you see?" She didn't, quite, but she went along with the idea; for one thing, it would be a good place to keep that bird he'd bought her from annoying the rest of the family, and for another she knew her private room made him feel better about having a world that she could never enter, a violent and brawling life that was to him what Viv's "sewing room" was supposed to be to her. Sometimes, after tying one on in Wakonda, Hank would arrive home in time to meet Joe Ben on his way to church, and he would go to where Viv lay reading on the low couch in her room and sit in the hard chair facing her while he told her about his night in town. Viv would listen, hugging her knees, then switch out her lamp and take him to bed.

These blow-offs in town never bothered her. In fact, the only quirk in her husband's personality that ever seemed to cause her remorse was Hank's teeth-gritting stoicism in the face of pain; sometimes as they undressed for bed she would break into furious tears on the discovery of deep line-cut festering red on Hank's thigh. "Why didn't you tell me?" she would demand. Hank would grin shyly. "Ah, 'tain't nothin' but a scratch." She threw her hands in the air. "Damn you! Damn you and your scratches to hell!" The scene always amused Hank and gave him such a glow of boyish pride that he went to great lengths to conceal his logging wounds from his wife; when a springback broke one of his ribs, she didn't know it until he took off his shirt to wash; when he lost his two fingers in the donkey drum he wrapped the stubs and didn't mention the accident until Viv asked him why he was wearing his work gloves at the supper table. Dipping his head with embarrassment he said, "Why, I guess I just forgot to take 'em off at the door . . ." and drew a glove from a claw so mangled and clotted with blood and cable rust that it took Viv a hysterical half-hour to get the wound clean enough to realize that the whole hand wasn't lost as well as three or four inches of the arm.

Sometimes Joe Ben's wife, Janice, would corner Hank and hold him grinning against a wall with her solemn owl-eyed gaze and chide him for not respecting Viv's secret spiritual needs and giving the poor girl a little more chance to be a wife.

"Don't you mean chance to be a nursemaid, Jan? I appreciate your good intentions but take my word: Viv is wife aplenty. If she needs to doctor something I'll get her a kittycat." Besides, he added to himself, for anybody to figure what the devil Viv's secret spiritual needs are or what to do about them you'd have to know her a hundred years. Have to be tuned in exactly to Viv's wave length. And Jan might be good at figuring people's needs but she wasn't *that* good. . . .

(But I got a big boot out of Jan that way. She was always corralling me in a corner with some of her big-eyed advice. Which I usually let slide off me like water off a duck. But when she come up to me that first morning Lee was at the house and told me to be real easy with the boy and I said, "Easy? what do you mean easy? I intend to get some work outa the cuss is what," and she said that wasn't what she meant, that what she meant was not to get into some kind of argument with him right off, I knew what she was driving at; better than she did, in fact. Because what with Viv and me getting into it the night before about her always wanting to fraternize with those harpies in town, and getting into it again that same morning as she headed for the barn in a huff, I was in a pee-poor mood. And that's the point: knowing this feeling like I did, I knew that if me and the kid started disagreeing about something I'd get an urge to pop somebody and it'd be just like me and that gleef in that bar in Colorado, only more so by a damned sight: I'd talk myself onto a limb again and end up getting pissed and kicking the living shit out of Lee . . . only this time it'd be worse than a little stretch in boot—we'd lose a badly needed woods hand. "What I mean, Hank," Jan said, "is you find something *safe* to talk about when you talk to that boy." I grinned at her and lifted her chin up with my finger and told her, "Janny lamb, you just ease yourself; I won't talk about nothing with him but the weather and the woods. That's a promise." "Good," she said and drew those waxy lids down over her eyes [I used to kid Joby about her being able to see through those lids like a frog], and headed off back to the kitchen to work on breakfast.

Soon as she left, Joby was on me about practically the same thing, only he wanted me to be sure I said *something* to Lee. "Tell him how he's growed or *something*, Hank. Last night you was about as friendly to him as a leper."

"By god, now," I said, "you an' Jan get together and rehearse this?"

"Just let the boy know he's home, is all. You gotta keep in mind he's one of the sensitives."

Joe went on off, leaving me kind of peeved—they act like the place was a grade school welcoming first-graders. I thought I knew what they were both angling at though. And I was already wondering how I was going to make it with another sensitive in the house, especially the way Viv'd been since finding out about the WP contract. I knew I was going to have to walk on eggs just to keep peace.

I walked on over to his room anyhow and stood there a minute, listening to see if he was up and around or not. Henry had give him a holler a few minutes before, but he could of passed that off as a bad dream, the way the old devil sounded with his calling; since the old man'd been laid up he'd been big on being the first one out of bed, storming through the house rise-and-shining till I could of choked the old bastard. Nothing galls a man more than being yelled out of bed by somebody all full of piss, vinegar, and the knowledge that as soon as everybody else is off to the job then he can cripple back to the sack and sleep till noon.

*The room is hard and dark, patrolled by the icy air circulating through the jammed window . . .*

I was about to tap on the boy's door when I heard him rustling

around, so I tiptoed back down to get shaved up for breakfast, thinking back on the first time cousin John came out from Idaho to work
for us and Henry went in to root him out in the morning. John'd
looked pretty bad when he arrived the night before—claimed he'd
swum his way across country on a great river of alcohol—so we'd put
him to bed before the rest of us, hoping he'd grow back together a
little bit with a good snooze. When Henry opened the door that
morning and went in, John reared up in bed like somebody'd shot
off a cannon, blinking his eyes and pawing at the air in front of
him. "What is it?" he said. "What is it?" The old man told him it
was three-thirty was what it was. "Jesus Christ," John said. "Jesus
Christ, you better get some sleep, Henry. Didn't you tell me we got
a hard day's work comin' up tomorrow?" And flopped right back
down. It was a good three days before we got John cooked dry
enough to look human, and he still didn't do us much good. He
just moaned and groaned around. That was before any of us realized
we were trying to run him without his fuel; just like his truck ran
better *with* Diesel than without, John functioned better with a tank-
ful of Seven Crown. One of the reasons for his drinking, Henry said,
was John's mama used to make the whole family get down on their
knees and pray like fury everytime John's daddy—Henry's first cousin,
I believe—would come home boozed, and John never quite got it
straight that they weren't thanking the good Lord for his blessing
same as they did at the supper table. So according to Henry booze
come to be sort of *holy* to him and with faith like that John grew
up religious as a deacon.

*The bed is a frozen shell, surrounding one kernel of warmth from
which you dare not move . . .*

John was a good worker. A lot more drunks are good workers than
people think. Maybe they need it like a medicine just like Jan every
day needs to take her thyroid pills to keep even-keeled. I remember
one day when we had to get John to drive the pick-up to town—the
day old Henry busted himself up slipping off that mossy rock and
Joe and me had to be in back with him to keep him from bouncing
and rearing around and jumping out. John, I remember, was the only
choice handy for driver. I thought he was going okay, but all the ride
in Henry keeps hollering, "I'll *walk* to town rather'n ride with that
damn ginhead. I'll walk, goddammit, I'll *walk*—" like it'd be easier'n
riding . . .)

*You try to shrink further inside that warm center, but the booming*

of old Henry's cast coming down the hall rips through your dark
armor of sleep like a cannonball. "Wake it an' shake it!" comes the
war cry following the initial knuckled assault on the door: Boom
boom boom! then:

"Wake it an' shake it! Wag it an' shag it! If you can't carry it
roll it out an' drag it hee hee hee."

Followed by more loud booming on the door and a high, malicious
giggle.

"Give me some whistlepunks! Give me some bully jacks! Give
me some fallers an' chasers an' chokersetters! Gawdamn; I can't run
a show without me some loggers!"

Gawdamn; I can't sleep without me some quiet!

The door thundered again. Wham wham wham. "Boy?" The house
shuddered. "Boy! Le's get out there an' take the shade offn the
ground. Le's get some daylight in that swamp."

Daylight is right, I mumbled into the pillow. Still black as the
holes of hell, and at any moment the senile old imbecile was going
to proceed to fire the whole house as a precaution against slugabeds
who might still harbor the ridiculous notion that the dead of night
was meant for sleeping. In that first reawakening chaos a quick glance
about at the morning proved as insufficient as it had the night before.
For once again I was able to establish the where but not the when.
Certain facts were apparent: dark; cold; thundering boots; quilts;
pillow; light under the door—the materials of reality—but I could
not pin these materials down in time. And the raw materials of
reality without that glue of time are materials adrift and reality is
as meaningless as the balsa parts of a model airplane scattered to the
wind. . . . I am in my old room, yes, in the dark, certainly, and it
is cold, obviously, but what time is it?

"Nearly four, son." Whomp whomp whomp!

But I mean what time? What year is it? I tried to recount the
facts of my arrival but they had come unglued during the night and
were too far blown in the dark to be readily recovered. In fact, it
took at least the first two weeks of my stay to gather all the balsawood
pieces—longer than that to glue them into any order again.

"Say, son, what are you doin' in there?"

Push-ups. My Latin assignment. The Blue Tango.

"You woke at all?"

I nodded loudly.

"Then what are you a-doin'?"

I managed to mumble something that must have satisfied as well as amused him because he rumbled on off down the hallway, snickering with diabolic glee, but after he was gone I couldn't get back to my warm sleep because it dawned on me that I seriously was expected to rise and go outside in that frozen night, and work! And with this realization I repeated his question to myself: What am I doing here? I had managed up until then to avoid this problem by treating it facetiously, as demonstrated above, or by passing it off with vague fantasies about heroically measuring up or righteously pulling down. But now that I was being confronted by the demon work—and at four in the morning—and could no longer procrastinate answering, which was it to be? I was too sleepy to make a choice and I had about decided to table the question for the time and sleep on it when the old poltergeist came thundering back into my skull to make the choice for me.

"Get up, boy! Wake it an' shake it. It's time to get to makin' your mark in the world."

*Lee rises abruptly from bed* . . . And, rather than risk his return, I struggled to me feet *he stares grimly at the door, his cheeks burning from the comment,* thinking, Yeah, Leland. If you're going to measure up it's time to get to measurin'.

I dressed and stumbled downstairs to the kitchen, where my fellow inmates were all elbows and ears over a checkered tablecloth covered with eggs and pancakes. They greeted me and bade me sit and join them in at least the last quarter of the meal. "Been waitin' for you, Lee," Joe Ben announced with a tangled grin, "just like one dog waits on another."

*The kitchen was calmer than it had been the previous night:* three of Joe's children were sitting on the woodbox beside the stove, engrossed in a comic book; Joe's wife was scraping the griddle with a wire brush; old Henry was one-handing his food skillfully into a set of false teeth; Hank was licking syrup from his fingers . . . a nice American breakfast. *Lee swallows hard and pulls out a chair, hoping it is meant for him.* But I noticed Hank's elusive woods nymph was still not present. "What about this wife of yours, Hank; hasn't Henry trained her to wake it and shake it?" *He sits, stiff-backed and apprehensive, hoping he makes a better impression than he did at supper* . . .

Hank seemed preoccupied; he hesitated answering and old Henry jumped into the breach. His face lifted from his plate like a cast-iron lid being raised. "Ya mean Viv? Why lordymercy, Leland, we kick her outta bed *hours* before the rest of us males stir a finger. Just like we do little Jan, here. Why, Viv, she's up, cooked this *breakfast*, mopped the *floor*, shelled a bushel of peas an' made us all a *nosebag* already. You bet; I taught this boy how to *deal* with women, goddammit." He snickered, lifting his cup, and a mouthful of pancake disappeared before a torrent of coffee; he exhaled loudly and craned backward to peer around the kitchen for the missing girl. The yolk of egg wobbled in the center of his forehead like a third eye. "I reckon she's someplace here if you want to meet her . . ."

"Outside," Hank answered moodily, "seein' to the cow."

"Why ain't she in here eatin' with us?"

"Damned if I know." He shrugged, then turned vigorous attention once more to his food.

The food platter was empty. Jan offered to prepare me a new batch of cakes, but old Henry insisted time was far too much at a premium and said I could get by this morning on corn flakes. "Learn ya to hop right up, by god."

"Some stuff in the oven," Hank said. "I stuck a pie tin of cakes in to keep warm for him, figuring he might not make the first round."

He took the pan from the black mouth of the oven and scraped the contents onto a plate for me as one might scrape leftovers to a pet. I thanked him for saving me from a fate of cold corn flakes, and cursed him silently for condescendingly assuming I would be late. *And again feels that flame redden his cheeks.* The meal continued, if not in silence, at least without benefit of words. I glanced at brother Hank a time or two, but he seemed to have forgotten my presence in the pursuit of some more lofty contemplation. . . .

(. . . of course, John made the drive okay, and the old man didn't walk to the hospital like he threatened, but it turns out that that ain't the end of it. By no means. When Joby and me go back to the clinic a day or so later, there John is, sitting on the front steps with his hands dangling between his knees, blinking up at us red-eyed as a white hat. "I heard Henry's goin' home today," he says. "That's so," I tell him. "He didn't break so much as he just knocked it outa line. They got him in a lot of plaster but the doc says it's mostly to keep him from rearin' around." John stands up and whops his palms on his britches. "Well, I'm ready whenever you are," he says, and I see that he's someway got the notion that Joe and me'd have to ride in back again to hold the old man down. Now, I got no desire whatsoever to ride in back again while Henry raves about John's driving, so before I think I say to him, "John, one of us'll probably be in better shape to drive; maybe you oughta sit this one out." Never for one instant imagining he'd be put out about it. But he is and bad. He bats his eyes at me three or four times while they run full of water and says, "Just thought I'd lend a hand," and goes shuffling off around the corner of the hospital, cut clean to the bone. . . .)

*The absence of talk fills Lee with almost uncontrollable nervousness. The silence is directed specifically at him, like a spotlight on a suspect in a police line-up, waiting. He recalls an old joke: "So you studied four years of trigonometry, eh? Okay, then, say something to me in Trigonom." They're waiting for me to say something to justify all those years of study. Something worthwhile . . .*

I concluded work on my pancakes and was in the process of finishing a cup of coffee when old Henry struck the table with an egg-dripping knife. "Hold on!" he demanded. "Hold on a minute." He squinted fiercely at me, leaning so close I could see where the vain old peacock had oiled and combed his bushy white eyebrows. "How big are your feet?" Puzzled and a little worried, I swallowed and managed to stutter out my shoe size. "We got to get you some corks."

He rose and rocked from the kitchen to search out the corks I obviously lacked; I sank back to my chair, overcome by the reprieve. "For a moment there," I said, laughing, "I thought he had in mind to cut my feet to fit the shoe. That or stretch them. A sort of pediatric Procrustean bed."

"What's that?" Joe Ben was interested. "A sort of what kind of bed?"

"Procrustean bed. Procrustes? The Greek bed freak? Who Theseus did in?"

Joe shook his head in awe, eyes agog and mouth hanging open as mine once must have hung for the tales of the north woods' legendary denizens, and I ended up giving a capsule lecture on Greek mythology. Joe Ben sat fascinated; his kids were drawn up from their comic; even his little doughball of a wife came away from her chores at the stove to listen; *Lee talks rapidly, his nervousness at first giving his speech an air of supercilious snobbery; but as he becomes aware of his audience's genuine interest the tone changes to enthusiasm. He*

*feels surprised and slightly proud that he can make an actual con-*
*tribution to talk around the table. This gives him a simple eloquence*
*that he has never—even in his dreams of teaching—imagined himself*
*capable of. The old myth feels fresh in his mouth, pure, then he*
*glances to the side to see if his half-brother is as enchanted as Joe*
*and his family—*but when I looked to see if brother Hank was picking
up on my mastery of mythology, I saw that he was staring with bored
vacancy at his dirty plate as though all this were either old hat to
him or just total nonsense—*and his inspired lecture runs down like a*
*punctured bagpipe . . .*

(So when John don't show up for work the next day I figured I
better head over and smooth him out. Joe says it might be tough
because he was truly hurt, and Jan tells me be sure—ifn I *do* smooth
him out—not to say something to hack him off again. I tell them not
to sweat it, that "I never saw nobody you couldn't bring around with
a little whisky, nor couldn't keep brought around with a little doin'."
I was right, too, that time; I found John sulled in his shack like a
whupped dog, but the promise of a whole case of Seven Crown
brought him right to the top. I wish it was always that easy. I knew
it was gonna take more than whisky to smooth over the sull I'd put
on Viv last night, and that the way I was feeling that morning, it
was going to take some pretty fancy doing to follow Jan's advice about
finding something safe to talk to Lee about. During breakfast I tell
him a little about corks, but it's just make-work talk, about how to
grease them and how wet shoes take to grease better'n dry shoes and
how the best application is a mixture of bear fat, mutton tallow, and
neat's-foot oil. And then Joe Ben claims it's just as good to paint the
whole boot with heavy floor paint and me and Joe get to arguing on
*that* old bit so I don't say any more to Lee. I wasn't sure he was
listening anyhow . . .)

Henry returned with my "corks"—spiked boots miserably cold and
stiff, obviously the recent home of migrant scorpions and rats—and
before I could flee all three set upon me and laced the leather horrors
to my feet. Then they draped one of Joe Ben's extra coats over me;
Hank handed me a battered metal hat with a dozen coats of vari-
colored paint peeling red and yellow and orange, like a chapeau designed by Jackson Pollock; Jan thrust a lunch sack in my hand; Joe
Ben gave me a pocketknife with eight blades; and they all stepped
back to view the result. Henry rolled a doubting eye, allowed as how
he guessed I'd hafta do till somethin' with more meat on its bones

showed up, and offered me a dip from his snuff can as a sign that I had passed review. Joe Ben said I'd do just fine, and Hank withheld judgment.

I was ushered out into a morning still totally dark save for a pale blue cast over the hills. I followed the silhouettes of Hank and Joe Ben down the invisible planks to the dock while the old man lurched along behind, slicing the dark in a distracted fashion with the misty beam of an enormous flashlight. While he walked he kept up a line of talk as aimless as the light: "That Evenwrite, now I don't trust him; watch for booby traps. When we get this contract done I think by god—say, what about the drums on that donkey? You boys watchin' out? Lord, I don't want to be buyin' new equipment. I was sayin' the other day to Stokes that that old donkey wasn't as old as this one and look at me still agoin'. . . . Say now, Leland, did I tell you about my teeth?" He swung the light to his face and I watched while he removed a moldy-looking mouthful of molars. "What you think about that for lucky?" He spread back his lips. "Only three my own teeth left—lookee here—an' two the sonofaguns meet. How 'bout that?" He laughed triumphantly and replaced the dentures. "Somethin' more'n just luck about it, too, Joe Ben tells me; it's a indication or something. . . . You, Joe, don't forget to lay the old oil on that boogin' donkey drum, hear me? It's good for another two or three seasons, treated proper. Whup. Don't care for the way the sky looks. Hmm"—grumbling, mumbling, "Ouch oh!" pausing occasionally to curse some paleolithic pain in his shoulder. "An' oh yeah, have Bob watch them scalers when he drives down; they're smooth as grease an' they'll cheat you ever' time you sneeze. Those boys of Orland's will be there from the mill to give us extra help, ain't that right? An' no coffee and bullshooting every twenty minutes. We ain't Wakonda Pacific yet. Keep everybody on the jump. We got only a month left to Thanksgiving, you realize, only a month . . ."

Keeping up a frantic free-association which he hoped would, by some miracle, save the day in spite of his monumental absence.

"Hey, did you hear me about that donkey, dammitall? That drum?"

Hank had been yanking at the starting rope of the outboard during the latter part of the harangue; only after the motor caught with a burbling roar and the rope had been carefully secured beneath the rear seat and the gas tank checked, only then did Hank indicate any awareness of the old man. "You know . . ." He flipped the mooring rope free and settled himself beside the motor, held out his hand for

the flashlight, which Henry relinquished with about as much enthusiasm as Napoleon must have shown giving up his sword on the
isle of Saint Helena. . . . "You *know* . . ." turning the light on
Henry and stopping whatever the old man was opening his mouth to
say as though the beam had knocked the wind out of his bony frame
". . . you are sure a noisy old fart this morning."

Henry blinked in the glare. He started to shield his eyes against the
light with his hand but decided this would be a gesture of weakness
unbefitting so noble a donkey, and lowered the hand, choosing instead to turn disdainfully away from the light and the sharper-than-a-
serpent's-tooth words of his disrespectful son. "Pshh." And thus did
he treat us to the magnificence of his profile framed there against the
dramatic backdrop of dawn. He stood there—majestic, striking, confident that Valentino could not come close to matching those steely
eyes, certain that when it came to classic facial proportion Barrymore
was not even in the running—and slowly, deliberately withdrew the
snuff can from the pocket of his robe, thumbed it open with one
hand, and placed a rolled ball of it in his lower lip . . .

"Just look at 'im," Hank whispered.

The long cowl of white hair like blown clouds; the firm jaw; the intelligent brow; the nose hooking down over the horseshoe mouth . . .

"Yeahhh," Joe breathed.

He remained profiled before us in the light's beam, aristocratically
austere, grandly aloof, as ludicrous as a buzzard, until Hank nudged
Joe Ben in the ribs and whispered again.

"My, ain't he handsome."

"Gosh, yes," Joe Ben agreed, "no getting around it."

"You think I dast leave a sheik like that home with my pore little
unprotected wife?"

"Can't tell," Joe answered.

"Mighty good-lookin' head of hair for a man that age."

"Oh yeah. Like a prophet, kind of."

The whole thing had the ring of long practice; I imagined a scene
not unlike this one went on nearly every morning. The old man tried
to remain aloof. But in spite of all he could do I could see the grin
creeping into the fierce features.

"And will you just *look*." Hank's voice was full of mocking awe and
admiration. "Just look how *fine* those eyebrows are groomed and
slicked up. Almost like he plucks them an' puts stuff—"

"Boogers!" the old man bellowed. "Sonsabitches! You ain't got no respect!" He made a lunge for an oar leaning against the boathouse, but Hank gunned the boat just in time and left the outlandish figure charging around the dock, so furious, so outraged, and so obviously pleased by the teasing that I couldn't help laughing along with Hank and Joe Ben as we pulled away up the river. *They swing out into the water, laughing. The tenseness that overcame Lee during his breakfast lecture begins finally to subside after the comedy on the dock, and Hank feels his concern for his wife's mood lessen as the boat leaves the house lights behind.* (We futzed around on the dock with the old man like we usually do, and I noticed Lee laughed, showing he's loosening up some. I think, Now's the time to make a move and try to talk with him. Now's the time forchrissakes to try to make some kind of contact.) *And as the dawning sky grows brighter the two brothers find themselves glancing quickly at each other and away, waiting . . .*

I had at first feared I might be embroiled in some small talk with Hank and my gnomish cousin, but neither of them seemed any more inclined toward conversation than they had at the breakfast table. The air was cold. All of us were content to let the motor hold forth in its rhythmical way while we drew our own thoughts about us against the ice-blue dawn just beginning to give the mountains shape. I tucked my chin into the sheepskin top of the jacket Joe Ben had provided and averted my face so the stinging mist struck my cheek instead of my eyes. The bow thump-thump-thumped against the river's surface; the motor warbled, a tight, high, full-throated whine underscored by the guttural churn of water; Hank weaved the boat up the river, responding to the grunted instructions of Joe Ben, who sat in the bow watching for floating snags. "Stump there, cut left. Okay." I felt warm and drowsy, entranced by the movement, the rocking . . . and the vicious, singing hiss of water speeding beneath the aluminum hull of the motionless boat.

(All that ride up the river I sit like a knot on a log, no notion in the world how to talk to him or what to talk about. I think the only thing I said during the whole trip was something about how pretty the morning was . . .)

Before me the dawn took on ghastly substance, becoming solid except for the trees and mountains ripped like jagged black holes to space. A dirty glaze spread over the water. An oilslick; it will explode at the touch of a match, a river of hellfire stretching to the horizon.

(You know? It's hard to talk to somebody you ain't seen in a long time and it's hard not to. And it's especially hard when you got a lot to say and no notion how to say it.)

We rocked forward in the boat, past phantom pilings suspended in mist, kerosene lanterns behind windows of stage-set house-fronts where wind-up dogs toll the watch beside muslin trees; past muskrats pulling a V of silver down into their underwater hideouts, and water-fowl, startled, splashing into the air dripping shiny intestines.

(And I'm right glad when we pull in to bank and take on Andy because I feel like the pressure's eased a little bit just having somebody else around and I can quit fretting about talking.)

At a perilous and tottering plank pier that continued out over the river like an extension of the path that came from the vine-tangled bank, we acquired another passenger. A droop-eyed, droop-mouthed, droop-shouldered hulk twice my size and not much more than half my age. He stumbled and stomped about the bottom of the boat with his spiked boots, almost upsetting the boat, while Hank intro-duced us. "This here is—sit down, Andy—this here is your cousin Leland Stanford. Down now, dammit"—like a bear that had been stricken with all the traditional clumsy woes of the archetype adoles-cent, he had acne, an Adam's apple and a timidity so stultifying that he was thrown into a fidgeting agony each time I glanced his direc-tion. He sat hunched between the peaks of his knees, rustling a brown paper sack that held a full-grown turkey at very least, possibly two turkeys. I was touched by his discomfort. "I take it, Andy," I ventured, "that you are part of the Stamper Industries?"

He was put suddenly at ease by my question. "You bet," he ex-claimed happily. "You bet I am." So at ease that he then fell im-mediately to sleep on a tarp at the bottom of the boat.

A few minutes farther on we stopped again for another passenger, a man in his late thirties, garbed in the traditional metal headgear of loggers and wearing a muddy pair of coveralls. "One of our neigh-bors," Hank explained as we glided toward him. "Named Les Gib-bons. A sawyer for WP, outa work from the strike. . . How's she goin', Les?"

An older, hairier, dirtier, and slightly smaller animal than our first passenger, Les was as garrulous as Andy was taciturn. His tongue worked continually to alternate a load of snuff and a charge of dia-logue so overdone in the colloquial vein that it was difficult to re-member this was a real person speaking real lines, not a character from an Erskine Caldwell novel.

"Not s' good, Hank," Les answered. "Not s' good. By dog, me 'n' the woman 'n' the kids, we done et the last measly bean 'n' chewed the last salty bone 'n' it shore beats me what this here world is acomin' to. Them u-nyn boys they don't do sompin' awful quick we jes' gonna be flat up agin it."

Hank shook his head, positively radiating sympathy. "I guess she's tight all over, Les."

"Ain't that a fack," Les said, and paused to lean over the side of the boat and work a gob of tobacco from between purple lips. "Don't look for no letup, neither, if ya ast me. Nope. Reason I'm agoin' inta town today is, well, that I hear tell there's road job hirin' on part time. Diggin'. Well . . ." He shrugged philosophically. "A beggar cain't be a chooser, I don't s'pose. You boys, now you, you're probably makin' hay, I bet. Eh? Eh? Pleased for you. Real happy an' that's a fack. You Stampers are good old boys. Yes, I'm really happy. But oh gawdahmighty but I surely do hate road work. An' that's the truth! They ever get you on the business end of a shovel, Hank? Oh, let me tell you, it' no work for a white man . . ."

The boat touched the other shore, and after spitting again—short, onto the seat—our passenger stood and disembarked decorously. "I thank you boys." He nodded to me. "Real happy to make your acquaintance, young fella. Well, I surely thank you. I do hate to put you boys out, but till I can get my skiff back from Teddy—"

Hank waved the gratitude aside magnanimously. "Not a word, Les."

"Just the same, Hank . . ." His hand inched toward a billfold that we all knew he had no intention whatsoever of opening. "Just the same I ain't one to be beholden. Let me—"

"Not another word, Les. Glad to help. I'd do the same for a white man."

They gave each other the pleasure of their smiles—Hank's grin wide and innocent, Les's like a broken clay dish—then Les clambered up the road, muttering thanks, ragged and humble as poverty itself, and climbed into a new Ford Fairlane convertible. "Can you hold 'er a sec, Hank?" he called back. "Mornin's are gettin' chillier an' sometimes the ol' ragtop don't start so good."

Hank nodded, amused, while little Joe Ben fumed at Les under his breath: "What you figure we could do for you, you cluck? give you a startin' shove with the boat?" Hank laughed softly. He idled the boat against the bank until Les got a reaction from his car; then we started up river again. It was light enough so I could see Joe Ben's face twisted into its own rendition of a frown.

"I'll slip up here one of these nights an' roll that machine of his into the river."

"Les is a good old boy, Joe, an' we wouldn't want to be party to any ill that come to—"

"Lester Gibbons is a cluck an' always has been! What about the time he took off a whole season an' left his woman to grub potatoes in Walterville? He oughta been tarred and feathered . . ."

Hank winked at me. "Does that sound like a Christian attitude to you, bub? Joby, it ain't like you to be hacked at poor old Les. What harm's he ever done us?"

"*Harm!* He'd cut your throat, an' you know it. Hank, sometimes I think you ain't got the eyes the good Lord gave a goose. Why, any man can see the way he's gunnin' for you. Yet you just fiddle along, swallowin' his bull."

"Joe's always been my big matchmaker, Lee. He got me into more scrapes than I can recall."

"That ain't so! That ain't so! It's just I sometimes try an' get you to face up to what you got to do. Oh yeah. Lee, he's the worst I ever seen for puttin' off till tomorrow what he already put off till today. Just like this business with Floyd Evenwrite; if you'd told Viv about it way back when you knew you was gonna have to, you wouldna had her angered at you now."

"Okay, Joe," Hank said quietly, strangely, "let's us drop that."

" 'Stead of lettin' it go till she *found out*, there wouldn't been near the fuss."

"Joe . . ."

"He's worst I ever seen, Lee. Especially when it's got somethin' to do with women that he—"

"Joby, I said drop it!"

The order was so charged with emotion that it caused all three of us in the boat to stare at Hank in surprise. He sat at the motor, grim and trembling. No one spoke, no eyes looked. And for a third time I experienced that feeling of combative elation that a long-shot challenger must feel when he notices a small but decided limp in his massive opponent's seven-league stride.

(The whole blamed trip. Just sitting there like a lump, trying to find the toehold to start with, trying to figure some way of working up to all the things I got to say, all the things I got to ask. But I can't make it. I introduce him to John when we pick him up in front of his shack, and John's able to get a hell of a lot more going with him than me. It seems they're both big on Seven Crown. John offers him a slash from the Thermos of the stuff he always carries, and they talk about how it is with a little coffee added. They got a common ground. Even Orland's three boys do better than me. When I wake them up from the rear end of the crummy truck and introduce them to Lee they're able to shoot the bull a few minutes, asking him questions about New York and what's it like, before they go back to sleep. Even them lugs.

I pour it to that old rattletrap. We're running a little late, what with waiting breakfast on the kid. The sun's already coming through the trees. We head out up Blueclay Road toward the North Spur of Breakneck, where the show is, and after about a half-hour bouncing and bumping and nobody saying word one to nobody else we get up to the site. The slashing piles are still smoking from yesterday's burning, and the sun's rose out of the branches and is promising to make a long hot sticky sonofabitch of a day of it. I slide out from behind the wheel and go around and open the door and stand there stretching and scratching my belly while the truck empties, kind of not looking at him. "What do you think?" I ask Joe Ben. "Did we or did we not come up with a fine day to welcome old Leland Stanford home to the woods?" Joe, he tips an eye up for a check with his Big Time Weatherman just to be sure and says, "Oh yeah! Maybe get a little on the toasty side before the sun sets, but the way I look at it all the signs point to a day with a heart of gold. Ain't that the way you read it, Leland?"

The boy is shaking like a dog shitting peach pits, still cold from the river ride. He frowns over at Joe like he isn't sure whether he's being spoofed or not, then he grins and says, "I'm afraid I failed to take any courses on astrological signs, Joe; I'll have to trust to your cially when they're aimed at him. He giggles and spits and goes to interpretation." This tickles Joe to pieces. Joe digs big words, espe-hauling out all the paraphernalia for the day—maps and hard hats and "Boy, be sure an' take these gloves!" and candy bars and snuff cans and pocket knives, and, naturally, the little transistor radio he keeps near him all day—passing them around like a munitions officer issuing arms before a big battle. He hands Lee his hard hat and goes prancing around, tilting his head this way and that to get a good look at the way it sits, saying "Um . . . oh yeah . . . say there . . . wait . . . here we go," and fooling with it till he gets it settled the way he wants it. Then he starts giving Lee a rundown on what to expect and what's happening and what to look out for working the woods.

"The main thing," Joe says, "oh yeah, the *mainest* thing . . . is, when you fall, fall in the *direction* of your work. *Conserve* yourself." He demonstrates how to conserve yourself by doing a couple of nose dives as we amble along. "The whole notion of loggin' is *very* simple if you get onto it. It comes to this: the idea is to make a tree into a log and a log into a plank. Now, when it's standin' up vertical it's a *tree*, and when it's laid down it's a *felled tree*. And then we buck it into lengths of thirty-two feet an' them lengths are *logs*. Then we drag them logs acrost to where the truck is and lift 'em up onto the truck an' then the truck drives 'em down to the bridge at Swedesgap where the government scalers cheat us an' then we take 'em on down to our mill an' dump 'em into the water. When we get enough of 'em in the water we drag 'em up into the mill and we cut 'em up an' we got planks, *lumber*." He stops to twiddle with the dial of his transistor, trying to pick up one of the Eugene stations. "Or, sometimes, instead of cuttin', we just sell the logs outright." I look over at him to see how he means that, but he's holding the radio to his ear. "Ah. Now it's comin' through. Oh man, Lee, you ever see the beat of one of these little outfits? Listen to that tone." He shakes his head at his little radio and twists the dial loud as it'll go. The tinny screech of some awful Western is squeezed out into the forest. "Makes the day a joy," he says, grinning till you'd think he'd pop; a little thing like that radio could give Joe Ben a thousand dollars' worth of kicks, just about any little thing could.

> *You broke my heart an' tol' me lies,*
> *Left me cold without good-bys;*
> *Oh, your frosty eyes . . .*

We stop walking right near where Andy's starting his chain saw. The saw chokes and barks and dies and barks again with a rising snarl. Andy grins over at us and hollers, "Commencin'!" cocks an eye up above for widow-makers, then touches the saw's blurred teeth against the flank of a big fir. A fountain of white fir sparks spew against the sun. We stand and watch him make his undercut and sight the tree. He's made it a little too much sloped, so he cuts him a dutchman and slides it in to account for the extra inch or so, and goes around to the other side and goes at it with the saw again. When the tree creaks and tips and goes whooshing down I glance over to check the boy and see he's impressed by it. That makes me feel better. I'd begun to wonder if it's possible at all to talk with him; I'd begun to wonder if maybe what a man learns over twelve years in a world so different is like a foreign language that uses some of the words from our world but not enough to be familiar to us, not enough so we can talk. But when I see him watch that tree come down I think, There's that; just like any man I ever knew, he likes to see a tree felled. There is that, by Christ.

"Well," I say, "we ain't makin' anything but shadows. Let's get hold of it." And we start walking again.

Joby leaves to fire up the donkey. Lee follows me across a clearing toward the edge of the woods. At the edge of a pile of slashing and dozed berry vine the clearing quits and the trees plunge into the sky. It's the part of the show I like best, this edge, where the cutting stops and the forest starts. I'm always reminded of the edge of a grain field where the reaper has stopped.

Behind us the donkey engine begins wheezing and gagging. I see Joe sitting like a twisted bird high up in his spiny nest of levers and cables and wires, grabbing at the throttle. The radio sits in front of him, sometimes carrying across to us, sometimes swallowed up by the noise. A ball of blue smoke explodes from the exhaust and I think the whole machine is going to shake itself to death. "That goddamned outfit should of been retired with the old man," I say. The boy doesn't say anything. We start walking again. Somewhere I hear the knock of an ax where John is chopping off branches. Like a wooden bell ringing. And that squeal of Joe's radio coming and going on little breezes. All these things, the way a day gets going, the sound and all, and seeing Lee dig that tree falling, make me feel a whole lot better. I decide maybe it's not going to be such a bear as I thought.

Overhead the highlines that swoop to the spar tree are commencing to bob and jiggle and strum the air. I point up at them. "That's your row to hoe, bub, that line. I aim to see if you can stand up under the strain of setting choker, by god, so just resign your ass to your fate." I'm meaning to rib him a little. "Course, I don't expect you to last out the morning, but we got a stretcher handy." I grin over at him. "That boy of Orland's is handlin' the other line . . . he can take over when you fall behind." He looks like he's being ordered up to the front lines, standing all at attention and his jaw set. I'm intending to kind of kid him but, try as I may, I can hear myself sounding just exactly like old Henry doing some first-rate ass-chewing, and I know I couldn't pick a worse way to talk to Lee. But I'm damned if I can stop it.)

"You ain't gonna like it at first. As a matter of fact you're gonna think I'm givin' you the dirtiest end of the dirtiest stick on the whole operation." (And he wouldn't of been far from the truth.) "But it can't be helped. The easier jobs, the machinery jobs, it'd take too long to teach you and they're risky even when a guy knows what he's about. Besides, we're hurting for time. . . ."

(And maybe that right there is why I couldn't help sounding angry, because of knowing just how tough setting choker was going to be on a tenderfoot. Maybe I really was trying to be extra tough and was hacked at myself for loading him with it. I do that sometimes . . .)

"But one thing: it'll make a man of you."

(I just don't know. All I know is I thought I was relaxing a little around him, then tied up, the same as I tied up trying to talk with Viv the night before, explaining our deal with Wakonda Pacific. Same as I tie up with anybody except Joe Ben; and me and him didn't really have to talk a whole lot . . .)

"If you can make it through the first few days you'll have it whipped; if you can't, well, you just can't is all. There's lots of other niggers can't cut it neither and they ain't all in Dixie."

(I've always had a tough time trying to talk to others without barking. With, say, Viv, I'd start out trying to sound like Charles Boyer or somebody and come off, every time, sounding like the old man telling Sheriff Layton how to deal with the boogin' Reds in this country, how to take care of them Commy bustards *right!* And believe me, sounding like that is sounding pretty damn hard. When old Henry got going on the Reds he could really come on fierce . . .)

"But all I ask is you give it a fair go for a while."

(Because Henry always claimed he was convinced that the only thing worse than Reds was Jews, and the only thing worse than Jews was high-and-mighty niggers, and the only thing worse than the whole lot of them was them goddamned hardheaded southern bigots he was always reading about. "Oughta poison everybody south of the Mason-Dixon line . . . 'stead sending Northern tax money down to feed 'em . . .")

"So if you're ready, grab hold of that piece of cable and drag it here. I'll show you how to look for a choker hole. C'mon, snap out of it. Bend down here an' watch . . ."

(I wouldn't argue much with the old man myself, mainly because I didn't know Reds here in America, and didn't feel much one way or the other about uppity jigs, and was just a little vague about what a bigot was . . . but I tell you, for a while him and Viv used to really lock horns about just that very subject, that race business. Really get into it. I remember . . . well, let me recall the thing that *stopped* the whole business. Let's see . . .)

"Okay, now, you watch this."

*Lee stands with his hands in his pockets while Hank explains the job with the slow patience of a man who is explaining something once and it had better be picked up because it isn't about to be repeated. He shows Lee how to loop the length of cable over a fallen and bucked log and how to hook the cable to the big line that runs in a circle from the pulley at the anchor stump to the rigging at the top of the spar.* ". . . and when you get it hooked you'll have to be your own whistle-punk till things level out. We're too short-handed for such luxuries. You savvy?" I nodded and Hank went on outlining my duties for the day. "Okay, listen." *Hank gives the cable a kick to make sure it is secure, then leads Lee up the slope to a high stump where a small wire runs in a gleaming arch to the donkey puffing and clanging seventy-five yards away.* "One jerk means take 'er away." *He pulls the wire. A shrill peep from a compressed-air whistle on the donkey sets the tiny figure of Joe Ben into action. The cable tightens with a deep twanging. The donkey engine strains; an outraged roar; the log lurches out of its groove and goes bumping up the hill toward the yarder. When the log reaches the spar they watch Joe Ben leap from the donkey cab and scuttle over the pile of logs to unhook the choker. Then one of Orland's boys creaks the neck of the yarder forward, like the skeleton of some prehistoric reptile painted yellow and brought fleshless to life; Joe Ben gouges the tongs into each side of the log and jumps clear as he waves to the boy in the yarder cab. Again the gigantic piece of wood lurches and is jerked into the air as Joe Ben hustles back to the donkey controls.* "Joe's bein' his own chaser. It's tough on him, but like I said, it can't be helped." *By the time the yarder has pivoted and swung the log onto the bed of the truck and nudged it into place, Joe Ben is back in the donkey and the cable is reeling back out again. It comes snaking through the brush and torn earth toward the place where Lee and Hank stand waiting.* I listened, hoping Hank would explain more about the task, cursing him for presuming he needed to explain as much as he had. We were standing alongside each other at the "show," going through last minute instructions before my big First Day . . .

(Viv, see, spends a lot of her time reading and is up on a lot of things—that's trouble right there, because there's nothing in the whole world makes old Henry madder than somebody, especially some woman, having the common gall to be up on a lot of things he's already got opinions on . . . so, anyhow, this once, they got into it about what the *Bible* of all things says about this race business . . .)

*They watch the cable draw nearer.* "Then, you see, when the choker gets close to where you want it, give her *two jerks.*" *The whistle peeps twice. The highline stops. The choker cable hangs shuddering in its own dust.* "Okay, watch now; I'll set it one more time for you."

(The old man, see, was claiming the Bible said the spooks were born to be bondservants because their blood was black like the blood of Satan. Viv disagreed a while, then got up, walked to the gun case where we keep the big family Bible with the birthdays in it, and went to flipping through with Henry just aglowering . . .)

*When Hank has repeated the procedure he turns to Lee* . . . "You got it now?" I nodded, determined and dubious. Brother Hank then took a wristwatch from his pocket and looked at it, wound it, and returned to the same pocket. "I'll check with you when I can," he told me. "I got to see about rigging a spar on that peak yonder this morning because we'll have to move the yarding and loading later this afternoon or tomorrow. You sure you got it now?"

*Lee nods again, his mouth tight. Hank says,* "Okeedoke, then," *and goes crashing off through the vine and brush toward the crummy truck.* "Hey." *A few yards away he stops and turns* . . . "I bet you didn't think to bring those gloves, did you? No, I mighta known. Here. Use mine." *Lee catches the wadded gloves and mutters,* "Thanks, thanks ever so much." *Hank resumes his crashing through the brush* . . .

(When Viv found what she's after in that big Bible she read, "The blood of all men is as one," and shut the Bible. And I tell you: that pissed the old man so . . . that I don't know if he would of ever spoke to her again, not another word ever, if it hadn't been for the lunches she started packing for us to take to work. . . .)

*Lee holds the gloves one in each hand, burning with frustrated and confused anger as his brother walks away: You prick, he calls word-*

*lessly after Hank, you pompous prick! Use mine, huh, as though he* *was giving me his right arm. Why I'll wager every nickel I can lay my* *hands on that he has at the very least a dozen such pairs in that truck!*

Hank finished his instructions and walked away, leaving me to have at it. I looked after him stomping off through brush and brambles, then looked at the cable he had left with me, then at the nearest log, and, fired by that long-shot challenger's elation that I had experienced earlier, pulled on my gloves and had at it . . .

*As soon as Hank is gone Lee curses again and jerks on the first of* *the gloves in a stylized parody of drawing-room fury, but the elegance* *of his style is marred when he is forced to inspect the second glove,* *and the fury turns abruptly back on itself when he withdraws from* *the last two fingers the dirty, sweat-packed cotton padding Hank uses* *to protect the ends of his tender stumps . . .*

The job was actually simple enough—on the surface—simple, backbreaking labor. But if there is one thing you learn in college it is that the first snowstorm is the most important—score high in your first test and you can coast out the rest of the term. So I had at it that first day with a will, dreaming that I might snow Brother Hank fast and measure up early and be finished with the whole ridiculous business before it broke my back . . .

*The first log he chooses lies at the top of a small knoll, in a patch* *of firecracker weed. He heads toward it; the little red flowers with* *sulphur-yellow tips seem to part to make way for him and the cable.* *He throws the bell around the end of the log that is lifted free of* *the earth where the knoll drops sharply toward the canyon, then* *secures it in its hook. He steps back to examine the job, a little* *puzzled: "There doesn't seem anything so difficult about this. . . ."* *and walks back to the jerk-wire. The whistle on the donkey peeps.* *The log tips and heads for the spar tree. "Nothing so very diffi-* *cult . . ." He turns to see if Hank has been watching and sees his* *brother just disappearing over another ridge where a second line leads* *from the spar tree. "Where is he going?" He glances around, deciding* *quickly on the next log he will hook. "Is he going to that other cable* *over there?"* (Yeah, it was the lunches that Viv packed . . .) *Hank* *passes the boy at the other anchor stump, telling him he'd better get* *it in gear, "Lee's already tooted one in" and continues on into the* *woods . . .* (Lunches, see, are about twice as big a deal in the woods as at home, because you get terrible hungry by noon; and the way the old man appreciates eating anyhow, they are like a Major League event. So when Viv took over the lunchbag packing from Jan—on account of Jan being pregnant, was Viv's story, but I've always suspected it was more to get back in the old man's good graces—well, Henry just somehow forgot all about Bibles and black blood. Not that Jan's lunches weren't all right, because they were; but that's all they were. Viv's lunches were always all right and then a good deal more than all right to boot. They were a goddamned feast sometimes. But more than there just being plenty, there was generally something special about them . . .)

*The second log goes as easy as the first. And as it is being unhooked he looks back toward the other anchor stump some hundred yards away on that other ridge. There still has been no whistle signal. As he watches he sees a figure struggling through a thicket of red alder, the cable still over his shoulder. Though the figure is not even wearing the same color sweat shirt, Lee is suddenly certain that it is Hank,* "Taking over the other choker job!" *The line above his head strums and with rising excitement he looks and sees his second log is unhooked and his cable is scrambling back to him. He takes it up before it has completely stopped and jogs, dragging the heavy cable as fast as he can, toward the next log, not even taking time to glance at the progress of the figure he supposes to be his brother . . .* (Something special and different in her lunches—something other than sandwiches, cookies, and an apple; something you could strut and brag about when you were sitting with a bunch of jacks eating out of their ordinary old nosebags—but, mostly, it was that Viv's lunches gave you a little piece of the day to look forward to in the morning and think back on in the afternoon. . . .) *The cable snags briefly, but he wrenches it loose. A berry vine trips him and he falls to his knees, grinning as he recalls Joe Ben's advice, but he is still able to secure the log and jerk the take-it-away signal just seconds before the second signal comes from the other ridge. In the distance Joe Ben's head swings back in surprise: he has been sitting, his hands already on the levers controlling the cables running to that southern ridge, not expecting a call so soon from Lee.* "That boy is really humping it." *Joe changes levers. Lee holds his panting, then sees the highline above him tauten and his log jump out of the vines: he is a log ahead, two if you count that first one! How about that, Hank?* (Her lunches sure changed the old man's point of view . . .) *Two logs ahead!*

*The next log has fallen on a clear, almost perfectly level piece of ground. Unhampered by vines or brush, Lee reaches the log easily,* noticing with elation that he is gaining on the other figure, who is fighting through the red alder again. But the very flatness of the ground beneath Lee's log presents a problem; how do you get the cable under it? Lee hurries along the length of the big stick of wood all the way to its stump, then crosses and hurries puffing back, bent at the waist as he tries to peer through the tangle of limbs lining its length where Andy's saw has stripped them from the trunk . . . but there is no hole to be found: the tree has fallen evenly, sinking a few inches into the stony earth from its butt to its peak. Lee chooses a likely place and falls to his knees and begins pawing at the ground beneath the bark, like a dog after a gopher. Behind him he hears the peep of the other ridge's signal and his digging becomes almost frenzied. The trouble was, with my plan to put in a good first day even if it broke my back: I almost broke my back that first day. . . . He finishes the hole and gets the cable through and hooked and jerks his whistle wire . . . But only during the first half of that first day. Then, panting rapidly, hurries to inspect the next log; "He should have told me about the holes, the prick. . . ." (And see, the funny thing is: it was also Viv's lunches that finally broke the ice and gave me the chance I was waiting for to talk with the boy . . .) The second half of the day went easier—because by then I had learned that I was breaking my back for naught . . . The line strums overhead. The cable comes back. The moss begins to steam softly on the old stumps . . and that I was never going to measure up to Brother Hank, simply because he had rigged the scale, making it impossible. As the sun gets higher and higher.

By the time Joe Ben blew a long, famished blast on the donkey whistle, indicating noon, Lee had regained his one-log lead over the other choker-setter. When the last thread of the whistle note raveled away into the forest Lee allowed himself to sink to the ground beside a stump. He looked blankly at his hands for a time without moving, then removed the gloves, a careful finger at a time. During the grueling morning he had forgotten the circumstances surrounding the gift of the gloves. Hank's remarks had vanished. So had the anger and the shame caused by the remarks. The gloves now existed pure and with no strings to the past and O Lord God, was he ever thankful that he had something to cover his soft, pink grad student's fingers! He had thought this a hundred times. Not long after Hank had left Lee had removed the heavy shirt to let the breeze dry off his sweat; the sweat wasn't much affected as he tugged, jerked, and hauled the unwieldly cable through a miasma of berry vine and fire slashing, but within a half an hour both arms were quilted from glove top to shoulder with a pattern of welts and scratches. The view he had of his stomach made him think fabric instead of flesh, a bright garment of patchwork skin stitched together with thorns. He put his shirt back on but an inch or so of wrist still showed between cuff and glove; occasionally he would pause, gasping as he waited for Joe Ben to reel the cable back out or for Andy to buck another fallen tree into thirty-two-foot lengths, and tenderly draw up a shirt sleeve and frown at that inch of bare wrist which was beginning to look like a scarlet bracelet: he hesitated to even imagine what his hands would have looked like without the heavy leather gloves.

He let his head tilt back until it rested against the ragged side of the stump. He watched the other men move through a haze of distorted distance toward the carrier that had brought them to this hell. He felt sick. He wouldn't have walked those ten wavering miles to that truck even if a hot steak waited for him. His stomach would never touch food again. He wouldn't move from the spot, though his leg was twisted painfully beneath him, though those bastard carpenter ants, big and shiny as carpet tacks, crawled through his shirt and across his sweating belly, and though he was sitting in a thicket of what was surely poison oak—what else? He sighed. Why try to gild this Dante world? he was resolved to never move again. He closed his eyes. The sound of Joe's radio was wafted intermittently through the trees:

> And in dreams I live . . . memory . . .
> Moon . . . splendor . . . love.

His breathing slowed. His glasses were being streaked with sweat, but he couldn't have cared less. He drew his eyelids over his mangled body . . . sliding backwards up a long, hot, glistening dream of a playground slide, tumbling over the top of the slide and down a thousand iron steps worn free of their nonskid texture by a century of sneakers, onto a gritty sandlot schoolyard. Where he was able to look from beneath the brim of a grade-school beanie at the names lettered on the side of the high-school gymnasium. WAKONDA HIGH SHARKS SPORTS RECORDS. And who there? Whose name on top of the list, record-holder for high jump? The same for pole vault? And for hundred-meter swim state record? The same name all the way on down. Whose? Shucks, you know whose. That's my brother Hank Stamper. And just you wait. When I get big. He told me. Teach me to. Someday, boy-oh-boy. Said he would. I can make. Body clean mind. But I kept up. One log ahead. By the gods did keep up with him today . . .

And the ants crawled over him. And Joe's little radio spun out in the hot air:

*Oh minny years ago in days of childhood . . .*

providing background accompaniment for Lee's dreaming, as well as for Hank's limber-legged stride.

*I used to play till shadows come:*

(See when lunch blew I walked back to the crummy, but Lee isn't anywhere to be seen. I pick up two sacks and tell Joe I'm going to look for the kid and I cut back and find him crapped out in the grass not a half a dozen steps from the anchor stump . . .)

*And heard my mother call at set of sun:*

Governor Jimmy Davis reminisced reverently with a steel guitar—

*Come home, come home,*
*It's suppertime.*
*The shadows lengthen fast*

—while Hank stood for a long time looking down on the boy's scratched and blistered features.

*Come home, come home,*
*It's suppertime.*
*I'm going home at last.*

In his sleep Lee sought to change and control his dreaming, as he was usually able to do, but his exhausted mind ignored his efforts and kept threatening to ramble off in its own willy-nilly direction through all sorts of best-forgotten childhood impressions. Unable to influence its meandering, Lee was just surrendering himself to the dream when one of the carpenter ant scouts cruising the area decided to test the terrain for logging potential.

(So I sat down near the kid and started eating, figuring let him rest, when all of a sudden up he comes with a squall like a wild man, whopping himself all over. When he stops I wipe my face on my sleeve and point towards his gaping shirt he's ripped half the buttons off.

"Something you learned in college, that strip act?"

"Whore of a bug bit me! Shit."

"Why listen there. He can cuss too. Don't that beat all?" I say and pick the second paper sack from the ground and hand it over to him. He's still rubbing the ant bite.

"I don't want that swill!" he yells, about half hysterical with getting woke up so unexpected. I grin at him. I know how he feels. I done that myself, asleep once and had a chipmunk get down in my boot . . . but I don't say anything. I shrug and put the sack on the ground and go back to my own lunch. The kid's embarrassed. The way I was this morning popping off at Joby. I don't act like I notice. I'm eating, humming a little, leaning back against the mossy padding of an old spongy deadfall. Things been moving along smooth and nice and with lunch and all I feel pretty good. Good enough I think maybe I can say a word or two to the boy without sounding like I'm sentencing him to be hung. Only thing I need is some way to start.

I go to picking through my sack and arranging boiled eggs, olives, apples, and Thermos in front of me on a piece of wax paper. He's acting like he's going back to sleep and don't want nothing to eat, but the sharp mustard-and-vinegar smell of them deviled eggs is ringing the air like a dinner gong. He sits back up and opens his own sack with one casual finger like, you know, he might . . . then he might not. "I guess I fell asleep," he says, looking at the ground. It's a way to let me know why he blowed up when I offered him lunch. A sort of explanation and apology. I grin at him and nod to let him know I catch it . . .)

> Ah got a radiation burn
> On my pore pore heart,

Joe's radio insisted. A jay screamed at them, hot and hungry as it watched them eat. Except for Hank's toneless humming as he chewed steadily at the venison sandwich, there was little other sound. From the truck where the other men ate, the bell-like combinations of talk and laughter and Western music stroked the air and reached Hank and Lee on rippling heat-warped waves. The radio played; the jay screamed. Sometimes Hank hummed along with Joe's radio; other times he whistled derisively at the bird. Neither of the brothers spoke again while they finished their lunches; they ate facing each other, but their eyes never met; when Hank looked up from his meal he scanned the firs behind Lee with exaggerated absorption, measuring, falling, bucking, and even sawmilling each tree with his eyes. Lee didn't look up. He concentrated on the packed lunch. It was obvious that this sack of food was another contribution from the girl he had yet to meet but who was constantly growing in stature in his estimation. The meal was prepared to keep a man going at a hard job—like a practical fuel for a machine—but there was also that extra touch again, that addition intended to lift anything, even a sack lunch, out of the commonplace. At the very bottom of the sack, wrapped in foil like a bright holiday surprise, Lee found a square of creamy brown candy filled with roasted filberts. Lee bit off a small corner and crushed it with his tongue. "Your wife's candy?"

Hank nodded. "That's why I generally eat apart from the rest of those snakes; they always looking to share Viv's dessert."

"It's very good."

Hank scanned the trees again for a moment, lips pursed in deliberation, then turned suddenly toward Lee and leaned forward. (Then while we were eating I just started talking . . .) Before him, his three fingers curled slightly as though he gripped an invisible object. "Listen, bub, what I did this morning? Let me tell you . . ." His voice was excited. *Lee listens with excitement to Hank's intense words, eager to hear what Hank has to say about the morning's choker-setting duel.* ". . . was top the spar where we are going to move. Oh man, let me see. . . ." *Hank's crippled hand continues to grip the air as he strains for the right words.* "Let me see, see if I can . . ." *Lee looks on, expectant and impatient, while Hank takes a package of cigarettes; he tosses one to Lee and puts another in the corner of his mouth.* ". . . see if I can give you some idea. Now. The tree you want for the spar is the biggest tree on the biggest hill you can find. It's gonna be like the main center tentpole of our circus. And it's gonna be the last one cut on the hill, see, the last one up there after we clear off the rest of the show. Okay? I get into this rig . . . oh, twenty pounds of paraphernalia, maybe more; handsaw, ax, hooks, rope, and throw a line around me and the tree an' up the big sonofabitch I climb, lopping off branches as I go." (And I get started telling him about rigging the spar. Just to have something to pass the time at first. Figuring that if he liked watching that tree felled when we first got to the show, he oughta like hearing about topping, too . . .)

"As you go up, you take in the line, around the tree. It gets shorter as the tree gets smaller. You're choppin'; one-handed; whack, whack, get the little limbs. Not many big limbs on a fir till right at the top but you still got to get the little ones, and keep an eye peeled where that safety line is because you get *that* with the ax, brother, wire center or no that could be *all* she wrote. Lots of climbers have chopped their line. That's how Percy Williams bought it, husband to one of Henry's first cousins. He cut his line. Hit feet first and jammed his legs all the way up to his shoulderblades. So you learn to watch out. Watch out those stobs we call gut-gougers. Watch out you get a good bite with your spurs or you slip and slide twenty feet and peel hide off your chest and belly and thighs like scrapin' a carrot. And you want to know something else, bub? You're scared as hell. They say that the first spar is the tallest but that's all hokum; *every* one you climb is the tallest. And Christ, this sonofabitch is a good forty thousand board feet."

(But see? When he looked at me, blank as ever behind those glasses, I realized he don't have *any notion* how tall this makes the tree. And that I didn't really have any way to tell him. And then it wasn't just a way to pass the time: I was wanting to *tell* him something about what was happening, to wake him up and tell him to take advantage, dammit! Even if it meant popping him in the nose like the guy in Rocky Ford. So I repeated, "Forty thousand *feet!*" He nodded at me again.) *Lee begins to wonder if Hank is going to bring up the subject of choker-setting at all.* (I'm a long ways from convinced by that nod, but I go on anyway: "Forty thousand *feet!*" and hoped; this time he nods like he gets the picture and I go on . . .)

"Anyhow . . . you get to where it's eighteen inches around and man, here comes the ride. Feel this breeze? Not so much down here, is it? But up there you're weaving around like a drunk man. You lash yourself on with a couple loops of slack and go to work with the short saw. Zsh zsh zsh . . . till you feel it start to crack . . . start to pull . . . eck, eckkk. . . . Okay, now, see if you can get this: as that thirty-so feet of top above you cracks and *leans*, it bends the tree *with* it . . . till you're leaned out, oh god, I don't know, maybe fifteen degrees off vertical is all it is but it *feels* like you're bent clean parallel with the ground! And when that top finally busts loose, whosh, back you come! And that tree waves you around up there like a football pennant." (I still knew he wasn't getting any notion of it—the feeling, the charge a man gets rigging a tree . . .)

Lee tries to step into the pause, starting to say something about his own particular morning in the woods. "I could have used a little of that wind down here. . . . Look." He pulls his soaked shirt from his chest with a thumb and finger. "You wouldn't have thought a Yale man had this much juice in him, would you? God. Whoever that fellow on the other choke chain was, he gave me quite a workout." And glances hopefully up at his brother . . .

(So I ask myself: how can I show him? how can I give him some notion? how can I snap him outa that fog without getting in some hassle with him?) When Hank makes no comment Lee lifts a pant leg to show a lump on his shin like a blue egg. He touches it with his fingers, grimacing broadly. "There was a moment, just after I acquired this little gem, when I'll have to admit I was just the teeniest bit tempted to chuck the whole business, chain and all, and let him have it. 'You've managed to break your leg,' I said to myself. 'Do you want to try for a compound fracture just to keep ahead of that other fellow?' Owee—" He blows on the wound. "Wowee, I'll bet that's a pretty color tonight. . . . See?" "What?" "Here . . ."

His attention drawn, Hank acknowledges the bruise with a preoccupied grin, but says nothing; the jay calls distractedly as Lee inspects the bruise on his shin . . . When the day was half over I was sincerely a little proud of my stamina, and actually expecting Brother Hank to give some small praise. Then suddenly Hank looks up from Lee's leg, snapping his fingers. (And then it came to me . . .) "Hey! I'll show you want I mean, bub; look here." (I hold out both my hands for him to see. As usual after topping I was all bunged to hell, raw and bleeding, and the gimp hand was swole across the knuckles like a piece of raw corned beef.) "See? that's what I mean: I was for chrissakes half-the-damn-way up that sonofabitch before I remember, sonofagun! no gloves! Halfway up. See what I'm drivin' at, now?"

Lee lets the pant leg drop and stares at the extended hands. The nausea that he felt after the noon whistle clamps again on his full stomach, but he fights it back. But quite the opposite of praise, I received a rundown of all the extra jobs Hank had completed while waiting for me to catch up . . . "You see what I'm driving at, bub?"

Hank repeats his question and Lee forces himself to meet his brother's eyes. "Yes, I believe I see what you're driving at," he answers, trying to keep the burning in his nose and throat from coming through in his voice.

(And when I ask him that he looks up at me really for the first time since he's come home and says, "Yes, I see." And for the first time since he's come home I think by god we're getting someplace. I think, He ain't completely lost to us, after all. College or no, we can still find ways of making contact. I think, Yessir! we still got a lot going. Joby and Jan was full of beans. Me and the kid's gonna hit it off just fine.) And the folly of my first half-day swept over me: He'll always be running ahead for me to catch up. He keeps changing the rules for the run, or the run itself. He's either running twelve years ahead of me, or the other direction, or claiming to be in a different race from what I am altogether. He challenges me to setting chokers, then after I've half killed myself informs me that he's been climbing trees. . . . He will never give me the chance! *The whistle on the donkey shrills a quick shave-and-a-haircut, and Hank takes his watch from his pocket. "Hell. It's goin' on two. We farted away an hour." He cups his hands to his mouth and shouts joyously toward the spar, "What say, Jooobee . . . ?" Joe Ben answered with shave-and-a-haircut on his whistle. Hank laughs. "That Joe . . ." He screws the lid back onto the Thermos. He scratches at his chin to hide a smile . . .* (That's what I thought. But then something happened. I asked the boy, "Wellsir, bub . . . what do you think after a few hours on the end of a choker chain?") *Lee has averted his face and is folding the rest of his candy carefully up in its foil. "I think," he says thickly, "it probably ranks with the cleaning of King Augeas' stables. I think dragging that ridiculous cable through berry bushes and thorn thickets is probably one of the most miserable, most tiring, most demanding and and and least rewarding jobs offered on this fucking earth if you want to know what I think of choker-setting!"*

(And what he answered was, "You can take choker-setting and the whole business and shove it up your ass!")

*They stood, with Lee's words still shaking the air between them; Hank squinting and taken aback momentarily; Lee trembling with outrage and trying to clean his glasses on his sweat shirt. And the jay, inspired by Lee's invective, it seems, screeches louder than ever from a scrub cedar not far away.*

(So there you go. Just when I thought we were in good shape. I just couldn't figure it. Well, Hank old sport, I say to myself, this'll give you something to puzzle over the second half of the day. And I headed on back to my rigging, leaving diplomacy to somebody else.)

*When the jay stops Lee raises his glasses and looks through them at his brother. "And that," he says with a shrug, "is what I think of your wonderful logging."*

*Hank smiles slightly, studying the tall boy before him. "Okay, bub, okeedoke. So now I'll tell you something. . . ." He takes his cigarettes from his pocket and places one between his lips. "Did you know that every woods-worker who ever barked a shin or broke a finger agrees with you?—when it comes right down to the nuts of it—agrees with you to a T? That it's one dirty, tough, miserable way to live. That it's about as dangerous a way to make your bacon as you can find. That sometimes you'd be better off chuckin' the whole scene and just flopping down on the ground."*

*"Then what possible reason—"*

*"Lee, I just gave you my reason. With that riggin' story. Or as close as I can come to it. And my reason is pretty nearly Joe Ben's reason or Andy's or even that bastard Les Gibbons'. What I was just studyin' about, though, bub . . ." he pushes the last of the scraps down into the sack and tosses the sack away down the hill ". . . was just what Leland Stamper's reason might be?"—hitches his pants and starts away up the slope, leaving the question dangling in front of Lee. "Let's go, you coons!" he calls across the distance toward the men around the crummy, clapping his hands together. "If we don't get him this round, we'll get him the next!"*

*And Joe's radio answers with:*

Mister engineer take that throttle in hand
'Cause this rattler's the fastest in all the land,
So keep movin' on . . .

The boy again watches him disappear over the southern ridge into the veil of green needles. The jay calls incessantly from the cedar, in a voice as coarse and dry as the afternoon heat. Lee cleans his glasses again: *have to get my regular ones fixed.* He doesn't move from his stump until he hears the other boy toot the take-it-away signal; then he sighs, stands, and walks stiffly to his cable, without even a look in the direction of the other choker-setter. *Screw him up there, whoever he is, blowing that damned whistle; he can bust his blood vessels if he is so inclined. I'm just going to make it through the day. That's all. Just make it through the day.*

Even so, even though I coasted from noon on, that first day still came about as close to undoing me completely, both physically and mentally, as any day had in almost a week. I didn't comprehend how devastating it had actually been until it was nearly over, until we had returned to the carrier and reversed our up-river process and arrived back at the house—under a sky as dark as the one that had bade us farewell that morning—and I had struggled up the stairs to my room. And bed. A sight even more welcome than it had been the day before. If the days progress in this fashion, I advised myself, I would do well to attend to whatever I have in mind before the end of the week, because I'll never last another.

*Lee lies on his bed, panting. Outside the silver chatter of stars anticipates the moon's arrival. Hank finishes securing the boat for the night and walks into the house. There is no one to be seen but the old man, seated before the television with his cast extended before him on a hassock.* "You here by yourself?" *Hanks asks. Henry doesn't turn his gaze from the flickering Western before him.* "Looks like, don't it? Joe and his are in the kitchen where I run 'em so I could get some peace. Viv, I think, is out to the barn. . . ." "And the kid?" "He drag-assed right on upstairs; you musta worked him some." "A little," *Hank answers, hanging his coat.* "I'll go tell Viv we're back . . ." (Puzzling over things the rest of the day didn't get me nowhere; by the time we got home the kid and I was just as hung with each other as ever, I hadn't come up with a thing to say to Viv, and I still had that feeling of exasperation. It looked like it was gonna be another long night. . . .)

In my sanctuary of a room I sprawled myself on the bed, just as I had twenty-four hours earlier—too shot down to even bother removing my shoes—but this time the innocent sleep would not come to knit up my ravel'd sleeve of care . . .

*Hank walks across the straw-carpeted floor of the barn and finds Viv lost in thought at the back door, a lithe silhouette against the blue-black sky, her hand resting on the door's big wooden pull-handle as she looks after the cow trudging darkly back out to pasture.* (Viv was in the barn when I got home; I was glad for that . . .) *He walks to her and wraps his arms about her waist from behind.* "Hi, honey," *she says and leans her head back against his lips.* (Because we get along better out there, it seems, like a couple barn animals. I go up to her and give her a little hug and see that she's come out of her sull pretty much, and's just a little blue is all . . .)

I lay there in the dark—wide-eyed and ache-headed, more than slightly delirious from exhaustion—recalling familiar demons that used to creep from the knotholes on the dingy ceiling above me. I had no wish to watch their activities, but neither did I have the energy to do anything about them. They wandered wild across the ceiling —wolves and bears stalking among sheep while the poor shepherd watches, watches helplessly, fagged and flaked and wanting nothing more than sleep . . . unable to let the marauders out of his sight for fear of his flock, unable also to rouse himself to its defense. I tried to force myself to the more pressing problems. Like: "Okay, now that you have decided it's no use trying to measure up to Brother Hank, just how do you go about pulling him down?" And like: "Why did you want to measure up to him anyway?" And: "Why is any of this crap necessary?"

*Viv turns inside the circle of his arms to press her cheek against his chest. "I'm sorry, hon, I was so ornery this morning—" "I'm sorry I was so ornery last night, chicken." "And as soon as the boat pulled out I ran out to wave, but you'd gone." He rolls a lock of her hair between his fingers. "It's just . . ." she went on, "that Dolly McKeever was one of the best friends I had in high school, and when she moved out from Colorado I was so looking forward to . . . having somebody to kind of chat with." "I know, chicken; I'm sorry. I shoulda told you about the WP deal right off, I suppose. I don't know why I never." He takes her hand. "C'mon now, let's go on in for some supper . . ." And on the walk to the house asks, "You got Jan, though; to talk with—how come you can't get anything goin' with ol' Janny lamb?" She laughs sadly. "Old Janny lamb is real nice, Hank; but did you ever sit down and try to talk to her? About just little things, say, like a movie you saw or a book you read?" Hank stopped walking. "Hey, just a minute. You know . . . ?"* (And seeing how blue she is is what gives me the notion. By god, I say to myself, by god, you got the answer to both your hassles. By god if you don't!) *"You know? I just thought of somethin': I think I know somebody you can chat with till the world turns blue, somebody you can really get things going with . . ."* (I'll just knock off trying to play diplomat with the two sensitives, I said to myself, and let them *entertain each other.*) As I lay there pondering these whys and wherefores concerning myself and Brother Hank, Goya's painting "Kronos

Devouring His Children" flashed across my ceiling along with all
the obvious oedipal implications; but I was somehow unable to
placate myself with second-rate psychological symbolism. Oh no you
don't, Lee baby, not this time. Certainly there were all the run-of-
the-mill Freudian reasons beneath my animosity toward my dear
brother, all the castration-complex reasons, all the mother-son-father
reasons—and all especially deep-seated and strong within me because
the usual abysmal longing of the sulky son wishing to do in the guy
who had been diddling Mom were in me compounded by the malevolent memories of a psychotic sibling . . . oh yes, I had numerous
scenes working on these multi-faceted levels—and any one of these
note-pad facts would have constituted reason enough to provoke
vengeance in the heart of any loyal neurotic—but this wasn't the
Whole Truth.

Also reason enough in my dislike for all he represented. It took
no more than that first day to bring back all his faults; sparse though
our communication had been it had taken only a few seconds at
each exchange of words to convince me that he was crass, bigoted,
wrongheaded, hypocritical, that he substituted viscera for reason and
confused his balls with his brains, and that he was in many ways the
epitome of the kind of man I regarded as most dangerous to my
kind of world, and certainly for these reasons should I seek his
destruction.

But still . . . not the Whole Truth.

. . . Frowning slightly, Viv turns to look at him; the light from
the kitchen window shapes his brow and jaw against the mountains;
"I know who you can get things going with about books and movies,
chicken . . ." For a moment the wild, almost childish flash in his
green eyes—a flash first seen through the bars of a jail—makes her
think he is speaking about the only person in the world that she
really cares to get things going with, but he says, "And that's the
kid, Lee, Leland. Viv, I'll tell you straight: I need your help with
him. Me and him have always been like pouring water in hot grease.
And accepted it. But now the business needs him to help us through
this deal. Will you go along with me on this? Kind of take him
under your wing?" She said yes, she would. "Fine. Dang, that takes
a load off me. Let's get on in." (But what I didn't think of was that
passing your hassles off on one another don't necessarily get shut
of them; sometimes it makes you a bigger one than your other two
put together.) "And maybe you can run up and get on a nice dress

*for supper, what do you say? Could you do that for me?" She says*
*yes, she could, and follows him on to the back door. . . .*

I knew that there was another, truer reason; a less concrete, more
abstract, tenuous-as-a-black-widow's-web reason . . . and I knew it was
akin to the feeling I had experienced when on our return from work
we picked up the esteemed Mr. Leslie Gibbons—dirtier, if possible,
than before—to ferry him from the road back across to his house.
"Stamper," Gibbons began after he arranged himself for the ride
across and cleared his throat of some terrible obstruction—his mis-
placed wad of snuff, most likely—"I seen Bigger Newton from Reedsport t'day. We 'uz aworkin' the same piece of pavement for a time
there . . . hot work, too, nigger work, that's what, nigger work,
ya know what I mean?"

Hank had watched the river ahead and waited. I noticed that, in
spite of Gibbons' casual, slightly insolent air, the man's grimy hands
were shaking in his lap. He kept wetting cracked lips with a tongue
pink and quick as a snake's . . .

". . . an' Big, he says he was boozed that night a month or so
back. You mind it? An' he says—this is Newton, you mind, I'm just
standin' an' listenin' and not takin' neither side—Big, he says you
took *advantage.* He says—ah Christ, how'd he put it?—he says, 'Next
time I run acrost Hank Stamper I aim to kick his ass till his nose
bleeds!' That was it; that's how he put it."

"He's tried about three times now, Les."

"*Shore!* I know that. But look here, Hank, them first couple times
he wasn't but eighteen or so. Snotnosed kid. Look here, I ain't takin'
sides but you want to keep in mind he's three years older now. An'
so're you."

"I'll keep it in mind, Les."

"He says—Big does—that you an' him have got a bone to pick.
Somethin' about that bike race you won down on the beach last
summer. He says you used them heavy treads for no other reason
than to kick sand on the other racers. Big's pretty sore, Hank. I just
thought to tell you."

Hank glanced sideways at Gibbons, smiling into his hand. "I appreciate it, Les." And, without taking his eyes from the river ahead,
leaned down with feigned absent-mindedness and took from beneath
the seat a Gardol can, shook it near his ear, emptied the few remaining drops into the gas tank—"Yes, I surely do." Then, just as Les was
about to speak further on the subject, Hank crushed the empty can
as though it were made of aluminum foil. The thumb and finger

simply came together with no apparent strain or effort. The metal seemed to offer no resistance. He tossed the can, looking like a metal hourglass, past Les's bulging eyes into the river and wiped his hand on his pants. This piece of theatrics was sufficient to keep Les silent the rest of the ride across. But when he climbed out of the boat he stood finicking with his tin hat, obviously wanting to say more; finally he blurted, "Saturday! Dang; nearly forgot. Hank, any you boys goin' into the Snag this Sat'day night? I'd be obliged for a ride across."

"Probably not this Saturday, Les. But I'll let you know."

"Will you? Will you sure enough now?" He was openly concerned.

"Sure, Les. We'll give you a call," Joe Ben reassured him quite tersely for Joe. "Oh yeah. Maybe even give Bigger a call too. Maybe even give 'em a call at the Snag so they can commence setting up *bleachers* and selling *tickets* and making *hot dogs*. Oh, we wouldn't let anybody miss it."

Les pretended to miss Joe's sarcasm. "Wonderful," he said. "That'll be fine. I thank you. I'm sure obliged to you boys." He pranced on up to the fence, calling his undying gratitude over his shoulder, thrilled to the core. And rightly so. Hadn't he been promised a trip to the future match where the notorious Big Newton from Reedsport was going to meet Horrible Hank in an attempt to break the title-holder's long winning streak as well as his neck? And repelled as I was by Gibbons' clumsy subterfuge and his sickening, two-faced good-fellowship, I knew I secretly rooted for his gladiator to put the champ down for the count. Les and I were heart to heart joined in this cause: we wanted the champ down simply because it was insupportable to us that he had the audacity to be *up* there—perched arrogantly on the throne, when we were not.

But even as I lay in bed confiding this to the ceiling, I knew I was not Newton the Nemean Lion with a record of barroom fights to rely on, nor was I Leslie Gibbons, who could be satisfied as a gibbering and drooling spectator sucking up vicarious kicks from the ringside. My part in the dethronement, the necessary abrogation, would have to be both passive and active at the same time: passive in the sense that I knew better than to wage open physical battle against my work-hardened brother—WATCH OUT warned my monitor in-side, my ever-alert distress signal that shouted FIRE at the first smell of a cigarette—and active because I *needed* the catharsis of being part of his overthrow. I needed to wield the torch, hold the knife. I needed the stain of his actual blood on my conscience as a poultice to draw out the pus of long cowardice. I needed the nourishment of victory to give me the strength I had been cheated of by years of starvation. I needed to fell the tree that had been hogging my sunshine before I even germinated. *My* sunshine, my need howled. Sun to grow on! to grow out of the shadow into myself! into me! Yes. And then—listen now—perhaps then, you poor runt, when you have brandished the torch! overthrown the champ! felled the tree! when the throne is empty and the sky overhead finally clear and the jungle finally safe for Sunday walk . . . perhaps then, you poor chicken-livered wretch EASY NOW you may be able to establish the Reason for Lee, you may even find the courage to live with that twisted corpse that has been lying in your brain since she dropped it there from the forty-first floor, lying in your brain there, rotting indomitably away like a clock ticking; and, Lee boy, if you can't measure up you'd better see to shortening the measuring stick down to your own size . . . because that clock is ticking right along.

*Viv walks upstairs to the bathroom. She removes her blouse and washes her face and neck. As she stands looking at her freshly dried features in the mirror—wondering if she should put her hair in a pony-tail for dinner or leave it down—she finds herself trying to recall if this is the same face she kissed good-by in her cracked mirror in Colorado. It really shouldn't be so very different from the face that looked out of that old oval mirror; she hasn't wrinkled—this climate is good for keeping down wrinkles, moist so much of the time—and she looks much younger than Dolly, whose birthday is a month after her own . . . but what about these stranger's eyes that sometimes look back at her? And did she really once kiss these alien lips? She can't remember. She turns from the mirror and picks up her blouse to hold across her breasts as she walks to her room—deciding Hank would rather she left it long, lots of hair hanging and swinging, as he puts it . . .*

For I was certain by now that no other elixir would heal me; no potion but victory would stem the curse and halt my slow ascent up the steps to my own forty-first floor. My whole future keened silently with suffocated need for that victory, my whole past screamed in fury for it . . . while across the ceiling overhead, with its stigmata of cavernous knotholes exuding forms hideous and vapors terrifying, walked the evidence of those very weaknesses that rendered my wrath impotent and my victory impossible. Watching helplessly, I was struck by the parodoxical beauty of the situation. It seemed to me that up there, projected overhead, was at once the absolute *proof* of my need for a victory over my brother as well as undeniable *evidence* of my inability to bring about that victory. The need instigated and paralyzed itself simultaneously. Helpless, I lay witness to my production: a panorama of unparalleled paranoia, as every neuron cowered in terror from its neighbor while the sheep were being slaughtered. WATCH OUT WATCH OUT WATCH . . .

. . . *She finds the table lamp in her room and switches it on and drops her blouse over her sewing chair. She sits down and pulls off her frayed tennis shoes, then removes her jeans. At the bureau she opens a drawer and removes a bra and half-slip. She pulls on the slip and reaches for the bra—thinking how ridiculous, with her build, to have to wear such nonsense . . .*

Then, at the moment, with exquisite timing, just as I was about to surrender to death by Status Quo, there came to me a sign, my pillar of fire leading to salvation, my torch . . .

A click in the next room sent a thin finger of light through that hole. The finger wrapped itself about my head and tugged. I lay still for a long time before I gave in to the pull of the light and let it draw my throbbing bones standing.

. . . *And, fumbling at her back with the task of hooking the fastening, biting at her lip, she becomes aware that she has been staring for some time now at the empty bird cage suspended from the ceiling. She ceases her fumbling and lets her hands and the bra drop gradually to her sides. In the cage a long solitary filament of cobweb hangs from the little swing, laden with dust. That's about as birdless as a cage can get, she thinks. Should have bought another bird. Hank had even offered once to drive her to Eugene for just that purpose. She always liked canaries. She should have got herself another one. She still could. The next trip to Eugene she could . . . She turns from the cage . . .*

I remember perfectly my first impression: that the girl—not the lamp behind her—was emitting the light. She stood there, motionless, her back to me, seemingly entranced by some vision across the room; clothed from the waist down in a beige-colored slip and nothing else . . . quite pale, quite slender, with wonderfully long sorrel-blond hair following the slender line of her head down over her shoulders—and she made me think of a burning candle. *She moves, tipping her head slightly forward.* Then she turned, and as she walked directly toward my spying eyes, *smooth almost hipless body, graceful wick of neck, pale unpainted face which seems to flicker and glow like a solitary flame* . . . I saw that her cheeks were wet with crying.

*T*ime overlaps itself. A breath breathed from a passing breeze is not the whole wind, neither is it just the last of what has passed and the first of what will come, but is more—let me see—more like a single point plucked on a single strand of a vast spider web of winds, setting the whole scene atingle. That way; it overlaps. . . . As prehistoric ferns grow from bathtub planters. As a shiny new ax, taking a swing at somebody's next year's split-level pinewood pad, bites all the way to the Civil War. As proposed highways break down through the stacked strata of centuries.

As a trilobite wades out of the paleolithic age and drags itself across the ruts of Breakbutt Road into the outskirts of town, and across a field of hop clover and beer cans, finally up the steps of the Mad Scandinavian's shack to stop and scratch at the front door like a dog wanting in out of the chill.

As an antique Indian with a face like an aerial photograph of a bombed-out city—Indian Jenny's father, incidentally—sits in a pine-log shelter back up fifty years of practically impassable dirt road, on a pine-needle floor with a greasy bearskin robe pinned at his wattled neck with a porcupine quill, intensely watching "Have Gun, Will Travel."

As Simone leans against her empty refrigerator, studying through the half-open door to her bedroom the little carved Virgin that studies her in turn, breathing the kitchen's odor of candlewax and wine. Who do they think they are, anyway? These Stampers? To make this bad strike?

As the rest of the town breathes their own passing breezes:

Willard Eggleston, in his theater's ticket office, counts the night's take. "If it don't get worse, if I can take in just this much a night I'll make it to the first of the year." Every night the take gets smaller. One night it will be too small.

Floyd Evenwrite waits nervously while Jonathan B. Draeger leafs casually through a stack of yellow papers.

Molly the hound watches the moon melt like wax, and feels the wax fall freezing on her hide, petrifying on her eyes and tongue . . .

*A point plucked any place sets all the currents and gales,*
*zephyrs and gales, vibrating delicately. . . .*

Joe Ben, out clamdigging one summer morning with his three
oldest kids, pauses in his giddy rushing from child to child to look
across the flats at a pack of bony hogs that comes sniffing from the
bam-tree thickets onto the mud. As he watches, a black swarm of
crows appear almost simultaneously from the top branches of a fir
grove; they sail screeching down to settle two or three apiece on the
back of each rooting hog. A hog grubs a clam or mud shrimp into
sight; a great squealing and squawking fight for the prize . . . a
bird flaps off laughing hoarsely to break his clam against the rocks
of the jetty. Joe Ben stands enthralled, palms pressing his skull—"*Oh*
*man! Oh boy!*"—as though to reinforce the walls of his bursting soul,
to take precaution against an explosion of joy . . .

Oh man, them *birds!* And them goofy hogs. . . . can you believe
it? Pap used to tell about that hog pack but I never myself laid eye
on them before. He said them birds been here long as the hogs, or
at least the bird kin long as the hog kin. All the way clear back to
1900. Oh man, Pap, what a kick you must've been, tearing around the
country seeing all these funny things and bouncing from bed to bed
with all those women. I wish, ah gosh I wish I might of knowed and
enjoyed you when I had the chance, might of freed myself earlier
from you somehow so's I could of give you the respect and attention
you deserved. What a kick it could of been, me and Hank and
Aaron's two boys bagged out on the floor while you'n old Henry sit
cooking your shoes on the stove, drinking green beer and smoking
cigars . . . fart and belch, fart and belch all night long while you
talked about the way it was . . .

Very swampy, son, back then. Arnold Eggleston and his brood
tried to settle Siskilou flat nineteen ought six or seven. Very swampy,
I recollect. Arnold put his hogs loose on the land to grub out
wapatoos an' skunk cabbages—I seen two them devils last week whilst
bringin' the boom down river—those type pigs with their ears slung
over their eyes like car fenders, an' they went wild. And mean, let
me tell you: Sam Montgomery, you recall, Henry? brother to Miss
Montgomery?"

"Betsy? Betsy Montgomery . . . ?"

"She was the first of a long line of the mattressback Montgomery
girls—"

"Never mind her, you foul-mouthed bastard, what 'uz you saying about Sam an' them wild hogs?"

"Yes. . . . One day me 'n' him was pirating drift logs off the flat and I 'uz doin' this or that an' all at once Sam commenced to holler, an' one of them devils had him down an' was workin' at him. I made a run to the skiff an' grab Sam's double-barrel he'd brung in case we get a chance at some mergansers. Sam's got the hog and the hog's got Sam. Over an' over they go, squalling an' cussin'! Mud and kelp and garbage an' god knows what all so's I can't make out *what's* about. "Shoot, dammit, *shoot!*" Sam yells. "I can't tell which is *what!*" I tell him. "Never mind that, dammit, just shoot into the *wad!*" So I run back a piece an' fly at the two of them on the ground there. *Whoo!* Both barrels. Hog turned loose an' lit out back to the thickets, an' I *swear* if Sam didn't jump up and tear off after him, cussing and screamin' that he was gonna break his skinny fuckin' back, an' I tell ya! if he didn't of trip over some roots I bet he'd of come mighty damn close. . . ."

"I remember Betsy Montgomery. I recall her *now*. I recall one time you traded Sam Montgomery a nearly full box of White Owls for the privilege of driving his sister Betsy to a dance up at Yachats and they were *my* White Owls too, by god!"

"Well." Ben shrugs and smiles at his older brother. "A cigar is just a cigar, but a good woman is a fuck."

The men guffaw and tip their foaming fruit jars; the boys lie full length on the wooden floor, chins on their crossed hands, grinning sleepily. Everyone has heard the story. Everyone has heard all the stories, even before they happen. At the stove Henry is recalling a tale told him by an oldtime hand logger who heard it from a one-eyed Indian, a folk legend . . . years of hard famine, game all gone, and the coyote god leads the men of the tribe to the beach as the waves recede revealing an abundance of food, warning that as soon as anyone picks up even the tiniest morsel the waves will start back; a hungry brave tries to sneak a clam into his loincloth and the coyote god catches him. The water begins to move landward again, explaining the origin of the tides . . .

On the riverbank the Indian storyteller materializes in full feathered dress; light from a driftwood fire illuminates eager ghosts dancing from a shiny, milkstoned eye; his stories, pure and comfortable and full of the fleshless fact of spirits, are still innocent of the demons to come from a far-away land called Hudson's Bay Company. His hand floats weightless in the night buoyed up on the heavy stream of his words; a circle of firelit faces listens. . . . A car's horn rings across the moonplated river and Hank rises from the supper table and crosses to the kitchen window. "Hush a minute; I thought I heard the old man toot. . . . Seems I been spending a lot of my time lately listening for that old fart to come home gassed and honkin'."

At home, wearing a green eyeshade on his bald head, Willard Eggleston writes a final figure at the bottom of a page full of calculation. "If I take in *just this much* next month, then maybe the overhead won't kill me. Just this much is all I need to overcome the overhead." But every month the figure to overcome is bigger. One month it will be too big. It seems to Willard he is always spending his time with figures too big or too little.

Indian Jenny's father rises with a grunt to stop the roll-over in his TV set. He spends a lot of his time adjusting his Westerns.

Viv reads, curled against a large satin-covered pillow on her makeshift couch. She spends a large part of her time reading. She didn't read nearly so much back in Colorado; and even during her first years in the house in Wakonda, when Hank brought her books down from the attic for the long lonely afternoons, she had had a difficult time getting interested—the books were so worn with other readings from other years that it didn't seem she should peek—but in the weeks spent in bed after she lost the baby she had forced herself to try, sometimes reading the same page over and over, until one sleepy afternoon something clicked, like a lock unlocking, and she saw those printed doors swing open on a vast house of words. She entered carefully, feeling that she was trespassing, knowing that this had never been her house and hoping almost that someone—whoever had lived here first—would come back and chase her out. But no one came, and she reconciled herself to living in another's house, and gradually came to understand and appreciate the beauty of the house's various furnishings. Since then she has amassed a large and erratic library. Books on all subjects—books hardbound and books paperbacked, some ragged with reading, some never opened—range over the wall at various levels on a unique bookcase forming a floor-to-ceiling fortress of words.

Once, as Viv tidied up her sewing before coming to bed, Hank stood before that fortress, rubbing his bare belly as he scanned the titles. He shook his head. He had long forgotten that the books were his idea in the first place. "All this," Hank said with a sweep of his arm, "all these books, all these buggy *words*." He turned and drew a finger down his wife's spine, producing a murmurous giggle. "Tell me, little girl: how's it possible all these words go in an' so piddling few come out?" He parted the bright glide of hair at the back of her head and examined her neck. "You must be so stuffed with words you due to *explode!*"

Viv shook her head, smiling with the pressure of Hank's chest at her back. "Oh no." She laughed. "No words. I don't think I even remember words. Sometimes I remember a writer's words—like a line he wrote that I thought was real nice—but those are *his* words, you see?"

He didn't see, but neither did he worry about it. Hank had adjusted to his wife's peculiarities as she had to his; if she was gone fifty per cent of the time, off someplace in another world while her body stayed behind humming over the housework, well, that was her world and her business. He didn't feel he had the ability to follow her into those reveries or the right to call her back out. What went on *inside*, that was nobody's business but whoever's it went on *inside* of, was the way Hank looked at it. Besides, the fifty per cent she gave him, wasn't that "a hell of a lot more'n most guys get outa their female even if they get the whole hunderd?"

"I couldn't say." Lee hedged at Hank's question. "I think it would depend on the female, and on which half she gave."

"Viv gives the best half all right," Hank assured him. "An' as far as the female goes, you tell me what you think along that line after you get a look at her."

"I'll do that"—still savoring that half-nude image seen through the hole not a half an hour before. "But do you think I'll be able to judge the whole 'hunderd' per cent without seeing all of it?"

Brother Hank's grin was swarming with secrets. "If you mean do you get a look at the whole hunderd of Viv, well I can't rightly say; that's up to her. But I got a hunch you might have to make do with the little bit showin'—like the legs an' face—and judge what's underneath like you'd judge how much iceberg's under water. Viv ain't one of these honky-tonk honeys I used to run with, Leland. She's shy. Joe says she's one of these 'still-water-runs-deeps.' You'll see. I think you'll like her."

Hank had straddled a chair near the foot of my bed and was waiting, chin on the chairback, while I dressed to come down for supper. And was being remarkably cheerful compared to the snarling silence that had flowed from him since my outburst over his rigging story at lunch. He had even gone so far as to bring me up a cup of coffee to rouse me from my stupor, little realizing that this particular stupor—unlike the faint that followed my first contact with physical labor earlier that day—had been induced by his wife's performance in tears and a half-slip. And along with the coffee a pair of clean socks. "Till we get your suitcase from the depot."

I smiled and thanked him, as puzzled by his change of mood as he must have been my mine. I knew my change was rooted firmly in reason: I had realized the imprudence of my afternoon of animosity—the clever assassin doesn't worm his way into the king's castle only to blow his chance of success by telling the king what he thinks of him. Certainly not. Quite the opposite. He is charming, witty, fawning, and he applauds the king's tales of triumph, however, paltry they may be. It is the way the game is played. And for this reason I was suspicious of Hank's generosity—I saw no reason for the king to seek the favor of the assassin, and I therefore advised myself I'd best watch out. He's being nice for some sneaky reason; beware!

But it is sometimes difficult to be very wary if people keep being nice to you, and I didn't know then that these underhanded tactics of niceness and warmth assailing my resolved revenge were to continue for so long.

So I drank the coffee and welcomed the socks—watching out, of course, for tricks—laced my shoes and combed my hair and followed him down to the kitchen to meet his wife, never for one minute imagining that the sneaky wench would be even more underhanded and nice and warm than her sneak of a husband, and even harder to watch out for.

The wench was turned to the stove, with that hair coiling down to her apron strings. And as lovely in the hard kitchen light as she had been in the mellow glow of her room. Hank pulled her toward me by the rear of the pleated skirt that I knew must be still warm from the iron; he turned her around by the sleeve of the blouse that had needed a button sewn on. "Viv, this is Leland." She brushed a lock from her forehead, offered her hand, and smiled a soft hello. I nodded. "Well, what's your judgment?" Hank asked, stepping back from her like a horsetrader from a prize two-year-old.

"I would at *least* have to check her teeth."

"I reckon we could see to that."

The girl swatted his hand from her. "What on earth . . . What's he been talking about, Leland?"

" 'Lee,' if you would."

"Or 'bub,' " Hank added, and answered for me. "Why, I ain't been talking nothin' but good about you, honey. Ain't that so, bub?"

"He said half of you was better than all of most women—"

"An' Lee said he'd have to hold judgment on that till he could see all of you, hon." He reached for the buttons of her blouse. "So if you'll just—"

"Hank . . . !"

She raised the spoon and Hank hopped agilely out of range. "But honey, we got to settle this thing . . ."

"Not right here in the kitchen." She took my arm coquettishly, lifting her nose at him. "Leland, Lee and me'll settle it some other time—all by ourselves." Then gave a brazen little toss of her head to seal the bargain.

"Done!" I said, as she spun laughing back toward the stove.

But neither the laughing spin nor the brazen toss could hide the blush that rose like a red tide—out of a bra that I knew was fastened left-cup-to-strap by a silver safety pin.

Hank yawned at his wife's flirtations. "All I ask is you feed me first. I could eat a snake. How about you, bub?"

"All I ask is the sustenance to climb those stairs back up to my bed."

"The fish'll be a few minutes yet," she said. "Jan has gone out to the barn for some more eggs. Ask Joe if all the kids are washed and ready, could you, Lee? And I think I hear Henry honking now; would you run across to get him, Hank?"

"Damn, but he's gettin' to be a regular tomcat . . ."

Hank left to start the boat and I went into the other room to help Joe Ben hose down his herd, with the treacherous smells and sounds and sights of that supper scene swirling about me like the background of a State Department propaganda film calculated to sell the American Way of Life to every hungry and lonely and homeless wretch in every hope-lost hamlet in every have-not nation in the world—"Don't listen to that Commy crap you dumb gooks, this is what we really live like in the good ol' Yew Ess Aye!"—and felt stir in my blood the first cancerous budding of an emotion that was not to go beneath the scalpel of sense until almost a month later, when it had almost got too firm a hold to remove . . .

*And Molly the hound tries again to rise, whimpering as her paws push at the cold earth; she stands a twisted second on all fours, but the moon is too cold and heavy and she collapses again beneath its frozen weight.*

And Teddy the bartender peers through his tangled neons at the darkening twist of river past the firehouse, and wistfully wishes it were January: *these Indian Summers, they are good for nothing but crickets and mosquitoes and old windbags dribbling out their money a dime at a time. Give me some rain, some bad weather, and watch me roll the dollars. Give me a dark smeary shiny night full of rain. That's when the fear starts. That's when you sell the juice!*

And Viv, through a lock of hair, watches Lee as he pats uncertainly at the dripping face of Joe Ben's girl with a towel. *He's never washed a little kid before in his life, she realizes; can you beat that? What an odd boy, so gaunt and ghosty sort of. With eyes like he's been to the edge and looked over . . .*

His shirt gets splashed as he washes the child, and he puts aside the towel to roll up his sleeves. Viv sees his inflamed skin.

"Oh . . . your arms!"

He shrugs and blows on a smarting wrist. "They were a little too long for my shirtsleeves, I'm afraid."

"Let me put on some witch hazel. Squeaky, honey," she calls to the porch, "would you toss in that bottle of witch hazel? Here, Lee, sit a minute. Old Henry hasn't come in anyhow. Sit here . . ."

She dabs on the liquid with a folded dishtowel. Pungent smells of spice and alcohol burn in the warm air of the kitchen. His arms lie on the checkered tablecloth, as inert as two cuts of meat on the butcher's counter. Neither of them speaks. They hear the approach of the motorboat, and old Henry's drunken singing. Viv shakes her head at the sound, smiling. Lee asks how she feels about having another animal to care for.

"Another animal?"

"Sure. Look at this menagerie." The singing outside is louder. "First, you have old Henry, who is bound to need a lot of attention—"

"Not really so much," she says. "He doesn't drink that much. Just when his leg hurts him."

"—I meant attention because of his accident, his age. And then there are the kids, you probably help take care of Joe Ben's kids, don't you? and all the dogs and the cow? And I imagine if the truth were known that even brother Hank has needed the gentle touch of witch hazel—"

"No," she muses, "he doesn't seem to."

"Anyway, aren't you somewhat discouraged when faced with another liability to do for?"

"Do you always consider yourself that? A liability?"

Lee grins at her, rolling his sleeves back down. "I think my question has priority."

"Oh"—taking a strand of hair in the corner of her mouth—"I suppose it *does* keep me on the jump, old Henry says that's the only way to keep from getting moss on your back—but when I *think* about it—"

"That's right! That's right!" The back door swings open and Henry enters, carrying his dentures in his hand. "I say in Oregon you got to keep on the jump . . . to put the hair on your chest an' keep the moss off your *rump*. Good evening, all, an' good health. Here y'go, girlie." He pitches the teeth to Viv; they hiss, grinning in the bright kitchen light. "Hose these off for me, willya? I dropped 'em in the yard there an' a goddam dog tried to put 'em on. Whup! See the way she nabbed them teeth on the fly there, boy? Keep 'em on the jump. Mm-mmm! I was right; I smelt that salmon bakin' clean back to the Evans place."

Viv turns from the sink, drying the teeth on a dishtowel. "Lee, now that I *think* about it," she says, as though speaking to the teeth; she lifts her head from her task and smiles at him. "I don't think I'll be discouraged . . . compared to *some* I could mention, you will be a pure joy to do for."

*Molly the hound pants at the moon with shallow, bright breaths. Teddy listens for rain. Lee—it is a month later—sits on his bed with his shoes off and his pants legs lifted gingerly from ankles inflamed by the half-drunk hunting trip he has just come in from, and he tells the anxious shadows that he can tend to his own cuts, thank you . . . "And with something far more soothing than witch hazel too!" On the table beside his bed three thin reddish-brown cigarettes are lying atop a cold-cream jar. A spiral notebook is waiting on a record jacket propped against his knees. A ballpoint pen and a book of matches lie in his lap. He gives the pillows behind his back a few settling punches, then, finally satisfied with the arrangement, he takes up one of the cigarettes and lights it, filling his lungs and holding the smoke a long time before he breathes it out with a long,*

hissing *"Yessssss."* *He takes another drag. As he smokes he scoots
deeper in the bed. When the cigarette is half gone he begins to write.
He smiles occasionally as he rereads a line that particularly pleases
him. His writing is at first neat and even, and the sentences congeal
without correction on the page:*

Box 1, Route 1
Wakonda, Oregon
Halloween

Norwick House
New Haven, Conn.

Dear Peters:
"Good God, betimes the means that makes us strangers!"
At which point, if you are up on Willy the Shake as you should be
with the o'crlooming approach of prelims, you should have replied:
"Sir, amen."
Did you? No matter. For in all good faith I must confess I'm not
myself certain which play the speech comes from. Macbeth, I think,
though it could as easily be from a dozen other histories or tragedies.
I have been home one month now and, as you can see, the dank and
drippy climate of Oregon has mildewed my memory and I substitute
surmise for certainty . . .

And Viv shooed them all from the kitchen ". . . or I'll never get
supper finished." And it happened, in the course of trying to bring
Joe Ben's kids to what Joe called "up next to godliness," Viv saw
the scratches on my arms. She dropped what she was doing at
the stove and insisted on treating me with some kind of folk medicine
that made me wish I had the scratches back, but I bit my tongue and
kept my cool, watching how much the girl enjoyed playing nurse.
Here, I thought to myself, is most certainly my weapon. Now how to
wield it?
So, my wounds attended to, I repaired to the living room to await
supper and to try to formulate a plan of use for this weapon. No, it
shouldn't be so difficult.
That first night my efforts were distracted by the old man. His
rattletrap energy made thought next to impossible. He clumped and
thumped up and down, to and fro across the overlarge room, like
an obsolete wind-up toy, useless and worthless, yet still not run down.
He switched on the TV on one of his passes; it began blaring patched

platitudes and keeping us up on the latest in the Great Deodorant War—"*Not* those drippy sprays, *not* those sssticky roll-ons . . . just a simple dab and be *sure* of all-day safety!" No one watched or listened; the machine's blaring was as senseless and as ignored as the old man's raving nostalgia, but no one presented a motion for silence. It was somehow obvious that any attempt to turn off either would have precipitated a squall of protest more devastating than both.

I tried to maneuver my brother into telling me more about his wife, but just as we were getting around to her the old man observed that there was some folks who preferred talkin' to eatin' but damned if he was one of 'em! And led an exodus into the kitchen.

The following day was more toil and exhaustion, much the same as the first except that I controlled my hostility toward Brother Hank. And he continued his goodwill campaign toward me. And the ensuing days found me thinking less and less about my forsworn vengeance and feeling more and more positive about my avowed enemy. I tried to rationalize this to my mental mediator when he warned me to WATCH OUT for the primrose path. I insisted that I had to devote my full attention during the days to the task of keeping out from under rolling logs, and in the evenings I was too wasted to think constructively of revenge—"And that's why I haven't come up with something yet." But Old Reliable wasn't put off that easily.

"Yeah, I know, but—"

BUT YOU'VE BARELY SPOKEN WITH HER.

"Well, that's true, but—"

ALMOST LOOKS LIKE YOU'RE AVOIDING HER.

"I guess it looks that way, but—"

I'M WORRIED . . . SHE'S TOO NICE . . . BETTER WATCH OUT—

"Watch out? What in God's name do you *think* has kept me away from her? I *am* watching out! Because she is too nice! She's warm and sweet and *treacherous;* I have to be careful about this . . ."

To tell the truth, in our common heart we were both worried. And afraid. Because it wasn't just Viv: the whole diabolical houseful was being warm and sweet and treacherous, from my serpent brother down to the littlest snake-in-the-weeds infant. I was beginning to care for them. And as that cancerous emotion swelled within my heart so did my poor heart's fear. Swollen heart. This is an insidious malady chiefly common in that mythical organ that pumps life through the veins of the ego: care, coronary care, complicated by galloping fear.

The go-away-closer disease. Starving for contact and calling it poison when it is offered. We learn young to be leery of contact: Never open up, we learn . . . you want somebody running their dirty old fingers over your soul's privates? Never accept candy from strangers. Or from friends. Sneak off a sack of gumdrops when nobody's looking if you can, but don't accept, never accept . . . you want somebody taking advantage? And above all, never care, never never never care. Because it is caring that lulls you into letting down your guard and leaving up your shades . . . you want some fink knowing what you are *really* like down inside?

And we might even add to this list the simple rule "Never Drink Past Your Limit."

For 'twas drink, I think, the dirty devil drink, that finally rusted through the last lock on the last door guarding my convalescing ego . . . rusted the lock and melted the bolt and sprung the hinges until, before I knew what I was doing, I was talking with my brother about my mother. I found myself telling him the whole story—the disappointments, the drinking, the despair, the death.

"I was real sorry to hear about it," he said when I finished. I had just completed my second week in the woods and we were celebrating the miracle of no-bones-broken with a quart of beer apiece. Hank had plucked a stick of kindling from the beaten cardboard box behind the stove and was curling long white strips from it with his pocketknife. "When I heard I wired back that there should be some flowers—a wreath, I think—did you see it?"

"No, I didn't see it," I told him somewhat coldly, angry at myself for telling as much as I had, angry at him for listening—"But then, there were such a number of wreaths one might easily have missed it"—but essentially angry with the memory of that one wreath. One wreath! Only one! Mother's family had chosen to ignore the death of this family disgrace—an educated Jezebel, they sniffed, a drinker, a dreamer, a dabbler in palmistry, phrenology, and promiscuity, a forty-five-year-old beatnik chick in black tights who not only had the indecency to blacken the family name by running off to the northern wilds with some old motheaten geezer and having a *kid* by him, but who compounded the shame by coming back and messing up her middle age as well, along with a sizable portion of the New York sidewalk—and as much as I had despised them at the time for refusing to send so much as a bunch of violets, I had despised Hank even more for his presumptuous wreath of white carnations.

It was late. We had switched from beer to wine. The place seemed hellishly calm. Joe Ben and his brood were spending the night at their new house, planning to meet the dawn with a paintbrush. Henry had climbed stairs to a rumbling wooden sleep. Viv curled on the couch next to Hank, a lovely puzzle, speaking only with wide amber eyes and her sweet little denim rump, until the eyes closed and she pulled a sheepskin robe over the rump and went diplomatically to sleep. The old house ticked like a great wooden, erratic clock and outside occasional drifting logs thunked against the dock. Underneath us between the floor and the ground hounds whimpered, heroes or cowards in personal dreams. Above, the old man threw some perfumed memory a bony screw. My brother sat across the room from me under a tassel-shaded floor lamp, whittling, he himself carved in shadow, varnished by light . . .

"Yes, there were a lot of wreaths . . ." I lied.

He tickled the wood with a glistening blade. "Was a pretty nice funeral, I bet?"

"Very nice, very nice," I allowed, watching the knife. "Considering."

"Good." *Thhht thhht.* "I'm glad." Curlicues of barbered pine fell like trimmed tresses at his feet. Viv wriggled herself deeper into the cushions, and I drank again from the gallon of the old man's blackberry wine. The liquid had been aprickle with thorns at the top of the bottle, lumpy with seeds at the shoulder, now, halfway down, it had smoothed out soft as cotton.

We waited for each other, wondering what on earth had prompted us to risk our cool by straying so far into long-forbidden territory, wondering if we dared throw caution to the winds and go even farther. Finally Hank turned the stick over. "Yeah, well, like I said, I was really sorry to hear about her."

I still felt a little of that first anger. "Yeah," I said. Meaning: You should have been, you cad, after the way you—

"Huh?"

The knife ceased its whispering, half a curl of pine lifting unfinished from the stick. I held my breath; had he heard the thought behind the words? WATCH OUT, Old Reliable warned, HE'S GOT A SHIV! But the knife moved again on the wood; the curl looped complete and fell with the others; my breath drifted out of my nostrils in a swirl of relief and disappointment. Blank expectations (what had I imagined he would do?) remained blank. The earth turned again (what had I imagined I would do?), continuing its falling circle.

The curlicues curled. I sipped again of Henry's homemade wine. I was sorry for my anger; I was glad he'd chosen to ignore it.

"Sack time." He folded the knife and with a woolen sweep of his stockinged foot swept the curls into a neat pile. He bent and cupped the pile and dropped it into the woodbox: tomorrow morning's kindling. He flapped his hands free of sawdust and sentiment, calluses husking against each other like wood against wood. "I believe I'll see if I can catch a few Z's; I told Joe I'd give him a hand at his place in the morning. Viv? Kitten?" He shook her shoulder; she yawned, showing a rose-petal tongue over bright white pips of teeth. "Let's head up to the sack, okay? You might as well make it too, bub."

I shrugged. Viv slipped past, dragging the sheepskin robe and smiling sleepily. At the foot of the stairs Hank stopped; his eyes lifted to mine for an instant— "Uh . . . Lee . . ." bright, green as glass, pleading for something, before they dropped to study a broken thumbnail. "I wish I could of been there." I didn't say anything; in that quick click-and-glitter of lifted eyes I saw a hint of more than guilt, more than contrition.

"I really wisht there'd been something I could of done." Meaning: Was there?

"I don't know, Hank." Meaning: You did enough.

"I always worried about her." Meaning: Was I partially to blame?

"Yeah." Meaning: We were all to blame.

"Yeah, well,"—looking down at the destroyed thumbnail, wanting to say more, ask more, hear more, unable to—"I guess I'll hit the hay."

"Yeah,"—wanting everything he wanted—"me too."

"G'night, Lee," Viv murmured from the top of the stairs.

"Good night, Viv."

"Night, bub."

"Hank."

Meaning: Good night but stay. Viv, silent and slim as a shaft of sleepy light, stay, talk more to me with your articulate eyes. Hank, forget my words behind my words, stay, say some more. This is our chance. This is my chance. Say enough more for love or hate, enough more to make me sure of one or the other. Please stay, please stay . . .

But they left me alone. They frightened, tantalized, excited me with contact, then left me alone. And confused. I think we approached each other that night and muffed it. He didn't venture further, and I couldn't. I look back on that evening through a film of mashed blackberries, trickling juices spiny and sour, as my brother

and his wife fade out up the stairs, into personal realities, to dream
dreams, and I think, We almost made it that time. A little courage
on someone's part and we might have made it. We were swollen and
ripe for an instant together, ready for picking, offering our store to
each other's hesitant fingers . . . a little tender courage at that rare
right instant, and things might well have turned out differently. . . .

*But the breath of memory still plucks such instants, setting
the whole web shaking. People fade up the stairs, but to
dream of each other's dreams; of days coming gone and
nights past coming; of hard sun-rods crisscrossing back
and forward across outspreading circles of water, meaning-
less-seeming . . . .*

From the dappled surface of the river a red-gilled, blue-green-striped
steelhead salmon explodes in a shimmering dance, gyrating wild in
glistening suspension, falls back on its side with a blistering crack,
and jumps again and falls, and jumps again—as though trying to
escape some terror pursuing it beneath the water. And falls and this
time darts to the bottom to lie behind a rock, with its stomach resting
exhausted on the sand and the sea-lice still gnawing its fin and gills in
spite of its efforts.

Swarms of black, squawking crows harass a herd of hogs. Green
beer sloughs in the throbbing stovelight. Indian Jenny's old man rises,
disgusted, and tries to clear up "The Sheriff of Cochise." Molly
watches her life pumping from her in clouds of white frost. Floyd
Evenwrite curses himself for not having made a better impression on
Jonathan B. Draeger, and curses Draeger for being so goddamned
biggity and making him feel like he had to make a good impression,
and curses himself for *letting* Draeger be so goddamned biggity as to
make him feel like he had to make a good impression. . . . Willard
Eggleston hopes. Simone prays. Willard Eggleston despairs. And a
Diesel freight running empty to Wakonda for the last of Wakonda
Pacific's stockpiled lumber at the Cascade Pacific yards honks for a
crossing, low and obscene, like the rutting call of a mechanical
dragon . . .

At a scarred tabletop near the front door of the Snag, sitting with a
cluster of cronies who are obviously more interested in his free beer
than in his talk, old Henry jiggles his ill-fitting dentures in his cheeks
and draws a deep breath. He takes another swallow from the pitcher,

holding it by the handle as though it were a giant mug; whenever he filled a glass, he has noticed, one of the audience at his table drank it, so he has resigned himself to the pitcher. He is relaxed, glowing, feeling his swelling belly push for another notch in his belt. For the first time in his life the old man finds the time to pursue his pitifully neglected social obligations. Almost every afternoon since his accident he has propped his plaster frame against the same beam near the Snag's front door, where he drinks, rambles about old times, argues with Boney Stokes, and studies the way the big iridescent-green riverflies electrocute themselves on the charged screen door.

"Hsst! Listen. I hear one—"

Teddy's electric killing device holds a great fascination for Henry; during some gusty preamble—eyes half closed, smile nostalgic with mellow reminiscence—he will suddenly freeze in midword. "Hsst! Hsst! Listen now . . ." He cocks a white-fuzzed ear toward the grid as some yet unseen victim buzzes closer. "Listen . . . Listen . . ." There is a sizzling spurt of blue. The parched carcass falls to join its predecessors on the doorstep. Henry cracks the tabletop with his cane.

"Son of a gun! You see that? Got a nother one, didn't it? Lord, lord, if they don't make some foxy outfits these days then I'll eat your goddam hat. Modrun scientific technologee: that's the ticket. I said so all along; ever since I seen the first winch an' cable rigged to snake out spruce I been saying so. Ah, I tell you we come a long ways. I can recall—an' I swear this is the truth—but you know it's goddam hard to believe the way it was sometimes, because things changing so all the time, every day . . . I still say we'll whip it Boney, you old sobersides—anyhow, let me think, it was durin' Coolidge, I think . . ."

*A young Henry with a fashionable black mustache skitters nimble as a squirrel up the trunk of a log lodged against a steep hill, and with hands like flickering steel frees drunk cousin Larimore from the tangle of oxen reins. A swift, grim, taciturn young Henry, carrying a compass in every pocket of his trousers and a boning knife in a scabbard on his boot . . .*

"Listen! Don't you hear? Ah . . . ahh . . . bing! There. Son of a gun, ain't that somethin'? Got a nother one."

At the back of the bar Ray and Rod, the Saturday Night Dance Band, dressed now in weekday Levis and work shirts, sit across from each other, writing letters to a girl in Astoria.

"How do you spell 'disparaging'?" Ray asks.

"Spell *what* . . . ?"

" 'Disparaging,' for the luvachrist; '*dis*-paraging'! Don't you know shit? *Dis*-paraging, like, say for an instance: 'I get a definite feeling he is writing you *disparaging* lies and remarks about me.' "

"Hold on a minute." Rod makes a grab for Ray's letter. "Who are you writing? Come on, give, give."

"Watch it, Jack. Just cool it with the hands. Just cool it, all right? Because I'll write to whoever I—"

"You're writing to Rhonda Ann Northrup!"

"—to who-goddam-ever I take a notion that—"

"Are you? Because the fur is really gonna fly if I find out."

"Now is that a fact."

"The shit is really gonna hit the fan."

"Is that the truth now."

"You better believe that's the truth."

They go back to their writing. It has been the same ever since they teamed up to play small-town dance bars eight years ago, fighting, bickering over the same woman, each confiding in her that before long he aims to split from that ginhead who's been holding him back, leave this mud wallow and make it big with Decca or Capitol or maybe even TV . . . at odds with each other eternally, yet eternally bound by failure and the need for some excuse for that failure. "If it wasn't for that danged tin-eared square holdin' me back, honey, I'd be long gone from this pesthole." They write laboriously with a grinding of teeth. After a moment Ray looks toward the other end of the bar, where old Henry is pounding home a dramatic point in his story by striking a chair with his cane; he spits between his teeth to the floor.

"Will you listen to that old fool carry on up there? You'd think he's deaf, wouldn't you? Loud as he talks? He rides right over anything anybody else might say, just like a deef man."

"Maybe he is. He's old enough to be deef."

But at the other end of the bar the old man's interest in the fate of certain flies shows a nearly superhuman acuteness of ear. "Listen! Hear him? Hear him? Assssh *bingo!*"

"Jee-zus *Christ!* Let me have a dime and I'll see if I can drown him out."

The jukebox whirs, caressing its coin, throbbing light and mechanical sound. Ray returns to this seat, whistling a memorized steel guitar intro between his big teeth:

A jewel here on earth, a jew-wul in heaven,
She's one of the diamonds around God's great throne. . . .

He is pleased with his tone. I'll be up there someday, he tells himself. "Grand Ol' Opry." Memphis, Tennessee. I'll make it. My day is coming. Leave these squares. Dust 'em all. Rod, old buddy, face it, your beat is beginning to drag like your butt. And Rhonda Ann, you're a pretty fair punch but nothing to write home to mother about . . .

"You boys mark it down," Henry exclaimed at the other end of the bar. "We are gonna whip it, we by god are *gonna!*" What it was that Henry was going to whip no one ever knew for certain, but of his convictions there could be no doubt. "All this new equipment, new methods . . . we are gonna lay it low!"

"How do you spell 'recently'?" Rod was now having trouble.

"The same as I did a while back," Ray told him. "A-yuk a-yuk." Yes sir man, dust 'em all. Memphis, Tennessee, make way for me!

"Our day is coming," Henry announced.

"No. Oh no no no." Boney Stokes, searching out tragedy the way a brush bear searches out garbage cans, found reason to rejoice his own way in spite of the rampant optimism. "No, we are old, Henry. Our day is ending, our skies are turning black."

Henry whooped his derision. "Bosh! Black? Just you look out yonder at that *glow-rus* sunset, does that look black to you?"

*Oregon October, when the fields of timothy and rye-grass stubble are being burned, the sky itself catches fire. Flocks of wrens rush up from the red alder thickets like sparks kicked from a campfire, the salmon jumps again, and the river rolls molten and slow . . .*

Down river, from Andy's Landing, a burned-off cedar snag held the sun spitted like an apple, hissing and dripping juices against a grill of Indian Summer clouds. All the hillside, all the drying Himalaya vine that lined the big river, and the sugar-maple trees farther up, burned a dark brick and over-lit red. The river split for the jump of a red-gilled silver salmon, then circled to mark the spot where it fell. Spoonbills shoveled at the crimson mud in the shallows, and dowitchers jumped from cattail to cattail, frantically crying "Kleek! Kleek!" as though the thin reeds were as hot as the pokers they resembled. Canvasback and brant flew south in small, fiery, faraway flocks. And in the shabby ruin of broken cornfields rooster ringnecks clashed together in battle so bright, so gleaming polished-copper bright, that the fields seemed to ring with their fighting.

This is Hank's bell.

He and Lee and Joe Ben watched the sinking sun as the boat rocked down the big river. It was the first evening in all the weeks Lee

had been working that they'd run the river home with the sun still
up to light their way.

This is Hank's bell ringing.

"We've been lucky," Hank said. "You know that? We've had
enough fall this year to make up for the last three early winters."

Joe Ben nodded avidly. "Oh yeah, oh boy yeah. Didn't I tell you it
was gonna be that way? Oh yeah, we're in the good Lord's pocket. Lots
of good log-cutting weather . . . say, didn't I say so this morning?
Was gonna be a bountiful day, a *blessful* day."

The little man thrashed ecstatically about the front of the boat,
jerking his torn face from side to side in a frenzied attempt to miss
nothing. Hank and Lee turned to share a brief grin of amusement
behind his knotted back. And also shared, in spite of themselves,
some of the very enthusiasm they were smiling about. For it *had* been
a blessful day, the *blessfullest* day, Lee had to admit, since he'd returned to Oregon. The day had started blessful, with the filbert- and
blackberry-filled coffee cake Viv had baked for breakfast, and had
seemed to get better as it went along; the air that greeted them in the
yard was cold and sour with the smell of apples turning to vinegar beneath the trees; the sky was clear but it threatened none of the previous week's stinging heat; the tide was coming in perfect and carried
them up river at top speed . . . then—and perhaps best, Lee thought,
perhaps the true beginning of the blessful day came when they had
given Les Gibbons his usual free ferry-ride across and deposited him,
still jabbering, on the bank near his car; he had turned to call over
his shoulder just how he wanted *once more* to say thanks and how
he wanted them to know he sure did hate bein' beholden an' sure did
hay-ay-ate!—had slipped, with his lips trailing the last word, scrambling like a drunken ape, back down the bank into the icy water
beside the boat.

Hank and Joe Ben howled with laughter as he surfaced, blowing
and cursing, and Les's phony good-fellowship shattered under the
laughter. He clung dripping to the side of the boat and screamed in
unleashed fury that he hoped the whole motherjumpin' Stamper
brood o' them was drownt! The whole horse-laughin' brood was
wrecked and killed and *drownt!* And good motherjumpin' riddance to
bad motherjumpin' rubbish—!

Lee had smiled at the man's uncontrolled frustration and then had
laughed out loud at the cool and Christian way his big brother had
fished him back into the boat and asked sympathetically, as a patient

policeman might question a hysterical child, did Leslie want to go wet into town like a rat fished from the well? Or did he want to be toted back across for a change into different clothes? "Because we'll sure wait on you, Les, if you want to go back up to your place and get into a dry outfit; whatever you say. . . ."

Les swallowed, and swallowed again. He pulled his blue lips back from his chattering teeth in a grotesque attempt to smile. "Ah, Hank, naw, naw I c-couldn't put you boys out th-th-thataway."

Hank shrugged. "Whatever you say, Les old buddy." Then with heavy concern Hank stepped out of the boat to lead the shivering man up the bank by the hand.

In spite of the delay the swift up-river tide seemed to double the speed of their boat and they arrived at the waiting crummy still way ahead of schedule. The crummy started easily. The civet cat that boarded under the hood fled in his usual humpbacked fit of pique but for the first time since he'd moved in fired no parting volley at his tormentors. Uncle John arrived without a hangover and cheerfully offered a stick of Beeman's to everyone; Andy played a gay tune on his mouth organ instead of his usual morning dirge as they drove; and just as they crested Breakleg Ridge a few miles from the show a big four-point sidled out onto the road and practically flagged them down. As they skidded to a stop, he sidled off the road to a leafy clearing, then waited politely for Hank to claw his little .22 Hi-Standard out of the toolbox and fit one of the half-dozen baby nipples he carried in the glove compartment over the barrel. The shot made a small spitting sound, shredding the nipple and nicking the buck's spine just behind the neck where Hank had aimed; the deer dropped like a puppet with its strings cut. Joe and Hank and Andy, working side by side with a speed that would have won respect at the gutting bench at the salmon cannery, bled the big deer, cleaned him, severed his head and hoofs, and had the evidence buried in less than five minutes. There was even a hollow stump next to the clearing the deer had chosen. "Mighty accommodating fellow," Hank acknowledged as he heaved the carcass into the hollow and covered it with a spray of huckleberry.

"Oh you dingdang right!" Joe Ben had said. "We're in God's pocket today. Ever'thing is gonna be milk an' honey! Ever'thing is gonna be abundant! Ever'thing is gonna be with us today 'cause ain't it obvious? Ain't it? The Holy Signals are on the Stampers' side today, you just watch if they ain't."

Even the donkey, even that vengeful conglomeration of wire and noise and time-brittled cast iron seemed to have been affected by the Holy Signals. During the whole day dragging two-ton logs back to the spar tree, while Joe perched on its seat, singing against the shriek of the engine, jamming levers, tromping pedals with the beat of the song as he played the machine like some infernal organ, it had broken down only once. There was a screaming jolt; the gears had frozen in the cable drum. But even then the Signals were consistent, the luck held; instead of having to shut down to send for parts, Hank waded into the trouble with a pair of pliers and a ballpeen hammer and overcame it in such short order that he'd scarcely used any of the usual names he kept reserved for the malingering machine. All the rest of the day it ran like a clock. In fact, all that day the equipment— the chain saws, the cat, the yarder—had behaved in a manner as polite and accommodating as that of the buck.

"Do you realize," Hank said, "that we sent eight truckloads down to the river today. By God, *eight*. That's the biggest cutting since— Lord, since I don't even remember, probably since we were working that state park where it was all roaded and flat, and I feel pretty good if anybody wants to know, pretty motherin' good!" He released the steering handle of the motor, and the boat rushed on straight as an arrow while he stretched and cracked his vertebrae. As he came out of the stretch he punched Lee playfully on the shoulder. "What about it, bub? How do you feel? You probably threw cable around more logs than ever before; you noticin' any repercussions?"

Lee rolled his shoulders against the pull of the suspenders. "It's strange," he reflected, half embarrassed. "I don't know, but I'm not *really* so tired, now that you mention it. Do you suppose I've become immune?"

Hank winked at Joe Ben. "You mean to tell me you don't feel like you'll 'expire of exhaustion' before you climb up to that room? Why, fancy that."

"To be perfectly honest, Hank, I feel halfway decent for the first time since I was sentenced to that cable."

Hank returned to his motor, ducking his chin and smiling into his fist. Lee saw the smile and added hurriedly, "But don't think I'm being lulled into some false sense of *optimism* by my recovery. Everything just happened to go well today. Pure coincidence. And it may happen again once in the next month, though I don't count on it. It may happen, another of Joe's blessful days, but would either of you care to bet some money that we have anything but the usual hell tomorrow? Care to bet we get another eight truckloads? Huh? I didn't think so."

Joe Ben aimed his finger at Lee. "But you got to admit this was a blessful day, don't you? Oh yeah!" Joe beat his fist gleefully in his palm. "You got to admit I was right about today's signals."

"Joby," Hank said, "I ever find the tiniest proof that days like this comes from mystical signals I swear I'll start goin' to church with you and help you figure the signals myself."

Lee shaded his eyes against the sun behind Joe's shoulder. "I will have to say, Joe, that the woods actually seemed more benevolent today. No vines reached to trip me. No branches tried to snatch my eyes out. And most of all, you know most of all what I noticed?—and I don't know if this means anything to you dedicated lumberjacks— but I noticed that all day long there were holes under all the logs. Saints be praised, holes! There is nothing more maddening than throwing a cable over a log the size of a Queen Mary, only to find you have to tear a hole under the monster to get the cable around."

"Oh! Hey by golly." Joe Ben laughed, pounding Hank on the knee. "You know what's happening? You see what's comin' over this boy? He's getting the call. He's hearin' the gospel of the woods. He's for-sakin' all that college stuff and he's finding a spiritual rediscovery of Mother Nature."

"Horse manure," Hank disagreed softly. "Lee's gettin' in condition is all. This is making a man out of him. He's toughening up."

Joe Ben barely paused. "Same thing, don't you see? Sure. Now, I want you boys to think about all the signals—"

"Horse manure," Hank snorted, interrupting Joe's expanding theory. "I still say all's happening is he's getting in shape. When he showed up here three weeks ago he was dying of diarrhea of the brain. Lord almighty, Joby, you give me three weeks to shape somebody up, hell yes the signals are going to be right!"

"Yeah but—yeah but those three weeks! wasn't they more'n sweat an' stumble? God helps them, don't it say, that helps themselves? You got to consider all the facets . . ."

And, shifting himself to a more comfortable position, Joe Ben folded his hands behind his head, gazed happily at the clouds over-head, and launched into an exuberant theory involving the physical body, the spiritual soul, choker chains, astrological signs, the Book of Ecclesiastes, and all the members of the Giant baseball team, who, it seemed, had all been blessed by Brother Walker and the whole congregation at Joe's request the very day before their current winning streak!

Lee smiled as Joe Ben talked, but gave the sermon only a part of his attention. He rubbed his thumb over the knobs of callus building in his palm and wondered vaguely at the strange flush of warmth he was feeling. What was happening to him? He closed his eyes and watched the last rays of the sun dance across his eyelids. He lifted his chin toward the color. . . . What was this feeling?

A pair of pintails flushed from the rushes, started up by Joe Ben's joyous arguments, and Lee felt the drumming of those wings beat at his chest in delirious cadence. He took a deep breath, shuddering . . .

*The river moves. The dog pants in the cold moonlight. Lee searches his bed until he finds the book of matches. He relights his minuscule cigarette and writes again, with it burning between his lips:*

And Peters, as you shall hear, more than memory is affected by this country: My very reason was for a time debauched—I was beginning to *like* it, god help me. . . .

The boat touched in against the dock. The hounds boiled from beneath the house. Joe Ben sprang out to grab the bow rope and flip it about a post. From the bank, plucking stiff and crinkly linens off the clothesline, Viv watched the three men step from the boat into the pack of dogs.

"You're early," she called.

"Early an' bright," Joe Ben called back. "An' it's been like that all day long. Brought home a little present, too."

She watched Hank and Lee have something from the bottom of the boat, wrapped in heavy tarpaulin. Hank settled it onto his shoulder and walked grinning toward her as the hounds leaped for sniffs at the bundle.

Viv put her hands on her hips, the sheets beneath one arm. "All right, what have we poached today?"

Joe came bounding up to Viv, bearing a swollen neckerchief.

"We run across another one of them horned rabbits up in the hills, Viv, and Hank just had to put him out of his misery. That's the kind of day I mean. Here." He thrust the neckerchief to her, pendulous and bloody with its burden. "We thought you might wanta fry up his liver for supper tonight."

"Get that dirty thing away from my *sheets* now. Hello, honey.

Hello, Lee; I see you have blood on your sweat shirt too; are you part of this felony?"

"Only before and after the fact; I allowed the crime and now I plan to partake of the spoils. So I'm afraid I'm innocent of nothing but the deed."

"Let's tote him on out to the barn and skin him out, bub. Joby, would you call Coos Bay and see they get to work findin' another screw gear for that bastardly drum?"

"I'll do it. I will do it. An' what about another couple chokers? The way Lee was throwing that one of his today it'll be wore about by the time we get a extra."

"Is the old man home, Viv?"

"Before dark? Before that crowd in the Snag goes to supper?"

Hank laughed, leaning into the weight of the deer as he mounted the ramp. "Well, you go on an' get that liver started; if the old tomcat ain't home by the time it's done, then we'll eat without him. C'mon, bub, if you plan to partake of this dog you better damn well plan on helpin' skin him. . . ."

At the Snag Indian Jenny bangs through the screen and stands blinking a moment as her sullen, mud-colored eyes grow accustomed to the light. She sees old Henry, then looks quickly away, momentarily confused. She sees Ray and Rod and makes for them past the row of barstools, moving purposefully, squat and blunt and pushing her cedar-hewn face before her as one might push a war shield. On this shield of cheekbone and forehead and chin are dabs of make-up that are arranged differently every day, though the expression beneath the make-up never changes. When her pension check arrives every month and she comes in to sit and celebrate the government's generosity by drinking one bourbon-over-snuff after another until a primitive council-fire music is kindled behind her dull eyes and she rises to shuffle about the room in a heavy-footed dance, and always stumbles and always falls . . . always across a table of fishermen or bushelers or truck-drivers who take no offense because they are always drunker than she (the townspeople talk of Jenny's canny skill at never falling over a man less drunk than she is), and then rises and takes a sleeve between stubby nail-painted fingers and squints into the face at the end of it: "You're drunk. You come on now. I'll take you home all right." But even then, with her prize in tow as she weaves out of the bar, the shield never changes, the expression stays, still somewhere between blunt ferocity and brute pathos.

Now she bears down on the Saturday Night Dance Band. They note her approach and smile their Saturday Night smiles; Jenny is a big tipper when she requests a song. Ray holds up his hand. "Hey there, Jenny girl." She stops inches short of bowling them over and blinks down, nearsighted and fierce from her near encounter with Henry.

"You boys play too fast last week. This week you play slower, you hear me? Then maybe somebody gets to dance except them little dittybops. Here. . . ." She dips into the pocket of her gold-fringed shirt and brings forth a snarl of bills. She separates two dollars and presses them firmly on top of the table as though gluing them there. "Slow tunes."

"Hey, Jenny girl; many thanks, many thanks."

"Okay then."

"And this Saturday we play so nice and slow you'll think we was drugged. Sit down a while, why don't you? Relax. Dig the juke—"

She has already turned and is purposefully heading for the door; a busy, purposeful woman with a tight schedule of errands just such as this to keep, and no time for jukebox folderol.

*When we was sixteen, we courted each other. . . .*

The insects up from the river to look over Teddy's collection of neons pop and sizzle against the charged screen. The theater marquee switches on, and a frightened-looking little man with a green eyeshade on his bald head hurries next door from the laundry to answer the phone ringing in the ticket booth: high-school kids calling from Waldport to see what's showing tonight. "Paul Newman and Geraldine Page in Williams' drama *Summer and Smoke* to be shown once starting at eight o'clock and sleeping bags cleaned this week only one dollar." Keep the morale up and the overhead down. He'll make it yet.

In his room at the Wakonda Arms Del Mar, Jonathan B. Draeger chews a Rollaid and rubs a salve into his chronic eczema, which has appeared this time on his neck. Last time the rash was on his chest and the time before on his stomach. Standing before the mirror, looking at his virile, masculine features topped by the close-cropped gray hair, he wonders if the next place it'll strike will be his face. "It's this coast climate. Everytime I come back I get it again. I rot like a dead dog."

Out in the bay the whistle buoy bobs moaning among the gentle swells, advising the fishing boats about the condition of the bar, and the tower on Wakonda Head lifts its four arms of light and begins flailing the rocks as darkness falls. In her room next to the clamflats Jenny stands motionless at the window, watching the out-of-work loggers searching the low tide with flashlights. "I bet they wouldn't even come in for a bowl of chowder. I won't even ask. But maybe I don't keep my place clean enough, huh?"—and sets about scrubbing her two sheets in the sink. In his bathroom, face contorted in an all-out effort to overcome his constipation, Floyd Evenwrite curses Jonathan B. Draeger: The big-ass, he didn't hardly look at the report! An' it covered the logging history of this area all the way back to the middle fifties! If that don't impress him, what will? In his tar-paper shack the Mad Scandinavian, having boiled the trilobite and eaten its meat, now makes an ashtray of its shell. In the kitchen Hank hushes the kids again to listen for the honk he thought he heard. In the Snag old Henry buys a bottle of illegal bourbon from Teddy and wraps it in yesterday's *Portland Oregonian*. He bids the few stragglers who haven't left for supper a grandiose good-by, then lurches out of the bar, rumbling his cast on the wooden walk, belching and cursing as he climbs into the mud-spattered pick-up and drives back up the river. "We whupped it, we did. You damn right." Then: "I sure hope somebody's there to hear me honk for a boat; I hurt too much to stand around waiting." He drives very slowly, leaned toward the head-lighted pavement. . . . His false teeth making wet bite-marks on the seatcover beside him. *And Molly's panting grows slower and weaker* . . .

It was Lee who finally heard the old man's honking plea drift from across the river. Lee had gone to the milkhouse for cream and was standing lost in thought at the river's dark edge. He had just finished the meal Viv and Jan had cooked; deer liver and heart fried in onions, and gravy made from the drippings . . . boiled potatoes and fresh green beans and homemade bread, and for dessert baked apples were waiting. Viv had prepared the apples by coring them and filling the holes with brown sugar and cinnamon redhots, then topping each apple with a slice of butter before she put them in to bake. During the meal the kitchen had been filled with the spicy smell of their cooking, and all the kids had squealed delightedly when she brought the square Pyrex dish from the oven. "Hot, now, hot, watch it." The apples sizzled in thick caramel-colored syrup. Lee had stared at the plate, feeling the heat of the open oven burn his forehead. "Hank," Viv asked, "or Joe Ben, would one of you mind running out to the milkhouse and skim off some cream?"

Hank had wiped his mouth and, grumbling, was pushing back his chair to stand, but Lee reached to take the tin spoon and bowl from Viv. "I'll get it," he had heard himself saying. "Hank killed our meat. Joe cleaned it. You and Jan cooked it—"

"I *salted* it," Johnny offered, grinning.

"—and even the apples, Squeaky went to the orchard for the apples. So I—" He faltered, feeling suddenly very foolish as he stood at the back door, spoon in one hand, bowl in the other, and everyone turned waiting toward him. "So I just thought—"

"*That's* the boy!" Joe Ben saved him. "Root hog or die. Cut bait or fish. Didn't I *tell* you, Hank? Didn't I say so about ol' Lee?"

"Bull," Hank scoffed, "all he wants is a chance to get outa this madhouse."

"No sir! No sir! I told you. He's shapin' up, he's comin' around!"

Hank shook his head, laughing. Joe Ben charged into a spontaneous theory equating muscle tone with divine intervention. And in the cool, dim concrete milkhouse, with antiseptic still standing in puddles on the concrete floor where Viv had washed up after milking, Lee leaned over a large stone crock and tried to keep his eyes from watering into the careful spoonfuls of cream he ladled into the bowl. That chlorine antiseptic is very bad for making the eyes water, he'd always heard.

He was returning from the milkhouse with the bowl of skimmed cream cradled against his stomach when the honking of the pick-up across the river stopped him. It came like a signal from a dream. Tentatively, feeling barefoot for the path in the dusk, he started once more toward the festive light of the back-door window. The honk came again, and he stopped, his face bent over the bowl of cream. A quail in the orchard called its mate home to bed with a low, seductive whistle. On a slide of light Joe Ben's irrepressible laugh spilled from the kitchen window, followed by the higher laughter of his children. The honk came again. His eyes burned where he had wiped them in the milkhouse. The honk came again, though he barely heard, watching the reflection of the moon stretch and shrink in the bowl of cream . . .

When I was young and walked this way—somber, sallow, and morose as a mudball—when I was six and eight and ten and thought my life doled out to me in mean, cheap distances ("Run down to the bottomland with this bean can, bub, and scrounge us some blackberries for our corn flakes." "Not me."), when I was a boy and should have sprinted barefoot in bib overalls along these ways where quails piped and field mice hid . . . "why was I kept in Buster Brown oxfords and corduroy slacks and a room full of big-little books?"

The moon didn't know why, or wouldn't answer.

"Oh, man, what happened to my childhood?"

Thinking back now, I see the moon quoting Gothic poetry to me:

> Even a man who is pure of heart
> And says his prayers at night
> May turn to a wolf when the wolfbane blooms
> And the autumn moon is bright.

"I don't care about what I'm going to turn into," I told the moon. "At the moment, I'm not interested in my future, only my fouled-up past. Even werewolves and Captain Marvel had a childhood, didn't they?"

"You know," the moon answered sonorously. "You know."

I stood with a bowl of fetched cream fragrant as alfalfa in my hands, watching the dark poultice of dusk draw bullbats from their hideaways, listening to their throated diving buzzes blending in years with that honking from across the river.

"Why was I spun into an upstairs cocoon? This is a land for childhood frolic, with forests dark and magical and shady sloughs alive with chubs and mud-puppies, a land in which young and snub-nosed Dylan Thomas would have gamboled, red-cheeked and raucous as a strawberry, a town where Twain could trade rats and capture beetles, a chunk of wild beautiful insane America that Kerouac could have dug a good six or seven novels' worth . . . why, then, did I refuse it as my world-to-grow-up-in?"

The question had a new and fearful ring to me. Always before, whenever I brooded in some moody apartment with some melancholy wine and let my mind wander back to stand gaping, perplexed and horrified, on the brink of my past, I was able to fix the blame on some convenient villain: "It was my brother Hank; it was my ancient fossil of a father, who frightened and disgusted me; it was my mother, whose name be frailty . . . they were the ones who tore my young life asunder!"

Or on some convenient trauma: "That tangle of arms and legs, sighs and sweat-wet hair telescoped through my bedroom peephole . . . *that* was what burned out my innocent eyes!"

But that doubting moon wouldn't let me get away with it. "Be fair, be fair; that event didn't happen until you were almost eleven, until a century of blooming cherry trees and dragonflies and river-skipping barn swallows had already danced past. Can you blame the first ten years on the eleventh?"

"No, but—"

"Can you accuse your mother and father and half-brother of more crime than is usually committed against *any* sulky son *anywhere?*"

"I don't know, I don't know."

Thus I conferred with the moon as October drew to a close. Three weeks after leaving New York with a suitcase full of certainty. Three weeks after infiltrating the Stamper castle with vague revenge simmering in my mind, three weeks of physical misery and wishywashy will, and still my revenge only simmered. Barely simmered, at that. In fact had grown rather cool. To tell the truth, had all but frozen in a corner of my memory; in the three weeks following my vow to pull Hank down, my intentions had cooled down and my heart warmed up, and a family of moths had taken up residence in my suitcase and chewed my slacks and my certainties full of holes.

So with the devil's-advocate moon grinning over my shoulder, with demure quails calling and bullbats diving and old Henry honking across the river that gurgled coyly to the stars, and with my stomach heavy with Viv's cooking and my head light with Hank's praise, right then and right there I decided to bury the hatchet. I would blame my sad beginnings on no fiend but my own. Live and let live. Forgive me as I forgive my debtors. The man who seeks revenge digs two graves.

"So all right."

Careless with victory, the moon leaned too far and fell into the cream. It swam there like half a golden macaroon, tempting me until I brought it to my lips. I opened my body to that fabled milk and that enchanted cooky. Like Alice I would expand, my life would now be changed. All those years barking various Shazams up the wrong tree—you'd think a foxy kid like me woulda known better. Magic words are too hard to come by, too tricky to pronounce, too unpredictable. Steady proper diet is the secret to growth. It *has* to be. I should have learned long ago. A sweet disposition, easy-going digestion, the proper diet, and love thy neighbor as thy brother and thy brother as thyself. "I'll do it!" I decided—"Love him as myself!"—and maybe that was where I made my mistake, right then and right there; for if thee is fashioning all love after that thee holds for thine own self, then thee had best make a damnably thorough inspection of thy model . . .

*Lee, in his cold room, smokes and writes; after he completes a paragraph he waits a long motionless moment before beginning the next:*

I have a difficult time knowing where to begin, Peters; so much has happened since I've been here, and so little . . . it all started so many years ago, and yet seems as though it only started this afternoon as I fetched a fatal flagon of cream for the baked apples. *Never* trust a baked apple, dear friend . . . but I suppose I should bring you more up to date before imposing any morals . . .

By the time I got back the kitchen was impatient with the smell of baked apple and cinnamon, and Hank was just lacing on his boots to come look for me. "Damn anyhow, boy; we decided you'd got et by the skeeters or something out there."

My throat was so choked with the heady effect of that milk and that moon that I could only respond by holding out the bowl of cream. "Oh, look," squeaked Squeaky, Joe's five-year-old, "*mus*-tash! *Mus*-tash! Uncle Lee has been into the cream. Mm-mm, Uncle Lee, mm-mmm on you"—and stroked her pink finger at me, shaming me into a blush that I am sure must have seemed far out of proportion to my crime.

"We 'uz just about to send the dogs out after you," Joe said.

I wiped my mouth with the dishtowel to hide the blush. "I just heard the old man sending the clarion call from across the bank," I offered as an explanation. "He's waiting over there now."

"And what do ya bet?" Hank said. "Oiled to the gills again."

Joe Ben rolled his eyes and wrinkled his nose in a gnome's grin. "Old Henry is big stuff in town these days," he said, as though personally responsible. "Oh yeah. They say the girls aren't nowheres safe near him an' that cane. But didn't I tell you, Hank? That there's to be trial and tribulation *and* suffering but, man, didn't I tell you? There *is* balm in Gilead. Oh yeah!"

"No fool like an old one."

Viv dipped a finger into the cream and touched it to her tongue. "Don't you start on my old hero now. I think that he has plenty of balm coming. He's worked, golly, how many years building up this business?"

"Fifty, sixty," Hank said. "Who knows? The old coon never lets on to anybody how old he is. Well, I bet he's over there crappin' bricks." He dabbed at his mouth with the sleeve of his sweat shirt and pushed back his chair.

"No, Hank, wait . . ." I heard myself saying. "Please. I'd like to do it"—surprising god knows which of us the most. Hank stopped, half up from his chair, and gawked at me, and I averted my face and went after my cream mustache with the dishtowel again. "I'll . . . I mean, it's just that I haven't had a chance to drive the boat since the day I arrived so I was thinking . . ."

I trailed off to an embarrassed dishtowel-muffled mumble under the glare of Hank's spreading grin. He let himself back down in the chair and tipped it back to look across the table at Joe. "Well by god, Joby, what do you think of that? First the cream, now the boat—"

"Oh yeah! An' don't forget findin' choker holes underneath all the logs, don't forget that!"

"—and this was the nigger we was scared to write 'cause he wouldn't never fit in with our illiterate make-do way of living."

"All right," I said, trying to shroud my pleasure in petulance, "if I'd known it was going to perpetrate such a stupid fuss—"

"No! No!" Joe shouted, scrambling up from his chair. "Here; I'll even go out with you and show you how to start the motor. . . ."

"Joby?" Hank stopped him, then coughed a clever cough into his smile hand. "I believe Lee can handle it on his own. . . ."

"Oh yeah, but Hank, it's night out there, with stumps big as elephants floating around—"

"I believe he can handle it," Hank repeated with bored nonchalance; he fished the key from his pocket and tossed it to me and tipped the chair forward again to his plate. I told him thanks, and outside on the docks silently thanked him again for understanding, and for having faith enough in his literate little brother's illiterate make-do to back up that understanding.

Dancing light in my stocking feet, I whizzed across the grass to the ringing reassurance of a full house of stars and down the plank in two springing leaps as the moon gave a bracing nod of encouragement—they were rooting for me all the way. I hadn't touched the boat's controls since my first bumbling attempt, but I had watched. I had taken notes. Stiff-lipped and set-jawed, grim and gritty as they come, I was ready for another go at making-do.

And the boat started with the first yank—as fir trees leaped cheering and stood waving madly with the warm chinook wind.

And the moon beamed like a junior-high-school coach.

I guided the boat skillfully across the spangled water, never brushing any of the mammoth-sized stumps the whole trip, aware of my audience, pleased with my performance under pressure, and proud of myself. How rare and beautiful in this day and age, I thought, is that simple combination of words—proud of myself . . .

*In a pool of frozen gold Molly the dog recalls through a haze the scaling excitement she felt hours earlier when she first realized that the only voice baying was her own, and the only pawbeats behind the crashing bear the sound of her own lonely crashing; warms herself for a moment at the memory.* In her bed deep and soft and white as sifted flour, Simone sleeps with a stomach full of esteem and dignity; she has not sold herself for meat and potatoes; she has not eaten all day; she fed her children with the last of the ham-hock soup and saved none for herself, and tomorrow she will drive into Eugene to seek a steady job; she has not weakened; and she has kept her promise to herself and her little carved Virgin. *In his room Lee writes: ". . . I humiliate myself even to admit it, Peters, but for a brief time I actually felt my activities here praiseworthy."* And in the garage by the landing old Henry is chided by a much soberer young Henry: "Stand up straight here, you old sot! Stop that infernal wobbling! You used to be able to down a quart of Ben's white dynamite and never bat an eye." "That's th' truth," old Henry remembers proudly, "I whupped it." And draws himself stiffly erect to go meet the boat . . .

When I reached the opposite shore I found our premonitions justified; the old man had obviously been enjoying the balm of Gilead for a good many hours, and had even been so thoughtfully kind as to bring a bottle of it home. He was a sight to behold. Like a victor he returned, singing, clumping, thrashing willy-nilly with his cane at the serfdom of dogs which clamored at his feet at the dock; like a Norse hero he entered his hall, glorified by scars and a nose red as the baked apples which graced his board; like a conquering warrior he bore the spoils of his campaign before him and called for glasses all around, kiddies too; then, like a venerable old warrior, he seated himself; loosed great blastings of wind from either end, sighed a well-deserved sigh, unhitched his belt, cursed the plaster armor that encased his right side, drew his teeth from a crumpled newspaper, and, adjusting same between his gums with the air of a dandy adjusting his foulard, asked when the goddam hell do we eat!

I was glad I had gone on first; his would have been a tough act to follow. He was in peak condition. The rest of us remained at the table while he ate the piece of deer liver Viv fried for him, laughing till we choked at his stories of the oldtime logging days, of bull-logging and horse-logging, of the year he had spent in Canada learning the trade in a camp forty thousand miles from noplace and where men were Men, goddammit, and women were the knotholes in slippery-elm logs! By the time he finished the last of the deer liver, the apples were warmed again and Viv gave them to us in Pyrex dishes and sent us from the kitchen so she could clear away the table.

In the living room Hank and I sat spooning cream into the hot, bubbling apples while old Henry continued his monologue. The twins sat at the old man's stockinged feet, eyes as round and wonderstruck as the white plastic disks of the pacifiers waggling in their mouths. Jan diapered the baby and Joe Ben stuffed Squeaky into flannel sleepers. The bottle of bourbon worked its way around the room, filling the corners and warming the cold little lonely shadows that hid in regions remote from the tasseled lamp. This lamp stood between Henry's thronelike armchair and the big woodstove, and the little area made up by these three—the chair, the lamp, and the stove—comprised the cultural center of the enormous room, and as the old man talked the rest of us pressed in from the yawning hinterlands to be nearer to this center.

Most nights Henry ranted about politics or economics, space travel or integration—and while his attacks on foreign policy were pure noise, his reminiscings were well worth listening to.

"We did it, we," he cried, warming up to his subject. "Me and the donkey. We whupped it, the swamp, the woods, all. Damn tootin'." The words rattled like wet dice among the loose dentures. He paused to arrange his teeth and his cast more comfortably. Chalk, I thought to myself happily, as the liquor rose to my eyes and brought him into looming focus, chalk, limestone, and ivory. Teeth, limbs, and head; he's turning directly from flesh legend to statue in one move, thereby cutting some park-commissioned sculptor out of a job . . .

"Let me tell you, me an' the donk—ah . . . What was I saying?

Oh, about them oldtime tales where we greased the skids and drove the ox and all that noise? Let me see now. . . ." He concentrated, zeroing in on the past. "Oh, I recall oncet about forty years ago: we had this slide, ya see, like a big greasy trough running from the hill down to the river, an' we was easin' the logs into the slide. Zoom! Hunnert mile an hour down to the river like a damn rocketship! Zoom! Kersplash. Float it down t' the mill, zoom, kersplash. So oncet we'd just got this one big bastard of a fir eased into the trough and she's just commencin' to start inchin' down before the big steep, an' I look an' here come that boogin' mailboat! Boy, howdy! I see we got a dead-center bead on her. That log'll break her clean in half. Oh mother, let me think: who was it run that boat? The Pierce boys, I think, or was it Eggleston an' his kid? Ah? Anyhow this is the picture; that log, it just can not be stopped! All right, amen to that. Cannot be stopped, but maybe slowed. So I quick as a flash pick up a water bucket and scoop it fulla dirt an' gravel an' I jump on that big devil before she gets up too momentium. And I ride her down, sprinklin' that dirt ahead of us in the skid trough to slow her. And sure it slowed her, you bet it did; maybe one gnat hair it slowed her down. Next thing I'm blazin' down that hill with Ben and Aaron hollerin' somewhere behind me, hollerin' 'Jump, you dumb nigger, jump!' I don't say nothin'—I'm hangin' on with teeth, toenails an' all—but if I could of I'd of told them You get on this here log goin' so fast everything's a blur an' let's see you jump! Yeah. See anybody nuts enough to jump, by god."

He paused to take the bottle from Hank. He tipped it to his indrawn lips and swallowed with an impressive gurgling; when he brought it down he held it to the lamp, making it slyly obvious that he had drunk a good two inches without wincing. "You boys like a little nip too?"—offering the bottle and making his challenge implicit by the bright green glitter in his old satyr's eye. "No? Reckon not? Well, don't say I didn't make the gesture." And started to tip the bottle again.

"But—but go on, Uncle Henry!" Squeaky could endure the old man's theatrics no longer.

"Go on? I'm goin' somewheres?"

"What happened?" Squeaky cried, and the twins echoed her plea. "What happened—happened?"

And little Leland Stanford, agog as any, soundlessly urged, Go on, Father, what happened . . . ?

"Happened?" He craned his neck about to check. "Happened where? I don't see a thing." Face as innocent as a billygoat's.

"About the log! the log!"

"Oh yeah, that log. Lemee see, by gosh. You mean, don't you, that log I was ridin' lickety-brintle down the slide trough to certain disaster? Hmm, let me see." He closed his eyes and massaged the bridge of his hooked nose in deep thought; even the apathetic shadows perked up and moved in closer to hear. "Well then, right at the last I come up with me a idea; I thought I'd try throwin' the bucket underneath the bastard. I pitched it up ahead in the trough, but the log shoved it rattlin' an' clatterin' along in front for a piece like that ol' bucket was a horsefly it was tryin' to brush aside—hey! sonofagun, that makes me think: have you boys checked that outfit Teddy's got goin' at the Snag for killin' bugs? Slickest-workin' piece of machinery I ever—"

"The log! The log!" cried the children.

The log, echoed the child in me.

"Hm? Ah. Yessir. Right at the last I saw there weren't nothin' for me to do but dive. So I give a jump. But lo an' behol', my gallusses is catched onto a stob! an' me an' that fir went shootin' off into the wild blue yonder, aimin' to tear hell out of the side of that mailboat—did, too, if you got to know; so me up there tryin' to be the big hero with the bucket was all just so much yellin' at the wind, 'cause it did! hit that boat and split it to kingdom come, letters flyin' in all directions like somebody'd set off a blizzard: letters, nuts, bolts, steamfittin's, kin'lin' wood, an' that boy steerin' it flung straight in the air—an' it was the Pierce boy, too, come to think of it, because I recall he 'n' his brother allus useta trade off makin' the runs and the one off duty got mighty sore about havin' to pilot full-time after his brother was drownt—"

"But what about you?"

"Me? Lord love us, Squeaky, honey, I thought you knew. Why, your ol' Uncle Henry was killed! You didn't think a man could survive a fall like that, now did you? I was killed!"

His head fell back. His mouth gaped in death agony. The children looked on, stunned to horrified silence, until his belly began to shake with amusement. "Henry, you!" shouted the twins, and each breathed a disappointed "Ahhh." Squeaky reacted with a hiss of outrage and fell to kicking at his cast with blue-flanneled feet. Henry laughed until tears poured down his gullied cheeks.

"Killed, didn't y'know? Killed yeee hee haw, dead YEE hee hee haw!"

"Henry, someday when I'm bigger you'll be sorry!"

"YEEE haw haw haw!"

Hank turned aside— "Lord; just look at him carry on"—to laugh into his hand. "The balm of Gilead is cooked his brains out." And Joe Ben lapsed into a coughing fit that took five minutes and a spoonful of molasses to subdue.

When Joe could breathe again Viv came from the kitchen, carrying a pot and cups on a tray. "Coffee?" Steam fell in an ermine mantle about her shoulders and when she turned her back to me I saw it was braided into her hair and tied at the bottom with a ribbon of silk. Her jeans were rolled to the swell of her calf; she bent to put the tray on the table, and a brass brad gave me a lewd wink; she straightened and a slight bind of denim made an interesting star of wrinkles. "Who likes sugar, anybody?"

I spoke not a word aloud, but could feel my mouth begin to water as she offered the cups around. "You, Lee?"—turning, with those feather-light tennis shoes sighing at her feet. "Sugar?"

"It's fine, Viv, thanks—"

"I'll get it for you?"

"Well . . . all right then."

Just to watch that brass brad wink its way back to the kitchen.

Hank poured bourbon into his coffee. Henry had a drink straight from the bottle to regain his strength after his untimely demise. Jan took Joe Ben's hand and looked at his wristwatch and announced it was time, past time for the kids to be in bed.

Viv returned with a cup of sugar, licking the back of her hand. "Got my thumb in it. One or two spoons?"

Joe Ben roused himself. "Okay, kids, move. *Up* them stairs."

"Three." I never took sugar in my coffee, never before or since.

"Three? Such a sweet tooth?" She stirred in one. "Try it like this first. I have very powerful sugar."

Hank sipped his drink, eyes closed, peaceful, tame. The kids trooped upstairs in a surly pack. Henry yawned. "Yessir . . . killed me dead." At the top of the steps Squeaky stopped and turned slowly and deliberately with her hands on her hips. "Okay for you, Uncle Henry. You know what,"—and walked on, leaving the air behind her pervaded with some awful fate meaningful only to her and the old man, whose eyes bulged wide in shammed terror.

Viv carried Johnny, tickling him with fuzzy breath down the back of his neck.

Joe held the twins by fat hands, patient with their one-step, step, one-step, step to the top of the stairs.

Jan snuggled the baby over her shoulder.

And I swelled, threatening to burst in an explosion of hearts, flowers, and frustration; love, beauty, and jealousy.

"Nigh'-nigh'. The baby waved.

"Night-night."

"Night-night."

Night-night, said a small voice inside, waiting to be cuddled upstairs. Frustration and jealousy. I blush to admit it. But as I watched that last pampered bundle disappear up the stairwell I could not help feeling a twinge of envy. "Twinge?" the moon mocked me through a dirty windowpane. "Looks to me more like a hammerblow."

"Yeah, but they are living the life I should have lived."

"Just little kids. Shame on you."

"Thieves! Stealing my home and my parental affection. Enjoying my unused paths and climbing my apple trees."

"A while ago," the moon reminded me, "you were blaming all your elders, now it's the children . . ."

"Thieves"—I tried to ignore that moon—"little fuzzy thieves, growing up in my lost childhood."

"How," the moon whispered, "can you be sure it is lost? Until you try to find it?"

I sat stunned by the insinuation.

"Go on," it nudged, "give it a whirl. Show them you still want it. Let them know."

So, with the kids gone and the old man nodding, I searched the room for a sign. My attention was caught by the sound of the dogs beneath the floor. Well, I'd made it with the cream, I'd made it with the boat . . . why not go the whole route? I swallowed hard, shut my eyes, and asked if they still used the hounds for hunting, still, you know, went on hunts—like they used to?

"Now and then," Hank answered. "Why d'ya ask?"

"I'd like to go sometime. With you . . . all . . . if you don't mind?"

It was said. Hank nodded slowly, rolling a hot spoonful of apple on his tongue. "All right."

A silence followed, identical to the one that had followed my offer to pick up Henry in the boat—only longer and stronger, because as a boy my aversion to hunting had been the most vociferous of all my aversions—and I once again reacted to my embarrassment at this silence with a flustered attempt at sophistication. "It's only that one should"—I shrugged, studying the cover of a *National Geographic* with bored authority—"*know* something of the area . . . besides, I've read all the decent paperbacks offered by Grissom's drugstore, and I saw *Summer and Smoke* on stage, so—"

"Where! Where!" Henry lurched to his feet like an old firehorse jumping to the bell, brandishing his cane and sniffing about for the flames. Viv uncoiled swiftly from the foot of Hank's chair and crossed to take his arm and ease him down again.

"The movie-picture show, Henry," she said in a voice that would have calmed Vesuvius. "Just the movie-picture show."

"What was I sayin'? Ah." He picked up the thread as though it had never broken. "About the old times. Say, them oldtime tales where we greased the skids and rode the oxen and all that noise? Hm? Them oldtime jacks in mustaches and ten-gallon hats carryin' a misery whip over their shoulders, you seen them pictures, ain't you? Lookin' all dashin' an' romantic? Well, them boys are good pictures in *The Pioneer* magazine, but I tell you now an' you can mark 'er down: *they weren't the ones!* that really rolled the logs. No. No sir. It was boys like me and Ben and Aaron, boys what not only had the grit but what had the sense to get hold of a *machine*. You're godblessed right! Let me say . . . hm, well now, roads? We didn't have roads worth sour apples, sure, but what did I tell 'em? Roads or no boogin' roads, I say, I'll take this here donkey machine any place you can take one them worthless tow-oxen of yours! Shoot; all I got to do is run a little piece of line up to a stump somewheres and pour it to 'er. Reel myself right up to where I want, then run a line to the next stump. Jumpin' the donk, we called it; cookin' with steam. Yessir, steam, steam, that's the business. You feed them animals of yourn bale of hay every other day at eighty, ninety cents a bale, and you know what I'm feedin' mine? Wood *chips*, and slashin', and *scrub oak*, and any other damn thing layin' around handy for the burnin'. Steam! gasoline! now *Diesel!* Yessir, that's the ticket. You can't whup the swamps with a animal. A animal is on the other side! You can't take much shade offn the ground with nutted ox an' a whittlin' knife! You got to have a *machine*."

His eyes brightened as he warmed again to his subject. He jerked upright in his chair and hooked a long bony hand in the invisible strap hanging before him. He dragged his body standing, a rickety stack of limbs and joints, teetering precariously on the edge of eighty and looking like the slightest breeze would turn it into a pile of rubble.

"The trucks! The cats! The yarders! I say more power to 'em. Booger these peckerwoods always talkin' about the good old days. Let me tell you there weren't nothin' good about the good old days but for free Indian nooky. An' that was all. Far as workin', *loggin'*, it was bust your bleedin' ass from dark to dark an' maybe you fall three trees. Three trees! An' any snotnosed kid nowdays could lop all three of 'em over in half an hour with a Homelite. No sir. Good old days the *booger!* The good old days didn't hardly make a dent in the shade. If you want to cut you a piece you can see out in these goddam hills you better get out there with the best thing man can make. Listen: Evenwrite an' all his crap about automation . . . he talk like you gotta go easy on this stuff. I know better. I seen it. I cut it down an' it's comin' back up. It'll *always* be comin' back up. It'll outlast anything skin an' bone. You need to get in there with some machines an' tear hell out of it!"

He lurched violently across the room, clearing his throat, wiping at the long cornstarch hair worrying his eyes, working his mouth in a grimacing mixture of anger and exuberance, of fury practically, of drunken, dedicated fury; he turned and came thundering back.

"Tear it out! Only thing! Chop out the big stuff and burn the brush, grub up the brambles and poison the vines. Goddam right. What if it *is* growin' back on you soon's you bat your eye? Screw it. You don't get it this round, get it the next. Yee HEE I useta tell Ben. Whoo Whooee. Goddam tootin'. Tear the livin' jesus outa it! You watch an' see if I—"

Hank kept him from falling. Joe caught the outflung cane. Viv hurried to his side, her face white. "Papa, Henry, are you all right?"

"I think he's just gassed, chicken," Hank said without conviction.

"Henry! Are you feeling all right?"

Slowly the old face lifted and turned toward hers; gradually the sunken mouth stretched itself into a grin. "Okay, now—" He fixed her with one searing green eye. "What's this about tryna sneak off on a coon hunt 'thout me?"

"Oh, lord." Hank sighed, releasing the old man and returning to his seat.

"Papa," Viv said with a mixture of relief and vexation, "you've just got to go to bed—"

"Booger the bed! What about a coon hunt? I asked!"

Joe Ben maneuvered him toward the stairs. "Nobody said anything about a coon hunt, Henry."

"Uh-huh, uh-huh, you think I can't *hear?* You think the old nigger is too deef, too stove up to go on a little hunt? We'll see about *that.*"

"Come on, Papa." Viv tugged gently at the sleeve of his shirt. "Let's me and you go upstairs to bed."

"Why, all right," he agreed with a sudden change of mood and gave Hank a wink so lascivious and led Viv so spryly up the steps that I told her I was giving her three minutes, at the most five, then I was organizing a posse to come up and rescue her from the old dragon.

We listened to him thundering and hooting overhead. "I sometimes think," Hank said, still shaking his head, "that my dear old daddy is slippin' his gears."

"Oh no." Joe Ben leaped to Henry's defense. "That ain't it. He's gettin' to be the town character, like I said. They're callin' him Old Wild and Woolly in Wakonda—kids pointin' at him, women sayin' hello to him on the street—and don't think for a minute he ain't lovin' every minute of it. Ah, no, Hankus, it ain't that he's really comin' apart—well, maybe a little, like his memory an' his eyes—it's more a kind of act, you see?"

"I don't know which is worse."

"Ah, Hank, he's gettin' a *million* kicks."

"Maybe. But dammit, the doctor put all that plaster on him to kind of anchor him. He said he wasn't really so bad busted up but if we didn't slow him down some he sure would be. Looks like, if anything, it revved him up."

"He's just holding his mouth right is all, enjoyin' his lot. Don't you think so, Lee? Oh yeah, listen to him rant an' rejoice up there."

I was pessimistic. "Sounds like he's rehearsing for a rape."

"Oh no. It's just an act," Joe insisted. "All just an act. If he's rehearsin' for anything it's for the Academy Award speech for the best actor of the year."

Above us we could hear the Academy Award candidate practicing diction as he called through spongy gums for Viv to get her puny ath back here an' quit bein' so blathted *perthnickety!* Viv appeared on the stairs, her hair disheveled and her pale cheeks flushed by the recent activity, and announced she was giving the rest of us one last chance to better old Henry's offer of two dollars and a pint of liquor. Hank said that was too rich for his blood but Joe Ben allowed that in as his woman had already petered out on him and gone to bed with the kids upstairs, he'd up the bid to two-fifty. I kept my wallet in my pocket, but as she passed me on her way to deposit old Henry's dirty socks in the laundry bag she asked if I didn't have a five spot I wasn't using. I told her to wait for next Saturday, payday.

"You could get a draw tomorrow," she hinted, blushing as she did with that anomalous combination of demure coquetry and brazen diffidence. "I could talk my husband into it."

"All right, tomorrow. Where shall we rendezvous?

She whirled away, trailing light laughter. "In town at the jetty. Tomorrow is the day I dig rock oysters at the jetty. Bring a hammer."

"It sounds romantic," I said and glanced about for brother Hank, to be sure it didn't sound too romantic. But he was just coming away from the window.

"You know, I been thinking," he said thoughtfully, "what with the big yield we had today we're standin' in pretty fair shape. An' we can't expect this kinda weather to hold. An' we're all about half lit anyhow. So how about we take them dirteaters under the house there out for a little run, just to limber up?"

"A hunt?" I asked.

"Yeah!" Joe Ben was ready.

"It's late," Viv said, thinking of us getting up at four-thirty for work in the morning.

"Just right," Hank said. "I was thinkin' we'd by god just cross off tomorrow as far as work goes. We ain't had a Saturday off in a long while."

"Good *deal!*" Joe Ben was beside himself. "Oh *yeah!* An' you know what tomorrow happens to be? Halloween. Oh yeah, it's too much: Halloween in town, a coon hunt, the old man bringin' home a bottle, Les Gibbons fallin' in the river . . . I can't stand it!"

"What about you, bub; you reckon you can stand it?"

"I wasn't exactly planning on a midnight stroll, but I think I'll survive."

"I tell you what, Hankus: Let's me an' you take out first around the hill an' get things goin'—them dogs'll be worthless anyhow for the first hour after this long a layoff—and Lee and Viv can go on up on top to the shack and wait till we tree somethin', then follow on down. No sense in all of us stumblin' around in the brambles. How's that sound, Viv? Lee?"

Viv was willing and I saw no way out of the trap I had fashioned for myself, so I said fine. Besides, I was looking forward to the chance of speaking with Viv alone. During the evening, along with my decision to bury the hatchet, I had resolved to use the impetus of well-being and whisky to tell all, to come clean. My grimy conscience begged for a thorough airing. I had to tell someone everything and had picked Viv as the most sympathetic ear. I would tell her the whole evil scheme, all my terrible plans. Of course, I might have to fill in here and there, pad out the abstract, chink in the unfinished details of the fiendish plot against my brother, but I was determined to reveal the truth to someone, though it meant lying myself blue in the face.

That, however, is not quite the way it turned out.

*Upstairs, the young Henry with a compass in every pocket and a knife in his boot reached down to grapple with the shirtfront of the old Henry, pulling him roughly standing. "Okay, old man, you can let them downstairs think you're fooled, but I'm blamed if I'll let you think you fooled yourself. . . ." The old man looks down at the soft doeskin bedroom slipper that covers his good foot, noticing how worn it is already just since that doctor gave it to him. A bedroom slipper, for the love o' Christ . . .*

As it turned out, I was never alone with her long enough to begin my fabricated confession— *"Because when we swore to beat it,"* the young Henry goes on *"we wasn't talking just about the first rounds, we was talking about the whole boogerin' fight! So get up from there . . ."*—because just as we were leaving old Henry decided that we couldn't possibly survive out there in the untamed wilderness without the blessing of his woods-wily presence. *In the front hall below they hear the light slipper's padding change to a heavy stomp counterpointing the rubber thud of the cast's crutch tip. "Listen there," Joe Ben says . . .* But, as it turned out, my father's presence was more a blessing than he ever knew; had I actually gone through with the ridiculous confession I was fashioning for Viv, I am sure I would have expired of sheer absurdity when later, back at the house after the hunt, my brother finally shed his phony foliage of olive leaves and forget-me-nots to reveal the true color of his nightshade heart—*"Listen there," Joe says. "Sounds like somebody for some reason is changed a slipper for a corknail boot. . . ."*—shed his foliage and showed his colors and proved himself once and for all deserving of whatever calamity I could conceivably perpetrate—*"Now who do you suppose,"* Joe asks aloud, *"could be snakin' down them stairs after us in one cork boot?"*—as it all turned out . . .

"I got a pretty fair notion who," Hank said. "What I'm wondering about is why."

He and Lee had been helping Viv into a pair of stubborn boots when Joe had heard that first boot-tread. Now they all stood listening to the somber approach of stealthy rubber creeping from the stairs toward the hall.

"Trouble sneakin' up on us," Joe said.

"Trouble is right," Hank said. "And with a snootful."

"Hank," Viv whispered, "couldn't he just go as far as—"

Hank cut her off. "I'll handle him."

She started to speak further but decided it would only cause more fuss. They were all standing in a row when Henry appeared. Viv saw him come clomping through the dark, struggling to work his plaster arm through the sleeve of a tattered elkhide jacket. She saw that he had pared away some of the cast at the elbow and wrist to give him more freedom of movement. He stopped before them in the hall, glowering.

"I couldn't get off to sleep, if you got to know." He looked from Hank to Joe Ben, challenging anybody to just by god try to tell him where he could go and where he couldn't. When no one spoke he resumed his struggle with the jacket. Viv leaned the .22-pump she was holding against the door and walked to give him a hand. "All right, then," he grumbled, "is they any of that likker I brought home left, or you hogs kill it?"

"You want some more of that rotgut?" Hank stepped forward to steady his father while Viv tried to work the sleeve over the soiled cast. "Why, Jesus, Henry, you can barely put one foot in front of the other as it *is*—"

"Get back away from me, blast it!"

"—so what you want to make yourself more a handicap for?"

"Get back, I say! I'll thank you to leave me dress my own self. Lord love us when the day comes that Henry Stamper is a handicap. Where's me some snoose, then?"

Hank turned to Lee. "What you say, bub? It's your show more

or less. You want to drag this old drunk cripple along or not?"

"I don't know. He's a sight. You sure he won't scare off the game?"

"Oh no." As usual, Joe Ben spoke in Henry's behalf. "Creatures been known to come for miles around when Henry's along. He *attracks* the game."

"There's something to what he says, Lee. You remember, Joe? The time we took him huntin' cat with us in the Ochocos?"

"All *right* now—"

"Left him leanin' against a tree—"

"I said all *right!* Viv, honey, you seen my snuff?"

"—an' he dozed off an' we came back into camp an' there was a scrubby coyote wettin' on his leg."

"I remember that. Oh yeah. Thought he was a tree."

Henry was concentrating on the cluttered shelf that ran head-high the length of the hall, choosing to ignore the conversation. "Just one can of Skol is all I ast an' we can get this circus on the road."

"So you see, bub, he may actually be an asset."

"Bring him along. Maybe we can use him for bait."

"I never in my life seen such a collection of crap." He rummaged through boxes of shotgun shells, tools, odds and ends of clothing, tennis shoes, paint cans and brushes . . . "Never in all my born days."

Viv raised herself on tiptoe and found a whole carton. She opened one can for him by running her thumbnail around the crack. Henry looked into the offered can suspiciously before extracting a pinch fastidiously between thumb and finger. "Much obliged," he said moodily. Turning his back on the others to confide to her in a low voice: "All I aim is just to walk up as far as the first flat an' listen to the dogs for a while. Then I'll come on back. I just couldn't get off to sleep."

She replaced the lid on the snuff and put the can in his jacket pocket. "It just hasn't been a night for sleeping," she said sympathetically.

Hank and Joe Ben went on ahead with the dogs and she hung back with Lee to keep the old man company. She preferred staying apart from the dogs, anyway. Not that she minded their baying—in fact, some had very musical voices—but their noise always so overwhelmed the other little noises of the forest night.

Henry had found a flashlight among the shelf's clutter, but it had burned out a few yards from the front door. He flung it away with a curse and they continued on in darkness up the path in the direction of the nearest hill. The clouds that had blazed so brilliantly at sunset now spread across the land, blackening the sky and bringing it down close over their heads. On all sides, just beyond the finger-tips, night hung in thick folds; even when the keen edge of the moon managed to slice itself a brief hole, its crippled light empha-sized, more than alleviated, the gloom.

They walked in a silent single file, with Viv a few yards behind Henry, and Lee bringing up the rear. The only thing Viv could see of the old man was the murky sweep of his cast leading the way toward the hill, yet she could follow him easily; there were perhaps a dozen paths up to the shack, and she knew them all by heart. Her first year in Oregon she had walked up to the shack almost every day, early in the morning or late in the evening. She had walked home from there many times in complete darkness after sitting through a long twilight. From the hill she could see the sun sink into the sea when the weather was clear, or hear the buoys out over the bar when it was stormy—the bell buoy clanging in slow cadence; the whistler keening mournfully as the waves tossed it about. Hank scolded her for choosing the early morning and the late evening for her walk, saying it would be warmer and clearer at midday. She tried it a few times but went back to her old schedule; in the eve-nings she liked to look seaward and see that perfectly round sphere sinking to meet that perfectly straight line—so different from the jig-jag line of the Rockies that her childhood sun had turned into a row of volcanoes, and so much simpler, like an orange ball rolling off the edge of a blue-green table—and in the mornings she enjoyed hearing the dark, mist-locked woods below her come awake for the day.

That first summer it came to be almost a daily ritual, her walk to the shack. After the men left for work she piled the dishes in the big sink to soak, filled a Thermos with coffee, singled out one of the dogs to accompany her, and hiked up to the shack to listen to the birds. The dog would sniff about the shack for a few minutes while she spread a big moss-covered stump with a piece of plastic bag she kept in the shack so she would not have to sit on the damp moss; then he would wet on the same wetting post and lie down to sleep on the same pile of burlap that the dog before him had used.

Then nothing else would be stirring—or so it would seem. But gradually her ears would pick out tiny rustlings in the vines nearby, where the grosbeaks were waking. A mourning dove would call unseen from the thicket below—a round, clear, bouncing note, as though a soft ball had been dropped on the lowest key of a xylophone: "Tuuu . . . tuu tu tu." Another dove would answer a distance away. They would call again, closer to each other each time; then they would emerge together from the mist, of the mist, gray, graceful, and be off together wing to wing like reflections of each other in a looking-glass sky. The red-winged blackbirds would wake all at once, like soldiers to Reveille. They would shake themselves from the barn grove and swing in a glistening pack to settle in the nearby bunch-berry vines, where they waited for the mist to lift from the cattails, singing incessantly or drawing the black feathers of their wings and tails slowly through their bills. With the bright scarlet amulets on each shoulder of their black uniforms they always made her sure that they were preparing for a review by the king. Then the blue grouse would drum away its kin, and the dowitcher would voice its piercing alarm at seeing the sun. The band-tailed pigeons would call seduc-tively from branch to branch, all with voices like Marlene Dietrich's. The flickers and sapsuckers would begin knocking the trunks of hem-locks for breakfast. . . . And after all the other birds were up and about their affairs—even after the jay, who would burst each morning from the mist, screeching in a blue rage at these damned *early birds* who never let a fellow finish his rest—the crows would make their stately entrance. From the tops of the firs they would swoop, laughing with a sort of pitiless amusement at the lesser birds, and circle away in a slow, disorganized flock bound for the mudflats, sometimes leav-ing her feeling strangely disturbed. Perhaps because they reminded her of the magpies from around her Colorado home—carrion-eaters, lining the rabbit-killing highways, living off death—but she thought there must be more to it than just that. Magpies were, all in all, rather silly birds. The crows, for all their raucous laughter, never seemed silly.

When the last of the crows had gone she would drink the coffee and return the plastic sack to the shed and start back, whistling for the dog. On the way back she would go by the orchard and kick the old cow awake, then go on to the house to clean up after break-fast. By the time she finished dishes the cow was lowing at the barn door to be milked.

When she milked again in the evening she often saw through the barn window the crows returning from their daily contest with the pigs; sometimes one or two were conspicuously maimed, or even missing. She didn't know about the pigs, how they were taking the contest, but, win or lose, the crows always laughed—the hard, old jaded laughter that came of looking at the world with a black and practiced eye. From the less skillful the laugh might have hinted of despair, or silliness, like the magpies', but the crows were masters of the wry outlook, and Viv never heard them but what she followed their expert lead and laughed along—they knew the secret of black, that it could not be made blacker, and if neither could it be made lighter, it could still be made funnier.

"What are you sniggerin' about?" Hank wanted to know when she carried in the straining cloth from the milkhouse to wash it on the back porch.

"Oh, I've got some secrets," she answered, amused by his curiosity, "some secrets of my own."

"Out yonder in the barn? So. You been meetin' some man on the sly up in the hayloft, is that it?"

She hummed mysteriously as she wrung the cloth out and hung it over a peg. "What man? You keep me imprisoned across this moat all day, forlorn, alone—"

"Uh-huh! So it's one of them *animals* out there? Which one, the tomcat? I'll wring the rascal's neck. Tell me which one them varmints been duffin' my wife. I got to know. . . ."

She smiled and started for the kitchen door. "You'll just have to wait another two months to see, I guess."

He caught the tail of her sweat shirt and pulled her backward to him until her rear pressed against his pants. He encircled her waist and slid his hand down the top of her jeans over the tight swell of her stomach. "I guess he'll be okay whatever," he said against the back of her head, "just so long's he ain't black; old Henry'll drown all of us if he's black, tomcat and all."

She arched her neck against him, thinking that it was nice to be young and pregnant and in love. She guessed she was very lucky. She had almost everything she wanted. She hummed and snuggled against him. And he nuzzled her hair. Then he pushed her away to arm's length and turned her so he could study her through squinted eyes. "I wonder—what it would be like, black?"

"The baby?"

"No, no." He laughed. "Your hair."

And through the darkening porch screen she could hear the crows settling into the tops of the trees.

As her time came closer she stopped climbing the hill, though the doctor told her the walk was probably doing her good. She didn't know why she stopped; she thought for a while it was because she was so interested in noticing all the movements inside her, but she decided later that this wasn't the reason or she would have started going again when the movements stopped and she knew the thing inside her was dead. When she received the examination some months later and was told that the operation was healed and she could resume her normal activities she went again to the shack. But it was drizzling rain and the only birds in sight were a flock of geese migrating down from Puget Sound, laughing a laugh she didn't understand, so she returned to her reading. She had gone only a few times since then, and it had been years since she'd used the particular path they were walking now, yet it was still surprisingly sharp in her mind. In fact, she would have liked to lead the way so she might have set a slower pace. Nothing would do for Henry but full speed ahead to show them he was still as fast as any man, plaster leg or no. Not that she couldn't keep up—it wasn't for that reason she wished he would go more slowly—but Lee was having a time of it in the unfamiliar dark. She could hear him struggling somewhere behind her as he fought the brush and berries on both sides of him. She thought of stopping to take his hand but decided against it, as she had decided against asking the old man to let her lead the way.

The three of them became gradually more and more separated. As Henry pushed ahead and Lee fell farther behind she was left more by herself in the dark.

After a few minutes she began to make out familiar shapes along the path and amused herself by identifying them. There was the patch of hazel bushes that grew along the orchard fence, there the dogwood, and the old lonely beech standing black and baffled against the purple sky, like an old bent-backed tramp a long way from home, waiting for Saint Vincent de Paul to bring him a suit of second-hand leaves. Close along the path she felt fern touch her ankles with wet fingers and sometimes heard the dry rattle of blue-vetch seeds in their little curled pods. From the bottomland, where trees resounded with the gleeful barking of the dogs, came a thick reek of jack-in-the-pulpit—skunk cabbage, Hank called it—and the sour-syrup smell of overripe blackberries. And over all these other plants, like a higher order of plant life, stood the fir—filling the sky with towering peaks, softly brushing its tart bright green fragrance onto the dark winds.

As the space between herself and the two men widened, Viv felt herself relaxing; until then she had not been aware of the tightness pinching her shoulders together and confining her lungs. She released her elbows and breathed deep, holding her arms slightly away from her body. From one of the hazels a wren called—"Tiu! Tiu!"—and Viv lifted her arms higher, imagining them to be wings. She tried pretending she was flying, but couldn't make it real the way it had been when she was a child; if it weren't for the boots! They weigh a hundred pounds apiece. If it weren't for the boots I could fly!

Hank always strapped her into boots before they went hunting; to him the woods was a battleground where you armed yourself with tin hat, leather gloves, and spiked boots, against an army of thorns. Then tromped through the forest. Viv would have preferred to fly through it; not high over it, like a hawk, but skimming through it inches above the ground, from rock to bush to tree, like the wren in the hazel. And for flying you needed wings, not spikes; tennis shoes, not hundred-pound clodhoppers.

A stifled cry from the path some yards back stopped her. She found Lee where he had strayed from the path into the fern. His hand trembled as she led him back.

"I stumbled when something flew against me," he explained in a whisper, more to himself than to Viv. "I think a moth . . ." A shudder stopped him. The very word, so softly whispered in the dark, fluttered against Viv's own cheek. "I know," she whispered back, "Sphinx moths this time of year. They scare me to death in the night." Her hand guided him along the path. "It's on account of they're white," she went on. "That's what gives me the willies. I know they're white, you see? But they feel dark."

"Yes, that's it," Lee whispered too. "Exactly."

"Hank kids me about it, but they just scare the daylights out of me sometimes. Br-r-r. And you know what else?" she went on softly. "Have you ever looked at one close up? On their backs they got a picture—I'm not kidding a bit—of a *skull*."

This time they both shuddered, like children who have managed to conjure up a fright.

The path started to rise and ahead of them they could hear the old man panting and cursing as he fought for footing with the rubber knob on the bottom of his cast. "Shall we give him some help?" Lee asked.

"Huh-uh. Not much further. He'll make it by himself."

"You certain? We couldn't help him? He sounds like he's having something of a time—"

"Huh-uh. You saw him with Hank and the coat. Let him make it by himself. It's why he came along."

"What is why he came along?"

"That, to do a thing he set out to do. Without help. The way you wanted to take the boat across alone."

Lee was impressed. "Madam," he said, panting. "I can't speak for—the middle-aged group—but I must say you are very—sensitive to the needs of crippled old men and frightened little boys."

"Why is it you always think of yourself as a liability or a little boy?"

"I don't. I was a liability when I first came. I don't feel so any more. But I'm still a little boy. Just like you're still a little girl."

The hounds bayed in the distance. "I haven't been a little girl in a long time," Viv said simply and Lee wished he'd kept his humor to himself.

At the top of the knoll a small fire crackled brightly in front of a three-walled log cabin. The knapsack with its delicious smell of tuna-fish and deviled-egg sandwiches dangled from the peg where Hank had hung it, and a large raccoon standing on its hind legs was reaching for that pack with both black hands as its shadow swayed lazily against the cabin's back wall. When Henry came into the fire-light the animal trilled a plaintive note inquiring the nature of this intruder's business. It dropped to all fours.

"Ain't you the one," Henry said. The raccoon stood looking at him, appearing perturbed at the interruption. "Don't you know you're supposed to be down in the slough-bottom givin' them dogs a run, not up here thievin' our grub—don't you know that?"

The raccoon knew of no such appointment. It rubbed its hands in the dirt, feigning interest in a nonexistent bug.

"Haw. Look here, kids; he just gonna give us the cold shoulder. He just gonna let us know what he thinks, us bustin' in on his business."

The animal rubbed a moment longer, then, seeing these three nuisances were not going to take the hint, puffed out its hair and humped its back and made a little mock charge at Henry. Henry laughed and kicked dust in its face. The raccoon uttered a series of huffing snorts. "Made you mad, huh? What's the trouble? Won't we go away and leave you to your thievin'?" Henry laughed again and kicked another puff of dust. Which proved too much for a nobleman of the raccoon rank. In a stiff-legged bound it caught the old man and wrapped all four legs around his cast as though prepared to crush it in the grip; Henry yelled and beat at the animal with his hat. The raccoon tried the plaster two or three times with its teeth, then gave up and ran off into the darkness, huffing and trilling righteously.

"By God." Henry leaned down to inspect the scratches on his cast. "Will you look at this. I bet that nigger has a thing or two to tell his buddies about the way a man is put together." He gave a stiff nod. "Well, Lee boy, I guess we better build up the fire some."

"To ward off further attack?" Lee asked.

"Damn right. He's so mad he's liable to be back with all *kinds* of pests. We're in grave danger."

Viv took his hand. "Seems like there's always some animal or other trying to get at your leg, doesn't it Papa?"

"All right now. A lot of you snotnoses are looking for trouble, ain't you? Just see if you can do something for your keep around here."

She found water in a ten-gallon milk can and started coffee while Henry and Lee dragged two gunny sacks of rubber duck decoys from the cabin and placed them near the fire. After she situated the pot in the coals she found her plastic sack and spread it on the ground. She sat down and leaned against the sack Lee was sitting on. During these chores none of them had spoken; now Henry loaded his lip up with snuff, scratched himself, and leaned forward to concentrate on the hounds, clearing his throat like a sports announcer before the game. "All right, you hear that?" The firelight carved from the darkness a red cedar relief of his face that appeared at times convex and at times concave. He ran his hand nervously through his long white hair as he talked.

"I don't mean them other suckers off yonder, but that way . . . listen . . . that ol' Molly dog talkin'? You hear *that?*"

Viv wriggled deeper into the sack's springy cushioning, situating herself for the discourse she knew to be coming. *And when she stops moving she realizes that the back of a hand has moved to rest lightly against the nape of her neck beneath her hair.*

". . . . Oh-oh, listen . . . she don't say fox, she don't say coon . . . I don't know about them other dirteaters but you can just mark it down in your little black book that Molly ain't talkin' like that about fox or coon; or deer neither, she never run deer. Ah . . . ah! Gawd-damn." Suddenly overcome with delight, Henry whacked his cast with the hard palm of his hand—"what she says is bear!"—and provoked a celebration of sparks from the fire with his cane. "Gawd-damn . . . a bear!"

He leaned forward, green eyes intent on the darkness beyond the fire. Below them, down river to the west, the other dogs were yelping in a pack; from the other direction, toward the mountain range, came a clear and measured baying, each bay distinct by itself, starting low, then breaking into a note high and keen and true as though blown from a silver horn.

"An' she's alone, Molly is. Them other dogs must be with old Uncle. Them other dogs generally follow Molly before they follow Uncle, but not when it's got to do 'th bear. An' Uncle, he don't want no more to do 'th bear, he got et up last year and lost an' eye over a bear, an' he says far as he's concerned Molly can have that bear all by her lonesome!" He laughed and whacked the cast again. "But listen there, boy, off down the slough—" He dug Lee in the side with his cane. "That bunch off down there, you hear the way they're yipin' and gripin'? All that fuss? Who they kiddin'? Yee hee. Oh, they know, they know. Damn, you can't tell me they don't. They're out with Uncle—after fox, most like—but listen how they feel about it. Listen how they carry on after that fox an' just Molly after that bear. . . ."

They all listened. Indeed, there did seem to be the unmistakable sound of shame hidden beneath their high, overhysterical barking, certainly a sound not in the barking of the lone dog.

"Where are Hank and Joe Ben?" Lee asked, and she feels the wrist move slightly.

"Damned if I know. I figured they'd be here waiting. But, now . . . what I reckon is, the pack there sounds like it tried once, then headed off again." He frowned, scratching the tip of his nose. "Yeah . . . I reckon Molly took the pack right off to that bear—uh-oh, hear that? fox is turnin'—and soon as Uncle saw what he'd got into he says, 'Let's go, boys. Leave that fool Molly to get et by bear if she so wants. Let's us go hunt some fox.' Yeah—an' that was that first big noise, at the bear tree when the pack was there. So what I figure is Hank and Joe headed off—*listen*—*to* get to the treein', but when the pack left, Molly couldn't hold the bear by herself . . . so when Hank an' Joe got there . . ."

He trailed off, mumbling to himself, nodding, opening his mouth to continue, then pausing to listen, eyes half closed and glinting green in the dark as he lip-read the hunt to himself. The fire spat and sizzled, opening pitch-pockets in the wood. The dogs' baying scrambled after shadows. And Viv sees those shadows flutter, black-plumed and black-beaked, just at the corners of her eyes. And hears their excited whisperings. And now feels the hand rotate tortuously until the tips of the fingers touch her throat. And does not move.

"What's happening now?" Lee asked with casual interest.

"Oh? Well, the fox—I reckon it's got to be a fox, the way they're moving around—he's cuttin' back an' forth, trying to back trail so's they won't pin him between the river an' the mouth of the slough. If he gets hemmed that way he'll have to tree or swim, an' there ain't any good holes or hollers down that direction an' lord does he hate to swim. If it was a coon he'd of cut 'cross the slough a long time ago, but fox don't want his bushy wet. An', over yonder, Molly . . . hm . . . she's moved back around the end of the slough and is cuttin' up to the high rocks. Hm. That ain't so good. But, listen . . ."

And she concentrates even harder on the sounds, already hearing far more than the old man. She hears the slough, the whistle and bell buoys, the last of the hillside flowers dying in the breeze—the drip of bleeding heart, the rattle of firecracker weed, the hiss of adder's tongue. Far off a fever of lightning takes a flash picture of Mary's Peak. She waits but hears no thunder. A curious breeze dashes out of the dark firs to rummage for a moment through the fire, then snatches her hair away from Lee's hand. A few strands blow into her mouth and she rolls them thoughtfully between her front teeth. Her wet boots begin to steam and she draws them back from the fire. She wraps her arms about her knees. The cold fingers against her neck move, growing hotter.

"Ah . . . what'll happen if he, if the fox, swims?" Lee asked his father.

"He swims the slough 'stead the river he'll be okay, but a lot of times they don't. Lot of times they head right 'cross the river; and that ain't so good for the dogs or fox neither one."

"Can't they make it?" Viv asks.

"Oh sure, honey. It ain't that far across. But somehow they get out in that water . . . and it's dark . . . and 'stead of going on across they swim with the current, swim and swim and never get to the other side, just keep right on agoin'. Listen . . . he's tryin' to make a run, cuttin' back to the north. That means they got him away from the slough and headed toward the river. They'll get him, ifn he don't swim."

The barking of the pack had reached a pitch that seemed way out of proportion to the size of the animal they were chasing—when compared to that relentless tolling of the lone dog after the much larger game.

"Keep right on agoin' to where?" Lee asked.

"To the ocean," Henry answered, "to the sea. Dang! Listen at the way them boogers are makin' over that pore little fox. Dirteaters!"

She feels that she should move from that touch—tend the coffee or something—but doesn't move. Henry listened to the pack's trailing with a displeased frown; this wasn't the way he liked to hear dogs work. They were making too big of some poor little runt of a fox. He leaned forward and spat his wad of tobacco into the coals as though it had turned suddenly bitter. He watched it sizzle and swell. "Sometimes," he mused, staring at the coals, "the salmon trollers pick up animals miles out to sea; deer, dogs, cats, lots of fox—just swimmin' around all by theirselves, miles and miles from shore." He picked up a stick and poked at the coals, deep in thought, seeming to have momentarily dismissed the hunt. "Once—oh, maybe thirty years ago, a good thirty years—I was workin' half-days on a crab boat. Get up about three an' go out an' help this old fart of a Swede haul up his crab pots." He held his hand out in the firelight. "Them scars there on my little finger? Them's crab bites, where the sonsabitches pinched me. Don't ever tell me crabs can't pinch. Anyhow, we was always running across animals swimmin' around out there. Foxes mainly, but some deer too. Generally the Swede would say leave 'em be, leave 'em be; 'No time to fool round, no time to fool round b'golly.' But this once we seen a great big buck deer, a real beauty, eight-nine points. And he says let's get that feller. So we get a line on him and haul him in. The Swede figures the buck's worth foolin' round b'golly because we can eat him, I suppose, so we get a line around his head and lug him on board. An' he just laid there. He was pretty nearly gone. Breathin' hard, rollin' his eyes scared to death the way deer do. But I don't know—not just scared. I mean it weren't like he was just scared of damn near drowning; or of bein' caught on a boat with people neither. Not that kind of just scared, as near as I could make out, but pure scared."

He jabbed at the fire, sending another fountain of sparks into the dark. Viv and Lee watched, waiting for him to go on. Feeling those sparks in her breast.

"Well, he looked so done in we didn't bother to tie him down. He was just layin' there sort of stunned an' so shot he didn't look like he could bat an eye. He laid there, didn't make a move till we got close to the beach on our way in; then, man alive, he was up and for a second there it was just hoofs and horns in *all* directions, then over the side. I thought at first the booger had just been *sullin'* till he got near enough to swim to shore. But that wasn't it. He turned *right around*, right into a incom' tide, and headed *right straight back out*, lookin' scared as ever. It kinda got me, you know? I'd always heard tell that deer and such went into the surf to kill the ticks and lice with salt water, then got swept out, but after seein' that buck I decided different, I decided there was more to it than bugs."

"More what?" Lee asked earnestly. "Why? Do you think—"

"Hell, boy I don't know *why*." He tossed the stick into the flames. "You got the education, I'm nothin' but a dumbass logger. I just know that I decided it didn't stand to reason a deer or bear—or say a fox, who's supposed to be a pretty smart customer—would drown hisself just to get shut of a few fleas. That's a purty stiff cure." He stood up and walked a few paces from the fire, brushing the front of his pants. "Uh-oh, listen there . . . they cut him off. They got the sucker now if he don't swim."

"What do you think, Viv?"

The slight pressing of fingers against her throat resumes. "Think about what?" She continues to stare thoughtfully into the fire, acting as though she is still drawn into the mood the old man has created.

"About this lemming instinct in certain animals. Why would a fox want to try to drown himself?"

"I didn't say they wanted to drown theirselfs," Henry remarked without turning around. He spoke in the direction of the barking dogs. "If it was just drownin' they was after they coulda done that in any pee hole or puddle. But they wasn't just drowning; they was swimming."

"Swimming to certain death," Lee reminded him.

"Might be. But that ain't drownin'."

"What else could it be? Even a human being has the intelligence to know that when he sets out deliberately swimming away—from the shore—that it is his obviously inten—" He stopped in midword. Viv feels the hand go bloodless and numb against her neck; startled, she turns to look at his face. There is no expression at all. For a moment he is gone from his face, as though he had fallen somewhere inward, away from her and the old man and the fire, into a remote pool of himself (However, as the evening turned out, everything worked for the best, and I gleaned from the experience a nice bagful of beneficial data which proved quite useful to me in experiences to come . . . ) until Henry interrupted him.

"It is his obvious what?"

"What? His obvious intention to not return . . . to the shore." (. . . the first bit of data concerned myself . . .) "So he, whatever he is, fox, deer, or despondent wino, *must* be intent on drowning himself."

"Might be, but look here: It's okay for the wino, but what's a old fox got to be so despondent about that he decides to cash it in?"

"The same thing! the same thing! (. . . and the witless depth into which I had allowed myself to be lulled since leaving the East . . .) "Don't you think a poor dumb beast has the ability to recognize the same cruel world as the drunk? Don't you think that fox down there has just as many demons to escape as the wino? I mean *listen* to that fox's demons. . . ."

Henry looked down at his son, puzzled. "That don't mean he's gotta drown himself, though. He could turn an' fight 'em."

"*All* of them? Isn't that just as certain as drowning? And more painful?"

"Might be," Henry answered slowly, deciding that, in as he couldn't figure the boy's goofy ways anyhow, he might as leave be amused by them. "Yes, might be. Like I said, you got the education. You're the *sharpie*, they tell me. But then *too*—" and with a nimble movement goosed Lee in the ribs with the cane —"that's what they allus told me about the *fox!* Yee haw . . ." He folded back to his seat on the sack, bawling his pleasure with Lee's violent reaction to the cane. "Yee haw haw haw! See him come outa his sull with a little prod there, Viv honey? See him hump up? Oh me: 'That's what they tell me about the fox.' Yee haw haw haw haw!"

. . . *Alone, under a needlepoint sky held up by the massive pillars of pine and fir, the dog Molly splashed through a narrow wash*

*beginning to ice at the edge with a lacy frill. She scrabbled up the*
*bank and thrust her muzzle into the fern and bushmonkey leaves,*
*dashing frantically to and fro after the lost scent; MOUSE MOUSE*
*DEER COON? MOUSE then bay-OOR BAYOOHR . . . ! In his*
*room Lee wonders how to include all the history that Peters will*
*need to make any sense of the situation.*

So very much . . . And I would apologize for my delay in writing
were I not convinced you would enjoy, much more than an apology, my
quaint explanation for this letter and the events that led up to it.
First, there was a great fox hunt during which I attempted to establish
contact with my brother's wife (you will understand why later, if
you aren't already guessing) and this chore left me somewhat unnerved. . . .

*And Viv, unnerved somewhat herself as she sits against her sack of*
*decoys with Lee's hand coming once more to life, wonders how to*
*stop the secret caressing without the old man's noticing, wonders if*
*she wants to stop it—*
"Say by golly, y' know?" Henry rolled his shoulders and watched
the braiding flames between the slits of his eyelids. "This brings to
mind, talkin' about fox hunts, a time some years back when Hank
was about ten or eleven or thereabouts an' Ben an' me took him
with us over to Lane County on a hunt that turned into a real doozer.
Y'see, there was this ol' boy over there we knowed that claimed he
had one *outstandin'* sharpie of a fox that he hadn't been able to
poison or trap or shoot, an' he would pay us five dollars cash to get
shut of the devil so's his pore poultry could get some rest nights . . ."
*—now she feels the hand slide further around beneath her hair to*
*cup her throat, fingers thin and soft beneath the new shell of calluses,*
*and Lee leans forward so his whispering is near her cheek:* "That first
day I met you, you remember? you had been crying—" "Shhh!"
"—and I still hear you cry at night sometimes . . ." *Oh! he can feel*
*that little vein there—*
"Now then, y'see, as I recollect it, little Hank, he'd raised from a
pup this young bluetick bitch—oh, about six or eight months old, a
nice little dog—an' Hank just thought the world of her. He'd took
her huntin' on his own a time 'r two, but never out with the whole
pack to show what she could really do. An' he thought this outstandin' fox was just the ticket . . ."
*—he must be able to feel how it throbs; why doesn't he stop?*

"Shh, Lee; Henry will notice. Besides, I hear you cry at night some-times, too." *Now the sparks race up to the dark! Like little fiery nightbirds—* "You do? maybe I should explain . . ." *—up and up and up and then gone, like little nightbirds—*

"But the things is, at just the time this ol' boy wanted us to come hunt down his fox, this bluetick bitch of Hank's she was right in the middle of heat an' havin' to be kept in the barn so's every mutt in the country wouldn't be after her. Hank, he still wanted to bring her along, sayin' that as soon's the hunt got goin' none the other dogs would pay any attention to her condition. But Ben, he says, 'Dammit, boy, don't try to tell your Uncle Ben about what a animal will frigging pay attention to and what he won't: those dogs would leave a whole *treeful* of foxes to mount that bitch of yours . . . I mean I *know* about these sorta things. . . .' an' Hank, he says that we didn't have to worry about *his* dog gettin' mounted, that she could outrun anything on four legs he didn't care *what* kind of at-tention it were payin' her . . ."

*—Henry is a nighthawk from behind, perched against the flames.* "Shh, Lee." "Don't worry about him, Viv—" *Doesn't he care if Henry hears?* "—he can't hear us; he's too wrapped up in his story." *Or doesn't he care to leave me alone so we can just watch the sparks, or listen to that faraway belling of that one lone dog* (scrabbling up loose dirt, sliding, leaning to corner a stump, a log up! *Molly soars over the deadfall in her path without breaking stride,* forepaws folded back against her scratched and bleeding breastbone, ears spreading for the jump like nicked wings; at the peak of her jump, across weightless expanse of brush, she saw him for the first time since he had broken through the pack—a round wobbling black ball flecked with the glisten of moonlight, boring ahead through the wet fern: bay-OO-OO-OOHRR!—then stretched forth her paws to catch the jar of earth running again) *that one baying dog so far away and so beautiful . . . doesn't he care?* "Viv, listen to me, please." "Shh, I'm listening to Henry's story."

"But Ben he says, 'Henry, I don't know as I'd let that boy bring that Jezebel along an' that's the truth—we'd be watchin' a rape instead of a hunt.' But Hank he says we just gotta let him bring her 'cause there won't be another hunt or another fox like this for her to learn on in years!"

*—the hand presses, slight desperate pressure:* "But I have to talk to you—to somebody . . . please. And I might not have another

chance." *But doesn't he feel that pounding there?* "No, Lee, don't . . ."

"Well, we fussed and fussed about it for a spell and anyhow what happened is Hank talked Ben into lettin' him bring her along just for the trip, just so's she could *watch* the hunt, not even run in it —an' Ben says all right. 'But listen here,' Ben says, 'you keep that whore up front in the cab with us on the trip over—sit her in your lap or something, just don't put her in back with all the other hounds; they'd be so rundown with screwing her that by the time we got across the hills to the hunt they wouldn't be able to see nothing but tail, or trail nothing but cunt! Assuming they had the strength left to run a trail at all . . . .' "

—*she tries to stop her ears against the words at her cheek*—"I must tell you something, Viv. About Hank, what I was planning to do. And why"—*against the needle-sharp hook of pain she senses lurking beneath the words, tugging at her flesh;* "It all started a long time ago . . ." *But in spite of her efforts to stop the words she can feel some of the need getting through: he doesn't need me that much, he couldn't*—

"So Hank's bitch rode up front all the way over, sitting in his lap. We got there an' it was just comin' daylight, I recall, sun was just comin' up. An' there was another fella there an' he had him six or seven dogs. An' when they saw how we's all favorin' Hank's bluetick— I mean had her up in his arms by god—they wanted to know what kinda damned animal we had that had to be treated so special. Hank says, 'The best goddamned animal of its kind in the state.' This feller with the other dogs, he winks at me an' says, 'Why, we'll just see about that!' An' goes into his pocket for his wallet and lays a ten-dollar bill on the car fender an' says, 'Right, here we go, sport. Ten to one. Ten dollars to your buck, my old *brake*-legged *beat*-up mongrel here finds that fox before your pedigree.' An' points over at his dog, about the finest-lookin' walker I ever see in my life with three or four these Kennel Club badges from field trials on his collar. Hank starts to eat pie about then an' say he can't let his dog run because of a game leg or some such an' this guy gives him the horse laugh an' brings out another ten-dollar bill an' plunks it down an' says, 'All right, *twenty* to one an' I'll hold my fleafarm *back* the count of fifty.' Hank, he looks up there at me an' I just shrug on account it's Ben's pick-up an' Ben's hunt, an' Hank's about to have him another slice of humble pie when Ben comes over an' puts a buck on the fender an'

says, 'You're on, old buddy.' An' this fella like to dropped his teeth
out. I mean a *fifty-count lead!* Lordymercy, that's way out yonder for
a dog even if she *is* in heat an' inexperienced! So this ol' boy has
talked himself into a bind. He swallers a time or two but he ain't
about to eat some of his own cookin', so he gives Ben a hard look an'
says all right . . ."

*—and as this need grows more intense so does a sensation of move-*
*ment, speed to come, impending declaration*—"The past is funny,
Viv; it never seems to let things lie, finished. It never seems to stay
in place as it should"—*until she feels that she is beginning to run*
*down an ever steepening hill and she must stop before the hill gets*
*too steep and she gets going too fast to stop: Oh. Look! A bit of the*
*moon; how pretty—*

"So we go on over through this fence to the other ol' boy's, the
farmer's, barn, an' he says we can drive most the way up this gully if
the fox runs that way, which he's like to do. An' he says we ought'n'
have no trouble picking up his trail 'cause he's all around the hen-
house every night. So Hank takes his dog on over to the fence and sics
her onto the scent 'n' off she goes sure enough at a real smart clip,
too. This fellow, he goes over there to the fence with his dog and fires
him up while Hank counts. Then off he goes! and a little bit after
that we let all the rest of 'em loose just to be shut of 'em. So this
fellow got in the pick-up with us an' we took out up this road *and I*
*swear we run them dogs for hours* in this little bitty ole canyon not
much bigger'n our own front porch. *Over an' around an' back an'*
*forth.* I told Ben, I says, 'That by god *is* about the smartest fox I ever
seen. How that bastard can keep ahead o' them dogs *this long without*
*treein'*—in a little bitty place like this—hell, I bet they wasn't a rod
o' area—little bitty stream—an' he just *kept goin'!*"

*—She lets her eyes unfocus. Look. That stick of spruce has feathers*
*of flame, spanning.* "And some things out of the past kept troubling
the present, *my* present . . . so much so that I felt I had to eliminate
the past, to *destroy* it. That's one reason for my tears in the night."
*But crying isn't really so different from singing. Sure. Or from that*
*dog's baying.* (Molly clawed spraddle-legged up the face of the rock
toward the sucking black hole where the bear had gone. She fell, unable to grasp the lip of the cavern as the bear had. She bayed and
leaped again, but this time skittered off sideways down between a
boulder and the rock wall, into a narrow stone slot squirming with
dark. She wrenched free, still baying, and ran to leap again. But felt

a sudden, searing weight at her hip hauling her back, jerking her back from the rock like a red-hot leash driven into her hipbone) *And crying doesn't always mean need—*

"Well, just like we was scared he'd do, the fox finally made a dash for it. We was up to one end of the canyon when we heard the dogs turn an' double back past us toward the farm. We swung the pick-up around an' headed after 'em, Ben at the wheel just apourin' it to her. We knew we had to keep purty good track after they passed the mouth of the canyon where the farm was, 'cause out past that was a lotta rivers an' roads an' stuff where they might run for days. So when we get to the farm at the mouth of the canyon we wheel up to the fence an' that ol' farmer that owns the place, he's standin' there lookin' after that pack of animals where they're foggin' it up the road to beat thunder. . . ." *But, oh, I wish he would please leave me alone.* . . . "And soon's we stop ol' Ben jumps out an' hollers an' asts the farmer, 'Say! was that them come right past here jest now?' And this old boy, this farmer says, 'It shore was.' And Ben jumps back into the pick-up, about to head on out after 'em, when just then Hank—it seems like he was in the back; must of been in the back, I guess, that other fellow we'd made the bet with was up in the cab with Ben an' me—when Hank says wait and hollers, 'Where was my dog runnin'? My bluetick?' The farmer, he kinda grins and says, 'The young bitch? Why, she was runnin' out in front, naturally.' An' this gets a rise outa the *other* old boy—him and his fifty bucks he stands to lose—an' he says, 'Did you see what position my *walker* was runnin'?' An' the farmer nods an' says, 'Why yessir, I did. Your dog was runnin' a good close third, just about neck-and-neck with the *fox!* With the fox!* Yee haw haw . . .'" The old man reared back and beat again at the fire with his stick. "Yee haw haw haw . . . neck-and-neck with the boogin' fox, y'see? Ben'd been right: hounds, fox an' all had all been so interested in a little nooky they'd the whole bunch of 'em been the livelong night runnin' the tail offn that pore little bluetick! Yee haw! Ben teased Hank about it for months, sayin' she'd probably whelp a litter of blueticks with big red fox bushtails! Oh me . . . oh haw haw haw!"

The old man shook his head, then pushed himself standing with the cane. Still chortling at his anecdote, he walked to the edge of the firelight; when Lee heard him peeing into the dry vetch he went on with his furtive whispering.

"So do you see, Viv? It's been like that all my life. Smothered.

Until I finally could see no reason to—to keep trying to breathe. Not that he was entirely to blame by any means, but I felt that unless I was *just once* able to have something over him, to beat him out of something, that I could never breathe. And that's when I decided—"

Lee ceased abruptly. He saw that she was not even listening—maybe had *never been* listening!—but was staring off into the dark as though in a trance. —*what's happened? Does he really need? Oh, it's the dog* (. . . Molly opened her mouth to bay but her tongue stuck hot to her teeth, and she fell back again); *she's stopped*—Not listening at all! She hadn't heard a word! In anger and humiliation he jerked his hand from her throat where she—where he had thought she had encouraged him by allowing the fingers to slip far into the neck of the shirt . . . just to let him make a fool of himself!

Startled by the abruptness of his action, Viv turned toward him questioningly, just as old Henry came back into the ring of firelight.

"Listen: that Molly dog, you notice? She's hushed. I ain't heard her call in a good while now." He was quiet a moment to let them listen, not quite trusting his own ears. (*The bear's shiny black eyes appeared in the moonlight over the rock, his face quizzical, almost regretful as he watched the dog. Fired by a thirst near to panic, she fled back down the ridge, seeking the wash she remembered.*) Convinced that they were hearing nothing he wasn't, Henry cast an expert's eye down the slope and decided, "That bear, he either lost her or he run her off, one of the two." He pulled his watch from his pocket, tipped it toward the fire, and made believe he could read it. "Well, that's the show as far as this nigger is concerned. I ain't about to sit up here and listen to them other dirteaters carry on about a little ol' fox. Sounds like they just about got him, anyhow. I'm gonna head on back is what. You kids suppose you'll come or stay a while?"

"We'll stay a while longer," Lee supposed for both of them, and added, "To wait for Hank and Joe Ben."

"Suit yourself." He took up his cane. "But they're liable to be a good stretch yet an' then some. G'night." He faded from the light, stiff and weaving, like an old ghost of a tree haunting the midnight forest in search of his stump.

Watching him leave, Lee chewed nervously at his glasses—good; now there would be no more reason for this spy-movie dialogue; they could just talk . . . *God, when he's gone, I'll have to talk!*—and waited for the sounds of his departure to cease.

. . . .*Molly half ran, half rolled back down the ridge. By the time she*

*found the wash again her hide was haired in flame, her tongue melt-ing—HOT HOT MOON HOT—and the thing hooked to her hind leg as big as leg itself now. Bigger. Bigger than her whole burning body.*
—As soon as the old man's crashing and cursing disappears down the dark hillside, Viv turns back to Lee, still with that startled, uncomprehending expression, waiting for an explanation of his violent withdrawal. And an explanation for the touch in the first place. His face is rigid. He has stopped chewing on the eyeglasses and he's taken a twig from the fire and is blowing on the end of it. His face. The cupping shield of his hand hides a glowing ember, but still . . . each time he blows his features are lighted from within by something a whole lot hotter than a spark on a twig. Like something inside there burning to get out, something burning, it needs so bad to get out. "What is it?" She reaches to touch his arm; he gives a short, bitter laugh and tosses the twig back into the fire.

"It's nothing. I'm sorry. For the way I acted. Forget what I was saying. I sometimes have these spells of compulsive truth. But as Lady Macbeth would say, 'The fit is momentary.' Regard me not. It's not your fault."

"But *what's* not my fault? Lee, what were you trying to tell me, before old Henry left? I don't understand . . ."

At her question he turns and regards her with amused wonder, smiling at his own thoughts. "Of course. I don't know what I was thinking of. Of course it isn't your fault." (Yet, as it turned out, it was very much her fault—) Tenderly, he touches her cheek, her neck where his fingers had rested, reaffirming something. . . . "You didn't know; how could you know?" (—though I had no way of knowing this at the time.)

"But didn't know *what?*" She feels she should be angry for the way he speaks to her and for—for the other things. . . . *But that awful burning hunger behind his eyes!* "Lee, please explain—" *Don't explain! Leave me alone; I can't be everybody's something!* "What was it you started to confess?" Lee walked back to sit by the fire. . . . *Molly dragged her body into the crackling water. She tried to drink and vomited again. Finally she stretched out on her belly, only her eyes and gasping muzzle above the surface: HOT HOT COLD cold moon MOONS HOT HOT HOT HOT . . .* He situated himself on the sack so he was facing her and took her hands between his. "Viv, I'll try to explain; I need to explain to somebody."

He spoke slowly, watching her face.

"When I lived here, as a child, I thought Hank was the biggest thing created. I thought he knew everything, was everything, *had* everything in this whole waterlogged world . . . except one particular thing that was mine. What this one thing is, was, doesn't matter—think of it as an abstract thing, like a feeling of importance, or sense of self—it only matters that I needed it, as any kid needs something all his own, *all*, and I thought I had it, forever, never to be taken from me . . . and then I thought he took it away. Do you follow me?"

He waited until she nodded that she understood—*his eyes softer now, tender, the way his hands were; but still the burning*—then went on.

"So I tried to get it back—this thing. I mean I needed it *more* than he did, Viv. But I found . . . even after I had it . . . that he was too much for me. It was never mine again, never all mine. Because I couldn't . . . ever take his place. See? I wasn't big enough to take his place." He released her hands and removed his glasses and massaged the bridge of his nose with thumb and finger (my failure to Come Clean that evening I blamed, of course, on Hank—) sitting in silence for a long moment before he continued. (—though I know now that she was as much at fault as my brother, or as myself, or as any of the other half-dozen principals in the plot, dead and alive. But at the time I was capable of no such painful insights, and quickly blamed the about-face I made in my march toward Brotherly Love on the brother I was marching to love, on my brother and on the Tin Pan Alley moon and his old hack magic . . .)

"And never being big enough to take his place left me no place of my own, left me no one to be. I wanted to be someone, Viv, and there seemed only one way to do it—"

"Why are you telling me this, Lee?" Viv asked suddenly, in a fearful voice barely louder than the breeze rustling the dry flowers behind her. Her voice seemed to come from a great, empty cavern. She was reminded of the hollow weight that had grown inside her when she had tried to give Hank a live baby. The memory filled her with nausea. —*He wants something from me. He doesn't know that the only thing I have left is the hollow of something gone*— "What are you telling me for?"

He looked back up at her without putting his glasses back on. He had been ready to go on by telling her how his whole return home had been motivated by the desire for revenge, how he planned to use her as an instrument in the revenge, how he had realized the error of his ways because of his growing fondness for all of them . . . but now he was stymied by her question: Why was he telling her? what reason had he to tell anyone, except, "I don't know, Viv; I just needed someone to talk to. . . ." (Not that she did anything antagonistic toward me—it certainly wasn't that—her blame lies in the way she tossed her hair back from her face, in the softness of her throat and the shine of firelight on her cheekbones . . .)

"But Lee, we're hardly good friends; there's Hank, or Joe Ben—"

"Viv, I needed you, not Hank or Joe Ben. I can't . . . look, I couldn't tell them the things I can tell—"

Something sounded in the darkness. Lee stopped, relieved momentarily by the distraction. Then from the direction of the slough bottom came a drawn-out "Heayoo-ooo . . ." and his relief turned to disappointment. "Damn. That's Joe Ben. They're coming back." He made a desperate calculation. "Viv, listen; let me meet you tomorrow, please, and finish this. Let me talk to you somewhere alone tomorrow."

"What do you mean?"

"Hey! I already have your invitation, if you remember right. To dig clams?"

"Rock oysters. But I was just kidding with you."

"I'm not kidding now. Meet me . . . where? On the jetty at the beach, was that it?"

"But why, Lee? You still haven't told me why."

"Because. I need to talk with somebody. With you. Please . . ."

She put on her teasing face. "Why, suh, a lady o' mah position—"

"Viv! I'm asking you . . . I need you!"

The hand swung her facing him, gripping her wrist demandingly; but her attention did not fasten this time on his fingers, or even on the eyes gripping with the same demanding pressure, but beyond the fingers, behind the eyes, where . . . she can see the concentrated strain of his need to be, see the agonizing, stiff labor of unfolding, of opening, of trying to proclaim, This is me! "Viv, please?"—like the efforts of a dark, diseased flower, too long in the bud, struggling to unfurl its crippled petals before a last-chance sun. And, watching, feels that desperate blooming draw for the air and water and light that was her bounty, feels it at the same time swelling to try to fill that icy bubble beneath her breasts. —Maybe. Maybe that is it. Maybe the hollow is not something gone, but something not given! "Viv, hurry . . . will you?" This is me, the flower pleads, drawing, and she feels herself just beginning to fly toward answering that plea when the vetch pods rattle the dark behind them and Hank shouts, "Here ya go; ornament for the aerial!" —and she flew instead to throw her arms about her husband, bloody foxtail and all. "Hank! Oh, you're back."

"Yeah, I'm back. But easy, I ain't been gone a month, you know."

Leaving Lee to kneel and hide his disappointment in the chore of tending the coffee. He bit his cheeks over the blurred sight of the girl forsaking him so quickly to run to the mighty hunter—(The dumb cow! I should have had more sense than to expect her to understand anything except how to run mooing to her bull)—and cursed the smoke making his eyes burn so. (Yet, taking everything into consideration, I still deem it a very interesting evening with some very interesting results: first, while the old man muttered and masticated beside us, and Hank and Joe Ben and the hounds chased smaller animals in the slough bottom, Viv and I had a most pleasant chat and seeded a relationship destined to bear a very tasty fruit for me later; and second, the excitement of the hunt prompted brother Hank to get even drunker later that evening, enough so to shake loose his hold on the mean streak he had been hiding since my arrival (also, I think he saw Viv and me getting a bit too cozy at the campfire for his liking) and he tried to provoke a fistfight with me back at the house, called me a "pantywaist" and other endearing terms when I refused to indulge him, and thereby snapped me out of my sentimental somnolence and put me back on my road to revenge once more after much time lost dawdling; and last, as well as foremost, the detailed scheme that I fictionalized to have ready for my Clean Breast of It All proved precisely the plan I had been searching for. A scheme meeting all the requirements: safe enough to pass the cautionary restrictions set up by Old Reliable WATCH OUT AT ALL TIMES; certain enough of success to give my workworn body the patience to last out the few weeks necessary to the plan's completion; diabolic enough to sooth my every mangled memory and vindicate each outraged obsession; and potent enough to stir up a spell capable of transforming a giant into a mewling babe . . . and vice versa.)

Viv realized too late how overdone her greeting had been, and looked to Hank to see if he suspected anything—*There is nothing to suspect, though; Lee was just talking, and not even making sense; I barely heard*—Hank was looking about the firelit area with a puzzled frown.

"I thought the old man was here," he remarked, watching her nervously.

"Henry just this minute left," Viv said.

"Most of the dogs are still out," Hank told them, coming to warm his hands at the fire. "On another fox, the way it sounds. But I thought I'd check here before we did anything else. Old Molly show up back here?"

"Hank doesn't care for the way she hushed so fast," Joe Ben explained gravely.

"We haven't seen her," Lee said. "Henry's conclusion was the bear either scared her off or lost her."

"Henry's full of beans. Molly ain't about to be scared off by any animal. Just about as unlikely, too, that she'd lose a trail hot as that one sounded. That's why her hushing so sudden worries me. Any of the other dogs, it might not. But Molly's too much dog to just hush like that unless she got into it some way."

The weeds rustled. "Here's Uncle and Dolly's Pup," Joe announced as two dogs slunk guiltily into the firelight, like criminals throwing themselves on the mercy of the court. "Little-bitty fox," Joe scolded, then, hands on his hips. "Chasin' a poor little-bitty fox . . . Why didn't you help out with that bear? Huh?"

Uncle slunk on into the shack and Dolly's Pup rolled onto her back as though her exposed undersides would explain the whole thing.

"What do you plan to do?" Viv asked.

"One of us ought to go look for her," Hank said without enthusiasm. More dogs were coming into sight now. "You all take the dogs, except Uncle, to the house; I'll take him on a leash and walk up toward the ridge."

"No!" Viv said quickly, holding onto his arm. They all looked at her in surprise. "Well, you'll be gone all night. She'll be all right. Come on to the house, now."

"What . . . ?"

*They stand, radiating out from the fire. A breeze shakes the weeds; and Lee shivers, hating her, hating them all.*

"Come on now. . . . Please?"

"I'll go look," Joe Ben volunteered. "I'm still up rearin', and Jan's asleep. Shoot, I'll find that dog in no time."

Hank was skeptical. "Last I heard her was east, up in the direction of Stamper Creek; you sure you want to head off up there by yourself?"

"You talk like I'm scared of ghosts or somethin'."

"Ain't you?"

"Goodness, no. C'mon, Uncle; we'll show 'em who's scared an' who ain't."

Hank grinned. "Right sure now? It's terrible dark, and remember what day it is now . . . last of October . . ."

"Foo. We'll find her. You go on back to the house."

Hank started to further tease his cousin but was stopped by the pressure of Viv's nails in his arm. "All right," he agreed hesitantly, then winked at Joe. "I don't know *how* come it is but every time the woman here gets a little sniff of alcohol she wants to celebrate."

Joe took a sandwich and a cup from the knapsack. "Oh yeah." He nodded out at the night beyond the fire. "No tellin' what a perceptive man's liable to find out yonder first wee small hours of Halloween day. *All* manner of things."

But once the others had left, his enthusiasm cooled quickly. "Dark, ain't it, Uncle," he confided to the dog tied to the shack. "Well, you ready?" When the dog didn't answer Joe decided to have another cup of the burned coffee, hunkering over the coals with the tin cup steaming between his hands. "Quiet, too. . ."

Though it was neither. The moon found holes in the clouds with skilled agility, making the forest glisten with frost, and the night animals, as though sensing their last chance of the year, were having a session equal to the event. The tree toads sang bright good-bys before burrowing into their nice snug mud; the shrews darted about the paths, uttering shrill squeaks of last-minute hunger; the killdeers flew jerkily from meadow to meadow, calling, "*Dee! Dee! Dee*," with clear, sweet, reassuring optimism about the state of this beautiful frosty night.

Joe Ben was not reassured; in spite of his show of bravery before Hank, rain or shine, fair or foul, daytime was his time. And the forest at night might be beautiful, but if it was dark how was a man to know that?

So he put off the search for the missing dog for one cup of coffee after another. Not that he was scared of the woods after dark—there wasn't a beast produced by all the northern wilds that Joe Ben would have hesitated tackling, barehanded, with every confidence of winning, day or night—it was that, some way or other, alone at night, with the prospect of walking up to Stamper Creek he got to thinking about his father. . . .

After a long time Molly moves, trying to stand in the shallow water. Most of the fire in her hips is out now. And the pain is numbed by the cold. And it is no longer unpleasant to lie in the water. But if she does not go home now she knows she never will. She falls a lot at first. Then she begins feeling her limbs again and stops falling. She frightens a possum right in her path. The animal hisses and rolls to its side, twitching. She walks past without sniffing it . . .

Because if there was ever ghosts in this world, then old Ben Stamper's ghost walked those woods out there right now, Joe was sure. It didn't cut ice whether that ghost happened to be solid or not—Joe had never feared harm from the corporeal side of his father—even when the man was alive. Ben had never threatened his young with physical violence. It might have been better if he had; the threat of violence can be escaped by simply getting out of range of it . . . but the threat Joe had felt it necessary to escape was the dark portent he had seen stamped into his father's face—like an expiration date stamped into a borrowed book—and since Joe carried the same face he had felt stamped with the same portent; changing the face had been the only way to change the stamp. "All right, Uncle, hush your whining; this one more cup and we'll have a look." So wouldn't it be a pity to be wandering around and it so dark that you couldn't see the change?

. . . She comes to the log she had jumped so easily before; now she drags her body over it, a leaden piece at a time: COLD. Cold little moon. Cold and hot and a long way. . . .

Joe cut himself a nice pitchy pine bough and shoved it down in to the fire. When it was blazing brightly he untied the dog and started off down the trail, leaning back against Uncle's pull. But those pine boughs don't work like they do in the moving pictures with the villagers out by the hundreds storming through the woods after some kind of monster that nabs the first guy without a torch and pinches his head off like a grape! Ten minutes later Joe was back firing up his torch again . . .

Hard and cold and small as a stone. Could just lie down. On the soft moss there. Sleep there. No . . .

This time he tied Uncle's rope to his belt and carried two boughs, one in each hand. And lasted twenty minutes.

Or under the tree in the pine needles. Tired and cold and burning a long way. Sleep for a long time . . . No . . .

The third time Joe and Uncle made it as far as the slough bottom.

The moon feinted this way and that, trying for a shot past the clouds. A beam of light threaded down through the trees and found a shrew ripping to pieces a frog twice its size, spotlighting them as though they were the main attraction of the evening. Uncle took one look and made a lunge that jerked Joe Ben free of his torches. They hissed to darkness in the deep, wet fern . . . *in the pine needles for a long time lie down, just sleep and not be cold or HOT ever again. No . . .* And it's black. At the house Viv cries with a feeling of terrific and uncomprehending release, trying to understand what has just happened between Hank and Lee downstairs. Hank fumes angrily in the kitchen with a beer. Lee stands at his window, looking out across the river. "Where are you, moon? You and all your nonsense about magic macaroons? I'd like a word with you, if you don't mind. . . ."

"Uncle! Father! Jesus!" Joe Ben stood petrified while Uncle consumed shrew and frog both. He tried some scripture— "Be thou a light unto my lamp,"—but it just didn't satisfy. Not when there was *. . . something out there!* something always out there big and black and waiting to pull you under . . . *where the MOON won't burn any more and the COLD and heavy hips won't drag. No . . . No!* Viv stops crying and turns to confront her room, where it seems she hears a mocking black-crow laugh somewhere behind her. There is just the empty cage. Old Henry, up in his bed, fights to whip a shadow with a knife in its boot, young, and nimble, and twice as elusive as usual because he dodges in and out of the years, first in the past then in the future where Henry can't even see the cheating young sonofabitch! And Lee finds his hack-magic moon hiding sheepishly behind a crackling cloud: I spat a contemptuous oath in his direction: *that* for your hearts and flowers and bury-the-hatchet baloney! And that for your dose of Alice's Patented Pituitary Stimulants you conned me into swallowing with a mouthful of cream—nothing but carnival hokum, medicine-show quackery that leaves a man worse off than he started!

Uncle began to whine at standing still so long, and Joe booted him in the rump to shut him up. The moon flashed off and on, signaling; in the mountains to the east silent lightning answered. Uncle whined again. "Shut up, dog! We're all in this thing together, every one of us. He's out there!" *HEAVY heavy COLD cold tired easy in the pine needles never cold any more. No! Yes; rest . . .* and Joe stood listening down into his fear for the booted tread of the man who never could walk the woods quietly—"But he won't come after me, the devil; he knows; he's waiting for me to come to him!"—and heard only the wind in the frosted red alder leaves. Lee turned from his window, leaving the moon and its medicine: *I was going back to good old Shazam or its equivalent. Maybe the right magic word was harder to find than the right magic macaroon, but let's face it, moon; those carbohydrates and polysaturates may put on weight and sweeten the disposition, but they've never been known to create instantaneous biceps of steel. I want power from my magic, not a pastry paunch. And lightning is one hell of a lot more powerful than leavening.*

That lightning left a taste of pennies and a slight ringing in the air. Joe swallowed the taste and stretched his neck forward to hear the ringing better. "Uncle! You hear that? You hear something just then?" . . . *and it's heavy heavy cold easy yes WHAT? yes just rest . . . hear WHAT?*

Down from the hill it came again, a thin, keen whistle that rose sharply at the end like a curved brush-cutting knife. "That's Hank at the shack!" Joe exclaimed. "Let's go meet him, Uncle, let's go!" Jubilant, they trotted back up the path in the direction of the sound as though the way had suddenly become brightly lit with flood-lights . . . *yes WHAT? Molly lifts her muzzle from her paws and turns her head stiffly toward the sound of Hank's WHISTLE WHAT? The air around smells heavy with BEAR, but the smell is not right now. This is the smell where the BEAR had first made a STAND. Right here. And she has run him. The WHISTLE cuts through the dark to her again WHAT? HIM? she pushes her front quarters up, and the one good hind leg, and starts WALKing once more HIM YES . . . WALK. As Lee prepares his writing tablet and rolls his three small cigarettes: "Dear Peters . . ." and Viv doesn't understand, doesn't understand . . .*

Hank was sitting on the sack of decoys, smoking, when Joe Ben came into the firelight. "Why, I sure didn't expect to hear you whistlin' at the night," Joe called jauntily. "I thought you'd be sawin' wood down there a long time ago. Oh yeah. I mean *I* woulda. Nearly dozed off just walkin' around . . ."

"No sign of Molly?" Hank continued to stare into the coals.

"Not hide ner hair. An' I combed the Stamper Creek territory high an' low." He took a deep breath to stop his panting, lest Hank know he'd run all the way back to the fire, and walked to tie Uncle back to the shack, watching Hank stare at the fire. . . . "An' what's gnawing your bones?" he wanted to know.

Hank leaned back, lacing his fingers about one knee. He squinted against the smoke of his cigarette. "Oh . . . me an' the kid kinda got into it."

"Oh, no, why?" Joe asked reproachfully, then suddenly recalling how fast Viv and the boy had jumped apart when they showed up, asked, "What about . . . ?"

"What about don't matter. Shit. Some little unimportant argument about music. That ain't it."

"It's too bad, too bad. You know? You and him been hittin' it off so good. After that first day, I said to myself, 'This here maybe was a mistake.' But then the ice thawed and everybody was goin' along and—"

"No," Hank told the fire. "We weren't hittin' it off that good. Not really. We just wasn't fightin'. . . ."

"You didn't fight now, did you?" Joe asked, afraid he'd missed something. "I mean a fist-feet-and-fur-flyin' fight?"

Hank continued to stare at the settling fire. "No, we didn't fly any fur. Just yelled back and forth some." He sat up and spat his cigarette into the coals. "But, by God, I think that right there is the bone that sticks in both our craws. Maybe that right there is the real thing that always keeps us from hitting it off. . . ."

"Yeah?" Joe Ben yawned, getting closer to the fire. "What's that?" He yawned again; it had been a full day and a fuller night for Joe.

"That we didn't fight. That he won't, and I know it and he knows it. Maybe that right there is the thing keeps us just like oil and water."

"That back East livin' is made a coward out of him." Joe's eyes had closed, but Hank didn't seem to notice.

"No, he's no coward. Or he wouldn't come on to where somebody's gonna bust teeth out for him someday. No. It ain't that he's a coward . . . even though he might think he is. He's big enough he knows he ain't gonna get too bad a lickin' even if he was whipped. I used to see him in grade school take crap off kids half his size, kids he knew couldn't whip him. . . . But even when he knows he ain't gonna get whipped, he acts like he knows he can't win neither!"

"That's right, that is right. . . ." Joe's head was beginning to wobble.

"He acts like . . . he don't have any reason, ever any reason, to fight."

"Maybe he don't."

"If Lee don't"—Hank stared into the fire—"then there's *nobody* does."

The vetch rattled and Uncle growled. Something moved at the edge of the light. Hank leaped to his feet. *TIRED tired cold but HIM!* The dog seemed to have two tails, issuing from hindquarters swollen large enough to handle even another two.

"Oh Jesus! There's a snake got her!"

*She tries to snap at them when they pick her up. She doesn't remember who they are. They are all part of it now. Like the MOON and the FIRE, and the LOG and the BEAR, all HOT COLD DARK in her fevered confusion, and part of the same big ENEMY the way the WATER has become part, and REST; even SLEEP . . .*

It is late. The big clock-in-a-horse ticks soulfully. With the station off the air, Indian Jenny's father can only sit and watch the blank screen that pulses before him like a filmed blue-white eye. Gradually from the eye troops a ragged line of disorderly memories and myths. They begin circling a pine-knot fire burning for sixty years. And finally sit where they please, overlapping each other like transparent years snipped from a cellophane calendar. "Once upon a time," says the milkstoned eye, and everyone leans to listen . . .

Henry bickers fitfully with a young shadow from the past. Lee strikes a match, fascinated. Molly whines, out of her head, in something's carrying arms. At the Wakonda Hotel, in the room they share, Ray and Rod haggle past midnight over the expenses they have incurred since coming to work for Teddy. Ray is trying to whistle Hank Thompson's guitar intro to "A Jewel Here on Earth," but he is sleepy and edgy and the wienies Rod boiled for supper on the hot plate, being so unruly in his stomach, make it hard for him to get the right tone. Suddenly he stops whistling and flings the handful of papers he has been reading into the basket.

"Fuck it! Fuck it all!"

"Take it easy, man! it's just this strike." Rod tries to soothe his friend. "Face it, man, until this motherin' *strike* is settled and there's more cash running loose, maybe we should take off to Eureka and make some bucks at your brother's parking lot. What do you think?"

Ray is staring at the battered guitar case showing from beneath his bed. Finally he holds up his hands and looks them over. "I don't know, man," he says. "Let's face it; neither of us is getting any younger. Sometimes I feel like just, oh . . . fuck it!"

At the dock in front of the old house Hank lays the unconscious dog in the boat and stands up. "Do me a favor, Joby; drive her to the vet's for me . . . ?"

Joe is surprised and suddenly wide awake. "What? I mean all right, but—"

"I want to cover the bank foundation tonight."

"*Again?* Why, you gonna check that foundation to death."

"No. It's just . . . Those clouds worry me."

"Well . . . okay." And, leaving Hank on the dock, as he guides the boat across the dark river, with his face in a bemused frown, like a scar over scars . . . Joe finds he is worried also—about something more than clouds, but not sure what.

Old Henry, in his rumbling bed, tosses and turns and talks to bygone beauties while his false teeth watch from their glass of water by his bedside. Viv hugs her pillow in the dark, wondering why isn't he coming to bed—tonight! to her! now!—and remembers spending night after night alone in her bed full of dolls "Way up yonder, top of the sky . . ." while her parents were away with the truck selling produce in Denver or Colorado Springs, and the dark room full of dolls' ears listening to every note: ". . . *blue jay lives in a silver eye.*" Joe climbs the stairs, already asleep and dreaming. Jan waits like a lump in a room full of lumpy sleeping bags, too shy in her flannel-nightgown sleep to entertain even the dimmest of dreams. Hank stands on the dock, rubbing his palms nervously up and down his thighs, lips tight. Lee sits wide awake on his bed with his shoes off, relighting his little cigarette and looking down at his long outburst of writing . . .

I would apologize for my delay in writing were I not convinced you would enjoy, much more than an apology, my quaint explanation for this letter: I have just come up to my room after a grisly hassle with Brother Hank, (do you recall? I think you made acquaintance with his ectoplasmic counterpart in a coffee house in the village) and I decided it would only be fair to give my nerve endings the solace of a joint. The pot was safe where I had secured it—cuddled in a cold cream jar at the bottom of the shaving kit Mona gave me—but where the bleeding papers: pot without papers, man, what kind of funny shit is *that?* It is beer without an opener. It is opium without a pipe. Our thermosed lives are, at best, nine-tenths of the time padded by vacuum and sealed by silvered silicon, but, for all their artificiality, we are generally able to find means for unstoppering them now and then, and enjoy at least some portion of addlepated freedom. Are we not? I mean, even the most square moral-ridden and socially-middled saddle-brow manages at *some* moment to drink enough to pop his stopper and enjoy a romp in the primroses. And that just with crude booze. So *how* can something so hip as a Pond jar full of pot be cursed to unfulfilled frustration by a lack of papers?

I rant, I rave with frustration. I even consider rolling it in magazine paper. Then . . . a flashbulb of remembrance; my wallet! Of course; didn't I put a pack of zig-zag gummed wheatstraws in my wallet that night we all got so zonked at Jan's and the three of us composed that immortal children's classic *Fuckleberry Hen?* I quick to my trousers and feel for my wallet. Ah. Ah yes. There are the papers, and there the typed story still folded about them—"See. See Rooster Booster run. See him jump Fuckleberry Hen. See him jam it in. Jam, jam, jam."—and what else flits out of the little package and flutters to the floor like a dying moth? A scrap of lipsticked Kleenex on which is written Peters' department phone number. I sigh. I languish with memories. Good old Peters . . . back there enjoying the good academic life. Hmm . . . y'know, do the tortured soul good to commune with him. I believe I shall drop him a line.

So, I transcribe here that line (if this damned unreliable ball-point pen stops skipping) while I blow up the three joints I have rolled. *Three,* I hear him gasp, *three* joints? Alone up in his room? Three?

Yes, three, I answer calmly. For after this particular day I feel entitled to the 1st, I want the 2nd and oh God I *need* the 3rd! The 1st is a just payment for being good and working hard. The 2nd for enjoyment. The 3rd is to remind me to never never never again be duped into believing anything but the worst of one's relatives. As a variation of W. C. Fields' great truth, How can anyone who likes dogs and little children be anything *but* all bad?

First, as I fire up number one, I will give you what brief history I can afford: since the day I fled the realm of the mind for that of the muscle I have been  cursed by having to pay homage to the wounds of both: physically, I have been forced for ten fiendish hours a day six solid days a week to subject my sinews to such sadistic stress as walking, running, stumbling, fumbling, falling down and getting back up and walking again as I all the while drag a rusty iron cable the obstinance of which is rivaled solely by the obstinance of the gargantuan log I am supposed to tie said cable around. I have had my bodily bones bunked and cracked, chunked and whacked by every rock stump root trunk within a fifty-foot radius as I fled that log so that cable wouldn't jerk it over me; I have had to stand there pant and fainting trying to endure berryvines, nettles, sunstroke, blisters, mosquitoes, no-see'ums and prickly heat in the brief respite alloted me while I waited for that cable to drop its log a hundred yards away and come hissing and snapping back for a new assault (something of Dante, don't you think?) I mean not only have I suffered all these physical horrors, but I *have*, if *anything*, in this land where I came to give my mind a rest, *increased my mental menaces a millionfold!* (Pardon my bad alliterative and endure my brief intermission while I um umm puff puff relight this joint . . . there we go.)

Dearest comrade, the point I wish to make with all this preambling penmanship is simply that I have been *far too* put upon to get either my lazy mind *or* my lazy ass to repaying your wonderful letter's most welcomed visit to this prehistoric land. Also, and at the risk of being honest, I actually *have been* more than ever beset by the slings and arrows of outrageous introspection . . . more than I was a month ago, even. (What did Pearson say about the apartment? Your other letter made no mention.) And for a couple of ironic reasons: you see, with the passing of these last few nightmare weeks here in this house I came to raze, living with these ogres I came to annihilate, I had contracted a malady I thought myself completely immunized against; I had come down with a bad case of Benevolence, with complications of Fondness and Distended Sympathy. You laugh? You snigger in your affected lipbeard that I could let my resistance run so low as to fall victim to that virus? Well, if you do, I can only point next door and smugly say, "Okay, my snide friend, you live three weeks in the same house with that chick and let's see if *you* can keep up your resistance!"

For I believe that 'twas she, the chick, the wildwoods flower wife of my sworn-destroyed brother, that stayed my vengeful hand and, till now, has kept my wrath from falling. Three weeks lost in my plot. Because, you must understand, it was *she* that my mind sought out as the undipped heel of my Achilles-like brother, and *she* was the only thing in the house which I hesitated to harm. This bind was brought to stalemate by the fact that my brother has been especially nice to me; I couldn't hate him quite enough to offset my fondness for the girl. It was even-steven. Until tonight.

You should, Peters, at this point, begin to detect the plot line even though you join the story one hundred pages deep. To sum up, in as you have missed the first four installments, there are only these facts to establish: Bitter Leland Stanford Stamper returns home intending to do his older half-brother some unconceived but horrible harm for diddling young Leland's mama, but in spite of his good intentions he has gradually been duped into sympathy for the arch step-fiend: we find Leland at the start of this episode, pitifully drunken and reasonless after an evening's sipping of this sympathy. Things look bad. It looks like he's going under. But, as you shall see, an unusual incident, almost a miracle, snaps our hero to his senses. It is this miracle for which

I now give thanks by lighting this second joint at the altar of the Great God Pot. . . .

We had just returned from a little foray into the woods and snacked on the leftovers of Viv's wonderful supper, and I had been waxing more and more banal as the evening wore on, and somehow the conversation between myself and my brother had wandered arm-in-drunken-arm through talk of school—"What actual *is it* you been studying?"—to talk of graduation—"Watcha aim to do with it to make a living?"—to talk of this and that and finally to the talk of music, of all things, Peters, *music!* To tell you the truth I can't recall how we arrived at the subject—alcohol, exhaustion and pot have eroded the edges from my memory—but it seems we were discussing (discussing, I wish you to note; we had even reached the point of *discussion* . . . a long way in three weeks from silent plotting of sinister doom) discussing the merits of life in the lovely but provincial West Coast as compared to the sophisticated but ugly East Coast when, in the course of championing the East, I mentioned that the *one* edge that the West Coasters must concede to the East was that it boasted far greater opportunities to hear good music. Hank was ready to concede no such thing . . . listen:

"Be easy," said he in his quaint way, "ain't you awriting your own numbers on the scale? What *you* reckon to be good music up against what *my* ideas are . . . might not fit all the notches. Just what do you mean 'good music'?"

I was in a philanthropic state of mind so for the sake of argument I agreed to meet him on a fair ground; remembering the old, remorseless driving rhythm and blues 78's of Joe Turner and Fats Domino that Hank used to assail my boyhood nights with, I agreed we would speak only of jazz. And after the usual amount of hemming and hawing and beating around the bush we got down to the thing all jazz enthusiasts are *always* working toward with their discussions; we went to get out our records. Hank commenced rummaging through drawers and boxes. From my suitcase upstairs I carried down my locked attaché case of favorites. But once again Hank and I realized very quickly that, even though we had arbitrated Jazz the Good Music we would discuss, we were still worlds apart as to what was Good Jazz.

(*They sat for a long time, across the room from each other, elbows on knees, head down . . . concentrating as though playing chess, the moves coming at the end of each band: Lee played a selection from Brubeck; Hank played Joe Williams singing "Red Sails in the Sunset"; Lee played Fred Katz; Hank countered with Fats Domino . . .*)

"That stuff of yours," said Hank, "sounds like the musicians all squat to pee. La lee la lee la lee."

"That stuff of yours," said I, "sounds like the musicians all suffer from St. Vitus' Dance. Bam bam bam bam, the epileptic stomp—"

("Now look a minute," Hank said, aiming his finger at Lee "what do you think them guys learn them horns for? Learn to sing that for? Huh? Well it ain't just to show how good they can finger the keys. Or to show how foxy they are at making some plumbline, T-square, to-the-inch . . . some kinda, oh, precision arrangement; da duh de da da; da duh dee da da . . . that crap. Bub, that sort of stuff might be a lot of fun for some white piano player who graduated from music college, something he can try 'n' work out like a crossword puzzle, but a man who learns to blow so he can blow jazz, he isn't worried what kinda grade some professor's giving him!"

"Why, will you listen to him, Viv," Lee said. "Brother Hank has let the cat out of the bag; he can articulate about more than the price of the cut fir per board feet or the wretched state of our donkey engine, or the 'sonofabitching' union! He does have the power of speech in spite of other rumors."

Hank dropped his head and grinned. "Shit now"—he rubbed the tip of his nose with the knuckle of his thumb—"I guess I did get up on a soapbox for a minute there. But I suppose, it comes down to it, there's a lot to what you say; it used to be that if there is one thing —other than the sonofabitchin' union—that I could get a good heat going on, it was music. We useta—me and Mel Sorenson, and Henderson and that bunch . . . Joe Ben, too, before he got saved so big—useta sit for hours in Harvey's cycle shop down in Coos Bay listening to this great collection Harvey played all the time . . . and you should have heard us then! We thought Joe Turner had come right outa heaven to give us the skinny. We thought somebody was finally playing OUR music—this was after listening to hillbilly-Western till we foundered. I mean there was sides taken, the Western fans and the rhythm and blues fans . . . we had real fights about it! We were ripe to fight about something anyway; I decided once that most of our bunch were mad 'cause we'd got cheated outa fightin' the Japs and Germans and didn't know yet we had Korea to fight about. So those first bop records made good causes." Hank let his head sink to rest on the back of the chair, closed his eyes on his reverie, and reminisced for a few minutes about obscure tenormen and

*drummers completely unmindful of the boneless dance of Jimmy
Giuffre on the phonograph . . .*

*"But you may be right," he said, finishing up along with the last
few bars of Lee's Giuffre record; "I probably haven't kept up with
what's been going on. But I know one thing: that old blues and
boogie and bop had some man to it.")*

And Hank said, "That manure they're playin' *there* hasn't got any
more balls than it does beat. I like somethin' with a little more *balls*
on it."

And I said, "Such a prejudice must limit you terribly."

And he said, "Are we gonna be like that?"

And I said, "I should think you would want to at least exclude such
things as the female sex from such a sweeping statement."

And he said, "I should think this outfit snuggling her little tail up
against me here would make a qualification like that pretty damned
unnecessary, but, if you are goin' to be hard-nosed about it . . ."

But I waved it off (see: still trying to be fair, a Good Guy) and said,
"Sorry, Hank, sorry." Then, my friend—to show you how grave my
affliction was, how deeply rooted the cancer—I went so far as to attempt to *repair* the rent my tongue had sliced in our tender new
fellowship. I said I had been only jesting and that, Sure brother, I
understand what you were talking about that music was meant for.
I told him that there were, in fact, two recognized schools of Jazz,
Black Jazz and White Jazz, and that what he was referring to as
*Masculine* was no doubt the Black Jazz school. I noted that I had
played only Brubeck, Giuffre and Tjader. But, here, listen to some of
this for Black Jazz: catch hold of *this!*

*(Lee riffled through the albums in his case, found the one he was
searching for, and removed it carefully, almost reverently. "You act
like it's about to blow up," Hank commented. "It very well might . . .
listen.")*

And I put on what? Of course. John Coltrane. "Africa Brass." I recall
no malice aforethought in this choice, but who can say? Does one
ever play Coltrane for the uninitiated without subconsciously hoping
for the worst? Anyway, if such was my wish my subconscious must
have been greatly pleased, for, after a few minutes of that tenor sax
ripping away at the privates, Hank reacted according to schedule.
"What kind of *crap* is that?" (Anger, frustration, great gritting of
teeth; all the classic responses.) "What kind of godawful manure pile
is *that?*"

"That? What are you asking? This is Jazz as black as it comes, black balls dragging the ground . . ."

"Yeah, but . . . wait a minute—"

"Isn't it so? Listen to it; is that precision la dee da?"

"I don't know if—"

"But listen; isn't it so?"

"That it has balls? I suppose . . . yes, but I'm not talk—"

*("So you may be forced, brother, to find a different prerequisite to found your prejudice on."*

*"But forchrissakes listen to that manure. Eee-onk: onk-eeek. I mean maybe he's got balls but it sounds like somebody's stompin' up and down on 'em!"*

*"Exactly! Exactly! Hundreds of years of stomping; ever since the slave traders. That's the story he tells! Not what would be nice . . . but the way it IS! The terrible, deadly way it really IS when you know you're surrounded by black skin. And we are all surrounded by that skin, and he's trying to show us some beauty in this condition. If you're incensed it's because he's being honest about our condition, because he's honestly describing the black and ball-stomping way it is, instead of being content to whine about it like those Uncle Toms before him."*

*"Bug, Joe Williams, Fats Waller, Gaillard, that bunch . . . they none of them never whined. They maybe griped but they did it with some joy. They never whined. By god if they did. And they never come on about, about . . . blackness and ball-stomping, neither—trying to make it beautiful, for shitsakes—because it ain't beautiful. It's ugly as sin!")*

Brother Hank then clamped shut his jaw and remained silent throughout the rest of the side, as I peeped at his stone-smiled obstinance through the fingers of my shading hand. Let me see, Peters! Was it then, during the tense listening, that I renovated my views of vengeance? Let me see? No. No, ah no. I still had not . . . Oh. It was—no . . . yes;—admit! admit!—it was, it *was* then, right after Coltrane, when Viv asked what to her must have been a perfectly innocent question, just a small-talk question to ease the strain. Yes; directly after . . . "Where did you get the record, Lee?" was the best the girl could do. Just a question to ease the strain. Perfectly innocent on her part. For if it had not been so innocent could I have answered with such little thought to what I was saying? "My mother gave it to me, Viv. My mother always—"

With such very little thought that I did not realize I had made the
blunder in his presence until he said Sure, until he said Sure, sure as
gods green apples I mighta known. Sure I mighta known because it *is*
just exactly the sorta dismal manure she'd go for, isn't it? Sure, listen
there—it is just the sorta manure Mother would—

Lee stops writing, abruptly jerking his face up from the page. He
holds his pen and sits for endless minutes with the little nub of a
cigarette cold between his lips, listening to the snaredrum sound of
a pine bough brushing in the breeze across his window screen. The
sound reaches him eerily, through twisting channels. At first it holds
no meaning and he thinks of it as a sound only, issuing from no
source. Then he catches sight of the dark movement of the branch
and fixes the sound; relieved that it is only a branch, he lights the
cigarette again and bends back to his paper . . .

But I'd best be on with it before it gets too late and too sleepy
and too high. I'd like to do the complete scene for you because I
know you would appreciate the nuances, the vicious undertones, the
pastels of hostility, but I'm—whup, wheep, whoop—getting too far
out to give these subtleties the attention they deserve.

So, anyway. All right. There I am with Hank hassling me about
my Mother. My mellow benevolence is shattered. The cold bitter light
of reason is beginning to peep through. The truce is obviously over.
Time to think again of the battle. I devise a plan to capture my intended weapon and immediately set about my campaign. . . .

"Well, Hank," I remark, sneeringly, "there are quite a number of
people well versed in music who might disagree with your evaluation
of current Jazz artists. So couldn't it be possible that you are being a
bit, shall we say bull-headed? narrow-minded?"

The victim blinks, surprised by Little Brother's testy tone. Could
Little Brother be spoiling for a fat lip maybe? "Yeah . . ." he says
slowly, "I suppose." I cut him off, going blithefully on. . . .

"On the other hand narrow-minded may be a dishonest label. It may
imply a specific not present. Anyway, that's not the point. We were
talking about balls, were we not? Balls standing—for the sake of argument—for manliness, strength, intestinal fortitude, etc. Well, brother,
do you think that just because a man has enough brains to play more
than bam bam bam bam—along with three blues chords and a half-
dozen notes—do you think this makes it impossible for him to also
have balls? Or does the presence of one eliminate the possibility of the
other?"

"Hold on." The victim sniffs, he squints. "Now wait." Perhaps like an animal he can sense the presence of a trap. But what he cannot sense is that the trap is set in reverse, to catch the trapper.

"Look at it this way," I continue, and begin offering newer, nastier arguments, "or what about this," I press on, "and will you at least consider *this*," I demand, parlaying one cutting point after another as I begin to put on the pressure. Not openly provoking hostility, not so Viv will recognize it, you see, but skillfully, shrewdly, with innuendoes and references to bygone events meaningful only to Hank and Myself. So that when I start dangling the bait he is ready.

"What do you mean Champion Jack Dupree is somebody's uncle Tom hushpuppy?" he demands, reacting to an incidental statement. "What do you mean about Elvis, too? while I'm at it. I know what's said about him but screw 'em I say. When Elvis started he had something, he had—"

"Tonsilitis? Rickets?"

"—he had more'n that asshole there playing hopscotch or whatever. Let me get that offa there. Christ, you've played ten sides, let me get a word in edgewise."

"*Don't!* Get your fingers off that record. I'll take it off."

"Okay, okay, take it off."

And so forth and so on with fists doubled and eyes red and I've got him. "Let me play it over Hank, then maybe you'll . . ."

"You put that goddam thing on again I'll so help me Christ—" "Prints! You've got all sorts of crud on it!" "Shit, I barely—" "I don't like *anyone* to touch my records!" "Well by *god* now . . . if you don't like it—" Shouting, standing up. Watch: Brother Hank is finally showing through. Just like Les Gibbons showed through what was truly inside. It's brother Hank skinned out of his tinfoil wrapper. Watch, Viv, look how he shouts at poor Lee when we argue. Look how he pulls rank of muscle. "—what you can *do* about it!"

See how unjust, Viv? Yet see how Lee tries to be fair though Hank grows angrier. Like a grade-school bully shouting Okay! It comes right down to it maybe I don't have a right! Watch: He is bigger tougher watch him Viv, because, bub, and if you don't like it *know do about it!*

And, see Viv, what *can* Lee do? What chance has he against this beast gnashing teeth before him this barroom brawler with commando training from Korea this bully Viv? What? Not a chance in the world and the poor boy knows it. He knows Viv, look, that any answer to Hank's challenge would be disastrous. Oh Viv, how awful it must be, do you see? for the boy to have to suffer the coward's shame, the craven's humiliation. He knows he is being a coward WATCH but he can't help it. Oh look, Viv, he *knows!* He knows! He's afraid to fight and he *knows!* How much more painful, do you see? how pitiful! How very terrible. (but *you*, comrade, you see, don't you, how very *clever*) as he bows his head in surrender suffers the degradation of mumbling an apology while *knowing* he is in the *right!*

But, oh Viv, right doesn't make might.

Hank stalks outside, victorious, adamant (trapped) Lee stands ashamed beaten (cunning) Viv watches (nibbling) at the miserable vanquished wretch, twice miserable for he was vanquished without a battle. Coward! Weakling! Loser! (fox . . .)

"I'm sorry, Lee. Hank . . . gets going like that sometimes when he drinks. I should have taken him up to bed earlier. But he seemed in such a good mood."

"No, Viv. He was right. He was perfectly right in everything he said."

"Oh he was *not!*"

"Yes. He was right and proved it. Not about the music. That's not important. But about . . . what he said."

"Oh Lee, he doesn't really think that."

"Thinks it or not, it's true." Look Viv, look at Lee needing so much. See how he is so small in the world. "It's true."

"It's *not*, Lee. Believe me. You aren't . . . oh, if someone could *convince* you—"

"Tomorrow."

"What."

"On our date tomorrow. If it is on again?"

"There never was any date. I just—"

"I thought so . . ."

"Now don't act like that, please Lee. . . ."

"How should I act? First you say—"

"All right. Tomorrow." See his face Viv? "If you think you need to . . ." See how much he needs? "I just wish I knew more, understood why you two . . ." There's a lot you don't know about him, Viv. That makes him even smaller. You don't know all his shame, you don't even begin to know. His shame is strangling him.

No, nobody's that ashamed.

Yes! you don't know. You just see the surface shame. Right now there is a second layer ashamed of the first, ashamed of being so weak as to use the shame, ashamed of his need to use the shame. And all his anger comes of it, his cleverness spawned of it, his hate . . . ah, his hate . . . like years ago? hating? as he looked through that hole? he looked, you know, so many times more than his hate needed . . . He came the first time and he looked and it was hate and he came the second time and it was shame for though hate made him big enough to watch what he had to watch the first time seeing the second time could not add more to hate for there was no more to be hated or seen than the first time and less to see the third time and less each time but hate no longer needed it. By the third time Shame needed it. Weakness needed it. Perversion needed it. And hate was stretched to cover everything. So see? All like that. Need Shame Weakness all boiling under that lid I am smothering of that lid hate and see I must must I must—"

The flow of ink ceases in midword but Lee writes on to the edge of the page before he notices the pen has stopped. Then shuts his eyes and begins to laugh, beside himself with amusement. He laughs for a long time and when his lungs are empty the echoes of his laughing rattle woodenly back from the pineboard walls. He fills his lung and laughs again, and again, until the laughter finally subsides into exhausted, hoarse wheezes.

He opens his eyes and looks about his bed vacantly until his eyes fall on the third cigarette. He takes it up gingerly between thumb and forefinger and places it between his lips with great care, as though the slightest jar might shatter it. After some difficulty he finds the matches. He lights the cigarette and draws slowly in. The walls of the room draw inward with the smoke. He holds the breath as long as he can, then lets it out with a low whistling sound and the room expands once more. He draws another. As he smokes he works to get the pen functioning once more. He pounds it against the paper, he tries running the point over the palm of his hand. Finally he remembers a trick Mona taught him and holds the point briefly in a match flame. This time it marks when he traces it across his palm.

He finishes the cigarette and bends to the notebook again, but he has forgotten what he was writing and can pick up no thread from the last few lines. He shrugs, and sits smiling. He sits motionless until a sound, at once far away and quite near, is heard above the brushing of the pine bough on his window. It is like the strumming of a great bass. And the brushes . . . He begins rocking to the beat. After a few more minutes the pen moves across the paper swiftly:

drums drums drums are death drums voo drums doo drums kha-a-a-a leading a rattling dance of skeletons through steamy green saxophones, through the screeching jungle. Gruesome, stark—he's right—godawful. And he is right, it is the very sort of manure Mother would buy. He is right and cursed right and damn him for it damn him to everlasting hell!

drums drums sucking drums ooze of mud, parched and moaning stones in sun, something swoops to scream at you with a brass beak honed like razor kha-a-a . . . and that's Coltrane, and that's Truth

. . . and that's true that that was mother and this is me and Hank's right and damn him for it damn him damn him damn . . .

dum . . . dum . . . dum dum EEkha-a-a-a there is blackness in his playing, blackness slashed apart with red. There is bleak and senseless pain. Warped and torn and gha-a-gasping lovely and yes also also ugly, grotesque, but then he makes it beautiful by convincing us it's true. Gawking mad and horrible, black apart with red, but that's the real face of it. And beauty must be made from what is really must be must be made

He pauses again when Hank stops whacking the big cable on the levee. He looks absently about him, clucking his tongue to remember something. Then Hank starts striking the cable again, more slowly. Lee's head begins to rock to and fro over the page, to a music swirling, broken and disjointed from the night . . .

*Black* crows. *Black* crows. *Over* the cornfield. *So* what they play. *So* What is the name I know the piece I got it now. Listen to them. Grim missionaries of *So* What! Three chocolate-coated vacuums calling *So* What!

All a drag man, all a hassle man, all too much not enough something else nothing at all *So* What!

All three ask it together, then each at a time, then all together again. SO WHAT? SO SO SO WHAT so so so what? All together, then the trumpet, then the tenor, then the alto, then all together again SOOOOOO what?

All three vacuums, transparent lips to the glass brass bells of three brass horns, sucking in at the three brass bells, fingering reverse indrawn music of despair, playing pictures on the desert SO what? tossed hot chance of skeleton dice over dunes sifting rust . . . burnt land, burnt sky, burnt black moon . . . burnt cities wind scattering hot memo papers no one to read them SOOO what? in houses sundered with big look and WHOOO what? . . . burn if don't shame empty up lay empty hot give stay SO loose what? look where is go is empty go so empty hot so frozen what and who

The pen reaches the bottom of the page, but he doesn't open the notebook for more paper. He sits, staring at a little hourglass-shaped patch of light cast onto his wall through a crack in his lampshade, very still, only his finger moving as he taps out slow rhythms on the paper. He sits until his eyes begin to water, then he gathers up the scattered pages of his writing and tears them into stamp-sized pieces, working on each with bemused interest until he has a lapful of confetti. He throws the torn paper from his window into the October breeze and returns to bed. He falls asleep watching the little fragment of light vibrate across his wall, thinking how much more efficient it would be filling an hourglass with photons instead of those unruly grains of sand.

$U$p river from the Stamper house and south, back into the sudden thrust of mountains, up the deep granite canyon of the South Fork of the Wakonda Auga, I know a place where you can sometimes sing along with yourself if you take the notion. You stand on a wooded slope overlooking the crooked little deep-green river far below, and sing into a lofty amphitheater of naked rock scooped from the steep mountain across the way: "Row, row, row your boat, gently down the stream . . ."—and just as you start on your merrily-merrilies, the echo comes in, "Row, row, row . . ." right on cue. So you sing with the echo. But you must be careful in choosing your key or your tempo; there is no changing of the pitch if you start too high, no slowing down of the tempo if you start too fast . . . because an echo is an inflexible and pitiless taskmaster: you sing the echo's way because it is damned sure not going to sing yours. And even after you leave this mossy acoustical phenomenon to go on with your hiking or fishing, you cannot help feeling, for a long time after, that any jig you whistle, hymn you hum, or song you sing is somehow immutably tuned to an echo yet unheard, or relentlessly echoing a tune long forgotten—

And the old wino boltcutter, who lives in this sort of world, not far from this granite cliff, and cuts his shinglebolts from logged-out slopes on the bank of that crooked fork of the Wakonda, gets cursing drunk to celebrate the coming thirty-first of October (the same way he paid tribute to the thirty other days) and spends his night in a Thunderbird dream joining those echoes in complete antiphonal choruses, singing against the scooped-out stone of his sixty years across a deep green river of wine, and awakes before daylight with a roaring in his ears. Just a few minutes before Viv dropped off to sleep, after tossing for hours trying to recall the words to a ridiculous childhood song: "Way up yonder, top of the sky . . ." The boltcutter coughs for a while, then sits up in his bed, giving up his songs to the museum dark: "It's all a lotta horseshit." And in her dreams Viv finishes her verse: " '. . . blue-jay lives in a silver eye. Buckeye Jim,

you can't go . . . go weave an' spin, you can't go . . . Buckeye Jim.'
A lullaby, Mother sings it to me when I am a baby. Who do I sing
it to, way up top of the sky? I don't know. I don't understand . . ."

Beside her, breathing deeply, Hank mirrors the image of an oft-
repeated high-school dream—to go on to college an' by Jesus show
the bastards just who's a dumbass jock an' who ain't—and down the
hall, still high as a kite though sound asleep, Lee thrashes about in a
bed full of roaches, crutches, and burnt paper matches, and, having
already chanted his own inquisition, judged himself guilty, and pronounced his sentence—death . . . by shrinking—he sets about composing a ballad to sing his praises after he is gone: a musical epic that
would commemorate all his heroic victories on the field of combat
and all his mighty feats in the arena of love . . . to the stirring beat
of drums drums drums . . .

> —And sometimes, as you sing, you cannot help feeling that
> the unheard echoes and tunes forgotten are echoes of other
> voices and tunes of other singers . . . in that kind of
> world.

At dawn the band of black clouds that slipped into town under
cover of darkness can be seen loitering on the horizon like unem-
ployed ghosts, impatient already for the day to be over so they can
get to their Halloween pranks. The lightning from the night before
now hangs upside down in the firs up in the mountains, waiting out
the day in electric slumber, like a recharging bat. And a scavenger
wind, ribbed and mangy, runs the frosted fields, whimpering with
hunger, cold and stiff and terribly lonesome for its buddy the bat
overhead there, snoring sparks in the tree limbs . . . in that kind of
world. Runs and whimpers and clicks its frost teeth.

As the aged and feeble sun slides up (cautiously, of course, in that
kind of world, and because it is Halloween Indian Jenny opens her
reddened eyes, even more cautiously. Sluggish and hung over after a
night dedicated to hexing Hank Stamper for refusing to let his
father marry an Indian . . . she rises from her freshly sheeted cot,
crosses herself providently, and, wearing nothing more than an arrangement of the knitted wool blankets the government last year
apportioned for her tribe (her tribe consists of herself, her father, a
half-dozen mongrel brothers getting steadily fatter somewhere in the
next county; the blankets consist of wool, also mongrel, but getting

steadily thinner), pads out across the chocolate-pudding mudflats to pay homage to the new day by reading from the Bible that waits beside the smoothed sawn plywood hole of her toilet. The Bible had come with the blankets and was a holy thing, like the plastic Jesus she'd stolen from the dashboard of Simone's Studebaker, or the bottle of aquavit that had materialized on her table one night after she had chanted out loud the mystic words from a dream about her father: she had called out the words in terror and halfhearted hope, and come morning, there the bottle had been, a talisman with a label in a magical language that she was never able to read. She was never able to reconstruct the chant, either.

Like the bottle, which she had forced herself to ration sip by pious sip over many months, the Bible had also enjoyed a long reign; she obliged herself, however cold the damp bay air, however uncomfortable the harsh edges of the plywood, to read the entire page before tearing it out. The religious discipline had paid off in kind. As she arranged the blankets about her heavy brown flanks and picked up the book she thought she detected deep within her a definite revelation that was certainly more than last night's pepperoni. But she jumped to no conclusions. For, while she was certainly a devout woman, given to diverse worships, she had more than once been disappointed in her spiritual experiments and hadn't really expected much action to come out of this reading business. She had entered into the Contract with the Book essentially because her subscription to *Horoscope* had run out and the bottle of Holy Aquavit had—quite unmiraculously, and in spite of all the best spells that the worst of Alistair Crowley could offer—run dry. "Read of this the first thing every morning," the man who brought her the blankets prescribed. "Read it religiously, all the way through, it shall touch your soul." Well, all right. It couldn't be as worthless as that Healing Prayer Cloth that she'd ordered from San Diego, and it couldn't possibly be as terrible as that jolt of peyote she'd ordered from Laredo ("Eat eight, mate," had been this cult's typed instructions, "and you got an Electra-Jet to Heaven"). So all right, she told the man and took the book, with a halfhearted show of gratitude, she'd try anything. But what she had lacked in enthusiasm she had made up for in staying power and now her devotion was beginning to show fruit. Now, eyes bulging toward the page as she shuddered, straining to rid herself of sin, she suddenly experienced a stinging needle of pain and saw—inside that little hut!—a beautiful spiraling of stars. Think of that, she marveled, shuddering once more, just think of that: she was only twelve days into Deuteronomy and already she had marked her soul! Now if she could just figure how to get these stars into her hexes . . .

Teddy the bartender prepares for the approach of All Hallows Eve by dusting his neon with a feather duster and removing the fried flies from his electro-kill screen with a Brillo pad. Floyd Evenwrite practices reading the preamble of International Woodsmen of the World aloud before a bathroom mirror toward the afternoon's meeting with Jonny Draeger and the grievance committee. The Real Estate Hotwire, always a shrewd cooky, greets the morning by soaping innocuous sayings on his own window, as he has done every Halloween for years; "Got to be one hop out in front." He snickers, smearing soap. "When the other galoots are just coming to the starting line, got to be two steps gone." He'd adopted this procedure after finding his window maliciously decorated one Halloween night with what he decided must have been paraffin of a most unusual type—"probably something manufactured by the government special" —for, scrub as he might, he had never been able to rid his window of the memory of that evening. Detergent wouldn't touch it; gasoline only hid it temporarily from sight; and even these many years later, when the light was right, the apparently spotless window would cast a dim but readable shadow on the floor before his desk.

With no small amount of research, he had established that the vandals who skulked this most unholy of October nights had a decided inclination toward panes unsullied and tended to bypass windows already soaped. A kind of unwritten law, he suspected: don't muck up a buddy's job. So he was determined to be one hop out in front with soap before the other galoots got to the starting line with more of that paraffin. So great was the triumph the Hotwire felt the following morn, when he came to find his windows untouched by any mark but his own, that he failed to notice that his was the only disfigured window on the whole street; owing to parties and apple-bobbings—initiated by the adults, the tamed vandals of those yestere'ens, for the purpose of keeping their offspring in out of the wet—paraffin, soap, and the whole art of window-waxing had gone completely out of vogue. Even when this was pointed out to him he refused to discontinue the precaution. "A stitch in time is worth a pound of cure"—he remembered one of Joe Ben Stamper's philosophies, scrawling wow across the glass with a flourish. "Besides, I ask you: who needs 'Zorro Go Home' two inches deep in paraffin right across their business?"

Joe Ben leaps from bed and confronts the Halloween Saturday

just about the same as he confronted any other Saturday when the Pentecostal Church of God and Metaphysical Science was holding services. Because, as far as Joe was concerned, every day could be Halloween if you held your mouth right. And Joe had a grin like a jack-o'-lantern. And, unlike the candle in the pumpkin he'd picked and fixed for the kids, the candle behind Joe's carved features needed no special occasion, no official day set aside for ghouls and goblins; it could be ignited by anything. Oh yeah . . . the discovery of a cricket in his drinking glass at the sink ("Good sign! You bet. Chinese say crickets bring all kinds fat luck.") . . . the number of Rice Krispies that might have snapped, crackled, and popped over the top of his bowl onto the breakfast table ("Four of 'em! See? See? It's the fourth month and this is my fourth bowl of cereal and Jesus said to Lazarus, Come forth. And ain't my name Little Joe, which is two and two or I'll eat my hat!") or kindled to a ruddy glow by nothing more than a simple sight that pleased his simple mind . . . such as the sweet pink flame of the morning sun through the window alighting on the sleeping faces of his children.

The kids usually slept scattered about the floor of his room in sleeping bags, just any old place, but last night they had quite unconsciously aligned themselves so that a single trickle of sun leaking through a single tear in a shade could skip from brow to glowing brow. And since no coincidences marred Joe Ben's auspicious world, this wondrous arrangement of faces threaded like pink pearls on the one tiny strand of sunshine was exactly the sort of datum he usually parlayed into a riot of prophecy, but this time the plain visual beauty of the sight so overwhelmed him that he was blinded to its metaphysical significance. He grasped his head in both hands to shore up a skull too thin to contain such high voltage. It would blow him to bits. "Oh God," he moaned aloud, closing his eyes. "Oh oh oh God." Then, recovering just as quickly, he tiptoed about the room in his skivvies, licking the tip of a finger and touching each of the five children as Brother Walker did in his baptism ceremonies. "No liquid nowhere in the world"—Joe paraphrased Brother Walker's philosophy—"is as big a deal in the eyes of our Saviour as good ol' human spit."

The impulsive baptism over, Joe scrunched down and crept back across the floor, striving intensely to make no noise, lifting his knees high and bringing his toes down with painful caution, elbows tight against his ribs like the plucked wings of a muscle-bound stewing chicken sneaking away across the kitchen floor behind the chef's back. At the window he let up the shade and stood fingering his navel while he grinned out at the waking day. He lifted his arms above his head, fists doubled, and stretched out his straightest and yawned.

Yet, stretched out or scrunched down, Joe still looked like some kind of poorly plucked fugitive from the butcher's bench. His bowed legs were lumpy with muscles cramped too tight against muscles squeezed too tight against other muscles; his back was pinched and knotted, and his stubby arms swiveled from shoulders which would have graced a six-footer but served only to distort a five-sixer.

When a carnival came to Wakonda Joe could barely wait to get down and give the weight-guessers fits; estimates would undershoot or overshoot the actual one-fifty-five by sometimes as much as forty pounds. He looked as if he should have been bigger or smaller, it was difficult to say which. Seeing him scampering about the woods, transistor radio bumping against his chest like an electronic locket, you might think he needed antennae, a glass helmet and a size four space suit.

Seeing him years before, still straight and graceful as a young pine, with the face of a teen-age Adonis, you would have thought him one of the most strikingly handsome young men in the world; what this Adonis had become was a triumph of indefatigable will as well as a showcase of perseverance. He seemed to have been issued a skin many sizes too small and chest and shoulders too large. Without a shirt he seemed to have no neck; with a shirt on he seemed to have on shoulder pads. Encountering this apparition in stagged-off pants and three sweat shirts chugging toward you on the boulevard, elbows out, balled fists chest-high, spread legs thrusting splayed boots against a springy earth, one might expect to see a halfback with the football sprinting close on his heels . . . were it not that the jack-o'-lantern lodged there between the shoulder pads made it extremely clear that it was not football that was being played, but some kind of queer joke . . .

On exactly whom was not quite so clear.

He pulled the shade back down. The shaft of light skipped again precisely across the sleeping faces, hesitating for an instant in the center of each little forehead to examine the drop of good old human spit. And as Joe struggled into his cold clothes he recited a prayer of thanks in a reverent whisper in the general direction of the chest of drawers, while the jack-o'-lantern looked on balefully with puzzled, sooty eyes and grinned a mildewed grin: a joke was being played, all right. That much was clear. And it might have been easier to figure on whom if Joe had refrained from grinning back.

Saturdays were busy for Joe. That was when he worked off his rent obligation. He had lived off and on at the old house across the Wakonda for most of his life, staying there as long as six or eight months at a time during his childhood, while his father gallivanted up and down the coast possessed with the frenzied squandering of a life that was burning a hole in his pants. Rent money was never mentioned or even considered; Joe knew he had paid old Henry ten times over with the countless hours of free overtime he'd put in at the show or the mill, paid board and room for himself and the woman and kids and then some. That wasn't it. To old Henry he owed nothing, but to the house, the house itself, to the actual flesh of paint and bone of wood of the old house he knew he owed a debt so large it could never be repaid. Never, never in a thousand years! So, as the day drew near when he would move into his own home, he had become a dervish of repairs, determined to make that deadline of never and repay that unpayable debt. Gleefully slapping paint or mending shakes, he rushed to square things with the pile of wood that had sheltered him so undemandingly for so long, certain sure, as he damned near always was certain of practically anything he decided was worth being sure of, that he would some way, right at the last, with a terrific spurt of last-minute nailing and puttying and calking, succeed in meeting that impossible deadline and pay off the debt he had already decided for certain sure was un-pay-offable. "Old house, old house," he crooned, straddling the topmost peak with a hammer in his hand and nails bristling from his mouth, "I'll have you shinin' like a new dime by the time I leave here. Oh, you know it. You'll stand a *thousand* years!"

He patted the mossy withers lovingly. "A *thousand* years"—he was certain. A lot of roof left to shingle and outside to shake in the three or four weekends before he moved, but he would finish, by gosh, by golly and—if it meant Sending Out for the Divine Help —by God!

The thought caused a little buzz of excitement to go through him; though he'd come pretty close, he'd never actually come to that point of really Sending Out yet. Oh, he'd prayed for things, but that's different, that ain't like Sending Out. You can pray for just about anything, but Sending Out for Divine Help!—well . . . it ain't ordering from Monkey Ward. It'll *be there*, don't ever doubt it a second—oh yeah—but you wait till there's something of a *size*, not just the donkey cable busted or a root hung in your—last night, now, last night with Hank so down from his argument with Lee, I come near to Sending—but I'm glad I held off. Only thing Hank has to do is quit worrying about it and go ahead and do what he knows already he's gonna do—like I knew he knew that he was gonna walk back out into the woods to look for old Molly because it's in him to do—to accept what he already knows is all he need do. . . . Yeah, I'm glad I didn't Send Out—because he'll come through even if he don't Believe, except I sure never seen him throwed before like Leland's throwed him. If he'd just quit patty-caking and accept what he *knows already*: that there's nothing but to go ahead and straighten the kid up when he gets outa line and Hank sure don't need anybody to Send Out for him some help when it comes to *that* sort of—But for a long time now, a year, since we heard about her killing herself—No, no that can't be, it's—ah—it's just that all this with the union, and then Lee too, he's throwed off kilter a little bit. He'll come back around, if he'd *just*—like anybody else destined to responsibility, like *any* of the chosen people—learn he's got to dig what he *knows already*, then everything's gonna be fine again—oh yeah—gonna be *prime* . . .

All this imprecise, rough-shingled thinking while the October sun pushed through the smoky blue layers of October sky, to bravely look toward November . . . and the black rat-pack of clouds, hiding on the horizon, seemed as far away as January.

Joe Ben scooted gradually along the peak of the roof, face bright orange, eyes clear green with white showing all around the pupil, and as he moved jerkily along, tacking down the new cedar shingles, he liked to look back occasionally at the bright contrast of new wood lined against old—the line ragged and rough, but bright nevertheless. He would study the line a moment, then set to again, hammering away at his rough-split shingles and whittling his rough-tooled thoughts, certain sure that everything would come along fine, be a gas, turn out prime . . . if you just held your mouth right and accepted what you knew already was gonna hafta be done. You *bet!* And if the joke was on Joe he was determined to be the first to laugh as well as the last to admit it.

At Viv's call to lunch Joe climbed down the ladder, content that he had fixed the roof and Hank's worries both at the same time.

There was nothing to it; just get Hank and the boy together and have everybody talk things out. Whatever was chewing at them, he was sure all it needed was a good healthy airing. They weren't neither of them nincompoops. They could surely see it wasn't any good going around with chips on their shoulders, they could surely see that. Nothing could be gained, and, if it kept on, Hank stood to lose sleep he needed to keep the job rolling. Lee stood to lose a mouthful of teeth. That was all there was to it. He'd make them see the lay of the land.

But after checking out the scene at the lunch table he decided to hold off for a few days on his suggestion for mediation. Hank brooded behind a newspaper with heavy, rumbling silence, and Lee, smoking and staring out the kitchen window with tragic, defeated eyes and an anemic pallor to his cheeks, didn't look capable of sustaining the shock of a haircut, let alone the loss of a mouthful of teeth. Looking at Lee, Joe was amazed that this could be the same person he had watched just yesterday scale a fifteen-degree slope at a run with a choker chain in his hand. He sure looked brought down and troubled, Lee did . . .

*Lee stares down at his plate, and the plate stares back from two wild egg-yolk eyes and wrinkles a bacon grin; like a mask of a skull the plate is . . . reminding him of another mask (the little boy stood looking at the mask, fighting tears) and another, long-ago Halloween (looking from the mask pathetically up toward his mother: "I can't see why I got to wear it—I can't see why I even got to go!" Hank took the mask from her and grinned at it. "Looks fine to me," he said). Lee stabs the yolk of one eye and stirs it over the bacon . . .*

"You better get hold of some of them eggs, Leland," Joe advised, "before you expire on the spot. Oh, I know what's botherin' you; you slep' too late. You oughta been up there on the roof with me, breathing of the firmament."

*Lee turns slowly to give Joe a trenchant smile.* "I was up there with you, Josephus. In spirit." *I had decided before coming to breakfast that it would best serve my plan to win Viv's simpathy by being bitter and hurt as a result of Hank's overbearing treatment of him last night.* "Yes, in spirit I was up there from the first crack of dawn and rattle of daylight. I was up there with you every stroke of that hammer."

Joe slapped his cheek. "I never thought for a second. And that's d'rectly above your room, ain't it? Oh man, you musta thought things was really comin' apart in man-sized chunks. You reckon you'll pull through? You still got just oh the *faintest* tremble to your lip. . . ."

"I *did* consider running to warn Henny Penny and Foxy Loxy," I laughed. In spite of my resolute bitterness, I couldn't help being amused by Joe Ben. "But I do reckon I'll pull through, though, shellshock notwithstanding."

"I'm truly sorry," Joe apologized. "I know how a man who's got to be woked up all the time durin' the week hates to be woked on the weekend when he doesn't got to."

"Apology accepted"—and wondered: But how can you know, Joe? How can you *possibly* know how I feel about being woked, Joe, when you've probably been up before dawn every day of your life?

Joe Ben constituted a phenomenon to me in more ways than one; quite apart from his appearance, he was one of those extremely remarkable beings whose hearts pump pure elixir of Benzedrine through a body made of latex rubber. Always high, always on the go, always looking overnourished and underfleshed, for all he ate. He devoted so much energy to his meals that one was apt to wonder how he kept from expiring in the very act of eating, like the car that died at the gas station because it burned fuel faster than the pump could deliver it.

*Having demolished the skull face on his plate, Lee pushes it from him, shuddering . . . (The little boy tried to ignore Hank's opinion of the mask: "Mother, I don't care about trick-an'-treating. If I don't care why do I have to—" Hank scooped him up before he could finish and perched him on his shoulder. "Bee-cause, bub, how you ever gonna get fierce, you don't learn to get out yonder an' meet the Hidebehind in his own territory? Takes some grit an' gumption, but it's gotta be did or you'll spend your life in a hole like a gopher. Here, stick this mask on; we'll get into town an' scare the pants off the folks.") and tries to ignore the unexplained threat from a plate of eggs. . . .*

"Joe," I said casually, after a small silence, "you know . . . I'm inclined to take you up on that offer you made me."

"Sure enough, you bet." Then asked casually, after a large mouthful of toast, "Just what offer was that?"

"To give me a chance to witness first hand the power of your faith in action, to visit your church for Saturday services . . . don't you recall?"

"Yeah! the church! you come! oh man *yeah!* But it ain't exactly a church, I mean it is a church, but it ain't exactly—you know, steeples and stained-glass windows and pulpits . . . it's more sort of a *tent* is what it actually is. A tent? huh?" He uttered a short laugh of dawning wonder. "Yeah, that's what it is—a tent—how about that?"

"Apparently your cathedral's architecture has never impressed itself on you before."

"But, hey, Lee, listen, one thing. Jan an' me wasn't planning to come right back out. It's Halloween, for one thing; I aim to give the kids a chance to trick-or-treat a little bit tonight."

"Yes, Leland," Jan corroborated in a small voice, "we'll be going over to our new place after church. To paint some in the kitchen. But you're of course welcome to spend the day there an' come back with us tonight."

"Shoot a monkey, yes!" Joe Ben snapped his fingers. "You ever paint much, Lee? Why it's a *gas*, you know? It's prime fun! Swarp swarp. A wave of the hand and bright *red!* orange! green . . . !"

"Off-white an' morning mist an' pastel green, Joe dear." Jan toned down his hues.

"Sure! But what do you say, Lee? If you can handle a brush—we'll give you a sort of try-out, to see if you're equal to it first—but if you are . . . it'd be a *nice* way to fill the wait."

I told him that I was afraid that, after a session with Brother Walker, I might be a bit too unsteady to wield a sure brush, but gave him the names of a few other fellows I knew who might be interested. . . .

"Joe Harper? Huck who? Lee, them boys *town* boys?"

"A joke, Joe, forget it."

Which he immediately did as he launched into an enthusiastic description of the plans he had for his bathroom's color motif: "A man, don't you agree, needs something to *look* at all that time besides white porcelain? Something wild, something gassy?"

I let Joe Ben and his wife discuss bathroom fixtures while I finished my eggs . . .

*. . . A threat that he finally attributes to the fear he had as a child of being forced to eat a raw egg . . . (from Hank's shoulder the little boy gave his mother a last entreating look, but she said only, "Have fun, Leland.") and to the fact that Hank is obviously still quite upset. . . .*

Joe was in high spirits even for Joe. He had missed the hostilities last night and had gone to bed ignorant of the redeclaration of the cold war between Hank and me, and had spent a night dreaming visionary dreams of brotherhood while his relatives wrangled below Joe's Utopia: a color-filled world of garlands and maypoles, of bluebirds and marigolds, where Man Is Good to His Brother Simply Because It Is More Fun. Poor fool Joe with your Tinker Toy mind and scrambled world . . . The story is told that when Joe was a child his cousins emptied his Christmas stocking and replaced the gifts with horse manure. Joe took one look and bolted for the door, eyes glittering with excitement. "Wait, Joe, where you going? What did ol' Santa bring you?" According to the story Joe paused at the door for a piece of rope. "Brought me a bran'-new pony but he got away. I'll catch 'em if I hurry."

And ever since then it seemed that Joe had been accepting more than his share of hardship as good fortune, and more than his share of shit as a sign of Shetland ponies just around the corner, Thoroughbred stallions just up the road. Were one to show him that the horses didn't exist, never had existed, only the joke, only the shit, he would have thanked the giver for the fertilizer and started a vegetable garden. Were I to tell him I wanted to ride to church with him solely to complete my rendezvous with Viv he would have rejoiced that I was cementing relations with Hank by becoming better friends with his wife.

*Lee sees Hank glance briefly at him from behind the paper, eyes troubled and mouth searching for a kind and prudent phrase that will make everything all right again. He cannot find it. The mouth closes in defeat, and before the paper is lifted again Lee sees an expression of helplessness that makes him feel both elated and somewhat troubled. . . .*

But I liked the little gnome too much to risk the truth with him. What I *did* tell him: "I don't mind, Joe, waiting till dark to come home. Besides, I think I heard—didn't I hear you say, Viv, that you were thinking about driving in for low tide this afternoon after some clams?"

Viv sat darning socks on a chrome kitchen stool with the toes of her tennis shoes hooked under a gleaming rung and a sock pulled over a light bulb. She drew the needle through the knot and brought the thread to her gleaming row of sharp little teeth *Snip!* "Not clams, Lee"—guardedly, looking into her darning box for another sock—"rock oysters. Yes. I mentioned that I might be coming in, but I don't know . . ." She looked toward Hank. The newspaper rustled across the table, straining its newsprint eardrums.

"Can I ride back with you? If you do come in?"

"Shall I pick you up at Joe and Jan's new house or where? If I do?"

"That'll be fine."

She slid the bulb into another sock; a GE eye winked at me slyly from a woolen rim.

"So . . ." I had a date. I stood up from the table. "Ready when you are, Joe."

"Right. You kids! Squeaks, get the kids in the boat. Get all your stuff. Hup! Hup!"

Wink. The eye was gradually stitched closed with white woolen eyelashes. Snip. "So I guess I'll see you later, Lee?" she asked with tense indifference and a white woolen thread hanging from her lip.

"Yeah, I guess." I yawned over my shoulder as I followed Joe out of the kitchen. "Later"—and yawned again: I could be as indifferent as they come.

*For a second, after Hank returns to his newspaper, unable to go through with his start, Lee longs to run to his brother and ask for his forgiveness and his help: Hank, pull me up! save me! don't let me die down here like an insect! (The little boy turned from his mother. "Hank, I'm awful tired—" Hank knuckled the boy's head. "Don't be a sissy now, sport—ol' Hankus'll keep the dark from gettin' you.")— but decides instead: The devil with him; what does he care? and clamps his jaw indignantly . . .*

In the front room Hank asked if I was planning on staying in town a while to hobnob with the hobgoblins after church. I told him I might, yes; he grinned—"Little of God, then a little of ghosts, is that it, bub?" as though our unfortunate argument were forgotten. "Well . . . keep a tight hold on it."

As a matter of fact, I thought, leaving the house, when it comes to being tensely indifferent, all three of us can swing it pretty skillfully . . .

*In the daylight sky outside, Lee finds the full moon waiting, like one who has stayed up all night to see the action and is not going to miss it now ("If you're ever gonna get through this ol' world," Hank told the child as they left the house, "you're gonna have to get big enough to take the dark of it.")—a daylight moon, staring at him even more fiercely than had the plate of eggs—and his indignation begins to quickly melt . . .*

As we drove the road to town, Joe was so enthusiastic at the prospect of a convert that he took it upon himself to relate to me the tale
of how *he* came to be saved. . . . "Come at me one night in a
*dream!*" he shouted, trying to make himself heard above the pick-up's
roar; though all the noise—the throb of the tires on the pavement,
the kids in back hooting Halloween horns and twirling ratchet-clatter-
ing noisemakers—somehow added to the effect of his tale. "Just like
it come to David an' them others. All day, all *week*, we'd been working a piece of swamp up a good deal north of here—oh, let me see,
this was a good seven, eight years back, weren't it, Jan? When I got
the call told me to join the church? In the early part of spring—and
the wind had been blowin' to take the hair right off your head. It
ain't so dangerous cutting in the wind as some say, especially you keep
a good track of what's what . . . check for snags with high limbs that
might bust off and like that—I ever tell you about Judy Stamper?
Aaron's little grandkid? She was just walking along one day, through
the state park back up river it was, too, and got hammered flat by a
spruce limb. In a *state park*, by gosh! Her mom and dad up and left
the country for keeps. Like to kilt ol' Aaron. Wasn't exceptional
windy, neithers, nice summer day—they was out picknickin'—she just
left the picnic table a second to go off behind the bushes to see a man
about a dog and *kerwhack*, just like that, dead as a doornail . . .
Man!"

He sat soberly shaking his head over the tragedy, until he recalled
the story from which he had digressed. "But, oh yeah!" A wide white
smile flashed from his orange face and he went on with the tale.

"It'd been windy, like I said, an' that night when I went off to
sleep I had this *dream* like I was up topping this spar and the wind
commenced to *blow* and *blow* till wasn't a thing still; *everything*
whirling this way and that and a great . . . big . . . voice booms out
*Joe Ben . . . Joe Ben, thou must be saved* and I said sure sure ain't
I been planning to all along? but let me first get this here tree topped
we're running way behind and here it is *March!* So I go back to
chopping . . . and that wind cranks up a notch. And the voice comes
again: *Joe Ben, Joe Ben, go get yourself saved* and I says okay can you
just hang on a second for chrissakes? Can't you see I'm bustin' my
butt hurryin'? And went to choppin' again. And then the wind *really*
cut loose! If it'd been blowing before, it was just warming up. Trees
come loose outa the ground and walked around the countryside like
dancers; houses went to whippin' past in the air; big old geese came
zipping by *backwards*. . . . And there I am, blowed out from that

tree stiff at an angle, hanging with just my fingernails. Flapping like a flag. *Joe Ben, Joe Ben—go get—*But that was enough for me. I jumped right up in bed."

"That's right," Jan confirmed. "He did jump right up in bed. In March."

"And I says, 'Jan, get up an' get on your clothes. We're gonna be *saved!*'"

"That's right. That's just what he said. To get up an'—"

"Yeah, just like that. We were livin' in the old Atkins place at the time, down river—just made a down payment on it, you recall, Jan? Couple months later, Lee, the old crackerbox just jumped in the river like a *frog. Just* one day *kersplash!* I swear, I no more thought it would cave off like that than I thought it could fly! But she did. Jan lost her mama's antique spinet piano, too."

"It did. I'd nearly forgot that. Just like a frog it—"

"So right the next day I went to see Brother Walker."

"After your house was lost?" I was a little confused by the chronology of his narrative. "Or after—"

"Oh no, I mean right after *The Dream!* And let me tell you. You want to hear something make your hair stand up on end? As soon, the very *instant* I took them vows, the very *instant* I took them vows and *drunk* that water diluted right from the River Jordan, you know what taken place? You know what?"

I laughed and told him I would be afraid to guess.

"Jan, she got pregnant with our firstborn is just exactly what!"

"That's so. I did. Right after."

"*Right* after," he emphasized.

"Incredible," I marveled. "It's hard to imagine an elixir of such potency. She became pregnant the *moment* after you drank the diluted water?"

"Yes sir! The very instant."

"I'd have given something to witness that event."

"Oh, man, the Strength of the Lord is a Caution." Joe shook his head respectfully. "Like Brother Walker tell us, 'God is a Highballer in Heaven.' A highballer, see, is a old loggin' term for a guy who did about twice as much as others. 'A Highballer in Heaven with a Lowballer in Hell!' That's the kind of talk Brother Walker uses, Leland; he doesn't come on with a lot of this highhanded crap other preachers talk. He lays 'em right on the *line!*"

"That's so. *Right* on the line."

*The pale daylight moon darts along through the trees, keeping them in sight. That drivel about men being affected by the full moon —wolfbane and so on—is nonsense, complete nonsense . . .*

Joe and his wife continued talking about their church all the way in to Wakonda. I had planned to beg off attending the services by developing a sudden headache, but Joe's enthusiasm was such that I couldn't disappoint him and was compelled to accompany him to the carnival grounds, where a huge two-masted maroon tent housed his version of God. We were early. The folding chairs placed in neat rows about the bright wood-shaving-strewn interior of the tent were only partly filled with long-jowled fishermen or loggers, haunted by their own dreams of windy death. Joe and Jan insisted on taking their usual seats in the front row. "Where Brother Walker really gets his teeth into you, Leland; c'mon." But I declined, saying I would feel conspicuous. "And, as I am a newcomer in the Lord's tent, Joe, I think it might be best to try my first sample of this potent new faith from the back row, out of reach of the good brother's molars, all right?"

And from this vantage point I was able to slip up the aisle a few minutes after services jumped off, without disturbing the worship of the red-faced believers or the rock-and-roll catechism that Brother Walker's blind wife was whanging out on her electric steel guitar. I got out of that tent just in time.

*Complete and utter nonsense. Those other times when the moon happened to be full, nothing but coincidences; coincidence and nothing more.* I say just in time because when I got outside I found a weird and whirly feeling sifting down on me from the thumb-smudged sky, a giddy and giggly sensation foaming up out of the cracked earth. Then it finally dawned on me: *Nitwit, you have a pot hangover is all.* The "aftergrass," Peters called it. Residual high that occasionally comes on about noon the day after blowing up too much of the Mexican laughing grass the night before. Nothing very dire. Compared to the living death of an alcohol hangover, this day-after high is a small price to pay for a night-before kick. There's no sickness; no headache; none of the baked tongue or bowled eyeballs that alcohol leaves one with—only a minor euphoria, and a dreamy, air-walking, time-stretching state that is often very pleasant. But it can tend to make the world appear a little goofy, and if one is in a goofy situation anyway—like a rhythm-and-blues church—it can tend to make it a lot goofier.

So I say just in time because when the high first started to come on
—to the tune of "Onward Christian Soldiers" played dance-time on a
steel guitar as Brother Walker screamed for converts to stand and seek
their salvation—I didn't relate it to being high the night before and,
for a few maddening moments, teetered on the verge of trooping forth
up that sawdust path to metaphysical glory.

In the lot outside I scribbled a note to Joe and placed it beneath
the wiper blade on the pick-up, asking that he forgive my early departure, saying I would have stayed but that "even from the back
row I felt the power of Brother Walker's bite; such holiness must be
taken at first in small doses." *He sees the moon again, reflected in the
pick-up window: You don't scare me. Not a bit of it. In fact, I'm in
better shape than during your quarter or half . . .* ("Here's as good
a place to start as any." *Hank stopped the pick-up and pointed to a
yard already choked with twilight.* "Just knock an' say 'Trick or treat'
is all there is to it, bub . . . head out.") *. . . because the chips are
falling my way for the first time in my life . . .*

I struck out for town, which seemed to lie hundreds of miles to the
north across a vacant lot. Banking slightly to the leeward, I turned on
an impulse from Alagahea Street down the long broken backbone of
Swede Row, trip-tapping along the old wooden-vertebrae sidewalk,
running my knuckles along the bleached picket ribs of the Scandinavian yards. *He keeps watch on it following ominously behind the
maple trees. . . . (The child lifted his mask and stared at the house.
"But we're at Swede Row, Hank! This is Swede Row!") He sees it
slide behind clouds. . . .* Christian Soldiers still marched Onward
across the scattered wood shavings of my tented skull, but from the
heathen Nordic yards skinny blond children with knees like door-
knobs peered out at me from behind godless Viking masks. "Look the
man. Hey, watcha scared of? Hey hey hey!" *Hell with you and your
macaroons and wolfbane. I'm in good shape; for the first time in my
life the faint odor of distant victory blows my direction (Hank
laughed.* "A Swede ain't no different from any other nigger. Now get
on; there's some other kids from your class goin'."); *so how can you
expect me to be coerced by a noon moon, and such a sallow one at
that?*

I stepped up my dreamy pace, eager to put behind me the noise, the
hubbub, the midway of bones and the whole Valhalla carnival, eager
to get across town to the long, withdrawing roar of bracing salt sea,
where Viv would be waiting with open arms and closed eyes. *Lee's*

steps fall faster and faster until he is near to running and his breath coming fast (The boy stood at the gate and looked into the murky, weed-lurking yard. At the very next house a Mickey Mouse and a masked cowboy no older than himself held forth sacks for the black-mailed booty. If they could do it, surely he could. He wasn't scared of the dark yard, not really, like he let Hank think, or of what he might find behind the door—just some old fat Swede fishwife. No, he wasn't really scared of Swede Row . . . but his hand wouldn't lift the gate's hand-carved latch).

The scene in town was as chaotic as the outskirts. A fever-cheeked real-estate man soaping his windows winked at me over a bar of Dial and hoped I was enjoying my stay, and a moth-eaten yellow rag of a tomcat tried to entice me into the alley to view his collection of dirty pictures. Boney Stokes stalked his shadow out of the barbership and into the bar, where he bought it a drink. Grissom frowned at my approach—"Here come that Stamper kid to read my books for nothing" —and frowned when I walked on past—"So! My books is not good enough for his educated tastes!"—and a miniature rubber-faced were-wolf leaned against the doorjamb, passing the time with a yo-yo while he waited for dark.

The sun is cold though very bright and sharp; the chrome ornaments on the cars stand out in glistening relief; atop the telephone poles the insulators gleam with brilliant emerald luminance of their own . . . but Lee walks with his eyes strained wide as though through a dark night (Finally the boy managed to get through the gate and across the yard, only to stop once more at the door. Fear paralyzed his fingers again, but this time he knew that the thing he feared lay not in back of that door, but behind him! back across that yard! waiting in the pick-up! Without thinking another second, he jumped from the porch and ran. "Bub, hold it. Where—?" Around the corner of the house. "Bub! Bub! Wait; it's okay!" Into the tall weeds, where he hid until Hank was past. "Lee! Lee-land, where you at?" Then jumped up and ran again, and ran and ran and ran) and already feels an evening chill in the afternoon wind.

Once more I accelerated my pace and when I glanced back over my shoulder I saw I had given the Christian Army the slip and ditched the Vikings and the real-estate man; the yellow tom still followed me, but his devil-may-care look of lascivious determination was beginning to tire. I turned from Main down Ocean Way, all but running, and was just complimenting myself on a clean getaway from all my demons when a machine swerved to halt on the roadbank, scratching gravel beside me like an amorous dragon.

"Hey, dad, we give you a lift somewhere?"

From a whiskerless face too young to buy beer glinted a pair of onyx eyes old before the Black Plague hit Europe.

"We're makin' the A and W, hey, dad. We'll take you that far. Climb aboard."

The molded white front door swung open to reveal a band sinister enough to make the masked Viking look like a merit-badge contender and the werewolf seem a whimpering old Dog Tray. A crew twice as frightening because they wore no masks or costumes. Terrors of teen-age fashion, dressed in their everyday Halloween best; a half dozen gum-chewing, toothpick-sucking, lipstick-nibbling oral compulsives, outfitted for an ordinary day with the gang. A carful of young America in living color, chemical monsters created by du Pont, with nylon flesh over neon veins pumping Dayglo blood to Orlon hearts.

"What's buggin' you, dad? You look rank. I mean you look rank!"

"Nothing. I'm just having a narrow escape is all."

"Yeah? Yeah? An' what happened?"

"I was on my way across town when I was captured by a band of aliens."

"Yeah? Brass band? Ball-point pens? Bamboo who? Who?"

A group giggle punctured by pistol cracks of gumfire unnerved me slightly, but I was nevertheless able to decipher their code.

"Bam-bee thee," I answered. "See . . . ?"

The giggling stopped, and the gum-cracking. "So . . . how's the life?" the driver inquired, after a cease-fire of silence.

"Rife," I answered, a little less enthusiastically this time. My coded witticism met with silence a second time, and something in the tone of this silence told me that my companions did not take kindly to squares turning their own slang back on them. So I kept quiet to let my benefactors concentrate on the road and their gum (Ran and hid, and ran again from alley to alley and shadow to shadow until he was confronted by the headlighted sweep of asphalt highway). After a few moments of gum-clacking the driver laid his hand on my sleeve.

"Well now. That church key, man."

I handed him the opener. He took it without thanks and went to work on a seed between his teeth with its plated point. I began to get worried. The air was charged with a sadism too overt to be imagined; I had got into hot water this time and no fantasy. There is a certain kind of impending violence that one can never mistake, no matter how rampant the imagination. But just as I was about to throw open the door and leap from the speeding car a girl leaned up from the back seat to whisper something in the driver's ear and he glanced at me and blanched, his maniacal leer changing to a little boy's ingratiating grin. "Oh . . . uh . . . but look, mister . . . unless you want a glass of root beer, I mean right now at the A and W up ahead, where can we drop you? Electric chair? Frigidaire?"

"There!" I pointed at a pair of fading ruts leading off the highway west into the push of green. "Right there!" (*The child lay in the ditch until his panting slowed; then he dashed across to a private dirt road hedged high on both sides with dense undergrowth*). Again on impulse, plus the desire to flee my newfound friends: "Right there will be fine, thanks. . . ."

"There? I declare. Nothing up that road but cedar keys and sand coons dunes. It's *wild* child out there." He slowed the car to a stop.

"It's wild in here," I noted, setting off a new sputter of giggling and opening the door to step out. "Well, I thank you . . ."

"You, hey. They say you're Hank Stamper's brother? Huh? Hey, well anyway, here's where you wanted out."

The driver waved with a casual lift of his hand, grinning in a way to let me know that for reasons unknown to me I was either very lucky or very unlucky to be Hank Stamper's brother.

"Blue-tail fly," he called meaningfully.

"Good-by."

The whitewalls jumped, spinning gravel back at me as the car pulled back onto the pavement and I scuttled into the underbrush before another carful of good Samaritans came along.

*Free from the car's predatory atmosphere, Lee tries once more to calm himself: What's the hurry? I have at least another hour before I meet her . . . loads of time (The boy walked through the overhanging dark, able for the first time to question his sudden flight; he knew that it hadn't been the house that he ran from, nor did he really fear his brother—Hank would never hurt him, never let anything get him—so what had he run from? He walked on, knotting his little features to understand his actions . . .) So, seriously now, what is the hurry?*

If I expected to find respite in Mother Nature's lush green arms I was disappointed. After continuing for a few minutes, the wobbling road petered out completely and I left the last human scatter of paintless shacks and geranium plants in coffee tins and entered the dense jungle that is found all along the Oregon coast wherever the sand dunes, driven up from the sea, have become mixed with enough organic material to support life. The span of this jungle where I crossed was no more than thirty or forty yards, yet my passage took an equal number of minutes, and the weaving vine maple trees with their supple limbs and pale fall leaves purified by sun and rain seemed no more natural than had the teen-age laboratory concoctions that had driven me to the woods.

*So, seriously, what is the hurry? It's not that late. But then . . . why does my chin tremble? It's not that cold (Why'd I run? I ain't scared of them Swedes. I ain't scared of Hank neither. The only thing I was really scared about was that he might be watching when I jumped or yelled or something . . .)*

Though it was still early it was already beginning to grow a bit dark. Clouds had moved in to take the sun from me. I stumbled forward toward a quiltwork of dim light filtering through the leaves. Once I broke through a garden of rhododendron and huckleberry into an oily purple-black bog, glassy with decay where decomposition spread in a thick film over the shallow water. Lily pads floated here and there and from a particularly foreboding mass of peat and pollution a disconsolate bullfrog cried, "Suh-WOMP! Suh-WOMP!"— with all the desperation of someone shouting "Murder" or "Fire."

I tried to skirt the bog, veering to the left, and at the edge, near the place where the frog had been voicing his plight, I found myself confronted by a community of strange, sweet-smelling tube-shaped plants. They grew in upthrusting clusters of six or eight, like little green families, with the oldest attaining a height of three feet and the youngest no bigger than a child's crooked finger. Regardless of size, and except for the broken-backed unfortunates, they were all identical in shape, starting narrow at the base and tapering larger toward the neck like a horn, except instead of the horn's blossoming bell, they turned at the last moment, bowing their necks, looking back to their base. Imagine an elongated comma, sleek, green, driven into the purple mud with its straightened tip; or picture half-notes for vegetable musicians, thicker at the neck than at the base, with the rounded oval head a swooping continuation of the neckline; and it is still unlikely that you have the picture of these plants. Let me say only that they were an artist's conception of chlorophyll beings from another planet, stylized figures half humorous, half sinister. Perfect Halloween fare.

*(So the only thing I was really scared of back at Swede Row was of Hank seeing me get scared. Now ain't that simply the most ridiculous thing? Sure . . . The boy laughed to find his fear so ridiculous, but kept walking away from the town just the same; he knew that what he had done had banished him forever from his home; he knew what old Henry and all of them thought of scaredy cats, even if the thing the scaredy cats were scared of was of being scaredy cats.)*

I plucked one of the plants from its family to examine it more carefully and found that under the comma's loop was a round hole resembling a mouth, and at the tapered bottom of the tube a clogging liquid containing the carcasses of two flies and a honey bee, and I realized that these odd swamp plants were Oregon's offering in the believe-it-or-not department of unusual life forms: the Darlingtonia. A creature trapped in that no-thing's land between plants and animals, along with the walking vine and the paramecium, this sweet and sleek carnivore with roots enjoyed a well-rounded meal of sunshine and flies, minerals and meat. I stared at the stalk in my hand and it stared blindly back.

"Hello," I said politely into the oval, honey-breathed mouth. "How's the life?"

"Suh-WOMP!" prompted the bullfrog and I dropped the plant as though burned and fled westward again.

*When Lee reaches the top of the dunes he shivers at the sight: a few hundred yards away the ocean lies, peaceful and gray, with its lacy edge turned back upon the beach like a chenille bedspread ready for night* (The moon led the boy across the dunes. A scant sliver of moon that barely lit the beckoning surf); *but there is the sand . . .*

I finally emerged at the base of a steep bank of golden sand and clambered upward on all fours, filling pockets and shoes. The Oregon dunes are of the finest, cleanest, and most uniform sand found in America; constantly moving, forever sifted by summer winds and washed by winter rains, and extending in some areas for miles without tree or bush or flower, too orderly to be the work of haphazard nature and too immense to be the product of man, they present an unreal world to even the casual observer—to my already cockeyed eye, as I achieved the crest of the bank, the dunes presented a terrain forbidding in the extreme.

*He trudges toward that bed's embroidered spread, heedless of his feet in his trancelike walking* (Halfway to the sea, completely alone on a bare, sweeping field of sand, the little boy vanished . . .) *and feels disappointed when he reaches the dunes' edge: What had I* imagined might happen, here in broad daylight out on a completely featureless field of sand? (vanished—into close and musty dark, vanished down into the black and moonless earth itself!)

At the edge of the dunes where the beach began, a sun-silvered pile of logs separated the sea's territory from the territory of dry land, like an absurd wooden wall. I climbed across it, wondering what I would do to distract myself and pass the hour until it was time to meet Viv . . . *When he reaches the beach he hopes that the terror provoked by the dunes will subside, but it hangs on and follows him down the beach like a piece of the clotted black clouds, crackling and hissing a few feet above his head. Pot hangover, he insists. Nothing else. Just get the old mind elsewhere. Come now, man, you can ignore a little old pot hangover* . . . To while away the wait I sailed rocks at the droves of sandpipers that stood motionless at the edge of the water, beaks to the wind like little weathervanes each mounted on one thin spike. I dug after the little pink-shelled sandcrabs and tossed them to the careening gulls. I rolled over humps of beach kelp and watched the blizzard of insect life that resulted. I ran full tilt along the foamed edge of the waves for as far as my poor tar-infested lungs would carry me; I engaged in frantic screaming matches with the gulls; I rolled up my cuffs and tied my shoes to my belt and splashed in the surf until my ankles became swollen and numb . . . *but every word he sings, every jump and gesture, seems to be an act making up a ritual for conjuring some fierce fiend out of the earth, a ritual he can't stop because every act calculated to stem its onrush to success turns out to be another part of some subconscious ceremony necessary to that success. As he comes closer and closer to the climax of this oceanside sacrament, it occurs to him that all his wild maneuvering might be re-enactments of childhood frolic: No wonder I'm getting the psychological jitters; why the deuce not? I'm sprinting hell-bent backwards. I'm taking a running jump at the womb. That's all it is.* Along with pot hangover. That's all (*Gradually, as the shock of the fall subsided, the little boy tried to move. He looked directly above him and found that he could perceive the passage of stars through a round hole far above his head, and as the wind shifted to blow from the rocky cliffs to the north at Wakonda Head, he found he could hear the angry pawbeats of an ocean frustrated at being cheated of a rightful prize by a hole in the ground*) and all I need to do to overcome it is find something of this tune to associate with. *He looks about the tuneless beach frantically* . . . and just then my eye happened to fall on a first-rate distraction: a car stuck in the seaside sand a quarter-mile south of me, down the beach, almost to the big breakwater jetty where I was due to meet Viv. And there was something very familiar about the molding and primer job on the car, familiar indeed; a first-rate way to pass the time, if I am correct. *(The boy lay at the bottom of a huge tube. A tube down into the earth. One of the chimneys of Hell! the boy thought, recalling old Henry's warning about devil's stovepipes out on the dunes where unwary wanderers might fall. Clear to Hell! the boy remembered and began to cry.)*

So I rolled down the pants legs and replaced the shoes and hurried down the beach. I was right, it was the carload of samaritans. My old friend the driver stood smoking calmly in complete disregard of the beseeching and baleful look of his sandlocked car, which stood trapped and helpless in the waves. He sighed at my approach. A cigarette package was rolled in the sleeve of his Dayglo pullover and his hands were thrust in the back pockets of his Levis. The skidding tracks along the beach told the story: they had driven to the Coast Guard station and down onto the beach, high on root beer and ripe for action. They had squirreled closer and closer to the ocean, taunting the tide, daring the waves, kicking sand in its gleaming teeth as though it were a ninety-eight-pound weakling. And had been caught. Planks and branches evidenced futile and frantic attemps to free the wheels. But no soap, the sand held fast. Now the tide was turned and it was the ocean's turn to tease closer and closer with excruciating patience. Footprints led up the beach, running for help, but unless that help arrived in the next few minutes it would be too late. Each snickering slap of water sank the right side of the car deeper into the sand. In five more minutes the foam would be chuckling against the differential. In ten, laughing against the door. In half an hour the waves would be roaring with triumph over the motorblock, into the wiring with the corrosive salt, ripping zebra-skin upholstery, breaking windows, and rolling the fuzzy dice hanging from the rear-view mirror. And in an hour would be rolling the whole car like a bathtub toy. *The car's passive acceptance of its fate touches Lee. The stoic wisdom of metal. He wishes he could be as calm (The wind gathered on the dunes. It blew over the tube with an intermittent wailing, a phantom pipe played by the wind and tempoed by the beat of a surf somewhere in another world. The boy stopped crying; he decided this couldn't be one of the devil's stovepipes; it was too cold to be part of Hell)—as calm and as accepting: wheels caught in a waiting grave, and with the moon full to boot. . . . He walks directly to the car . . .*

The driver eyed my approach but didn't speak. "Hey, man," I called, "what's the bubble?" *Say trouble, Lee implores the boy silently.* "What's the clatter?" *Please say matter, Lee begs as longingly as the doomed car, please say something friendly.* I stopped walking. His cronies, standing ten yards back up the beach in the midst of a collection of trunk paraphernalia—jack, spare tire, blankets, golf clubs —looked slowly from me to their leader.

"Mr. Stamper," he purred when a little space opened in the ocean's roar. "You arrive just like a hero. All you Stampers are heroes, they say. So, hey, you bring along a shovel? A chain maybe? Maybe you called us a tow truck. You call us a tow truck by any chance, Mr. Stamper? Or you got help on the way?"

"Nope. Just strolling past, enjoying the beach all alone."

Alarmed by his sugar-and-venom tone, I quickly realized that this scene might constitute more of a distraction than I had bargained for. "Well, blue-tail fly," I said cheerily and tried to walk on past. *Lee stands, looking beyond the kid's Dayglo shoulder in the direction of the whistle buoy calling plaintively out in the dark water (The little boy could occasionally hear the buoys out in the bay's mouth, and sometimes the sound of Diesels going past on the highway . . . but as time passed he came to devote all his attention to the star-dotted coin of sky above him: it seemed to be growing lighter near one edge . . .)* But as I passed him he reached out and laid a freckled hand on my arm to stop me, keeping his face turned slightly away; brilliant stigmata of whiteheads decorated his rosy cheek. When he spoke I noticed a decided change in his attitude since our earlier encounter. There had been cruelty, but now something had turned it to hate.

"Gee, Mr. Stamper. Where you going? Didn't we give you a hand in need a while back? Don't you suppose you might help us?"

"Sure"—brightly, cheerfully. "Sure, what can I do? Should I phone for a truck? I'm going toward civilization. . . ." I gestured vaguely toward town. "I'll send someone."

"Oh well I jes' guess not," Dayglo crooned. "We already sent somebody to telephone. Can't you help some *other* way? You being a Stamper and all?" His fingers tenderly rolled the fabric of my jacket. "Sure," I exclaimed. "Sure, I'll do what I can but—" Too bright now, too cheerful. I laughed nervously, and the fingers tightened on my arm.

"You sure happy about something, Mr. Stamper. What is it you so happy about?"

I shrugged, knowing by this time that any answer I gave would doubtless be the wrong one . . . *A cluster of sandbirds flickers past Lee's head like leaves in a whirlwind; he watches them with remote interest as they wheel in a sharp turn and settle all together at the edge of the waves a few yards from the car. They go immediately to work as soon as they all light.* (Yes! *the boy exclaims.* Light! *He was positive of it now . . . way up through the tube, right over at that one edge of his little spot of sky: light! a Heavenly light! dimming out his allotment of stars as it moved ever so slowly through the sky. . . . A light was coming and was going to stop directly above his hole, just for him!* "Help me, O Heavenly Father, O God. You can do it, I know You can. Help me . . .") So I vowed to keep quiet, but that little nervous giggle escaped from me again.

"Oh boy, Mr. Stamper here is got a good sense humor, seein' our car in this fix!" And I felt the hand grow even tighter on my arm. . . . *Almost oblivious now to the hand, Lee watches the little birds work the runneling beach: How their poor bonded lives are written for them . . . everlastingly tuned to the pitiless sea, immutably timed to the measured echo of the waves.* "An', y'know, guys, the way I see it, a fellow like Mr. Stamper with such a good sense humor about our fix he should be able to help us *outen* it, I see it that way."

I didn't see it at all that way, but I didn't voice my dissension. I half turned to gauge the distance to the jetty, but the driver's gum-cracking henchmen read my look and shuffled over to cut off any attempt at a sudden break, and I began to feel properly trapped (*At the bottom of the hole the boy's eyes burned from long minutes without blinking. His numbed legs had collapsed unnoticed beneath him and his crumpled skull mask dangled from his neck like an amulet. The aching cold in his fingers was forgotten as he watched the light in the sky overhead move closer to his restricted line of vision.* "I'm ready, Father in Heaven. O please. Come take me. I don't want to die in this old hole. I don't want to go home ever again. Just come and take me with you, O God . . .") and also for the first time properly afraid; I'd heard tales of these beach hooligans and their ideas of sport. . . . *Lee shakes his arm free of the driver's grip and moves a few steps closer to the sea. He feels tired, almost sleepy. He looks for the daytime moon but the clouds have blown across it. He looks back at the busy detail of birds working the dangerous* surf; *their hectic pecking and hunting makes him more tired than ever* . . . "Gosh, I mean, you're a Stamper, Mr. Stamper; a Stamper oughta be able to help us out." . . . *He sees the birds as slaves, slaves to the rocking waves.* "I mean, now say, for instance Hank Stamper, I bet he could just put a big strong shoulder agin our car and push it out with one heave." *Slaves, birds in bondage to the waves. Run run run down the beach right at the edge of the receding wave peckety peckety peckety after sand fleas turn around run run run back before the next wave rolls salty death over you* . . . *over and over and over.* (*The little boy prayed fervently in his constricting dark, as the wind blew a hymn over the top of the hole, and the light came closer, brighter* . . .) "An' if Hank could do it I bet you could do it too, hey? So let's see you put a shoulder an' try. Come on, hey?"

I saw there was nothing to do but humor my tormentors and hope that they would grow tired of the game; so I rolled my pants legs another roll and walked around to the seaward side of the car. The water was like cold knives against my ankles. I put my shoulder against the rear fender and made as though I were shoving. . . . *Slaves to the waves; pause too long pecking out a morsel from the running sand and WATCH OUT all the others turn run run run back except one careless bird, and when the wave rolls back a gray-speckled dot kicks desperately to free its wing from the sand before the next wave run run run up turn run run run back* ("O Father in Heaven I see you comin' I'm waitin' I'm waitin'!") *turn run run run* . . . "You gonna have to do better than that, Mr. Stamper; Hank Stamper'd be downright ashamed, you goin' at it so puny an' the water getting so high." . . . *One of the other birds comes across the drowned wad of feathers and pauses for a fraction of a second before running on in his eternal game with the waves; can't stop! no time to mourn! sand fleas or starve! No time, no time!* (*The light brightened. The boy could see one edge of it, like the tip of a great glowing finger crooking to him from the sky!*) "Mr. Stamper, I don' even think you're tryin'. We'll have to help you out." I felt the icy rasp of salt water scrape my throat, and the first choking of panic. "C'mon, you can try!" . . . *He feels tiredness creeping up his bones like the cold; he tosses his head and spits a mouthful of water. The birds, why do they do it? He thinks of the Darlingtonia he picked earlier. They aren't like the birds, they can afford the luxury of patience. They can wait. And if one doesn't attract his quota of flies and starves, it is only the dropping of a leaf. The plant still lives, the roots still live.*

But that little bird was just one and when he drowned, that was it, that was all of him, the one little bird. He lost. The wave wins, the bird loses.

And the waves always eventually win. Unless . . .

"Right down here, Mr. Stamper, your shoulder." My mind became frantic as I felt more hands on me. . . . *Unless you play it smart, unless you acknowledge your fate and accept it. Like the car. . . .* "Get your shoulder here, Mr. Stamper."

"You better not . . . my brother will . . ."

"Your brother will what, Mr. Stamper? Your brother isn't here. All alone, you said." . . . *He doesn't struggle against them; they begin to weary of the sport without a struggle* . . . "My goodness, you got wet, Mr. Stamper." . . . *And even when they step back he doesn't try to come out of the water that is breaking waist deep* . . . "You must really like the water, Mr. Stamper." . . . *He turns instead toward the incoming froth of the waves, looking out at the beautiful line of the horizon, then at the frantic efforts of the silly birds. All the poor silly devils need do is run run run and then wait* . . . *for that cold final crack to stop the whole insufferable hassle. A half-dozen steps and you end this frantic game. You don't win, but you don't lose, either. A stalemate is the best you can hope for, don't you see? The very best* . . .

"Look."

"Who's that?"

"Oh Christ-o-Friday. It *is* him. . . ."

"Split! Everybody split!"

The driver leads and the others follow, sprinting off toward the dunes. Lee doesn't notice them leaving. He is tossed off balance by a wave. He is completely under for a moment, and when his face rolls into the air once more, serene and thoughtful, he sees again that tranquil horizon: *You come into this scene begging for quarter. Silly bird. You spend all your time calling King's-X, hoping to halt the game temporarily. You could learn from the fox and his sharpie ways. Screw it. Forget King's-X. Stop the game completely, stop the frantic hassle. Call it a draw while there's still a chance. WATCH OUT. No; concede. WATCH OUT! WATCH OUT! WATCH OUT! YOU CAN'T DO THIS TO ME! Just see if I can't. I concede* . . . "Lee!" *I call it a draw* . . . "Bub!"—*and walks toward horizon, into the lifting white embrace of the water* . . . "Goddammit anyhow—" . . . *into the rolling gray What?* "Lee!"

"What? Hank?" I pushed myself up from the sand where the Dayglo Gang had thrown me. "Hank?" And through the lace of foam frozen briefly in the air, I saw him coming over the rocks of the jetty. Not running yet; walking fast but not running. His fists clenched and his arms swinging and his boots spitting sand, but not running. They ran, the Plastic People, all five of them, they ran as if the devil were after them. But Hank just walked. He never for a moment blew his cool. . . . *Through distance and his foam-flecked glasses, Lee watches the scene on the beach. He watches the teen-agers flee as Hank closes the distance ("O Heavenly Father, I see your old light coming!") He is still being wallowed about by the waves out past the car as he watches Hank come. He makes no move toward deeper or shallower water—but, wait a minute! what's Brother Hank doing out here in place of his wildwoods wife?—no decision until an overpowering curiosity finally breaks the deadlock and he begins floundering awkwardly through the snowy foam toward the beach where Hank waits with his hands in his pockets.* All right, it may be a frantic hassle but you can call it a draw some other day . . . not even to come into the water to my rescue did he blow his cool; *but, wait a minute: what's he doing out here instead of . . .* he just stood on the bank with his hands in his pockets, watching me fight my way out of the surf. "Damn, Lee," he encouraged me when I got close enough, "if you ain't about the poorest excuse for a swimmer I ever saw, I'll eat my hat."

I couldn't even make a clever reply. I plopped to the sand, gasping and spent and feeling as if I had swallowed my weight in salt water. "You could . . . have . . . at least—"

"I tell you one thing that would help," Hank said, grinning down at me; "you'd do better wearing a *bathin'* suit 'stead of corduroy pants an' a sports jacket next time you go swimmin' with your friends."

"Friends?" I wheezed. "They were a gang of toughs . . . trying to kill me. You were almost too late . . . they might have . . . drowned me!"

"Next time I come I'll bring a bugle an' blow the cavalry charge. What reason did they give, by the way, for the drownin'?"

"A very good reason . . . as I recall." I was still lying on my side with the waves lapping hungrily at my feet, and I had to think a moment before I could remember what that very good reason was. "Oh yes . . . because I'm a Stamper. That was their reason."

"Reason aplenty, it seems," he said, and finally condescended to lean over and help me to my feet. "Let's get over to Joby's an' get you in some dry clothes. Boy. Look there at you. That's something. How a man can be damn near drowned by a gang of toughs and still never lose his specs. That's truly something."

"Never mind that. What are you doing here? What happened to Viv—the rock oysters?"

"I got the jeep parked just back of the driftwood there. Come on. Look out, grab your shoes! That wave like to got 'em . . ."

*By the time Lee has retrieved his shoes Hank has already started back up the beach, in the same hurrying walk: Where did you come from, brother, like a Mephistopheles in logging boots? (Out on the dark dunes more and more of the light showed in the hole; the little boy beat at his cramped thighs with mounting anticipation: "Yes! Yes! Yes God yes!"—more and more, brighter and closer, slowly . . .) Why did you come instead of her?* "What are you doing here?" I repeated, jogging to catch up with him.

"Something's come up. Joe Ben tried to find you after church but you'd gone. He gave me a call on the phone. . . ."

"Where's Viv?"

"What? Viv couldn't make it. I asked her to stay and help Andy tally up the booms . . . 'cause the heat is suddenly on. Joe phoned to say there was a meeting of Evenwrite and the boys, and the top union dog of the whole business. He said that they got the whole story about our deal with WP. Everybody knows. An' that the whole town's got their tit in a wringer." . . . *You were jealous, Lee decides triumphantly; you had misgivings about letting her come in to me! (Slowly brighter and closer . . .)* "So you came?" I asked, feeling my disappointment turn to a covert elation. . . . *And your jealousy has given me strength to make the moon wait another month.* "In Viv's place?"

"Christ yes I came in her place," he answered, flapping his hands against his pants legs to rid them of the sand that he'd picked up helping me to my feet. "I told you that once. What's the matter'th you? one them punks bust you across the head or something? Come on! Let's get up to that jeep; I want to get into the Snag an' see how the winds are blowin'."

"Sure. Okay, brother." I fell in behind him. "Right with you."

My pot hangover disappeared, and, in spite of the cold, I was blooming with sudden enthusiasm: he had come in her place! He was already sweating the possibility of a scene! My feeble embryo of a plan was proceeding better than I had hoped . . . *They move up the beach. Hank in front and Lee grimly shivering behind: We are joined, brother, shackled together for all our lives, just as the birds and the waves are immutably tuned together, in a song of patience and panic. We have been tuned thus for years, me piping and pecking after morsels while you crashed and roared* (Closer and brighter, the light almost there now; the little boy held his breath at the approaching glow of salvation . . .) *but now, brother, the roles are switching, and you are beginning to plaintively pipe the tune of panic and I am beginning the melancholy long withdrawing roar of patience . . . and I faced the future with a confident smirk.*

"Right behind you, brother mine. Lead on. Lead on. . . ."

Lee's steps stretch out to keep up with Hank. Indian Jenny prepares her soul for another attack on her manless world. The old bolt-cutter empties his last bottle of Thunderbird and decides to start for town before full dark. The clouds swarm up from the sea, black-booted and brave with the coming of night. The wind springs up from the slough bottoms. The dunes darken (*the boy watches the light*). In the mountains past the town, where the streams grow thirsty for winter, the lightning uncurls and begins to flutter in the fir trees, white-orange and black, for Halloween . . . (*Then, finally, after cold minutes or hours or weeks—he has no idea—the earth above the waiting boy has moved far enough. The light is in full view. And the glow of salvation is nothing but that same moon that led him across the dunes, a thin paring of moon that has gradually centered itself in his meager patch of far-off sky*) . . . in that kind of sky . . . (*Leee-land . . .*") in that kind of world.

"Leeee-land; oh, Leeee-land . . ." The boy doesn't hear; he stares at the moon, a thread-thin crescent hanging there between the stars like the last of a faded Cheshire cat—everything gone but the black reminder and the jeering grin . . . and this time the boy's weeping is not of the cold or the fright of falling into a dark hole, or of anything else he has ever cried about before . . .

"Leeeeelan' boy, answer me . . . !" The call comes again, nearer, but he doesn't answer. He feels that his voice is trapped like his weeping, beneath a cold lid of wind. Nothing can ever get out.

"Leland? Bub . . . ?"

The hole sinks deeper and deeper into the earth and is just beginning to strangle his consciousness when he feels something hail against the back of his neck. Sand. He raises his eyes up to the hole: The grin is gone! A face is there!

"Is that you, bub? You all right?" And a flashlight! "Gawdamn, bub, you gave me a real run for my money!"

With no tool but his pocket knife it takes Hank most of an hour to cut the limbs from a little scrub pine that he dragged onto the dunes. He works as near to the mouth of the hole as he feels safe, so the boy will be able to hear his labors. As he works he tries to talk constantly, keeping up an unconcerned-sounding flow of jokes and stories and shouted commands to the hound—"Come back here an' forget chasing those rabbits, you ol' potlicker!"—that listens, puzzled, from the spot where Hank tied him before starting. "Dang that ol' gadabout dog." He clucks loudly, then crawls to the hole on his belly again to check on the boy, whispering, "That's the kid. Sit good an' still. Don't fret. But don't rustle around down there any more'n you have to, neither."

He bellies back from the hole and returns to his work on the little pine; his nonchalant and rambling narrative is just the opposite of his frenzied hacking and whittling.

"Say now, bub, you know? Ever since I got here I been thinkin' . . . that this whole situation sure does put me in mind of something. An' it just now come to me what it was. It was the time old Henry and your Uncle Ben an' me—I was just about your age at the time, too, I guess—all drove over to Uncle Aaron's place up in Mapleton to help him dig a big hole for a outhouse. . . ."

He works swiftly but carefully at the tree; he could remove the branches more quickly by breaking them off, but then they would break off next to the trunk . . . he has to leave enough sticking out for the boy to hang on to, but not enough to scrape the sides of that hole—any little jostling could bring it all down.

"Your Uncle Aaron, you see, couldn't do with just any old five-or six-feet hole under his crapper—he wanted it deep. He had got it into his head some way that if it wasn't deep enough the roots from the garden could get to it an' he'd end up with carrots tastin' like turds. Now. Hang tough a minute; I'm gonna bring the ladder an' try to get it down."

He slides toward the hole again, dragging the tree with him; the branches have all been removed except those opposing each other, and these have been cut off a few inches from the skinny trunk. The result is a wobbly ladder some thirty feet long. Without standing, he up-ends the tree and begins to lower it very carefully down, talking all the while.

"Well, so we went at that hole, the dirt just aflyin' because it was loamy an' pretty soft diggin'—feel the ladder yet, bub? you holler when it gets down to where you can feel it—an' pretty quick we'd dug down about fifteen feet— Don't you feel it yet, for chrissakes? I'm prodded up against something."

He pulls the light from his pocket and shines it down; the butt of the trunk is resting against the boy's leg. "My leg's too cold, Hank, I didn't feel it on my leg."

"You mean you can't climb out on it?"

The boy shakes his head. "No," he says without emotion. "I can't feel my legs."

Hank shines the light around the tube; it might stand another hundred years or it might cave in in another ten minutes. Likely ten minutes. He can't chance going for help; he'll have to go down and carry him out. He scoots back from the hole and turns over on his back and comes at it again, feet first. An inch at a time he lowers himself through the opening.

"So we'd dug down fifteen feet . . . an' Uncle Ben an' Uncle Aaron was at the bottom, Henry an' me up top haulin' off the dirt . . . easy, easy does it . . . then Uncle Ben says he just had to go to the house for some water, would be right back, he says. Ah, gotcha, bub. Now; can you hang onto my belt?"

"I can't feel my fingers, Hank. I think my fingers died."

"You just dyin' a little bit at a time, huh?"

"My fingers and my legs, Hank," the boy answers flatly. "They died first."

"You're just cold. Here. Let's see what we can work out. . . ."

After some effort he removes his belt and loops it beneath the boy's shoulders; he ties the end of it through the leather trade patch at the back of his jeans and begins a slow climb back up the cramped tube; only during this climb does his casual tone flag. "Okay. Now listen, Lee: I didn't figure this scrub pine supportin' anything but you, not me an' you together. So help by climbin' if you can. But if you can't help, for Jesus H. Christ don't go to kicking and squirming! Here we go. . . ."

He emerges into the wind and straddles the hole, standing. As he draws the boy up after him by the belt he feels the sand surrounding the hole begin to crumble. He takes a breath and heaves, falling backward and pulling the boy onto him. From the hole there is a soft thump and for a moment a dusty cloud of rotten wood smell hangs above the sand, then is chased away before the sandslinging hoofs of that gritty wind. "Let's get our asses gone from here," Hank says in a hollow voice and starts back across the dunes with the dog at his heels and the boy piggyback.

"I reckon you know what you got into," he says after a few minutes of silence.

"A devil's stovepipe, I guess."

"Yeah. That's what the old man calls them. I didn't know there was any left. You see, bub, this here was a pine forest a long, long time ago. These dunes didn't useta be here, just trees. But the winds kept bankin' the sand higher and higher and finally covered up the forest. Clean to the top of the trees. And the trees eventually rotted out, leaving these *hollows* where they useta be, maybe just barely covered at the top. An' you stepped into one. A pretty good one, too, thank your lucky stars, because most people who fall into a stovepipe pull the stovepipe in after 'em an' then . . . But what I want to know is what in the goddam hell were you doin' out here anyway, headin' across the dunes to the ocean in the dead of night? Huh? Tell me that."

The boy doesn't speak; his face is cold and wet against Hank's neck, and the dilapidated mask flaps about them on its elastic string. Hank doesn't ask again.

"Anyhow, you ain't never to come out here again. The devil's stovepipe ain't none too pleasant a place to spend a night, even Halloween. It's lucky, too, I had me this old bluetick dog because the wind had blowed away all your tracks. . . . Yeah. Oh! Say now —about what happened to ol' Uncle Aaron the time he got in dutch in a hole. See, in the barnyard where we was putting in the hole, there was this old horse that Aaron kept around for his kids to ride, a old blind gelding who was twenty years if he was a day. Aaron'd had him all his worthless life, that old horse, and wouldn't get shut of him for nothing. So that old horse knew ever' inch of that barnyard, from the house to the fence and the barn to the pigpen. We kids used to put us on blindfolds and gallop him to scare ourselves, but he never hit a post or nothing. Well, anyhow, while we was there digging this outhouse hole, none of us'd even thought about that horse. Except Uncle Ben. And that was just the sort of thing Ben could think of. When he come up out of the hole for a water break he hollers back at Aaron and says, 'Henry and the boy are going with me for a sip, Aaron; we'll be back shortly!' He pulled us

off a piece from the hole and put a finger to his lips to me and Papa
and says in a whisper, 'Okay, now, shush. Watch this.'

" 'Watch *what*, you damn fool?' Papa says, and Ben says, 'Just keep
shushed an' watch this . . .'

"So Papa and I stood there. Ben went to trotting across the barnyard at that hole, pawing the ground with his boots and snorting.
Keeping back far enough to where Aaron couldn't see him. He even
kicks a couple clods into the hole.

" 'Whoa!' Aaron yells. 'Whoa! Get back there, damn you, get
*back!* You'll fall in here on me! Get back.'

"Ben kept it up, knocking more and more clods down. Aaron kept
hollering whoa, louder and louder. Then all of a sudden the damnedest thing you ever saw; there was some scrambling and scuffling down
there, and then zoom up out of there Aaron come! fifteen sheer foot
of dirt, and not a rope nor a ladder, like a man shot out of a cannon.
He never did know how he managed it. Papa and Ben hoorawed him
about it all the way to the house and back. And you know, when
we get back, what do you think? Down at the bottom of that hole
there's this old blind horse, sure enough, dead as hell."

When I finished telling little Lee that tale about the horse I had
expected him to laugh, or call me a liar, or something. But he didn't
twitch a muscle. And I'd expected him to be scared stiff when I got
him out of that dune hole, but he'd fooled me there too. He didn't
act scared at all. He was limp and relaxed—peaceful, kind of. . . .
I would ask him if he was okay and he'd say he was fine. I asked
him if he was scared down there and he said for a while, and then
he wasn't. I asked him how come? I said, "Boy, I was scared from
the second I went down that hole on that pine ladder to the second
I come out." And he thought for a while and said, "That canary I
had? I was always scared somebody would leave a window open and
a cold wind would kill it. And then the wind did kill it and I wasn't
scared any more of that." And he sounded darn near happy about it.
And now, when I ask him if he wasn't scared of them punks that
was giving him a hard time there on the beach, he acts the same
way, giddy, like he'd been drinking. I ask him, "Didn't them fool
kids know that car could roll on you out in the surf that way?"

"I don't know. Perhaps. They weren't exactly worried about it."

"Well, weren't you?" I ask him.

"Not as much as you were," he says and sits there grinning with
his teeth rattling together from the cold while I drive to Joe's place;
he looks pretty pleased about something. But for all his grins and

good humor I can't shake this nagging notion that he'd come to the ocean for the same reason he was headed across them dunes as a kid, and that I maybe had something to do with it this time too. Maybe the fuss I had with him last night after the hunt, maybe something else. Lord knows.

I fill him in a little on what's happened since this morning, how Evenwrite has come back with another report, so that people all know where the bone is buried now. "That's probably one of the reasons them punks was giving you a tough time."

"And that explains their change of attitude," he says. "They gave me a ride earlier this afternoon and they weren't exactly pleasant, but neither were they trying to drown me—they must have heard the news at the root-beer dive. Maybe that's even why they came driving down on the beach, to find me."

I tell him that could well be. "We're none too popular around town right now. I wouldn't be a bit surprised but what somebody on Main Street starts taking pot shots at us just for general purposes," I say, only half kidding.

"So naturally that's right where we are going: to Main Street."

"That's right," I tell him. "To Main Street quick as we finish over at Joe Ben's."

"May I ask why?"

"Why? Because I'm goddamned if I'm gonna let a bunch of niggers tell me whether I can come into town or not, I don't care how hacked they are at me—tell me whether I can have a Saturday-night drink in a public bar."

"Even if you weren't planning to have that Saturday-night drink in the first place?"

"Yeah," I tell him; I can tell by the way he starts using his prissy tone that he can't see my real thinking on it, no more than I can see his thinking on wanting to take a long swim in the cold ocean "—that is right."

"Curious," he says. "And is that why Joe Ben called you? Because he knew you wouldn't want to miss a chance to come into town and take advantage of the public hostility?"

"That's right," I tell him, getting a little hacked. "There ain't nothin' I like better than walkin' into a room knowin' everybody there would like to take a pot shot at me. You bet. I like to take advantage is exactly right," I tell him, knowing he ain't going to see it anyhow.

"I understand perfectly; it's like the madman who goes over

Niagara Falls in a coffee can because that's as good a way as any to get dead."

"That's right," I tell him, knowing he don't understand it at all —that it's more because it's as good a way as any to stay alive. . . .

*And as they hurry across the dunes toward town, matching steps in their haste—Hank in front with Lee close behind (and silent lightning fluttering softly out ahead of both of them)—the first drops of rain, like a thousand eyeholes opening on the white mask of sand, come winking down, and the eelgrass sways to a soundless tune. . . .*

> *Which brings to mind one more notion to add to the bit about Singers of echoes and Echoers of songs: the notion of Dance. Not the weekend dance in the Saturday-night sense, where you two-step to music you've heard before and always know—even if only in a cellular way— just about where your two-step is headed . . . but the Daily Dance with the wilder step, to a tune as soundless as the eelgrass tune, to an echo of a song or a song still unechoed. A dance where you can never really have much notion where you are headed. You can trip off to places so wild and so wiggy that you don't know where you are until you get back.*
>
> *And sometimes not even know you tripped off at all because you never get back to know that you've left . . .*

And when Brother Walker had unplugged the organ and turned off the current of his wife's electric guitar and finally brought his roaring sermon to a sweaty stop, all the dancing tripped-out congregation blinked and sighed and ruefully returned to the world of their week-day selves . . . except Joe Ben, wild-stepping and still sky-bound, with eyes that showed white all the way around the green iris and a soul that soared to a currentless music Sunday through Saturday. And never knew he was tripped-off at all.

When he left the tent with his family in tow he walked to the pick-up and found Lee's note, but before he had time to decide what to think about it one of the fellow followers of the faith had been so swept up by the services that he had felt called upon to put aside his natural antagonism toward the Stampers and bring it to Brother Joe Ben's attention that a certain meeting was to be held shortly at the grange hall: "A meetin' I bet is due to really affect you sonofabitching Stampers, too . . . this afternoon, with Evenwrite an' the Strike Committee an' Mr. Jonathan B. Draeger *hisself!*" he wanted Joe to know. "An' if what comes to light in the course of this meeting is what we all expeck to come to light, Brother Stamper, then you heartless sonofabitches better be prepared to suffer the conch-aquences!"

After the man stalked off, Joe stood for a time considering the information. If the conch-aquences of what come to light in that grange-hall meeting could affect him and the family so, well then maybe he just should observe that meeting personally. . . . It seemed the least he could do, after that church brother'd had the common decency to tell him about it.

He looked about briefly for Lee, then piled Jan and the kids into the pick-up and drove them out to the new house, where he left them with instructions for painting, then headed back to town. He returned to Wakonda by a wonderfully devious and roundabout route, angling closer and closer with meticulous caution until he had slipped up on the bayward side of Main Street without a soul the wiser. He parked the pick-up in the great banks of seeding Scotch broom behind the cannery and had a final cigarette while the bursting pods fired rattling shots at the windshield. He finished his cigarette, stepped out into the sunless afternoon, flipped up the collar of his leather jacket, and began sneaking up on Main Street as if he were stalking a wild and wounded beast and afraid of its turning and charging.

The Scotch broom gave him cover until he reached the fishbone-strewn dock beneath the cannery. This concealed him up to the corner where the fire station was. After that it was clearing; the open stretch of Main yawned before him.

He hitched up his trousers and struck up a merry whistle and stepped onto the walk, trying to affect an air of casual and purposeless strolling. He even found a beer can to kick along.

He strolled safely past the Sea Breeze Cafe, past the soaped window of the real-estate office, past the five-and-dime, where a pasted display of black cats made of construction paper and pipe-cleaner whiskers observed his nonchalant stealth with respectful orange eyes. He cut across the street so he was opposite the Snag and walked on, his hands in the chest pockets of the cracked leather coat and his scarred face bent toward the cracked walk. He walked with a forced slowness that emphasized more than concealed his urgency. When he had passed and was out of sight of the Snag's front windows he looked furtively up and down the block, then broke into a run back across the street. He settled again into his slow, casual walk, his back hunched and slanted slightly and his bowed legs taut with restraint. When he reached the place where the alley ran back beside the grange hall, he stopped, stepped completely off the sidewalk out into the gutter, squinted a casual eye down that alley like a town-league pitcher looking to a catcher for signals . . . looked over his shoulder left, and over his shoulder right, checking the Snag up the street at third and the clouds leading off of first base down the street, then practically leaped out of sight into the narrow alleyway, as though the pitcher had suddenly decided he could dash unnoticed past the batter, ball in hand.

All in all, he could not have drawn more attention to his actions with flags and cannonfire, but it was fortunately nearing dinnertime, with the Saturday ball game on TV and the sky dim and nobody on the streets to care about his actions anyway. Still, he stood with his back against the plank siding of the grange hall for a moment and listened for footsteps. The only sound came from the whistle buoy in the bay and the famished wind scratching in the garbage. Satisfied, Joe hurried on to the rear of the hall and leaped silently to the top of a woodbox and walked along it to a window. He looked through the window at the dim rows of folding chairs, then raised the pane a few inches, carefully. He tried for a moment to squat comfortably under the open window, gave up, and jumped down from the woodbox and heaved a great chopping stump up. It hit with the sound of a bass drum, and the open window banged shut. He climbed back on the woodbox, reopened the window, pushed the stump beneath it, and sat down to wait, with his leather elbows on his knees and his chin in his hands. He sighed and for the first time wondered why for the love of God in Heaven was he doing this, sitting here waiting to hear what he and Hank had both known for months was due to be said? Why? And why worry about how to tell Hank? or what Hank would do? Hank'll just have to pull himself together and tell them, "Up yours," like he knew already he would. Like Hank knows already he will have to tell them when they finish all the bullshooting and horseplaying that they are going to have to do in there. Like Hank has always had to do when all's said and when all's done, on account of that's his place, no matter how he don't like it. So why does Hank waste his time stewing about it?

I always say to him it is our lot to accept our lot and the best way to accept that lot is back off and see what a ball it is, I tell him, back off and see what a boot in the rear it is! Because it *is*, it *is*, if you just back off and look at it with your mouth held right. And Hank *could* be gassed by this lot, he could, just like he likes having to milk the cow sometimes. Don't I tell him so about a thousand times a day? Be gassed and happy and running around and loving every bit of it and even the bad stuff like this if you *just hold* your *mouth right*, Hankus. Now I don't expect you to know the Redeemer liveth like I do, but you *do know* what's coming up right here on earth, because I can always see in your eyes how you *see already*. So how come, when you can see already what's coming up ahead and know *already* what you're gonna have to do about it, why don't you save yourself all this fretting and cut across to what you *see coming* and do what you already know has to be done . . . ?

But, then, I don't know about that neither. Maybe *not* being able to cut across to what he *sees already* is part of that lot he's got to accept. Because I recall what almost happened the one time, when we was sixteen or seventeen in high school, and he almost cut across to what he could *see already*, instead of going all the way around. Seventeen. Right the first few days when we're enrolling for our senior year. We drive up and park his cycle in front of the front steps where everybody hangs around waiting for the eight-o'clock bell to ring. The guys are there, in blue and white lettermen's sweaters, thick-weaved wool all messed up with initials and numbers and badges and golden-ball emblems and any other decoration they can sew or pin on. Standing there, they look like generals in some kind of slouchy army, leaning back to watch, reviewing the troops passing by. And a new guy on the steps too, a visiting general, with a yellow and red Lebanon High letterman's sweater with just one decoration, just one, just a pair of tiny brass boxing gloves. There's no boxing allowed at Wakonda, so he stands out with that one decoration.

Hank isn't wearing his sweater. He says it make him feel rinkydink.

Guy Wieland gives Hank a corny wave he learned from pictures in *Life* about teen-agers. They don't wave to me. They don't know why Hank troubles with me. Guy waves. Watcha say, Hank? Not a whole lot, Guy. Oooh, feel that rubber tire there; pretty soft, ain't it. Might be, Guy. Oooh, can't have that. How was the summer, Hank? How? You felt, didn't you? Pretty soft. . . . I bet it was, Hank; oooh, feel that rubber tire; I bet you didn't do anything all summer. I *bet* you didn't do anything all summer except you and that hot-britches stepmama of yours all the time—

Hank looks up into Guy's face and smiles at him. Just a little smile and nothing mad or threatening about it. Just the littlest smile, *pleading*, to tell the truth, with Guy to lay off because he's tired, the smile says, after a whole summer of just that sort of thing and fighting about it. Soft and pleading. But, pleading or no, there's threat enough in that smile to shut old Guy Wieland off *stone cold*. And Guy fades back out of the way. There's a minute with nobody talking and Hank smiling down again, like he was so embarrassed he could die, then, all of a sudden, the new guy from Lebanon steps forward to fill in the place Guy just emptied. So you're Hank Stamper? Smiling himself, just like in the Westerns. Hank looks up and says yeah, like in the Westerns. Yeah, Hank says, and I say to myself *right at that instant* that Hank *knows already* what's going to one of these days have to happen. Hank grins at the new guy. And his grin is just as tired and pleading and bashful as it was for Guy Wieland but I see he *knows already*, too.

We stand around. Behind us, out on the playground, this year's yell squad is practicing.

Guy comes back up and says Hank, this is Tommy Osterhaust from Lebanon. Hank shakes the hand. How's it going, Tommy? Pretty fair; how about you? Tommy—you know, don't you, Hank?— made All-District last year at Lebanon. No foolin', Guy, is that right? Yeah; yeah; so with you and Cyrus Layman and Lord and Evenwrite and me *and Tommy too*, tell me we won't have some depth in that backfield! Huh, tell me.

I lean against the cycle ticking itself cool, and listen to them talk football, watch the way this Tommy Osterhaust studies Hank's forearms. From the playground come the scattered voices of touch football, keep away whatever, and the yell squad *two four six eight who do we appreciate*. I lean there, wait, watch everybody else wait too. They fart around awhile. Guy clears his throat and finally gets around to it. He flips the little boxing gloves on Tommy's jacket with his finger. You know, don't you, Hank, that Tommy is the big boxer *too*? No foolin', Tommy, is that right? I spar around some, Hank. You must be pretty good to get that medal, Tommy. Yeah, Hank, I spar around little bit now and then . . . we had a championship team in Lebanon. Tommy was captain, Hank. You guys don't box? It's against the rules, Tommy. Do you know, Hank, that Tommy here took All-

District and State and—which was it?—was either third or runner up in Northwest Golden Gloves! Third, Guy, just third; I really got my ass waxed when I got up with those Army guys from Fort Lewis. Hank—you know, don't you, Tommy?—Hank took the one-sixty-seven division at the state wrestling meet in Corvallis last year. Yeah, I guess you told me that before, Guy. Oh boy, oh boy, tell me we won't push Marshfield around this season like they was paper dolls; a *boxing* champion!—Guy takes Tommy's sleeve—and a *wrestling* champion! He takes Hank's sleeve, pulls them close. Tell me we won't!

I start to say now go to your corners and come out fighting. But I see Hank's face and I don't say anything, I see his face and hush. Because that is all it would take. I know that look. With the grin white right at the edges like the muscles in his face holds each end of his mouth and wrings the blood out of it. I know the look and I know already and get set. Hank smiles that smile and watches Tommy; he's already gone through the whole act, past the first few ignored remarks and past the bumps in the hallway and past the dirty playing on the field, and past whatever the final insult will be, to the place where they get down to what he *knows already*, what everybody knows *already*, will have to happen. And Hank is ready to get it over with. Because, after a whole summer of being teased and fighting, he is tired of it, sick and tired of it all, and any part of it he can bypass is fine with him. He smiles at Tommy and I see the cords in his neck start lifting his arms up. Behind us those scattered dumb girls *two four six eight* with Tommy distracted for just a hair to turn and listen, and he don't have the *vaguest inkling* that the fight which he plans on happening three or four weeks from now is already *right this minute* ringing the bell *round one* and no preliminaries. And I lean and watch the cords lift Hank's arms up, like number-ten cables lifting a log up to a truck. I'm the only one knows full-scale what this means. I know how unnatural stout Hank is. He can hold a double-edged ax straight out arm's length for eight minutes and thirty-six seconds. The closest I ever seen anybody else come to that was four-ten, and he a rigger thirty-five years old, big as a bear. Old Henry says Hank's so godawful stout because something odd happened to Hank's muscle tissue because of all the sulphur his first wife, Hank's real ma, ate while she was pregnant with him. Hank grins when Henry says this and says must be. But I think different. I think there's a lot more to it than that. Because Hank didn't set that eight-thirty-six record until the day Uncle Aaron kidded him about some jack in Washington holding a double-edge out there for eight. Then Hank did it. Eight-thirty-six by stopwatch. And no sulphur, neither, so that's not it. Whatever the reason, I do know he's god-awful stout and if he clips Tommy Osterhaust while Tommy's looking off there at the yell squad he'll split him like a mule kicking a watermelon, but I don't say anything, though there's still time. Maybe I don't say anything to stop it because I'm tired too, of just watching, of having to watch Hank wade through all the horse manure. Because back then I'm not accepting my lot and enjoying it and getting a gas out of it. Anyway, I don't say anything.

So if it wasn't for the eight-o'clock bell rings just at that instant Hank would have sure as shooting caught Tommy Osterhaust from his blind side like a mule kicking and would sure as shooting busted his skull like a ripe melon.

Hank knows it too, how close he come. When the bell stops him, his shoulders sag and he looks at me. His hands are shaking. We go to class and he doesn't say anything to me till lunchtime. He's standing at the cafeteria fountain, looking at the water running, and I come up. Ain't you gonna get in line for chow? I'm gonna cut the rest of the day, Joby. Can you get you a ride home? Hank, you—Or look, I can leave you the cycle and hitch a ride, if—Hank, I don't give a hang about the cycle; but you—Didn't you see this morning? Didn't you, what almost happened? Boy; I don't know what's the matter with me. Hank, listen. No, Joe, I don't know what's the matter . . . am I getting punch-drunk? Hank, now listen. I would of creamed him, Joby, you know that? Hank. Listen. Listen, ah, listen.

He stands there, but I can't say what I want to. That was my first time back to school with my new face, and I'd changed outside but it hadn't come inside yet. So I didn't have the words to tell him what I knew. Or maybe I don't *already know* then. But I couldn't tell him that, listen, Hank: maybe whosoever believeth that Jesus is the Christ is born of God and everyone that loveth him is got of him. That maybe someday the morning stars sing together and some-day all the sons of God'll holler for joy and someday maybe the wolf *is* going to dwell with the lamb and the leopard lie down like a kid and maybe someday everybody'll beat their swords into plow-shares and their spears into fishhooks and all that sort of thing but *until that time* you might as well take what the Lord's judged is yours to do and *do* what the Lord has already decided is yours to do and have a gas with it! Do I know that then? Maybe. Down in the middle of my heart, maybe. But I don't know it to tell him. So all I can say is Ah ah ah listen Hankus listen Hank while he watches the water run.

So he goes on home and he doesn't come the next day, or the day after that, and then at practice Coach Lewellyn wants to know where's the big star and I tell him Hank is under the weather and Guy Wieland says more likely under the bedspread, and all of them except the coach laugh. And after practice I take the activity bus instead of walking to the motel where me and Pop are staying those days back then. The bus goes past the motel, but I don't like to ask to be let off there. Through the window I see my daddy in the kitchen as the bus flashes by, head back in the lamplight with his teeth like quicksilver grinning at somebody I can't see, Lord only knows who this time. But it gets me thinking. You sow the wind you're going to have to reap the whirlwind. There's no getting away from it, not for Papa or me or anybody, and not for Hank neither, and he and that woman sure been seeding wind enough not to have much gripe coming about how much he has to reap. Maybe I'll tell him that.

At the landing I stand and holler until I see a light show in the boat shed and he comes over to me in the motorboat. Hey look, is that you, Joby? Yeah, I came up to see if you'd died or what. No, dammit, I just been holding things down while old Henry's gone to Tacoma on a timberland contract. Hank, Coach Lewellyn was asking if— Yeah, I'll bet he was asking. I told him you was sick. Yeah, what did you tell that Tommy Osterhaust? Huh? Never mind.

He stoops down and picks up a handful of flat rocks and goes to skipping them across the water, one after the other in the dark. Lights blink around in the house over there. I get me some rocks and I skip rocks for a while. I came out to talk to him but I knew already before I even got off the bus that we wouldn't talk, because we never do. We've never been able to talk. Maybe because we've never had to. We growed up close enough we pretty much know what's happening. He knows I'm out here to say to him you might as well come on back to school and get on with it because you and Tommy Osterhaust are going to fight it out sooner or later. And I know he is already answering sure but didn't you see the other day how I can't do it sooner and I can't take all the bullshit that goes before the later. I don't care about the fight. Oh, yes I do care. But I mean I don't care about the actual hitting and getting hit so much as I care that

I *always* have to be goddammit working up to *fighting* with some-guy-or-other!

(And always will, too, Hank, right up from then till now and from now till doomsday, so you might as well accept what you know already and see what you can find about it to have a ball with. Always will, with Tommy Osterhaust or Floyd Evenwrite or Biggy Newton, or with the falling-apart donkey or the berry vines or the river, because it is your lot and you know it is. And I guess it is your lot as well that you got to do it by the rules, because if you'd caught Tommy Osterhaust the other day while he was ogling the yell squad you'd of killed him and for no reason at all.)

But I don't say anything. We skip rocks a while longer, and he takes me home on the cycle. The next day he's at school. And after school he draws his practice togs and we all go out to the field and sit on the ground while Lewellyn tells us all about his college days for about the dozenth time. Hank isn't listening, it looks like. He's digging turf from his cleats with a stick, tired of Lewellyn's bull. Everybody else really listening to Lewellyn tell how we're a fine bunch of young men and he's gonna be proud of us come what may this season because he knows win, lose, or draw we'll be good sports and a credit to Wakonda High. I see Tommy Osterhaust, who hasn't heard all this before, with his mouth open like he tastes the words, nods every time the coach says something he likes. Hank stops digging at his cleats and throws away the popsicle stick. Then he turns and happens to see the way Tommy eats up Lewellyn's words. And men, the coach says, and men . . . I want you to remember this always: You are like sons to me. Win, lose, or draw, I love you. I love you boys like sons, win, lose, or draw. And I want you to remember this: what that grand old man of football said. Grantland Rice. Remember this poem. Remember this.

Then he closes his puffy eyes like he'll pray now. Everybody is still. The coach sounds like Brother Walker's blind brother, Brother Leonard the Seer, when he gets up to talk. Remember this, men, the coach says, remember this:

> For when the One Great Scorer comes to *write*
>  against your name,
> He marks—not that you won or lost—but [the
>  coach draws a breath]
> But how . . . you played the game!

And Hank says, just loud enough, bullshit.

The coach doesn't act like he heard. He never does. Because right behind his head is that big scoreboard donated by the Rotary, and all the records list down along it Hank Stamper, record-holder in this, Hank Stamper, record-holder in that, on almost every other name, so he knows better than argue with it. But Tommy Osterhaust turns and glares at Hank and says I don't think that's very funny, Stamper. And Hank says I almost give a rat's ass what you think, Osterhaust. And so forth and so on until the coach stops it and starts the practice.

After shower everybody's ready. Tommy Osterhaust talking low with a bunch of guys next to the foot-powder trough. Hank and me get dressed by ourselves, not talking. After we get dressed and Hank combs his hair we all go outside together and they fight in the gravel at the bus stop. And all the rest of the year everybody blames Hank for Wakonda High's not winning district title and maybe even state, like we might of done if Tommy had been capable to play for us. And for a long time after that the talk in the Snag was that Hank Stamper would never of made the Shriners' All-Star team if Osterhaust had been back there to divvy up some of the running. Hank never say anything about it even when they told him to his face. Just grins and shuffle his feet is all. Except one time. When me and him and Janice and Leota Nielsen all go out on the dunes and get drunk on wine and Leota brings the fight up because she'd been going with Tommy. We all think Hank's passed out on the blanket with his hand over his eyes. I'm trying to tell her what really went on, that Tommy had been spoiling for a fight from the first day he set eyes on Hank and that it was really *him*, not Hank like everybody always says, really Tommy that wanted the fight. Yes, but, but just because Tommy *wanted* to fight I don't see . . . well, if Hank didn't really want to do it why did he beat him up so terrible?

I start to say something but Hank beats me to it. He doesn't even move the hand off his eyes. He says Leota, sweetheart, when you come after me to do it you don't want me doing some half-assed job, do you? Leota says what! And Hank repeats the same thing— you want the best I can put out, don't you? Leota gets so upset we have to take her home. At her door she turns and hollers back, what do you think? you're God's gift to woman? Hank don't answer but I holler some things at her that she doesn't understand. About how she's just like Tommy Osterhaust, only doesn't fight as fair. I should

keep still. It was the wine. I yell and she cries and yells some more;
then her big brother comes out on the porch and he gets into it,
hollering. He is one of Hank's motorcycle buddies. Once they gypsied
all the way to Grand Canyon. Now listen here, he says. Listen here,
Stamper, you sonofabitch! He doesn't understand. Hank tells me to
drive the hell on. We pull out. He knows already about the brother
but he doesn't want to think about it yet. He can't let himself think
about it yet, though he sees already there's another scrap brewing.
But that he's got to let it brew its course or everybody will figure
him more a bully than they do already.

So . . . I guess . . . I ought'n' to look for him to be any different
with this business with Leland. He won't cut across to the place
where he *knows already* he's going to have to knock the boy's ears
down. Because he way down keeps hoping it won't come to pass. He's
*got to* keep hoping these things won't come to pass. Or get hard and
lonely as a old pit dog.

Oh, Hankus . . . Hank . . . I always say to you the thing to do
is accept what your lot is. But that's pure bull when I come down to
it. Because you can't accept that you can't quit no more than you
can quit, and you can't cut across to what you know already no
more than you can keep from hoping that what you already see coming
won't ever come. Because they are the same thing, every bit the same
exact thing. . . .

"This meeting will now come to order! Everybody rise and pledge
'legiance . . ."

A gravel rapped. Joe Ben started up from his stump and then
leaned back toward the open few inches of window. The hall inside
was lighted now and most of the chairs were full. Howie Evans
rapped the speaker's stand and repeated, "This meeting is going to
come to order!" He nodded and from a chair behind him Floyd
Evenwrite rose with a handful of yellow papers. Floyd pushed Howie
Evans aside and spread the papers on the stand.

"What is happening is this," he said. Outside the window Joe
Ben zipped his windbreaker higher and smelled the first far-away
sprinkling of rain . . .

The old boltcutter finishes unloading his load of split wood at the
shingle-weavers, and finds that he must sit down on the running
board for a minute to rest before he can make it the few yards to the
office to collect from the foreman. The smell of liver and onions

reaches him from the house out behind the mill where the foreman and his wife live. He wishes he had a woman back at his house up the canyon, to fill the air with smells like liver and onions. He has wished the same wish before, of course, many times; even, in his drunker moments, has given the idea of marriage some drunken thought . . . But now, as he tries to stand, the full force of his years strikes him at the small of his back like a sixty-pound maul, and for the first time he admits to himself that the wish is hopeless: he will never have that woman: he is just too old—"Ah well, it's best to live alone anyways, what I say"—too rotten worthless dirty old.

The clouds swarm past. The wind rises. Lee fights his way through the frog-infested swamp, bound for the sea. Jenny considers trying another trip to the Bible, for good measure. Jonathan Draeger listens to the men's overdramatic reactions to the news of the Stamper deal with Wakonda Pacific and writes: "The lowest of villains will push man to greater heights than the tallest of heroes."

And by the time Floyd Evenwrite has swung into the summation of his exhaustive case against the Stampers, the spy for the other side is beating it up the sidewalk to make a report to headquarters, all concern for caution left back in the alley among the careless litter of garbage. He must phone Hank, tell him quick—but quiet, too. . . . His espionage work would give them a little edge over the union only if they kept it quiet; the union wouldn't know that they knew. . . . But he must call right away! And the phone in the Snag, if not the most private, was certainly the closest. . . .

"Evenwrite told the whole story and then some," Joe let Hank and everybody else in the bar know. "And them as was able to last out Floyd's bull and get the drift sounded pretty salty. They says if you was going to be a leech on the town's blood that the town was gonna have to treat you like a leech. Pretty salty. They said you better keep outa their way, Hank. So what you think you'll do?"

And when he hung up thought he heard someone in the bar ask what went on at the other end.

"Hank says he just might have to come in to town tonight an' see about that," Joe announced belligerently. "Oh, you betcha; anybody who supposes Hank Stamper is gonna be scared into hiding out up in the hills just because a few people shakes their fists at him is got another suppose comin'."

Ray, the talented half of the Saturday Nite Dance Band, barely looked up from his scotch—"Big deal"—but at the other end of the bar Boney Stokes had more to say. "A pity, a pity . . . that Hank should have been ruint by the upbringing of his prideful father; with all his energy, he could have made a real contribution to society, not just be a clod washed out to sea. . . ."

"Watch that, Mr. Stokes," Joe warned. "Hank's no clod."

But Boney was beyond warning; his eyes were fixed on tragedies beyond the walls. " 'Therefore never send to know for whom the bell tolls,' " he tolled sonorously through his dirty handkerchief; " 'it tolls for thee.' "

"It tolls for horseshit," contradicted a thinner voice from a gray beard at the back of the bar, thinking of liver and onions. "All horseshit. You're alone all your life an' you darn sure die alone, what I always say."

Back with Jan and the kids, Joe Ben was able to contain his excitement only by venting it through a paintbrush; even then each minute dragged on him like an anchor dragging through gumbo mud. And by the time Hank showed up, with Leland shivering in tow, Joe had given all the window frames two coats of morning-mist white and was mixing up a third.

There were no extra clothes for Lee, so while Joe took the children around the area with their Halloween masks and paper sacks, and Hank drove to the A & W for hamburgers-to-go, Lee sat wrapped in a paint-spattered drop cloth before a panel heater, wishing he were home in bed; why Hank felt it necessary that he accompany them in their showdown tonight at the OK Saloon was a mystery. I'm a delicate sort of flower, he reminded himself wryly; perhaps he wants me around in case something starts, in hopes I'll be trampled underfoot—what other reason could he have for insisting on my coming along?

Hank would have been hard put to supply a reason himself, though he knew it to be true that Lee's presence at the Snag tonight was important to him . . . maybe because the kid needed to see first-hand what kind of world was going on around his head all the time without him ever seeing it, the *real* world with *real* hassles, not this fairybook world of his that he was having most of the time like a kind of *nightmare* that him and his kind'd made up to scare theirselfs with. Like that spooky crap he played the night before that he called music, when anybody could see that there wasn't any more tune to it than there was sense. Maybe that's one of the reasons for dragging him along to the Snag with us . . .

"Here's a burger, bub. Choke it down." He caught the white paper sack that Hank tossed him—"I want you to see how woods folks here deal with their hassles"—and ate, watching Hank with puzzled wariness (what *kind* of hassles?).

. . . Or it maybe was because I wanted the boy to have a try at going over this Niagara Falls in this coffee can with me just this one time, so he could see that this madman he was talking about could do even more'n come out of it alive—he could get a laugh or two out of the trip as well. (What *manner* of hassle are you referring to, brother? I wondered, as my confident smirk changed to a weak and worried smile. Not, by any chance, a hassle such as someone making a play for one of the woods folks' wildwoods wife?)

By the time we finish our burgers and fries, Lee's clothes are pretty well dry and Joe Ben is commencing to run circles around himself to get going. Joe just come back in from taking Squeaky and the twins and Johnny out around the area, and he is ready to do some tricking-or-treating of his own. Joe was always big on seeing a fuss if it was me getting fussed.

We drove up to the Snag in the pick-up because the jeep didn't have the box up and the night looked a little upsy-daisy for open-air driving, what with it clear one minute with a nice little quarter-moon in a calm sky, and the next minute lightning and blowing flurries of rain and sleet. (These questions didn't penetrate my earlier feeling of minor victory until Hank made such a point of bringing me to the Snag . . . then I began to come down from my cloud and get worried.) There are so many cars on Main we have to park all the way back to the firehouse and walk to the Snag. The place is running full tilt, with light and noise and people slopping clean out across the sidewalk into the street. The two guitar-players are doing "Under the Double Eagle" with their amplifiers turned to the limit. I never seen the place so booming. The stools at the long bar are filled completely, with men even standing turned sideways in the little spaces between the stools. The booths are filled, and Teddy's got one of the waitresses over from the Sea Breeze helping him with the drinks. There are men standing the length of the shuffleboard and the bowling machine, men at the toilet door and men at the bandstand, and loud groups gathered drinking beer in every smoky niche and cranny all the way back to the bus depot. (And something in Brother Hank's grim and grinning manner turned my worry to fear.) I'd had a notion it might be crowded, and I was prepared for it being wild, but the reception I get when me and Joby and Lee come in catches me clean off guard. I was halfway looking to have them go to throwing chairs and tables, and when they wave and grin and sing out howdies instead, it really throws me for a little while.

I walk past the shuffleboard and guys I barely know go to shouting acknowledgments at me like I was visiting kin. A place clears at the bar for the three of us and I call for three beers.

(My first thought was that Hank planned to call me out and humiliate me in front of the throng, administer in public a verbal flogging for my adulterous inclinations . . .)

Old buddies come up to slap my back and snap the elastic cross of my galluses. Motorcycle buddies come around to ask me how I been. Marine Corps buddies I ain't heard from in years stop by for a long-time-no-see. Dozens of guys: "Hey, what's happening, Hank, you old coon? Long time, by gosh. How's it hangin'?" I shake the hands and laugh at the jokes and watch the faces bob around in the mirror behind the picket row of bottles.

Not a one of them says a thing about our contract with WP. Not a solitary one!

(But after minutes passed without incident, I decided not: Brother Hank has something worse in mind, I decided.)

After a bit the greeting eases up and I get a chance to take a better look around. Boy! Even for a Saturday night, even for a Saturday night in the Snag in Wakonda, it's still a doozer. There's at least a two-cord truckload of guys at every table, hollering and laughing and sucking down the beer. And, by golly, there's maybe twenty-five women! More women than I ever saw in the Snag. You're usually lucky to have a Saturday with one woman to every ten men, but tonight there's at least one to four.

And that's what puts me onto what's happening: women don't come out in a pack like this to a bar unless there's going to be a good band, or a raffle, or unless there's a sure fight. Especially a fight. Nothing like the possibility of a little scuffle to bring out the ladies. Squeakers and squealers, squallers and squawkers, I've seen every high-heeled and red-sweatered one of them at some time or another boring in on some drunk Dempsey in a hard hat who's just punched down her daddy, swarming all over the poor guy twice as murderous as daddy did. Just like at the rassling match. You ever notice the first three rows at ringside at the armory are always filled with nothing but red mouths like gouged screams, hollering to *strangle* that dirty villain up there, kick his *head* off?

(Something even more edifying than humiliation WATCH OUT! more pointed than a word-whipping! Hank, Joe Ben, everyone in the bar seemed to be awaiting the arrival of the lion I was to be thrown to RUN WHILE THERE IS TIME!)

If I was a rassler I bet I'd have some real nasty dreams about those first three rows. Matter of fact I'm liable to have some real nasty dreams about this bevy of sweeties right here before the night's over.

I order me another drink, this time whisky, Johnny Walker. Why is it, I wonder, I always buy good liquor if I'm expecting a fuss. Usually it's beer beer beer, one after the other, nice and mellow and slow.

(MAKE A BREAK FOR IT!)

Maybe it's because beer *is* slow; and that I need something faster than that.

(RUN! RUN, YOU FOOL! CAN'T YOU SMELL THE CROWD'S BLOODLUST?)

Bay-*bee*, but she is fierce in here tonight! Did all these high-spirited coons come down just to watch somebody stomp the shit out of me? Why, it makes a man humble and a little proud, it does for a fact.

(But just as I was about to bolt for the door NOW, FOOL Hank succeeded in once more shattering my certainty . . .)

I lean over to Joby, who is still puzzled by our reception. "You figure it out yet?"

"What? *This?* Me? No, by golly, I sure ain't."

"Well, I just bet you that new spinnin' reel of yours against my old one that we can expect a visit from Biggy Newton before the night's out."

"Oh," Joe says. "*Oh!*"

(. . . by telling Joe Ben that the crowd was not lusting for my blood, after all, but for *his* . . .)

Les Gibbons pops up beside us with strawberry preserves all over his mouth. I wonder who he got to tote him across so he could make it in. He shakes hands all around and orders a beer.

(. . . and making it clear that the awaited lion was the sworn challenger I had so often heard mentioned: the illustrious Biggy Newton.)

"Hank," Lee asks me, "what precisely is your relationship to this illustrious Mr. Bignewton?"

"It's a little hard to say, bub . . . precisely."

Les pushes in. "Big he says that when Hank—"

"Les," Joe says, "nobody ask you"—which shuts him up. Joby never has cared a whole lot for Gibbons, but lately he's been a damn little wildcat on him.

"You might say," I tell Lee, "that our relationship is one of these things where this here town ain't big enough for the both of us."

(So I was once more without benefit of any logical reason for my presence in the bar—puzzled and perturbed, and at my wit's end to find an explanation for my apparently pointless paranoia.)

A lot of people standing around whoop and laugh at this. But Les is very serious. He turns to Lee and says, "Big, he says that your brother here took advantage. In a motorcycle race."

"That ain't it," Joe Ben says. "Big is mad, Lee, purely because he says that Hank violated a girl friend of his three or four years back. Which is a ball-face *lie* in my estimation, because this girl had long before that been violated."

"Will you listen to *this*, Lee. By god, Joe, where do you get off tryin' to discredit some of my prime trophies? Unless"—I give Lee a wink—"unless perchance you got some first-hand facts as to who copped little Judy-girl's cherry?"

Joe turns red as a beet, and, with his face, that's a sight to see. I always rib him about Judy because she used to be so hot for him in high school before he got cut up.

Everybody laughs some more at what I say to Joe.

I start seriously trying to explain to Lee Biggy Newton's real and deepdown reason for hounding me, when, right in the middle of my third whisky and what I consider a pretty goddam honest and eloquent explanation, in stalks old Big hisself.

(It was some minutes before the key to solving this puzzle presented itself.)

Ray and Rod finish off a song.

(It walked into the bar, the key did . . .)

It hushes down a little in the bar, but not much.

(. . . or, more accurately, it stalked in—like a Kodiak bear someone had succeeded in partially shaving and getting into a dirty sweat shirt . . .)

Every one of them in the whole bar knows that Big's walked in, and that here comes the whole reason for getting out in the weather tonight with the old lady's teapot change for beer, and every one of them knows every other one of them knows it. But do you think they'd ever let on to the guy standing next to them that they got anything on their mind tonight but a glass of beer and maybe a game of checkers? Got any but the noblest intentions? Not a word of it, not a word.

The music starts back up.

> *Candy kisses, wrapped in pay-per,*
> *Mean more to you, than any of mine. . . .*

I order me another shot. Four's just about right.

Evenwrite comes in, looking constipated; there's another man with him in a suit and a clean-shaved, intelligent face, like he thinks he's going to be entertained by a string quartet.

Big turkeys around the floor awhile like he always does. Playing the game, too. Never letting on I'm on his mind. In fact, the only guy in the whole place saying anything about what's in the air is that guy mocking me from the mirror there behind the bottles—sucker. He wants another whisky, but I know better. Four's enough, I tell him. Four's just right.

I look at Big and he's black and grimy from construction work and big sure enough. A huge round-shouldered hulk of a kid, built a lot like Andy is built, only bigger than Andy. Six three or so, thick eyebrows powdered with road dust, heavy beard, greasy black arm hairs every place but the palms of his hands. Slow-looking *But not so much as he used to look* stomping around in his corks *Watch out for those; he put those on; he don't wear corks on road work* and tin pants and a hard hat *Mistake there, Big ol' boy; I ain't going to conk you but I might jostle that topper down over your eyes just a bit* and one of Teddy's rum-soaked crooks sticking out of his teeth.

(This prehistoric biped in a sweat shirt made a preliminary circle of the ring before he confronted Hank. Hank went on drinking after the entrance of this challenger—a prehistoric biped and an extremely proficient-looking pugilist.) *Yeah; four good shots is just about right.* (Brother Hank didn't look in the beast's direction, or openly watch him make his lumbering preliminary circle around the arena.) Pretty soon ol' Big he ambles his way over to us. . . . (And even after he had walked over to us and made his challenge, Hank pretended to be surprised by his presence.) "Hey, by gosh! Biggy Newton! What ya say, Big, babes? I didn't see you come in. . . ." *Hell, I seen every dirty inch of his ninety-board-foot body . . .* and we talk it over a little like a couple high-school kids. (They greeted each other with sweet smiles and salutations, as friendly as rabied wolves.)

"Haven't seen you in some time, Big; how's it hanging down Reedsport way?" *I wonder . . . does the kid see?* (Then, just before the eruption of the actual fight, I noticed Hank glance in my direction.) "Ah, not too bad, Big, how about you? How's your daddy?" *Does he see, I wonder, how Big outweighs me a good thirty or forty pounds?* (Hank had just the barest suggestion of a smile on his face, and a look in his green eyes that asked again the question: You want to see how the woods folks deal with their hassles?)

"Yeah, you're lookin' right in the pink, Biggy."

(And it then became quite obvious to me: Hank wanted me to witness first-hand the wrath to come should I continue my advances toward his wife. SEE? I TOLD YOU. RUN WHILE THERE IS TIME! My paranoia was exonerated.)

I sip my drink and shoot the bull with Biggy, like we're enjoying the best of relations. "You been around Harvey's cycle shop much lately, Big?" *Big ain't a bad old boy. You see, Lee? In fact, it comes right down to it, I think a lot more of him than three-fourths these other niggers in here.* "I been tied down pretty tight of late, Biggy, maybe you heard . . . no chance to go cycling." *You see, Lee? You see? He's a damn sight bigger'n that punk trying to mess you up in the surf this afternoon . . .* "Yeah, pretty tied down, Big. But I'm glad to see you, I sure am." *Hm. That goddam crazy feeling again: some galoot about to knock my brains out, and I feel like I want to play patty-cake with him.* "Had a lotta cats to kill, Big, lotta logs to cut." *. . . But you see, Lee? I ain't running out to sea from him, I don't give a shit how big he is: he can whip my ass but he can't run me out to sea!*" "Ah, now, Big, don't be like that. . . ." *That crazy feeling; I got to keep telling myself he's just waiting to kick my frigging teeth down my throat or I'm liable to throw my arm around his shoulders like he was my best buddy.* "You know how ol' Floyd likes to blow things up; I ain't keeping you out of work. As a matter of fact I hear they're jumping up and down for men out at WP. I hear there was a bunch of fellows walked out on a strike or something like that, y'know?" *Look here, Lee; you think I'm gonna let him run me, I don't care how the fuck big he is? Even he's my best buddy, you think I care I break his grubby neck? Ain't he looking to break mine?* "So you could get mill work if you was a mind to, Big." *But ain't they all Look here, Lee looking to break mine?* "Course, if you're partial to swinging a pick . . ." *So you think I care I scuff a few noses Look here, Lee, he can whip me but he can't run me! while I'm* defending my own? Even my best buddy? "You don't say so, Big. My, but that's a shame. . . ." I have to keep telling myself *And if he don't run me he don't ever really whip me, do you see?* You think I give a shit I blind I kill the dumb bastards? Any the dumb bastards, best buddies or no? I owe it to them not to give a shit *do you see?* They all come out all hope to see me get my neck broke get killed! ". . . if that's how you feel about it, Big, ol' buddy, then I'm ready any time you are."

(I watched as Hank stood, strangely peaceful, and let the challenger deliver the first blow. It was almost his undoing. He was spun completely around and into the bar; his head struck the wood with a thick sound and he fell to his knee RUN FOOL! WATCH OUT! and the Bignewton was on him before he could rise . . .) *You see, Lee? All every one dirty whining sniveling pricks vicious red-sweater cunts grubby faces far back I can remember blame me Me, Lee, do you see?* (this time hitting him high on the cheekbone and rolling him face forward on the floor) *assholes who couldn't pour piss outa a boot is my fault—Oh Christ, Lee, do you see?* (and from this position he twisted his head toward me WATCH OUT! WATCH OUT! seemingly to make certain of my presence) *all yelling stomp him stomp the hardnosed motherfucker—Oh Christ, Lee!* (He looked at me from the floor, his head twisting back, asking the question now with one green eye WATCH OUT RUN! the other blinded with blood . . .) *all yelling kill him because I won't run the sonsabitches Lee! you bastard!* ( . . . and, before I could think—because of the noise, the beer I'd drunk, perhaps because I wanted him beaten further—WATCH OUT, HANK! I heard myself shouting encouragement right along with Joe Ben GET UP, HANK, GET UP GET UP GET UP!) *sonsabitches you think I care please let me hate them Lee you see I can* (and, as though he had been waiting for my signal, he rose GET UP trailing blood HANK HANK and an awesome war cry . . .) *YOU you think I care hate I please them! owe them not run* ( . . . to prove himself HANK YES HANK HANK! every bit as primitive . . .) *please hate! care do you? them sonsabitches!* (as the prehistoric biped) *THEM NOW do you? CARE please KILL THEM!* (and even more proficient YES HANK YES a pugilist!) *let me do you THEM kill NOW NOW NOW . . . !*

The lightning has left, leaving in its wake a spasmodic black mist that darts fitfully from hilltop to valley and back again. The old boltcutter walks mournfully up the path from his garage to his cabin; he doesn't even bother bringing along the case of wine . . .

Lee rides home in the back of the jeep while Joe Ben drives silently. They have left the pick-up at Joe's house with Jan. The erratic rain whips at them and Lee holds his face out in the wind left over from Halloween, hoping his mind will be blown clear of the beer and whisky he drank after the fight. He sits in the back of the jeep on one side of Hank, supporting him when he lists toward the floor. Hank hasn't spoken since they left the bar, and though his eyes are closed, it is difficult to know for certain if he has passed out completely because, in the flickering little dashlight that is fixed openly to the front of a jeep's dashboard, his face appears to be animated—alternately going blank, then smiling at some humorous memory. Lee studies the obscure expression, wondering, Is it an actual conscious smile, or just a swelling of the lips? . . . It was hard to be sure, considering the condition of the rest of brother Hank's face—it was like trying to read a letter after recovering it from a muddy bootprint.

In fact, the whole evening was difficult to read. I was less positive than ever about what he had hoped to accomplish by taking me to the debacle. But one thing was certain: If he had wished to show me —as I half suspected—that I had better watch my step in my relationship with certain female parties because, if provoked, he was capable of violence . . . then he had at least proved his capabilities in that area most successfully.

"I have never," I said to no one in particular, "in all my life, witnessed anything, anything nearly so vicious, so brutal . . ."

Hank didn't move, and Joe Ben said only, "It was just a fight, a plain old fist fight, and Hank whipped a fella."

"No. I've seen fist fights before. It wasn't that. . . ." I paused, trying to clear my head enough to phrase my feelings. I had drunk more than I intended after the fight, trying to blot the scene from my mind. "It was like . . . when that man knocked him over the chair, then, like Hank went insane, *berserk!*"

"Big is a pretty big boy, Leland. Hank had to come on pretty strong to take him. . . ."

"Berserk! . . . like some kind of *animal!*" And wished I had drunk more.

The car drums through the night. Joe Ben stares solemnly ahead. Hank slumps against Lee's shoulder, appearing to sleep. Lee watches reruns projected slow-motion against the dark, rain-glutted clouds that sweep overhead, and wishes more than ever that he had spent the day home in bed.

Joe Ben parks the jeep outside the garage on the gravel, to make less distance to carry the drunken Hank to the boat. Hank mumbles and groans all the way across. At the dock in front of the house he rouses himself enough to awkwardly kick the pack of hounds aside so he can walk to the end of the planks. There he strikes a match and sways out over the oily black water to study the depth marker on the piling. . . .

"Not tonight, Hank." Joe took his elbow. "Let's leave it go tonight. . . ."

"Now, now, Joby . . . the rains've commenced. We got to be ever on the alert, you know that. 'Ternal vigilance is the price." He cupped the match's frightened little flame and bent close to the dark mark that indicated the water's peak. "Ah. Just two inches from last night. We're in God's pocket, men. Carry on."

They guided him on up the incline as he kicked and shouted at the overjoyed hounds. . . .

The boltcutter climbs into his bed without taking off his wet clothes. It has commenced. He hears the rain on the roof, like soft nails being driven into the rotten wood. It has commenced, all right. And it'll go on now for six months.

Indian Jenny recalls a prediction and regards the rain as an omen, but falls asleep before she can remember the rest of her prediction or interpret the omen's meaning . . .

In his cold room at the end of the long meandering hallway old Henry lies, quilted over by old odors of sweat and fungus, of ointments and sour breathing—"A man he can keep hisself"—grinding his two-teeth-that-meet against each other in his sleep. He has been disturbed by the dogs' barking. He grumbles and frets, fighting to hang onto the sleep and keep back the pain that pounds like the surf all day against the woody shore of his body. He doggedly refuses to take the doctor's sleeping medications—"Smearin' up my vision"—and sometimes goes for nearly a week before he passes out. Now he grumbles and curses in an in-between fog that is not quite sleep, not yet consciousness.

"Damn the goddamn," he said softly.

"Grab a root an' dig," he said.

The barking ceased and he became calm and still and stiff beneath his green blankets, like a tree fallen and covered where it fell by a spreading moss . . .

Joe Ben stands alone in his room, wondering if he should stay the night or go back in to Jan and the kids; the strain of indecision knots his features. He wishes somebody would give him some advice on these heavy questions.

On the bureau the jack-o'-lantern, half covered now with fine gray-green hair, has sunk into a puddle of clear, viscous liquid. It watches Joe struggle with his problems and grins a mildewed grin, looking like a happy drunk exhausted by his revels but not yet completely passed out; if the pumpkin has any advice, he is just too shot to give it.

In his room Lee lies, hoping he will not be ill. The last three weeks wheel around his bed in full carrousel gallop. "Whirlies," he diagnoses, "pot hangover." Every event, every bruise and scratch and blister comes cavorting past, all made with intricate detail by a skilled Swiss woodcarver. They pass in review for him like a carved cavalry. He lies dreamily in the center of the wheeling display, trying to decide which steed he will be riding tonight. After some minutes of careful scrutiny he chooses "That one there!"—a high-prancing filly with slim flanks and sleek withers and a flowing golden mane, and leans to whisper in her lifted ear: "Really, you should have seen him . . . like a primitive animal . . . brutal and beautiful all at once."

And at the other end of the hall Hank sits slumped in a straight-backed wooden chair with his shirt and shoes off, breathing loudly through a clotted nose while Viv dabs at his cuts with cotton dipped in alcohol. He flinches and jerks and giggles at each touch of the cold cotton, and tears flow red down his cheeks. Viv catches the blood-stained tears in her cotton.

"I know, sweetheart, I know," she croons, trailing her slender fingers over his arms, "I know"—caressing and rubbing him until the tears stop and he lurches upright. He stares blankly about him for a moment. Then his eyes clear and he slaps his belly.

"Saynow." He grins. "Why, look who's here." He flips the buckle of his belt and works at the buttons with swollen hands. Viv watches, aching to come to the aid of those drunken, fumbling fingers. " 'Fraid I might've tied one on tonight, did Joe Ben tell you? Was compelled to kick the tar outa Biggy Newton again. Oh . . . you an' Andy get that tally sheet for the booms? Fine. Oh lord, me for some Zs." He drops his trousers and falls into bed. "I'm sorry, honey, if I was any trouble to you. . . ."

She smiles down at him—"Don't be silly"—shaking her head. Her hair sweeps out with the movement and she catches a lock in her lips. She stands looking fondly down at him, watching sleep slacken the jaw, loosen the lips, until the face of Hank Stamper is replaced by that of a long-lost somebody—the Somebody she fell in love with, the face she first saw lying unconscious and bleeding on a dirty cot in her uncle's jail—tired, and tender, and a very vulnerable face.

She pushes the annoysome hair back from her face and leans close to the sleeping stranger. "Hello, honeybunch," she whispers, as a child whispers to a doll when she doesn't want anyone to hear because she is too old for such baby stuff. . . . "You know? I tried to remember the words of a song today, and you know, I couldn't remember? It goes: 'Away up yonder, top o' the sky . . .' and I can't remember what else. Can you? Can you?"

The only answer is the labored breathing. She closes her eyes and presses her fingertips against her eyelids until the dark is filled with whirling sparks, but the bubble beneath her breasts remains cold and hollow. She presses harder, making her eyeballs shoot with pain, and harder still . . .

While Hank dreams that he is at the top of his class and nobody is trying to pull him down, nobody is trying to push him off, nobody but himself even knows that he is up there.

*A* curious, bizarre, diabetic ex-anatomy prof who now runs his own curious curio shop on the coast highway near Reedsport, to vend his own bizarre brand of hand-carved myrtlewood anatomy, substitutes for forbidden liquor kicks the little gray-blue tomb-blue berries gathered from the deadly-nightshade vines that grow near his shop. . . . "Just a sort of belladonna cocktail," is how he allays the shocked concern of his beer-drinking friends. "One man's poison is another man's high."

Teddy, the part-time bartender and full-time owner of the Snag, though he might have been compelled to take open issue with the woodcarver's choice of cocktails, would have been, of all the men in Wakonda, the man most likely to believe in the woodcarver's principle. For the town's leanest days were inordinately Teddy's fattest, the town's darkest nights his brightest. He turned more liquor Halloween night at the crowd's disappointment than he would have sold if Big Newton had knocked Hank Stamper's head off . . . and the Halloween rain that brought a deluge of despair down on the striking loggers the following day brought a jingle of joy from Teddy's till.

Floyd Evenwrite's reaction to the rain was somewhat different. "Oh me, oh me, oh me." He woke late Sunday morning, hung over and suspicious of the effect of last night's beer on his bowels. "Look at it come down out there. Dirty motherin' rain! An' what was that dream I had? Something bound to be awful . . ."

"This country will rot a man like a corpse," was Jonathan Draeger's response when he looked from his hotel window onto a Main Street running an inch of black water.

"Rain," was all Teddy had to say, watching the falling texture of the sky through his bedside lace curtains. "Rain."

Those Halloween clouds had continued to roll in off the sea all the rumbling night—a surly multitude, angry at being kept waiting so long, and full of moody determination to make up for time lost. Pouring out rain as they went, they had rolled over the beaches and town, into the farmlands and low hills, finally piling headlong up against the wall of the Coastal Range mountains with a soft, massive inertia. All night long. A few piled to the mountaintops and over into

346

the Willamette Valley with their overloads of rain, but the majority, the great bulk of that multitude gathered and blown from the distant stretches of the sea, came rebounding heavily back into the other clouds. They exploded above the town like colliding lakes.

The garrison of speargrass that picketed the edges of the dunes was beaten flat by the clouds' advance guard; with the fallen green spearpoints pointing the way the attack had gone by graying dawn.

A torrent of water that ran from the dunes back to the sea, in measured sweeps, as though enormous waves were combing overhead and breaking far inland . . . swept the beaches clean of a whole summer's debris by gray daylight.

And along parts of the Oregon coast there are clusters of seaside trees permanently bent by a wind that blows everlastingly landward across all the Oregon beaches—whole groves of strangled cedars and spruce bent in an attitude of paralyzed recoil, as though frozen by a dreadful Medusa revealed centuries ago by lightning . . . and by midmorning of that first day after October, the little short-tailed mice that dwelt between the roots of these trees had crept from their homes and, for the first time in local remembrance, were moving in droves east, toward higher ground, afraid that such a rain would surely raise the sea and flood their burrows. . . .

"Oh me, oh me; the mice are leavin' their holes. We're in for a bad one," was the way Evenwrite viewed the migration.

"The rodents are moving into town to winter with the riffraff," Draeger decided moodily, and wrote "A Man Is Known By The Mice He Keeps" in his notebook.

"I think I had better go down and open the place early this Sunday," Teddy decided and hurried to the bathroom mirror to see if he needed a shave this week.

At the moorage that first day the old Scandinavian fishermen watched the black rolling of clouds overhead and added extra hawsers to their boats. In her shack near the clamflats Indian Jenny melted pitch, candlewax, and an old pocket comb on the stove, used the mixture to calk gathering wet spots in her ceiling, pressing the searing gum into cracks and holes with her broad, shovel-callused thumb as she hummed tonelessly along with the lonely drone of rain. On Main Street the townspeople sprinted from awning to awning with lowered heads, dodging puddles, skirting the spew of rainspouts. As frantic and as flustered in their movements as the drenched mice fleeing the safety of their burrows; even the oldest of mossbacked residents was bewildered, even the stanchest logger generally proud of his laconic acceptance of weather—"Can't never get wet enough for me!"—and his endurance of legendary rains of the past, even these veterans appeared shaken by the sudden, determined ferocity of that first day's rain.

"Comin' down like a cow wettin' on a flat rock," they called to one another. "Like ten cows. Like a goddam *hundred!*" they called as they dashed from awning to doorway, from doorway to awning.

"I hear it's a record," they assured one another all afternoon over beers in the Snag, "a goddam record."

Yet when the report came in over Teddy's bartop radio at the end of the day, the precipitation count was by no means a record. "Four inches recorded since midnight." It wasn't even phenomenal. "Jus' four inches? That all? I mean, that's a lot of rain, surely, but I tell ya! the way it was coming down out there today didn't ack like four inches, it acted like four goddam *hundred!*"

*Just four inches,* Teddy thought sarcastically, *just four little inches.*

"I think somebody made a mistake," Evenwrite thought moodily. "Those smartasses down at the Coast Guard station, where do they get this crap, draw a number out of a hat? Shit, the ditch out behind my place had a good foot of water in it by noon! What makes those smartasses think they can measure water any better than anybody else?"

*Four inches of rain*—Teddy simpered—*and the fear hidden all sum-summer shoots up and blooms overnight.* He floated soundlessly about the dim avenues of his bar, like a plump little water spider in a white apron and shirt, black slacks and tiny pointed crepe-soled shoes, *Blooms all funny-colored and different-shaped,* tending his web with remote servility. *But all the colors and shapes spring from that same weed of fear. . . .* His small dark lips pursed in a practiced smile, and his tiny black eyes noticing everything in the whole dingy expanse of his barroom limits—the man fingering the coin-return slot on the juke, the trio in the booth near the back stubbing cigarettes out on the table, the feet getting heavier, tongues getting thicker . . . seeing everything except the grained bartop or rows of glasses at which he polished constantly. *And that weed is rooted in all of us. It is in me as well as in Floyd Evenwrite or Lester Gibbons. But I am different. I know that it is not brought to blooming by the rain. It is brought to blooming by nothing more than stupidity. And the native dirt here is rich in stupidity.*

Teddy considered himself something of an expert on fear and stupidity; he had studied them for years. He had a constant supply of specimens. Now he shifted his covert gaze to watch Jonathan Draeger, the union official that Evenwrite had called up to help with this strike foolishness, come through the arch of neons wearing a hat and a very light blue overcoat. Teddy's eyes followed the man's confident, well-fed movements as he removed the hat and coat. He had noticed him last night and had been curious about his calm interest in the brawl. Like himself—and perhaps Hank Stamper—this Mr. Draeger didn't seem to fit into the same category as the rest of the specimens. There seemed something special about him that set him apart. Teddy felt himself different from the rest of the town because, while he might harbor a natural seed of fear like the others, he had the shrewd patience and intelligence to keep it from sprouting. Hank Stamper, on the other hand, was neither shrewd nor intelligent, but by some quirk of nature completely fearless. This Draeger was certainly this and more. . . . "Good evening, boys"; Draeger greeted the largest table and its assembly of citizens. "It appears we are having us some weather. Four inches to date, the paper said. . . ."

"Where'd they get their figures," Evenwrite demanded, "this 'four inches to date'?"

Draeger hung up the coat and hat and carefully brushed his trousers free of rain before answering. "From the United States Department of Weather Service, Floyd," he explained, giving Evenwrite an understanding smile. *He is shrewd, this Mr. Draeger. He also appears intelligent; that certainly sets him apart. Fearless, too, maybe . . .* "Why do you ask, Floyd? Had you estimated more than four inches?" . . . *but there is something more.*

"Um . . ." Evenwrite grunted at the question and shrugged sullenly. He was still hung over. And he wasn't so goddam sure anyhow that he liked the way this goddam bigcity big-ass in his suntan and slacks was *responding* to the *gravity* of the situation. ". . . I didn't say I estimated at all, Mr. Draeger."

"Of course. I was just joking."

*Something that sets him apart from the rest of these brainless fools, but from myself and Hank Stamper too.*

"It *did* seem more than four inches," the Real Estate Hotwire admitted. "But you know what *I* diagnose it, Floyd? You want to know? It was the *shock* effect, that's what. Days of sunshine, the good weather that we had all the way to November kind of *constituting* a

soporific, do you get what I mean? Then *blooey*, the sky falls on us."
He tilted back in the chair and his easy-going, affable Rotarian laugh
spilled from his throat—"So we're all running around like Chicken
Little with her head chopped off. . . . Haw haw haw." A laugh calculated to warm the cockles of every cold wet heart in the house; and
maybe stimulate a little confidence in the land-buying situation. "So
that's all it was. Nothing to be alarmed about. We were running
around telling ourselves the sky was falling. Haw haw haw." The
others all laughed and agreed with the shrewd explanation; that must
have been it, the surprise effect, the suddenness . . . then the laughter stopped and Teddy saw them turn questioningly toward the smiling
Draeger. "Don't you diagnose it like that, Mr. Draeger?"

"I'm sure that must have been what happened," he reassured them
as Teddy watched. *All the others are afraid of the night, of the dark
outside; I know they are . . .*

"I ain't so sure that's what happened," Evenwrite said suddenly,
looking down at Draeger's hands on the table; the hands were resting
one on top of the other, nails clean, cuticles groomed, like two pompous and pedigreed show-dogs. He looked at his own hands and they
seemed knotted and ugly, like mongrels made all red and hairless with
mange—"No, I don't think so"—but mongrels or not he was by god
if he was gonna run them outa sight under the table!

"No? Then what better explanation do you have, Floyd?" *I know
these others, animals, all scared of the forces in the dark; that's why
they buy TV sets, and buy Buick cars with red and green lights blink
off and on in the holes in the hood . . . that's why they flock to my
neons. Like bugs attracted to streetlights, to fire. Anything to get
out of the dark . . .*

"Yeah, Floyd; you ack like you got somethin' on your chest."

"Yeah, Floyd . . ."

Evenwrite compressed his face into a pinched labyrinth of terrific
concentration. He *did* have a better explanation, goddammit, if he
could just put it the right way. He'd worked on it all night. It was a
hell of a lot more than surprise effect, and there damned well *was*
something to be alarmed about. All night long he had worked on
the feeling—after the sight of Stamper clobbering that muscle-assed
Newton had faded from his consciousness—lying half awake, half
asleep, half drunk in his pitch-dark bedroom, trying to put his finger
on an insistent and ominous worry, trying to make out the whispered
warning beneath the rain, like cold wet lips against his ear—what was

that dream? what was it somebody just whispered?—and by noon when he climbed from bed he had deciphered the wet warning.

"Look," he started, trying to choose his words. "This rain coming like it did and . . . *upsetting everybody like it did, is a lot more than just a all-of-a-sudden change of weather. As far as us woods boys are concerned—an' the rest of you who make a livin' off the woods payroll—this rain coming might as well be an atom bomb."*

He forced himself to not look at Draeger. He licked his lips and went on.

"This rain might as well be a tornado or an earthquake as far as us boys are concerned. And is liable to be just as tough to survive." Don't want to lay it on too thick, but they got to realize, goddammit . . . *he's* got to realize! "You think about it a minute you'll know what I mean." He's got to see this ain't just one of these pipe-smoking parties like he usual sits in on, diddling in his notebook like he's got all the goddam time in the world. "And you'll see how come I been tryin' to light a fire under you before it's *too late* to survive."

The men all took a drink, to reinforce themselves against whatever event Evenwrite's ominous statement suggested they might be too late to survive. *Yes; all of them flee the shadows for the light. Some more, some less than others* . . . Then, just as Evenwrite opened his mouth to cap his build-up, the glass door rattled and Les Gibbons entered as though on cue. Everyone turned to watch Les's lumbering dance as he shook the rain from his clothes. Evenwrite groaned at the disturbance, but Les didn't get the hint; he stood slapping his soaked hat against his thigh, enjoying the spotlight his interruption had created. "That there river, fellas, she's acomin' up an' that's the truth. Boy howdy! I like to not made it. I tole the woman not to expect me back till mornin', maybe, if it gets worse. So I hope somebody can put me up. Huh? Ifn I can't make it back?"

Evenwrite's annoyed face suddenly brightened as he saw a way to salvage his point. "You drive in, Les? Up to Scaler's bridge an' across?"

"I sure didn't! My car ain't give me any service at *all* ever since I lent it to my wife's kid brother. Ruint it, I reckon. No, that's why I say I barely made it: I had to give Stamper a phone call to come up and tote me across in his boat, an' you know? I thought for a piece there the motherjumper wasn't even gonna? Then he sent that Joe Ben 'stead of comin' himself, like he couldn't waste his time on a ol' boy up agin it."

Evenwrite tried again. "But someone drove you home by way of

Scaler's last night, Les . . . how is it you didn't call whoever drove you then?"

"Why, I just didn't consider it safe, Floyd! My yard's warshed clean away. Never did that before, even in 'forty-nine. So I had my doubts about sections o' that road from my place to Scaler's. No time for the water to soak, y' see, fellas; what with this much rain all to once after such a long dry—"

"Ex-actly!" Evenwrite brought both fists down on the table with such sudden violence that Les stumbled backward over a chair. "What I was trying to tell you boys . . . just *exactly!*" Now by god we'll just see about a better explanation. "You don't know this, I guess, Mr. Draeger, but you boys, you know as good as I do, if you stop to think about it, what this hard rain comin' down on bone-dry ground will do! What it will do to haulin', to *the whole of woods-workin'*, if we don't get on the ball and be goddam quick about it. I mean *do* something!"

He nodded, letting them think about it. Les stood stiff and uncomfortable, immobilized by the legs of an overturned chair and the passion in Evenwrite's words. He had never seen Floyd so forceful. None of them had. They watched him in uncomprehending silence; he strained his features before going on, the way some men clear their throats:

"Because this ain't just a rain, boys . . . it's like the start of a execution." He stood up and walked away from the table, rubbing the back of his thick neck. At the bar he turned. "A execution! A goddam knife tearing out ever' goddam road on this side of the valley! Anybody want to cover my ten dollars that the Breakleg Spur is still in after that night of rain? Anybody want to try to take a crummy up to Pacific Camp or Feeny Creek by way of Spur Nineteen? I *told* you, goddam your thick heads"—his own round head swung from man to man—"and I tell you again, that if we ain't back up on those slopes this *very goddam week!* this very sonofabitchin' week, that, strike or no strike, picket or no picket, you can just mark her down that we'll be spending every Monday mornin' for the rest of this fuckin' winter driving to Eugene to pick up unemployment checks!"

He turned his back on the men and stood for a moment, feeling the men watching him, and Draeger watching all of them. Well, that oughta satisfy them as a better explanation.

He waited, expecting Draeger to make a comment, but the silence he had wrought held, so he pushed it to its limit. He let his shoulders rise and fall in a heavy sigh. He rubbed his neck again. And when he turned back around, his red rubber-ball face had been arranged in sagging lines of fatigue and sacrifice. Teddy watched in the bar mirror *All like frightened insects as Evenwrite returned to the table . . . and of all of them Evenwrite is the most frightened.*

"Boys . . . I mean . . . you *know* the story, don't you? You know what I'm talking, what I *been* the fuck talking about for a week now! An' even before then I warned 'em, Mr. Draeger, I told 'em about my suspicions . . ."

*The one acting the toughest and the bravest, and the one most afraid of the forces of the dark . . . is Evenwrite.*

"Up till yesterday I kept that report secret, waiting till I was sure I was gonna get another copy . . ."

*Gibbons there is the scaredest-looking, but he's too stupid to be as scared as he looks.*

"Up till yesterday afternoon you boys thought we were in pretty fair shape. I couldn't get any action stirred up with all my claims about the Stampers, could I? You thought: 'Hang on a while more.' You thought: 'WP can't hold out much longer; they got to have the logs. They got to have a cold deck stockpiled for spring work.' You thought we had 'em by the short hairs, didn't you? Because a lumber company, it just ain't going to make any money, you thought, without it has some lumber to sell! You thought: 'Okay, so Hank Stamper is makin' hay while his sun shines, but that's no skin offn our noses. Live an' let live. Can't knock a man for fightin' for his honest dollar,' you thought, now ain't that so?" He paused to glare about at the men; he hoped Draeger noticed how they one and all—even the Real Estate Man and that brother-in-law of his—dropped their eyes before his accusing gaze. *Willard Eggleston, on the other side of Gibbons, he might be almost as scared as Floyd Evenwrite, though he does not make as much commotion.* "Yessir . . . 'Can't knock a man for fightin' for his honest buck,' you thought."

Floyd had started to settle back into his chair. Now he jumped standing again. "But that's just it, goddammit anyhow! All this time he wasn't just makin' his honest buck. While he was runnin' around grinnin' at us an' shakin' our hands he was cuttin' our throats, just like that rain out there now is cuttin' our log roads!"

*All of them, talking about rain and logging roads, when it is really the dark; if I were to cut the lights in here the whole lot of them would surely die of fright . . .*

Now Evenwrite was working to his climax; he was bent into a slight crouch, and he had let his voice become soft the way he'd seen Spencer Tracy do when he was whipping the cattlemen to action. "An' I tell you boys this, you can mark her down: if we don't some way talk that hardnosed so-and-so into breaking that . . . under-handed contract with Wakonda Pacific, if we don't put the bind on them lard-butts owners like our strike was intended to do—get them running circles around themselves down there in Frisco and LA 'cause they need logs and lumber for the spring and they can't stop to haggle about what they're paying to get 'em—and if we don't do this right soon, like before a couple of weeks of rain washes the roads so bad they can't be fixed, you boys might as well tell your women either get used to the state's fifty-two forty a week, or go to looking for you a different line of work!" He nodded with grim finality at his audi-ence and, at last, turned triumphantly toward the isolated chair back from the others, where Draeger sat like a noncommittal casting direc-tor at an audition. "And ain't that the way you see it, Jonny?"— flushed with confidence and drenched with sweat from standing too near the stove. "Ain't that just about the way you'd sum up our position?"

Teddy watched. Draeger smiled pleasantly, giving no indication of what he thought of the performance. *The whole lot of them except this Mr. Draeger.* He looked thoughtfully down into his pipe. "What is it you are proposing, Floyd?" *This Mr. Draeger, he is really different.* "What are you proposing, Floyd?"

"A picket! I'm sayin' we throw a picket around their mill. We shoulda done it a week ago, but I wanted to wait till you got here."

"What do we list as our complaint?" Draeger asked. "Legally, we aren't able—"

"Legal be damned!" Evenwrite erupted uncontrollably—not nearly as uncontrollably as his tone indicated but, by godfrey, it's time to get off the pot! "Legal be screwed!" Draeger seemed mildly surprised by the outburst and held his flaming match motionless above the bowl of his pipe. "I mean, Jonathan—we got to get back to work!"

"Yes, of course . . ."

"An' we got to do something about it."

"Perhaps . . ." Draeger frowned slightly as he sucked the pipe to life. "At any rate, do you have men willing to stand all day out in this weather?"

"Shoot, yes! Les! Arthur, what about you? The Sitkins boys, they ain't here but I'll guarantee that they'll stand. And me."

"Before you jump into this wet—and illegal—ordeal, I would like to make a suggestion, if I might."

"Jesus Christ—!" Like I ain't been waiting a week for you to do something to earn your salary. "Sure we'd like to hear a suggestion."

"Why don't we talk things over with Mr. Stamper first? Maybe save a lot of walking around in the rain."

"Talk things over? With Hank Stamper? You saw last night how the Stampers talk things over, like goddam savages. . . ."

"I saw last night a man finally provoked into teaching a bully a lesson; what he did didn't strike me as being particularly unreasonable. . . ."

"Unreasonable is a word Hank Stamper was toothed on, Jonathan; talkin' with him is like talkin' to a signpost . . . didn't I go to him first off I got that first report? And I get what kind of reasoning? Dynamite throwed at me."

"Still, I think I would like to take a little ride up and ask the man if he wouldn't reconsider his position. You and I, Floyd . . ."

"You and me? I'm damned if I'll go up to that place tonight."

"Come on, Floyd; the boys will think you're afraid to be out after dark. . . ."

"Jonathan . . . you don't know. He lives on the other side of the river, for one thing, an' no road in."

"Isn't there a boat we might rent?" Draeger asked the room in general.

"There's Mama Olson," Teddy answered quickly and avoided Evenwrite's dark look. "Mama Olson, down at the cannery, sir, she'll rent you a motor rig."

"But it's raining out there," Evenwrite wailed.

"She'll rent you rain gear too," Teddy added, a little astonished by his own outspoken suggestions. He came gliding out from behind the bar to trip the lever in back of the pay phone. He held out the dial-toning receiver, smiling passively. "You can call her from here."

He watched Draeger nod a polite thank you and rise from his chair. He handed him the phone, almost bowing as he did. *Yes. I do not understand why yet. But I know that this Mr. Draeger is no ordinary man. He is decidedly intelligent, and sensitive to a high degree, I am sure. And he may even be fearless, too.* Teddy stepped back from the phone and stood, his little hands beneath his apron, watching the way all the others waited in respectful silence while Draeger got Mama Olson's number from the operator and placed his call, like dogs waiting in mute and unquestioning obedience for the master's next move. *But he is also something more; yes, something wonderfully special . . .*

> Alongside the statement about one man's poison being another man's high, one might as well add that one man's saint can be another's sore and one man's hero can turn out to be that man's biggest hang-up.

And it was beginning to look to Evenwrite as though the hero he had so long awaited to come smooth out this Stamper hassle was turning out to be as big a hang-up as the hassle he had come to smooth.

He and Draeger were putting doggedly up the river in a boat that looked none too sound, with an outboard motor that looked even less reliable. The rain had let up and leveled out to its usual winter-long pace . . . not so much a rain as a dreamy smear of blue-gray that wipes over the land instead of falling on it, making patient spectral shades of the tree trunks and a pathic, placid, and cordial sighing sound all along the broad river. A friendly sound, even. It was nothing fearful after all. The same old rain, and, if not welcomed, at least accepted—an old gray aunt who came to visit every winter and stayed till spring. You learn to live with her. You learn to reconcile yourself to the little inconveniences and not get annoyed. You remember she is seldom angry or vicious and nothing to get in a stew about, and if she is a bore and stays overlong you can train yourself not to notice her, or at least not to stew about her.

Which was what Evenwrite attempted to do as he and Draeger rode up river in the open launch they had rented from Mama Olson. He succeeded in ignoring the actual raindrops and was partially successful in his attempt to keep from stewing about the damp wind, but try as he might, he couldn't overlook the stream pouring down his neck and into his pants. They had been better than an hour coming from the moorage at Mama Olson's dock at the cannery to the Stamper house, twice as long as it should have taken because he hadn't thought to check the tides and catch an up-river flow.

Evenwrite hunched near the motor in chilled silence; at first he had been angry with Draeger, who had suggested paying Mr. Stamper this senseless social call; he then became furious with himself, not only for forgetting to check the tides but for insisting to Draeger that they go up in a rented boat instead of driving up and honking for Stamper to come across and get them at the garage. ("He might not come across to pick us up when we get there," he had told Draeger when the man had asked about driving to the Stamper house, "an' even if he *does*, the bastard might not take us *back* across"—knowing better, knowing Hank would have greatly enjoyed this sort of chance to be neighborly and helpful, would probably have been just nice as pie, the sonofabitch!)—and, finally, he had become absolutely *enraged* with Mama Olson for loaning him a poncho that was so frigging full of holes it practically drowned him and ruined his goddam pack of cigarettes. (But by god if you ever catch Floyd Evenwrite begging for anything, be it smokes, matches, or that plastic tarp he's sitting on and me soaked to the goddam skin!)

Draeger sat barely visible in the twisting dark in the bow of the boat with his pipe bowl turned upside down against the rain, saying nothing to make the trip any more enjoyable. (In fact, the *sonofabitch never has anything to say!* other'n "Let's talk things over." And I'm getting tired of that.) How Draeger had risen to the top in the labor business was something Evenwrite found increasingly hard to comprehend. There seemed to be nothing to him but front. He hadn't done a goddam thing about the strike in the whole time he'd been in town, after being a week late to boot—just walked around nodding and grinning like a nincompoop. (Except—it's funny—except all the time he's taking *notes in that little book*.) He hadn't asked a thing about the minutes of the walk-out meeting (but funny thing is *you feel he's already got it wrote down*) or about the morale of the members after a long strike, or the dwindling strike funds, or any of the stuff Evenwrite had been prepared to answer. (Like he thinks he *knows so goddam much* he don't have to stoop to ask question of *dumbasses like us!*) One thing, though, that Evenwrite had to give him credit for (now he might think *just because of some goddam college-degree friend in Washington or something* that he can come around here *expecting us to kiss his feet* . . .) and that was the man's impressive and calm way of handling the members, (. . . but he'll see he's got *another think coming*). Also Floyd had to admire the way he kept them in line, the way he kept them aware that he was the man at the controls (I'll have to learn how to bring that off) and that they were just the rank and file (*that's only way to command any kind of respect and get any kind of discipline* outa the bunch of knot-heads).

So Evenwrite fumed and fretted, worshiped and hated all the silent trip up the river, and wished Draeger would say something so he could grunt just enough answer to show that Floyd Evenwrite didn't give a good goddam for him, he didn't care if he was president of the whole United States!

The window lights of the house came into view. "Balls," Evenwrite said finally, without being asked, making the word a general, all-encompassing denouncement. He swallowed hard: he was cold, he wasn't looking forward to this meeting, and he was longing so for a cigarette that the smoke from Draeger's pipe was bringing tears to his eyes.

They tied the launch to the marker at the dock and stepped out into a smothering dark that reminded him of the flashlight left lying in the front seat of his car. "Balls again," Evenwrite said, more softly. Draeger wondered if they shouldn't call to the house for a lantern but Evenwrite vetoed the idea: "You don't catch me asking for a lantern" and added in a terse whisper, "They probably wouldn't bring one out anyway."

With the running lights of the boat extinguished, and the kitchen window cut off behind the thick vine hedge, the darkness was terrible. Each match they tried hissed out immediately, as though pinched by invisible wet fingers; they gave up all hope of light and began shuffling blind along the slippery, slopping planks, hearing the river inches away in the night. Evenwrite led the way inch by inch, feeling ahead with his feet, both arms extended well in front of him. They both remained perfectly silent, as though coerced by the shushing of the rain, until Evenwrite ran his forehead into a piling pole; it was so inconceivable to him that any innocent object of the night could get past his double straight-arm guard that he thought someone lying in ambush had clubbed him. "Dirty bastard!" he cried, throwing both arms about his mysterious assailant. Who was clothed in a garment of cold, wet slime and barnacle shells. "Oh!" he cried again a bit too loud, and from beneath the house came a black boiling of frenzied beasts, roaring down on him pitilessly. "Oh dear Lord," he whispered as the unseen pack bore down, rumbling the planks with a rhythm of galloping claws, baying, snarling and yipping. "Oh dear Jesus."

He released the post, threw both arms instead around Draeger, and clung there in shameless terror. "Oh me, oh me, oh me!"

With the beam of his flashlight Joe Ben found them clutched thus, swaying in the rain as the dogs surrounded them in a frenzy of delight and welcome. "Why, look here," Joe called good-naturedly. "Why, it's Floyd Evenwrite an' a *date*, I guess. Come on inside, fellows, where we got a nice fire goin'."

Evenwrite blinked stupidly at the light, becoming more and more certain that his most pessimistic reservations about this excursion would undoubtedly be realized.

"Sure!" Joe called once more. "Whatever you're doin' you can do better in the warm."

Draeger untangled himself from Evenwrite's grip and smiled back at Joe. "Thank you, I believe we will." He accepted the invitation as pleasantly as it had been extended.

In the living room Viv brought them hot coffee. The old man spiked the coffee with bourbon and offered them cigars. Joe's oldest girl dragged chairs up close to the stove for them, and Joe was so concerned that they might catch their death—"Out there froze, huggin' each other for a little warmth"—that he dragged out a great pile of blankets for them.

Evenwrite refused everything and suffered the humiliation of this mocking hospitality in silence. Draeger suffered not at all; he took the spiked coffee and cigar, complimented Joe Ben on his lovely children and old Henry on the quality of his smokes, and humbly asked Viv if she would be so kind as to fix him a teaspoonful of soda in a half a glass of lukewarm water: "For a cantankerous stomach."

When he finished the soda water Draeger asked if Hank Stamper might be bothered for a few moments—they had a proposition for him. Joe told him Hank was out on the bank, checking the foundation, right at present. "You boys care to wait here for him? He's liable to be a while out there—or you want to go out and discuss this proposition with him in the rain?"

"Oh for heaven's sakes, Joe," Viv scolded. "It's miserable out there. He can come in for a while. I'll give him a call. . . ."

Draeger held up his hand. "Please don't, Mrs. Stamper. We'll go out and talk with him." Evenwrite gaped, unable to believe he was hearing it. "I don't like to interrupt a man's work."

"By godfrey, Draeger, what are you saying?"

"Floyd . . ."

"But, Christ, this stove here . . . an' you want to up and—"

"Floyd."

They went out, with Joe Ben behind them like an usher, waving the flashlight in a frenetic tempo to his soliloquizing about the sudden rain, the landslides, the rising river, and had Floyd been playing with dynamite of late? They wound a zigzagging plank walk and found Hank in a poncho and rain pants, dangling a lantern bail in his teeth while he lashed a timber firm against what appeared to be a railroad tie that had washed up recently and was being inculcated into the rest of the formless reinforcing. One side of his face was still bloated blue from the fight and a piece of adhesive dangled uselessly from one end over a cut on his chin. Evenwrite introduced Draeger, and Hank shook his hand. Evenwrite waited a few moments, expecting Draeger to state their business, but Draeger had stepped back from the light, and Floyd realized he was even gonna have to do the goddam *asking!* He swallowed hard and began. Hank took the lantern from his mouth while he listened.

"Let me see if I got you right," he said when Evenwrite had finished. "You want me to go in the house and call Wakonda Pacific and tell 'em no dice on the three million feet I cut for 'em, and to show your appreciation you boys'll help me peddle my logs someplace else?"

"Or," Draeger offered, "we'll buy the operation from you outright."

"Who? The union?"

"And some of the citizens of the town."

"Fancy that. But the thing is, Mr. Draeger—an' Floyd, you know this—I can't possibly do such a thing. It ain't all mine to sell. It belongs to a good many of us."

Evenwrite started to answer but Draeger interrupted. "Hank, think of this." Draeger's voice was sterile, carrying neither veiled threat nor solicitous entreaty: Evenwrite noticed that Hank was watching the man closely. "A good many people in town are dependent on that mill reopening."

"Yeah!" Evenwrite came back. "So like I started to say, I know you can't possibly *not* do such a thing, Hank, not and still call yourself a Christian. There is an entire town off there depending on you. An *en-tire* town, your home town, the fellows you grew up with, played ball with . . . an' their wives an' kids! Hank, I know you, boy; this is ol' Floyd, remember? I know you ain't one of the lard-butts in Frisco or LA, bloodsucking your fellow man. I know you can't allow that town of men, women, and children to go hungry all winter to line your pocket."

Hank dropped his eyes, amused and a little embarrassed by Evenwrite's rhetoric. But he shook his head, smiling and shrugging. "They won't starve, Floyd. Some of 'em might miss a couple payments on their TV or—"

"Goddam your soul, Stamper—!" Evenwrite pushed in between Draeger and Hank. "You can see what a bind we're in. And we ain't about to let you keep us eatin' dirt."

"Floyd, I just don't know." Hank continued to shake his head, looking down at the dangling ends of wire where he'd been wrapping the timber. One of his fingers was bleeding slowly down his arm. "I don't see what I can do. I'm in a bind too. Our whole business, the whole shebang, is tied up in those booms up at our mill."

"Hank, could you hold off and sell later?" Draeger asked. "Just until the strike was settled?" Truly an odd voice, Evenwrite had to admit, something about it pure and tasteless, like eating snow or drinking rainwater. . . .

"No, Mr. Draeger, I couldn't; didn't Floyd here show you all that research he did? I'm over a barrel myself. The contract reads delivery by Thanksgiving; we get them logs down by Thanksgiving or the deal is void. We break terms and the price is throwed open. They could pay us what they please. Wouldn't even have to pay us at all if they wanted to be ornery about it—could just sue for fraud an' take the logs."

"They couldn't take your booms! You know damn well—"

"They might, Floyd."

"No judge and jury would find for 'em!"

"They might. You can't tell. And even if they didn't, what am I going to do with twenty acres of logs floating on the river? Our little craphouse mill couldn't handle a quarter of 'em, working night and day all winter . . . even it did we might not be able to market the lumber if we did get it cut."

"You could market it." Floyd was sure.

"How? The big companies got all the construction contracts already sewed up tight."

"Hell, Hank, use your damned head." Evenwrite was charged with sudden enthusiasm. "You could sell to the outfits Wakonda Pacific was planning to sell to. You get it? Sure. Them outfits'll need buildin' material come spring, and man, look, *there's* where you clean up! You cut out WP and since they don't have the wood they can't meet their contract and you sell to the contractors for *twice the profit!* Hey boy, there we go." He turned to Draeger, smiling triumphantly. "What you think of that, Jonny? There's our answer. Hell, now, why didn't I think of that before? Why didn't I *think* of it?"

Draeger chose to let the question pass, but Hank's face came up from examining his cut finger and he regarded Evenwrite's enthusiastic features with obvious amusement. "Probably, I'd say, Floyd, you didn't think of it for the same reason that you didn't just now think that if I let WP go back to work then they'll be able to supply their contracts themselves."

"What?"

"Look, Floyd. The reason you *don't* want me to sell to WP is so *they'll* go back to work and cut their *own* logs. Right? And mill their *own* lumber? To meet their *own* contracts?"

"I don't see . . ." Evenwrite furrowed his brow and a rivulet of water shot down the furrow and off his nose.

"It's like this, Floyd." Hank tried again, patiently. "I can't sell to contractors that WP failed to fill contracts for if you guys go back to work and—"

"Oh man, don't you see, Floyd?" The material was too rich for Joe Ben to stay out of. He popped into the circle of light, his eyes blinking glee. "Don't you see? Oh yeah. See. If we break our contract so you get your contract then *they* can meet *their* contracts with the contractors that you are saying we can contract to if we—"

"What? Wait a minute—"

Hank was trying to keep his amusement from becoming even more obvious. "Joe Ben means, Floyd, that if we let you guys go back to work we're eliminating our market."

"Yeah, Floyd, see? Oh, I admit it's deep. If we let you cut *their* lumber, then *our* lumber we aim to sell to *them* . . ." He took another breath and tried to start anew but gave way to a snorting explosion of laughter instead.

"Screw all this," Floyd growled.

". . . or if we let you keep *our* lumber"—this was the sort of material that could keep Joe going for days—"from becoming *their* lumber so your lumber can become *their* lumber—"

"Screw it." Floyd hunched his shoulders against the lantern light and clamped his jaw. "Just screw it, Joe Ben."

"You can always sell lumber," Draeger said simply.

"That's right!" Evenwrite saw an opportunity to regain lost ground. He took Hank by the arm. "That's why I say screw all this bull. You can *always* sell lumber."

"Maybe . . ."

"Goddam you now, Hank, be reasonable. . . ." He drew a deep breath in preparation for another assault on Hank's stubbornness, but Draeger cut in abruptly. "What are we to tell the people in town?"

Hank turned from Evenwrite; something in the tone of Draeger's question stripped the situation of humor. "What are you gonna *what?*"

"What are we to tell the people in town?" Draeger asked again.

"Why, I don't care *what* you tell them. I don't see—"

"Are you aware, Hank, that Wakonda Pacific is owned by a firm in San Francisco? Are you aware that last year a net of nine hundred and fifty thousand dollars left your community?"

"I don't see what skin that is—"

"These are your friends, Hank, your associates and neighbors. Floyd tells me that you served in Korea." Draeger's voice was placid . . . "Do you ever think that the same loyalty that your country expected of you overseas could be expected of you here at home? Loyalty to friends and neighbors when they are being threatened by a foreign foe? Loyalty to—?"

"Loyalty, for the chrissake . . . *loyalty?*"

"That's right, Hank. I think you know what I'm talking about." The soothing patience of the voice was almost mesmerizing. "I'm speaking of the *basic* loyalty, the *true* patriotism, the selfless, open-hearted, humane *concern* that you always find welling up from some-place within you—a concern you might have almost forgotten—when you see a fellow human being in need of your help. . . ."

"Listen . . . listen to me, Mister." Hank's voice was taut. He pushed past Evenwrite and held his lantern close to Draeger's neat-featured face. "I'm just as concerned as the next guy, just as loyal. If we was to get into it with Russia I'd fight for us right down to the wire. And if Oregon was to get into it with California I'd fight for Oregon. But if somebody—Biggy Newton or the Woodsworker's Union or anybody—gets into it with *me*, then I'm for *me!* When the chips are down, I'm my own patriot. I don't give a goddam the other guy is my own *brother* wavin' the American flag and singing the friggin' 'Star Spangled Banner'!"

Draeger smiled sadly. "And what of self-sacrifice, the true test of any patriot? If you really believed what you say about yourself, Hank, you would be in for some pretty shallow patriotism, some pretty selfish loyalty—"

"Call it whatever you want, that's the way I intend to play it. You can tell my good friends and neighbors Hank Stamper is heartless as a stone if you want. You can tell them I care just as much about them as they did about me layin' on the barroom floor last night."

The two men held each other's eyes. "We could tell them that,"

Draeger said, still smiling sadly at Hank, "but we both know it would be a lie."

"Yeah, a *lie!*" Evenwrite burst out of his angry reverie. "Because, goddammit, you can *always* sell lumber!"

"Christ Almighty, yes, Floyd!" Hank turned on Evenwrite, relieved in a way to have someone to shout at again. "Sure I can sell lumber. But wake up and die right! use your damn head! Look!" He grabbed the flashlight from the still laughing Joe Ben and shone it down at the surging river; the black water eddied about the beam of light as though it were a solid pole. "Look at that push down there! Look! After just one day of rain! You think I can wrestle those booms of mine through a winter of *this?*" I'll tell you something, Floyd, old buddy, to make your trip worth while. Something to make your damn constipated heart bust out singing. We just might not make that deadline, you ever think of that? We still got another half-boom to fill out before we make our run. Another three weeks, and some of it the shittiest type logging in the world; we go up in the state park to finish off with. Steep logging, goddam *hand*-logging! just like they did sixty or seventy years ago, because the State won't let us bring cats and donkeys in for fear we might skin up some of the goddam mountain greenery. Three weeks of flooding and primitive logging, an' we're liable to fall short. But we're gonna work our asses at it, ain't we Joby? And you boys are welcome to stand there and talk about men, women, and children, friends and neighbors and loyalty and that crap till the cows come home, stand there and talk about how they are gonna lose their TV sets this winter, and how the poor folks got to eat . . . but goddammit I can tell you this, that if *they* eat it's gonna be for some reason other'n me, or Joe Ben or the rest, some reason other'n us playin' Santa Claus! Because I don't give a *goddamn!* for my friends and neighbors in town yonder; no more than they give a damn about me." He stopped. A cut on his lip had reopened, and he licked at it gingerly. For a second, in the circle of the lantern's saffron light, the men waited. No one looking at the others.

Then Draeger said, "Let's go" and Floyd Evenwrite said, "Yeah, back where there's still some brotherhood in this world," and they picked their way in the dark back along the plank. Behind them Evenwrite heard a choking laugh start up again—"Break our contract to meet your contract so we can sell"—and heard Hank join in the laughter. "The toplofty cocksucker," he said. "He don't know it yet, but he's real due to be brought down a few pegs."

"Uhuh," Draeger agreed, but his thoughts were obviously else-where.

At the boat Evenwrite snapped his fingers. "Damn. We should've asked him—" Then stopped cold. "No, no, I'm goddammed if I will."

"Should have asked him *what*, Floyd?"

"Never mind. Nothing."

"Nothing?" Draeger seemed amused and in even better spirits than before they had made this dumb-ass trip. "Ask him nothing?"

"I guess nothing. I knew better. I knew it was like talkin' to a signpost. We shouldn't of come. We should of knew better. That's *exactly* correct: we should of asked him *nothing*."

Evenwrite untied the back rope with blind, frozen fingers and climbed into the launch. "Darn," he muttered to himself, feeling his way to the back of the boat. "I should of asked him anyway; he couldn't of said more than no. And he *might* of come through, just out of contrariness. Then at least the trip wouldn't been a *complete* goose-egg. . . ."

Draeger returned to his seat in the front of the boat. "The trip wasn't a goose-egg, Floyd," he mused aloud, "not a goose-egg by any means." Then, as an afterthought: "Should have asked them what?"

Evenwrite gave the motor rope a furious yank. "For *smokes!* We should have asked him for smokes is what."

He got the motor started and swung the little running light away from the dark into the murky fume of rain, turning down river, he realized with a groan, just in time to buck the incoming tide.

By the time Teddy saw Evenwrite and Draeger crossing the street back to the Snag, all the other men had gone home. From his lair of colored light near the front window he watched the way the two men moved after they entered the bar, studying them with veiled intensity: *Floyd is uncomfortable.* Evenwrite examined the wet ruin of his clothes with irritated and jerky pluckings. *He is changed some since he came out of the woods and into the white-collar world*, like a molting chicken that longed terribly to pluck at the annoying itch of its feathers, yet feared just as much to be naked. *Floyd used to come in from work like the animal he is, wet and weary and not worried about it; a stupid animal, but a comfortable one* . . . He finally sighed and loosened his belt so he could sit without having his wet slacks cut him in half . . . *Now he is just stupid. And scared. Floyd has added to the normal fear of the dark a worse fear: the fear of falling.* After folding his pudgy hands across his stomach to try to conceal the bulge that had been building steadily since he had been voted into that white-collar world, Evenwrite sighed again with discomfort and disgust, and frowned across the table, where Draeger was still carefully hanging his overcoat. "All right, now, Jonathan . . . all right." *And worst of all, he is too stupid to know he isn't high enough to fall very far.*

Draeger finished with his coat, then unhurriedly brushed the rain from his slacks; when he was satisfied he pulled out a chair and sat down and placed his hands on the table, one on top of the other. "All right?" he said, *This Mr. Draeger, though, he's up in a position of some height,* looking as neat and composed as Evenwrite looked disarranged. All right what, Floyd?" *So why doesn't he act afraid of falling?*

"What? All right what the fuck are we gonna dammittohell *do* is all right what! I mean to say, I'm *waiting,* Jonathan. Christ, I been waiting a week for you to show up around here an' go to earnin' your pay. . . . I waited yesterday when you said hold off until you looked over the situation, an' I waited today while you took a little joyride up to the Stamper house, an' now I want to know what you aim to *do!*"

Draeger reached into the breast pocket of his jacket for his tobacco pouch. "Do you suppose you can hold off until I fill my pipe?" he asked pleasantly. "And order a drink?" Floyd rolled his eyes and sighed again. Teddy came gliding out of his lair to wait beside the table. "I'd like a whisky if you don't mind," Draeger said, smiling up at him, "to take off the chill of that little joyride. You, Floyd?"

"Nothing, no," Evenwrite answered. Draeger said "one" with his lips adding, "I. W. Harper's," and Teddy melted backward into the throbbing light. *Not any fear of dark, not any fear of falling . . . like he knows something the rest of us don't.*

"Now, Floyd." Draeger puffed his pipe to life. "Exactly what is it you expect me to do? You talk as though you expect me to hire a gang of labor goons and go back up there and burn the Stampers out." He laughed softly.

"That don't sound like such a bad idea, for my money. Burn his whole by god business, mill, trucks, an' everything."

"You're still thinking in the thirties, Floyd. We've learned a few things since then."

"Yeah? Well, I've yet to see them. Leastways in the thirties they got results, those old boys did. . . ."

"Oh? I'm not so sure. Not the *desired* results, anyway. Those old boys' tactics quite often tended to make the opposition set its jaw and dig in firmer than ever—ah, here we are. . . ." He moved his arm to allow Teddy to place the shot glass of whisky in front of him. "Thank you—and, oh, Teddy—could I have a glass of water?" He turned back to Evenwrite and went on. "And, in *this* particular case, Floyd—unless I'm completely off base about Hank Stamper—I can think of nothing that would make the opposition set its jaw any firmer than burning his 'whole by god business.' . . ." He picked up the shot glass and smiled into its amber contents reflectively. "No, I don't think one could choose a worse method against this man. . . ."

"I don't follow you."

"I think you do. You know this man better than I do. If you wanted him to travel east when he had it in his mind to go west, would you get behind him with a whip and try to drive him your way?"

Evenwrite thought a moment, then slapped the table. "By god yes, I would! If he was heading toward walking all over me coming west. Yes! Even if it meant—even if it might mean him raising a fuss . . ."

"Raising quite a fuss, too, in all likelihood, isn't that right? A long and costly fuss, you could be sure. Even if you finally got your way. Because this man obviously thrives on physical opposition. He can understand it. He's oriented to react like a boxer. If you hit him, he'll hit back."

"All right, *all* right! I'm tired of hearin' what Hank Stamper'll do. I want to know what *you* aim to do now that you got him figured so good."

Teddy slid a small glass of water onto the placemat in front of Draeger and stepped back, unnoticed, watching. *What is it you aim to do?* "To be perfectly frank, Floyd, I think all we need to do is wait," he said—*What is it you know we don't?*—and tossed down the shot of whisky.

"Screw that!" Evenwrite shouted. "We *been* waiting, like I said, for too damn long as it is! Oh me, Draeger, don't you under*stand*? What I been saying about this rain? We *can't* wait much longer or there *won't* be no work no way goddammit, can't you *see*?"

Evenwrite's face looked as though he might explode in tears of rage and frustration. He'd *never* had to deal with a man like this! *What is it, Mr. Draeger?* In all the years of woodsbulling drunk riggers and lazy bushlers and government scalers who cheated you blind and owners who wanted done yesterday what was humanly impossible to have done tomorrow—*What is it you have over poor stupid Floyd, Mr. Draeger?*—in all them years foremanning all them sonsabitches, never one of them as unreasonable as this! *What is it you know?* Or leastways never one of them who *frustered* him so. "I mean can't you *see?*" Maybe it was the *surroundings;* hadn't he always managed dealing with sonsabitches out in the brush?

Draeger took a small swallow from the water glass and set it down. "I understand the weather problem, Floyd; I'm sorry if I implied doing absolutely nothing; I know you have your back against the wall so to speak . . . but when I said wait, I meant only to hold off taking any action that would only make Mr. Stamper more obstinate."

"Hold off till when? Till spring? Summer?"

"Until we find some way to make clear to him just how his stand is harming his friends." He had taken a ball-point pen from his pocket and was studying the tip of it.

"Hank Stamper don't have any friends," Evenwrite muttered; then, trying to resume his old woods-bossing manner, demanded scornfully, "You mean you don't even have some kind of *plan* for straightening this out?"

"Not exactly a *plan*," Draeger answered. "Not yet, anyway."

"Nothing but wait, huh? Is that it? Just wait?"

Draeger was doodling on the placemat, absorbed in his thoughts: "For the time being, yes," he said.

"Well, what do you know about *that*. Like we couldn't wait ourselfs, without any help from a college graduate making ten thousand a year of our goddam money . . . what do you think of that?" When Draeger gave no indication that he had heard, Evenwrite went on. "Anyhow, if it's all the same to you, I think me and the boys will get our horsewhip and tend to making this horse turn around and go our direction, while you're waiting."

Draeger looked up from his doodling. "Pardon me?"

"I said me and the guys are gonna go ahead and handle this thing. Plain and simple. With our plain old dumb-ass head-on approach."

"That being?"

"Why, a picket to start with. Like we shoulda done the first thing . . ."

"You can't legally—"

"Legal be damned!" Evenwrite interrupted, momentarily losing his cool. "You think Hank Stamper's gonna call the cops in on us? Or that any of 'em would come if he did? Huh?" He felt his frustration mounting again, but this time he closed his eyes and drew a deep breath to try to stop his outbreak of anger; there wasn't no sense letting the sonofabitch know he was getting under his hide. "So we'll just . . . all right start off tomorrow . . . with a picket." No sense acting like a goddam heathen . . . he'd show them that Floyd Evenwrite could by god be poised and passionless too, in any sonofabitching surrounding! "Then we will see what we will see."

Draeger watched him for a moment, smiling his sad smile, then shook his head. "I suppose there's nothing I can say to—"

"To make me hold off any longer? No." He shook his head in turn, calm and self-contained as they come. "I suppose there ain't." Yessir, as self-possessed as the best of them . . . except, for a little itch troubling his throat, a *cold* picked up on that goddam cold-ass boatride, most likely. Hell!

"Do you think," Draeger wanted to know, "that you will be doing anything more than mollifying your natural punitive desires?"

Evenwrite cleared his throat. "I think by god—" and had started to let the sonofabitch know—in a completely self-contained and self-possessed fashion—just by god *exactly* what he thought, before he recalled that he could never remember for certain whether "punitive" meant weak and sick-looking or strong and sharp-smelling. "I think *that*"—and what in the living hell was "mollify"?—"that uh under the circumstances . . ."

Still, he kept his cool; he didn't panic. He closed his eyes and drew a deep breath and launched a sigh that would reveal to all concerned how simply overcome he was with disgust for this whole conversation . . . but halfway through this sigh he was stricken by that old familiar tickle deep in his throat: oh no! Not here; not *now!* He couldn't sneeze *now*, just as he was getting such a good grip on the situation! He clenched his teeth. He clamped his lips tight. His face swelled out red and desperate from his wet collar, like a prewar inner tube bulging out through a split in the casing just before it burst . . . not *now!*

Because he hated to sneeze indoors. Ever since childhood Evenwrite had been afflicted with a sneeze of such magnitude that it could have turned every head for blocks in his direction by virtue of volume alone, but more than that—above and beyond their acoustical power—his sneezes distinguished themselves by carrying a message as well, always the same message, forceful and invariable: as though he had stopped whatever he'd been doing and shouted—at the top of his lungs—haw . . . haw . . . hot SHIT! In the woods this resounding declaration had been a cause for kidding and fun, and even a bit of unconfessed pride. In the woods. But somehow it didn't go over as well in other areas. In church, or at a meeting, when he felt a sneeze coming on, he was always torn between letting it—hoping those present would either miss the message or excuse it—and bottling it back in his mouth. Each method had its drawbacks, to be sure. That was to be expected. But this time he suffered the drawbacks of both: while he managed to stifle the first half, the "hot" half, behind his bulging lips, the second half, the "SHIT" half, exploded forth clearly and resonantly in a cloud of saliva that settled like a mist over the whole table.

Teddy, on his way back to the bar, paused to see how Draeger would handle this situation. The man looked quizzically across at Evenwrite, then returned his pen to his pocket and picked up a cocktail napkin to carefully wipe a place on his coat sleeve. "Of course," Draeger went on amiably, "every man to his own opinion, Floyd"—as though nothing whatsoever had happened.

Teddy nodded, impressed, and continued on around the end of the bar—*What is it he has learned to put him so far out past the others?*—and Evenwrite, wiping a watering eye with the knuckle of his thumb, wished he was out of there and *home* goddammit, where his clothes didn't bind him so and a man could sneeze without worrying about it.

"And look here, Floyd." Draeger put down the cocktail napkin and gave Floyd a neat, reassuring nod. "I hope you understand that I sincerely want you and 'the guys' to succeed with your head-on approach. Because, confidentially, there is nothing I would like better than to tie up this business here and get back down south; you see," he confided in a whisper of mock-intimacy, "I get athlete's foot up here. But, ah, in as I have already paid a week's rent on my hotel room, and in the event your approach does not prove completely successful, I believe I'll stay around. . . . Is this fine with you?"

Evenwrite nodded. "Fine with me," he answered flatly, making no attempt to regain his state of grim determination. The abortive sneeze seemed to have drained all Evenwrite's spirit. His eyes were watering, and he felt a cold building for certain now, far down in his lungs like a gathering volcano; he just wanted to get home to a hot tub and a bit of Vicks VapoRub in the water. That was all he wanted. He didn't want to fuss no more tonight. . . . "Yeah, that's fine, Draeger. An', like you say, if our approach don't work, well then, we'll just come over an' ask you for some of your help." . . . But just wait by god till tomorrow when he got his zip back; then he'd show the bastards!

Draeger stood up. He picked up the placemat he had been scribbling on and looked at it, smiling, then put it down and took his wallet from his pocket. "It's still raining; do you have a car here? I could run you out to your house in mine. . . ."

"No. Don't do that. It ain't but a few blocks."

"You're certain? I don't mind, really. And you look as if you could use—"

"Yeah, I'm certain."

"Very well, then." Draeger pulled on his overcoat and flipped up the collar. "I'll see you tomorrow probably?"

"Probably. If I got anything to report. Yeah, tomorrow."

On his way out Draeger handed Teddy a dollar bill for his drink and told him to keep the change. Evenwrite grunted a "G'night" and pulled the door closed behind him. Teddy moved to his end of the bar, near the window. He watched the two men walk their different directions, their backs glowing with the stain of his neons. When the glows faded, as dark rain washed the stains off, Teddy circled his bar and locked the door and pulled down the shade with "Sorry CLOSED" printed on it. He switched off the three smoky overhead lights and most of the neons, leaving a few for night lights. In this undersea gloom he made a silent round of his saloon, unplugging the pinballs and the bowling machine, switching off the bubbling jukebox, clearing tables, emptying ashtrays into a large coffee can. Back at the bar he untied his apron and dropped it in the laundry bag that Willard Eggleston's helper would pick up Monday morning. He removed all the bills from the cash register and added them to a roll in a large conch-shell lamp, where they would wait for banking day a week from the coming Monday. He flicked the switch under the bar that put the silent sentinel of the burglar alarm on guard over all his doors and windows and grills. He dusted roach powder along the baseboard. He turned off the blowers on the oil heater and turned the oil down to a trickle. . . .

And only then, after he had looked all about him, turning in a circle in the red and amber light to be sure he had finished with all the chores he could think of, only then did he go to the table where they had been sitting to see what Draeger had written on the placemat.

The Snag's placemats were of corrugated paper, embossed with a silhouette of a topper just completing the saw-through of a spar tree, the top of the tree just beginning to tip as the topper reeled back, gripping his rope. Teddy held the mat to the light. Draeger's doodles seemed quite ordinary at first: The tree had been striped like a barber pole—how many times had he seen *that* one?—and the logger's eyes had been blacked out and a beard added; and a few crude popcorn-shaped objects had been placed about the paper sky to portray clouds. . . . Then, down in one corner he saw three lines of writing, in a sharp, precise hand so small Teddy almost missed seeing them:

Teddy: I'm afraid you mistakenly served me Bourbon De Luxe instead of I. W. Harper. I just thought you would want this called to your attention.

Teddy stared at the inscription in thrilled, unblinking wonder, *What is it? what is it about you?* until his eyes began to burn from the strain and the mat in his hand began to flutter in the light as though a red wind were blowing through the empty bar.

At home, in his bathroom, Evenwrite sat on the clothes hamper in his shorts and undershirt, waiting for the tub to trickle full. It took hours nowadays to pull a good hot bath. They needed a new water heater, had for a long time. In fact—he sighed, looking about him—they needed a lot of new things; even the bottle of Vicks had been empty.

He had taken a big cut in money when he had accepted the head job at the local; the job didn't pay near what he'd been drawing as the first push for Wakonda Pacific. But he'd be damned if he'd try to hold down his union job and work the woods at the same time, the way a lot of local officials did. You couldn't do worth a shit at neither job if you did. And both positions meant too much to him for that.

He prided himself in knowing that both logging and labor were in his blood, though the price of this pride came high. His granddad had been a big man in the very start of the movement, in the IWW, the Wobblies. He'd been personal friends with Big Bill Haywood; a photograph of the two of them hung on Floyd's bedroom wall: two mustached men, each wearing a large white button with the words "I AM AN UNDESIRABLE CITIZEN" pinned to his pea-jacket, and held between them a circular picture of a grinning black cat, the Wobblies' sabotage symbol. His granddad had given his life both in deed and in fact to the movement: after years of work as an organizer he had been killed in 1916 in the Everett Massacre, championing the union man's right to free speech in that Washington milltown. Penniless, his grandmother had returned to her family in Michigan with her young son, Floyd's father. But the son of a martyred Wob wasn't about to settle down in tame old Michigan; not when the fight still raged. After a few months the boy had run away, back to the north woods and the work the old man had died for.

By the time he was twenty-one this stocky, thick-featured redhead —called Knob, because of the predominant Evenwrite feature of a head set without benefit of neck on heavy round shoulders—had chopped a reputation for himself as one of the fiercest, fence-nail-chewingest, carpet-tack-spittingest men in the woods, both as an all-around dawn-till-dark diehard logger and as rip-roaring loudmouth of a labor visionary, a Wob that his old man—or even Big Bill Haywood himself—would have been proud of.

By the time this redhead was forty-one, he was a skid-road alky with a rotting liver and a broken heart, and no one in the world proud of him.

The Wobs were dead, gone, crushed between the thundering collisions of the AFL and CIO, discredited as Communist (though they had spent more fighting the "Red Dawn" than the other two unions combined), and the woods Knob Evenwrite had loved were rapidly filling up with exhaust smoke where there had once been only clear, pine-winy air, and the rough diehard loggers he had fought for were being replaced by beardless boys who learned their logging from textbooks, and smoked instead of chewed, and slept between snow-white sheets just like they thought lumberjacks had always slept that way.

There didn't seem anything left but to get married and drown the disappointed memories.

Floyd never met the young diehard fire-eating Knob, not face to face, though he often felt that he knew the young man better than he knew the dejected spook in the fire-eater's cast-off skin who staggered about the impoverished shadows of their three-room shack in Florence, intent on drinking and dying. For some nights, when his father came home from his boiler-tender's job at the mill, he would do more than just drink and die. Maybe on these nights something had ripped some old memory loose from the bottom of his father's past, or it might be that he had witnessed some capitalistic injustice at the mill that relit the fire-eater in him, but on these nights the man would sit in the kitchen, telling young Floyd how things used to be, how they by god woulda handled a injustice like that back in the days when the air was still clear and the Wobs still stalked the woods! Then the cheap liquor that usually brought nothing but silence and eventually sleep would, on these special nights, stir up the sleeping zealot imprisoned behind the blue-veined bars of sick flesh, and Floyd would see the young Knob Evenwrite rise up from the rubbish and walk forward to glare from the cell's two eyeholes and shake at the hellish blue bars like an enraged lion.

"Listen, kid, it all boils down to this," the lion would sum up the situation. "there's the Big-Asses like them, an' the Little-Asses like us. It's easy to tell who's on whose side. There's just a few Big-Asses; they own the world an' all the corn. There's millions of us Little-Asses; they grow the corn an' all go hungry. The Big-Asses, they think they can get away with this because they think they're better than the Little-Asses—on account of maybe somebody died an' left them a lot of money so they can pay the Little-Asses to grow their corn for them, an' pay 'em what they want to pay. We got to haul 'em down from that, do you see? We got to show them we're just as important as they are! Everybody is as important as they are! Everybody grows corn! Everybody eats it! Simple as that!"

Then would leap up to sway about the room, roaring fiercely:

"Which side are you on?
Which side are you on?
When we all line up in the bat-tul . . .
Tell me which side are you on?"

Floyd's mother and his two sisters cringed from the rare roaring visits of this lion. His two sisters blamed the devil for these spells of violent nostalgia; his mother maintained that it was the devil, all right, the devil in a pint bottle without a label! But young Floyd knew it was something far stronger than a bogeyman from the Bible, or from a bottle either; he knew that when his father's past roared out through the old stories about injustices overcome in their fight for shorter hours and longer lives, and through old songs about the impossible utopias they had worked to realize, he could feel in his own young blood the roaring cry for justice and see rise again in the distance those blazing utopias that his father's whiskied eyes perceived—though the boy hadn't touched a drop.

Of course, these nights of passion were rare. And, like his mother and sister, Floyd could despise the worn-out fanatic who kept them locked in poverty, the husk of a man who nightly drank himself into a senseless sleep to keep from having to face all the bewildered, groping ghosts of his stillborn dreams and extinct ideals, but just as he could hate the old man he could love the tough visionary who had dreamed the dreams and forged the ideals—though this young visionary was responsible, he knew, for the fanatic's worn-out husk that he hated.

His father died during Floyd's freshman year in high school—burned to death on a mountaintop. The man's drinking had finally reached the point of making him incapable of even tending a boiler. After a long winter of unemployment some old friends had found him a job as a fire lookout on the highest mountain in the county. He left for the job with his spirits high. Everyone had hopes that the lofty solitude, and the month-long periods without access to any kind of alcohol, would ease old Knob of his anguish and perhaps even start him on the road to a cure. But when a party of firefighters reached the smoldering ruin of the lookout shack, they discovered not only how mistaken those friends had been but how the fire had started as well: in the ashes of the shack they found the exploded remains of a makeshift still. Every available container—from the coffeepot to the chemical toilet—was filled with a fermenting mash concocted from potato peelings, salmonberries, wild barley, and a dozen different kinds of flowers. The condensate worm had been fashioned by laborious coupling of empty rifle cartridges with their caps poked out. The firebox was of stone and mud. The boiler had been wrought from beaten stovepipes. Then the whole affair had been riveted together with tacks, and with staples, and with bleak, unimaginable desperation. . . .

It appeared that the betrayed ghosts of old dreams and ideals, however bewildered, could grope their way up even the highest mountain in the county.

The two sisters left home after the funeral, bound for a holier land, and the mother, who had spent the last years of her husband's life hiding his label-less fruit jars from him, began bringing the bottles from their hiding places and took up right where old Knob had left off. Floyd managed to support his mother's sorrow as well as put himself through the rest of high school (through to the midpoint of his senior year, actually, when his last football season ended). The only job that afforded him the hours and the money for this was a shady arrangement he made with a gyppo outfit that was running log trucks so ancient with loads so big that none of the union men would touch them and none of the state patrolmen would leave them alone, so the runs had to be made in secret, in untraveled areas from the gyppo's show to the mill, and in the dark.

"Scabbin'!" Floyd used to call out in the night during an over-loaded lights-out drive down a mountain road where state cops might wait up any side spur and black death over any part of the road's narrow shoulder, "Scabbin'! For a goddam gyppo outfit who won't meet union regs! How do you like *that*, old man Little-Ass?"

He hoped the old man could hear him. He hoped the old bastard was spinning in his drunkard's grave to hear his son blaspheme so. For wasn't it the old bastard's fault—and the union's too—that he had to be out there every other night like this, risking life and limb? None of the other kids, with their level-headed feet-on-the-ground daddies— even those whose daddies had been killed in accidents—had to take such risks to get along, because none of them had fanatics for fathers. So wasn't it the old fanatic's fault that he was out on some garter-snake road with no lights three hours a night, just when he should be resting up for a big game the next day?

The question he never asked, though, was why he didn't quit the team and get a regular job after school. He never let himself ask why it was so important that he get out on a stinking mudwallow field three hours a day and try to kick the stuffing out of all the other bastards, smartasses who acted like it was a federal crime having an alky for an old man. . . . He never did ask himself that.

When he left high school Floyd went straight to the woods for work. For daylight work! no more living by the dark of the moon for Floyd Evenwrite! And since he was goddamned if he was gonna join the Teamsters or any *other* goddam union just so's he could jockey a truck, woods work was the only choice left him. Being non-union, he had to work twice as hard to survive a layoff. In fact, his anti-union feelings were so strong that he was soon noticed by top brass in the show—old woodsmen who still figured a man oughta be his own man, no organization to back him up!—and it didn't take these old timers very long to recognize this young tight-muscled redhead as prime potential for foremanning work. After two years he made cutting boss, from choker-setter to cutting boss in two years, and in one more year he was top push of the whole outdoor operation.

Things were looking rosy. He married a girl from one of the county's big political families. He bought a house and a good automobile. Big men in the community, mill-owners and bank presidents, began to call him "sport" and "Red" and invite him to join service organizations and participate in drives to provide money for decent living quarters for the Indians. Things were certainly coming along.

But there were nights . . . when his sleep was troubled by a ringing roar, and days when a bum deal was given some fellow worker by one of the lard-butts who never stepped outside his office except to walk down to the bank, when Floyd would find his thick red hands rolling and unrolling in musclebound outrage, and his thick red ears echoing old battle tunes:

> Which side are you on?
> Which side are you on?
> In this war for life and liberty,
> Which side are you on?

Gradually he found himself less and less on the side of management and more and more in sympathy with the workers. And why the hell not? Foreman or no, wasn't he a worker himself, when you come down to it? The son of the son of a worker to boot? He gained nothing by whipping the men to better production; he had no finger in any of the pies when the profits were cut up at the end of the year; he worked his hours and drew his wages and felt the slow abuse of logging make its inevitable marks on his body, on his only skilled instrument of any value to the owners, just like the other stiffs. So why the living hell *shouldn't* he feel the workers' jolt? Not that he was ready to throw his lot in with the union—he'd had enough of that crap to last him a good long while, thank you, so he'd just pay a fee and sign a paper and stay inactive—but oh *me!* did it piss him off to see a man, say a old bushler or the like, *a man fifteen motherin' years devoted to the same motherin' company!* turned out cold by some new mechanical gadget . . . oh, that did get his blood up!

The lion's roaring began ringing in his head louder and louder, and he couldn't keep the owners from hearing it. They couldn't consider letting him go—he was far too good a foreman to lose—but they could become decidedly cold after so many of his tirades against unfair treatment of the men; no more "sport" or "Red," and the service clubs dropped his name from their rosters. But others were also aware of the roar. One noon the men came to the solitary stump where he was eating his lonely foreman's lunch—six of them, coming from the clearing down the slope where all the rest of the crew joked and horseplayed during sandwiches and Thermoses of coffee—to tell him that they, the crew, which was large enough to compose three-fourths of the local, had talked it over and were voting him president at the next meeting if he would consider taking the job. Evenwrite sat in mute, open-mouthed amazement for a long minute: voting him, a foreman, *their* foreman, to be their local's president? And then stood up and removed his company-issue hard hat, threw it to the ground, and announced with tears in his eyes that he would not only consider it but he was quitting his job as of right now!

"Quitting?" the owners had asked later at the mill. "I don't understand, Floyd; why quitting?"

"The men want me for local's president."

"Yes. I understand that. But that's no reason to chuck your job; that's no reason for quitting. . . ."

"All right then. Not quitting, if you don't like that word. Let's just say I'm leaving your side so's I can finally get started working for my own!"

Even now, as he recalled the event, his eyes began to water. He'd never in his life been so proud. He'd gone to that first meeting with his head up and his shoulders back, figuring *now*, by god, *now* he was gonna show them, the ones who'd shot his grandfather dead for sticking up for his American rights, the ones who'd sandbagged the Wobblies into an ignoble back seat in the thirties, who'd forced his disillusioned father to a shameful life and a humiliating death, who'd put him—just a high-school kid!—behind the wheel of an overloaded truck long past the age of safety so's they could hell around in a new convertible every year off the money his risks had made them! The ones who thought they were better, the *Big-Asses* . . . goddam if he wouldn't show them!

Yet, after more than a year at it, what had he done? What could he point to? His eyes began to water faster, and he felt that warning tickle scrape in his throat. He plumped heavily down from the clothes hamper and took a sip of water to quench the tickle, then removed his shorts and undershirt and stepped into the tub. It wasn't nearly as warm or as full as he liked it—no good old Vick's neither—but it would have to do. He sighed and leaned back, searching for the comfort he used to find after a long day in the woods. But the water just wasn't warm enough.

As he lay with his eyes closed, the scene at the Snag suddenly leaped back into his thoughts. Draeger. Damn, it was hard to know how to take that man. It seemed so strange to Floyd that they should both be on the side of labor. Try as he might, he couldn't imagine Jonathan Bailey Draeger in there in the thick of it when the Wobs were winning those first terrible and costly victories . . . imagine him in there with pamphlets and sabot shoes, with ax handles and peavey poles, busting heads and risking his life for the right to stand up on a box in a company town and say what he thought, or for equipment safe enough it wasn't going to kill you before you drew your time, or even imagine him doing a little reckless and mocking act of rebellion such as wearing a button proudly proclaiming himself one of the citizens that President Teddy Roosevelt had labeled as citizens who, if they weren't guilty of any crime, were nevertheless "undesirable" as far as the USA was concerned. No, not Draeger, not this fastidious know-it-all who'd obviously never had on a pair of corks in his life, or swung a double-edge when every swing felt as though it was sinking three inches deep into a head three feet thick with last night's liquor, or sat for hours at the end of a day with a needle under a bright lamp, digging the jaggers and berry thorns and cedar slivers out of tired fingers. . . . Not Jonathan Bailey Draeger.

Without any warning the tickle flared hot and crackling in his throat again. He didn't try to stave off the sneeze this time. He let it roar through the house in all its full-volumed magnificence; it might wake the family but at least they'd know who was up and fooling around at this hour; they'd know the old man was home. It left him tingling all down his arms and thighs. A good sneeze was damn near like when you got your rocks off. It left a man feeling like he'd sure enough had something happen to him.

After a minute Larry, his four-year-old, appeared at the bathroom door, rubbing the matted red hair where his head had lain on the pillow. Evenwrite scowled at him.

"Here now, you little skunk . . . you ain't supposed to be up an' roaming around."

"Hello, Daddy," the boy said sleepily. He stepped closer to the tub and looked down at the bubbles in the stiff fuzz that swarmed from his father's heavy shoulders down over his chest and belly like a mantle of thick orange moss. "I heard you an' I woke up," the boy explained.

"Do you have to pee?" Evenwrite asked.

The boy thought a while, looking at the hair, then shook his head. "No."

"You sure?"

"I done peed once tonight."

"Good fellow."

"Where'd you go, Daddy?"

"Daddy had to see a man about some business."

"Did you win?"

"It wasn't a poker game tonight, skunk. Now you get on back to bed."

"I peed before I went to sleep."

"All right, good boy. Now back to bed."

"Good night, Daddy."

The boy scuffed out of the bathroom with short splay-footed steps, his round shoulders rolling with the walk: an infant parody of the bearlike Evenwrite movement. When Floyd heard the bedsprings squeak he reached out and pushed the bathroom door closed so the light or another sneeze wouldn't wake the child's brothers or sister. He slid down in the tub until the water came over his lips. His ears were submerged. He left just enough of his nose out to breathe. He closed his eyes again. Did I win, he thought, laughing warmly to himself at the boy's imitation of the mother's irritating question: I suppose he sees my whole life away from home as one big game of penny-nickel-dime draw. And that's about it, too, you come down to it, playing the crummy cards you was dealt and betting on better cards to come. Bluffing and bullying when you're short, laying back when you're long. . . .

As he dozed, his thoughts returned again to Draeger. One thing, he promised himself, one thing, though: I ain't gonna tell my kids one side or the other . . . because it's getting so you can't hardly be sure . . . any more . . . who's the Big-Asses and who's the Little-Asses . . . who's on whose side . . . or who's winning . . . any more . . . or even who you want to win for sure . . .

Before noon of the next day, Monday, Evenwrite had called the two mute Sitkins boys, Howie Evans, Mel Sorenson, and Les Gibbons. They arrived, except for Les, in time for deerburger and potatoes. They could see the picket signs Evenwrite had made standing against the wall like arms stacked before a battle.

"Sit down, boys," Evenwrite told the four men. "Have some chow. We'll wait a while longer for Les, then head on out. Boy"—he winked at them over the meat—"I tell you, I don't know where we'd be during this strike it wasn't for all the sidehill salmon I been catching."

No one laughed. "This picket," Howie said, "you sure Draeger knows about this?"

"Sure as shooting," Evenwrite said brightly. "I let him know last night that we was capable of running our own affairs if he wasn't going to get off the pot. . . ."

"I don't know." Howie hedged. "My old lady won't like it if I'm doin' something illegal—"

"Legal be screwed! We're doin' something *right* for a change, and legal be screwed!"

"But what about Hank?"

"What about him? What can he do? What is there he can possibly do about a picket?"

"I don't know," Howie muttered, standing. "You never can be sure . . ."

A half an hour later the pickets were plodding back and forth in front of the office at the mill. Orland Stamper came out and stood a moment looking at them, then returned to the shrieking mill.

"He's gone to get word to Hank," Howie said unhappily.

"So what if he does?" Evenwrite demanded. "Howie, I swear you do overestimate that bastard . . ."

The next time the log truck arrived from the show, Hank and Joe Ben alighted from its cab before it drove on to dump the logs in the river. The plodding men watched guardedly from beneath their metal hats as Hank and his little companion sat on the bench beneath the mill's sheltered porch, viewing the parade. Half an hour passed. Hank smoked, grinning, leaning forward with his elbows on his knees and his hands dangling between his legs; Joe Ben provided some march music with his little transistor radio. Finally, to Howie's relief, they saw Hank turn and whisper something to Joe and Joe erupt with laughter, then dash from the porch to a battered pick-up and drive away toward town. When the log truck returned again, Hank bade them all a pleasant afternoon and climbed into the cab. They didn't see any more of him that day.

"We got him," Evenwrite crowed, back at home that night with a new bottle of Vicks. "They got to have supplies. They can't run a show without supplies. An' what supplier, what good teamster is gonna cross our picket line with gas or oil or parts, huh? Tomorow or the next day will tell the tale."

Tomorow told it. When Floyd arrived with his pickets the next morning they found a television mobile unit from Eugene with a portable TV camera, two photographers from the *Register Guard*, and Indian Jenny. And that night the front page carried the heading: PICKETS PERPLEXED BY MYSTERIOUS MATRIMONY—*which one is happy groom?* And the six-fifteen TV news carried a picture of a woman with a shape like a stone and a face like a baked yam walking alongside a line of pickets, in poncho and rubber milking boots, just what the pickets wore, carrying a sign on a stick just like those the pickets carried. Their signs proclaimed: UNFAIR UNFAIR. Her sign added: JUST MARRIED. No one volunteered for picket duty the next day.

They met this time in the Snag. Behind the bar, completely absorbed in the polishing of a shot glass, Teddy seemed to barely register their called requests for drinks.

"What tactics are you proposing this time, Floyd?" Draeger had entered without anyone's noticing; he stood near the bar, opening a newspaper. "No fire, I hope?"

"You'll see, by godfrey. We're tired of foolin' around. You'll see."

"Fine," Draeger said pleasantly and sat down. "Let me know how it all turns out." And arranged his paper before him and leaned over it. "A bourbon," he said without looking up. "I. W. Harper's." Teddy already had it poured.

"Okay then," Evenwrite said in a terse whisper at his table. "About ten. I'll call Sitkins. Mel, you call Howie and ask him. Ten, then." The men nodded back, sitting in grim silence around the table, chewing the rims of glasses, not even breaking the serious mood of the approaching night to kid Teddy about his watered drinks. The talk went on until it was time to go to supper.

A half-dozen resolute and stouthearted men met that night in Evenwrite's front room over a case of Olympia quarts and devised a plot to slip out to the Stamper mill and hacksaw the cable bolts linking the surrounding logs that penned the booms together. "Stampede them logs downstream like they was wild horses!" Les Gibbons exclaimed, pounding the floor beside him with a beer bottle. "'N' if we're lucky they'll rip out the *whole rat's nest* of the motherjumpers as they go stampedin' past!"

"And we can drop a few blasting sticks amongst the booms to give them a good start." Evenwrite could feel his heart beginning to hammer.

"Attaboy! Now we're pickin' cotton!"

"Maybe even let a stick or two drop right in the mill." Yessir, *this* was the way to get things done, old-fashioned or no!

"Now we're talkin'!"

Gibbons struck the floor again. "Awright then, we gonna *talk* sic 'em or we gonna *do* sic 'em?"

"*Do*, goddammit'hell! Jus' like commandos. Let's go, let's go!"

They managed to get one boom opened before the slippery, lurching logs spilled Evenwrite and two other men into the freezing black water. These three unfortunate commandos were swept off into the dark and, after a moment, could be heard cursing and shouting from a flooded clump of bam trees where they clung, too far from solid land to risk swimming, too cold to wait for one of the others to drive into town for a motorboat. There was no choice but go into the mill and phone for help from the nearest boat.

"What'll we tell him?" Howie Evans whispered as he stood, humpbacked and cold, dialing the flashlit wall phone in the mill.

"Tell him we need help quick to keep three men from perishing!"

"But I mean . . . what about the *logs?*" Howie whispered, holding his hand over the mouthpiece of the phone.

"McElroy is out there now wiring the cut back together. In the dark maybe he won't notice a few logs missin'."

Hank arrived, as eager to help as ever. With his flash he and Joe Ben found the three men in the leafless thicket of bam saplings. The bony saplings rattled and clattered as the current swept through their skinny trunks, making them appear as cold and miserable as the shivering men who clung to them. They all three were prepared to start talking as soon as the boat achieved the security of solid land; each had created his own elaborate and logical-sounding reason for being out so late, so far from town, and so near the property of their enemy, but when Hank didn't ask for reasons, did not even seem inclined to ask for their reasons, they wisely chose to keep silent, realizing that any alibi or excuse they offered would be received probably without question, maybe even without comment, and certainly without belief.

"You boys looks a little wasted, Floyd. . . . I tell you, come on here in the mill an' we can get some coffee going."

"No." Evenwrite declined. "No thanks. We got to—"

"I'd offer you some hard stuff if I had some. Seems a shame. Joby, we ain't got any brandy or bourbon, do we?"

"I'm afraid not. Not here. Some at the house, though, if you'd care—"

"That's okay. We got to be going."

"That's too bad. I hate to be a bad host. But say, I tell ya what: you come back tomorrow night an' we'll see if we can't be better prepared."

The three men stood in a line, waiting the way children wait before the principal's desk. "N-n-no, thanks, Hank," Les chattered. "Uh—uh—we wouldn't want to put you out."

"Les, by god, you should be gettin' *accustomed* to this water."

"Yeah. Ain't that the truth, Hank. Well, by gosh, I don't have to tell you how obliged. Anyhow. I guess we ought to be goin'."

"Who's out there on the road in the car? Some others? Floyd, you'll tell 'em, won't you, that I'm sorry I wasn't better prepared. Will you tell 'em that? And tell 'em we'll sure see to getting in some brandy or the like for the future."

All the next day Floyd spent in the bathtub, and used the whole new bottle of Vick's. It was Thurday before he made another attempt to dissuade Hank. Alone this time, he drove up to Scaler's bridge and parked his car out of sight up a back road; while the government men were talking with John Stamper in the little shack, he slipped out on the blind side with a hammer and a bag of tenpenny spikes. He managed to get four of the spikes driven out of sight beneath the bark of the logs before the sound of the shack door opening ran him back to the bushes. He waited there in the rain, shivering and chewing at his lip, until the truck went back up and returned with a new load; then he popped out again to plant a few more spikes. He knew he might have to mine hundreds of logs in this way to be sure of getting one into the mainsaw's teeth, because most of the logs were being boomed up to be sold to WP. And so what if WP loses a few blades too? Serve both the sonsabitches right.

He worked all day, and when dusk settled he complimented himself on a job thoroughly done. He dragged back to his car and drove into town. He ate the cold left-overs in the kitchen, then drove on in to see if news of a Stamper breakdown had yet reached the Snag. It had. Along with the news that the Stamper mill workers were all being transferred to woods work for the rest of the year. "McElroy said that Joe Ben said," the first man Floyd met told him, "that Hank is got sawn lumber aplenty and was just *looking* for some excuse to move his whole crew into the woods to get at this WP contract."

Evenwrite didn't say anything; he stood, silent and chilled, wondering why he wasn't more surprised by the news.

"An' you know what?" the man went on. "You know what me 'n' the boys an 'a lot of others reckon?"

He shook his head slowly. "No. What is it you 'n' the boys reckon?"

"That Hank Stamper hisself brought off this breakdown for just such a reason. It's just like him to pull a trick like that."

Evenwrite agreed and turned to go. He had almost reached the door when he heard his name called. Draeger was coming out of the toilet, buttoning his jacket. "Wait, Floyd. . . ." Dumbly, and still without surprise, he watched the man's amiable face growing larger as it approached him down the double row of booths. "Wait just a moment." Like one of the head-on shots of trains in a movie show. "I have something here for you." Stopping a moment at a booth to pick up something, then looming forward again, not like something really moving closer but like one of them pictures of trains projected on a screen, crashing larger and larger onward without moving a goddam bit. "Hank Stamper was by looking for you. . . ." Till it's right on top of you, blacking out the whole screen with its crashing, right on over you and it still ain't moved; you ain't even felt it. "He left a gift for you."

"Huh?" He shook himself from his reverie. "Gift?"

"This. Hank Stamper asked if I wouldn't give this to you. He said he was by your house but you weren't there, so he came to the Snag. Here."

He took the brown bottle-shaped paper sack from Draeger by the neck, looking down at the twisted top.

"Aren't you going to open it? I must say you have more restraint than I do. A gift drives me nuts until I see what it is. The difference between a married man with family and a bachelor, I suppose. . . ."

"I know what's in it," Floyd said in a flat voice. "It's a bottle. So. Hank Stamper just come in? An' said, 'Give this to Floyd Evenwrite'? Is that what happened?"

"No. He told me to tell you—ah, what was it? I've lost the exact words but he said something like, let's see—it'll surprise you—"

Floyd watched the man pause to recall a message that he knew was no more lost to Draeger than it would be a surprise to him. "Oh yes,

Hank said, 'Give Floyd this brandy for me along with my sincerest thanks.' Or something to that effect. Aren't you going to open it? There's something else in the sack. I could hear it tingling about. . . ."

"No, I guess not. I know what that is too. It's nails."

"Nails? Like carpentering nails?"

"That's right."

Draeger smiled and shook his head in amused puzzlement and winked at Teddy. "These boys up here are sometimes blamed difficult to fathom, aren't they, Teddy?"

"Yes sir." *I doubt that any boys anywhere are very difficult for you to fathom, Mr. Draeger.* . . .

The following Saturday night brought in another topnotch crowd. The long room pulsated with light blue smoke and the heavy blues beat of Rod's guitar (Teddy had been forced to offer the band an additional three-fifty apiece to come in; although the deluge of despair didn't hamper the alcohol sales, it stopped completely such frivolities as the tips that usually accounted for the bulk of the band's take); the music flowed as melancholy and as free as dark draft beer. Ever since the November dark had settled down from the clouds the men had been swarming to the flickering lure of his neons like moths in a July twilight. Teddy rippled back and forth from tables to booths to bar in his crepe-soled haste—a plump, silent scurry that seemed actually the antithesis of movement—emptying ashtrays, filling glasses, spiriting away loose change with covert skill, and, tonight, barely hearing the old charge that he had been once again filling his empty Jack Daniels bottles with cheaper liquor. The charge was levied against him with such regularity—"Bust your fat little ass, Teddy, what sorta crap you giving us *now!*"—that he was sometimes afraid he would lose control and shout to the rooftops how much truth was in what the idiots considered merely a teasing accusation.

". . . I mean, Teddy boy, I ain't one to complain about you cuttin' expensive liquor with cheap—you *know* that; I'm about as easy a man to please as you'll find any place, no highfalutin tastes or that sorta thing—but I will by god draw the motherin' *line* on havin' my bourbon diluted with Mennen's Skin Bracer!"

And the men would laugh, craning heads from booth and back bar to enjoy Teddy's blushing reaction to the joke. It had become a once-, sometimes a twice-a-night ritual. In fact, he recently had become so tired of being accused of diluting with Mennen's that he was currently contemplating just that. Not that it would make any difference: he knew that there wasn't a man among them with taste civilized enough to tell anything more than the temperature of a liquid, just as surely as he knew that not a one suspected the truth of their jest. When he was reminded of this, the knowledge would fill him both with fury at the indictment (They have no right making such slanderous charges without proof!) and with a contempt that made it possible to keep the fury in control (Morons, if they only knew . . .)

Lately, however, when confronted by the charge, the fury had become almost unmanageable: he would flutter his lashes and blush and mumble out a frightened denial, all the while vowing behind his fawning stammer: No more Ten High for these morons. They do not deserve it! Not even Bourbon De Luxe. From now on the Jack Daniels these morons get will come right out of a fruit jar and I hope they all go stone blind!—still apologizing out loud, of course, "Sir, I am very sorry." and offering to stiffen the drink with another jigger free on the house. "Please, sir, let me—"

The moron would always wave the offer aside—"Ah, fergit it, Teddy, fergit it. What the dickens: it 'uz worth the shavin' lotion just seein' you blush so pretty"—and, quite often, drop a few pieces of change on the bar with a kind of nervous magnanimity. "Here . . . keep the gravel."

And the men would laugh. And Teddy would ripple away in his buoyant shoes with a sixty-cent tip and a weak smile drawn like a curtain over a mouthful of hate, to the far end of the bar, where he would stand sulking and hurt and furious, waiting for the healing light of his neons to give him relief. Here was his peace and his sanctuary, the only comfort in his solitary and friendless world. And lately, while his business was better than ever, and although his belief in his superiority in a world of terrified nincompoops was beyond doubt, he had needed an increasing amount of this hissing comfort: there were nights, after standing, head bowed and humble before the drunken spray of one of his funnyman patrons, when he found himself forced to convalesce for half an hour or more at this end of the bar, smiling, with one hand lightly on the bartop, like something needing the protection of a shell—for half an hour before the throbbing lights could massage away the outrage. During these periods he would seem quite unchanged, greeting each new arrival with his usual formal manner, fiddling with the long key-chain that looped across the round bulge of his apron, calling out the hour when asked . . . and even if any of the customers had chanced to observe him closely, as he stood there with different hues of red and orange and magenta fluttering across his blank face—

"Teddy, goddam you little octopus, could you come down here outa your cave and pour some of that clear-looking stuff out of that Gilbey's gin bottle into this glass of mine? There's a good boy . . ."—even so, they would have attributed the color to nothing more than the pulsing neons.

But this night, in spite of an uncommon collection of bruising insults, Teddy spent very little time recuperating under the light of his neons. In the first place he was too busy: the disheartening news of the Stamper lumber-mill crew's move up to the woods had kept him pumping liquor almost as fast as had the Stamper-Newton fight a week before; and this time he hadn't called in the waitress from the Sea Breeze to lend him a hand. So he was far too busy scurrying after orders to afford himself the luxury of pouting under his lamps whenever one of the morons made some remark. In the first place.

And, in the second, didn't really need the balm of his lights as much as usual: not only was he especially soothed by the muted pitch of worry that rose from each of the tables blending with the rising smoke—"Teddy, goddammit, I tell ya . . . somethin' is haywire here. . . ." "Yes sir, Mr. Evenwrite." "Somethin' terrible wrong . . ."—rose blending to hang congealed and blue all over the room . . . but he was already in a delicious state of thrilled anticipation owing to a phone call he had received that afternoon from Jonathan Draeger: after telling him that he was calling long distance from Eugene and asking that he do him a favor—"I'll be there this evening; would you please see if you can keep Floyd Evenwrite indoors and out of trouble until I arrive?"—Draeger had put Teddy in a heart-thumping swirl by adding, "We'll show these muscleheads just what a little thoughtful patience can accomplish, won't we, Ted?"

All the rest of that afternoon and evening that tiny intimacy had glowed in Teddy's chest. We, Draeger had said; we! Such a word, coming from such a man, could outshine all the neons in Oregon!

Evenwrite had come in after supper, a little before seven, with his face redder than usual and his breath laced with the sweet smell of brandy. "Yeah, somethin' wrong . . ." he announced again, knotting his features terribly.

"What's that, Mr. Evenwrite?"

"Haw?" Evenwrite looked up, blinking stupidly.

"You said something about something being wrong . . ."

"Hell yes, somethin' wrong. With this *drink*, I was talkin' about! What'd you think I was talkin' about?"

In response Teddy lowered his lashes and gazed at the wienie-fingered, rusty-knuckled paw resting on the richly grained surface of the bar. Beside this monstrosity his own curled hand—eternally bluish from so many hours in the wash-water cleaning glasses, the flesh appearing to approach transparency the way meat does after pickling—looked even bluer and smaller than usual. He waited timidly, face bent in an attitude of abject and persevering embarrassment. "What about it, sir? the drink . . . ?"

"Well, right this minute it's *empty* is what about it. You could fill it back up for a start. That'd help some."

Teddy brought out a bottle and refilled the glass; Evenwrite picked it up and started to walk back to his table.

"Oh. That will be fifty cents, Mr. Evenwrite."

"Fifty cents! You mean to tell me you're askin' money for this stuff? Teddy, I wasn't planning to drink it, I was goin' into the head and give myself a shampoo with it."

Teddy looked back down. The men at Evenwrite's table laughed, always welcoming the comic interlude Teddy brought to their serious, grim, down-to-business discussions. Then Evenwrite guffawed himself and slapped a four-bit piece down on the bartop as though squashing a bug. Teddy picked it up gently and carried it to the cash register, relishing an exquisite and curious new fear just garnered from the emotional clutter of Evenwrite's face, *This is one thing, Mr. Draeger, that sets you apart from me and the muscleheads both:* carefully rolling the new specimen over and over with a connoisseur's studied appreciation. . . . *I can just escape fear; you can create it.*

At all the tables grouped about the table where Evenwrite was holding forth, the conversation followed essentially the same lines, starting with they'd never thought it of Hank Stamper, double-crossing his neighbors like he's done—"Old Henry, maybe, but Hank's always been a pretty good ol' boy himself"—on to "What the devil? You can't expect to get a peach offn a thorn-apple bush, can you? Just because Hank ain't all the time juiced out tellin' about how you got to have a armor-plated hide to make a go of this business, like the old man all the time is, don't mean he ain't blood of blood and flesh of flesh." And eventually on to "There's no two ways about it that I can see: Hank Stamper's indicated where he stands and he's just got to be showed the error of his ways."

Evenwrite led the charge in this last maneuver. "And I for one say," he shouted, jumping to his feet, momentarily enlisting the room's attention with eyes glazed and red as hard candy and a nose plugged near to bursting, "say that a bunj of us go out there and put Mister Hank Stamper *straighd!*" He wiped his nose on his sleeve and added, "Right by god *gnow!*"

There was a brief flurry of agreement, "Yeah, straight . . . right now . . ." but Teddy knew the bar was too comfortably warm and bright and the night outside too miserably cold and wet for this flurry to flare into action. It would take a lot more talk and drink before Evenwrite could lead any sort of mob out into the rain. Still, the ways things were going, he *did* wish—

The door opened and, like an answer to Teddy's unfinished wish, Draeger entered. Hardly anyone but Teddy noticed, the others devoting attention to Evenwrite's bloodshot eyes and plugnosed speech. Draeger removed his overcoat and hat and hung them by the door, then seated himself at a small empty table close to the oil heater. He held up a finger and said, "One," silently to Teddy, then turned to watch Evenwrite's neck heave and swell in his plea for action.

"We been beatin' too long around the bush with them, tryna be *legal,* and *fair* . . . well, I ask you, they been fair with us? They treated us *ride?*"

There was more yelling and some scraping of chairs. But Teddy, carrying whisky and water, peeked from beneath his lashes at Draeger's pleasant, understanding face and saw that Draeger was no more worried about being trampled in a riot than he was. *If anybody here is going to whip up a riot, it is not going to be Floyd Evenwrite.* He placed the glasses on the table; Draeger tasted the liquor and smiled up at Teddy.

"My old man," Evenwrite was shouting, "always said that if the workingman *wants* something in this world then the workingman has to *get* it. . . . *Ride?* Goddab ride . . ."

Draeger swallowed the rest of his drink, then sat, studying the facets of colored light in the shot glass while Evenwrite banged about the tables, cursing and taunting the men, red-faced with diluted liquor and imagined power.

"So whadya say? Who says we get with it? Huh? Huh?" Most of them said yeah, get with it, but none of them moved. "Whadya say! Whadya say! Ride on out there and we'll—" He blinked, concentrating fiercely, damn it all, he *had* for a shake there had his finger on it. "And we will just the whole bunch of us we'll—"

"Swim across the river like a pack of beavers?" The heads turned from Evenwrite to Draeger. "Stand on the bank and throw rocks? Floyd, you sound like you caught a cold somewhere."

Evenwrite refused to turn to the voice. He wanted to ignore it now, just as he had been expecting it all evening. He snatched up his empty glass and glared at it as though the calm, deep words were issuing from its crystal mouth.

"Use your head, Floyd," Draeger continued. "You can't stir up these people into running out to that house like a bunch of fools out of a cowboy movie, even if we could find a legal way, because in the first place—"

"Legal again!" Evenwrite shouted at the glass. "What the shit's legal got to do?"

"—because," Draeger went on, "in the first place we couldn't get across the river as a group. Unless you think Mr. Stamper would ferry us across two or three at a time. Now, I don't really know the man"— he smiled about at the room—"but from all I've heard I don't think I'd care to go across as an emissary and request that he bring enough of us across to make up a mob. Of course, Floyd may be so inclined. I hear he's more skilled at this sort of thing than I am."

The men laughed uncertainly, puzzled by the calm tact of this man. They waited, watching him at his solitary table toying with his glass. But when he didn't go on, the crowd turned its attention back to Evenwrite, who still stood clutching his empty glass. Evenwrite felt the attention burn at his back: balls. He'd been going good before that bastard had showed up; real good. But some way Draeger had made him the fool again, though damned if he could see how. He tried to study the fact for a moment, then gave up and vented his frustration on Teddy by demanding a free glass on account of dammit for all the juice he'd throwed down in there tonight if it'd been *real* stuff he'd be drunk on his ear, now ain't that so? Without comment, Teddy refilled the glass. Evenwrite drank it with a gulp, not even closing his eyes, then smacked his lips thoughtfully. "Pigeon piss," he decided and spat in the direction of the spittoon. There was a little wave of laughter, still uncertain. The men looked back and forth from their president to their representative, waiting for the next move. Draeger seemed unaware of the silence that had risen up after his entrance; he peered through the little glass he twisted in his fingers, his eyes patient as his smile. Evenwrite leaned against the bar. He knew he was on the spot. Draeger had made it his move. He rubbed his neck and finally broke the quiet by throwing the glass at the brass pot wired to the corner of the bar and shouting "Pigeon piss" again. "That ain't whisky, that's pure hundred-fifty-proof pigeon piss." There was more laughter and he turned then toward Draeger, confident again. He was leaning slightly, eyes very bright. "Okay, Jonathan Bailey Draeger, since you're so fuckin' smart let's hear what you say we should do. You called this walkout the first place. Ain't that so? Since you're so smart, okay let's hear what you're gonna do to get us outa this mess. I'm jus' a dumb-ass sawyer! I mean, nobody pays us dumb-asses to think. Since you're so smart—"

Draeger brought the glass down on the cocktail napkin on the Formica table top; there was a muffled yet resonant click, sounding at once distant and very near, like a click heard under water. "If you'll just sit down and take it easy, Floyd—"

"Ho ho. Don't you Floyd old boy me, Jonathan Bailey Draeger. Legal? All right, if you want to be legal then, you know and I know what we gotta do. Maybe we beat our gums here the rest the night but we *know!* An' me hollering to go out there after Stamper was a dumb-ass thing, sure . . . *but not no more dumb-ass than you suckin' us into this strike none of us wanted!*"

"Floyd, to hear you tell it last August you boys were all starving to death."

"Last August you told us we'd settle without a walkout!"

"Are you scared to gut it out, Floyd? Scared you might miss a couple of paychecks?"

Draeger still spoke so softly that it was difficult to tell if the voice came from him or not. Evenwrite's voice grew louder to overpower the silence that Draeger had brought down on the room. "No, I ain't scared to miss a couple of paychecks! I done it before. All of us have. We've struck before and we've gutted it out. We've gutted it out since the days before the Wobs came to back us up. And we'll do it again, won't we, boys?" He looked about at the men, nodding. The men nodded with him, watching Draeger. "You're damn right. We ain't scared to gut it or miss a couple paychecks, but we ain't scared to back off when we're dead whipped, neither!"

"Floyd, if you'll—"

"And legally, if you want to be that way about it, we are *whipped!* Whipped comin' an' goin'." He stopped speaking to Draeger and turned toward the men again, wiping his nose. "I been wantin' to cash it a long time now. It was the wrong time of year to walk out; we all knew that—hell, middle of winter, not a whole lot in the strike fund—but Draeger figured if he could just swing this one he was on his way to him a big spot, make a goddam king or something of hisself. . . so he got us—"

"Floyd . . ."

"Draeger, if you're so fuckin' smart—"

"Floyd."

*Click.* Again that light, restrained touch of the glass against the table, as light as a hammer cocking. The heads swung back to Draeger. *I see now; now I understand. . . .* From behind his bar Teddy marveled at the man's power and timing. . . . *You know how to wait. As soon as you started speaking . . . watch these idiots draw in toward you without leaving their places, straining without motion toward your voice as metal particles strain in toward a magnet . . .*

"Floyd . . . doesn't the foreman from the Stamper mill, Orland Stamper, live right next door to you?"

*. . . Straining in to you without even moving; it doesn't make any difference what you say. Because you are one of the forces yourself, a force, and that's what matters. Not what you say. Like Walker the Healing Preacher is sometimes a force. But not that way either, because you know more than Brother Walker and his God put together . . .*

"And Sitkins, you and your brother, I heard you both have children in the same class as some of the Stamper children. It seems I recall hearing that. Those kids are just kids, aren't they, just like your kids?"

*. . . You know what it is—the cold force in the dark—that makes people move. And that you don't have to have all those drums and guitars and organ music to make the idiots dance. You know that Brother Walker's God is just a straw God, a make-do doll to wave in the face of the true All-Powerful. . . .*

"And the Stamper wives, aren't they just women? Worried just like any women about how their house looks for company? What the new hairdo is?—and, boy oh boy, have you men seen some of those styles?—just like any woman, the Stamper wives?"

*. . . A make-do deity doll, not even as powerful as the other make-do gods like What the Fool Next Door Thinks, and The Great Things to Be Done . . . none of them a fraction as powerful or terrible as the Force that created them, the Fear that created them.*

"Men . . . Floyd . . . there are one or two things to keep in mind: that it doesn't make any difference what their name is—they want the same things from life that you want, the same things you men fought for when we put this union together, the same things you want now . . . because it's *natural*."

*. . . . Natural for animals to bunch together for protection. You don't need drums and guitars. No. All you need is just to have people around with the natural fear, like all a magnet needs to be a force is just the pieces of iron to pull against.*

"I take my stand behind the human heart, not alongside violence . . ."

*. . . Not be right or wrong or good or bad, just be pulling. In a minute the idiots won't even be listening, they'll just be pulling. They don't have to think. Just be afraid naturally and pulling together. Like specks of mercury rolling into the big piece. Like little specks of mercury rolling into bigger specks and then bigger and then just one piece, and nothing to be scared about or hurt about because you're just a piece of a bigger piece getting bigger rolling across the land into an ocean of mercury . . .*

"So here is what I've been doing the last four days, over in Eugene—toward the benefit of all, with no violence, no bloodshed . . . I've been appropriating funds from the union treasury . . ."

*. . . And you know all this, Mr. Draeger. It is the thing that makes you special. And you have the courage to use it. I can only stand awed by the true All-Powerful; you can use it. You are beautiful . . .*

"What are you driving at, Draeger?" Evenwrite asked, feeling suddenly tired again.

"Not quite all we need, perhaps," Draeger continued as though he hadn't heard Evenwrite, "but I am sure some local businessman with a little capital and a shrewd investment eye can raise the rest of the money. . . ."

"Muddy for what, Draeger?"

Draeger smiled sadly at Floyd. "You've got a dilly of one, haven't you, Floyd? Too bad; especially since we have to take us another little joyride up the river and have another talk with Mr. Stamper."

"Now just a goddam *minute!* I know this man, he's less likely now than he was a week ago to change his—" Evenwrite squinted at Draeger. "Money for *what?* I asked."

"We are going to buy the Stamper Enterprises, Floyd, lock, stock and barrel, kit and kaboo—"

"He won't sell," Evenwrite said, a little desperately. "Hank Stamper? Never . . ."

"I think he will. I talked to him on the phone. I quoted some figures that he would be a fool to pass up—"

"He said *yes?* Hank *Stamper?*"

"Not absolutely, no, but I don't see what would stop him. He'll never get a better offer." Draeger turned back to the others, shrugging. "The price will be a little stiff, men, but he had us by the short hairs, as Floyd puts it. It will still work out to our advantage: the business will be owned locally, in conjunction with the union; the investors will share in the profits; the Wakonda Pacific will be over a barrel. . . ."

Teddy listened through his thoughts to the muffled, distant voice and fell in love from behind his barricade of rainbows.

Evenwrite leaned against the bar, stunned completely sober. He didn't listen to the rest of the excited questions, or Draeger's optimistic plans. For a while, the prospect of another river trip almost jolted him out of his stupor, but when he raised his head to protest he saw all the other men so enthusiastic that he couldn't bring himself to speak. And when Draeger left in the direction of Mama Olson's he put on his coat and docilely followed along.

On the street outside he shook his head and repeated, "Hank Stamper . . . just won't sell."

"What difference?" Draeger said happily. "We aren't even going to make an offer."

"Then where we going?"

"Just for a walk, Floyd. A stroll. I just thought folks would be more inclined to *believe* we made that offer if we strolled down toward the docks. . . ."

"Believe? What are you talking about? Hank Stamper'll never believe we went up to his place just because we—"

"But he'll be the *only one* who won't believe it, Floyd." He chuckled, confident. "By the way, do you play cribbage? Fine game for two. Come on; I have a board up in my hotel room. . . . There should be just about enough time to teach you while we supposedly have another 'joyride.' "

And back in the bar Teddy, standing in his spot by the window, is the only one to see them double back from the docks and duck into the side door of the hotel. *You are a force, a force.* He nods slowly when the light switches on in one of the hotel's upstairs rooms. Why, it's almost like Mr. Draeger *wanted* him to see the ruse; *You know I always stand by this window . . .* it's a real confidence! *"We," you said to me . . . "we"*—and feels his plump little body stretch nearly to bursting as his initial admiration and awe swells to love and beyond —to adulation, to worship.

*W*hen my father mustered out of the Navy in 1945 we moved from a fair-sized town near Mare Island, where he had been stationed, to the "Old Jarnaggan Place" in the Willamette Valley—a two-story farmhouse thirty miles from Eugene, where Daddy had a job, fifteen miles from Coburg, where I would attend the third grade, and a good million light-years from the highway, where the nearest other human being could be found. Electricity had penetrated as far as the kitchen and living room, but to illuminate any of the rest of the house one needed to go through the entire Coleman lantern bit, replete with ash mantles, a nickel-plated handpump, and white gasoline which was considered too dangerous for a third-grader who should be old enough by now to sleep in the dark, for goodness' sakes! And my second-floor bedroom was indeed dark. Damned dark. A back-country night in a one-window room during a tar-bucket rain, in the sort of dark where nothing at all happens when you open and close your eyes. There is simply no light. But, like water, this thick dark affords tremendous conductivity to sounds of unknown sources. And after I had lain three or four bulge-eyed hours of my first night in my new bed, I began to perceive one of these very sounds: something hard, heavy, and horrible, rumbling and thudding insanely from one side of the hall to the other, coming steadily closer. My head lifted from the pillow. I stared in the direction of my door, filling the void with demented monster crabs and drunken robots as the noise came relentlessly on through my door, into my room. . . . (I recall thinking when I discovered Edgar Allan Poe's world some years after: Yes; this is sure the way it sometimes is!) I lay with my head lifted. I didn't call out; I felt totally bereft of voice, the way you feel when you try calling out of the confines of a dream. And as I waited an odd, recurring light at my window began to illuminate the room—a brief, quick glow, separated by long intervals of identically timed darkness. The rain had stopped and the clouds lifted, allowing the sweeping beam

*of a beacon from a cropduster's airfield to swing across my
upstairs window (I traced down this mystery light weeks
later); from the stroboscope impressions given me by this
periodic flash I was able to solve my mystery: a small rat had
scored a large walnut from the storeroom down the hall and
was trying to corral it against something solid so he could
gnaw through its stubborn shell. The nut kept skittering
away from the rat's teeth, and the rat kept chasing after it
and rolling it back against the wooden wall, which amplified
his gnawing like a sounding board. Teamed thus, the two
of them had worked their way from the storeroom, along
the baseboard, all the way to my open door. Just a mouse,
that light showed me, just a little old field rat. I breathed
and let my head fall back to the pillow: just a mouse
chewing a nut. That's all. That's all it—But what's this
light that keeps flashing past like a ghost or something
flying round and around the house looking for a place to
get in? . . . What is this awful light?*

The same November rain that drove the mice from their holes and
beat the eelgrass flat also stirred up the mightiest flock of migrating
geese the coast had seen in centuries. At night, above the lullabying
roll of the wind and rain, the ring of their voices could be heard, the
free, bright, yodeling toll of Canada honkers. They were stirred south
all the way from Dawson Creek by the storm, feeding in the oat-
stubble by day and flying southward by night; and the great honking
set up by this nightly flight came pealing like mountain bells down
from the peaks of the wind, through the clouds, and into the little
muddy towns that line the coastal flyways.

When most of the citizens of these little towns woke to hear
them tolling past their rooftops, they only heard "Winter is here,
winter is here," like a taunting, malevolent chant, over and over;
"Winter is here, winter is here . . ."

Willard Eggleston, the bald and bespectacled brother-in-law of the
Real Estate Hotwire in Wakonda, listens more carefully one quiet
night through the chipped round hole that opens from his ticket
window onto a street wet and shiny with the light of the theater
marquee, and remarks to himself and the empty street: "The geese
have their special secrets too, I bet. They are singing out all the
secrets of the dark, and no one to listen but me."

And when Lee happens to hear a small flock flying over the parked carrier wagon where he sits, at the stumpy edge of the logged-off show, waiting for Hank and Joe Ben and Andy to finish burning the slashing, the sound prompts him to remark in a letter he is writing to Peters in an old ledger he discovered under the seat:

> We are kept on the move by continual reminders of the lateness of the hour, Peters: nature signals to us in her numerous ways that we'd best get our ass in gear while we can, because the summer is never going to last, my darlings, never. Just now a flock of geese passing over calls out to me "Go south! Follow the sun! If you wait too long it will be too late." And I get all manicky just hearing them. . . .

But Hank hears the geese call a dozen different thoughts, stimulating a dozen dozen feelings—envy and resentment, worship and bitterness—making him long to join in their reeling southward song, cut loose, leave! A variety of thoughts and feelings, flowing and blending and breaking apart in sudden octaves, like the sound that set them off . . .

The towns listened to the geese tell them, "Winter is here," that first week, and despised the geese for rubbing it in. All the little coast towns listened, and all despised the geese in those first dingy November days. Because the irrevocable fact of winter is never a particularly rosy picture (But this winter, here in Wakonda, it's gonna be worse even than the last), and these first nights of November are always tough because they are a preview of a hundred such nights to come (Yeah, but, this time it's special tough, because we got no job, no income, no roll socked away for the rainy days this time . . . here in Wakonda) . . . does anyone ever like harbingers of such tidings?

And winter was certainly there. All along the coast that first week of November, while the geese swept noisily down from the north, a flock of darker clouds swept viciously in from the sea's western horizon. The clouds combed overhead and broke against the mountains like waves breaking, and the water ran back toward the sea . . . clouds like waves breaking, or like clawed hands thrust grasping up from depths to furrow the earth with gray-nailed fingers. Like the hands of something trapped and determined to claw its way up on land, or pull the land down beneath the sea. The hands reached up and out, to Breakleg and Breakrib, to Mary's Peak and Tillamook and

Nahamish, to west-facing slopes along all the coast, and the blind fingers scratched bleeding gullies in the slopes. These gullies bled into bigger gullies, bigger gullies into freshets dry all summer, freshets into ditches choked full of Canada thistle and buffalo weed, and these ran into Elk Creek and Lorain Creek and Wildman Creek and Tyee Creek and Tenmile Creek; sharp, steep noisy creeks, looking like saw-teeth on the map. And these creeks crashed into the Nehalem and the Siletz and the Alsea and the Smith and the Longtom and the Siuslaw and the Umpqua and the Wakonda Auga, and these rivers ran to the sea, brown and flat with the clots of swirling yellow foam clinging to their surfaces, running to the sea like lathered animals.

"Winter is here," the geese proclaimed, flying from river to river over the little towns, "winter is here." A winter just like last year (But last year we was able to blame them Reds and their bomb tests, screwing up the weather), and just like the winter before that (But *that* winter, think back now, there was all them *hurricanes* down in Florida that blew us up more than our share of rain), and just like the winters a thousand years before these little coast towns ever existed. (But those years were just winters, those towns just towns . . . *this* year, I tell you, in Wakonda, things *is* truly different!)

In the bars and bowling alleys the men of these little towns packed snuff under stained lips and cleaned their ears with matchsticks, gave each other stiff, knowing nods as they watched the rain hopping in the street, and listened to the geese. "Lots of rain. Listen at them boogers shag it up there—*they* know it's a lot. It's all them frigging *satellites* the government keeps shooting up in the air, is what's causing it. Just like you shoot a cannon inta the clouds to get rain. That's who done it. Those numskulls in the *Pentagon* made a *slip-up!*"

The geese might claim that it was winter just like the year before, just like a thousand years before, but these little towns found it helped to survive an unpleasant inevitability if you regarded it as a slip-up and found something to blame it on. It eased the outlook a little if you had some scapegoat to point a finger at: the Reds, the satellites, the hurricanes down south. . . .

The logger men in these little towns could blame the construction men: "Loosenin' the dirt with all them damn roads you're buildin'!" The construction men could blame the logger men: "You, you ax-happy nuts, takin' out all the brush off the watershed, layin' the mountainsides naked . . . what can you expect?"

The younger people found ways to blame the older generation, who had borned them into this mess; the older people blamed the churches. The churches, not to be outdone, put it all at the feet of the Lord: "Oh yay-us, *now!* Haven't I been saying so? Havn't I *now!* again and again, warned you to stand up in His light *now* and live by His laws *now* and not chance His *awful wrath?* Yay-us *now!* Now *look*: the Arm of the Lord is on its way; the *floodwaters* chastiseth!"

Which is just another way of blaming, and perhaps the best way, because there is solace and a certain stoical peace in blaming everything on the rain, and then blaming something as uncontrollable as the rain on something as indifferent as the Arm of the Lord.

Because nothing can be done about the rain except blaming. And if nothing can be done about it, why get yourself in a sweat about it? Matter of fact, it can be convenient to have around. Got troubles with the old lady? It's the rain. Got worries and frets about the way the old bus is falling to pieces right under you? It's the ruttin' rain. Got a deep, hollow ache bleeding cold down inside the secret heart of you from too many deals fallen through? too many nights in bed with the little woman without being able to get it up? too much bitter and not enough sweet? Yeah? That there, brother, is just as well blamed on the rain; falls on the just and unjust alike, falls all day long all winter long every winter every year, and you might just as well give up and admit that's the way it's gonna be, and go take a little snooze. Or you'll be mouthin' the barrel of your twelve-gauge the way Evert Petersen at Mapleton did last year, or samplin' snail-killer the way both the Meirwold boys did over to Sweet Home. Roll with the blow, that's the easy out, blame it on the rain and bend with the wind, and lean back and catch yourself forty winks—you can sleep real sound when the rain is lullabying you (But I tell you things is *different* this year in Wakonda) real nice and sound . . . (because geese ain't *letting* us sleep, and the Lord ain't *taking* the blame, not this year, in Wakonda . . .)

Because that year, in Wakonda, the citizens truly weren't being allowed the easy out. They weren't being allowed to lean back as the days passed and nights slid by. They weren't being allowed to make themselves comfortable by blaming it on the rain, or on the Lord, or the Reds, or the satellites.

Not when it was so goddam evident, so right-before-your-eyes obvious, that in Wakonda, that year, the town's worries and woes were being caused by nobody else but that goddam hardnose up the river!

And rain is one thing and, fine, maybe you can't do nothing about the weather except yak about it, but Hank Stamper is a *different* breed of cat from the rain! And you can maybe put the blame on the Arm of the Lord those years when that arm puts a stranglehold of frost on the woods so tight it freezes all the way to your pay envelope, and maybe you can roll with the blow of the wind if there's nothing else except the wind blowing . . . but when the arm is the arm of Hank Stamper strangling off your income, and you damn well know that the blow is being dealt by the *fist* on that arm, then you find yourself having a pretty hard time blaming your woes on anything *other than* that arm!

And a harder time than that leaning back and catching forty winks when there's geese going by in a steady stream telling you, "Winter is here and you better get the lead out and *do* something about that particular arm . . . !"

Willard Eggleston plans to do something, all right, but he isn't saying what. He finally closes the ticket window and switches off the marquee, tells the projectionist to cap it up and climbs the balcony stairs to let the solitary young couple know the picture has ended. In the lobby he pulls on his overcoat and rubbers and opens his umbrella and walks out into the rain. The geese remind him again of the secret that he isn't telling, and he stops for a minute to look wistfully through the window next to the theater into his laundry and wish his old confidante was still there (even though he *wouldn't* have been able to tell her this) like she used to be. Oh, those were the days of secrets, those good years before the coin-operated Laundromats had come to change his life and before his wife and brother-in-law had pushed him into buying that movie-show house for what they called "real prudent real-estate reasons, Willard; it's right next door and you wouldn't want a Laundromat concern picking it up, now, would you?"

He laughed to remember that. Now that you mention it, he thought, tracing his fingers along the familiar glass door of his old laundry, I don't think I would have cared. Even if it had been likely. He knew that wasn't their real reason for pushing him into the sale. He had known better at the time: his wife's brother had simply been interested in moving a worthless property, and his wife had just wanted to move Willard. After ten years she had finally grown suspicious of the extra time he spent at night in the laundry with Jill Shelly—"that little bar of dark soap you call your 'assistant.' What is it she *assists* with, I'd like to know, that takes until all hours of the night?"

"Jelly and me just sort clothes and talk—"

"Jelly? Jelly? Blackstrap Molasses would be more appropriate. Or Tar . . . why don't you call her Tarbelly?"

Funny, Willard thought, because it had been his wife who had first called the young girl "Jelly"—more a sarcastic comment on the child's fleshless frame, he was certain, than a mispronunciation of her name. He had never called her anything but Miss Shelly before, just as it had never occurred to him to chat with the girl during their late working hours until his wife accused him of it. Now he wished he'd been accused much earlier, and of much more; look at all those years wasted when she was nothing more than a skinny black girl, all knees and elbows and teeth . . . why hadn't he noticed her value until his wife called his attention to it?

"I'm tired of it, do you understand me? You think I don't know what goes on back there in all those dirty clothes?"

Perhaps it was because his wife insisted so much on acting the part of the overbearing spouse that he had found it easiest to play the dominated husband and wait for her to call the shots. He didn't know. But before his wife had been so kind as to suggest it, he and the girl had had nothing at all going in the dirty clothes except dirty clothes and silly little secrets.

Although that had been quite a bit, he realized, now that it was gone for good; that was the part he liked best to remember, the dirty clothes and the silly secrets. It had started that way, showing each other little treasures of information they discovered in the town's dirty laundry, then working together to interpret their findings. Gradually they got to be able to read a soiled slip as though it were a syndicated gossip column. "Look here what *I* found, Will. . . ." She would come to him, proudly bearing a coupon for a prescription for an oral contraceptive found in the pocket of Pucker Pringle's coat. "Now who in the blue-eyed world would of *thought?* And such a good Catholic besides."

He might counter with a spot of lipstick found on Howie Evans' undershirt, and she would come back with the cuff of Floyd Even-write's new trousers, caked with the dawn-blue mud like a fellow might step in out in them old mudflats around Indian Jenny's shack . . .

Oh, those may not have been the best nights, he conceded, but they were the nights he liked best to recall. Strange as it now seemed to him, looking through the window of a business he owned but no longer ran, at piles of laundry that had been coldly sorted by some unappreciative and heartless hand, the memory of those long-ago nights giggling over the town's telltale stains still held more warmth than the memory of nights much more recent and far warmer. Those early nights had been his. No one had suggested they study those stains. For nearly five years he and the girl folded sheets and sewed buttons, matched pennies to see who would go across to the Sea Breeze for Cokes, and satisfied themselves with such intimacies as those which could be read aloud to one another from other people's letters found in other people's pockets.

And never shared a single secret of their own until his wife practically insisted on it.

Then, for a few marvelous, frantic months, they had shared two secrets: the first on top of the pile of unfolded sheets that came nightly from the drier, fragrant and fluffy and white, like a great bed of warm snow . . . and the second beneath the dark blanket of the girl's skin, warmer even that the pile of sheets, and growing.

"And when you get this movie house, Willard, I think it would be a very wise plan to get you a new assistant, too; employing the only darky in town hasn't been the *best* way to get new customers, by any means; also, I would imagine she might like to be with her own, for a while. Why don't you see if she wouldn't be interested in going back to wherever it is—she must have a family—that she came from?"

Again, it seemed, his wife had come up with just the right suggestion at just the right time. Jelly laughingly agreed that it was considerate of her, all in all, and that it might be wise indeed to spend a few months up in Portland visiting with the folks, "long enough leastways that when I come back I can tell everybody about this *wild* marriage I had with this sailor who drowned at sea, me just bringing the poor lad's child into the world. Sure; everything'll work out hunky-dory. I think your wife *always* has some wise ideas."

Everything did work out hunky-dory. Not a suspicion in town was aroused, not an eyebrow lifted: "About Willard Eggleston? An' that chocolate drop worked for him? *Never*, in a hundred years . . ."

And, while she didn't even know where Jelly had gone, once more it was his wife's idea that he take trips to Portland every month or two to screen the pictures he wanted for the theater. Hunky-dory as you could ever wish for. Never even a slip to make the bank-messenger curious, as though the whole conspiracy had been planned for him, and worked out to the last detail.

Jelly was even considerate enough to schedule the birth of the drowned sailor boy's child to coincide with one of his screening trips to Portland: Willard arrived at the Burnside Infirmary and asked about the Shelly girl just in time to have a colored intern tell him she was fine and point to a glass case being wheeled from the delivery room. He leaned to look through the glass at a child so wild-looking and fierce, so absolutely individual with his conglomeration of characteristics, that it was all Willard could do to keep from spoiling everything by announcing, "That's my boy!"

Now, hardly a year after the birth, he was able to find only the feeblest residue of that moment of terrible pride. He found it hard to bring his mind around to admitting that the thing had ever happened, that these two most important people in his life even existed. Especially since the strike; at first he had seen them almost weekly, when he was still doing well enough to send three hundred a month without its being missed. Then another Laundromat opened, and the best he could do was two-fifty, then two hundred. And since this strike he had been forced to borrow on theater and laundry both to be able to send them a hundred and fifty. He couldn't face a son so fierce, so wild-looking, when a hundred and fifty dollars a month was the best he could do as a father.

And today he had received a letter from Jelly telling him that she knew how hard it must be, with the conditions and all, for him to keep slipping her money . . . so she was thinking of marrying. "A Merchant Marine, Will, most the time at sea and he don't have to know one single thing about anything me and you do while he is gone. Then we won't keep on being a burden and a drain on you, you see?"

He saw. Things were still working out hunky-dory for his protection. His world had been kept under his hat so long that pretty soon no one would even need to worry about somebody's finding out; there wouldn't be anything under there to find out. If he didn't take steps it would all never have been, like the sound a tree doesn't make when it falls in the forest and no one is there to hear it.

Willard stepped back from the laundry window to leave and was stopped by his dim reflection in the glass: hardly there at all, a ridiculous little character with a receding chin and eyes swimming nearsightedly behind glasses out of style years ago, a cartoonist's wash-drawing of the capital-H henpecked husband, a satirist's two-dimensional straw man designed to convey at first glance a two-dimensional personality that everyone knows everything about before it even opens its straw man's mouth. Willard wasn't shocked by the image; he had been aware of it for years. When he was younger he had scoffed to himself at all those people who treated him as though he really were this image he projected—"What do I care for what they see? They think they know the book by its cover, but the book knows what it is." Now he knew better; if the book never opens up and comes out, it can be warped to fit the image others see. He remembered Jelly telling of her father . . . a shy and gentle man until a car's windshield branded him from chin to ear with a scar that raised the hackles of any strange Negro in a bar and provoked policemen to frisk him every chance they got: once a gentle man, he was now serving twenty to life for killing an old friend with a razor. No, a book wasn't invulnerable to the appearance of its cover, not by any means.

He took a parting look at the reflection—not a figure adapted to having a burden or a drain put on it, that was certain—then moved on off toward the streetlight on the corner. This funny-paper image is so complete and so consistent, he thought, it's a wonder the rain doesn't just wash me away down the gutter like a old paper doll. It is, for a fact, a real wonder . . . that I haven't been washed down a long time ago.

Yet, when he turned the corner and walked away from the light, his shadow stretched before him, black and solid. So he wasn't quite disengaged from his world. There was still something. His two-dimensional perfection was still marred, he knew, by the memory of a skinny colored girl and an ugly and outraged baby: they were the blood and heart and bones that kept him from collapsing flat. But that blood had grown thin and the bones transparent, and the heart small and riddled with holes the way a plant grows, kept untended too long from the light.

And now she had written that she was planning to marry her sailor boy, just as she said in their whispered fantasy, so she and the child would need less of his tending than ever. He had written back begging her to wait: There was something he could do; he'd be thinking about it for some time, couldn't tell her, but take his word, please, just for a few days, wait!

As his shadow stretched on to nowhere down the wet sidewalk, he became aware of the geese again. He lowered the umbrella to hear them better, lifting his face to the rain: You birds . . . you aren't the only ones with secrets to tell.

Though it did seem a terrible shame that he couldn't find some soul to share this final secret with. Just one person who would never tell. A real shame, he thought, lifting his umbrella again and continuing on with his face wet with rain, envying the geese their invisible confidants in the winnowing dark overhead.

Whereas Lee, being long on confidants and short on courage, envies them their outspoken, and terse, honesty.

"Fly now! Delay later!" they tell me, Peters, which leaves me feeling that if I hang around here too much longer I will begin to take root right through the hobbed soles of my boots. "Fly! Fly!" they cry, and I raise my feet up from the muddy floor of this vehicle just to play it safe. . . . What is there about our generation, man, that makes us sweat this root scene so much? Look at us: we wander across America in dedicated droves, equipped with sideburns and sandals and a steel-stringed guitar, relentlessly tracking our lost rootbeds . . . yet all the while guarding against that most ignoble of ends: becoming rootbound. What, pray, is it we hope to do with the object of our search if we succeed? If we have no intention of attaching ourselves to these roots, what use do you suppose we have in mind? Boil us up a tea and use them, like sassafras, as a purgative? Stash them away in the cedar chest with our high-school diploma and prom programs? It's always been a mystery to me . . .

Another straggling flock came over, sounding quite close. I looked up from my ledger and out the peephole I had rubbed in the fogged windshield; the sky was filled with the same twilight of rain and smoke that had been hanging over the carrier like impatient six o'clock kept waiting ever since noon. The geese must have passed within yards of me, but not so much as a gray ripple broke that twilight's surface. There was a feeling of curious doubt building in my mind about these phantom birds, like that sensation one gets hearing a canned audience on TV: in days and days of hearing thousands and thousands of them pass overhead, I had actually seen only one.

The honking faded off where Hank and Joe and Andy were working. I saw Hank stop work, listen, start off toward the donkey after his shotgun, change his mind, stop, and stand ready for their appearance, barehanded and cruel-looking in his hood and smoke-blacked face: Watch; he's going to spring into the air and snag one on the fly the way that ape in the New York zoo used to catch pigeons . . . rip them to feathery shreds before he hits the ground!

But he relaxed and straightened back up; he hadn't seen them, either. He might have mighty leaping powers, but his eyes couldn't penetrate that Oregon twilight any better than mine.

I looked back down at my obscure pencilings in the ledger; I had been beating around the bush for a half-dozen pages of discursive philosophy and foolishness, trying to explain to Peters why I had tarried in Oregon so much longer than I had predicted. For days I had been afflicted with a malady of hesitation, and I was having the devil's own time explaining it to Peters, not having got around to understanding it myself. The germs responsible for this current attack of procrastination were a good deal more difficult to isolate than those that had finally been wiped out during that argument following the fox hunt. That earlier attack had been much easier to diagnose; even before the fox hunt I halfway understood why I'd slowed to a sodden stop: at *that* time I had been so uncertain of myself, my scene, and my whole scheme in general that slowing to a stop meant mainly that I didn't know where the hell I was headed in the first place. Not so, this time, not so at all . . .

Unlike my previous paralysis, this time I knew exactly where I was going, precisely how I would get there, and, most important, *this* time I had a clear idea what the realization of my objectives would accomplish.

Like all schemers, I relished the fantasy more than the finished work, and for this reason I had labored overlong, savoring my own craftsmanship (I knew I had; I don't believe we can afford to pass over the grade-school kicks our daydreams offer), but the scheme had long since been finished and put into action; in fact, the campaign itself was nearly completed. Everything was ready. All precautions taken, all arrangements made. All the plastic bombs placed and awaiting my hand on the plunger. Had been waiting now for a number of days. Yet, I hesitated. Why, I demanded rhetorically, why wait at all . . . ?

Lee is piqued and prodded by the sound of the geese, but Hank listens with a different ear. All his life he has been affected by the sound of game birds, hunting and watching and associating their calls with other events until he could peg the feeling to come before the bird made a sound, but of all upland birds and all the waterfowl, and all their numerous sounds of migrating, nothing even came near to giving him a feeling approaching the soaring, pure, lonely sensation from hearing a Canada honker . . .

Widgeons, for instance, when they came in low, beneath the dawn—in scrambling clusters of six or seven—their melancholy whistlings could make a man feel a little sorry for them poor, foolish ducks who get so rattled by shotgun fire they fly in a circle around and around over your blind, watching their number reduced at each pass . . . but that was about the size of it: a little sorry. Mallards you could feel more for. A mallard is sharper than a widgeon. And prettier. And when they come in at dusk, cautious, clucking and quacking, yelling down at your spread of decoys for the come-on-in signal, orange feet reaching out to catch the shock of the water, heads flashing the last bit of daylight, not purple, not green, not quite the acetylene blue of a cutting torch, a color almost a sound it's so bright: ringing of bits of tinted glass against each other in the wind . . . When a mallard comes in you can feel for him that kick you get watching fireworks web the sky with color. Seeing something pretty. The way you feel watching a chinee rooster explode out of the maize in the afternoon, and kind of the way you feel when you bring down a wood-duck, which is actually a far prettier bird than a mallard but it's not a prettiness you see in the air because a wood-duck's always glimpsed dodging and whizzing through the trees; you don't generally even know he's a wood-duck until you pick him up out of the water. Then he's pretty, all scarlet and purple and white, like a clown with feathers, but then he's dead, too.

Cinnamon teal can make you feel foxy if you hit one, foolish if you don't, because they're little and tricky and have a nasty habit of coming right past you about two feet off the ground at about two hundred miles an hour through the air. Coots can make you ashamed of yourself for creaming a dozen of them on the water after you get tired of them farting around your blind; the brant goose can give you a kind of laugh, him such a big bird with such a hoarse little squeak; and, boy oh boy, the cry of a *loon* when you're out at night with the dogs and you hear that bastard calling across the dark slough—a sound like something lost and lonesome and stark gone crazy in a stark old world where it always knew it didn't belong—that sound can give you the willies so bad you don't know if you care to go outside in that stark old world ever again.

But there's nothing, there's none of the birds and all their whistles and squeaks and quacks, that can get to a guy like hearing a Canada honker go past the rooftop on a stormy night. For one thing, you can't help feeling a little sorry for the poor devil, out there trying to fight his way through that muck. For another, you can't help feeling a little sorry for your own self because you know when the weather gets bad enough to run off a bird as big as a Canada goose that winter has set in sure enough . . .

But mainly—I mean aside from the pure pleasure—I think you feel just a teeny bit *cheated* when you hear a honker. Because for all that you got going for you as a human—a warm bed, a dry place to stay, plenty to eat, plenty things to entertain you . . . for *all* that, you still aren't able to fly; I don't mean like inside an airplane, but just you yourself, make a run out into the air, and spread out your wings, and *fly!*

Anyway, I was happy to hear them arrive. I heard the first of the migration come over the foundation when I was out hammering up some spare six-by-eights I'd brought home from the mill account of they was too knotty to sell . . . come flying over about forty, fifty feet off the water—low enough I was able to pick out a couple with that big eight-cell flashlight Joe Ben'd left with me—and I was so happy to hear them I hollered out and told them so.

Geese arriving always catches a man by surprise some way. Probably because they're gone so long and last such a short piece when they do show back up; a couple weeks is about all the passing ever takes, a dang short time compared to how long it takes a lot of other things to pass, short enough I would of never in a hundred years imagined I could get tired of hearing their honking. It just wouldn't of seemed possible. It'd be like imagining getting tired of the rhododendron flowers in the dozen days they bloom every year, or like getting tired of that one magic day of silver thaw we have every dozen years that turns the dirty old world all the way from rusty tow-chains and the needles on the long-leaf pine to a bright, tinkling crystal. . . . Now how could a man get drug with *that kind* of short-term treat?

That first flock passed on up the river and I decided it was time for me to move on too. The only reason I'd stayed out on the embankment as long as I had was to cool off a little after Evenwrite and this Draeger'd put my nose out of joint coming out and *asking* me sweet as you please if I wouldn't consider breaking my contract with WP, so's not to be a mean old man to the union . . . right out and asking, then Evenwrite for chrissakes acting like he was *disappointed* I didn't say yes! It made me see red for a minute there. I was even scared for a minute that Floyd and me was on our way to locking horns right on that catwalk, and I tell you: to be honest about it I was in no particular mood nor condition for another hassle, not the day right after my fight in the Snag with Big Newton, anyway. . . .

I rounded up my paraphernalia and took it out to the toolhouse. Between there and the house I heard another couple smallish flocks. And after I was up in bed and the lights was out, I heard a fair sized bunch. The advance guard, I figured; first ones to be shooed down from Washington by the storm. The main of them from Canada won't be making it through till around Thursday or Friday at the soonest, was what I figured, and went off to sleep. But around one or two that night—Monday morning, actually—one by *Jesus* of a flock went over! In the *thousands*, it sounded like. And I decided then, well, maybe they was *all* shooed out at the same time. Too bad. That means they'll pass through all in a bunch this year, be all gone in a night or so . . . because that is at least half the geese in the *world* going over up there right now.

But I was wrong again; they went over at that rate, in that size flock or better, night after night after steady night, from that first Monday in November dang near to Thanksgiving. Gave me some bad nights. Like that first week when Evenwrite decided to declare whole-hog war on us with pickets and midnight sabotagings and what-all, and I needed whatever few hours of rest I could grab in the sack, and I'd be laying there, about to drop off when a flock'd come by so loud and so low they'd lift me right up off the bed.

Yet and all, after a week of them hollering, I was still a little sorry when Joby finally got woke up enough to their presence (Joby could sleep through the presence of a full-scale artillery attack, I swear if he couldn't!) to come down to breakfast all hot to kill us a honker for supper. "No lie, Hank; there was a *tremendous* big flock went over . . . just a *tremendous* big flock."

I told him I'd been laying in bed all week trying to go to sleep with big flocks going over just as tremendous.

"Well, then, there you go! Don't you reckon you laid awake listening to enough of 'em to earn the eating of one?" He went to hopping around the kitchen in his sock feet, holding his hands at each side of his head. "Oh *yeah*, Hankus; I thought a long time about it, and today is the day: a wind like that wind last night, see now, is bound to scatter some of the flocks, what do you think? Yeah, boy, I bet there's dozens of poor old lonely geese out there this morning, flying up an' down. . . . Huh, what do you think?"

He turned to grin at me from across the kitchen, still shifting from foot to foot and holding his hands against the side of his head in that excited, little-kid way he had. (*Joe stands there looking . . .*) He knew how I felt about shooting geese; even if I'd never come out and said so, he knew I didn't care for seeing them killed. (*Joe stands there looking at me. Worried about something more than taking a shotgun to work. Something's funny.*) Not that I've ever had much patience with the kind of pantywaist who says, "Oh, how can you kill the cute little deer? How can you be such a brute and a coward?"

. . . I don't have much respect for this sort of do-good thinking because it's always seemed to me a whole lot more cowardly for a man to have nothing to do with the meat he eats except picking it up out of a supermarket meat section all sliced and boned and wrapped in cellophane, looking about as much like a pig or a cute little lamb as a potato does. . . . I mean, if you're going to eat another living creature, I figure you at least should know he was once living, and that somebody had to kill the poor devil and chop him up . . .

(*Viv comes in from upstairs. Joe looks quick at her, then back at me.*)

But people never think that way about hunting; it's always "brute and coward" the hunters are called, by some Eastern prick who thinks pheasants are found under glass, plucked and already full of stuffing. (*Something's funny . . .*)

"What do you think, Hank?" Joby asked again. I took a seat, kidding him by dragging it out. I told him that one thing I thought was that he looked like he was standing on the foul line about to take a free throw with his noggin, the way he was holding his head. He took his hands down. "I mean about taking along a *shotgun?*" he wailed.

"Sure, why not," I told him. "You ain't disturbed one single honker feather in twenty years of hunting, so I don't suppose I'll have to be doing any retrieving today." And he said, "You wait an' see . . . I got a feeling . . ."

Well, as it turned out, like it usually did with Joby's predictions, it wasn't his day after all: we didn't see goose one all that day. It wasn't my day either: that was the day Evenwrite spiked our logs and tore a six-hundred-dollar two-way carriage saw to pieces for me. Matter of fact it wasn't even Evenwrite's day: that breakdown gave the excuse I'd been waiting for, a good reason to move the mill crew to the woods. I didn't tell them then, though. I let them go on home the rest of that day, figuring to start them Monday. They weren't going to be red-hot for it.

So everybody came out sucking hind tit that day, except that honker Joby'd sworn to kill for supper; wherever he was, he got off easy. At the supper table that night Joe explained what had went haywire with his prediction. "The mist was too thick for good visibility. I hadn't allowed for the mist."

"Always my trouble ex-*actly*." The old man put in his two bits' worth. "I'd allow for the wind an' the drop, but sonofagun if I was ever able to allow for that *mist!*"

We razzed Joby about that a while. He said okay, just wait till tomorrow . . . "Tomorrow *mornin'*, if I read the signals correct, it's gonna be *colder!* Yeah . . . wind enough tonight to scatter the flock, cold enough in the morning to keep down the mist. . . . *Tomorrow* is the day I bag my honker!"

It was cold enough that next day, all right, cold enough to freeze your balls off, but it still wasn't Joby's day. That cold kept off the mist but it kept the geese huddled someplace to keep warm, too. There had been honking all night, but we didn't even *hear* a goose that day. It got colder. By night it was cold enough it even showed signs of clearing. When I told Viv to give the relatives a call and have them all drop out for Sunday dinner the next day, I told her she better mention to them all to put in some anti-freeze, the way the mercury was going down. I damn sure didn't want any of them not making it out to the meeting; they all had a pretty good idea what was coming, anyway, that I was planning to tell them we were moving everybody to woods work, "An' knowing how much a lot of them hate outdoor work," I told her, "I know better'n to give any of them the chance to miss the meeting by saying their radiator froze up. . . . I'd at least like to get enough cars parked at the landing over there to let that damned Evenwrite know what he's up against."

After lunch that Sunday me and Joby took the guns and hiked to the slough to see if any of the geese had lit in down there. I got a load of widgeons, but that was all we saw. We got back to the house about four, and when I rounded the barn and looked across at the landing I could barely believe my eyes: there was cars packed over there thicker than I'd seen in years and more coming. Most of the Stampers within fifty miles showed up, whether they were connected with the lumber end of the business or not. I was surprised to see so many turn out on such short notice, and a lot more surprised than that at what a friendly, easy-going mood they were all in. That's what really floored me! I knew they must have a notion of some kind what I was up to, but they all acted like maybe they was tired of mill work anyhow and looking forward to a little stretch out in the good old fresh air.

Even the weather took a turn toward an easy-going mood: the rain eased down a lot, even though the mercury had come up a good deal since morning. And the sun was showing through now and then the way it will sometimes at the start of the wet season, shooting all of a sudden between two clouds so the hills sparkle like they was sprinkled with sugar. By dark the rain had quit and I could occasionally make out a piece of the soggy moon. The wind laid down and bugs started showing up with the people. Nobody asked what the meeting was all about, so I didn't say anything. We all just hung around on the porch while people showed up, talking hounds and recalling great hunting nights of the past and whittling white strips from the kindling near the woodpile; the ones that didn't whittle stood at the screened wall watching the children spin each other around on the tire swing Joe'd made in the toolshed out of the rain. I went out and plugged in the big three-hundred-watt porch light, and the men standing on the bank near the incline cast shadows all the way across the river against that cut stone embankment above the railroad. Every time another car full of new arrivals swung onto the gravel across the way those shadows would kind of fold over it to see who it was just showed up.

"It's Jimmy! Ye gods if it ain't," the shadows would holler across. "Jimmy, oh Jimmy . . . that you?"

A voice would come floating back. "Somebody gonna come over here an' tote me across, or do I wade?"

Then one of us would get up and ramble down the planks to the boat and pick up the newcomer, bring him back to stand around the porch to talk hounds and whittle and guess at the next car that stopped.

"Who you think this time? Martin? Hey, Martin, that you?"

I just stood around enjoying it. The voices stretched like the shadows, becoming huge across the water as it got darker. It made me think of the way it used to be on Christmas and other get-togethers when us kids would sit in the porch windows and listen to the men laugh and lie and holler across the water. Back when the shadows were always big and the mood always seemed easy-going.

They kept coming. Everybody was all grins and greeting. Nobody asked what was up, and I didn't volunteer the information. I even held off starting the meeting, waiting to see if any stragglers were showing up, I told people, but really because I hated to get around to business and foul up the whole evening. But after a while it got me so curious I went upstairs to ask Viv what she might of said over the phone to get so many people out in such a good mood.

The kid was there, laying belly down on her couch, stripped to the waist; Viv was working at the big cloudy blue welt below his right shoulderblade where he'd got tagged a day or so before. (*The room is hot, full of the stink of wintergreen. It reminds me of a locker room.* . . . *"How's the back, bub?" I say.*

*"I don't know," he says. His cheek is on his arm with his face turned toward the wall. "Better, I guess. Until Viv began her ministerings and massagings I had given it up as a complete loss; now I think I might salvage the spine."*

*"Well," I tell him, "you keep on the bounce out there you won't be gettin' bopped by springbacks." He don't answer. I can't think of anything else to say for a minute. The room is tight and strange. "Tomorrow* . . . *anyway, bub, tomorrow we'll have a good number of extra men up there, so you can take it pretty easy. You can maybe do some driving till it quits paining," I say. I unbutton my jacket, wondering why is it always so hot in a room when he's in it? Maybe he's got thin blood* . . .)

I walked over and asked Viv, "Chicken, can you remember what you said when you called the kinfolks last night?" She looked up at me, lifting her eyebrows the way she would when something puzzled her, made her eyes look big enough to fall into. (*She's got on Levis and the green and yellow striped jersey pullover that someway puts me in mind of bam trees on a sunny fall morning. Her hands are red from the analgesic. Lee's back is red* . . .)

"Golly, hon," she said, thinking. "I can't remember exactly. Just what you asked me to say, I think: that they all should come out about suppertime because you had a few things to go over since this breakdown. And to check about the anti-freeze . . ."

"How many calls did you make?"

"Oh, four or five, I guess. Orland's wife . . . Netty . . . Lou . . . and asked them to make some calls. Why?"

415

"If you'd been downstairs in the last hour you'd know why; we got every shirttail cousin in the country down there. And all of them acting like it was their personal birthday party they were attending."

"Every one?" That got her. She raised up off her knees, wiping hair off her forehead with the back of her arm. "I didn't get groceries enough for more than fifteen or so . . . how many do you mean by every one?"

"A good forty or fifty, counting kids."

This really brought her to her tiptoes. "Fifty?" she said. "We've never had fifty people, even on Christmas!"

"I know, but we do now. And all of them happy as clams—that's what I can't explain . . ."

Then Lee said, "I can explain it."

"Explain which?" I asked him. "How come they're all here? Or how come they're all so happy?"

"Both." He was laid face to the wall on that day-bed affair of Viv's. (He scratches the wall with his fingernail.) "It's because," he said, without turning over, "they are all under the impression that you have sold the business—"

"Sold it?"

"That's right," he went on, "and as stockholders—"

"Stockholders?"

"Yeah, Hank. Didn't you tell me that you made each man that ever worked for you a stockholder? In order to—"

"But sold it? What a minute. What are you talking about sold it? Where did you hear about this?"

"Grissoms'. Last night."

(He never moves, laying there turned to the wall. I can't see his face. His voice sounds like it could come from any place in the room.) "What the hell are you talking about!" (I want to grab him and roll him toward me so bad my hands are shaking.)

"If I remember correctly," he said, "Floyd Evenwrite and this other cat—"

"Draeger?"

"Draeger, yes, came up in a boat to visit you last night with—"

"Nobody was out here last night! Wait—"

"—with an offer to purchase the whole business with union funds, and the help of some of the local businessmen—"

"Wait. Hell's bells, I see now . . . them bastards!"

"—and that you drove a hard bargain and got a good price."

"Them snake-bellied bastards! Yeah, I see now. This Draeger musta thought of this—Evenwrite ain't got the brains. . . ." I stormed around a while, pretty hacked off, then turned back to where Lee was still laid facing the wall. For some reason this hacked me off more than ever. (*He hasn't so much as twitched a muscle. Damn. Viv's got it so hot in here with the electric heater humming. And that smell of wintergreen. Damn. I want to throw ice water on him. I want him to yell, get excited, wake up, come to life. . . .*) "Why in the shit," I said to him, "didn't you let me know about this before *now?*"

"I guess," he said, "I presumed that if you *had* sold the business you would probably already know about it."

"But what if I hadn't?"

"You would be just as apt, it seems to me, to know that, too."

"Hell's *bells!*"

Viv reached out and touched my arm. "What's the trouble, honey?" she asked. The only thing I could say was "Hell's tinkling *bells!*" and stormed around the room some more. What could I tell her? (*Lee is turned to the wall, tracing the edge of his shadow with a matchstick. I don't know.*) What could I tell any of them? "What is it, honey?" Viv asked again. "Nothing," I said. "Nothing. . . . But just what does a man *think* of somebody who's supposed to be giving him a big red apple and puts him to work pruning the apple tree instead? Huh?" I walked to the door and opened it a little and listened, then I came back. (*I can hear them down there waiting. It's so hot in here, and that smell . . .*) "Huh? How would you feel toward somebody who'd pull such a dirty switch on you?" (*I just don't know. He just lies there. That electric heater purring.*) "No, Evenwrite don't have the sense for something like this. . . ." (*I just want to wake him up. It's so mothering hot . . .*) It's this Draeger. . . ." (*Or I want to lie down myself. I don't know.*)

Finally, after I'd fumed and fretted enough, I did what I'd known from the first I was going to do: I went out in the hall to the stairwell and hollered for Joe Ben to come up a minute.

"Whatsay?" I heard him holler from the back porch where the kids were.

"Never mind whatsay, just get up here!"

I met him out in the hall and we went into the office. He was eating the pumpkin seeds hollowed from the jack-o'-lantern, all big-eyed and curious about me calling him. He was wearing a necktie for the occasion, a big blue silk affair he'd had since high school with a hand-painted picture of a duck on it that he was real proud of; the tie was all twisted around and two buttons were off his white shirt from roughhousing outside with the kids. Just to look at him, standing there in that godawful tie and a pumpkin-seed hull stuck to his lip and his hand in his shirt front fingering his navel, it tickled me so that it took the edge off my mood. And anyhow, now that I had him up here, what was it I wanted from him? I don't exactly know what good I thought he could do with that bunch down there, but now that he was there I could see what good he could do me.

"You know," I said to him, "when we seen them cars, an' I told you that I was damned if I was able to understand such a turn-out?"

He nodded. "Yeah; an' I told you that it was the ee-on charge the atmosphere gets when it's cold, puts people in a better mood."

"Ion," I corrected him, and went on. "But I don't think that fully accounts for it." I walked over to the desk and got out the pint I keep in there for bookkeeping work. "No, not completely," I said.

"Yeah? What else?"

I took a little sip and offered him the bottle. "They're all out here because they think I sold the business," I told him. I told him what Lee'd said and how I figured Floyd Evenwrite and this other dude started the rumor. "So all those friendly folks of ours down there think they are in on the pie-slicing; *that's* why the whole afternoon's been smiles and shoulder-slapping, not from ions."

"But what for?" he asked, blinking his eyes. "I mean what for would Evenwrite—?"

"Evenwrite wouldn't," I said. "Evenwrite wouldn't have the sense. Evenwrite is more inclined toward planting spikes than planting rumors. No; it was this Draeger."

"Uh-*huh*," he said, punching his fist in his palm and nodding; then he went to blinking agan. "But I *still* don't see what they was hoping to get outa that . . . ?"

I took back the bottle, in as he wasn't using it. I had me another sip and screwed the lid back on. "Just more pressure," I said. "Like a squeeze play . . . a way to make me look more the villain than before, even to my own folks."

He scratched at his bellybutton some more, thinking about that. "All right. I can see that, yeah; I can see how it ain't gonna make some of the boys none too happy to be told they're gonna be moved to work the woods when they was thinking the work was all over . . . and how some of them might hardtime you a little. . . . But I just don't see for the *life* of me what good Evenwrite and Draeger thought it would do *them*."

I grinned at him while I put the bottle back in the drawer and slapped it shut. "Why, by gosh, I don't see neither, Joby," I said and wiped off my mouth. "Now that you mention it. No good at all. So let's get on downstairs and see how we stand up under a little hardtiming. Let's get on down there and show those dirteaters who's one of the Ten Toughest Hombres This Side of the Rockies."

He followed me out of the room, still shaking his head. Good old Joby. Why anybody, dirteaters or no, would have to be showed something so obvious was way beyond him. (*That heater is still humming when I go past the door. Viv is gone, down in the kitchen helping Jan. But Lee is still there. He sits there on that day-bed couch with that thermometer hanging out of his mouth, cleaning his glasses on one of her silk hankies, looking at me with that innocent look nearsighted people have with their glasses off. . . .*)

None of the folks did handsprings over the news, but Orland and his wife was the only ones that really hardtimed me. The rest just moped around smoking cigarettes while Orland claimed he was damned if he could see where I got off trying to dictate to the whole county, and his wife kept yapping That's right! That's right! like a hysterical lap dog.

"Of course you—out here in the sticks like a hermit—you don't have to worry about neighbors!" he kept telling me. "You don't have a teen-aged daughter who comes home crying because the kids in school won't vote her into the Y-teens."

"That's right!" his wife barked. "That's right! That's right!" She was one of these little-bitty women with bulgy, bright eyes and too big teeth pushing out of her lips, like she was about to jump right out of her hide at you.

"We also have a share in this business," Orland said and waved around at everybody. "We also own stock! Shares! But do we get a chance to vote like other shareholders? Hank, I don't know about the rest here, but I certainly don't recall casting any vote of any kind for this deal with Wakonda Pacific. Or for going up to the woods and working for such a deal!"

"That's right! That is right!"

"A share gets a vote; that's how it's supposed to be done. And my share votes we take this offer Evenwrite and these people are making!"

"I've yet to hear this offer Evenwrite and those people are making, Orland," I told him.

"Yeah? Maybe that's so and maybe not. But a considerable lot of the rest of us have heard it, and it sounds considerably better than anything you've offered."

"That's right!" his wife barked. "That's right!"

"Orland, it seems to me that you—and that considerable lot of the rest of you—that you would all be a little slow in wanting your jobs sold out from under you."

"We wouldn't lose our jobs. The union doesn't want to put men to work in our jobs, just back to their own. We'll keep our jobs, it's just they would own the operation."

"The union not wanting to put men in our jobs sure comes as a surprise to me—considering how they been on my ass for years to get me to hire somebody other than family—but I do have to hand it to them for working it out so complete, jobs guaranteed and all. Did Floyd tell you this? My, my; I wouldn't thought he concerned himself so over us. Was that who you heard it from? Floyd Evenwrite?"

"Never mind who I heard it from, I have faith in the particular party's word."

"You can afford to. It ain't likely they'd fire you and have to train another sawyer. . . . But some of us others might be a little easier to do without. Besides, you wouldn't want to sell the old Stamper operation down the river after so many years of faithful service to us, now would you?"

"So many years us serving the *business*, is what you mean. Ancient machinery, buildings . . . why, we're still working a high-lead show, for the love of Pete! We'd be *wise* to get out from under it while the getting's good—"

"That's right!"

"—and I cast my vote to *sell!*"

"Me too! Me too!"

Some of the others started to stir around, talking about voting, and I was just about to say something when the old man suddenly appeared. "How many sheers you got to vote with, Orland?"

He was standing in the kitchen door, eating a drumstick. I hadn't even seen him come back from town; somebody must have ferried him over while I was upstairs. He was wearing the shirt that he'd won off Rod the guitar player once in a game of dominoes, a black rayon job wove all through with strips of tinfoil thread so when he moved it shimmied against his hard little gut like a burlycue costume. I saw he'd cut off more of his arm cast to give his arm more freedom with a bottle, and that he was feeling his oats. He took another chomp out of the drumstick and asked, "How many sheers some of the rest you boogers got? Eh? Eh? A hunnerd between the whole lot of you? Two hunnerd? You got any better'n two hunnerd, I sure will be surprised. Yes sir, I will be surprised. Because I don't offhand recall—the old nigger's memory ain't what it was, I admit—but, see, there ain't but about twenty-five hunnerd sheers in all, and I'm blamed if I recall turin' loose any of my twenty-one hunnerd in the last year or so. . . . Hank, you sell any that hunnerd you useta have? No? Joe Ben, how about you?" He shrugged, then took the last bite off the drumstick and scowled down at the bone. "Lordy, but this is fine chicken," he said and shook his head. "It sure looks like we oughta bought more, though, for a bunch this size. Because somebody's gonna be short."

But not many hung around to eat, just Andy and John and one or two more. The others gathered up their coats and kids and followed Orland out to the dock, not having much to say, like they was stunned. I walked out with them and told the mill crew to meet at Scaler's Bridge at six in the morning and they could ride up to the show on John's truck. This set Orland off again; he said he was damned if he'd ride the back of a log truck in the confounded rain! . . . But I went on like I hadn't heard him, telling them how much we had to get done and where and by when, and mentioned that it was getting close on to the end of the year and that the men who hung in with me and didn't miss any work—unless they were sick or like that—could probably look for a nice fat bonus at Christmas. Nobody said anything. Even Orland hushed. They stood around the dock while Big Lou yanked at the boat motor . . . just standing quiet and watching the perch nibble at the trash floating through the circle of dock light on the water. The motor caught and I said good night and I moved on back up the incline to the yard. Then, I just had reached the door when I thought I made out a far-off honking. I stopped and cupped my ear to see if I was right, and finally heard for sure a big flock way off to the northeast over the mountains. Joby'll be glad to hear that, I thought, and started to go on in. I had the door open when I heard the crowd down on the docks go to talking. They thought they'd waited long enough, that I'd gone in—I was out of sight up behind the hedge and they didn't have a notion in the world that I could hear them. Not just Orland and his wife, either, everybody. I listened a minute to their voices rattle around in the cold, all jumbled and excited and salty-sounding, all saying something different, but it all coming out the same, somehow. Like a round sounds with the singing all mixed. I'd hear one guy start on a particular gripe about the way he was being treated or the way he wouldn't be able to face the people at church, and then all the others would come in on it like a chorus. And they'd keep that going until some other guy would come up with a variation; then they'd all take that up. And Orland's wife's voice, high and clear above all the rest, going like a pile driver: *That's right! That's right! That's right!*

Actually, it didn't surprise me much what they were saying—it was about what I figured all of them'd been thinking all along anyway—but the longer I listened the less it sounded like they were even talking, let alone saying anything. The longer I listened, the weirder the sound got. Usually, when you listen to people talk, you're where you can see *what* is coming out of *who*. Kind of hook the voices up with the faces and keep them separate that way. But when you can't see the faces, then the voices get all mixed together, and the talk isn't exactly talk any more, not even a mixed-up round . . . it's just a mish-mash of noise coming at you, without any individuality, damn near without source. Just a sound, feeding on itself the way a sound will when you get a microphone picking up its own broadcast so it goes running in circles faster and faster and faster into finally just a high, tight whine.

Eavesdropping has always hacked me, but I didn't even think of this as eavesdropping, because it honestly didn't seem that I was listening to a lot of people talk. It was just one sound, not a lot of people, just one building noise; and suddenly I realized it was getting louder and louder every second!

Then I woke up to what was happening: those damn geese! While listening to the crowd on the dock I'd clean forgot about the geese. Now they were going right over the house, raising such a din I couldn't even hear the people any more. Just more of those old honkers.

I laughed at myself and headed on into the house; I was reminded of what Joby's old man used to say about distraction, and how effective the spell of distraction was on women. (*I go into the kitchen. They're already eating . . .*) Ben always claimed a woman was the easiest distracted of animals. He claimed he could walk up and go to talking to a woman, get her distracted, "and have her so hooked on the noise I was making that she wouldn't even know I was in her drawers until I hushed talking to come!" (*Lee isn't at the table. I ask if he's going to eat tonight or not. Viv says that he has a temperature again.*) Well, I don't know how reliable Ben's claim was, but having that flock of geese get right overhead before I noticed them convinced me of the effectiveness of distraction in general, and that it worked on men as well as women. I wished, though, that it was the geese distracting me from Orland and his wife and all the rest goddam griping relatives, instead of vice-versa. (*I tell her that everybody is running a fever this particular night, and Lee oughten think he's special or let it keep him from eating. She says she has a plate set back for him that she'll take up to his room . . .*) I remember wishing, in fact, that the geese would do more than just distract me; I was peeved enough with the relatives at the time that I wished the geese would get loud enough to drown them out completely! But that was still before the flocks really hit their peak; that was before I got as tired of the geese as I was of the people, before I got to wishing they would all shut up altogether.

(*. . . I sit down and go to filling my own plate. I ask Joe Ben to pass me the chicken platter. He picks it up and starts to pass it. There's just a back left. He sees this and pulls back the platter and says Here, Hank, here, take this breast I don't really want it I'm saving up for that old honker I'll get me tomorrow so why don't you go ahead and—He stops too late; I look around to see what's wrong. Then, I see. The plate she's set back for him on the warming shelf with all its chicken. I take the back and start eating. Everybody starts eating again, watching their plates. Then there is nothing but eating sounds for a long stretch before the people start talking again.*)

By that second week in November that year, all the little towns along the coast had become peacefully reconciled to the rain: they had elected, judged, and found it responsible for most of their troubles, and found responsible for the rain itself such impervious scapegoats as the satellites, or the Soviets, or their own secret and sinful ways; they had found something out-of-reach to blame and no longer minded the geese reminding them that "Winter is here, citizens, winter is sure enough here."

All the little towns except Wakonda.

Wakonda, that year, hated the geese more than ever for their infernal night-long nagging about winter. The citizens weren't being allowed the customary peace of blaming, like the other towns. These citizens of Wakonda, while they had judged and found their scapegoat every bit as responsible as the scapegoats in other towns, for some reason hadn't had much say in their scapegoat's election; and the particular candidate that had been forced upon them that year—

for all his stand-offishness and his hardnosed obstinate ways—was just too damned *available* to be classified as out-of-reach and passed off as impervious.

So the second week of rain brought to Wakonda none of the traditional fogginess that descended on Coos Bay, and Winchester Bay, and Yachats and Florence and all the rest of the muddy little coast towns where year after year citizens with drowsing but dreamless eyes drift foggily through their winters in a state of near-hibernation. Not to Wakonda, not that November.

It brought instead to the town a wide-eyed insomnia, a great nuisance of geese, and a wild sort of grim and giddy spirit of dedication to the town's Common Good—a spirit the likes of which the coast hadn't seen since those big sky-watching sea-scanning war-effort days back in '42 after that single Japanese plane fire-bombed the forest outside of Brookings to give the Brookings area the distinction of being the only American shore ever to suffer a foreign air attack. This sort of distinction is bound to provoke a certain amount of community feeling; the bombing and the strike, while they exhibited very little in common outwardly, were in a way quite similar in that both had the effect of making the citizens feel, well, feel just a bit . . . special? No; more than special; let's admit it: it made them feel downright *different!*

And there is nothing like feeling special for hustling a citizen out to round up every other comrade he can locate with a corresponding feeling; there is nothing like a sense of *difference* for getting a man lined up, shoulder to shoulder, with everybody as different as he is, in a dedicated campaign for the Common Good; which means a campaign either for the ramming of that difference down the throat of an ignorant and underprivileged and *unholy* world—this is only true, of course, in the case of a bona fide *holy* difference—or, at the other extreme, a campaign for the stamping-out of the thing that caused the damned difference in the first place.

Meetings sprang up everywhere there was room and warmth enough, like mushrooms after lying dormant for months waiting for proper conditions. Everyone convened. Old hatchets were laid aside for the duration of the campaign. The young saw eye-to-eye with the old, the women stood solidly behind their men. The loggermen consorted with the construction men (although the roads still scarred the loggerman's slopes) and the construction men with the loggers (though a lack of trees still left the roadbuilder's efforts vulnerable to slides and settlings), and the churches went easy on the sinners. Folks had to get solidly together! Something had to be done! Something *bold!*

And Jonathan Draeger, seemingly doing nothing but chat pleasantly during those days of crisis and insomnia, skillfully helped all the folks get solidly together, and gently aimed them toward the *doing* of that bold something.

All except Willard Eggleston. Willard was too deeply involved in the preparations toward the doing of his own bold something to be expected to pick up on Draeger's subtle, tossed-off hints aimed at putting the pressure on Hank; Willard just had too much of his own aims to see to during those first weeks of November, too many documents to prepare in private and too many last-minute papers to sign in secret, to have time for writing nasty letters or going out of his way to snub Hank's wife on her visit to town. No; as much as he might have liked to join in the campaign, Willard would have to shirk his civic responsibility. He felt his time too dear, too personal and precious; at the most he couldn't have devoted more than a few paltry seconds to the Common Good, though he knew the cause just and worthy. A pity, a real pity . . . He would have liked to help.

Yet Willard, in a few seconds, unknowingly did more for that good than all the dedicated hours of the rest of the citizens put together.

When he reached his house the geese were still confiding with one another louder than ever in the dark overhead. The rain had grown heavier. The wind had become bolder, stronger, rushing at him from side streets with such ferocity that he had been forced to fold up his umbrella to keep from losing it completely.

He closed the picket gate behind him and cut across the yard to the garage, going in the side door and sliding around the hushed black form of the car and into the house through the kitchen to keep from waking his wife. He tiptoed through the dark kitchen to the utility room that served as his office and pulled the door carefully closed. After listening a moment and hearing nothing in the house but the dripping of water from his coat onto the linoleum, he flicked on the light and walked to put the umbrella in the laundry tray. He sat down at the desk and waited until his heart ceased banging at his temples. He was glad he'd made it without waking her. Not that his wife would have spoiled things if she had awakened—he often came in this late; nothing strange—but she sometimes got up and came out to sit in that awful old ratty red housecoat on the stool in front of

the heater, her hands laced about her knees and all bent forward like
a shabby flamingo, to watch down her nose as he figured the profit
and overhead in the ledger, sniffing and scowling and demanding to
know what his plans were for keeping them out of the poorhouse.

That was what he was afraid of tonight, how he might respond to
her inevitable demand to know what he intended to do. Generally he
would only shrug in henpecked silence and wait for her to provide
an answer for him, but tonight he had something he could tell her—
and he was afraid, for want of someone to listen, he might do just
that.

He opened the desk drawer, removed the ledger, and noted the
night's meager take, being sure to keep the tickets and concession
separate. He closed the ledger and exchanged it for a brown manila
envelope full of policies and legal documents; he pored over these
for nearly a half-hour, then returned them to the envelope and pushed
it far back in a bottom drawer and piled other papers on top of it. He
took a sheet of paper from a tablet and wrote a short letter to Jelly,
explaining that he would see her and the boy after Thanksgiving instead of the day after tomorrow, because he'd made a mistake about
the meeting of Independent Theatre Owners and it was to be in Astoria in the morning instead of in Portland. He folded the letter and
put it in an envelope and addressed it. He stamped it and sealed it and
closed it inside the ledger so it would look as though he had forgotten
to mail it (that letter was going to do some toward showing the old
flamingo her husband wasn't quite the spineless rock-oyster she'd always called him); then he took out another sheet of paper and advised
his wife his cold was much improved and that he thought he would
drive on to Astoria tonight instead of sleeping a few hours and getting
up early in the morning. Would have phoned about meeting change
but hate to wake you. Weather might be worse in the morning the
way it looks. So think it best to leave now. Will phone all the news
tomorrow. Everything changing for better I am positive. Love, etc.

He propped the note against the inkwell and returned the tablet to
its drawer. Sighed loudly. Folded his hands in his lap. Then, listening
to the solitary peck of water dripping from his coat onto the linoleum,
began to weep. In complete silence. His little chin fluttered and his
shoulders jerked with the violence of his sobbing, but he made not
the slightest sound. This silence made him weep harder than ever—
it seemed he'd been crying in secret for years—but he knew he wouldn't
let himself be heard. Especially now, no matter how it hurt to keep

still. He was too practiced at keeping hidden within the black india-ink outline of his looks to ever destroy the effect of letting anyone know he could cry. It was arranged that he keep still. In fact every-*thing*—he looked at the neat note, the tidy desk, the umbrella in the laundry tray—everything was always so arranged, so worked out. He wished he'd been either a bit less thorough, or a bit more. He wished he'd arranged it so there had been at least one person available to cry out loud to, *one person* to share his secrets with. But there just hadn't been time. If he had just been allowed to take his time and work things out more carefully, he might have devised a scheme capable of doing all that this one would and still let people know what he was doing! let *someone* know what he was really like. . . . But this strike, coming when it did, and that Stamper making it go on and on until the money was all gone . . . there just hadn't been time to work out something so fancy. All he could do was use his natural resources, his weak-kneed look, his wife's belief in his cowardice, and especially the image of him held by the whole town: a rock-oyster, a creature soft and white living inside live rock and the rock more alive than its tenant . . . all he'd had time to use was this image, and never let a soul know what he was truly—

He ceased the noiseless crying, raising his head: Stamper! He could tell Stamper! And because Hank Stamper was somewhat to blame for what had—was very *much* to blame! Yes! Who's fault was it that things were getting too tight for people to spend money on dry-cleaning or movie pictures? Yes; *very much to blame!* enough so he *deserves* to be told just what *extremes* his hardnosed obstinance can drive a man to! enough so he *can be told* and be trusted to keep the secret! because Stamper *can't tell* anybody else what really happened! because what happened is *his fault!* Yes! Hank Stamper! He's the one!—because he was to blame, and others would know this if he told, Hank Stamper could be trusted to keep the secret . . . *compelled* to keep it.

Willard leaped from the chair, already composing the phone call, and headed back to the garage, leaving that coat dripping behind him. No longer concerned with silence, he heaved up the door of the garage and slammed the car door shut loudly as soon as he was behind the wheel. His hands shook so with excitement he broke the key chain starting the car and backed over his wife's pyracantha bush on the way out. He was burning with excitement at the prospect of telling someone, bursting with enthusiasm for his plans. He saw the light blaze on in the bedroom window as he stopped in the street—good thing he'd decided to make his call from a booth instead of from his own phone—and, as he trod his headlights on bright and put the car into forward, swinging past his wife's startled bedroom window and into the street's double-barreled rifling of rain, he couldn't help giving the old flamingo an impudent parting volley of horn blasts . . . "Shave and a haircut . . ." Perhaps not the all-illuminating farewell he would have preferred to leave her with, but enough, along with the letter in the ledger, to leave her wondering, enough to leave her forever with a bulge of doubt troubling her newspaper-flat picture of the man she thought she had known for nineteen comic-strip years, and perhaps even enough to give her an inkling of what that man in turn actually thought of her.

". . . six bits."

In his own letter in his own ledger, up in the woods, Lee struggles with a stubby pencil to illuminate his own particular reality to someone else—"Before moving on to farther-out explanations, Peters . . ."—secretly hoping in this way to throw a little light on the dim puzzle of his life for his own benefit:

Do you recall, Peters, being introduced to this oracle? I believe I called him "Old Reliable," as is my wont when bringing him into society to meet my friends: "Old Reliable, The Sentry of my Besieged Psyche." You remember? I said that he was my faithful and constant lookout for danger, perched atop the loftiest mast of my mind, sweeping the horizon for any sign of disaster . . . and you said he looked like nothing more than plain old paranoia to you? I have said the same about him a time or two myself, I must admit, but, all name-calling aside, experience has taught me to trust his call of WATCH OUT to be as infallible as radar. Whatever perceptions he uses must be as sensitive to the slightest radiation of risk as a Geiger counter, because when his signal advises WATCH OUT it has always turned out that the advice was always founded in fact. But this time, as I ready my plan, for the life of me I can *not* see the danger he warns of. WATCH OUT, he screams down, but when I ask "Watch out *what*, old friend? Can't you point to the danger? Can't you show me where I have left room for the slightest element of risk? You've always been able to pick out the pitfalls before. . . . Where awaits this peril you proclaim so positively?" In answer he only squawks WATCH OUT! WATCH OUT! over and over like a hysterical thinking machine, unable to point to a thing. Can I be expected to stay my hands much longer on such flimsy advice? Maybe the old fellow has flipped; maybe there is no specific risk, and the overall radiation of the scene has become high enough to blow his wiring and set him to hallucinating horrors that never existed at all. . . .

Nevertheless, Peters, I'm still spooked by him enough to hesitate: while I have seen my sentry fail this once to point out the peril, I have yet to see him be mistaken about a peril's presence. So I make some conjecture on my own; I ask myself, "Now just what could happen to me if I go through with this?" And the only answer I can truthfully make is, "Viv. Viv could happen to you. . . ."

But unlike the time before, when I did not want to hurt her, this time I am hung-up with the possibility of *helping* her and the gratitude that might result. This is why I was coming on about roots and our generation's aversion to being tied down: Perhaps I have become fond enough of this girl (or fond enough of this girl's *need* for what I have to offer) that I stand a chance of being caught. Perhaps Old Reliable is warning me of a treacherous tarbaby trap, that Viv is a sticky pickaninny of a woman who is just waiting to turn a fond touch into an attachment so black and unbreakable that a man would feel forever horrible and eternally—

The pencil lead had dimmed almost completely into the chewed wood; I stopped and reread the last few lines of the letter, then penciled through them with anger and shame and the very last of the protruding lead, telling myself that even Peters—as emancipated as he claimed to be from caring about cracks to do with color—still didn't deserve to be subjected to such tasteless tar-colored metaphors: "No reason to risk hurting a friend's feelings," I told myself, but I knew that I had crossed out the statement in the interest more of honesty than of diplomacy. In the first place I knew that there was nothing farther from the truth than a description presenting Viv as a sort of glue-ball female, and that there was even reason to suspect that any attachment occurring between us, be it black or be it unbreakable, would have made me feel quite the opposite of horrible.

I gnawed a bit more lead into view on the stub of pencil, turned to the next page in my musty-smelling ledger, and tried again:

In spite of this girl's Al Capp cover story, Peters, she is a rather extraordinary person. She told me, for example, that her parents were both college grads (killed in a car accident when she was in the second grade) and that her mother had taught keyboard for some years. At Juilliard, no less.

Again I stopped, snapping the ledger shut on the pencil in my disgust and breaking its lead; while this statement about her parents was at least accurate, it still seemed a long way from telling any sort of truth about the girl I had come to know. It was still part of the intellectual smoke-screen put up to shroud the true scene, and the true emotions I had felt growing since the night that circumstances— and an SOS from some hapless saboteurs up the river—gave Viv and me the first chance since the fox-hunt to be alone together.

I had perhaps been the only one still awake in the rain-battered old house when the phone rang. Unable to sleep as a result of too much hot lemon-tea sloshed to soothe an irritated throat, I was passing the caffeined hours propped up under the covers beside my bedside lamp, trying to collect some new meanings from the depths of some old Wallace Stevens poetry (as we grow more literate it seems we mature mentally in our collecting, passing from the kid stuff of stamps and bubble-gum cards and butterflies to the more adult items such as "deep meanings"), when I heard the ringing start downstairs. After a dozen or so nail-loosening rings, I heard the unmistakable hard-heeled thudding of Hank's barefoot tread as he worked his way along the hall and down the steps. In a moment the tread came back up the steps and past my door to Joe and Jan's room, then returned, accompanied by the erratic hop-step-and-stumble of Joe Ben's walk. The feet hurried downstairs and donned boots; I listened, wondering what strange midnight doings were afoot and—after I heard the boat start outside and roar off up river—afloat.

All this strange and sudden activity seemed even more pregnant with possible deep meanings than Stevens' poetry, so I switched off my light and lay back to try to plumb the depth of these midnight doings. What was up with all this barefoot roaming? Where were those feet going in that boat at this hour? And, snuggling deeper into my drowse, I was just getting the boots laced onto the feet of my own fantasies—"Perhaps the call told of a great forest fire and Hank and Joe Ben . . . no; too wet; . . . a flood, that's it. Andy has called to say that a terrible forty-caliber rainstorm is strafing the land and splintering the trees and tearing the machinery to shreds!"—when a soft click snapped my eyes back open and a thin needle of light stabbing my bed told me that Viv had turned on her lamp in the room next to mine. . . . Going to read until he gets back, I surmised. This means either he is to be gone only a short time and nothing to worry about, or a long time and maybe she'd better wait up.

I wrestled with my curiosity a few minutes, then got out of bed and pulled on an old army surplus raincoat in lieu of a bathrobe; neither a fitting nor stylish attire to call at a young lady's room, but it was a choice between the raincoat, the still damp work pants spread out before the heater, or the pegged and pressed slacks hanging in my closet, and somehow the raincoat seemed the least ridiculous of the three.

My choice turned out to be a fortunate one; when she said, "Yes?" to my knock I opened the door to find her in almost complete accord with my apparel: she was on the couch, surrounded by pillows and lamplight and an overcoat even bigger and harsher than mine. And much heavier. A black wool job of obscure extraction; I suspected that the coat had once belonged to old Henry or someone even taller; its folds and fabric were so dark that it lost all outline against itself, becoming a featureless clot of sooty black from which was thrust a gleam of face and two slight white hands holding a paperback novel.

The coincidence gave us a chance to laugh, a chance to cut through the distances that ordinarily take hours to overcome before you can feel anything in common. The raincoats afforded us an in-commonness to start from. "Very pleased to see that you are hip to the latest thing in casual wear," I told her when our laughter had stopped, "but I feel that you—ah—should see your tailor about the fit," I said, and shuffled a sneaky yard into the room.

She lifted her arms and studied the overwhelming sleeves. "You think so? Or should I wait till I wash it and see if it shrinks?"

"Yes. Better wait; wouldn't want it to be too small for you."

We laughed again and I advanced another dozen inches. "Actually," she explained, "I do have a housecoat, but I never wear it. I believe it was a gift—it must have been a gift—from Hank for my birthday or something right after I first came out here."

"It must be a sight to behold, this gift, if you wear that tent instead. . . ."

"No," she said. "It's all right. For a housecoat. But, you see . . . I had an aunt that was in a housecoat all the day long, morning to night, never got into anything else till night, when she got fixed up to go to Pueblo or someplace . . . and I promised myself Vivian, honey, when you get big you go nakedy before you run around in a old housecoat!"

"My reason precisely," I replied, "for not wearing a smoking jacket." I assumed a look of lidded reverie. "Yes. Had an uncle. Same way about *his* dress. Always in this ruddy old tweed, getting cigar ashes in the sherry; smelling up the house; shedding. Damn nuisance."

"My aunt had terrible breath . . ."

"Oh, my uncle's breath would sometimes asphyxiate entire rooms full of poor souls unaccustomed to his stench."

"Did he always leave the sleepy in his eyes?"

"Never removed it; let it build up in the corners of his eyes over the weeks until it was heavy enough to fall out in walnut-sized chunks."

"I wish we might have got them together, my aunt and this uncle of yours; they sound made for each other, don't they? Too bad that she couldn't have married a man like him. With those cigars," she remarked wistfully. "My aunt had a perfume that she wore that would have gone perfect with his cigars. What will we call your uncle?"

"Uncle Mortique. Mort for short. Your aunt?"

"Her real name was Mabel, but I always called her—to myself, I mean—Maybelline . . . because of all the eye make-up she used."

"Uncle Mort . . . ? meet Maybelline. Now why don't you two go on off someplace and get acquainted? There's good kids . . ."

Sputtering giggles like silly children, we went on to wave the pretended pair out of the room, bade them not hurry back, then—"There goes a real cute couple,"—closed the door behind them triumphantly.

With the little trip ended, we were for a moment without words. I sat down on the big piece of driftwood. Viv closed her paperback. "Well," I said, "alone at last"—trying to draw out the joke. But this time the response was forced, the giggle much less childlike, and the joke not nearly so silly. Viv and I were fortunate to be able to kid with each other; as with Peters, operating within the limits of humor and make-believe afforded Viv and me opportunities to laugh and make jokes, put each other at ease with pretense; and with this system we could enjoy a relationship without too much worry about commitment. But a system made secure by the protective plating of humor and pretense always runs the risk of having its protection get out of hand. A relationship based on jokes invites jokes; jokes about anything—"Yes," Viv said, in an attempt to reinforce my attempt, "alone at long last,"—and jokes about anything are now and then bound to cut too close to the truth.

I saved us from the fate of hangnail-tending and lint-picking, by remembering what I had come calling to ask about in the first place. The mysterious phone call, she answered, was almost as much a mystery to her as to me. Hank had stuck his head in the door and told her he had to go up to the mill to fish some of his friends and neighbors out of the river, but he hadn't said who they were or what they were doing at the mill at this hour. I asked if she had any ideas what it was all about. She said no ideas at all. I said it certainly is peculiar. She said it sure is. And I said especially this late at night. And she said and it raining so bad and all. And I said we'll probably find out in the morning. And she said yes, in the morning, or maybe when Hank and Joby get back. And I said yes. . . .

And after another small silence I said that the weather doesn't seem to be easing up any. And she said the radio says a new low's moving down from Canada, be like this another week. And I said that's sure happy tidings. And she said isn't it, though . . . ?

And then, we just sat. Wishing we hadn't been so wasteful with our topics, realizing we had exhausted all the excuses and that if we were to talk it would have to be plunge right into the subject of each other—the only topic left in common—or not talk at all. I stood up, and shuffled backward toward the door, preferring at this point to take the second alternative of not-at-all, but before I could finish my good night Viv took the plunge.

"Lee . . ." She paused a moment to debate something with herself, while she tilted her head and studied me with one blue eye peeking over the coat's black collar. Then all at once asked me point-blank ". . . what are you doing out here? with all your learning . . . education, out here spending your time wrapping a dull old cable around a dull old log?"

"The cable and the log are not that dull"—I tried to clown my way through—"not when analyzed in their truer, their deeper meaning, as sexual symbols. Yas. You must keep it a secret, of course, but I am out here on a grant from the Kinsey foundation, doing research for a book on the Castration Complex of the Choker-setter. Fascinating study . . ." But she had asked the question out of serious curiosity and she was waiting for a serious answer.

"No, I mean it, Lee," she said. "Why are you out here?"

I began racking my brain and kicking my rear for not having anticipated this inevitable question with a good, ready-made, and logical-sounding lie. Damn stupid oversight! And this brain-racking, or the rear-kicking, or both, must have produced an expression of considerable anguish, for Viv's head immediately straightened out of its questioning tilt and her face filled with sympathy. "Oh. I didn't mean to ask about something . . . about something you—"

"It's okay. It's not that kind of question. It was just that—"

"No; it *is* that kind of question. I could see it. I'm really sorry, Lee; I do that sometimes without thinking. I had just been wondering why and thought I'd ask; I wasn't intending to pick at a purple place. . . ."

"Purple place?"

"A bruise, a hurt place in somebody's past, do you know? Well . . . see, in Rocky Ford, my uncle used to run the jail . . . and he used to tell me that I ought to talk with the prisoners a little when I brought their food because they—he was a good man about things like this—because the poor men felt low enough already without me acting stuck-uppish. Mostly drifters, tramps, drunks; Rocky Ford was a big railroad town once. And he was right, my uncle, that they felt low enough. I would listen to them, their stories and how come they were in jail and what they were aiming to do, and *really* get involved, you see? And then my aunt would see this and come in and sit on my bed at night and tell me that I was maybe fooling those poor men or my uncle, but *she* was onto me. *She* knew what I was, she'd say— whispering, sitting there on my cot in the dark—that I was one of these *carrion-bird people*. Like a magpie or a raven. Somebody . . . just interested in picking at the purple places in people's past, she'd say, not at their healthy places, just at their hurts . . . that she was *onto* me and that I'd better watch out." Viv looked down at her hands for a second. "And a lot of times—I'm still not sure—I thought she was right." Then back up at me: "Anyway, do you see what I mean? about purple places?"

"No. Yes. I mean yes I see what a purple place is and no you didn't hit one with your question . . . all right? Why I couldn't answer, Viv . . . I don't really know *what* I'm doing out here, fighting dull old logs. But then I didn't know what I was doing back at school, fighting dull old poems and plays written by dull old Englishmen, either . . . making believe I cared about it all so a committee of dull old professors would authorize me to teach the same rot to more young fellows making believe so more committees would authorize them to teach more fellows, and so on to the last syllables of recorded time. . . . Didn't it bother you? having your aunt accuse you of preying on the jailbirds?"

"Terribly," she answered, "for a while, anyway."

I sat down again on the driftwood. "It's one of the worst sort of binds you can be put in, you know," I informed her, in a voice I'm sure must have made me sound as though a record number of similar situations had made me the world's foremost authority on the resulting hang-ups. "The binds—I mean a *bind*; the binds sounds like something caused by nitrogen bubbles in your ego—a bind is when you are put in a damned-if-you-do-damned-if-you-don't situation. In your case, for instance, you were made to feel guilty if you didn't listen to the prisoners, and guilty if you did."

She listened patiently but didn't seem very impressed by my diagnosis. "I felt something like that, I guess," she said, and smiled, "but you know, it didn't bother me too long. Because I found out something. I found out little by little that whatever either my aunt or uncle were after me about didn't really mean anything but that they were onto themselves about it already. That aunt of mine; boy, she used to wear make-up all week long so terrible thick that—well, she started about Wednesday layering it on, and she *never* washed, and every day she slapped down a new layer. Until Sunday. Then on Sunday she kind of *peeled* it off to go to church. And after church she was so holy she'd follow after me for *hours* to see if she could catch me putting on some lipstick so she could make a big fuss." Viv smiled, remembering. "Boy, she was a case; I used to hope she'd skip a Sunday—sleep through to Monday or something—because I knew two weeks' worth of make-up and she'd set up like a statue. Especially as hot as it got around there. Boy oh boy." She shook her head at the memory, smiling. Then yawned and stretched, becoming lanky, her lanky cowgirl arms lengthening up out of the sleeves. Arms still stretched, she said, "Lee, if it really isn't prying . . . was it always dull, your studies? Or did something happen to take the life out of it?"

I had become so engrossed in the shy outpouring from her world that the sudden cut back to me and mine once more caught me off guard; and I stammered out the first answer that came into my mind. "Yes," I said. "No," I said. "No, it wasn't always dull. Not at first. When I first discovered the worlds that came before our world, other scenes in other times, I thought the discovery so bright and blazing I wanted to read everything ever written about these worlds, *in* these worlds. Let it teach me, then me teach it to everybody. But the more I read . . . after a while . . . I began to find they were all writing about the same thing, this same dull old here-today-gone-tomorrow scene . . . Shakespeare, Milton, Matthew Arnold, even Baudelaire, even this cat whoever he was that wrote *Beowulf* . . . the same scene for the same reasons and to the same end, whether it was Dante with his pit or Baudelaire with his pot: . . . the same dull old scene . . ."

"What scene is that? I don't understand."

"What? Oh, I'm sorry; I didn't mean to come on so jaded. What scene? *This* one, the rain, those geese up there with their hard-luck stories . . . this, this same world. They all tried to do something with it. Dante did his best to build himself a hell because a hell pre-supposes a heaven. Baudelaire scarfed hashish and looked inside. Nothing there. Nothing but dreams and delusion. They all were driven by the need for something else. But when the drive was over, and the dreaming and the deluding worn out, they all ended up with the same dull old scene. But, look, you see, Viv, they had an ad-vantage with their scene, they had something we've lost . . ."

I waited for her to ask what that something was, but she only sat silently, her hands folded on the black overcoat.

". . . They had a limitless supply of tomorrows to work with. If you didn't make your dream today, well, there was always more days coming, more dreams full of more sound and fury and future: what if today was a hassle? There was always tomorrow to find the River Jordan, or Valhalla, or that special providence in the fall of a sparrow . . . we could believe in the Great Gettin'-up Morning coming some-day because if it didn't make it today there was always tomorrow."

"And there isn't any more?"

I looked up at her and grinned. "What do you think?"

"I think it's pretty likely . . . that the alarm will go off at four-thirty, and I'll be down making pancakes and coffee, just like yes-terday."

"Pretty likely, sure. But let's say Jack comes home unexpectedly, all miffed at the steel magnates, his back aching and his vigor gone, and finds Jackie and Barry making it in his rocking chair . . . then what? Or, say, Nikita has one vodka too many and decides what-the-hell, then what? I'll tell you. Zap; that's all it takes. The little red button and zap. Right? And this little button makes a definite dif-ference in our world; in our generation, ever since we've been old enough to read, our tomorrows have been at the mercy of this button. Well . . . at least we've quit kidding ourselves about the Great Gettin'-up Mornin' acoming someday; when you can't even be sure of having that 'someday' come along, you have the devil's own time convincing yourself of that Mornin'."

"Is it that?" she asked in a soft voice, once more examining her hands, "not being sure of that 'someday'? Or is it not being sure of having that 'somebody'?" Her face raised, framed by the contrasting black of the overcoat's collar.

The best I could do was respond with a question of my own. "Have you ever read Wallace Stevens?" I asked, like a sophomore on a Coke date. "Wait. I'll get you this book. . . ." And I fled to my room to recuperate. The light from the hole showed me the book on the bed, open to the poem I had been reading. I pick it up, keeping my place, but hesitated to return. For a moment I stood, sucking at my cheeks, still feeling that glow, then, like Nikita after too much vodka, decided what-the-hell and tiptoed quickly to the hole in the wall.

She hadn't moved from the position I'd left her in, but her expression had changed to puzzlement and some concern for this nut next door who flea-hopped from room to room, from glib despondency to tongue-tied frustration. Safely separated by the wall, I found my cool returning. In another moment I would be able to go back in there and be as unruffled as Oscar Wilde at a tea. But as my cool came back, so did the sound of the motorboat. I barely had time to run back in with my book and point out a couple of poems she *must* read —"Be patient with Stevens; don't force him; let him force you"— and make it back to my room before I heard those hard-heeled bare footsteps mounting the stairs again. And I lay awake for hours, hoping another phone call would give me that opportunity to be alone and unruffled with her.

As it happened that opportunity, by my own doing, became less and less likely as the days passed and the scene at the house grew stickier, until it was finally apparent that it would only happen if I made it happen. "That chance is now at hand," I wrote to Peters in my ledger, after gnawing another slight point on the nub of the pencil,

and all I need do is screw my courage to the sticking point and take that chance. But still I hesitate. Is it courage that I lack? Is that the explanation for my warner's WATCH OUT? In these days when a man's courage hangs between his legs and can be read like a thermometer, do I hesitate going through with my plan because simple old masculinity doubts make me afraid to risk sticking my courage to the screwing point? I don't know, in truth I just don't know. . . .

And in her room with Lee's book of poetry Viv tries to decipher the sense of vagueness that bathes her like diffused light. "I don't understand," she says, frowning at the page. "I just don't understand. . . ."

And down the hill from the carrier Hank steps back from the sizzling pile of burning trash to listen to the sky. Another low-flying flock is coming over. He runs to get his gun, then stops, feeling foolish. What the hell. . . . There wasn't a snowball's chance in hell seeing a goose through that smoke and rain. Let alone hitting one if you saw him. And the way things had been going since that meeting with the relatives—all the hassles by day and the honking by night—if I'd got that shotgun I might of just gone to throwing buckshot in the sky like a wild man, whether I saw anything or not. . . .

The day after that meeting with the relatives Joe Ben was up bright and early getting some shells ready, because it "looked like his day for sure." He was prying open the tops of some Super X magnums and pouring out the B-Bs and filling the shells back up with chunks of these pencil sinkers he'd cut up; long strips of lead about as big around as a pencil, all chopped into pieces about a fourth-inch long. I told him he was wasting his time today, as foggy as it was, but he said he might get a chance coming home tonight because the fog would be rained down by then and he figured we'd get to come home early because of all the help we'd have now that all the mill crew was gonna help out. He was right about the fog but wrong about getting done early; only about two-thirds of the crew showed up—the rest had just the most awful colds, they told me—so it was pitch-dark by the time we started back.

That night a couple more phoned while we were eating to say they had fevers and couldn't make it, and I told Joby it didn't look like he could expect anything more than just morning hunting the next day either. He just looked up from his supper plate and shrugged and said it wasn't gonna take more than morning hunting when the holy signs all lined up just right; when that time come along his old honker would be good as in the pot, he said, then leaned back over his plate and went to packing away the potatoes to fortify himself for the coming of that great lining-up of holy signs. (All through the meal Lee keeps sniffing and rubbing his eyes. Viv says they should take his temperature. He says he's all right; this is just his way of expelling excess moisture, like a dog sweating from his nose. Before we go to bed Viv goes up and brings down the thermometer and gives it to him. He sits reading the paper with the thing stuck out of the corner of his mouth like a glass cigarette. Viv reads it and says he has about a degree, not anything fatal. . . . He asks if he couldn't have a glass of hot lemon tea, that his mother always gave him hot lemon tea when

he was coming down with a cold. Viv goes and makes it. She brings it in
to him and he sits by the stove in the living room sipping the stuff,
reading her some poems from that book . . .)

Apparently, the signs didn't line up for Joe worth a darn the next
day; it wasn't only foggy as ever, but only about a third of the crew
showed up this time. And it was worse still the next day, and the
next, and Joby was about to give it all up when one night toward the
end of that week there came another big blow and a lot of geese
going over, and in the morning it was cold and clear enough you
could look out the kitchen window and see car lights going by across
the river. It was raining, but not too hard, and even in the dark you
see up in the sky well enough to make out the grocery flag on the
pole.

"This is the morning, Hank, abso-*lutely*, you just wait and see if it
ain't. Everything is right; a storm, wind, lots of honking in the night,
and now the mist is down. . . . Oh yeah, everything is right!"

He was standing by the breakfast table oiling his gun, all excited
(*There's something funny*), while we waited for Viv to get the food
on. (*There's something funny again.*)

"Oh you know it," he rambled on, "I bet there's some poor old
lonely lost honker out there calling for his brother geese and just
needing to be put out of his misery. . . ." (*I turn in my chair and
look around the kitchen. Viv is at the stove. Jan is slicing ham for
sandwiches. The old man is out the back door somewhere, hawking
and spitting. I cut in on Joe Ben's ramblings:* "Talkin' about brother
geese," *I say,* "where's the boy this morning?"

*There's a minute nobody says anything. Something is funny. Then
Joe Ben says,* "Lee'll be right along, I imagine; I hollered at him just
a bit ago when I come past his room."

"He wasn't up?" *I say.*

"Well . . . he was dressing," *Joe Ben says.*

"Well he'd better get to shagging it," *I say.* "He's gettin' harder to
get movin' every morning."

"He told me," *Viv says,* "that he didn't feel too good this
morning. . . ."

"Now is that the truth? Joe an' me out last night till midnight
hammering on that foundation, an' Lee don't feel good! That's something. . . ."

*Nobody says anything. Joe Ben comes and sits down and Viv comes
over with the skillet. She takes the pancake turner and hikes some*

sausages on the plate for me. I go to eating these. It's hot in the kitchen and the windows are all steamed shut. Joe Ben's got his radio turned on. It'd be nice to just sit here and read the paper . . . pleasant.

Lee comes into the kitchen just as I'm getting up from my plate. "Let's move it, bub," I tell him. He says all right and I go out to put on my boots. There's something different happening but I don't know what, or more there is something different going to happen and nobody knows for sure what. . . .) "Yes siree bob!" Joby said, clashed the pump of his old J. C. Higgins 12-gauge a time or two. "You know how I know it's my day? Because I gave up coffee today, been intendin' to a long time, Brother Walker says it's a sin. So by gosh I quit, an' I'm ready to get my goose."

Well, Joby was nearly right this once; it sure enough should've been his day to get him that honker. Everything was just as right as he said. I went outside to start the boat while Lee ate, and I saw why it was so clear. The rain and cold had sort of beat that mist down out of the sky. It was packed down on the river thick as snow and about four feet deep. I couldn't even see the boat; I had to feel around to get it started. Lee and Joe come out and we headed out, traveling through that mist like the boat was submerged and our heads was periscopes. Joe was still beating his gums about what fat times he had ahead by now, not even about the goose he was going to get; as far as he was concerned that goose was good as in the pot, a settled issue, and he was going on to new glories.

"Fat times ahead," he was saying. "Oh yeah. Not many more trips up in this boat. What do you figure, Hank? Another day or so at Breakleg, then clean-up, and that's her for ridin' this boat up river in the cold and dark, you boys realize that? That one more day or so is the last of this, the last we'll ever have to look at those stump-jungles? Few more days, then we got easy street at that state park, cuttin' those big old easy sticks like we was tourists gatherin' huckleberries."

I told him, "You'll think gatherin' huckleberries after about ten hours' work out there twisting a screw jerk. Working that park with all the goddam restrictions they put on us'll be just like going back a hundred years."

"Oh yeah, but," he said, closing one eye and holding up his finger, "but at least there won't be no more fightin' that donkey; you got to admit not having to fight that donkey is gonna be a gas."

"I ain't admitting anything is gonna be a gas until I try it out. What about you, bub?"

Lee turned and gave me a flimsy sort of grin and said, "Not when the only advantage seems to be the elimination of a piece of modern machinery . . . that doesn't sound like much of a gas. . . ."

"*Modern?*" Joe whooped. "You ain't had to ride that monster you call a 'modern machine,' Lee; that outfit was wore out and old when old Henry was still a boy! You ain't looking at the *bright* side. Remember, 'I had no shoes and complained till I saw a man griping about his feet.' "

Lee shook his head. "Joe, if I didn't have shoes and saw a *basket* case, I still wouldn't have solved my own footwear problem. . . ."

"No; no, that's so; that wouldn't solve your problems. . . ." He thought a second, then he brightened up: "But you got to admit seeing a basket case, it would distract you from it a little bit!"

Lee laughed, giving up. "Joe, you are incorrigible, completely incorrigible. . . ."

Joe said thank you to that and was so flustered at being so flattered he didn't say anything else until we got to the mill.

The fog around the mill was packed just as thick as it was at the house. It was lighter out now and we could see it better, and that mist looked more than ever like snow. I swung the boat in to about where I judged the dock to be, hoping there hadn't been any change since I last saw the landing. Andy was standing there, alone and looking tired. He'd been standing guard at the mill every night since Evenwrite had tried to loose the booms. It'd been his idea. I'd given him a sleeping bag and a flashlight and the old eight-gauge goose cannon Henry'd ordered once from Mexico a long time back before everything under a ten-gauge was made illegal. Hell of a gun, used a shell about the size of a beer can and you had to pass the stock under you armpit and brace it against a tree or a rock to keep the recoil from breaking your shoulder; I'd told Andy why I gave that gun to him instead of a 30-30 or something easier handled, was that I didn't expect him to kill anybody defending the place, to just fire that monster in the air if there was trouble and help would come running, probably all the way from the Pentagon with the racket it made.

Andy caught the rope Joe pitched him and pulled us up to the dock. I thought at first he was looking so drug account of he wasn't getting a good night's rest in the sleeping bag, but then I saw it was something else. He was alone.

"Hey," I said, standing up in the boat. "What's the story? Where's Orland and his two boys? Lard-assing in the mill there out of the wet while they leave you to hold the boat for 'em?"

"No," he said.

"What'd they do? Decide to ride up with John on the truck?"

"Orland an' the others ain't coming to work today," he said. He stood there holding onto that rope leading down into the fog to the boat, like a big old bashful kid hold of something he can't understand. "I'm the only one going. And . . ."

"And. . . ?" I waited for him to get on with it.

"Orland called to say him and his boys all got the Asian flu. He said a lot of folks in town got it, Floyd Evenwrite, and Howie Evans and—"

"I don't give a shit about Floyd Evenwrite and Howie Evans," I told him. "What about our bunch? What about Little Lou? Did he call? And Big Lou? Shit fire, Orland's boys; now wouldn't that frost you? And what about John? He got the sour-mash flu, I imagine, an' can't even drive the truck up there?"

"I don't know," Andy said. "I just heard the phone in the mill ring and I taken the messages. Orland said—"

"What about Bob? I suppose he's got the *ingrown toenails* or something. . . ."

"I don't know about what he's got. I told him we still had a lot of logs to go to make that contract, but Orland said not to expect sick people to—"

"Well shit fire," I said. "That just about makes the lot of 'em, don't it? First it's Big Lou, then Collins, then that damned fiddlefooted brother-in-law of Orland's who wasn't worth a goddam anyhow. Now Orland and his boys. I'm goddamned but I never thought they'd fade so fast with just a little rain and hard work."

And Lee said, "The thanes fly from us," or some such crap.

And Andy said, "It ain't just the rain and hard work, Hank. You see, there's a lot of folks in town saying they don't like what's—"

"I don't give a *goddam* who likes what and who don't!" I told him, louder'n I'd aimed to. "And if the folks in town think this is gonna make me short on that contract, then they take me for a whole lot more fool than I am. Next time anybody calls in how sick they are by god just tell 'em that's all right that's just fine, because your old Uncle Hank made a *mistake* keeping count an' we'll make it just fine with the four or five of us."

Andy looked up. "I don't see how," he said. "We got this whole boom to fill an' then two more."

"One more," Joe Ben said, giving Andy a big wink. "Folks got to get up pretty early to get a jump on us. Long time ago me and Hank started slipping logs in that slough up behind the house at night, pulling a few at a time with the motorboat. Oh yeah, people got to get up pret-tee ear-lee!"

Andy grinned, and I told him to get on in the boat. I could see he was pleased that I had that other boom hid, that we still had a chance to make our contract. Really pleased. And that got me to thinking just how many people wasn't going to be the least *bit* pleased. A god-awful amount, I realized. This made me feel funny, thinking for the first time just how many there was *didn't* want the contract made. I just sat there a minute, studying about it, looking out across the mist toward the anchor pilings up past the mill where the booms were snubbed. And then I got this goofy urge; it's hard to explain, but all of a sudden I found myself wanting to see those booms again, wanting to see them so goddam *much* right then that I felt like I was going batty! There was a hundred and fifty or two hundred yards between us and those pilings, covered with mist like a big blanket of dirty snow. Underneath that blanket was the booms, better than four months backbreaking ass-bleeding labor, millions of board feet of lumber, thousands of logs out of sight under there, nudging and scraping and rubbing against each other as the river current moved past under them so they were making an actual sound above the motor and the rain . . . a kind of a surly, complaining murmur, like a big throng of people muttering to each other.

I didn't have any real need to check them logs. I told myself that. Even if they were covered with mist I still knew them damn near by heart. I'd watched them stand as a forest when I first took a drive up to see if I wanted to make a bid, seen them all thick and green, like a big piece of green herring-bone wool. I'd watched them mown from the sky. I'd bucked and chokered and yarded and loaded them. I'd heard the way the branding hammer sounded against them with a woody *thock* when I knocked a big crooked S into the end of each log; I'd heard them rumble off the truck into the water. . . . Still, listening to them out of sight there some way made me doubt what I knew. I wanted to grab that layer of mist by the edge and jerk it up for just a moment, like jerking a carpet up from the floor so you could see the pattern underneath. I wanted to look at them. For just a second. Like I maybe needed the sight to reassure me—not that they were still there—but that they were . . . what? Still as *big* as I remembered? Could be. Maybe I wanted to see that they hadn't been gradually worn and eroded by the continual rubbing and grinding, down to the size of saplings and pile posts.

Andy got himself settled. I shook myself to try to get shut of my foolishness and turned back to the motor. But just as I started to throttle the motor Joe Ben gave a hiss like a snake and grabbed me by the sleeve and pointed off up river.

"There, Hank, *there*," he whispered. "What'd I tell you?"

I looked. A lone honker, separated by the storm just like Joe'd figured, was flying dead for us. Everybody froze. We watched him come, stretching his long black neck from side to side as he searched around him, flapping along, honking over and over the same question. "Guh-*luke*?" he would honk, then be still and listen a while before calling again. "Guh-*luke*?" . . . not exactly afraid, not the way I've heard other geese call when they were lost. Different. Almost human, the way he was asking it. "Guh-luke . . . ? Guh-*luke* . . . ?"

It was a sound like . . . I remember thinking . . . a sound kind of like Joe's little girl Squeaky made the time she come running in from the barn hollering that her special cat was in the bottom of the milk can drowned and *where was everything?* She wasn't crying or carrying on, just hollering *my cat got drowned where is everybody?* She wouldn't calm down till she'd gone all over the whole house and talked to everybody and seen everything. That was the same notion I got hearing that lost goose honking: that he wasn't so much just asking where the lost flock was—he was wanting to know where the river was, and the bank, and *everything* hooked up with his life. *Where is my world?* he was wanting to know, *and where the hell am I if I can't locate it?* He had lost his way and was out there flying the river, out of his head looking for it. He was trying to check around quick and get everything in its place, like Squeaky had needed to do when she'd lost her cat, and like me wanting to see them logs again. Only with me, I couldn't figure what I thought I'd lost: no cats that I could think of, and I don't know as I was missing a flock . . . or ever even *had* a way. But I still knew the feeling. . . .

While I was studying about this, I heard Joe whisper, "Meat in the pot," and saw him reach down into the fog for the shotgun. (*The black barrel of the gun comes up out of the mist. The goose doesn't see us. He keeps coming.*) I watched Joby run his finger down the muzzle, checking for a mud clog—an unconscious habit that anybody picks up after years of squatting in a muddy duck blind. He drew in his breath . . . (*The goose swells closer to us. I move my face inside the rubber poncho hood to see if the kid is watching. He ain't even turned toward the goose. He's turned looking at my face. And he's grinning.*) . . . then, just as the goose comes within range, I said, "Forget it." "What?" Joby said. His jaw dropped a foot. I said again, as casual as I could, "Forget it," and gunned the motor out into midstream. The goose veered sharply overhead, making a slight whistling sound with his wings, he was so close. Poor Joe just sat there with his jaw hung open. I knew he'd be pretty disappointed— bagging a Canada honker is a pretty big deal; more buck deer are killed every year in Oregon than Canada geese, because geese don't decoy worth beans and if you set out to slip up on a flock in a field you're in for about a three-day crawl through the mud with the wily bastards always keeping just a hair out of shotgun range . . . pretty near the only chance you got is to luck onto one, and that happens about as much as lucking onto a pirate chest. So Joby had every right to be disappointed. Anybody would, if someone screwed up his first and maybe only chance for a honker.

He sat there watching that big pearl-colored bird fading off into the sky till it was out of sight. Then he turned and just looked at me. "What's the sense?" I said to him; I turned away from his look and watched the bow split the fog. "We couldn't of located him in this crappy fog even if you did knock him down, could we now?"

He still just sat there with his trap open, looking for all the world like Harpo Marx.

"Well, Jesus H. Christ!" I said. "If I'd known you wanted to just *kill* a goose I wouldn't of stopped you! But I thought I heard you say 'bag' one. If you're just looking to kill something, maybe you'd like to go out on the jetty this weekend with the 30-06 and shoot some of the seals playing in the bay? Okay? Or dynamite some trout in the sloughs, maybe?"

That got him. Les Gibbons used to dynamite the deep sloughs above our place and gather the fish in a boat. Once Joe and me skin-dived to the bottom of one of these holes after a blast, and there was dead trout piled up down there by the hundreds; only about one out of fifty floated up. So when I mentioned dynamiting fish, that really got him. He closed his mouth and looked sheepish. "I didn't think, Hankus," he said. "An' I forgot how you hate to see a animal killed an' lost." I didn't say anything and he added, "Especially the way you feel about the Canada goose race. I just didn't follow your reasoning right off. I got all in a boil seeing him. Wasn't thinking good. I understand now."

I left it at that, with him thinking he understood a reasoning that I could barely follow myself. How could I expect him to understand that my feeling toward the goose as a race was doing a slow but sure turnover—what with squadron after squadron of the bastards ruining my sleep—and that it was this one particular lost goose that I didn't want shot because he sounded like he was asking *Where is everything? Where is everything?* . . . how the hell could I expect poor rattleheaded Joby to understand that?

In town the arrival of the Asian flu only served to bring the citizens more tightly together in their campaign: "*Another* cross to bear but if we just all stick together in the fight any cross comes along will surely be bearable." Snuffling and coughing, they continued to stick together. Eyes rimmed with misery and backs bent beneath a whole truckload of crosses, they trudged to front doors of Stampers living in town and reminded wives to tell their husbands to let Hank Stamper know what folks thought about him trying to set himself up against friends and neighbors, against his very home town! "No man is a island, honey," they reminded the wives; and the wives told the husbands, "No woman is going to stand for this sort of injustice, I don't care if you do lose your Exmas bonus!" and the husbands phoned the house up the river to say the Asian flu made it impossible to come to work.

And when all the Stamper wives had laid down the law, and all Stamper husbands in town had contracted the flu, then the citizens carried the battle to the enemy himself. "No sir, no man is a goddam island," they let Hank know on the phone, "not you nor nobody!"— all hours of the night. Viv stopped answering the phone during the day (she had already stopped going into Wakonda to shop, and was even experiencing chilly stares when she went as far away as Florence); she even asked if they might not have their phone disconnected. Hank only grinned and replied, "What for? So's all my friends and neighbors can say, 'Stamper has had to shut his phone off; we *must* be getting *to* him'? Kitten, we don't want to get our good friends an' neighbors all het up over nothing, do we?" He had acted so amused and nonchalant about the whole business that Viv couldn't help wondering if he actually meant it. Nothing seemed to get to him. He seemed more impervious than ever, even to that flu bug; he snuffled a little bit, naturally (he always snuffled a little bit, though, because of his broken nose), and sometimes he came home sounding hoarse (from hollering at the rest of the sick slackers, he told her in a joking boast), but he obviously wasn't nearly as ill as the others. Everybody else in the house, from the baby all the way to the old man, was having stomach aches and lung congestion. Nothing serious—Lee got better and worse; Joe Ben took three aspirins when his sinuses hurt him, then swore off artificial medicines as soon as the headache let up enough for him to remember his church's doctrine of faith-healing; Jan spent a night vomiting out the window to the dogs below . . . nothing serious, but everybody had been bitten deep enough by the bug going around to show a *few* symptoms. Not Hank. Hank just kept chugging along day after day without signs of a let-up. Like a machine. She couldn't help wondering sometimes whether he was made out of flesh and blood and bones, like the rest of them, or out of workboot leather and Diesel fuel, and blackjack oak dipped in creosote.

Viv wondered at Hank's uncanny strength; the old man bragged about it every chance he had to get to town; even Lee had occasion to doubt the existence of the weakness that he was dedicated to prove, to his brother and himself:

A further possibility, Peters, is that I may be holding back my Sunday punch because I am afraid that Hank will not be fazed by it. Thus far my belief in the iron man's vulnerability is based only on a few uncertain glimpses of rust spots. What if these spots are the whole of his weakness? What if I had been wrong in my whole precept and he actually turns out to be invulnerable? It would be like working for years developing as ultimate a weapon as one could conceive, only to find that the target was completely unscathed by it. Such a prospect might give a fellow pause, don't you think?

In fact, it was Joe Ben, whose faith in Hank's invulnerability had been a long-time joke, who was the first to glimpse for certain those spots of rust. He saw these spots in the way Hank brooded over his supper coffee, in the sharp way he spoke to Viv or the kids, in a dozen places. Joe tried to avert his gaze, and most of the time managed to smother his misgivings under surges of enthusiasm, but it was these same surges that began to gradually reveal to Hank the very misgivings Joe was trying to smother.

They were all tired and edgy with overwork. By the end of that week there were only five left working: Hank and Joe, Andy, Lee, and, surprisingly, John. John was the only outsider relative left (Andy was never considered with the "outsider folks"; while he was a more distant relation than most, his absence from the job would have surprised everyone as much as Joe Ben's would have), and Joe could see that John was beginning to get the itch to join the other defectors. The five of them had worked doggedly all that day, falling and cleaning up the few logs still standing in their spread, until they were numb with cold and fatigue. They had finished all the cutting and hauling; nothing was left but the clearing required by the Forest Service. Not the sort of work for a trucker, Joe knew, but he knew as well that Hank needed the help of everyone, including John. They were all standing near Hank at the spar tree, looking out across the slopes they had cut. It was already growing dark, the night drifting down with the rain. John made a circle to check his load, then mounted to the cab and waited. Joe watched Hank draw at the cigarette angling out of the corner of his mouth.

"Take us most of tomorrow to doze the place clean and set the slash to burning," Hank said. One eye was squinted against the cigarette's looping smoke. "We'd of got to it today if we'd had one other man helpin'. That means we're gonna be short a day an' maybe have to work this weekend."

Joe watched the others. "Andy, you make it this weekend?" Hank asked while he continued to look down the slope. "I know that'll be twelve days straight for you, without a let-up, but whatcha say?"

The boy was leaning against the muddy side of the carrier, stubbing out a hole in the ground with the toe of his boot. He lifted a shoulder in a shrug and said without looking up, "I can make it."

"Good goin'." Hank turned toward the log truck, where John sat looking straight ahead through the clicking wipers on the windshield. The smoke of John's cigar rolled from the open window and up to mix with the flutter of exhaust. He was waiting for Hank to repeat his question. When Hank only looked at him he began to fidget with the choke knob, then finally blurted out, "Hank, look here: you don't need me up here tomorrow for burnin' slash. And I hate to chance the rig on this road more'n I have to, the way the bedrock's washing loose."

The motor of the truck idled; a sleepy, restful sound; smoke rose from the stack to blend with the rain and oncoming night. Hank continued to watch John narrowly until he went on. "Blast it . . .

the way I see it you boys'll be falling direct to the river at this state-park deal, without much use for a trucker." He licked his lips. "So the way I see it . . . Thanksgiving on its way and all . . ."

Hank waited until the man's voice trailed to a stop. "Okay, John," he said evenly. "I reckon we can get by. You go ahead an' tie one on."

John was stung by this for a moment, then nodded and reached for the gear. "I might do just that." Joe Ben climbed into the carrier and started the motor, wondering at Hank's noncommittal acceptance of John's desertion. Why hadn't he pushed John more? They needed every man they could get, and Hank could have put a lot more squeeze on than that . . . how come he didn't? On the drive back down Joe opened his mouth a number of times to ask something about it, something funny to take the gloom off, but always stopped when he realized he couldn't think of a funny thing at all.

After supper Viv wanted to phone Orland and his family to ask how they felt. From behind his newspaper Hank said, "I guess not, Viv. I guess we'll find out in good time."

"But I think we should find out *now*, Hank, in case . . ."

"I don't believe we better call," he said. "That Asia flu is damned contagious; we wouldn't want to pick up somethin' over the phone from Orland."

He gave a short laugh and went back to his paper. Viv wasn't ready to drop it. "Hank. Honey, we should *know*. There's the kids, and Janice. And Lee had that temperature last night and tonight he had to lie right down after supper, so I know he doesn't feel so good—"

"Lee still doesn't feel so good, huh? Along with Orland? And Big and Little Lou and the rest? Doggone, sounds like a epidemic."

She ignored his sarcasm. "And I think we should find out from Olivia what the symptoms are."

Joe was on the couch, helping Jan get the kids in pajamas. He watched Hank put down the paper. "You want to know what the symptoms are? Hell, *I* can tell you what they are: the symptoms are clear as glass. First, see, it rains. Then it gets a little chilly. Then it gets muddy and tough goin' on the hills. Then one morning you get to thinking how much nicer it'd be layin' in bed all day with your finger up your ass instead of goin' out in the goddam woods workin' yourself punchy! Those are the symptoms, if you want to know. In Orland's case I got a notion there's probably some special complications, like living next door to Floyd Evenwrite, but as far as just the *usual* symptoms go, you can't miss 'em."

"What about a temperature? Don't you think a three-degree fever means something?"

He laughed and picked up the paper again. "What I *think* don't means beans, so we'll just leave that out. I mean I could *think* all sorts of stuff; in the Marines I used to think maybe the guys who got put on sick call by rubbin' a thermometer on their pant leg wasn't so sick as they'd like you to believe, but I couldn't be sure of that. So let's just forget what I think and I'll tell you what I *know*. I know we ain't calling Orland; I know I'm going up to the bedroom to finish the paper if you think I can make it without *catching* something in the drafty hall; and then I know—shit, never mind." He rolled his paper into a tight club and started for the door; at the stairwell he stopped and turned and pointed it back at the table. "I know this too: I'm going to finish out that last boom, it don't matter if I come down with flu from every country in the world. And if Orland or Lou calls, you can tell them that!"

He whapped the paper against his thigh and turned to tromp on up the steps. From the couch Joe listened to the stockinged feet striking the floor overhead, loud as old Henry's cast and just as hard-sounding. And didn't he sound plenty hard just now, tellin' us what to say to Orland? You bet he did. . . .

But, just as Joe knew that those feet banging around upstairs were bare, for all their hard and booted sound, he knew that there was something bare about Hank's hard talking too. Something naked-sounding about the voice . . . Joe frowned for a moment, searching for a way to explain the sound to himself; a slight cough from upstairs gave him the chance: Not naked, he insisted to himself in an attempt to find peace with his worry . . . no, not naked, *raw!* Throat all raw. Cold, that's what made him sound like he did. Raw. Yeah. Have to see that he takes care of that bad throat, I will. . . .

Upstairs, Hank's attempt to find some kind of peace didn't meet with much luck. First off, the sports page had been left downstairs. (*The kid is down there.* . . .) Then there wasn't enough hot water left from dishes to take a decent shower. Then those damn geese were out there again so thick and heavy and hullabalooing that I found myself wishing to beat heaven that Joe Ben'd not only laid into that one lone honker when he had the chance earlier but into every other goddam goose that had come over since! Then, to top it all off good, those mothering phone calls started up again. They was worse than the geese. At least the geese didn't insist you get out of bed and walk all the way downstairs to say hello, like the phone-callers did. I tried to get Lee to handle some of the calls for me, seeing that he was downstairs anyhow, but he claimed he wasn't feeling up to it (*he's lying on the couch, sucking that damn thermometer*); Joe was more than willing to answer a few for me but I told him it was a shame but he didn't have the knack for such chitchat. (*After about the third trip down I ask the kid if he can't see his way clear to let me have the couch so I could be near the phone. He says yes and starts upstairs.*) Joe wanted to know what that knack was we had that he didn't, and Lee stopped on the steps and told him it was the ability to be nice to somebody at the same time you're cutting their throat. "You're one of the few people left without the ability, Joe," Lee told him. "Be proud of the lack. Don't force such rare innocence into extinction any quicker than necessary."

"What?" Joe said, looking over at me.

"He means you're a poor liar, Joby," I told him. "Not many of you left. It's almost as good as bein' 'incorrigible.'"

"Oh," he said, then, "*oh!* Well, in that case"—he swelled up his chest—"I reckon I *should* be proud."

"If not proud," Lee said, "at least thankful"—and headed on upstairs (*Viv comes in from the kitchen, drying her hands. She asks where Lee went with the thermometer. I tell her upstairs . . . and she goes on up after him*), leaving Joby standing there pleased as a frog eating fire.

By the time the calls slacked off everybody was in bed but me and the old man (*Viv doesn't come back down. They're up there together. I can hear Lee's voice reading that goofy poetry . . .*); the old man was asleep in his chair by the stove and every time the phone'd ring he'd jump like he'd been goosed. (*She calls down that she's going on to bed. I say okay, an' what about the kid? She says he's already in bed, feeling pretty rocky. I say okay, I'll be up after while.*) Finally the ringing got too much for Henry and he hauled himself on up to his room and left me there to chew the fat with all the folks phoning to let me know what a *boon* I was to the community and what an *inspiration* I was to the impressionable young kids, and that sort of thing. Gradually the calls got farther apart, and the geese let up a little, and I dozed off. I must've slept an hour or so, dead to the world, then the next thing I was over at the phone table in a kind of stupor like I'd been bopped a good one or something. All I knew was that I was sweated clean through my clothes from sleeping so near the stove, and my eyes was burning and my head ringing and I was jerking the phone out of the wall.

I didn't know for sure what it was had woke me, or set my ears to whanging. When you doze off someplace strange, not expecting to, it takes a second to get straight. Especially if you been sleeping too warm. But it seemed it was more than just that. It seemed like I'd got a call from somebody. Something real screwy. But I wasn't sure, not till the next night, actually sure whether I'd heard that call or dreamed it or what.

I carried the phone back to the couch with me and sat down and shut my eyes (*There's still a light on upstairs*), trying to remember if somebody'd called and what he'd said (*What time is it?*), but it seemed like the words just blew in and out of my head like pieces of torn newspaper. (*The light's coming from Viv's room it looks like*) I wasn't able to get a thing straight; I was just too goofy-feeling and wrung out to know if I'd got a call.

I stood up to go up to bed and looked down at the phone. "Well, by god, there's one thing I know," I told myself, while I wound the wire around the phone and put it on the TV set on my way to the stairs. "That is if I get any more calls I'd be pretty damned sure they come from too long without sleep and too many nights with geese, not from the goddam telephone."

(*She's in bed but she's left the light on in that room of hers. I go down. That heater is going too. I go in and flick the heater off and start to turn off the light. Then I see that thermometer; it's sitting right beside that poetry book he reads out of. Up on the sewing-machine case. Right near the edge. I bump the case and the thermometer rolls off. It hits the floor sparkling like a icicle hitting a rock. I sweep the sparks under her cot with my foot; then I turn out the light and go on down to bed.*) "I have seen things, Peters, I have seen a few things . . ."

. . . Lee went on to write in his ledger:

And, while I have only had uncertain glimpses at the iron man's rusty moments, they are glimpses that you would consider quite convincing if you could have seen them yourself. For example, the tremendous significance behind an act such as the deliberate destruction of an innocent little thermometer . . .'

I stopped writing, once more struck with the near-impossibility of communicating a scene so complex with a pencil so short. Too much went to make up the situation, both above and under the surface, too much to circumvent in a letter.

Watching Hank through the hole and seeing him break that thermometer had come very close to pushing me to my final stroke. The morning after, when the old man's wake-up war-whoop knocked me from sleep, I awoke still trying to decide. Everything awaited my go-ahead. The scene with the thermometer proved this. So I tried a few practice coughs, and was checking down into my poor fevered frame to see if I was anywhere near well enough to have the energy to fake illness, when Joe Ben came bouncing in to try to coax me from bed by promising me an easy day of work. "Just burning today, Leland," he announced, "no more cutting, no more cable-pulling, no more choker-setting. Just lighting a few little fires is the all of it! Come on up. . . ."

I groaned and closed my eyes to try to shut out my tormentor, but Joe was never one to give up easily.

"It's just woman's work, Lee boy, just old woman's work!" He pranced about the bed in his heavy wool socks and canvas trousers. "Nothing to it a-tall! You'll probably even find it interesting. Listen. We doze up the ol' slashin' in a pile. We squirt it with coal oil. We light it on fire. We sit around chewing the fat and toasting marshmallows. What could be easier?"

I opened one doubting eye. "If it's all that easy one might think you two heroes could manage it alone without half trying. And let me sleep, please, Joe. I'm dying. I'm riddled with viruses. Look"—I ran out my tongue for Joe Ben to examine—"thith look like I care about marthmellowth?"

Joe Ben took my tongue daintily between thumb and forefinger and leaned close. "My, would you look at the tongue on this animal," he marveled. "Looks like he's been eating chalk. Hm, well . . ." Joe Ben turned toward the door. Hank had come up silently to stand looking in. "What you think, Hankus? Lee maintains he's suffering bad and wonders why we don't burn the job trash without him? We could probably handle it, me and you and Andy. We won't have nothin' to do but clean up. We won't be able to get any cuttin' done up river today nohow. We could leave the boy here to gather his resources for . . . we could, ah . . ."

Joe Ben ceased abruptly, it was as though he'd just seen something invisible to our less sensitive eyes. He blinked rapidly, took another quick look at Hank leaning against the doorjamb nonchalantly paring his fingernails with a pocketknife, then looked back at me. Then he seemed to come to some decision and suddenly reached out and snatched off my blankets.

"But then again," he reflected, "on *second* hand we can't have you *sufferin'* cooped up here in this room all day long. It'd hang you up. You'd get the wearies. Tell you what, Leland. You come along with us just for *moral* support, and just sit around and watch; what do you say? Oh yeah, that don't need a healthy tongue, just watching. So *up! up!* We can't leave you to waste away. 'Rejoice in thy youth, an' let thy heart cheer thee in the days of thy youth,' or something like that." He thrust a handful of clothes at me. "Let's go. We'll get the boat warmed up for you. Hank, tell Viv to butter him up some toast. We'll make it. Yeah. We're all in God's great pocket."

While I finished breakfast, Hank waited silently at the kitchen window, looking out through a hole he had rubbed in the steamed glass; the condensed beads of water gathered and ran in a slow-motion parody of the rain's fervid pattern on the other side of the pane. The kitchen was hot and silent except for those tiny rain sounds: the monotonous drumming on the porch roof, the sluggish gushing as the downspout flushed into the worn ditch that ran down to the bank, the endless reiteration of rain spattering against the window . . . all sounds that served to sink one into that state of drowsy fascination that Oregonians label "tranquilitis" or that Joe Ben titled more graphically "standin' an' starin'." I finished eating but I didn't move, nor did Hank notice. So lost was he in his thoughts that he might not have moved for another twenty minutes if he hadn't been startled awake by the shiny rubber apparition of old Henry carrying a lantern from the barn. Hank stepped backward from the windows, yawning. "Okeydoke," he announced, "let's move it." He went striding into the hall, calling up the dark stairwell. "Get my shotgun too today, will you, Joby?" He took a poncho from the nail. "And better wrap a plastic laundry sack or somethin' around them." He came back into the kitchen and picked up his calk boots from beside his chair and gulped the last cold inch of his coffee. He started again for the hall, passing without looking at me. "Hurry the grub, bub. Let's get the show on the road."

"Let him finish his breakfast," Viv said brightly. "He's a growing boy."

"He get up with the rest of us, he'd have time for three breakfasts." He picked up his lunch sack and went again into the hall, where he sat down on the bench to lace on his boots.

The screen of the back porch squeaked and through the window of the kitchen door I could see the old man in his glistening rubber garment, looking like a creature left over from a black-lagoon movie, doing his outlandish utmost to drag a muddy nylon parachute in out of the rain. I watched this unusual struggle with interest and curiosity but little sense of involvement: that one of the inhabitants of this den had need of a parachute was of only the barest concern to me, and that it was important for this parachute to be in out of the elements I never for a moment doubted, but neither did I feel the slightest obligation to go out and give the old man a hand with the battle. So I did not move. I was really feeling too ill to want to move.

But when I heard a thud of boots behind me and another call to "get the show on the road," I began to stir; for, while I felt no more obligation to help get the show on the road than to help get the parachute on the porch, I knew I couldn't in this case be faithful to my sluggish disinvolvement; it was necessary in this case not to appear too sick; at least not so sick as I felt. The necessity of presenting this image of false illness put me in something of an ironic bind. Because while everyone thought my complaints fake and my ills fraudulent—like the mysterious virus maladies of the other relatives who had phoned in nightly since the meeting to advise us they could not help on the job because they were dropping like flies—I was, in truth, so sore I could barely move and so sick I could barely fake it. My only recourse was overacting. So I moaned dolorously at Hank's call, rubbing my sinuses with one hand, my back with the other. "Well," I sighed, "another day, another dullard."

"Do you feel better?" Viv asked.

"I feel like my entire cerebrum has become waterlogged." I stood up slowly, shaking my head from side to side. "Hear it? Slosh, slosh, slosh."

She moved close, watching the hallway door. "I told him," she confided in a whisper, "that he was out of his mind taking you back up there today. You had almost a three-degree temperature last night before you went upstairs, a hundred and one point four. I'd take it again this morning but the thermometer's missing."

"A hundred and two . . . Is that all?" I grinned at her. "What a paltry score. I'll hit a hundred and three tonight or hang up my togs. Look out the window, there; perfect day to set a record. So have the thermometer ready"—at the same time making a mental note to be sure in the future to keep a more careful watch on the mercury. Three degrees is a bit high to be a good malingering temperature. I couldn't have her thinking I was truly in a faulty physical condition.

Conditions of that physical nature can be cured with pills and penicillin and other chemical curatives, whereas areas correspondingly
faulty but definitely *non-physical* responded only to the medication
of love.

"Let's make it," Hank's voice called from the doorway. I limped
out of the kitchen with every cell in my body screaming a protest at
the misery that lay ahead. Not much longer, I kept reassuring myself;
if I can last another day or two I'll be forever finished with the whole
excruciating nightmare. . . .

In spite of Joe's efforts, the trip to the job seemed even more
silent than the day before. Andy was alone at the mill again; this
time Hank didn't ask about the others and Andy looked relieved that
he had been spared answering. When they reached the job nothing
was said to Lee about helping. He remained in the carrier at the
base of the spar, appearing to fall asleep immediately, with his arms
crossed and tucked in the folds of the mackinaw he wore, and his
chin pushed deep into the sheepskin collar. When Hank returned
from the top of the spar, where he had been unsnapping the rigging
cables, he noticed that the crack in the rear door had been chinked
with a piece of burlap and the windows of the carrier were fogged
with breathing.

Andy swarmed the small tractor over the hills, between rocks
and stumps, pushing the bark and branches and deadwood into piles.
The machine hurried back and forth through the dingy rain with
its little loads rolling and cracking ahead of it, looking like a big yellow crab busy tidying up the floor of its undersea home. Joe Ben followed after the tractor with a forest-fire fighter's tank filled with a
mixture of gasoline and oil and sprayed a dirty stream into the piles
of rubbish, then set the piles afire. He went about his work with
fervor, panting, sweating, running from pile to pile as he saw a fire
about to flicker out beneath the rain; a comic fireman engaged in a
life-or-death battle with perverse blazes which not only defied his
attempts to extinguish them, but roared their defiance in the face
of his puny hose. His face was blackened and rutted with sweat and
rain under the brim of his rainhat. The scars appeared to have all
shifted into a vertical order. And with his back humped to the
weight of the tank he looked like a troll or gnome of the woods.

Hank worked with the machinery, securing the yarder and donkey
by packing all the open parts in grease and tying canvas over the
engines. When he finished he loaded one of the olive-drab fire-fight-

ing tanks with oil and gasoline from the big drum resting in the mud beside the yarder, strapped the tank to his back, and went to help Joe.

By midday a dozen fires screwed thin black columns of smoke into the rain. Over the warbling sputter of the cat motor there was a sound like a wind through the branches of a forest no longer there; a phantom wind, blowing through the ghosts of the trees that had stood on these slopes; this was the sound of the rain steaming in the fires. When one of the fires seemed to have burned out, Andy rooted it over with the blade of his cat, and it burned again, and when the fire died down again he spread it until the ashes were scattered smoldering and hissing among the stumps.

They worked past lunchtime, partly because by the time it was noon they saw that they could finish the job in another few hours— "Let's just keep at 'er, Joby, whatya say?"—and partly because Hank made no move toward the spar where the carrier sat holding their lunch buckets behind steamed windows. When the clean-up was finished they all stopped at once, without a signal or word, as men stop at the end of of a baseball game. Andy switched off the cat, and the motor gave a short, baffled gasp, turned over a few more times, and gasped again, unable to believe its day was finished so early. It finally stopped, to stand inert and patient, and in the after silence the little hissing burst of the raindrops steaming on the motor seemed far louder than the detonations the cylinders had made. Andy remained motionless on the seat, staring out through that steaming. Across a canyon Hank and Joe Ben stood next to each other on the rise opposite the spar, the tanks still strapped to their backs. Joe looked thoughtfully down at the land they had opened to the sky to see if things had been improved or not.

The hills were dark and torn. The fires still hissed, but the rain was beginning to get the top hand, beating the coals into the reddish-brown mud. The stumps stood arranged in stark, surprisingly ordered patterns now that the vine and slashing that had concealed these patterns was burned away. Joe Ben followed the pointing smoke finger of one fire to the sky. "Y'know . . . it might be letting up, do you reckon?"

"I reckon we may as well give up dreaming it's gonna let up," Hank said, "and get to fixing that donkey."

"Now what we need to fix that donkey for?" Joe wanted to know. "We can't use it on this next job."

"We'll need it fixed so it can pull itself up on the truck, won't we?"

"I suppose, yeah . . . But why we so pressed to get it fixed now for?"

"Why not?"

"Be dark in a little bit." Joe listed one reason.

"We can use the drop light. We won't need Andy, I reckon. I'll tell him to snooze in the carrier with Lee if he wants."

Joe sighed, resigning himself to hunger and cold. They fell quiet, looking out across the hacked landscape. "Always puts me in mind of a graveyard," Joe Ben observed after a time. "You know, tombstones? Here lies so an' so, here lies Douglas Fir, Born the Year One, Chopped Down the Year Nineteen Sixty-One. Here Lies Ponderosa Pine. Here Lies Blue Spruce." He sighed again with poignant remorse. "Ever since I can recollect, it's brought that thought to mind."

Hank nodded a halfhearted agreement, but Joe noticed that his attention was directed more toward that crummy wagon uphill than than the stump field down the gully. "Look over yonder at Andy." Joe pointed the nozzle toward the dark figure seated motionless on the tractor. "I bet he's thinking the same thing, looking out at a logged-off show. Thinking, 'How Them Mighty Are Fallen.' "

Hank nodded once more and began working the tank from his shoulders, still not taking part enough in the discussion to satisfy Joe.

"Still . . . I suppose that's one of the things that keeps men knocking their brains out at this profession," Joe supposed in a serious tone.

"How's that? Turning forests into cemeteries?"

"No. Seein' 'How Them Mighty Are Fallen.' Didn't you ever note how a fellow, I don't care how long he's been at it, will stop what he's at whether he's peein' or pullin' cable, to turn and watch and see a tree come falling down?"

"You better believe it. That's how he keeps drawin' air. His life depends on him keeping one eye peeled."

"Oh yeah, oh yeah, there's that. But even it's on a completely different *slope* he'll turn to watch. Even a half-mile off. Even he's on a clear hill with no trees even *close* to worry about, he'll always raise up to watch. Don't you? I always do. Even ol' Bottled in Bond John with a hangover that's splittin' him in half, whenever he hears somebody holler, 'Tree' or 'Down the hill' he'll raise clean up and turn clean around to look and he wouldn't do that some mornings if somebody yelled, 'Naked lady.' "

Hank slid the tank off and helped Joe Ben off with his. They carried their tanks by the canvas straps, walking down the hill in the direction of the donkey. Hank's long legs reeled smoothly out in front of him like ropes that stiffened at just the last moment to hold his weight; Joe Ben, taking two steps to Hank's one, followed down the hillside in a jerky, bowlegged skitter, lifting each foot quickly as though the mud were hot. He kept quiet, hoping Hank might be drawn into the talk of watching the mighty fall; it was the sort of rich ground that gave Joe possibilities to raise and crossbreed his own peculiar strain of parables. He waited, but Hank seemed off in thought. Joe tried again.

"Yes, by gosh . . . I think I have hit on something."

"Hit on something what?" Hank asked, amused by the profundity of Joe's tone.

"About people hot to see a tree felled. Oh yeah. I think there is something going there. There's a passage in the Book that says, 'The righteous shall flourish like the palm tree: he shall grow like a cedar of Lebanon.' That's Psalms, and I know I got that one right because I paid very special attention to it when Brother Walker talked on it. Because I thought what the everloving dickens is a cedar got to do with a palm? Besides, I don't remember any cedars around Lebanon, damn sure they's no palm trees. I thought a good while about it. That's why I'm sure of the line."

Hank waited in silence for Joe to cut in closer to his point.

"So anyhow, if we say that the righteous are like trees, an' say people do like to see trees felled, then it comes to people are hot to see the righteous felled!" He paused a moment to let the power of this logic sink in. "It follows right to a T. Think about it: somebody always tryin' to do a good man some dirt. Some Whore of Babylon is always hustling the Man of God, ain't that so?" As he warmed to his sermon his little blackened hands began jumping about in front of him and his eyes brightened. "Oh yeah. Oh man yeah! Wait till I pass this on to Brother Walker. It works right to the hair. Remember Rita Hayworth in that Sadie Thompson show? She was for falling that preacher's cedar tree even she had to gnaw down like a beaver. Same thing in Samson and Delilah. Sure. And even Brother Walker: remember three-four years back when that baloney was passing around about what does he do with those women who come to his house private to receive the Spirit? Shoot, he had to discontinue them prayer meetings, remember? The talk got so bad . . . not that Brother Walker wasn't maybe guilty of what was said—what the dickens, Spirit's Spirit, I always say, for whatever it takes to get it into you—but the point is them *women* weren't complainin', were they? No. Just the *people*, the people trying to fall the Tree of Righteousness. Oh yeah, oh *yeah!*" He hammered his thigh with a sooty fist, so pleased and enthusiastic about his remarkable analogy. "Don't you agree that's a lot to it? People likin' to watch the trees come down? That they is a natural hell-driven desire to see the righteous fallen?"

"I suppose," Hank agreed, with one eye blinking against the smoke of his cigarette.

Joe Ben thought he detected a slight lack of enthusiasm in that agreement. "Well, don't you?" he persisted. "I mean that people just *naturally* sinners at heart got to chop down the righteous to keep from *feeling* like sinners . . . now don't you?"

They had reached the bottom; a stream of coffee-colored water floated chunks of ash along the canyon. Hank wiped his hand on the belly of his sweat shirt and took his pack of cigarettes from his pocket. He offered one to Joe, but Joe declined, saying cigarettes were now lumped in with coffee as taboos at his church. Hank took a cigarette from the pack, lit it with the butt, and flipped the butt into that stream. "Joe," he said, "I don't know about a natural hell-driven desire, but I don't think people give a tinker's damn that a tree is righteous or not when they fall it. A man wouldn't walk across the street to watch you chop down a little pisspot cedar, I don't care if it was blessed by Brother Walker till it stunk of holiness."

He meant to let it go at that, but Joe's hurt silence demanded more.

"But them same people, they'd come for miles to see somebody chop down that tallest-tree-in-the-state up yonder in Astoria." He shifted the weight of the tank to his other hand and took a long, jumping step across the stream. "Nope"—he started up the slope toward the donkey—"it ain't the righteous, it ain't that," he said with finality. "Now; what do you say we get at that bastard of a donkey before it falls into a junk heap."

Joe Ben followed in silence. At first, he was merely disconsolate that such a prime subject had been done in so prematurely, but as he continued to think about Hank's statement while they worked on the donkey, his disconsolateness began to change, to a sort of perplexed anxiety, to that feeling quite close to panic that he had experienced earlier that morning at the house when he saw Hank's face looking through the door at Lee in bed. The two of them battled the inevitable decay of the piece of machinery in silence for a time, speaking only when they needed to call instructions or requests for tools to Andy, who sat up in the operator's seat; finally Joe could no longer contain his anxiety.

"*Choice* days ahead," he announced suddenly. "Oh yeah!" Then paused to wait for Hank's reaction. Hank was hunched over the capstain of the donkey as if he hadn't heard. "You bet!" Joe went on. "Little bit more of this an' we'll be on the shady side of easy street. We'll be—"

"Joby," Hank said softly, stopping work but not moving as he spoke into the greasy clutter of machinery. "Let me tell you something. I'm tired of it. Tired. And that's the God's truth."

"Of the rain? The breakdowns? Shoot yes, you're tired! You got every reason in the world—"

"No. You know I ain't talking about the rain or the breakdowns. Hell, we've *always* had rain and breakdowns and I'm *always* tired of that. . . ."

Joe Ben felt a little thing start running inside of him, slow at first then speeding up very fast—how? he wondered, how can you get tired?—like a lizard or a shrew or something, a little thing running around and around inside while he waited for Hank to go on.

"A guy gets fed up," Hank said. He had raised his head now and was looking up at the black crisscross of belts and cables of the donkey. "Fed up to his ears. Forever going down the street and hearing the locks snap shut in front of him like he was some kind of bogey man. Real *tired*, you know what I mean?"

"Sure," Joe said. He constricted his bowels to stop the scurrying, "but—"

"I mean, gets tired having people phone him about what a hard-nose he is."

"Sure, but . . ." He felt woozy, dizzied by the sound of Hank's words, the way he'd felt coming out of the ether in the doctor's office after they'd stitched up his face. ". . . Well, sure a man gets tired of it . . ." He shrugged: How *can* he? "But, well, you know . . ." When it was obvious to both of them that Joe was not going on, they bent back to work on the capstain.

After a while Hank stood up with a mashed finger. Grimacing, he looked at the red beginning to bead over the grease of his knuckle. (*The whole day up there . . .*) He looked about the wet ground for a rag and remembered the only rags were up in the crummy where Lee was (*He's spent the whole day sitting up in that outfit. I can't keep making him do that. Not just to keep him away from home),* then doubled his fist and pressed the cut into the blue-gray mud ridged up by the cat treads. (*Because there is bound to come a day . . .*)

Darkness fell fast while they waited for Andy to rig the light. (*I can't keep him away forever . . .*) The machinery became ominous and threatening in silhouette. The steel-ribbed yarder reared against the stiffening sky, thrusting its neck into the moiling twilight like a prehistoric creature. The cat tractor hunkered motionless in the mud, a patient, brute form watching them work. "I don't know," Hank said suddenly, stopping work. "Maybe we been kiddin' ourselves about it. Maybe we made the whole town mad at us for nothing. This rain ain't easin'; the spurs are washing out; we still got those last booms to finish. . . . An' even if we get 'em finished, with the weather like it is, an' no help, an' nobody in town willin' to rent us a tug . . . maybe we don't have a snowball's chance in hell driving them down river to the mill."

"Why, man?" Joe was aghast. "Why, listen to you!" His scratchy voice stood out sharp against the soft rain sounds. "Why, how can we miss? We been fat an' happy as babies up to now, ain't we? We can't miss! Now, let's get at this devil. . . ."

"I don't know." Hank stood, looking up toward the crummy. (*Just can't keep track of him all the time. Sooner or later I'm bound to be off someplace else. . . .*) and sucked at his finger. "A bit ago you was all for heading home . . ."

"Me? Leaving a job undone? That was somebody else. . . ."

Andy finally rigged the wires, and a light bloomed suddenly at the end of a black cord. He hung the light out over Hank and Joe Ben; it swung pendulously back and forth, provoking a terrific struggle of shadows on the granite outcropping behind the donkey. Joe blinked in its glare for a second—"and as far as the contract goes . . ." then flung himself to work on the machine, talking all the while. ". . . Oh, yeah, we just can't miss. Look, look at all the signals we got. Just look."

Hank removed his cigarette from his mouth and looked toward the knotty figure jabbering away as it worked; he was amused and a little puzzled by Joe's sudden intensity. "Look at what?" he asked.

"At the *signals!*" Joe declared without looking up from his work. "What about Evenwrite an' his bunch getting throwed in the drink when they tried to cut our booms? Or the big saw bustin' at the mill just when we needed the crew to help . . . yeah, I know they didn't last long, but the saw *did bust!* That you *got to* admit!—let me see that Allen wrench. If old Jesus wasn't on our side would he flung those birds in the water? Or broke that saw? Would he?" His voice rose as his theme developed. "*Oh*, I *tell ya*, the way I feel we just can *not* miss! We're in God's pocket and he's been breakin' his back to let us know it. We can't disappoint him. Man, look. *Look here!* See? I got that capstain to fit by gosh just like *that.* Try her out, Andy! Oh yeah, we'll get home an' get us some sleep and get up at that state park in the mornin' while it's still dark and log more board feet than anybody ever logged in one day before in *history!* Hank, I know! I know! I *feel* it like I never felt nothing else before in all my life! Because I—*whups*, hear that? Hear it? What did I tell you, purring like a kittycat—*leave it run*, Andy boy—because I mean on *top* of all those other signs and the like—*wait; swing the light closer so's we can get our tools up*, Andy—on top of those signs—an' I seen signs in my time, but nothing ever to hold a match to all we been getting—*on top* and *more important* . . . I been experiencin' a tremendous *power* building in me the last few days like I could just tear out those old firs up in that park and *toss* 'em to the river like *throwin' the javelin* . . . and I just *now* been able to figure out *why!*"

Hank stood out of the way, grinning, as he watched the little man hustle the tools together, like a squirrel gathering nuts. "Okay, why?"

"It's *because*"—Joe caught his breath—"like the book puts it: 'Whosoever shall say *unto* this mountain be thou removed into the sea an'—uh-uh, yeah—'an' *shall not doubt* that those things which he hath sayeth shall *come to pass*, why, man, that guy is gonna have just exactly what he sayeth!' Hey, boy; you didn't know I knew that one, I bet. Anyway, what I'm saying, is this *power* I been feeling is because I *don't doubt it!* See? See? An' *that's* why I know we can't miss. Dang! Quick; grab that hard hat of Andy's where it's blowin' away. . . ." He scrambled after the spinning aluminum hat and caught it before it hit the ground. He came panting back to where Hank stood grinning. "Hot dog and man alive," he exclaimed studying the swinging trees to cover the flush of embarrassment brought on by the open fondness of Hank's grin, "she is a windy one tonight, friend; oh yeah."

"Not as windy as some," Hank judged, telling himself that as winds and friends went, all in all, a man could do a whole lot worse than old Joby and the storms he blew. A whole hell of a lot worse. Because even when he was as obvious as a forty-mile-an-hour gale you still couldn't help wanting to go along with him. Most people, when they tried to cheer you up, didn't make fools out of themselves; they could be a lot more subtle about it than Joe could with his prancing and hollering, but they couldn't be nearly as successful. I think this was because he *didn't* try to be subtle; he didn't care if he made a fool out of himself, just so long as he made you happy with the fool. And as we hurried around, buttoning up the show for the night, I was so tickled at him working to improve my mood that I clean forgot for a while what'd caused the mood in the first place. Right up to when we headed up to the crummy I couldn't remember (*He's sitting there awake; I tell him to scoot over . . .*); then I heard a flock of geese off down country and toward the town and I remembered just exactly what was bugging me (*I ask him what he'd been doin' to pass the day. He says writing. I ask if it was more poetry and he looks at me like he doesn't have the vaguest inkling what I'm talking about*), because hearing them geese is just like the phone ringing; even with the wire tore out it's still the same yammering, the same crazy pestering and wheedling, even if I can't make out the words. And hearing the geese, and thinking about the phone wire being tore out . . . that screwy phone call from the night before finally came back to me. It had been dangling just out of my memory's line of vision ever since last night, like one of those dreams when you can remember the *feeling* but not the dream.

I started the crummy and headed off to the boat at the bottom of the hill, trying to get the memory straight. The whole conversation started coming back to me, clear as a bell; I *still* wasn't sure right then whether it had really happened or was just a dream, but, real or a dream, I could remember it damn near word for word.

It was from Willard Eggleston, the little gink who used to run the laundry. He was all keyed up and excited and so screwy-sounding I thought at first he was actually drunk. I was still about nine-tenths asleep and he was trying to tell me some story about him and the colored girl that used to work for him, and about their child—this was what made me think he was drunk—about the *child* the two of them had had. I just listened for a while, polite, like I did with the other calls, but after he rambled on long enough I began to see this wasn't *like* the others; I began to see he wasn't just calling to give me a hard time, that there was something else on his mind behind all of his rambling and roaming talk. I let him go on; pretty soon he drew a long breath and said, "That's the story, Mr. Stamper; just like it happened. Every bit the truth, I don't care what you think." I said, "All right, Willard, I'll go along with you, but—" "Every word of it the Lord's pure truth. I know, I *personally* know, so I don't care if you go along with me or not—" "All right, all right; but you had more on your mind when you called than telling me how proud you are to be able to sire yourself a pickaninny—" "A boy, Mr. Stamper, a *son!* and not just *sire* him; I was able to pay for his way in the world like a man should for his son—" "Okay, have it your way: a *son*, but—" "—until you went and made it impossible for a fellow to make profit enough to pay for the overhead—" "I might hafta be *showed* just exactly how I did that, Willard, but for the sake of argument—" "You've all but bankrupted the *whole town*; do you need to be showed that?" "All I need is just for you to get on around to what you had on your mind when—" "I'm doing exactly that, Mr. Stamper—" "—because there's a lot of other anonymous callers these days waitin' their turn at me; I don't want to tie up the line too long with one when so many—" "I am not anonymous, Mr. Stamper; I want you to be sure of that; this is Eggleston, Willard—" "Eggleston; all right, Willard, now just what is it you had to tell me—other'n your secret loves—at, ah, twelve-twenty-two in the morning?" "Just this, Mr. Stamper: I'm on my way this very moment to kill myself. Ah? No wise comment? This wasn't what you expected, I'll bet? Not from Willard Eggleston, I'll bet? But it's as true as I'm standing here. You'll see. No, don't try to stop me. And don't try to phone the police, because they couldn't reach the place before I do anyway, and if you phoned they would know I phoned you, wouldn't they? And that I phoned to tell you it was your fault that I was forced into—" "Forced? Willard, now listen—" "Yes, *forced*, Mr. Stamper. You see, I have a very large policy with double indemnity in case of violent death, naming as beneficiary my son. Of course, until he's twenty-one it will—" "Willard, those companies don't pay on suicide!" "That's why I can't have you telling anyone, Mr. Stamper. You see now? I am dying for my son. I've arranged everything to look like an accident. But if you were to—" "Willard, you know what I think?" "—to *tell* anyone about this phone call then I would have died in vain, wouldn't that be true? And your guilt would then be doubled—" "I think that you been seeing too many of your own movies." "No, Mr. Stamper! You wait! I know you people think that I'm totally without courage, that I'm just 'that spineless Willard Eggleston.' But you'll see. Oh yes. And don't bother trying to stop me, my mind is made up." "I ain't trying to stop you from anything, Willard." "You'll see *tomorrow*; oh yes, you'll see what kind of spine—" "I ain't trying to stop anybody from anything, but you know, that looks to me like a pretty poor excuse for spine as far as I'm concerned—" "It's no use trying to talk me out of it." "What I'd call a man with spine is a man able to pay for his kid by *living* for him, no matter how hard it comes—" "I'm sorry, sorry, but you're just wasting your breath." "—not by dying for him. That's a lot of crap, Willard, dying for somebody." "Just whistling at the wind, Mr. Stamper." "That's the one thing that everybody in the world can do, ain't it, Willard? is die . . . living is the hassle." "No use, Mr. Stamper, not the slightest. I've made my decision." "Well, good luck, then, Willard. . . ." "There's no way anyone can—what" "I said 'Good luck.'" "Good luck? Good luck? Then you don't believe I'm going to do it!" "Yeah . . . I think I do; I think I probably do. But I'm tired, and not thinking too sharp, and 'good luck' is about the best I can offer." "The best you can offer? Good luck? To someone who—" "Christ almighty, Willard; you want me to read you a page of scripture or something? 'Good luck' seems as good as anything in your case; it's better than 'Have fun.' Or 'Bon voyage.' Or 'Sweet dreams.' Or just plain old 'Good-by.' Let's leave it like that, Willard: Good luck, and I'll toss in the good-by for good measure . . . okeydoke?" "But I haven't—" "I got to try to get some sleep, Willard. So, with all my heart, good luck—" "—completely finished telling—" "—and good-by."

"Stamper!" Willard hears the phone buzz in his ear. "Wait, please. . . ." He stands in the booth, surrounded by his three dimly lit reflections, listening to that electric hum. This isn't the way he planned it; not at all. He wonders if he should call back, make the man understand! But he knows calling back won't do any good because the man obviously does believe his story, whether he understands completely or not. Yes. There is every indication that he believes him. But . . . no evidence at all that he was concerned; not even the *slightest!*

Willard returns the receiver back to its black cradle. The phone thanks him for his dime with a polite clatter as it drops the coin from the points into the box. Willard stares at the phone for a long time, not thinking of anything at all; until his breathing fogs the images from the glass walls and his feet and calves go to sleep.

Back in his car he starts the motor and turns up Necanicum Street toward the coastal highway, driving slowly through the twisting rain. The enthusiasm he felt at his house is all but gone. The anticipation dampened, the adventure of the night blunted. By that man's cruel indifference. How could the devil not care? How could he have the heart to not care even the slightest? How could he have the *right!*

He reaches the highway and turns north, traveling along the edge of the dunes in a gradual rise toward the palisades where the Wakonda lighthouse stirs the thickening sky. The muffled cadence of the surf to his left annoys him and he turns on the radio to drown it out, but it is too late to pick up local stations and the terrain is becoming too hilly to pick up Eugene or Portland; he switches it off. He continues to rise, following the flicker of white guardposts that line the cliff side of the highway; he is too high now to hear the surf, but a feeling of annoyance continues to nag at him. . . . That Hank Stamper and his talk about spine; what kind of way is that for a man to react to such a desperate phone call, just brushing it off with a good luck and good-by? . . . What gave him the *right?*

By the time he reaches the stone-fenced view point near the top his chin is quivering, and by the time he is approaching the turn the hot-rod crowd calls Bustass Curve, his whole body is quaking with grim outrage. He drives on past the turn. He has half a mind to go back and make another call, by golly! Even if the man doesn't understand completely, he has no right to be so heartless. Not when he is so much to *blame!* him and the rest of that bunch. No! No, he certainly does not!

Willard pulls into the drive that leads off to the lighthouse, and backs out, turning around. Fuming with indignation, he heads back toward town. No, by golly; no right! Hank Stamper is no better than anybody else! I have every bit as much spine as he does! And I will prove it! To him! And Jelly! And everybody! Yes I will! And I'll do everything possible to help drag him off his high horse! Yes I will! I promise, I *swear* I will . . .

And, hissing down from the palisades along the wet, winding pavement, swollen with anger and determination and life, Willard goes into a slide on the very turn he had picked weeks before, and unintentionally keeps both his appointment and his promise. . . .

"Oh . . . heard tell over the news, I did . . . you recollect that puny little drink of water owned the laundry till he took over the picture show a year or so back? Willard Eggleston? Well sir, they scraped his carcass offn the rocks out by Wakonda Head this mornin'. Slammed through the guard rail, he did, sometime last night."

The old man followed this piece of information with a loud belch and returned to the less spectacular gossip about the townspeople's trials and tribulations. He hadn't expected any of us to pay the news much attention; the man was too vague an entity to concern any of us. Even Joe, who usually could be counted on for elaboration about any of the local citizenry, admitted that he knew about as much about the unfortunate carcass as I did: that the little man sold tickets to the movies and had displayed about as much life as did an arcade fortune-telling dummy in his little glass case. Nobody knew much about him. . . .

Yet the news of this lifeless thing's death doubled Brother Hank over like a cannonball to the stomach, producing sudden coughing and a sheet-white face.

Joe's immediate diagnosis was "Bone in the throat! Bone stuck in the throat!" and he was out of the chair like a shot and banging away at Hank's back before any of the rest of us even had time to suggest a cure. The old man's opinion was "Leave off poundin' on him, for god's sake . . . all he's doin' is gettin' set to sneeze"—and he held his snuff can in front of Hank's mouth as though the snuff might coax the reluctant sneeze forth with its aroma. Hank pushed both Joe and the can away.

"Damn!" he declared. "I'm not trying to choke or sneeze, neither one! I'm all right. I just had a tinge in my back is all, but Joe beat it to death."

"Are you sure you're all right?" Viv asked. "What do you mean, a tinge?"

"Yes, I'm sure." He insisted he was perfectly all right and, much to my disappointment, neglected to answer her second question (I would have enjoyed knowing what a "tinge" was myself), choosing instead to get up from the table and stride across to the refrigerator. "Don't we have a can of cold beer on the place?"

"Don't have a can of no kind of beer." The old man shook his head. "Not beer, wine, nor whisky, an' I'm drastic low on snuff, by god, if you want to hear some *real* tragic news."

"What's the matter? I thought we had a standin' order at Stokes's?"

"I guess you ain't heard," Jan said. "Henry's old friend Stokes has cut us off. Stopped delivery."

"Friend? That ol' spook? Shoot, I ain't no more friend to that—"

"Stopped delivery? How come?"

"He said it was because there wasn't any other stops out this way for his delivery truck to make," Jan answered from beneath her eyelids. "But the real reason is—"

Hank slammed the refrigerator door. "Yeah; his *real* reason is . . ." He picked up the clock from the stove and looked at it; everyone waited for him to go on; even the kids had stoped eating and were exchanging the scared glances kids exchange when the *big folks is actin'* funny. But Hank decided not to go into real reasons: "I think I'll go on up and hit the sack," he said, putting the clock back.

"An' miss *Wells Fargo?*" Squeaky asked incredulously, lifting an eyebrow. "You don't ever miss *Wells Fargo*, Hank."

"Dale Robertson'll have to handle *Wells Fargo* without me tonight, Squeaks."

The little girl pursed her lips and lifted both eyebrows at that; oh boy, the big folks was *really* actin' funny tonight.

Before he left the kitchen Viv hurried across to feel his forehead, but he said all he needed was a decent night's little sleep without phone calls, not a head rub, and clumped on up the stairs in his boots. Viv looked after him, worried and wordless.

And her worry and wordlessness worried me. Especially the wordlessness, in view of Hank's footwear: it was as unusual for cork boots to pass the first step without Viv's calling out, "Boots," as it was for Dale Robertson to ride the *Wells Fargo* stage without Hank sitting glued to the TV set with Squeaky on his lap. I couldn't understand my brother's funny actin' any more than Squeaky could (I did know, however, that it was no more brought on by a mere lack of sleep than by bone in the throat; his reaction to the theater-owner's death was so classic a reaction to bad news that he might have taught Macduff a thing or two) but I was very quick to pick up on Viv's concern.

"He's more a man than I am," I said with grudging good nature, "because I certainly could use a head rub."

She seemed not to hear.

"Yes. I admire the man his health. . . ." I stood up, groaning. "He was able to make it up those stairs, at least."

"You going up to bed too, Lee?" she asked, turning at last to me.

"Going to attempt it. Everybody wish me luck."

She was looking back at the stairwell again. "I'll drop around to your room in a bit," she said absently, and added, "I wish I could find that thermometer."

So, with mysterious WATCH OUT still echoing in my head, I vowed that the time had come. Tomorrow was V-day, without fail. And if I could not understand the qualms I felt, I could nevertheless still understand that a dilution of Viv's concern was in the offing unless I moved quickly. I could still understand that if one is to alter iron at all he'd best strike while that iron is still hot. I didn't need a thermometer for that. . . .

The old house is noisy even without television. The children talk in whispers, and the rain outside seems to whisper back, but the geese call full-throated and brazen as Hank lies listening. . . . (*I don't even bring a paper to read. I just hop right in the sack. I'm about asleep when I hear the kid come up and go on down to his room. He's coughing a little, sounds about as real as the cough Boney Stokes been putting on thirty years. I listen to see if anybody else comes up, but there's a flock goes so loud I can't hear. Thousands and thousands and thousands. Flying round and round and round the house. Thousands and thousands and thousands. Banging against the roof, crashing through the walls till the house is full of them gray feathers beaks at my ear hard and hollering at me beating chest and neck and face hard whacking wings of thousands and thousands louder than—*)

I woke up, feeling like something was haywire. The house was dark and quiet and at the foot of the bed the glow-dial clock said it was about half past one. I laid there, trying to figure what had woke me. The wind was blowing outside, crashing rain against the window so hard it sounded every once in a while like that old river out there was rising up in the dark and striking at the house like a big swaying snake of water. But that wasn't what woke me; if I was woke up by every little wind kicking against the window I would of died of exhaustion years ago.

Looking back, it's easy to figure what it was: the geese had all shut up. There wasn't a sound, not a hoot nor a honk. And the hole left in the night by their honking was like a big roaring vacuum; enough to wake anybody. But at the time I didn't realize that. . . .

I slid out of bed, taking it real easy to keep from waking Viv, and I got hold of the six-cell light I keep in the room. The way the weather was carrying on out there I decided I maybe ought to have a look at the foundation, seeing as I hadn't checked before going to bed. I walked over to the window and put my face up near the glass and shined the light off in the direction of the bank. I don't know why. Laziness, I reckon. Because I knew that even on a clear day it was next to impossible to see the foundation from that window on account of the hedge. But I reckon I was just punchy enough to hope this time it would be different and I would see the bank and it would be fine. . . .

Out past the glass there seemed to be nothing but rain being whipped around in long filmy sheets, like the banners of the wind. I was just standing there, stroking the beam of that light back and forth, still about half sacked-out, when all of a sudden I see out yonder a face! A *human* face! floating out there on the rain, wide-eyed, wild-haired, with a mouth twisted in horror like a thing been trapped outside in the storm for *centuries!*

I don't know how long I stared at it—maybe five seconds or five minutes—before I gave a yell and jumped back from the window. And saw the face mimic my actions. Oh! Oh for chrissakes . . . It's just a *reflection*, nothing but a reflection. . . .

But so help me god, it was about the wildest thing I ever had happen to me; the worst scare I ever had in my life. Worse than in Korea. Worse even than the time I seen the tree falling at me and I tripped right underneath it and fell next to a stump and the tree hit that stump like a two-ton maul driving a stake; the stump was pounded a good six inches into the ground but it protected me so I didn't suffer no more than the loss of my breakfast. That particular incident shook me so bad I laid there without moving for a good ten minutes, but I tell you so help me *god*, that wasn't nowhere near the scare I got from that reflection.

I heard Viv hustle around behind me. "What is it, honey?"

"Nothing," I told her. "Nothing. I just thought for a minute there the *bogey* man was after me." I laughed a little. "Thought the old boy had come for my ass at last. I looked out the window to check the foundation, and there the sonofabitch was, face looking like death warmed over." I laughed again, and finally turned from the window and walked to sit on the edge of the bed beside her. "Yessiree, a regular fiend in the night. See him yonder?"

I shined the light up toward my face again so's Viv could see the reflection for herself, and made a face at her in the window. We both laughed, and she reached out to take my arm and hold it against her cheek, the way she used to do when she was pregnant.

"You were tossing and turning so; did you finally get to sleep?"

"Yeah. I guess them geese finally give up tryin' to get in."

"What woke you, the storm?"

"Yeah. The rain woke me, I imagine. The wind. She's walkin' and talkin' out there tonight. Dang. I bet that river's comin' up, too. Well, you know what that means . . ."

"You're not going down to *check*, are you? It's not that bad. It's just blowing a lot. It couldn't have come up so much since you checked after supper."

"Yeah . . . except I *didn't* check tonight after supper, remember? I had a bone in my throat."

"But it was all right when you came home from work; that was just before supper. . . ."

"I don't know," I told her. "I *should* go check. It'd be safest."

"Honey, don't," she said and squeezed my arm.

"Yep, one hell of a scare," I said, shaking my head. "Most like it was the *dream* had a lot to do with it; getting me ripe for a scare, sort of. I'd been dreaming again that college dream again, you know? Only this time the reason I quit wasn't because I was just too duncy to hack it, but because *Ma'd* died. I come home from school and found the old lady dead, like the time when I was a kid. It happened just like it really did: I found her bent nearly double, with her face in the launder tray. And when I touched her she tipped sideways and banged to the floor, still bent, like she was frozen bent, like a piece of a root. 'Probably a stroke,' was what Dr. Layton said. 'Probably suffered a stroke while she was washing and fell in the water, drown before she could come to.' Hmm. . . . Only in this dream I'm not a kid; I'm twenty or so. Hmm. . . ." I thought about it a minute, then asked Viv, "What you suppose, Doctor; am I completely schitzish?"

"You're completely nuts. Get under the covers. . . ."

"Funny, ain't it . . . the geese hushing up all at once. I almost think that's what woke me."

Looking back, I know damn well that's what woke me.

"That or the rain knocking to remind me I ain't checked the foundation tonight . . ."

Looking back, a guy can always pick him out some top-notch reasons to explain what happened. He can say the reason he woke up like he did was because the geese hushed; and the reason that reflection spooked him so was the dream he'd been having leaving him in a kind of spooky frame of mind . . .

(*I sit there on the bed, listening to the rain. I can feel her cheek pushed up against my bicep, all warm and smooth, and her hair falling down in my lap. "I'm sure it's all right, honey," she says. "What's that?" I say. "The foundation," she says. . . .*)

A guy can even look back and see that the thing that happened the next day at work was because of them dreams and reasons, along with thinking about that nut Willard Eggleston, and with all that week working so hard and not sleep enough when I got home . . . he can look back and say there was the why of it . . .

(*I shake my head. "I don't know," I say. "I know I ought to go down there and check, just run a light over the waterline to see how things are . . . but oh lord god," I say, "how I hate the thought of pulling on a pair of ice-cold boots and go slopping out in that soup . . ."*)

Even that flu bug that was going the rounds, a fellow could add that on, looking back . . .

(*I reach over for my trousers off the back of the hard chair. "Especially," I say, "the way my kidneys are giving me hell. . . ." "Your kidneys?" she says. "Yeah, you remember, they used to bother me some just after we was married; Layton said it was from riding all the way across the country on the cycle with no support on; floating kidney or something was what he called it. Hadn't troubled me none for the last couple years. Till today. I skidded offn a peeled one and whanged hell outa my rear end and back—" "Oh," she says, "bad? Let me look." She flicks on the bed light. "It's okay," I tell her. "Sure," she says. "Sure, it's always okay with you." She sits up and gets hold of the scruff of my hair and pulls me back over on the bed. "Now roll over to your stomach and let me look."*)

Yeah, a fellow can look back and add up all the reasons and say, "Well, it ain't really so hard to figure how come I was so punchy and so logy, and so careless out working the state park the next day, what with all the hassles banging at me so long; no, not really so hard . . ."

(*She pulls up my undershirt. "Hon-ey! . . . it's all raw." "Yeah," I say into the covers, "but nothin' to fuss over. Nothing you can do with a bruised butt anyhow but pee blood for a few days while it heals. I tell you, though: you might see can you unravel some of the kinks in my shoulders while you got me here. . . okeedoke?"*)

But just the same, being able to look back and give reasons and all that still don't do much toward making a man proud of what happened because of them reasons. Not if he can look back as well and

see how he could have kept it from—no, not could; look back and see
how he by god *should* have kept it from happening. There's shames a
man can never reason away, though he looks back and piles up reasons
over them forty dozen deep. And maybe those are the shames a man
never should reason away . . .

(*She gets up and goes to the dresser for something and switches on
the electric heater on her way back. She's wearing the nightgown with
the one broken strap. I smell that she's got the analgesic before it
touches my back. "Boy," I say, "that's all right. I sure didn't realize
how knotted up I was." She hums along with the electric heater for
a while, then commences to sing in just this least little whisper possible. "Redbird in a sycamore tree-ee, singing out his song," she sings.
"Big black snake crawls up that tree and swallows that poor boy
whole." "That's nice," I tell her. "Dang, that's nice. . . ." She rubs
round and around and around; and it is nice, it's very nice . . .*)

Hank breathes deeply, his lips damp against the back of his forearm as he lies on his stomach. The hands slither over him like a warm
and fragrant oil. The heater beside the bed purrs pleasantly, glowing
at him from across the room in a deep orange spiral. Viv sings:

> "Bluejay pulled a four-horse plow
> Sparrow why not you-oo?
> 'Cause my legs is little an' long
> An' they might get broke in two."

He rolls to his back. In thick, warm oil. And reaches his maimed
hand languorously up to take the dangling strap and pull her down
toward him . . .

> *Wild geese flying through the air*
> *Through the sky of blue-oo . . .*

The rain strikes against the window and draws back and strikes
again without effect. The wind strums the four insulated power lines
that swoop over the river to the house, making the house hum in deep
response. Hank falls asleep with the lamp still burning and the heater
still purring, and the slim liquid hands once again flowing warmly
across his back . . .

> *They're now a-floating where the south sun glows*
> *So why not me and you. . . .*

*S*ometimes—after futile all-nights—deserts fill my work-
house and smoking sand gets in my eyes . . . and I must
split the swollen cabin to check the dawn, to find: the
creek still parties with the moon . . . the thrusting pine
and whippoorwills still celebrate the sun.

It generally works, and things are cool, but sometimes—
after cutting out—nothing out there happens but the
night. And those days were best forgotten.

In the morning Lee refused absolutely to rise from bed; there
would be no carrier to sleep the day away in at the new grounds, and
he was damned if he'd get out of the house just to sit like a mudflat
indian under a rubber poncho, frustrated and frozen, while the rain
slowly washed the remaining shreds of his life downhill into the
river. He was determined to remain firmly in bed; no amount of per-
suasion on Joe Ben's part was going to work this morning. "Lee, boy,
think of this." Joe raised a finger significantly. "You don't even have
to ride the boat up river this time. We're taking the pick-up all the
way to the job." Then the finger began to jab, icy and insistent—
"Come on. Hop up; get up now—"

"What?" I was shaken from warm dreams of victory by that cold
little jab of reality. "What? Get up? Are you serious, Joe?"

"Certainly," he told me seriously, then launched a new sales
campaign.

Through a scrim of sleepy I saw Joe Ben's fanatic eyes crackling
green at me from their orange rims. A happy Caliban. He was offering
me some kind of nice little excursion in the pick-up. I half listened,
sitting up and reaching for another handful of aspirins from the dish
beside my bed. All night long I had been chewing them like salted
peanuts to foil any attempt a thermometer might make to reveal my
actual sickness.

"Josephus," I interrupted, "a ride in the pick-up somehow just does
not compete with the ride I'm now taking. Have a handful of aspirin.
Get a nice buzz on." I leaned back and pulled the covers over my
head, remembering that this was the day I had chosen for my assault,
for the final step in my plans. To stay home. With the remembering,
excitement began to run through me, but I managed to keep my

474

voice appropriately weak and muffled. . . . . "No, Joe. No no no, I'm sick sick sick"—and at the same time allow just enough of an edge of malicious amusement show to let Joe know better. I reasoned that Brother Hank had sent him on this mission to my bedroom, for I was positive that Hank too understood the importance of this day. Everything had led up to it. It could not be denied. At long last it was inevitable that I would have to spend the day home from work . . . alone . . . except for the old man, who slept most of the mornings and sometimes a good part of the afternoons if he didn't go into town, and for Viv. The thought of my brother's anxiety lent a new dimension to my undercover excitement, as well as a glow to my frozen extremities. "Forget it, Joe. No. I'm not going." I burrowed deeper.

"But Lee, boy, you might be *needed!*"

"Joe, stop, you're getting my rear cold. Be*sides*"—I raised an edge of the sheet to eye him meaningfully—"just why is it that my company is so important? Needed? I don't recall being needed before. Why now, Joe? Why now does poor Hank feel it necessary to have me continually in sight? Is he afraid to leave me alone? Some harm come to me, perhaps?"

"What are you talking, poor Hank?" He jerked away my quilt; "Hank don't have nothing to do with my comin' up here; what's wrong with you? Hank don't give a snap one way or the other. No sir! I came up here *thinking* you'd be interested—as a scholar—*interested* in the way logging was one time performed. History, man, yeah, history right out there! Come on with us, what do you say?"

I laughed and struggled to repossess the quilt from Joe. "Joe, tell Hank that as far as history goes, that I—as a scholar—don't give a snap one way or the other myself. Night-night." And drew my head back into the warm darkness, pretending to sleep . . .

Joe Ben turned and walked away from Lee, scratching the tip of his nose with a broken nail. Out in the hall he saw Viv coming out of old Henry's bedroom. His face brightened and he took her hand. "Viv, honeybun, I—we all—we need you to *do* a thing for us! Need it real bad. The old boy up and around? He was gonna give us last-minute advice on handlogging. Oh yeah. Anyway. Look, we need somebody to run us up to the job in the pick-up and then get back to town and get a set of cotter pins soon's the stores open. Need 'em bad, honeybun. Now you been close to Leland and all . . . *also!* I think the boy should drop in on Doctor Layton. I don't like the sound of that throat."

She smiled at him. "You're one to talk about the way a throat sounds." Joe's voice would frighten a bear.

"Me? The trouble is—didn't I ever tell you this?—the doctor didn't beat all the phlegm outa me when I was born. It ain't a sickness with me. I'm too lovable to be sick. But what do you think about Lee?"

"I don't know, Joe," she answered. He went on talking and she waited to see what he was getting at. Viv knew when Joe Ben was rearranging the truth to his own ends; everyone generally knew except Joe. Even when the reasons behind his rearrangements were obscure, people usually went along with Joe because they had learned that in the end his reasons were always unselfish. When she saw he had finished his jittery outburst, Viv nodded and agreed to talk with Lee, though she was still in the dark about his motives. Frowning, her slim light brows drawn together, she went to Lee's room and knocked on the door.

"Lee?" *Thump thump thump.*

"Who's there?" I mumbled from beneath my quilt. "Go away." Hank will now have to try himself, I thought, since Joe has failed, and maybe get angry enough at my malingering to lose his cool. *Thump thump?* The door opened and I steeled myself. WATCH OUT. Zero hour. If he did lose his cool the game would be mine. He was approaching the bait once more; the trap lay in readiness. All he needed to do was get a *little* angry, just enough to poke the trigger (my nose, I hoped; please my nose and not my lovely teeth, after all those years of braces and agony having them straightened). I would squeal in terror. Viv would rush to my aid, defending me against the cad, soothing my poor nose as he fumed with frustration . . . and the game would be mine, nothing left for me but to take her away.

So imagine my shock when I saw, instead of Hank, it was Viv who lifted that quilt to peek in.

"Morning," she piped. "No," I groaned. She was insistent. "Morning, Lee; up up up." "Can't," I groaned again, but she said I *must* get up. To go to town. She told me she would worry unless I went to see a doctor about my throat and the swollen glands in my neck. "So up, Lee; I don't plan to take no or can't for an answer. Get some warm clothes on while I tell Hank to wait"—and left before I could protest further.

Puzzled, I managed to drag myself from the warm bed and shuffle down to another morose breakfast in the steamy kitchen. The tinny music of Joe's radio only emphasized the silence. I ate slowly, curious, completely at a loss to understand her insistence on medical attention. Did she also object to my being left behind? Could she be worried about being alone with one so obviously harmless? Impossible. I ruminated slyly over my oatmeal and was right on the verge of making crafty alterations in my plans—Viv could drive me in; my fever, you know, feeling a bit giddy—when a second unforeseen event turned up to further complicate matters. Old Henry, all decked out in his going-t'-town best, came rumbling down the steps, hawking terrific hornlike blasts from an early-morning larynx as he struggled to pull on a heavy sheepskin-lined parka. . . . "Here we go, bullies, here we go." I sighed. It was going to be that sort of day. . . .

"Yep, here we go. Today we really whup 'er, boys! Hm. Look at the rain. Fine-looking weather. Goddam, looks almost like you was aimin' to run off without me."

They all turned from the table to watch the old man work to pull on the parka; when he turned they saw he had removed his arm cast. . . .

"Henry," Viv, she says to me when she sees. "Oh, Henry." She's standing at the table, about to give Leland some sausage, when she points at my wrist with the fork. "All right," she says. "What did you do with it?"

"Goddam thing came off whilst I slept, if you got to know," I tell her. "So when I heard you talking I thought to myself: Henry, you better ride into that doctor with Leland to see about should you maybe take the one off your leg." I knocked agin the pant leg with my knuckles to show them how holler it sounds. "Hear that? I ain't sure but the damn leg rotted clean away in there. So I'm goin' along, if nobody minds too much."

"Okay," Hank, he says. "Let's get with it. We ought to make it there right at daylight."

Joe Ben, he rides in the back of the pick-up with the equipment. Hank, he drives. Beside Hank, Leland, he sits, nodding with his eyes closed, and next to the door I sit, trying to get squirmed around to some comfortable position for the goddam booging plaster leg. On the ride up to the new show site I try to give the boys some notion of what to expect up there today. Explaining as much as I can about handlogging, about this and that, about a man really *oughten* to be cutting in this wind and rain but since you can't get around it then you got to more'n *ever* pay attention to the drift of the rain, to the gusts you see off in the distance comin'—you can see 'em, off there, shakin' the tops of trees like some big goddam invis'ble *bird* flyin' at ya—an' watch those 'cause they can *kill* ya . . . but you mainly got to be watchful *after* the stick is on the ground whilst you're buckin' it because you are fallin' the bastard to slide anyhow an' she ain't always so polite as to wait for ready set go . . . and you mainly *most of all* need to study the trough she ought to take down hill, an' *there's* where a man needs to know his beans!

"Takes some experience, huh?"

"Yes sir! Know his *onions!*"

My fossilized father has taken it into his head that he had to ride into town with us, and nothing would budge him. During the pick-up ride he talked on and on, rocking back and forth with his left hand cradled against his chest. The hand was blue and thin-looking, more like the limb of something ripped untimely from the womb than the hand of an octogenarian. He rocked the hand, cooing over it in a bemused, sing-song way as we drove toward the state park. When he spoke of some particularly exciting aspect of logging the hand stirred restlessly. I watched its fetal movements, wondering what I would say to the doctor at the hospital . . .

"Needs be on the jump every second, a man does . . ."

They reached the end of the paved road. Hank consulted a section quadrangle map to see that it matched the section marker tacked to the tree. "Hold it here . . ." (Figuring that I'd best double check before we started work: *tired and none too clear-headed . . .*) "What's that section shingle yonder read, Joe?" (I didn't want to have the hill cleared, then find I was cutting the wrong forest. Joe called back a number and it checked; this was our show. "Better look around, bub." I nudged Lee upright. "Better wake up and watch the turns or you won't make 'er back to the highway, let 'lone be able to drive back up here tonight to pick us up," I told him. *He looks at me. I don't know. I just feel tired.*

The pick-up rocked and pitched up a steep pan of streaming ruts, then leveled off and traveled for a few minutes along the ridge before I stopped it out on the lip of a rim. I opened the door and took a look down: below us, down one steep sonofagun of a hill through the shaggy trunks of firs, was the river. I pulled on the emergency brake and put the pick-up into neutral. "This is our slope," I said. "The

state park commission want these trees cleared to give tourists a view
of the river. I imagine from this high they can see the coast from
here too. Can you find your way back, bub?"

"I'll be along with him," the old man said, before Lee could
answer, "and I could get back here with my head in a sack." The old
man's voice had grown real calm as we got closer to the site. There
was none of that tomfool childish sound been in his talk of late. And
when he looked off at the tree trunks, the huge looming trunks
never seen anywhere any more except in government parks, his face
set up hard and his old toothless mouth pulled down. "I can show
him the way back here in pitch dark an' hurricane," he says and gives
the kid another nudge . . . )

"What?" Once more I was jolted awake. Just as Hank had predicted, we had reached the work site in a dead heat with gray
dawn. Henry had reached into the cab to goose me awake for a look.
Through the window I saw firs fingering the interminable rosary of
rain. The old man stood, talking and pointing down through a
shaggy opening in the forest. Hank got out and walked to his side,
leaving me to sit in the muttering pick-up. Joe Ben was shivering
from his long ride in the back, anxious for the old man to finish his
gabbing so he could get to work and warm up, but Brother Hank's
attitude toward Henry had become very attentive, almost respectful
for some reason. Their conversation drifted in through the heater
vents under the dash . . .

("Blamed right; worked many a slope just like this one forty
years ago."

"Fierce terrain."

"Worked many a one fiercer," the old man let me know.

"Hear you tell it, this country use to all be eighty-degree slopes
with earthquakes and geysers," I said, shucking him a little. He
frowned and scratched his wet old noggin.

"I can't call to mind any geysers right off," he said. "But I admit
earthquakes plagued us some." And we both laughed a little, taking
it easy while Lee came to enough to manage driving *Why can't he
wake up?* and while Joe drug the stuff out of the back end . . . )

At the rear of the pick-up, a ways apart from Hank and old Henry,
Joe Ben was already unloading the gear; the saws and gas cans stood
already against the fender and he was dragging out the old wooden
hand-carved screwjacks and leaning these alongside the sleek and
shiny Homelite saws, hurriedly, ready to get with it, hot to get at

it and show old Hank that by golly just me and him is enough and *then* some! So I shag that gear out like a tiger. Hank and Henry talk. The kid gets out but he don't offer to help. He just stands watching, coughing occasionally into his fist like he's about to drop dead on the spot. Behind me there with Hank the old man stands at the edge of the road—that limp hand cradled in his other hairy claw— looking off down the hill—the rain swirls about the trees, the sound of gullies being dug into the mountainside is like the sound of a busy highway roaring past somewhere nearby—Hank and me'll show 'em. The old man raises his hand to point to an outcropping of mossy rock. "Set up over yonder," he says to Hank. "Start low close to the river an' work up. These here bastards are big. We won't need but a day or so cuttin' to fill the contract."

"How about stopping time, do you reckon?" Hank asks. "We don't want to float logs past Andy in the dark, do we?"

The old man wrinkles his face, thinks about that a minute. "That's something, that is something . . . let me see, from here it'll take oh, a good hour'n half to float to him. Now, the river's high and the tide's ebbin'. Say one good hour, you say so Joe Ben?" I tell him sure and he says, "So stop cuttin' one good hour before dark, 'bout tide change." He turns and starts back toward the pick-up. "I'll see that them cotter pins get back up here quick as possible." He catches Lee by the sleeve and shakes him.

"You alive, boy? Or you need some ass-kickin' to bring you to? Get in there. You drive. Let's wag it an' shag it. Say, by the by, Hank . . ." The old man aims his finger at Hank. (As the pick-up was backing up and turning, leaving me and Joe in the rain there, Henry rolled down the window and called back, "What the hell you mean *any* goddam way, runnin' down so low on cotter pins? Do I hafta do *all* the thinkin' for this worthless outfit? Do I hafta do *all* the goddam figgerin'?" Then they faded off. *There the kid goes. Back to the valley, there he goes. . . .*

Joe Ben grinned at me as the pick-up drove off with the old man still calling. "Hardboiled ol' owl, ain't he?" Joe said and started dancing off toward the outcropping Henry had pointed out, rearing to get at it. *I follow after the squeak of Joe's radio. Like in a dream. Can't seem to get my mind off that pick-up, on my business. And we headed out . . .*)

On Main Street old Henry went into Stokes's Hardware—hoping I'll run onto the old spook, sort of—for them cotter pins. Leland, he stays behind in the pick-up to wait for me. Stokes ain't there, but the nigger behind the counter, he's damned rattled to see me. He kind of shudders when I ask for the pins, and starts to tell me sorry, Mr. Stamper, but Mr. Stokes said no service . . . so I say piss on him I'll serve myself, and look and find the size I want and pick them from the shelf myself before the proprietor can think of a good answer to that. "Much obliged," I tell him real nice. "Just put 'em on the Stamper tab." And I go back out and get in the pick-up, where the boy's setting there waiting. "Let's go, son. Before we get accused o' robbery."

In town, after a brief stop for parts, Henry dropped me at the doctor's office to drive on to the Snag, where he said he could "pass the wait profitably." I told him I would wait in the outer room if he wasn't back when the doctor finished with me, and I walked to the desk; a forty-five-year-old Amazon in white informed me that I would have to wait, asked me to be seated, then glared at me for an hour over the top of a magazine while I fought sleep on a septic-scented couch and wished I could join my old father at his place of profitable waiting. . . .

After I drop the kid at the doctor's I decide to drive on to the Snag for a little slash. See what's the news. Mainly me, it looks like. My coming in kind of stirs things up a mite, but I say piss on 'em and head for the bar. I have me two whiskies while I read the scribbled notes pinned up there near the door, advertising all kinds of paraphernalia, and I'm about to get me a third when Indian Jenny comes driving through the door like a big old cow. She blinks around and sees me and she comes bearing down on me with fire in her eye.

"You!" she says to me, "you all, your whole family, you, you're bad as hell on us, being so stubborn."

"Jenny! By god now, you like a drink? Teddy, see what Jenny here'd like." I act like everything's normal as pie, just like I done at Stokes's. I'm darned if I show them I know better. Maybe I don't hear so good no more, but I can still keep up appearances. Jenny, she takes the glass Teddy brought but she don't let it soothe her down none. She sucks it down without taking her eyes offn me. Seems to me she's awful caught up in something don't have any bearing on her. But then, she's never gone overboard for me. When she's done with her whisky she sets down the glass and says, "Anyhow, you can't make delivery anyhow. Not by Thanksgiving. Nobody can."

I just grin at her and shrug like I ain't got no more idee than a duck what she means about Thanksgiving. Wondering what's eating at her, by god. Maybe without a little cash floating around and niggers here not able to get drunk, she's been having a tough time getting victims. Could be. This business is affecting everybody, I reckon. Maybe the way it's affecting Jenny is giving her the hot britches. She keeps glaring at me; then she says nobody can make it by Thanksgiving and I tell her I am awful sorry but I just cannot make out what she is driving at. She tips her glass again and puts it back on the counter. And then says again, "No, you won't make it." This time in a spooky goddam fashion that someway bothers me, by god. Enough I have to ask, "What you mean I won't make it? I don't know what you're talking about. Besides, what's to stop me?"

And she says, "I get my revenge on you, Henry Stamper . . . I been working with bat bones all week. . . ."

"So bat bones is gonna stop me? Boy howdy, and you Indians—"

"No. Not just bat bones, not only. . . ."

"What else, then?" I ask, getting peeved a little. "What is this thing you got workin' for you so fierce?"

"The moon," is all she says, "the moon," and walks back in the direction of the women's toilet, leaving me standing there studying that one over . . .

The other citizens in the bar went disappointedly back to their drinks and their conversations; they had thought for a minute that Jenny might really light into the old turtle. But no, they decided, when she'd left, just more of her bull about the moon and the stars. . . . So they dismissed her and drew finger patterns on the formica tabletops with the condensate from their drinks and wished something would happen.

Only Henry, with his lean, slanting back to the room, gave serious thought to Jenny's words. The moon? He finished his drink slowly. . . . "The moon, huh?" he said again to himself, frowning. Then, slowly, reached for the wallet from his pocket. "What if . . . ?" He took a tiny book from one of the wallet's compartments and riffled through the pages, stopping, running a cracked black nail down a list of tiny numbers. "Let's see. November; what if—" Then abruptly shoved wallet and book into his pocket, lurched out through the door to the pick-up. "Christ . . . what if she hadn't said something?" He drove east, out of town, without pausing for stop signs or even considering going back to the doctor's office for Lee. When he passed the mill he swung off to the side of the highway and called out to Andy, "How they doin' up there?"

Andy was dragging a huge log into place with a peavey pole; the small motorboat he was using to retrieve the logs as they showed up in the river chugged through the opening in a boom. "Pretty good," the boy called back. "About ten. An' bigger'n any I ever see before."

"How's the river mark? Up, ain't it?"

"Up a scosh, yeah; why? It ain't up much, not near enough to trouble us. . . ."

"But it's still ebbing fast, ain't it? While it's rising? Ain't that right, it's ebbing"

Before Andy answered he stood up in the boat bottom to look across the surface of the water; chunks of bark and debris were indeed still moving rapidly down river toward the sea. Slightly confounded now, he turned the boat and putted to check the marker on one of the check-pilings to be sure he hadn't misread the depth. No; he'd been right. It was rising, and at a fair clip, though the river was still ebbing fast. "Yeah," he called slowly over his shoulder, "it's running out an' rising at the same time. Uncle Henry, what you make of that? The water coming up while the river's running down?"

But the old man had already thrown the pick-up back into gear and was picking up speed on the highway up river. The moon. The moon, huh? Well, maybe so the moon. Well, okay, the moon. But I can whup it too. I by god can whup the moon too. . . .

When the Amazon in the nurse's uniform finally led me to the doctor's office for examination, the doctor wasn't even concerned enough over my pitiful fever-racked frame to be present; in fact, it was the Amazon that ministered to me, and I didn't see the good doctor himself until she had completed my treatment and showed me to another office where a mountain of flesh trapped within a white smock whistled and sighed from an ancient swivel chair.

"Leland Stamper? I'm Doctor Layton. You got a minute? Sit down."

"I have a minute, probably more, in fact; I'm waiting for my father to return for me, but if it's all the same to you, I think I shall continue to stand. I'm paying homage to the penicillin shot."

The doctor grinned at me through his purple jowls and held out a gold cigarette case. "Smoke?" I took one and thanked him. While I lit the cigarette he leaned torturously back in his chair and regarded me with that look generally reserved by deans for wayward sophomores. I waited for him to get into whatever it was he was planning to lecture about, wondering if he didn't have better things to do with his valuable time than to waste it on a young stranger bent on adultery. He ponderously lit his own cigarette, then leaned back like a white blimp exhaling smoke. I tried putting on my best look of annoyed impatience, but something in his manner, in the way he relished the pause, turned my impatience to discomfort.

I naturally assumed he had called me in to make a citizen's appeal to brother Hank through me, as most of the rest of the strikebound town had been doing to every available Stamper, but he took his cigarette from his fat red butt of mouth and said instead, "I just wanted to have a look at your face was all. Because your *posterior* has a certain nostalgic significance; your posterior happened to be one of the very first in a long line of posteriors that I had the opportunity to whack. You were born my first year practicing, you see."

I told him he could have seen the article itself a moment ago if he'd been on his toes.

"Oh, posteriors don't change much. Not like faces. How's your mom, by the way? I certainly hated to see you two leave here when—"

"She's dead," I said flatly. "You hadn't heard? Not quite a year. Now, if there's nothing else?"

The chair squeaked and complained as he leaned back forward. "I'm sorry to hear that," he said, tapping the ash into the wastepaper basket. "No, that's all." He looked at the chart the nurse had given him. "Just come back in three days for a follow-up. And watch out. Oh, and say hello to Hank for me when you—"

"Watch out?" I stared at him. The fat face underwent an abrupt transition before my eyes, from clod of a doctor to arch-criminal in white. "Watch *out?*"

"Yes, you know," he said; then, after a knowing wink, added, "for exhaustion, cold, et cetera." He coughed, frowned at the cigarette, tossed it in the basket with the ashes, as I tried to fathom just how deep the knowing went beneath that wink. "Yes, you can lick this thing," he said with heavy overtones, "if you don't let it catch you with your pants down."

"What thing?"

"This Asian flu bug, what did you *think* I meant?" He regarded me innocently from beneath eyelids bloated and positively drooping with wickedness. I was suddenly certain that he knew everything, the whole plan, the entire intended vengeance, everything! In some diabolic Sydney Greenstreet fashion, he had amassed a complete brochure of all my activities. . . . "Maybe we could have a chat the next time you come in, huh?" he purred, lips dripping innuendoes. "Until then, like I said, watch out."

Terrified, I hurried out to the waiting room, with his echo pursuing me like a hound baying watch OUT . . . OUT . . . OUT . . . What was happening? I wrung my hands. What had gone wrong? How had he known? And where was my father . . . ?

On the slope Hank stopped the shriek of his saw and tilted the metal brim of his hat back to watch the lean, stiff-moving figure of old Henry work its way down a switchback deer trail, curious and amused (but, as a matter of fact, none too surprised that the old man had come back out. I had been halfway suspecting as much since I'd saw him look over the set-up and watch Joe unload the old-time equipment. I'd halfway figured he'd get into town and get a little juiced and decide to come back out and show us how it used to be done. But, as he got closer, I noticed he looked pretty sober, like there was more on his mind than just futzing around shooting the bull and getting in everybody's way. There was something about the way he moved that I recognized as special, about the way he hustled—a mixture of worry and joy and excitement as he jerked his neck and tossed the white shock of hair around where it kept getting washed down in his eyes. It called to my mind the kind of grim giddiness that I hadn't seen in him in god knows how long, years and years, but that I recognized right off, even fifty yards off and him in a leg cast.

I stopped my cutting. I laid my saw down, lit a fresh cigarette off my stub, and watched him come . . . scrabbling, grabbing vines and roots as he heaved that stiff leg before him—heave, then lurching forward, pole-vaulting forward almost over that muddied cast, finding a foothold with the one good, cork-booted leg, then throwing that cast ahead of him again—relentless and grim and comical all at once.

"Whoa back a little," I hollered up the hill at him. "You'll pop a gasket, you old fool. Slow down. Nobody's after you."

He didn't answer back. I hadn't expected that he would, puffing and panting like he was. *Where's the kid?* But he didn't slow down, either. *What's he done with the kid?*

"Lee up in the pick-up?" I called again and started angling toward him. "Or was he so goddam sick he couldn't even make the ride back with half a dozen cotter pins?"

"Left 'im," he said, short of breath. "Town." He didn't say anything again until he reached the log I had been bucking and leaned his hip up against it for a rest. "Ah, lor'," he gasped. "Ah, lor'." For a minute I was worried: his eyes were rolling; his face was as white as his hair; his throat seemed clogged . . . he tipped his pink old toothless mouth up to the rain, sucking in great breaths of the wet air. "Ah, lor' almighty," he said, finally getting a good breath. He ran a tongue around his lips that looked like a tongue out of a boot. "Shoo! Took 'er faster'n I planned. Shooee!"

"Well, Jesus H. Christ I hope to shout," I said, relieved as well as a little hacked off at being so worried. "What the shit do you mean, come ball-assin' down that hill like a wild stallion? I'm damned if I want you poppin' some gasket where I have to tote you back up to that pick-up. You'd be heavy with that load you got on." I could see he'd had him a couple by the way he was colored up, but he was a long way from drunk.

"Lef' the boy in town," he said, standing up and looking around him. "Where's Joe Benjamin? Get him over here."

"He's the other side of those outcroppin's—what the hell's wrong with you, anyhow?" I saw he was steamed up with more than Teddy's whisky. "What happened back there in town?"

"Give Joe Ben a whistle," he told me. He walked a few steps from the log, surveying the lay of the land. After looking it over he says, "You workin' land too level. No good now. Too much effort to get the bastards moving. We'll move on, down yonder past that little swale, where it's steeper. It's dangerous, but we're in kind of a bind. Where the hell's Joe Ben!"

I gave Joe another whistle. "Now cool off and tell me what you're so steamed up about."

"Let's wait," he says. He was still puffing pretty bad. "Till Joe Ben gets here. Here's the pins. I left in a hurry. I didn't have time to pick up the boy. Whooee. My lungs ain't so good any more. . . ." And I saw there wasn't any sense doing anything but wait. . . .)

After another hour spent in that pungent waiting room, an hour of pure terror and paranoia spent pretending to read back issues of *McCall's* and *True Romance* under the nurse's supervision and wondering just how much that devil of a doctor knew, I resigned myself to admitting that the old man wasn't coming back for me and that perhaps the doctor didn't know anything. I faked a yawn. I stood up and blew my nose loudly on a handkerchief so overused that the Amazon winced with disgust at the nasty old thing. "Could get yourself some paper from the john," she advised me over the top of her magazine, " 'n' throw that unsanitary thing away."

A dozen parting replies passed through my mind as I pulled on my jacket, but I was still too cowed by my recent experience with the woman and her needle to be able to voice them. Instead I paused at the door and meekly announced I was going to walk downtown. "If my father comes back, could you please tell him I'll probably be at Grissom's?"

I waited for an answer. She did not seem to have heard at first. Her face did not rise from the book, but as I stood there, like a schoolboy waiting to be excused, the curl of her slurring voice traced the curl of her lip perfectly. "You right sure you can make it without fainting again?" She licked her thumb to flip a page. "And don't let the door slam."

Between my clenched teeth I cursed her soundly, as well as the hypodermic, the doctor, and my thoughtless father, cursed them all and threatened dire revenge for each and every one in his turn . . . and closed the door behind me with a coward's care.

In the puddled walk outside the clinic I stood wondering what to do, feeling completely foiled. My chances to get Viv alone seemed to grow slimmer and slimmer. How would I get back out there unless old Henry came back? And yet, without thinking of it, when I started for town I avoided the only street on which he might drive if he came to look for me, taking instead, "for old time's sake," the old broken walk that would take me past the schoolhouse . . . "in case that doctor comes looking."

Sulking, furtive, alert—hands hanging cold and cocked at my sides instead of warm in my pockets—I advanced cautiously through billowing rain down a long row of memories, ready for anything. The rickety, slithery wooden walk took me past forlorn fishermen's shacks ominous and smoky and quilted with assorted patches made from snuff-can lids and flattened Prince Albert tins: There the Mad Scandinavian lives; "a baby-eater," my schoolmates used to claim as they tossed apples at his windows; "you skeered, Leland?" . . . past the cottage where the janitor had lived with all the rumors that janitors always live with, past the squat brick furnace building that heated the school, past the shaggy wall of stacked waste lumber that fired the furnace . . . and, strangely, I didn't relax my caution most of the long walk. Then, when almost at once my groundless fears did leave me—why so scared? How stupid I had been, thinking that jowly fool knew anything; what a stupid worry!—I realized that I was standing in front of the schoolhouse, my age-old citadel of Learning, of Truth, and my sanctuary. But fear was not replaced by peace: as I strolled along the walk edging my sanctuary's play yard, my alert pose turned to one of slouching dejection and remorse as I trailed my knuckles along the cyclone-fence enclosure past a school I'd never belonged to, past a playground loud with lunch-hour memories of teams I'd never played on. Through the fence, I saw I was passing the baseball diamond. Where the "big kids" had played when I was a first-grader; where the "little kids" played after I reached grade four . . . "Little kids?" Hank once asked. "Yeah, you know, the *dumb* kids, the stupes who couldn't enjoy a book in all their lives." Now this old rationalization seemed pitifully thin to me; big kid or little, first grade or fourth, Leland, old chap, you know you would have given your whole collection of Edgar Rice Burroughs to have joined that noisy, disorganized group. Isn't that so? Isn't it! As I looked through the dripping crisscross of wire to the runneling field I found myself wryly asking When do I get to play, fellers, when do I get chosen? Everybody's had a turn but me. Come on. Choose me for a change.

The fellers hung back. No nine-year-old demagogue of the diamond rushed forward, freckled with good old American sandlot sunshine, to point with the greasy finger of a fielder's mitt and say, "I choose you for my team." Nobody shouted, "You're needed, Leland, you'll come through strong in a clutch."

But fellers, I pleaded into the whorled ear of rain, fair's fair, now, isn't it? Fair's fair?

Yet, even in the face of that time-revered truth, the phantoms hung back; fair might be fair and all, they couldn't argue with *that*, but when it came to first basemen—or second or third—they wanted a cool head and a brave heart, not some dang punk who throws his fist up in front of his specs every time he sees a fast one skipping in his general direction.

But guys . . .

Not some dang sissy who falters, fidgets, and finally faints dead away and wakes up five minutes later with his trousers around his ankles and an ammonia capsule under his nose—just because a nurse pricked him from behind with a little penicillin.

Wait, fellers; it wasn't just a prick. The needle was *this* long!

This long, the sissy says. *This* long. Willya listen at him.

It was so! Please, fellers . . . maybe home base?

Home base. Willya just *listen* at the pantywaist. . . . C'mon; let's get at it . . .

They shifted back into time and I walked on again, past the ball-field while the wind booed and the rain hissed through the chicken-wire backstop and the regular team held down sodden home plate against all comers. I turned toward town, away from the school where I had received straight A's in everything but recess. Some sanctuary. Oh, sure, my fear had been pacified by the sight of that institute of learning—at least I no longer expected the doctor to swoop down on me like a fat vampire; for, like a church, the school served as my defense against such demons—but in the demon's place grew a terrible emptiness, a great malignant vacuum. No demons, but no teammates either. Seemed it was always like that.

A person might almost think they were one and the same. . . .

On the slope Hank smoked in patient silence beside his father while he heard the dissonant squeak of Joe Ben's little radio draw closer through the dripping firs. (The old man still stood leaned up against the log, working his jaw in thought; his white hair was plastered to his bony skull now and hung streaming from the back of his head, sort of like wet cobwebs. "Steeper land like that over yonder," he kept mumbling. "Hm. Yeah. Over there like that. We can get half again the cutting. Uhuh. I bet we can. . . .")

I was a little awed by the change that had come over the old coon; it seemed that the cast had broken to reveal a younger and at the same time more mature person. I watched old Henry appraise the land and announce which trees we was gonna cut, how, in what order, and so forth . . . and I got to feeling like I was seeing a once-familiar but almost-forgotten man. I mean . . . this wasn't the old yarn-spinning, bullshitting character that had been thundering damn near unnoticed through the house and the local bars for the last six months. Not the noisy joke of a year before either. No, I realized gradually, this is the boomer I used to follow on cruising walks twenty years before, the calm, stubborn, confident rock of a man who had taught me how to tie a bowline with one hand and how to place a dutchman block in an undercut so's the tree would fall so cunthair *perfect* that he could put a stake where he aimed for it to fall, then by god drive that stake into the ground with the trunk!

I kept still, looking at him. Like I was scared if I said something this phantom might disappear. And as Henry talked—haltingly, yet deliberate and certain all the same—I felt myself commence to relax. Like I'd had a couple quarts of beer. I let my lungs pull deep and easy and felt a kind of repose, almost like sleep, go running through me. It felt good. It was the first time, I realized, that I'd felt relaxed in—oh, Christ, except for last night with Viv rubbing my back—in what seemed years and years. Hot damn, I figured; the old old Henry is back; let him hold the handles a spell while I take a breather.

So I didn't say anything until Joby was almost there. I let him carry on for a while with his instructions before I reminded him that that slope me and Joby'd been working was exactly the one he'd pointed out for us to work that morning. "Remember?" I grinned at him. "You said just down from that outcropping?"

"That's all right, that's all right," he says, not the least concerned, and went on to say, "But I said that account of this place was *safest*. An' that was this morning. We ain't got time for that, not no more, not now. Down yonder she'll be a little trickier, but we can fall half again the bastards we can fall up here. Anyhow I'll tell you when Joe gets up here. Now hush and let me think a minute."

So I hushed and let him think, wondering how long it had been since I'd been able to do *that* . . . )

I left the school and playground and spent most of the rest of that lonely morn over dreary cups of drugstore coffee brought me by a dour Grissom who seemed to hold me solely responsible for his lack of business. During this time I revised and revamped my demon-teammate theory—improving on symbolism, sharpening the effect, stretching it to cover all possible woes. . . . I could stretch it far beyond grammar school. All through prep school I avoided that playground, all through college I had stayed safely in the classroom, secure behind a bastion of books, and played no base at all on the field outside. Not first or second, not third. Certainly not *home*. Secure but homeless. Homeless even in the town of my home-town team, with no base to play. No arms in all the wet world to enfold me, no armchair by the cozy fire to hold me. And, now, on top of it all, I was *deserted*, deserted at the hospital, left to the merciless hoofs of galloping pneumonia, by my own pitiless father. Oh, Father, Father, where can you be . . . ?

"Gettin' drownt," I tell Hank. "Out in the weather thisaway, I should of brung more better gear." I lean my bum hip against the log again to take the weight offn the cast and I take me a little knit cap from my pocket and pull it on. It ain't gonna keep my head dry none, but it'll soak up enough rain to keep it from running into my eyes. Joe Ben, he comes scrambling up the hill practically on all fours, looking like some kinda animal scared outa the ground. "What's up? What's up?" He looks from Hank to me, then settles himself on the log and looks down the direction we're looking. He's itching to pieces to know what's up but he knows he'll get told when I'm ready to tell him, so he don't ask again.

"Well sir." I pat my old cap into place and spit. "We got to finish our cuttin'," I tell them, "an' finish it today." Just like that. Hank and Joe Ben light up cigarettes and wait to see what it's all about. I say, "It's full moon, an' a poor time for it. I bet this mornin' was a good minus-one-five or minus-two tide. Real low. When we left the house this mornin' the river shoulda been low enough to show barnacles on the pilings, ain't that so? With a tide so low? Huh? But did we see any barnacles? Or did anybody look . . . ?" I look right at Hank. "Did you check the marker at the house this mornin' against the tide chart?" He shakes his head. I spit and look disgusted at him. Joe says, "What's it mean, anyway?" "What it means," I tell them, "is the game is all, is jick, jack, joker, and the game for Evenwrite and Draeger an' that bunch of goddam feather-beddin' so-slists is eg-zactly what it means! Unless we really get in high gear. What it means . . . is there must be damn heavy rain up country; there's more water comin' out'n the upper branches'n anybody figured. We're in for maybe one sonofabitch of a flood! Not tonight, probably, no, I doubt it tonight. Unless she really cuts loose a storm. And she could, but let's say not. Let's say it keeps on like it's goin'. By tomorrow or the next day nobody'll be able to hang onto a boom of logs, not us nor WP. So we got to deliver before it crests. Now. Let's say, oh, say, it's about ten-thirty now, so that means eleven, twelve, one, two . . . so let's say we get two of the bastards an hour, pushin' it, two of these. . . ." I take me a look up one of the firs standing there. She's a good one. Like they used to be. "At seventeen board feet, times two, times—what did I figure? five hours' cuttin'?—times five hours, say six hours; we can have Andy to stay up all night at the mill with a boat and spotlight watchin' for the latecomers . . . yeah, we can do that. So. Anyhow. Figuring six real highballin' hours of cutting, nothin' goes wrong, we—let's see now . . . hum . . ."

The old man talked on, darting the brown tip of his tongue over his lips and occasionally pausing to spit, speaking more to himself than to the others. Hank finished his cigarette and lit another, nodding now and then as he listened (content to let the old guy call the shots and run the show. Damned content, to be honest with you.

Henry kept rambling on. After telling Joe and me all the details and outlining to us all the dangers and doubts, he finally got around to allowing, "But, yessir, we can hack it," like I knew he would. "With even a little margin, if we hump our tails. 'N' then tomorrow we got to rent a tug an' run the booms down to Wakonda Pacific, quicker the better. Not wait for Thanksgivin'. Get 'em off our hands before we lose 'em. Well . . . be tight, but we can whup it."

"You bet!" Joe said. "Oh yeah!" Business like this was right up Joby's alley.

"So . . . ?" the old man said, talking straight ahead. "What do you say?"

I knew it was me he was asking. "Be tough," I tell him, "with Orland and Layton and the others buffaloed by Evenwrite and the rest of the town. I mean, it'll be tough making a drive on that high a river, with that many booms and us so shorthanded. . . ."

"I know it'll be tough, goddammit! That ain't what I asked. . . ."

"Hey!" Joby snaps his fingers. "I know: we can get some of the Wakonda Pacific foremen!" He's excited and chomping at the bit. "See, they got to help us, don't you see? They don't want to lose their winter millwork. With Mama Olson's tug, and some of them WP bosses, we'll be pretty as you please, right in the good Lord's warm little fist."

"We'll take that jump," the old man says, pushing himself up from the log, "when it comes up. Right now I'm sayin' can we cut our quota today? All of it. Just us three?"

"Sure! Sure we can, oh yeah, there ain't nothing—"

"I was askin' you, Hank. . . ."

I knew he was. I squinted through the blue film of cigarette smoke, out across the fern and salal and blackberry, through the brute black straight trunks of those trees down to the river, trying to ask myself, Can we or can't we? But I didn't know; I just couldn't tell. The three of us he said. Meaning two and one old man. Two tired jacks and one old crippled man. It's crazy, and I said to myself, and I knew I should say Nothing doing to the old man, say it's too risky, forget it, flick it. . . .

But some way he didn't seem like an old crippled man to me then. It wasn't like I was standing there talking with the wild and woolly town character any more, but with some fierce young jack who had just walked up out of the years ready to spit on his palms and take over again. I looked at him, waiting there. What could I tell him? If he says we can whip it, all right, maybe he knows, let him take over. "I'm askin' you, boy. . . ." Because all I know is that the only way you can keep this jack from out of the past from trying to whip it was with a club and a rope, so I say all right. "All right, Henry, let's try it." *You probably know more about this kind of logging than me and Joby put together. So all right, head out. You run it. I'm tired rassling it. I got other things on my mind. You take it. Me, just turn me on and aim me. That's how I'd like it, anyhow. I'm tired, but I'll work. If you take over. If you just turn me on and aim me it's fine and dandy with this boy . . . )*

After Grissom had the effrontery to ask me to pay for the magazine I spilled coffee on, I decided to go mope elsewhere. I crossed the street and entered the Sea Breeze Cafe and Grill, the very apotheosis of short-order America: two waitresses in wilted uniforms chatting at the cash register; lipstick stain on coffee mugs; bleak array of candy; insomniac flies waiting out the rain; a plastic penful of doughnuts; and, on the wall above the Coca-Cola calendar, the methodical creaking creep of a bent second hand across a Dr. Pepper clock . . . the perfect place for a man to sit and commune with nature.

I climbed onto one of the leatherette stools, ordered coffee, and purchased freedom for one of the penned-up doughnuts. The shortest of the waitresses brought my order, took my money, made my change, and returned to the cash register to play her accordion of neck to her bored companion . . . never really acknowledging my presence to herself. I ate the doughnut and reiterated my woes with fresh coffee, trying not to think ahead, trying not to ask myself, What am I waiting for? The second hand creaked a meaningless dirge. An ancient refrigerator complained in the cluttered kitchen, and the second hand cranked out a dreary fare of short-order time— tepid seconds, stale minutes, the drab diet that He Who Hesitates must always be satisfied with . . .

As the rain quickened on the slopes the three men set about work. Hank jerked the starter rope on his saw and wondered why the saw should feel so feather-light *(just take it over and it's dandy with me. . . .)* when his arms felt so heavy. Henry walked the length of the log, looking for a place to set a check, and wished he'd brought a plastic bag or some damn thing to wrap around his cast so's it wouldn't soak up water and weigh him down even worse than ordinary. On the other hand Joe Ben, leaping back downhill to the log he had been working on when interrupted by Hank's whistle, felt as though the mud caking his boots was actually becoming lighter. He felt even more nimble and buoyant than usual. Everything was going fine. He'd been worried over something earlier that morning—can't even *remember* now—but everything was turning out just the way he liked it: old Henry's dramatic arrival, the news of the tides, the planning in terse, muted voices, that brass-band feeling rising among them, beating out we *got* to make that first down, we *got* to, and you block for me, Joby, and I'll tear 'em apart! Yeah boy! That brassy beat of high-school idealism and determination that he liked best of all: beating out we got, got to, *got* to! over and over until the words became we will, we will, we *will!*— and when I put my hand on the log and vault over it I feel like if I don't hold back I'll just sail right off in the sky—the log's ready to go—it was ready when Hank whistled—all the dickens needs now's a good shove to get it over the rock it's hung against. Let's see here . . .

Joe circled the end of the log and looked at the jack. It was screwed out to its maximum length, with one end anchored against a rock and the other biting into the bark of the log. To unscrew it meant that the log would fall back a few inches while he anchored the jack against another rock. "Bug that," he said aloud, laughing, and told himself, "Don't give a *inch!*" He wedged his compact little body in on top of the jack, with his shoulders against the rock and his boots against the log. I give a yeah-h-h *shove be thou you* dickens *cast* into the uh uh *sea!* Yeah! She teeters over the rock, rolls against a stump picking up speed, spins off the stump, and slides straight as an arrow *whew* down the hill to within a bare half-yard of the river! Good deal, I'd say. "Hey . . ." Joe stood up and shouted over his shoulder at Hank and old Henry, watching him. "See *that?* Oh man; no sense messin' around, the way I see it. Now, you fellas want me to kick *that* one downhill and save you the effort?"

Laughing, he skidded down the slope with the jack light under his arm and his boots flying. And the little transistor bumping and squeaking against his neck . . .

*I know you love me*
*An' happy we could be*
*If some folks would leave us alone. . . .*

All righty now—I *screw* the jack short again and *wedge* it under the log and *twist!* He watched the butt of it bite the juicy bark. The wooden screw of the implement lengthened out with his cranking. The log rolled a few feet, paused—*this* time she pitches crashing through shredding fern blackberry vines and *into* the river. Yes sir, all righty, *there!* He picked up his jack, slung it across his shoulder by the strap, and swarmed up the hill on all fours—who-so-ever!—snorting and whooping as he came, like a water spider fleeing to high ground. His face was scratched and red when he reached the second log, where Hank worked the saw. "Hankus, ain't you finished bucking this thing yet? Henry, it looks like me'n you have to carry our load an' then some to make up for this loafer!"

Then vaulted over the log, the mud on his boots turning to wings: and whosoever shall not doubt in his heart, he will, by golly, he *will . . . !*

In her shack Indian Jenny hummed over an astrologer's chart that was patterned mysteriously with glass rings *interlacing!* Lee sipped coffee at the Sea Breeze. At the house Viv finished up the last of the dishes and wondered what to start on next. With Jan and the kids staying at the new place, there's not so much rush. And it's nice to set my own pace. I enjoy Jan and the kids here, and I'll miss them when they move into the other place, but it's nice to be here and set my own pace. Boy oh boy, is it quiet just here alone . . .

Standing in the center of the big living room, watching the river, feeling distracted and flushed, anxious almost . . . like I'm expecting something to happen. One of the kids to holler, I guess. I know what'll calm me down; take a nice long hot soak in the tub. Aren't you the Miss Lazy Britches? But gee, is it still and quiet . . .

Hank wiped his nose on the wet cuff of his sweat shirt sticking from his poncho, then grabbed the saw again and dug into the trunk of the tree before him, feeling the relaxation of labor, of simple uncomplicated labor, run through his body like a warm liquid. . . . (Like a sleep, sort of. More relaxing than some sleeps a guy could name. I never minded work so much. I could of got along right well just doing a plain eight-to-five with the bull telling what to do and where to do it. If he had been a decent bull and fairly reasonable about that what and where. Yes I could of....) Everything was going pretty good. The logs fell good and the wind stayed down. Henry helped where he was able, picking the trees, figuring the troughs, arranging the screwjacks in place, using his experience instead of bones he knew were brittle as chalk . . . wheezing, spitting, thinking a man *can* whup it, even he don't have nothin' but knowhow left, even his legs like butter and his arms and hands like cracking glass and he don't have nothin' but his knowhow left—he can *still* help whup it! Downhill Joe Ben paced off twenty-five steps and cut through his log, feeling the screaming vibration of the chain saw tingle up his arms and accumulate in his back muscles like a charge of electrical power . . . building, yeah, rising oh yeah and a *little* more and I'll just *grab* this log up and *bust* it over my knee! Watch if I don't. . . .

On the counter of the Sea Breeze Cafe and Grill was a selection box for our youth's music. To pass the wait (I told myself I was waiting for my father to show up at the Snag across the street) I took a survey of what Young America was singing these days. Let's see . . . we've got Terry Keller "Coming with Summer"—very neat —a "Stranger on the Shore" called—s'help me—Mister Acker Bilk. Earl Grant "Swinging Gently"; Sam Cook "Twistin' the Night Away"; Kingston Trio "Jane Jane Janing" . . . Brothers Four . . . Highwaymen (singing "Birdman of Alcatraz," a ballad, based on the movie, that is based on the book, that is based on the life of a lifer who has probably never even *heard* of the Highwaymen . . .) the Skyliners . . . Joey Dee and the Starlighters . . . Pete Hanly doing "Dardanella" (how did that slip in?), Clyde McSomebody asking "Let's Forget about the Past" . . . and currently number one, at least in the Sea Breeze Cafe and Grill, a waitress with three pounds of nose under thirty ounces of powder accompanying herself on a tub of dishes while she sings "Why Hang Around?"

I muttered in my coffee cup. "Because I'm waiting for my daddy to come get me." Which convinced no one. . . .

The hillside rang with the tight whine of cutting; the sound of work in the woods was like insects in the walls. Numb clubs of feet registered the blow against the cold earth only by the pained jarring in the bones. Henry dragged a screwjack to a new log. Joe Ben sang along with his radio:

> "*Leaning, leaning,*
> *Safe and secure from all alarms . . .*"

The forest fought against the attack on its age-old domain with all

the age-old weapons nature could muster: blackberries strung out
barbed barricades; the wind shook widow-makers crashing down
from high rotted snags; boulders reared silently from the ground to
block slides that had looked smooth and clear a moment before;
streams turned solid trails into creeping ruts of icy brown lava. . . .
And in the tops of the huge trees, the very rain seemed to work
at fixing the trees standing, threading the million green needles in
an attempt to stitch the trees upright against the sky.

But the trees continued to fall, gasping long sighs and ka-whump-
ing against the spongy earth. To be trimmed and bucked into logs.
To be coaxed and cajoled downhill into the river with unflagging
regularity. In spite of all nature could do to stop it.

*Leaning on the ev-ver-last-ting arms.*

As the trees fell and the hours passed, the three men grew accustomed to one another's abilities and drawbacks. Few words actually
passed between them; they communicated with the unspoken language of labor toward a shared end, becoming more and more an
efficient, skilled team as they worked their way across the steep
slopes; becoming almost one man, one worker who knew his body
and his skill and knew how to use them without waste or overlap.

Henry chose the trees, picked the troughs where they would fall,
placed the jacks where they would do the most good. And stepped
back out of the way. *Here she slides! See? A man can whup it goddammit with nothin' but his experience an' stick-to-'er, goddam if
he can't.* . . . Hank did the falling and trimming, wielding the
cumbersome chain saw tirelessly in his long, cable-strong arms, as
relentless as a machine; working not fast but steadily, mechanically,
and certainly far past the point where other fallers would have
rested, pausing only to refuel the saw or to place a new cigarette in
the corner of his mouth when his lips felt the old one burning near—
taking the pack from the pouch of his sweat shirt, shaking a cigarette
into view, withdrawing it with his lips . . . touching the old butt for
the first time with his muddy gloves when he removed it to light
the new smoke. Such pauses were brief and widely separated in the
terrible labor, yet he almost enjoyed returning to work, getting back
in the groove, not thinking, just doing the work just like it was
eight to five and none of that other crap to worry about, *just letting
somebody turn me on and aim me at what and where is just the*

way I like it. The way it used to be. Peaceful. And simple. (*And I ain't thinking about the kid, not in hours I ain't wondered where he is.*) . . . And Joe Ben handled most of the screwjack work, rushing back and forth from jack to jack, a little twist here, a little shove there, and whup! she's turnin', tippin', heading out downhill! Okay—get down there an' set the jacks again, crank and uncrank right back an' over again. Oh yeah, that's the one'll do it. *Shooooom*, all the way, an' here comes another one, Andy old buddy, big as the ark . . . feeling a mounting of joyous power collecting in his back muscles, an exhilaration of faith rising with the crash of each log into the river. Whosoever believes in his heart shall cast *mountains* into the sea an' Lord knows what other stuff . . . then heading back up to the next log—running, leaping, a wingless bird feathered in leather and aluminum and mud, with a transistor radio bouncing and shrill beneath his throat:

> *Leaning on Jee-zus, leaning on Jee-zus*
> *Safe an' secure from all alarms . . .*

Until the three of them meshed, dovetailed . . . into one of the rare and beautiful units of effort sometimes seen when a jazz group is making it completely, swinging together completely, or when a home-town basketball squad, already playing over its head, begins to rally to overtake a superior opponent in a game's last minute . . . and the home boys can't miss; because everything—the passing, the dribbling, the plays—every tiny piece is clicking perfectly. When this happens everyone watching knows . . . that, be it five guys playing basketball, or four blowing jazz, or three cutting timber, that *this bunch—right* now, right *this* moment—is the best of its kind in the world! But to become this kind of perfect group a team must use *all* its components, and use them in the slots best suited, and use them all with the pitiless dedication to victory that drives them up to their absolute peak, and past it.

Joe felt this meshing. And old Henry. And Hank, watching his team function, was aware only of the beauty of the team and of the free-wheeling thrill of being part of it. Not of the pitiless drive. Not of the three of them building toward a peak the way a machine running too fast too long accelerates without actually speeding up as it reaches a breaking point that it can't be aware of, and goes on past that breaking point, accelerating *past* it and *toward* it at the

same time and at the same immutable rate. As the trees fell and
the radio filled in between their falling:

> Leaning on Jee-zus, leaning on Jee-zus,
> Leaning on the everlasting arms.

The fogged glass door of the Sea Breeze Cafe and Grill swung
open and a pimpled Adonis came in out of the rain and seated
himself down the counter from me, openly contemplating the heist
of one of the three-week-old Hersheys beside the cash register—
could get him two months for petty theft, and more acne.

"Mrs. Carleson . . . I'm thinkin' on drivin' up river to Swedesgap to see Lily and I'll be goin' past Montgomerys' house if you'd
care to visit your mama"—one eye on the stale chocolate, the other
on the staler waitress.

"No, I guess not right now, Larkin; but I thank you for the offer."

" 'S okay." *Snatch!* "Well, I'll see you later."

Our eyes met as he turned from the counter, and we each grinned
sheepishly, sharing our mutual secret guilts. He hurried on to his
car, where he hesitated outside the café for a few minutes, worrying
about my discretion, wondering if he should come back in and pay
for the snatched Hershey before I snitched. *And the trees fall, in
the forest, and the rain slices the sky* . . . while I hesitated *inside*
the café, worrying about my own discretion, wondering why I kidded
myself about waiting for my long-lost father . . . *In the forest, bent
over a log, old Henry skillfully wedges a screwjack between stump
and log that's just exactly by god how I useta do it even if I maybe
ain't so spry as back in them days* . . . and wondering *also* why I
didn't get up and go outside and ask the pimpled thief for a ride.
Why not? He's going to the Montgomery place, right past our
house; he would have to oblige me, with all I have on him! *Joe Ben
runs downhill, leaping the ferns, right on the heels of a sliding log,
setting his jack almost before it stops, because there ain't no sense
lettin' up if you don't doubt, because if you don't doubt you are
already in God's fur-lined pocket* . . . So I slid from the leatherette
stool, dug a handful of change from my pocket to pay my bill, and
hurried toward the door—determined to make the move before the
heat of my decision cooled . . . *And Hank rips his saw free from
a huge moss-covered trunk just as it starts to tip, steps back to watch
the top far above him lean, wave, faster, gasping and whistle, suck·*

*ing* gray *rain* after *it just the way I like to see it, simple and straight
and* whomp! *Who knows a better life?* . . . thinking as I hurried
out, Viv, here I come, ready or not! "What?" Viv says, but it's
just the dogs at the porch door wanting dinner. She puts down her
broom, wiping back her hair. Lee flips up his collar as he steps
into the rain. The pimpled boy panics at his approach and spins
away with the car. Hank kills his saw to refuel it. Lights a new
cigarette, starts the little quarterhorse motor again. Old Henry jug-
gles at his snuff can, his hands cold and stiff. Joe jumps, trips, falls
and takes a strip of hide off his chin with the grooved dial of his
little radio, switching off the music. A moment's hush runs like a
fuse through the wet sky. They each pause and notice the pressing
silence, then make ready to move again, forgetting it. Lee starts
walking along the gravel, east. Viv feeding the hounds. Hank thumb-
ing the chain oil button on the saw. Henry packing his charge of snuff,
wheezing and spitting. Joe Ben turning his radio back on, convinced
that the fall has by golly *improved* the reception . . . to Burl Ives:

> *When you walk the streets you will have no cares*
> *If you walk the lines and not the squares.*

Then, as though the fuse had burned away, the forest ended its
brief hush.

And a wind, heavy with rain, came up from the river through
the fern and huckleberry like a deep-drawn breath; and "*as you go
through life make this your goal* . . ." and Hank feels the air about
him swell with that wind, gathering with it, just as he rocks the
saw free from a limb he is bucking off the fallen fir, looking up,
frowning to himself before he even hears it listen! the maddened
snapping of bark someplace else moving, he turns back to the log
in time to see a bright yellow-white row of teeth appear splintering
over the mossy lips to gnash the saw from his hands fling it furiously
to the ground it claws screaming machine frenzy and terror trying
to dig escape from the vengeful wood just above where old Henry
drops his screwjack *Gaw* when mud and pine needles spray over
him like black *damn!* rain an' even if I don't *see* so clear as I used
to there's still time to get *down* the hill Joe Ben hears the metal
scream behind a curtain of fern but if you *never doubt* in your mind
*where's Hank* spins away leaving his log and turn me on and aim
me is all I want still peaceful, relaxed like sleep from eight to five

without thinking or I'd said *Nothing doing* to see the log springing suddenly massive upright pivots on Henry's ARM GOD my good one goddammit GOD GOD just leave the old nigger enough to whup it enough arm that he'd been using to fix his screwjack it waves limp then disappears a second beneath the row of teeth before the log springs on downhill massive upright like the bastard is try-ing to stand up again and find its *stump!* a swinging green fist slams Hank's shoulder goes somersaulting past upright like the bastard is so mad getting chopped down it jumps up chews off the old man's arm clubs me one now tearing off downhill after "Joe! Joby!" the last of us and Joe Ben's hand parts the fern there's this *blunted* white circle fanged jagged spreading toward him larger and larger down the mud-trough *oop* springs backward from the fern over the bank not really scared or startled or anything but *light* like the mud on my boots turned to *wings* . . . and hangs in the air over the bank for an instant . . . a jack-in-the-box, bobbling . . . sprung up from his box and dangling backward above the tangle of vines . . . face sudden clown red the color of the old man's arm now crushed flowing all the way to the boogerin' *bone* . . . hangs, sprung up, for an instant, with that ugly little goblin face red and still merry grinning to me that it's okay Hankus okay that you couldn't of been thinkin' that limb you cut off would of done this then falls cut loose slapping back to the muddy bank outa the way if it wasn't "Look out!" for that screwjack "Look out!" don't worry Hankus face still red like the old man's GOD you booger, leave me some-*thin'* to fight with the ARM GOD my one good ARM *Look out!* just don't worry Hankus just never doubt slaps against the muddy bank right in the path LOOK OUT JOBY slaps and rolls as the runaway log thunks the log he'd been working with his screwjack jolts sideways rearing above ROLL rolls still light-feeling confident almost safe half into the river almost but slamming down, the log, across both legs, and stopping.

> *As you walk through life you will have no cares*
> *If you walk the lines and not the squares. . . .*

There was again the near, the more than silence: the radio; the hiss of the rain on the conifer leaves, the river sucking at its banks. . . . Hank stood, reeling, the only movement in the fern, dizzy from the blow—waiting—that he'd received in his back. Everything was still now—waiting—crystallized and set in dead soundless calm, like a dream stone set in a dream ring. "When you go through life make this your goal." (Except it wasn't a dream, just crystallized calm. *For I'm wide awake, so wide awake my brain has run off and left time behind. Time will start in a minute; time, will start, in a minute. . . .*) The thought continued to echo softly. "Watch the doughnut, not the hole." (*In a minute, in a minute. I been asleep. I just woke but time ain't started yet. In a minute that branch there'll spring back and those mallards froze in the air'll go on flying and the old man's arm will bleed and I'll holler my ass off. In a minute. If I can just break loose, then in a minute I'll*) "Joe!" (*in a minute I'll*) "Joby! Hang on, I'm comin'!"

He ran down the gouged rut of mud and leaped the bank of berry vine and saw Joe Ben sitting in water to his shoulders, looking as though he were holding the log on his lap. His narrow back was toward the rutted bank, and he smiled out across the river toward the mountains. He was resting his chin on the bark, in no apparent pain. "Man oh man, she really came barrelin' after me, didn't she?" He laughed softly, strangely calm. *Like me,* Hank thought; *time hasn't started for him yet. He don't know yet he's in trouble. . . .*

"You bad off, Joby?"

"I don't think too bad. She lit on my legs, but the mud under me there's soft. I don't feel like I broke anything. Didn't even bust my radio." He twisted the dial; Burl Ives still strummed out across the water:

> . . . *in golden letters three foot high*
> *Is this phil-os-o-fee.*

There was—waiting together—an odd and honest moment before either of them spoke again.

> *When you walk the streets you will have no cares*
> *If you walk the lines and not the squares. . . .*

Then . . . Hank moved suddenly. "Hang on," he said. "Let me get up there after the saw."

"What about the old man? I heard him yell."

"It mashed hell outa one arm. He's passed out. Let me get the saw."

"Go on and see to him, Hank. I'm not hurtin'. Don't get in a stew about me; you know what I told you? I been promised to liye till eighty and have twenty-five kids. See to the old man while you're gettin' that saw. And be careful."

"Be careful?" Listen to the crazy outfit. "Five kids he's got and he tells me to be careful. You bet," I told him and headed back up the slope. I was gasping so I almost conked out by the time I made it back up to Henry. "Whew; too frantic . . ." I told myself to ease off, that we was in a little tight but we'd make it. Ease off and be calm about it like Joe. I forced my lungs to breathe deep and slow and tried to make my hands stop trembling. "Whew lordy . . ." Cool, cool and slow. Just don't sweat it. Go slow. . . .

While his head rang and his heart rattled out a code he was still—waiting—trying to pass off as nonsense, as panicked nonsense.

On a mound of pine needles and mud the old man lay like a broken gull. I knelt and looked at the crushed arm. Well . . . it was in bad shape but not bleeding too hard. I took my handkerchief out of my pocket and put a tourniquet at the armpit and the blood stopped gushing so big. That would hold till I could get him up the hill to the pick-up. Be a job, toting him up. But then maybe Joby's legs are all right and we can rig up a stretcher and we can both carry him as soon as I saw that log off. "That log." In a minute I'll go back down and saw through that—"but that *log!*" In a minute I'll—"That log on Joe . . . in the water!"

Hank's head jerked up. That rattling was like a frantic telegraph. The message crystallized everything—the waiting over—before his eyes once more: *That's* why I couldn't ease off! I knew, back down there. I knew. Just like I knew before that log sprung in the air that there was trouble. Just like I knew clear back last night that I'll—Oh, Christ, that log, the way it's laid!

With a cry he grabbed the chain saw and once again ran stumbling down the gouged trough, charging through the vines and springing fern down toward the bank, where Joe Ben lay trapped . . .

Walking the roadside gravel from the restaurant east toward the old house, resolved to make my own way now that I was in motion, even if it meant walking the whole eight miles, I found myself enjoying a satisfying symbiosis with the rain: I was walking from the rain, along with it. This meager assistance of water blowing against my neck piqued my determination: I can make it, I grimly told myself, I *shall* make it. And this way I didn't have to think about the ordeal ahead, only the struggle getting there. I trudged onward and up-river-ward, resolute and relentless, never even once sticking up my thumb to hitch a ride: I can make it, by gosh, and—if you don't count the rain—by myself by gosh. . . .

Hank bounded through the bank brush, right out onto the log; he could see the water had already risen a few inches up Joe's back.

"Glad to see you," Joby said. "Gettin' a little deep all of—"

"Joe! I can't! The log here!" I fumbled with the starting rope of my saw, damn near raving. *My hands are shaking again.* "I mean I won't be *able* to cut—I mean look at the goddam waterline where I have to—" The saw whirred. Joe's face darkened when he saw what I meant. The log was deep enough in the water that I wouldn't be able to cut through it without submerging the saw's motor. That's why I couldn't make myself cool down. I knew, before, up the hill, that I couldn't cut it. Maybe before then. "Look out," I said anyway. "I'll see what we—"

Again Hank jabbed the guard prongs of the saw into the bark and tipped the whirring teeth. Joe clinched his eyes as the chips and sawdust flew past him into the berry vines over his shoulder. He felt the chips of bark sting his cheek briefly, then heard the saw sput and gurgle, then stop. It was quiet again; the rain and radio—*As you go through life make this your goal* . . . Joe opened his eyes; out across the river he could see Mary's Peak blurred by rain and the fast-falling dusk. But anyway. Whosoever don't doubt . . . *don't hafta worry.* Hank tried to jerk the saw free to start it again, but it was stuck.

"No good anyway. Never do it, Joe."

"Look, Hankus, it's okay." *Whosoever knows in his heart.* "I know it's okay . . . because look: *all* we got to do is wait. An' have a little faith. Because look, man: things is already seen to. Ain't this tide coming up gonna float this thing offn me in a minute? Oh yeah, now *ain't* it?"

Hank looked at the log. "I don't know . . . the way it's sitting. It's got to do some rising before it'll lift."

"Then we'll do some waiting," Joe Ben said confidently. "I just wish I'd waited one day to swear off smoking. But I can stand it."

"Sure," Hank said.

"Sure. We'll just wait."

And waited. While the sky before them, over the river, thickened with rain, and the forest behind shushed the wind to listen to the tinny music reeling out below. While freshets gushed icy mud into gullies, gullies into creeks, along banks wattled by erosion.

While the waves, back up the coast at the Devil's Jailhouse, thudded higher and higher toward escape up the cancered rock wall, and the clouds combed overhead, in from the sea over the surf, and broke against the high slopes to rake back the way they had come.

While Viv rose from a hot tub of water and hummed herself dry before an electric heater in a room that smelled of rose oil.

And while the distance between the old house and my rain-soaked and relentless shoes clicked steadily away, my resolution mounted: Eight miles through this rain, eight miserable miles . . . why, if I can make that, I can make *anything* . . .

Hank tried to set the screwjacks to move the log, but they only twisted into the mud.

"What we need is a horse," Hank said, cursing the jacks.

"An' then how?" Joe asked, amused by Hank's frustration at the log. "Hook on and drag it over me up the hill? No, what you need is a *whale* in the river yonder to pull it off that way. You bet. Know where we can rent a good stout whale broke to harness?"

"How you doin'? You feel it lightenin' any yet?"

"Maybe some. I can't tell. Because I'm cold as a witch's *tit*, if you got to know. How much has it come up?"

"Only another couple inches," Hank lied and lit another cigarette. He offered Joe a drag, but Joe, after eying the smoke, allowed as how he'd best keep his promises to the Lord, things being the way they were. Hank smoked in silence.

The kingfishers waited ceremoniously on the branches over the river.

> . . . *watch the doughnut, not the hole.*

When the water reached Joe Ben's neck Hank dived under the surface and braced his shoulder against the bark and tried to budge the log. But it would have taken a two-hundred-horse Diesel to move that weight and he knew it. He also knew that the way the log lay, slanting up the bank, it was going to take considerable water to float it off. And when it did move it was likely to roll up bank, more onto Joe.

Occasionally a kingfisher would dive, then return to the branch without chancing the water.

Joe had turned down the radio and they talked some now. About the old man lying up the hill under Hank's parka, about the job and how they'd call J. J. Bismarck, the head man at Wakonda Pacific, first thing they got to a phone and score some non-union help for the run tomorrow.

"Maybe get old Jerome Bismarck hisself out there in corks doin' the river-run twist—wouldn't that be a sight to behold? J. J. Bismarck floppin' around in the water, all four hundred pounds of him? Lord, Lord . . ."

Hank laughed at the thought. "Okay, buster, but let me call to your attention the first time you tried to pond-monkey. Remember? Right in the middle of January, and there was ice all around the logs?"

"No. No, I don't recall nothing about that. Not a thing."

"No? Why, I guess I should refresh your memory. You'd put on about a dozen sweat shirts and a set of rain pants and a big mackinaw—"

"Nope. That wasn't me. I never owned no mackinaw. Some other boy . . ."

"And first jack outa the box you fell in and went down like a rock. Just one little whoop. And it took half the mill crew to haul you out, you weighed so much. I like to died laughing."

"Somebody else. I'm *always* light and agile. And, anyhow, what about you the time you was wearin' that scarf that Barbara knitted for you and it got caught in the chain saw—for a while there we didn't know whether you was goin' out by hanging or *decapitation!* How 'bout *that?*"

"You remember that time the wrestling team drove to Bend for a dual match—talkin' about clothes—and big old Bruce Shaw brought along a *tuxedo* because the coach told him to dress?"

"Lord, Lord—Bruce Shaw . . ."

"Bruce the moose—he just kept growing."

"Ain't that the truth! Oh yeah. He was in our congregation for a while, did I tell you that? Falling down and talking in tongues. Dangerous to get too close; he was bigger'n he was in high school."

"Lordy that was pretty big. He was two-eighty or -ninety then. . . ."

"After he quit comin' to services I lost track of him. What come of him, hear tell?"

"He got in a bad car wreck seven or so years ago . . . Hey, I ever tell you? I run into him, not long after that very wreck, I guess, over in Eugene at Melody Ranch. I saw him at the dance and said hiya Bruce, friendly enough, but he was salty as hell about something, just scowled at me like he'd break me in *half*. And—listen to this, I never told you this—I got a real skinful that night, one of the fullest ever. That summer, home from the service. Really bombed. I *shoulda* passed out, but I made the mistake of thinking I was up to maneuvering *around*, you see. So I left the dance and went out and started walking, see, and this *tree* accosted me, man, kept me pinned down for hours. Because I'm really loaded and . . . it's dark and late . . . and I'm walking along and I come up to this tree—with sap running down on it, just *standing* there. It's old Shaw, big as life and twice as ugly. Shaw, I'm certain of it; old Bruce the moose . . . and man, he looks *bad!* He's got his shirt off and his arms all spread out and he's got scabs all down the front of him. I stand there and say, 'Hey there, Shaw, how's it hangin'?' Nothing. 'What's happening lately, Shaw boy?' He still don't say nothing, but man he *looks bad.* I ask him how things are up at the dam where he was working and how is his *girl*, and his mom, and I don't know what all, and he just *stands* there—big and bad-looking. So finally—after I've been shivering in front o' him, thinking he's after me for some business I can't even recall—I go to sliding around him. I sorta put myself in my pocket and slide *away* around him and on down the street, and I don't know old Shaw's a tree till I see he's still standing there in the morning."

"Oh yeah? You never told me that."

"Swear to God."

"Jesus. Pinned down by a tree."

While they were laughing the squeak of the radio suddenly stopped. "Oh dadgum; I forgot to take my radio from around my neck. Dadgum . . . it's ruint. Now don't you laugh, dang you. I thought a lot of that little outfit." Then broke into giggles himself.

But without his radio Joe's laughter gave to chattering. Hank's laughter only increased. "Whoee. After you braggin' about not breaking it when a log rolled over you; now you dunk it . . . oh lord, oh me. . . ." Joe tried to join him. Their laughter stretched out across the water. The kingfishers watched from between solemnly hunched shoulders. As they were laughing a sudden gust of wind blew a small wave into Joe Ben's mouth. Joe choked and spat and laughed some more . . . then turned to ask Hank, in a voice too full of kidding, "Now you ain't about to let this here old river just up and *drown* me, are you?"

"This river? Why, by gosh; is Joe Ben Stamper worryin' this old river? Sounds screwy. Because man, I thought all you had to do was call your Big Buddy and He'd just aim His finger an' the water'd just hallelujah *snap* back away from you."

"Yeah, but I've explained this: I hate to *bother* Him if some of us can handle it. Hate to call anybody out in this stuff, especially Him."

"Okay; I can see that; He's probably got a lot on His mind."

"You bet. It's a busy season, Christmas coming. Then all them trouble spots. Laos, Vietnam . . ."

"And lots of goiters to tend to in Oklahoma. Oh, I can see how you'd hesitate . . ."

"That's right. That's right. Oklahoma needs Him special this year. I believe Oral Roberts has got Him signed on down there right now, shooting a TV series. But the thing is"—Joe raised his chin to avoid another small wave—"this dang *water* keeps gettin' up my nose. I'll tell you what, Hankus: maybe you better hustle up to the pick-up after a length of hose . . . it might just be a while before this log begins to float."

You'd never thought it possible, but Joby was commencing to sound worried. "What is this noise?" I ask him. "Is this the boy who says, 'Accept your lot and hold your mouth right!' . . . scared of a little wet? Besides, Joby, it's a good three-fourths mile up hill to that pick-up; you want to be alone all that time?"

"No," he says very fast, and quotes: " 'It ain't so good that man should be alone.' Genesis. Just before He whopped up Eve. But, still and all, maybe you oughta run get that hose. . . ."

I splashed into the water beside Joe and stood with my hand resting on his shoulder.

"No," I told him. "It's a fifteen-minute run up to that pick-up and a fifteen-minute run back and at the rate the—well, one thing; I'm just too *wore out* to go runnin' around here and there, this way and that, at your every little whim-wham. An' you can't run your neck out like you are much longer neither. You remember that leatherback terrapin we caught in the slough bottom once? An' put in a tub with too much water—two, three inches—and nothing for him to climb up on? He didn't drown, you remember? He stood on the bottom of the tub and stretched his neck for so long and out so far to breathe that he *stretched* himself to death. . . . And, where I ain't worried that you'll drown, there *is* some chance to might stretch yourself to death." Joe tried to laugh, then shut his mouth before another wave got him. "Anyhow, that log should come up from there right away. An', if worst comes to worst, I can always give you mouth-to-mouth till it rises."

"Well, sure; sure, that's the truth," he said. "I hadn't *thought* of that." He brought his lips together for a bit as the water lapped up to his face. "Oh yeah; you can always give me mouth-to-mouth."

"Just so long as you don't get *worried* under there . . ."

"Worried? I ain't worried. Just cold. I know you'll do somethin'."

"Sure."

"Just like we used to trade off with one aqualung under water."

"Sure. It's no different."

"Just like it."

I stood there in the water beside the log, shivering.

"All a man is ever got to do is hold his mouth right an' keep his faith. An' wait . . ." He clamped his mouth.

"Sure," I finished for him while the wave passed. "Just wait. And think about good times ahead."

"Right! And—boy oh boy—Thanksgiving in a few days," Joe remembered, smacking his lips. "That's something, that's good times. 'N' this business will be all over. We'll have to really do something *full-size* for Thanksgiving."

"Damn right."

Just stood there and shivered, feeling like maybe the time for doing something full-size had long gone. . . .

The kingfishers waited. . . . The rain buzzed pensively against the river, adding drop after drop . . . while Hank spent the last darkening hours of that day clinging to the bark of the log, the sharp brown fingers of the current dragging at his legs—shivering at first, then cold beyond cold and no longer shivering—carrying lungs full of air to a face invisible beneath the water. . . . All Joe has to do, he told himself, is keep from panicking, keep up his spirits.

Joe seemed in the best of spirits. Even after his little scarred face had been submerged Hank could still hear sputtering giggles, and when he ducked his face under still feel that goofy, half-wit grin against Joe's lips. The situation seemed so bizarre to them both that for a time they felt silly and foolish and made the job of transferring the air more difficult and dangerous with their laughing, both realizing it, but unable to stop.

For a time they were unable to think of anything except sonofagun I bet we look like fools; I bet if old Henry up there came to an' saw this we'd never be shut of him kidding us, not in the next hundred years. And, for a time, even after all the situation's ludicrous humor was exhausted for Hank, he still could feel the amusement beneath the water. This kept his hopes alive; *as long's the little fart is laughing under there we'll make out. I can carry him air all night if it comes to it. As long as he's got faith enough to see it's funny. As long as I still feel him grinning. That's what'll save his ass, him still getting a boot out of being in a bad fix; him still holding his mouth right.* . . .

But beneath the water, in the close, cold dark, the fix was as bad as it was above. And as humorless. More so, actually. Still . . . there was something funny happening. Not funny the way Joe liked, but funny like it was somebody else's joke. And the laughter was no more his laughter than the grin was his grin. They came from someplace else. They had started coming over him right after the water completely covered his face. Black and cold. Shock and horror, then . . . this funny thing swimming up out of the dark. Like something'd been there all along and just waiting for it to get dark enough. Now, in tight silence beneath the water, Joe feels it trying to fit into the skin of him, trying to eat away the thing *he* is inside, and fit into *his* skin. A black, laughing cancer trying to take over the shell of him. He doesn't like it. He fights to stop it by trying to think of brighter sides. *Like Thanksgiving just a couple days off. One of the best of all times, any time, and this time due to be one of the best of the best of all times. Because this WP deal will be finished; we'll be able to take a breather. With smells all morning. Sage and onion dressing in the turkey. Punkin pie with allspice. Watch the doughnut.* Then sit around the stove in the living room, fart and belch, fart and belch like it used to be. Watching the ballgames on TV and drinking beer and smoking cigars. *No, no beer or cigars. I forgot. Not the hole.* No coffee neither. *Don't laugh. Because a man,* Brother Walker says, *builds his mansion in the sky out of the lumber of Good Living as you walk the streets that he saws here on earth. Lays up his treasures in Heaven by not partaking in—don't laugh now you will have no cares—by not indulging in—don't you laugh because you start laughing pretty quick I choke then I never catch up* . . . *Besides. There's nothing funny. Not under here. Look: I'm a little worried—and not the squares—and I'm cold; and I hurt. That's not funny. I want to go home. I want to go to my new home and put on the clean suntans Jan's ironing for me and* have the twins sit on my belly and Squeaky show us what she drew today in drawing. And all them things. I want . . . cranberries and mincemeat. Oh yeah! And sweet potatoes with marshmallows—don't laugh—with marshmallows baked on top and turkey . . . Don't laugh I want it *again!* Don't you laugh it ain't funny never to taste sweet potatoes baked with marshmallows on top again! But don't you want *watch the doughnut* that cigar too? *Yes!* but dang it a man's got to build his mansion out of! Sure but you tell me—*don't get me laughing!*—wouldn't you rather have that cup of hot coffee now that you didn't—*don't, dang you!*—didn't have this morning? *No! Not the hole.* And don't laugh I know you now *get outa here*— or that Judy girl who was always—*get outa here, Devil!*—putting the ray on you in math class? *Satan! Satan! I know you and don't laugh*— you know me—*you black Devil*—you know better than that now *Devil! The Good Lord in His goodness He leadeth me through the valley of the shadow!* Come on now, sonny, don't make me laugh; you know better than that bullshit. *It ain't funny! Or bullshit. I'll hack it out if I just don't go to doubting.* Oh yeah, sure you will . . . *I will! Whosoever believe that he don't laugh!* Sure you will just like you hacked me out with a brush knife *it ain't funny* no but it still gives a fellow amusement *don't laugh you you cheated me* no you cheated me *no no they* yeah yeah that's what I mean it was *Him and them* yeah that's what's so *don't do it!* baloney what's the *Oh oh oh no* difference? See? See? If we all got cheated? *But the cigars!* Oh yeah, I missed the smokes but *And o my god I liked coffee* oh yeah me too but *that's what's so goddam funny so blessed funny so oh oh . . . oh . . .*

A bubbling of hysterical mirth erupted in Hank's face just as he was bending to deliver another breath to Joe. It startled him so he lost his lungful of air. He stared, frowning, at the now placid spot where the strange laughter had exploded. Then gulped another lungful of air and plunged his face into the water, feeling with his lips until he found Joby's mouth . . . open in the dark there, open and round with laughing. And huge; like an underwater cave, it's so huge, like a drain hole at the world's deepest bottom, rimmed with cold flesh . . . so huge it could empty seas.

And the current swirling down in a black spiral, filling it to laugh again.

He did not attempt to force his cargo of air into that lifeless hole. He withdrew his face slowly and stared again at the surface

of water that lay featureless and unruffled over Joe. No different
from any of the rest of the surface, all the way across the river, all
the way out to sea. (*But Joe Ben is dead, don't you realize?*) The
clicking was going again—waiting—louder and harder. And a fuzziness,
too, and nausea. (*The little sonofabitch is dead. And yet, the little
goblin is dead don't you see? in spite of the sudden rolling pitch
of nausea, above that ballooning sense of loss that you always feel
right after somebody close dies but he's dead, Joe Ben is dead, don't
you understand, I experienced a sort of feeling of relief. I was tired,
and it was almost over, and I was relieved to know I would be able
to rest before much longer. Waiting. Tired for a long time. Just a little
bit more, just get the old man up to the pick-up and in town to some
help, and maybe then it will be over. Finally finished. After going
on now for Christ how long? after going on now for at least . . .
since I saw the old man coming down the hill from the pick-up
this morning, looking all worried. No. Before that. Since earlier this
morning, or last night waking up and seeing my reflection. No. Before that, too. Since Joby first got me out for football and made me
his hero. Since he first jumped into the ocean that time to make
me outswim him. Since the old man nailed that plaque on my wall.
Since Boney Stokes bugged old Henry about his old man. Since,
since, since . . .*) until—standing there, waiting, still looking at that
spot of water—his burning lungs broke the backrushing stream of
thoughts, "But you're dead, Joby, you bastard oh damn you you're
dead"—and he blew out the stale air in a loud, gasping sob . . .

As it grew darker along the highway more and more kindred souls
motoring in my direction up river pulled over to ask if they mightn't
give me a lift. I refused politely and continued stoically on with a
delicious air of martyrdom about me. The walk had become more
and more religious to me; a pilgrimage with built-in penance, taking me to my mosque, my shrine of salvation, and at the same time
punishing me with rain and cold for the sin I planned to commit
when I got there. And, believe it or not, the closer I got to the
house the slower fell the rain and the warmer felt the air. Quite
a change, I thought, from streets filled with sleet and demonic
doctors . . .

(After climbing up onto the end of the log still sticking out of
the water, I noticed for the first time since the accident that the
weather was clearing off a little; the wind had died down almost
complete, and the rain was beginning to ease off. I rested a minute

or so on the log there; then I got out of my back pocket some big cable staples and a crescent wrench I was carrying. I found Joe Ben's hand floating in the dark. I pulled the sleeve up over the limp hand and rolled it back into a thick cuff. Then I nailed it to the log. I found the other hand and did the same; it was clumsy work, hammering the big staples through the heavy fabric with a crescent wrench, about half under water to boot. I took out my hanky and tied it to that branch, the one that had whacked me. When I was finished I stood up, and already I could feel a little movement beneath my feet as the rising current lifted at the log. "If Joe could have hung on another twenty minutes or so . . ." Then I jumped from the log into the tangle of vines and made my way through the forest toward the place I had left the old man.

The climb up the hill to the pick-up shook the old man to consciousness. He rolled his poor old head back and forth in the dark while I was starting the motor, asking, "What? What, dammit all?" and, "You got the cast on the wrong ruttin' side er somethin'?"

I felt I should say something to reassure him but somehow couldn't make myself speak. I just kept saying, "Hang tough, hang tough." I drove the pick-up back down the hill, listening to the whimpered questions like they were coming from a long ways off. When I reached the highway the questions stopped and I could tell by the breathing that he had passed out again. I said thank the Lord for small favors and tore out west. I reached into my breast pocket after my smokes and it wasn't cigarettes at all: it scared me; it was that damned little transistor radio and it had dried out enough to peep a little when I touched it. I throwed it from me and it landed next to the door, going off and on with pieces of Western music. "*Keep movin' on—*" it played. "When they get you goin' they really keep at you," I said out loud. The old man answered, "Grab a root an' dig,"—and I really tromped down on her. I didn't want any more of *that* than necessary.

The rain slowed to a mist and had quit altogether by the time I swung the pick-up into the mill yard. The clouds above were beginning to break up and in the pale moonlight I could see Andy leaning on his peavey like a sleeping heron. I got out and handed him the two candy bars I'd found in the jockey box.

"You got to stay out here all night," I told him. My voice sounded like it was coming from someone standing in the shadow beside me. "Most of the logs rode the current up. You won't see no more probably for three or four hours, till the tides change again. And get every log that comes past, all of them. Every one, you hear me? And watch for one flagged. Joe Ben's nailed onto that one, drowned."

Andy nodded, wide-eyed, but he didn't say anything. I stood there a minute. The overcast had thinned and split above us and was beginning to curl up and pull apart into dark clots; the full white circle of the moon came out now and then between the clots. The dripping berry vines that grew along the plank walk from the mill to the moorage looked like banks of crumpled foil. I saw Andy look at the blood-drenched arms of my sweat shirt, wanting to be told what had happened, but there again—just like back at the slope— I couldn't bring myself to speak. I turned, going back along the planks toward the idling pick-up without saying anything else. I just wanted to be away from people. I didn't want to have to avoid answering questions about what happened. I didn't want the questions.

I barely slowed down as I approached the house. Just enough to glance over and see that the light was still on in Viv's room. I better call her when I get into town, I figured. Jan, too; call them from the hospital. But I knew I wouldn't.

The little radio had finally stopped playing. It was warm in the cab now, and quiet; just the tires ripping along the pavement as I passed our garage, and a sound beside me from the old man like a wind going back and forth over old dead leaves. I was tired. Too tired to mourn or care about what had happened. I'll mourn later, I figured, I'll—"What!" I'll mourn later when I get time—"What?"—after a rest I'll—"What! It's him!" Then I saw the kid, just as I went past the garage. Walking along the highway headed for the house, *not at the hospital, not in town, but here, now, there, back there at the garage, back there getting ready to go down to the launch and across to the house! Damn. They really keep at you. When they get you going they really keep right at you. . . .*)

By the time my damp pilgrimage ended and the garage came into sight it had stopped raining, my nose no longer ran, and a wind had sprung up and showed signs of blowing the skies clear. Yet my old anxiety was returning, barking WATCH OUT WATCH OUT over and over, and this time giving as a reason to hesitate the dangerous lateness of the hour: THEY WILL BE RETURNING; THEY WILL CATCH YOU. . . . But, where I might have procrastinated another hour away haggling with this thought, the reason eliminated itself for me: just as I stepped from the highway to the graveled drive I caught sight of brother Hank himself zooming past in the pick-up, face fixed with the obvious intention of going all the way into town—to look for the old man, I was certain.

That sight scuttled my new excuse; and, never once wondering how Hank had acquired the pick-up without old Henry's driving it to him, I made for the launch, unable to come up with any reasons not to. "Here's your chance to get into the game," I told myself, "with security insured and no tricky grounders or pricky needles."

And tried to convince myself that I was pleased that events had laid the way so open for me.

Indeed, the way seemed to be becoming more open, and more lovely, by the moment. The clouds, suddenly shriveled and empty, were returning on the wind over the treetops back to sea to reload, leaving the land to frost and the boat motor dry when I removed the tarp covering. The moon ran like quicksilver on the motor, guiding my hands to the right instruments; the rope pulled smoothly; the motor started the first try and held, even and full-throated; the mooring rope came loose with a single flip and the prow swung pointing at the house, as sure as a compass needle. And from the glisten of frozen forest across the river I could hear the bugle of an elk, possessed by lust or a cold bed, I didn't know which, but I know those high skirling notes marshaled me forward like a tune from a satyr's pipe. The light from Viv's upstairs window rolled a glowing carpet out across the water to me . . . ushered me dimly up the stairs . . . seeped warmly from beneath her door. Everything was perfect; I will be a veritable stallion, I told myself, Casanova personified . . . and had already knocked when a new fear smote me: *but what if I can't make it!* I TOLD YOU TO WATCH OUT *what if I start to come on like a stallion and can't get it up!*

I was petrified by the prospect; with no luck along that line since way back before Mother's suicide, and months even since my last painful attempt, what reason had I to expect success this time? perhaps *that's* why I have been holding back so long; perhaps it is this pain I have been warned to WATCH OUT for; perhaps I should—

But when a voice called, "Come in, Lee," from the other side of the door, I knew it was too late to use this reason to run, even if the reason had been real.

I opened the door and poked in my head—"Just for a quick hello," I said, and added matter-of-factly, "I walked out from town, now I—"

"I'm glad you did," she said, then added in a lighter tone, "It was getting a little scary out here all by myself so long. Boy! Are you drenched! Come sit by the heater."

"I became separated from Henry at the hospital," I offered lamely.

"Oh? Where do you suppose he went?"

"Where can one ever suppose old Henry goes? Maybe after more of the balm of Gilead. . . ."

She smiled. She was seated on the floor before the humming orange heat of her coiled heater with a book, wearing a pair of tight green capris and one of Hank's plaid woolen shirts that itched itched itched against her skin, I was positive. And the glow of the electric coils made her face and hair shimmer with a deep fluid opulence. "Yes," I said, "I suppose he must have stopped by Gilead for more balm. . . ."

After our initial howdy-do's and what-do-you-supposes, and that stretched instant of silence, I indicated her book. "I see you're still bent on improving your mind."

She smiled at the volume. "It's the Wallace Stevens." She looked back up, asking forgiveness. "I don't know that I'm getting all of it—"

"I don't know that anybody is."

"—but I *like* it. It—well, even when I don't get it, I still feel certain ways when I read it. Some places I feel happy, some places I feel all funny. And then"—she dropped her eyes again to the book resting in her hands—"sometimes I feel pretty awful."

"Then you are most certainly getting it!"

My enthusiasm hung there for another silence with egg on its face; she looked back up. "Oh say, what did they say to you at the doctor's?"

"They *said*"—I tried to change from enthusiasm to comedy again—"in so many words: 'Drop your pants and bend over.' And the next thing I knew they were pumping my lungs full of smelling salts."

"You passed *out?*"

"Cold."

She laughed softly at me, then became confidential, lowering her voice. "Hey now; I'll tell you a little something, if you promise not to plague him about it."

"Cross my heart. Plague who about what?"

"Old Henry. After his fall off those rocks. See, when they brought him in from the show he cussed and carried on just terrible while he was around here, then, when we got him to the doctor, he went tough as nails. You know the way he can be. He didn't make a peep while they were lookin' him over—except for joking with the nurses and kidding them about being so antsy with him. 'Ain't nothin' but a busted wing,' he kept saying. 'I had twicet as bad—twicet as bad! C'mawn, git the booger put back in place! I got to git back to work! Yarrrr!' "

We both laughed at her gravel-voiced impersonation. 'But *then*," she went on, becoming secretive again, "they brought out a needle. Not even very big, but big enough. I knew how he felt about needles and I saw the old fella just go white as a sheet when he saw it coming. But he wasn't going to let on, you see? He was just going to keep up his front. 'C'mawn, c'mawn, c'mawn; stick me with that outfit so I can get back to business!' he kept growling. Then, when they *did* shoot him—after him bein' so tough and so brave in front of them over his broken bones—he just flinched and made a face. But we heard something; and when I looked over I saw he'd wet all over himself and it was running down his *leg* all over the *floor!*"

"No! Henry? Oh *no*, Henry Stamper? Whoo! Oh god . . ." I laughed more than I could remember laughing in years. The thought of his funny surprised face reduced me to a soundless quivering. "Oh god . . . that's beautiful, oh my god . . ."

"And . . . and—oh listen," she went on in a whisper, "when we went to get him into pajamas—oh listen—after the shot had knocked him out . . . we saw that wetting himself wasn't *all* he'd done."

"Oh lord . . . oh that's marvelous, I can just see it. . . ."

We laughed until we reached that awkward emptiness that follows long laughing, like the emptiness that follows a long roll of thunder; then we were silent again, and uncomfortable, and terribly, deafeningly aware of the thought in both our minds. But what's the sense in trying? I demanded of myself, staring at the lock of hair which ran like a glowing arrow down the side of her averted face into the neck of her shirt. . . . What's the sense in dreaming? You can't make it, that's all. It's all part of the way you have worked it out. You should have known all along that the selfsame weapon of weakness that was to win you victory over Brother Hank would be incapable of partaking of the fruits of that victory. You should have known that the spoils which you won from him with limp impotence could never be taken with the same tact. . . .

I stood there, then, looking down at this girl's shy and unvoiced and obvious offering of herself, trying to be philosophic about my organic inability to accept the offer . . . while the very organ in question rose to refute this newest of excuses and demand with pounding insistence the chance to *prove* his ability. I stood there, with all obstacles at last removed and nothing separating me any more from my most desirable goal but the space of a few feet—all reasons removed, all excuses exhausted—and *still* that voice in my head refused to let me go: WATCH OUT WATCH OUT, it chanted. But for *what?* I demanded, almost sick with frustration. Please, tell me; watch out for *what!*

JUST DON'T DO IT, was the reply; IT WILL BE A BAD SCENE. . . .

For *who?* I'm safe, I *know* so. A bad scene for Hank? Viv? For who?

FOR YOU, FOR YOU . . .

So, when I had suffered this period of silent standing sufficiently, I sighed and mumbled something about well, it would probably be best—oh, for my cold and all—if I went on in to bed. And she nodded —face still averted—yes, that's probably true . . . well, good night, Viv . . . Good night, Lee; I'll see you, I guess, in the morning. . . .

With her eyes downcast for my cowardice as I slunk from the room. With my stomach sick for failure and my heart dying with shame for an impotence that could no longer even be blamed on impotence . . .

(I stopped the pick-up out in front of the hospital, and when I picked up the old man to cart him into the emergency room, I saw his arm had come all the rest of the way off. It dropped out of the ragged sleeve to the street like a snake coming out of its skin. I left it lay. I couldn't fuss with it now. *There is something else, if I could just remember* . . .

The night attendant stopped me and started to say something, then looked at the old man. His pencil fell out of his hand. I told him, "I'm Hank Stamper. This here is my old man. A log rolled on him." And I put the old man on a bed and went over and sat down in a cushioned chair. The attendant was asking questions that I didn't care about answering. I told him I had to get gone. He said I was nuts, I had to stay till the doc come. I said, "Okay. When Doc Layton gets here wake me up. Soon as he gets here.

And we'll see. Now. Take this old man somewhere and give him some blood and leave me alone."

When I woke I thought for a second that no time had passed, that I'd just blinked and that attendant had merely aged and put on about two hundred pounds and was still asking the same questions that I wasn't hearing yet. When I seen it was the doctor I stood up. "Now," I told him, "all I want to know is do I need to give him some blood?"

"Blood? Lord, Hank, what's wrong with you? You're in about as much condition to give a pint of blood as he is. What happened out there?"

"He's all right, then? The old man?"

"Sit down. No, he isn't all right, for chrissakes. He's an old man and he's lost him an arm. What in the name of god are you trying to rush off to that's so—"

"But he ain't dead? He ain't goin' to die tonight?"

"He isn't dead—Lord knows why—but as far as— What's the matter with you, Hank? Sit back down there and let me get a look at you."

"No. I got to go. In a minute I will—" *I'm late for something, sleeping like that.* "I got to in a minute—" *In a minute I'll remember what it is. I pull on my hard hat and feel for cigarettes.* "Now," I say.

*The doctor's still waiting for me to explain.*

*"Now, you think he'll make it?" I ask him. "Is he still out? I reckon he would be, wouldn't he? Well . . ." I look up at the doctor's face. What's his name? Now I know this man, knowed him for years, but I can't recall his name to save me. "Ain't it funny how quick you get out of touch?" I say to him "Now. If that's it, I got to get that pick-up and—"*

"Well, for chrissakes," the doctor said to me, "he's going to drive home. Look here, let me look at that hand, anyway."

It was the cut I'd got working on the jetty some days before; it had opened and was bleeding. "No," I said slowly, trying to remember what it was I was late for. "No thanks, I can get my wife to tend to that for me. I'll call you about old Henry in the morning."

I headed out the door. The arm was still laying there on the sidewalk beside the pick-up in a puddle. I picked it up and tossed it in just like it was cord wood. *What was it? In a minute I'll—*

On the way back through town I stopped at the Sea Breeze to

ask where the kid was. "Don't know," Mrs. Carleson answered, more sullen than usual, "jest he ain't here no more." I didn't feel like pressing it so I walked on up the street to check the bar. No one there had seen him. Before I could leave, Evenwrite eased up to me and said something at me. I just nodded and told him I didn't have time to fool with him right then and headed for the door. This Draeger guy was sitting there and he smiled at me and he said hello. He said, "Hank, I feel I should warn you that your casual presence in town is more dangerous to you than you—"

"I'm busy," I told him.

"Certainly, but stop a moment and consider—"

I walked out along Main. I wasn't sure where I was headed. *In just a minute I'll remember . . . somewhere I have to go.* I went to the Sea Breeze and started to go in and then I remembered that whatever it was I had asked about in there, they didn't have it. I started back for the pick-up when three guys I never saw before in my life come out of the alley by the grange hall. They pull me back in the alley and go to working me over. I think for a minute, they're gonna kill me, but then I knew that they weren't. Some way I knew. They just weren't working at it hard enough. They took turns holding me against the wall and belting me pretty good, but not like they really aimed to kill me. And I wasn't really giving them my undivided attention; *just a minute I'll*—I was about to sit down and just let them have their way when up the alley came Evenwrite and Les Gibbons and even old Big Newton, hollering, "Hang on, Hank! Hang on, boy!" And I'm damned if they didn't run off these three other guys and help me up from the ground. Dang, Les said; those must be that bunch of yahoos from Reedsport again, we heard they was spoiling for you . . . and I thanked them and Evenwrite says people got to stick together and I thank him. They help me out to my pick-up. Les Gibbons even says he'll drive me home if need be. I tell him no, I don't know that I'm going that way, but thanks just the same, I'm in somethin' of a hurry to— what? well, in a minute I'll—I told the boys so long and started the pick-up and headed off, feeling lightheaded and pleasant, floating, sort of. Some of that fever going around, I suspect. But what the devil? it ain't so bad, a little temperature . . . like Joby always says, accept your lot and swing with what you got. And a runny nose is maybe a damn nuisance, but a fever is a cheap drunk . . . driving up Main. It was funny; I felt that there was an errand or something that had slipped my mind *in just a little bit I'll* but I was damned if I could remember what, exactly. So *in a minute I'll*—I headed out up river, figuring I might as well go home as long as I couldn't recall what it was I was supposed to see to. I just drove, slow and easy, watching the white lines blink past and the clouds blowing in the moon, not trying to think.

And I didn't recall what was on my mind till I pulled the pick-up up to the garage, and that reminded me of seeing him *and I don't recall all of it till I look out across the moonlit river and see the launch is tied over there now, across the way, and that now there's two rooms lit over in the house instead of only one . . .)*

After leaving Viv with her poetry and her disappointment, I went to the bathroom, where I drew out my teeth-brushing as long as possible and spent a good five minutes examining the skin of my face to see how the burn had healed. In my own cold quarters I undressed slowly, putting off getting into bed until the cool of the room forced me between the covers. Finally I turned out the light. The darkness exploded into the room; then, slowly, the moon cast a blue-white beam across my quilt, chilling my cheek and intersecting that thin finger of light that came from the hole in the wall. Have to fill that hole, I thought to myself. I'll have to fill that hole. Someday soon I will have to do that for good. . . .

Then, like that exploding darkness, the shame rose again and surged over me with the same sickening force that had years ago left me with drumming headaches and vomiting . . . the same force, years before, in the same bed . . . always after (oh God, I had never made the connection before!) always the day after I had watched through that spyhole the passion that I was then, was *still* incapable of competing with. Now that point of light had found me again. I cringed back into the bedclothes; it seemed to be chopping away at me, at the worthless flesh of me. A scalpel of terrible light, causing actual physical *pain!* I lay writhing beneath it, feeling no longer shame but only pain. Perhaps when shame grows too much for the soul to hold, it expands to sicken the flesh itself with a disease as palpable as cancer, and as deadly. I couldn't say. Not then. Only that it was a very real hurt and rapidly growing in proportion . . . I realized I was crying, not at all silently this time. I clutched my head in time to catch a thunderclap of pain that shook water from my forehead and eyes. I clenched my teeth and rolled groaning into a ball, readying myself for the blow to my stomach. I shuddered with deep, clutching sobs. . . .

And it was this way, a whimpering wad of childhood misery

under a quilt, that she found me. "Are you feeling sick?" she whispered. She was beside my bed. The pain behind my eyes disappeared at the glimmering sight of her. The sickness in my chest fled instantly before the light brushing of her fingers . . .

Outside, the river rocked between mountain and sea, suspended momentarily between tide and flood, motionless but for a spreading moon-rippled wake. The clouds hurried along, back to the sea. The pick-up eased lightless and quiet into the cavernous garage . . . (When I saw that the launch was gone I don't know what got into me; *you'll make it across* because I decided to swim, rather than call for the boat. *You'll make it.* Now from the garage across to the dock in cold water is no slouch of a swim, even when a man is feeling his oats. And I was tired clean through, tired enough I should never have tried. But the funny thing is after I dived in and started swimming I didn't get any tireder. It took hours, it seemed like, of hard swimming, but I never got any tireder. I was out there and it was like that old river was a hundred miles across—blue-silver, cold—but I knew I would make it. I remember thinking: *Look at you: you'll make it all the way across here when you couldn't make it up that hill for a air hose for Joby. You'll make it across here not because you're strong enough but because you're weak enough* . . .)

Then, of course, after she had touched me, we made love. The scene no longer needed the impetus of my contrived plot. I no longer moved the scene; the scene moved me. Quite simply, we made love.

(*You'll make it acrosst* . . .)

We made love. How pedestrian the words look—trite, worn, practically featureless with use—but how can one better describe that which happens when it happens? that creation? that magic blending? I might say we became figures in a mesmerized dance before the rocking talisman of the moon, starting slow, so slow . . . a pair of feathers drifting through clear liquid substance of sky . . . gradually accelerating, faster and faster and finally into photon existence of pure light.

(*Tired and beat as you are, you'll make it acrosst, you big stud swimmer you* . . .)

Or I might instead list impressions, images still brilliant, flashbulbed forever by the white arching of those first touches—the first look after the woolen plaid was parted to show that she wore no brassiere; the slight shy lifting as I pulled the coarse denim from her hips; the supple line starting at the point of her back-thrown chin, pulsing down between her breasts to her stomach spotlighted by that beam from her room . . .

(*You'll make it acrosst because you ain't strong enough not to,* I kept thinking as I swam. And I recollect this one other thing, a notion that came to me when I climbed out of the water: *that there ain't really any true strength* . . . and as I climb the steps: *there ain't really any real strength* . . .)

Yet it still seems to me I best communicate the beauty of those moments by repeating, quite simply, we made love. And consummated there a month of quick looks, guarded smiles, accidental brushings of body too open or too secret to be mere accident, and all the other little unfinished vignettes of desire . . . and, perhaps most of all, consummated the shared *knowledge* of that desire, and of that returned desire, and of the juggernaut advance of that desire . . . in a silent inward explosion as my whole straining body burst like fluid electricity into hers. Shared, consummated, resolved; in a joyous sprint side by side up the steep slope to the topmost brink, vaulting out . . . the weightless glide . . . the soaring motionless through light-year distances of skin-tight space; gliding down, gradually back . . . to the tick-tock of majority-vote reality, to the timid squeak of bed, to a LISTEN dog barking outside at the voyeur moon . . . and to the LISTEN WHAT? pressing memory of a strange sodden *tread* that I thought I had heard WATCH OUT somewhere frighteningly near ages, hours, *seconds* before!

To finally opening my eyes and finding Viv brushed only by the soft, wide stroke of moonlight, and the spotlighting beam from the hole in the wall extinguished!

(*No, not the strength I always believed in; I kept hearing in my head—not strength like I always thought, I could build and thought I could live, and thought I could show the kid how to live* . . .)

The total revelation of what had happened during our love-making blasted me so hard I was nearly knocked right back into that outerspace safety of orgasm. I had been confident of my security behind the moat. *Positive* of it. It had occurred to me that he might return before I was finished. I had half hoped he would. But when he returned he would be across the water. He would honk for the boat. I would take it across to him. Sure, he would be suspicious—me alone there in the house with his woman all those hours—be almost certain, in fact. But *almost* was all I had planned on. Not on his swimming the river and creeping up the steps like a thief in the night. Not on his actually stooping to *spying* on me! My Captain Marvel brother, peeking like a pimp through a knothole? Brother Hank? Hank *Stamper*?

Can't a fella bank on *anyone* any more?

(*No, there ain't any true strength; there's just different degrees of weakness . . .*)

I lay paralyzed, with Viv still in a swoon beneath me. One part of my brain was remarking with academic detachment: "So *that's* how he used to know I was watching; my room would cast a corresponding beam into the next-door dimness, which went out when interrupted by something solid, like my head. How stupid of me." While another, louder part kept screaming at me: RUN, YOU FOOL! WATCH OUT! FLEE BEFORE HE COMES FOR YOU RIGHT THROUGH THAT WALL! HELP! WATCH OUT! HIDE! JUMP! . . . as though the wall were going to crash at any instant to reveal a swaying lock-kneed monster, myself springing nude out into the cold moon and falling to the mud below in a splintering shower of crystal . . . HIDE! WATCH OUT! FLEE!

Yet gradually, as the initial shock subsided, I remember being overcome by a gloating sense of remarkable good fortune: sure . . . why, this is too perfect! This could mean victory beyond my wildest dreams, vengeance beyond my wickedest schemes. Shall I? I debated. Dare I? Yes . . . never give an inch, as they say . . .

"Never," I breathed to Viv before I had a chance to back out. "Never in all my life"—not loud, just loud enough—"have I had it happen like *that*."

She took the cue beautifully. "Me neither. I didn't know, Lee . . . so wonderful."

"I love you, Viv."

"I didn't know. I used to dream . . ." Her fingers traced my spine and came to rest on my cheek. I wasn't to be distracted. "Do you love me too, Viv?" I could *feel* the breath stop beyond that wall; I could hear the tunnel roar of listening strained through the hole to catch her whisper. "I love you too, Lee."

"This may sound inappropriate at the time, but I need you, Viv; I love you very much, but I need you very badly."

"I don't understand." She paused. "What are you asking?"

"I'm asking you to come away with me. Back East. To help me finish school. No. More than that: to help me finish living."

"Lee—"

"You said once that perhaps I needed Somebody instead of Something. Well, you're it, Viv; I don't know that I can make it without you. I mean it."

"Lee, . . . Hank is . . . I mean I—"

"I know you're fond of Hank," I cut in quickly; I was into it now and nothing to do but drive on through. "But does Hank need you? I mean, oh, Viv, he can get along without you, and we both know it. Couldn't he?"

"I imagine that Hank," she mused, "could probably get along without anybody, if it came to it."

"That's right! He could! But not me. Oh, Viv, listen." In my fervor I rose to my knees on the bed. "What's stopping us? Not Hank: you know if you ask for a divorce he'll consent. He wouldn't hold you here against your will!"

"I know that"—still musingly—"he's too proud to do that sort of thing; he would let me go. . . ."

"And he's too strong to be hurt by it."

"It's hard to say what hurts him. . . ."

"Okay, but even if he is hurt, won't he survive it? Can you imagine a hurt he wouldn't survive? He's arrogated to himself the powers of Superman, and he believes it. But Viv, I'll tell you; listen. I came out here at the end of my rope. You've given me a knot to cling to, to survive with. Without that knot, Viv, I just don't know, I swear to god I don't. Come with me. Please."

She lay for a while, looking out at the moon. "When I was a kid," she began after a pause, "I found a rope doll, an Indian doll. I liked it better than all my other dolls for a while, because I could pretend it was anything I longed for it to be." The moon stroked her face through the pine bough on the window; she closed her eyes and from the corners tears ran into her pillowed hair. . . . "Now I don't know what I love any more. I don't know where the thing I make-pretend leaves off and the thing that's really there starts up."

I started to tell her that there was no line between the two, but stopped myself, not knowing what make-pretend virtues she had fashioned for my brother. And said instead, "Viv, all I know is that I can't be noble about this. Only desperate. I need you to live. Come with me, Viv, come away with me. Now. Tomorrow. Please . . ."

If she answered my pleading I did not hear her. I was no longer paying any attention to her. My listening, as well as every spoken word, was now directed toward that hole which had suddenly opened again to light. Viv, intent on my words, had not noticed. I started to go on when I thought I detected that same sluggish tread that I had previously heard, moving away from the wall, out of the room . . . into the hall now . . . now into his room, where he will sit, stricken, on his bed, eyes glassy, hands slack in his lap . . . all right, Superman; it's your move. . . .

A thin groan shot down the corridor, followed by peals of retching. And another, even sicker groan. "Hank!" Viv lurched sitting with a startled cry. "That's Hank, what is he—? What's *happened?*" Then ran from the room, drawing the wool shirt about her, to find out.

I was somewhat slower dressing. My head rang with anticipation and I smiled as I walked the dark hall toward light fanning across the floor from their bedroom door. I knew what had happened: he's getting sick, losing his lunch. He's carrying on with moaning and coughing and all the other theatrics traditionally used by children seeking repossession of sympathy. Yes. I knew: an exact duplication of the scene I used to enact, with identical motives and intentions.

There was just one thing left now, one short speech, and my overthrow would be complete.

I walked slowly down the hall. I was savoring the words I had prepared for what was to be the greatest put-down in history; as my long-ago words had come back to me at the bottom of that postcard this phrase was Brother Hank's own put-down returning to roost after all these years, like a homing pigeon equipped with the murderous beak of a hawk. "Musta been somethin' gawdawful rich"—I tried the line half aloud, practicing it for my entrance "to make you so gawdawful sick." Ah, it was perfect. It was beautiful. And I was ready. I stepped into the room where Viv sat holding to Hank, who had slipped half to the floor in an effort to stick his head into a vomit-covered metal wastepaper basket. His sopping shirt clung to his pathetically shaking shoulders, and the back of his head was matted with river scum. . . .

"Well, brother. Musta been somethin' gawdawful rich," I incanted ceremoniously, giving the phrase the magical sound afforded words due to effectuate all kinds of miraculous change, "to make you so—"

"Oh, Lee, Hank says—" My incantation was cut short, first by

Viv, then by the sight of Hank's head rising and turning slowly to reveal a cheek swollen blue over one eye and lips torn ragged as though by the force of his retching. "Oh, Lee, Hank says that Joe Ben . . . Joe and the old man . . ."—turning, slowly, until his good eye could fix on me, cold and green with knowing—"that Joe Ben is dead, Lee; that Joe's dead; and maybe old Henry"—mouth opening to a black, guttering tongue and unintelligible words. "Bub—bub—there ain't, bub—" Viv caught him; "Call the doctor, Lee; somebody beat him all up."

"But there . . . ain't any real—"

But whatever he was trying to say was lost in more retching.

(*But if the strength ain't real, I recall thinking the very last thing that day, before I finally passed out, then the weakness sure enough is. Weakness is true and real. I used to accuse the kid of faking his weakness. But faking proves the weakness is real. Or you wouldn't be so weak as to fake it. No, you can't ever fake being weak. You can only fake being strong. . . .*)

Downstairs, at the telephone talking to the doctor, without thinking of it, I completed my magic words. "How does he look?" the doctor asked. I answered, "Why, Doctor, I would say he looks sick" —adding, without realizing until later it was the end of my incantations, "gawdawful sick"—finishing the phrase, like Billy Batson, gag ripped from his mouth, finishing the last half of a broken "Shazam!" that all-powerful word that would transform Billy, to the accompaniment of lightning and thunder, from a drab and puny runt into that great and all-powerful orange giant, Captain Marvel. "Yes, Doctor . . . gawdawful sick," I said.

And my bolt of lightning was right on time, spilling suddenly in all the western windows like moonlight through clouds. And my clap of thunder roared deafeningly through the house, echo-chambered from upstairs by a wastepaper basket. Everything was in order. But, unlike Billy's, my transformation failed to materialize. I don't know what I expected—perhaps to actually find myself swollen to Captain Marvel magnitude, flying away replete with cape, spit-curl, and neon-orange leotard—but as I stood there, holding the buzzing phone at my side, hearing the overacted melodrama being coughed and sobbed out upstairs, I knew that I had in no way achieved the stature I had subconsciously dreamed that my revenge would bring about. I had very successfully completed my ritual of vengeance; I had accurately mouthed all the right mystical words . . . but instead of turning myself into a Captain Marvel, as the ritual and words were supposed to do according to all the little-guy-beats-big-guy tradition . . . I had merely created another Billy Batson.

Then, finally knew what I had been warned to WATCH OUT for.

(And if you can only fake being strong, not being weak, then the kid has done to me what I set off to do to him! He's shaped me up. He's made me to quit faking.

He's straightened me out.)

*S*uburban survivors of Hiroshima described the blast as a "mighty first boom, like a locomotive followed by a long, loud train roaring past, fading gradually away to a murmur." Wrong. They describe only the ear's inaccurate report. For that mighty first boom was only the first faintest murmur of an explosion that is still roaring down on us, and always will be. . . .

For the reverberation often exceeds through silence the sound that sets it off; the reaction occasionally outdoes by way of repose the event that stimulated it; and the past not uncommonly takes a while to happen, and some long time to figure out.

. . . And the citizens of the little West Coast towns, not infrequently, needed some time to even begin recognizing that it had happened, let alone to get around to figuring it out. For this reason their centennials are never a great success—many oldtimers from bygone times are reluctant to admit those times are gone by. For this reason a nondescript bog in a meadow is still called Boomer's Ferry . . . though Mr. Boomer, his cable-drawn ferry, and the wide slough that once floated them, have long since sunk into nondescript mud. For this reason it takes almost a day after the rain has stopped in Wakonda for the men to straighten up out of their hump-shouldered shuffle, almost a day after the wind has quit whipping the water before the women remove the newspaper calking from beneath doors. After one whole rainless day they are willing to say that it by god *might* be clearing up at that, after a rainless day and night the men and women are even compelled to go so far as to admit that it has *stopped*, but it takes the mentality of a *child* to think that the sun might actually come out, here, in November, right in the dead of winter.

"Look: the old sun might come out, and it almost *Thanksgivin'*. How come? It never did *that* before . . ."

"Old sun is gonna come out to *look* is how come . . . to see is it springtime yet," was how the phenomenon was interpreted by a Siuslow Street Grade School meteorologist in galoshes and mud-daubed tresses. "To see if it is time to have springtime is how come . . ."

"Ain't," a junior colleague, behind her one whole grade and a boy at that, had the gall to dissent. "Ain't it a-tall."

"The ol' rain some way quit rainin', see, an' the sun he waked up an' he says, 'It quit rainin' . . . maybe time for spring. I better see. . . .' "

"That ain't it," he kept on, "that ain't it a-tall."

"And so," she went on, ignoring him, "and so . . ." She drew a deep breath and lifted her shoulders in a gesture of bored certainty. ". . . the ol' sun is simpah-lee come sneaking out to see what *time* it is."

"No. That . . . just . . . ain't . . . it. Not a-tall."

She tried to remain silent, knowing it was best not to dignify these sillies by replying, but the mysterious measured tone of his statement, suggesting knowledge of other data, had anticipated and cleverly baited that silence. The muddy meteorologist detected a vacillation of faith in her audience—too much vacillation to simpalee ignore.

"*All* right, smarty-pants!" She turned on him. "You tell us how come there's sunshine out an' it almost Thanksgiving."

Smarty-pants, a big-nosed, big-eared skeptic in taped-together eye-glasses and a screaming Nylaglo raincoat, raised his eyes and looked gravely up at the seminary watching him from the creaking merry-go-round. They waited. The pressure was on. There was no two ways about it: he'd opened his mouth one time too many and now he had to put up or shut up, and he was going to have to put up some extremely persuasive logic to overcome the girl's lead, for not only was she backed by some pretty sound argument and her own bright red Frisbee, which she tossed and caught at unpredictable intervals; she was a second-grader to boot. He cleared his throat and called on authority to help make up the gap.

"My daddy said last night, my *daddy* said . . . that it's gonna be clear sonofabitchin' skies now that the sky's cleared."

"Poot!" She wasn't one to fall for a closed argument. "But how come?"

"Because—my *daddy* said—" He paused, kneaded his brow to re-call the verbatim beauty of the reason, darkening his countenance and simultaneously building suspense with a devastating sense of timing. "Because—" His face cleared; the old memory had come through once again. "That hardnosed Stamper bunch is finally knuckled under, is what." He delivered the clincher. "Because that sonofabitchin' Hank Stamper is *fine-a-lee* called off his deal with Wakonda Pacific!"

Right on cue the sun slid above a cloudbank, sharp, keen, and freshly bright, to illuminate the playground with an icy white glare. Without another word the girl turned and galoshed off toward the swings, whipped and knowing it; it was a great loss of prestige, but there was simply no way to dispute the statement of authority when it was being seconded by the actual appearance of the party in question. No, she was forced to bow to the truth: the sun had come out because of the capitulation of the Stampers, not because it suspected an early spring.

Though, in fact, it did seem very much like spring. Dying dandelions woke to that keen-edged sun and managed a last bloom. Beaten grass lifted straight. Meadowlarks sung in the cattails. And by noon of that second rainless day the town was so thick with the warm, steamy air of Oregon springtime that even the adults recognized the presence of that sun.

The sun tried to draw off some of the moisture that had gathered in its brief absence. The roofs steamed. The walls steamed. The railroad ties in weed-grown fields steamed. In Swede Row off Nahamish Street, where the fishermen lived, their drab shacks, primerless and paintless and soaked through and through, gave off such a cloud of hissing silver mist that the whole row appeared to have caught fire from the unexpected arrival of the November sun.

"Bitchin' weather, don't you say?" said the Real Estate Man on the South Main sidewalk as he strode, with his coat over his shoulder and good times just around the bend, beside Brother Walker of the First Pentecostal Church of God and Metaphysics. He drew a great lungful of optimism, puffed out his chest to the sun like a chicken drying its feathers, and repeated, "Bitch-*ing*."

"Ah." Brother Walker was not very enthusiastic about this particular description.

"What I *mean* is"—damn these guys make a guy feel like he can't let go and talk American—"is this kind of climate in late November is truly *extra*-ordinary, *extra*-ordinary, don't you agree?"

Brother Walker smiled. That was better. He nodded. . . . "The Lord is merciful," he announced with confidence.

"You bet!"

"Yes, yes, merciful . . ."

"Big times coming," was the Real Estate Man's evaluation. "We're out of the woods; around that old corner." He was tingling with joy and ease; he thought of all the little Johnny Redfeathers he had carved recently, how their faces had grown so like Hank Stamper's that he had almost gone bats. Now all that was over. And just in time. "Yep. Prosperity round the bend . . . now that everybody's been set to rights."

"Yes . . . the Lord is merciful," Brother Walker said again cheerfully, adding this time, "and eternally *just*."

They strode on down the puddled walk, a dealer in dirt and a peddler of sky, chance comrades for a while because of their shared destination and their corresponding views of destiny, both beaming their brightest and dreaming of great transactions of earth and air—tingling and cheerful, real pinnacles of optimism, masters of the bright outlook . . . but still only amateurs compared to the dead man they were on their way to bury.

At the parlor Lilienthal studies old snapshots and adds last hurried touches to make this loved one look just as natural as life. He wants everything in this ceremony to be *especially* just as natural, so the kin won't object to the bill: the bill is padded heavily to cover the loss he took the day before by burying that miserly Willard Eggleston and the poor old drunk who used to cut shingle bolts; a ranger had found the old man passed on in his shack and brought him in, and a coroner is legally *bound* to attend to such deceased finds, though the poor souls are without a relative to their name and have been passed-on for a week. . . . So Lilienthal takes extra pains and special efforts with *this* loved one, partially to pay for, partially to make up for, the treatment that other hunk of rotten meat received yesterday. . . .

At her shack on the clamflats Indian Jenny sits on her cot in a position as close as she can come to the full lotus. She has been meditating ever since the news of the accident reached her; now she is stiff and hungry and she suspects that a family of earwigs has taken up residence in the back of her skirt. But she waits, motionless, and tries to think as Alan Watts told her to think. Not that she has much hope any longer of solving her problem by this method; mainly she is just dallying: she just doesn't want to go into town yet for further news. Further news, she has realized since hearing of the developments up river, cannot possibly be anything but *bad* news . . . and she doesn't know which will dismay her most, hearing that Henry Stamper still lives or hearing that he has died.

She closes her eyes and redoubles her efforts to think of nothing, or almost nothing, or at least of nothing as unpleasant as her aching thighs, or Henry Stamper, or earwigs . . .

At the Wakonda Arms, Rod looks up from his newspaper to see Ray come buck-and-winging through the door with his cheeks glowing and his arms filled with green-papered bundles. "*Puttin' on my white tie . . . gettin' out my tails.*" Ray tumbled the load onto the bed. "Fish and soup, Roderick my man, fish and soup this p.m. Cash, too. Teddy paid, after nearly two months; it's a drag that poor little Willard wasn't around to enjoy the event, after bugging us about our cleaning bill for so long. Too bad, Willy-o; you'd of waited a few days, you could of split fulfilled." He clicked into his dance step again, skipping over to the chest of drawers. "But look here, I got to get hold of the old ax. Come to daddy, baby; I got to get the old phalanges limbered. . . ."

Rod watched from the bed as Ray pulled the guitar case from beneath the chest of drawers. He gave up on his paper, but for all Ray's buoyant good tidings, he decided to hold his finger on his place in the want ads. "What you coming on so about?" he asked as Ray began tuning the instrument. "Hey! Did Teddy finally agree about upping our cut?"

"Nope." *Ting ting ting.*

"You heard from that moneypockets uncle of yours? Huh? You heard from Rhonda Ann in Astoria? Damn you, if you and her—"

"Nope, nope, nope-a-dope." *Ting ting ting-a-ting.* "Baybee! does a change in weather like this screw up the ol' strings." *T-eeng t-eeng.*

Rod rolled to his hip and spread the newspaper against the sun streaming through the dust-starched curtains, returning to the want ads. "Then if you're tuning that outfit planning a gig tonight, you might's well figure on pickin' lead and bass both. 'Cause man I mean screw it. I'm not taking it . . . ten bucks a night and no tips for a month, I don't hafta take that sound and I told Teddy so."

Ray looked up from his tuning, his face a wide grin. "Man . . . tell you what I'm gonna do: just because I'm such a sterling fellow, tonight . . . you can have the whole ten and I'll be happy with the tips. Cool?"

No answer came from beneath the paper, but a suspicious silence.

"Cool, then, okay? Because I tell you, Roderick. There's things you ain't heard and veins you ain't got your fingers on; it's gonna be tips up the geetus from here on out and loot and luck all the way to Nashville. Hoo-hoo! I don't know about you, but I'm goin' to the moon, you sour-mouthed pessimist. To the moon. Dig?"

From beneath his paper the pessimist remained silent, digging only that the last time Ray came buck-and-winging into a hotel room to go to coming on like this the nut had ended up, instead of in Nashville, on the emergency ward in a stinking little hospital outside of Albany or Corvallis or someplace like that, with a hose down his big mouth after a fistful of Nembutals.

"Get up from there, man," Ray shouted. "Get shuckin'. Get out your machine an' let's get the kinks loose. Get your chin off your chest and get on the sunny side of the street and pack up your troubles. . . ." *Chang:* C-chord. *Chong:* F, G-seventh, G . . . " 'Cause, man, it's—" *Chang:* C-chord again and *"Blue skies, smilin' at me . . . nothin' but blue skies—"*

"For maybe one or two days." A voice rose from the want ads and clouded the air with dismal forecasts of approaching low fronts. "For maybe one or two crummy days, *then* what kind of motherin' skies?"

"Go ahead." Ray grinned. "Sit there under a paper and rot. This boy's gonna get his pickin' and strummin' hand sharpened up and take it straight to the top. Tonight's the start. Sweet joy and victory is gonna fill the old Snag tonight, you see if it don't. Because, man" —*chang tink a tink*—*"Nothin' but blue skies . . . do I skooby-dooby see E E E . . ."*

In the Snag, Teddy looks at the blue sky through his cold scribble of neon and has a slightly different reaction to the unusual change in weather. . . . Blue skies isn't barroom weather. You need rain for bringing in the drinkers; this kind of day people drink lemonade. You need *rain* and *dark*, and *cold.* . . .*That's* the stuff to start the fear running, to keep the fools drinking.

He'd been concerned with fear and fools ever since Draeger had told him with a wink the day before that Hank Stamper had just called to say that the shooting match was done. "The 'shooting match,' Mr. Draeger?" " 'The whole by god shooting match,' as Hank put it. He said that because of 'developments,' Teddy, he couldn't see how he could possibly make his deadline. Developments . . ." Draeger grinned proudly at him. "I told you we'd show these muscle-heads, didn't I?"

Teddy had responded with a blush and some mumbled agreement, pleased that Draeger had chosen to be so intimate with him, but, all taken into consideration, rather saddened by the news that the whole by god shooting match was ended; the trouble with the Stampers may have hurt the rest of the town, but it had certainly kept his own till ringing. He would miss that sound. . . . "What'll you do now,

Mr. Draeger?" And miss even more this forceful and wise and hand-some relief from all the fools that patronized his place. "Go back to California, I suppose?"

"I'm afraid so." Draeger's cultured voice had been a delightful inter-lude—intelligent, calm, kind but not pitying like the others. "Yes, Ted, I'm off to Eugene now to tie up some things, then I'm coming back to share Thanksgiving with the Evenwrites, but after that . . . it's back to sunny southland."

"All your . . . all the trouble up here is cleared up?"

Draeger grinned across the bar, laying down a five for his I. W. Harpers. "Wouldn't you say so, Teddy? Keep the change—but, all kidding aside, wouldn't you say it was cleared up?"

Teddy nodded resignedly; he'd always known Draeger would show the muscleheads. . . . "I guess so. Yes. Yes, I'm sure it is, Mr. Draeger . . . the whole by god shootin' match, all cleared up."

Now, only a day later, Teddy wasn't so sure. The let-up in business that he'd expected to accompany the town's good fortune had yet to begin; it should have started, by his reckoning, as soon as the flush of victory had been drunk away last night. But, if anything, business had *picked* up instead of let up. When he consulted the neat set of records he kept in his head, and checked under "Quarts Consumed per Customer," he found that individual consumption was up close to twenty per cent over last week, and, while he couldn't be sure of "Customers per Cubic Foot per Hour" until the peak time tonight, all indications pointed to a top-notch crowd. At the rate men were dropping in already, it looked like the Snag would be filled tonight.

But, unlike Ray, Teddy knew his customers too well to ever believe that sweet joy could fill a bar. Or victory either. Teddy knew that it took something much stronger than those two watery reasons to fill a bar. Especially with the weather so nice. If it were still raining, he mused, looking at his neons dead and powerless under the bright sunshine, I might understand. If it were raining and dark and cold, then I might know what was forcing them here, but with weather like this—

"Teddy, Teddy, Teddy . . ." At one of the tables near the win-dow, Boney Stokes squinted against the sun. "Shouldn't we have us a shade or blinds or something to pull over that terrible glare?"

"I'm sorry, Mr. Stokes."

"A curtain or some-thing?" His meatless old hand pawed at the light. "To protect tired old eyes?"

"I'm sorry, Mr. Stokes; I sent the blinds off to Eugene for cleaning when the rains started. I just never in a hundred years thought we'd get any more sun, I sure didn't. But let me see . . ." He turned to the laundry box behind the bar; in the mirror Boney's reflection blinked hollowly after him. Stupid old eyes, always looking for something to whine about . . . "Perhaps I might be able to pin up some cloth and help?"

"Okay, you do that." Then Boney craned his neck, squinting at the street. "No. Wait. Best not, I reckon. No. I want to be sure and see him when he drives out to the cemetery. . . ."

"Who's that, Mr. Stokes?"

"Never mind. I just . . . don't feel like attendin' the funeral— my lungs and so on—and I want to watch them drive by to the buryin' ground. I'll just sit here. I can endure the glare; I reckon I'll just have to. . . ."

"Very well."

Teddy returned to dishtowel to its box, glancing again at the reflection of the skinny man. Repulsive old specter. Stupid old eyes, cold as marble; and vicious, too, in a stupid way. Boney Stokes's eyes never have seen anything but rain and dreariness, so it's no mystery *him* being in here on such a pretty day; he's seen nothing but fear all the days of his stupid life. But these others, all these others . . . "Teddy! Get your pink little rear in gear, by gory; there's drinkin' to be done!" He rippled soundlessly down the bar with his pink little rear switching in tight black trousers, toward the draft taps where a crowd of sweat-shirted shamblers had gathered again already with empty glasses. "Yes sir, what'll it be, sir?" But what about all these others? No fear seemed to cloud their fool's firmament, or no more than usual anyway. . . . What drove *these* men in, like cattle to the barn in a thunderstorm, on this crystal-clear day? Could it be that his cherished equations and formulas of man, based on years of correctly relating alcohol intake to fear output, were finally being proved imperfect? For what awful fear could possibly lurk beneath all this noisy joy and victory? How could a storm strong enough to drive such a large herd into his long, barnlike bar be thundering behind all this blue sky and sunshine?

Evenwrite, panting at the bathroom mirror, finds himself wondering along about the same lines as Teddy, only with less eloquence: Why ain't I happy with how things worked out?—as he arranges the oversized knot on his tie to try to conceal the unbuttoned gap in his collar. "God! Damn! Dammit!" But *why* ain't I pleased . . . ?—wrenching at the collar furiously.

He hated white shirts anyhow, never had liked 'em, wouldn't even wear the things to big muckymuck meetings—frig 'em; they ain't no better bird just because they can afford better feathers!—and he didn't see why he couldn't use the same argument on a dolled-up corpse. His wife saw differently. "Maybe poor Joe Stamper *won't* kick about your blue Catalina Casual with the stripes, but *I* wouldn't go to a funeral dressed like that *dead!*"

He'd argued, but he saw her point, and he'd been forced to dig down through the drawers after the shirt he'd been married in, only to find that the goddam *collar* had shrunk a good goddam two inches.

"Jesus, Mama," he called out to his wife, leaning from the bathroom door, "what'd you wash this shirt in to shrink it so bad?"

"Your *white* shirt?" his wife called back. "Hasn't been *near* water since our first wedding anniversary, buster. When you got drunk and decided that if a man was high enough he didn't need *no such stuff* and tossed it in the punch."

"Yeah, well, if that's so . . ." he trailed off weakly, jerking the tie unknotted to start over. Then why ain't I happy with how things worked out?

Simone, on the other hand, lighter by the fifteen pounds she had always promised herself that she would lose (the weeks of virtue had rendered her poor enough to keep that promise), looks back over her shoulder at the reflection of her nude ass in the cracked full-length mirror in her closet door, and wonders if she didn't look better sinfully plump than morally trim. Well, it's hard to say, nude; perhaps new clothes—her old wardrobe hung on her like dreadful old sacks! —perhaps if she could afford one of these smart new *short* things and a—

She stopped. She walked to the dresser and felt again in the empty Marlboro box, avoiding looking at the dresser mirror, trying to forget her wardrobe; this kind of thinking, it could do nothing but make her sad all over again for the appearance she made in those hateful rags. Why torture yourself drooling after thousand-franc cakes when six hundred francs was all you had? But she liked pretty things. And she detested her clothed look, so much so that she frequently spent her hours in her room naked to keep from seeing her baggy image in the mirror. And now, now, it seems—she turned to confront the reflection full front, head tipped and one hip thrown forward—that

even *this body*—unless that crack distorted more than she thought—
is becoming no longer a *pretty thing to see!* It's all wrong. The . . .
the *bones* push out. The *flesh*, it is become too small. . . . *I need
money* . . .

Simone was thankful that the Holy Mother was closed in the
closet so that the evil desires did not cause Her sorrow; the poor
Virgin, how such desires must pain Her! But one *cannot* help wishing
sometimes, damn it, that one could afford something decent, just
one *pretty thing* to fit right . . . it didn't seem fair for one to have
to endure the double humility of having both clothes too large and
flesh too small.

The sun shines. The wood steams. The sapsuckers rap happily on
the softened scrub-oak trunks. Men straighten up and women fill
their washing machines in these little coast towns. But in Wakonda
there is some dissent against this mood (and outside of Wakonda, up
river, in the Stamper barn . . .) and some gloom in all the sunshine.
Even Biggy Newton, who had leaped about the water in the drainage
ditch like an overjoyed whale when his boss had strolled by the job
to let him know that old Hank Stamper had finally throwed in the
towel . . . even this swollen boy, pledged to the last ounce of his
stunted intelligence as Hank Stamper's arch enemy, found himself
feeling less and less overjoyed. As he got drunker and drunker in the
Snag.

Big had not always been big; at thirteen he had been Ben, Benjamin Newton, an average lad of normal size and sense. Then fourteen
had pushed him up over six feet, and fifteen had carried him on up
to six-six and left him with less sense than he'd had at twelve. By this
time he had acquired a number of managers, and they could lay
claim to at least part of the credit for Biggy's first-rate progress. Older
men, these managers—uncles, cousins, and job friends of his father's
—had devoted a lot of time to the big boy's training. A lot of
time to training and a *precious* lot to conditioning. And by the time
he'd reached his full growth, he was so well conditioned that he was
as sure as they were that he was the bully of the woods, the thick-
headed heavy who'd bust up any block who got in his road. And
after busting up enough of these blocks he'd become good enough
at his role that his road began to be avoided. Now, barely voting age,
he faced the bleakish future of the bully with no blocks left who'd
get in his road and nothing to bust up. He hulked over his dark beer
in the Snag, brooding about the years ahead, and wondering why all

them managers who'd started slapping his back and buying him drafts when he was fifteen hadn't prepared him for this inevitable blockless day.

"Hot diggity *dawg!*" Les Gibbons, one of the crowd at Biggy's table, lurched up out of his chair, overcome with emotion and Seven Crown. "I do feel fine. I feel just *real* fine, to be siffically honest. . . ." He tossed down the last of his drink, then wagged his head about in search of some way to demonstrate just how fine he really felt. He decided throwing his glass at something was the only way to give them some idea. He aimed for the eagle in the big Anheuser-Busch clock above Teddy's mounted Chinook salmon and hit the fish square in the eye, spraying glass and old fish scales over a booth full of tourists in deer-hunting garb. They started to protest, but Les stopped their objections with a steely-eyed stare. "Yessir!" he crowed. "I feel *fine!* And like a pur-ty tough bird, too."

Big could hardly stir himself enough to raise his head for a look at this bird; and after he looked he didn't even bother speaking. Boy, if this Gibbons was the toughest block a crowd this size could offer to bust, then his future was bleakish for *goddam* sure. Dammit anyhow. . . . What does a guy *do* . . . when his purpose in life peters out? when he ain't fit for marryin' or bein' friends or for nothin' but bustin' up one certain somebody? And that certain somebody's just finked out? Big ground his teeth: Stamper, dammit anyhow, how *could* you be such a bad ass, so downright *thoughtless* as to cop before them managers got me a replacement trained?

( . . . Up river, in the barn, Hank hears Viv's call stretch out to him from the house. She is ready to leave. He stands up and releases the old redbone hound whose ear he has been doctoring. The dog shakes himself with a great dusty flapping of ears and lopes eagerly out of the dim barn into the sunshine. Hank returns the swab-stopper to the bottle of creosote and sets it up on the shelf with the rest of the various animal medicines. He brushes his hands on his slacks, picks up his jacket, and starts for the back door that leads out of the barn, down to the dock. Outside, the sun strikes his barn-accustomed eyes and momentarily blinds him. He pauses, blinking, while he puts on his sports jacket, thinking *Dang . . . wouldn't old Joby be pleased to see what a fair day we got for his funeral?*)

"Yes, merciful." Brother Walker picked up the conversation again. "Merciful, just, and *fair* . . . is what the Lord is. That is why I cannot be too stricken by Brother Joe Ben's death. Grieved, if you know what I mean, Mr. Loop, but not *stricken*. For I feel that the Lord needed the use of Joe to make Hank Stamper see the Light, so to speak. That is why, like I was telling the little woman this morning, 'I cannot be too stricken by poor Brother Joe Ben's death, much as we all will miss him . . . for he was an *instrument*, an *instrument*.'"

"A real squareshooter," the Real Estate Hotwire felt moved to add. "Right down the middle. Myself, I was never actually very closely acquainted with ol' Joe, but what I seen always struck me that he was a *real squareshooter!*"

"Yes, yes, an instrument."

"A real right-down-the-center guy."

The conversation faded again and they continued toward the funeral parlor in silence; Brother Walker was looking forward to the funeral. He knew that enough members of the Faith would be there to insist that he say a few words about Brother-in-the-Faith Joe Ben after the Reverend Toms finished, and the prospect of saying a few words to all those polished seats, those somber clothes, the organ, the drapes, to all the plush and pompery of conventional religion, always made him a little schoolgirlish. A tent, he knew, could certainly be the House of the Lord as well as any building, and as long as he held with the Faith—which did not hold with any gaudy show of mourning—he was compelled to frown on the orthodox Christian funeral; but frown as he might, he was always secretly pleased when one of the deceased's kin insisted—as one of the deceased's kin invariably did—that, with all due respect for the Faith's teachings, still perhaps a funeral *should*, just for appearances, be held at a funeral parlor. And in spite of all its ostentatious, gaudy, and disgusting pageantry, you couldn't deny that that pale gray drapery lining Lilienthal's Funeral Parlor was acoustically superior to canvas as a backdrop for the Word of God. Yes, a tent could most certainly be a House of the Lord as well as any fancy building, but it was still just a tent.

(*Wouldn't old Joby have a field day with these kind of sunshiny signals? I thought to myself, just standing there, looking at the sky . . . wouldn't he bust a gut? Then I heard Viv call again and headed on to the boat . . .*)

Simone works futilely with scissors and needle. Indian Jenny sighs and untangles her legs and arranges them full length on her cot heavily. Oh, she isn't *giving up* on her projects—she reaches for the copy of *The Search for Bridey Murphy* lying on the shack floor—she is merely changing her approach once more . . .

In their hotel room Rod gives up on the want ads and reluctantly unsnaps his guitar case to join this madman roommate of his in rehearsing.

Behind his sunlit scrawl of neon tubes Teddy listens to the rising pitch of laughter and merrymaking and tries to plumb the dark well it rises from. What are they afraid of *now?* Evenwrite gives up on his tie: a white shirt, o-kay, but that was compromise enough . . . *no by god chokerope,* and that's final! Simone hears the doorbell ring and hurries to answer it before it wakes her six-year-old from his nap; disgustedly she wraps a faded chenille housecoat about her body and checks the empty cigarette box one last time as she leaves the bedroom. Big Newton drinks his tasteless beer and orders another, feeling more bleakish than ever . . .

(Across the river, at the garage landing, I held the boat steady while Viv stepped out of the boat with the hem of her skirt held in one hand, watching that she didn't get any mud on her high-heeled shoes. She crossed the gravel, then headed on up to the garage and waited there for me to tie the boat up and drag a tarp over the motor. The sky looked clear, and maybe that tarp wouldn't be necessary, but one thing you learn young in this neck of the woods is not to be sucked in by a little fair weather. "Never trust the sun no further than you can throw it," the old man always said. I took my time lashing on the tarp in spite of the sunshine, and even though we was running a little late. I took my time and got it right and let her stand there . . .)

The Real Estate Hotwire waves at someone down the street. "There's Sis. Hey, Sissy, wait up." And they step up their walk to reach her. The Real Estate Man took her arm. "You positive you feel up to this, Sissy? This close after Willard's?"

She blew her nose through the veil. "Willard always had the finest opinion of Joe Ben. I feel I should go."

"There's a girl. You know Brother Walker, don't you? Of the First Church and Christian Science?"

"Metaphysics, Mr. Loop. Yes, we saw each other at—the other day. May I say again how sorry I am, Mrs. Eggleston." Brother Walker extended his hand along with his condolences. "These last few days . . . have been a cross for many of us."

The Real Estate Man squeezed her arm. "But we're through it, now, isn't that so, Sissy-little? We're around that corner."

They resumed walking. Sissy-little wished she were alone with her brother so she could tell him about this awful thing the insurance company was trying to do with her Willard's money. The Real Estate Hotwire wished he'd sold Willard a better package than that theater, as long as it looked like it was coming back to him anyway. And Brother Walker wished he'd worn less sedate garb. As they walked he watched the healthy bounce of the Real Estate Man's once-muscular breasts through the casual blue polo shirt and wished he'd dared a bit of casualness himself. It would make a nice picture against all the rest of the stiff and formal trappings. He wondered . . . perhaps he could remove his dark serge coat and loosen his tie; on a day like this, who could blame a man for being a little informal? Even a man of God? It would be one way to show all those who were not Brothers or Sisters just how the Faith stood on appearances, show them he was a regular guy. He might even remove his tie completely. Wouldn't Reverend Toms, with his french cuffs and his double-breasted black and his hanky-in-the-pocket, wouldn't old Biddy Toms go into a flap when he was replaced by an open-collared white shirt that delivered a better eulogy in a more resonant voice? A regular flap?

"Ohyas," he said, "a time of great trial for many of us."

(I got the boat secured good and walked up to the garage. Viv was waiting to see what I planned to drive into town; the jeep had that damn top on it I never liked, but the pick-up was still a mess from driving old Henry to the hospital—I hadn't done anything about cleaning it up but for taking out that arm. So I said let's take the jeep. And you drive, okay? I don't care to. . . .

I never minded driving the jeep during the summer, it's wide open and wild in good weather; but with that damned top on for winter, it makes the thing like a tin coffin on wheels, hardly any rear or front vision at all and just a couple slits in the side so you can see out that way. Not the sort of thing I like to ride in anyhow, especially to a funeral.

Viv got in behind the wheel and went to grinding the starter. I leaned back and tried to rub me a spot to see out through that plastic-covered slit in the door. . . .)

When Floyd Evenwrite leaves the house, wearing a tie, on his way to warm up his car, he meets Orland Stamper walking to his own car, as groomed and grumpy as Floyd himself—". . . yeah, it took some doin', Orland . . . but, shit, he *needed* brought down a peg or two."

"If he'd been brought down sooner," Orland said harshly, "Janice would have her a live man today instead of something swole up over at Edward Lilienthal's. We're just lucky his hardheadedness didn't get more of us hurt. . . ."

"Yeah . . . too bad about Joe Ben. He was a good old boy."

"If Hank'd been brought down that couple pegs just one *day* sooner . . . them five little tykes'd have a daddy instead of a piddling little four-thousand-dollar policy. The old man'd still have two arms. . . ."

"What's the word about old Henry?" Evenwrite asked.

"Comin' along, they say; comin' along. Hard old coon to kill."

"What has he said about his pride and joy knuckling under to the union? Looks to me like that alone would be enough to kill the old coon. . . ."

"Why, to tell the truth, I don't know how he took it. I didn't think about it. Maybe they ain't even told him."

"Bull. Somebody'd sure have told."

"Maybe not. Hank's give orders nobody's to get to see him. Maybe the doctor wants him to get his strength back before he hears the news."

"Uhuh . . . an' *then* you know what. He'll go to frailin' whoever's knob happens to be closest. Personally, I was Hank, I'd tell him before he got able to swing that cane of his again."

"With one arm gone clean," Orland said, "and the other just fresh out of a sling, I'd venture Henry Stamper's knob-frailin' days are a thing of the past."

"*Never saw the sun*," Ray sings, "*shining so bright . . .*"

"I ain't givin' up," Jenny vows.

"Teddy . . . ?" Boney Stokes calls. "What's the time?"

"Twenty till, Mr. Stokes," Teddy answers.

"They should be comin' past in about twenty minutes, then. My, my; that awful sun . . . you should think about putting up an awning, Teddy."

"Yes, I guess I should." Teddy returns to his spigots. It is still picking up. If it continues he will have to call in Mrs. Carleson from the Sea Breeze to help tonight. He should have already made the arrangements, but he still is unable to believe that such weather and well-being could stimulate so much business. It goes against all he has learned . . .

(Viv let go the jeep's starter and took off her white gloves—the wheel and gear shift are wrapped with friction tape—and handed them to me so she could wrestle the jeep without getting them dirty. Neither of us said anything. She was fixed up real nice for the occasion; she'd worked half the morning getting her hair stacked onto her head like a coil of gold ropes—I swear to god the only thing a woman'll spend more effort getting ready for is a wedding—but by the time she got that coldblooded bastard choked, started, killed, started again, into low, killed again, and finally out on the road, the golden coil was on its way to coming unwound. I watched her but I didn't put my two cents in. I didn't even tell her to throttle it with the choke. I just sat there with them gloves in my lap figuring it's by god *time* somebody besides me learned to tote and roll . . .)

"I ain't quitting," Indian Jenny assures herself when she shuts her book and puts it down, "just resting." She closes her eyes, but the image of a green-eyed, proud-eyed young logger with a bristling mustache will not let her sleep.

Simone answers the door and . . . why, Howie Evans! "Yeah, Simone, I'm just wondering . . . if you might not join me at the Snag tonight?"

"No, Howie. I am sorry. Look at me . . . can I go into public like *this?*"

He shuffled uncomfortably for a moment, started to make a wisecrack, then grinned and said, "Well, who knows? Maybe a fairy godmother er somethin' will come through, huh? Anyhow . . . we'll be seeing you?"

"Perhaps. . . ."

He was gone before she could say good-by. . . .

The Real Estate Man and his bereaved sister leave Brother Walker when they reach Lilienthal's, to go talk something over. Brother Walker searches the crowd for Janice—she will need him in this hour of need, certainly—and is astounded at the number of people who have turned out to pay their last respects to poor Joe. He'd no *idea* Brother Joe Ben had been so well loved by his neighbors . . .

(Viv or me didn't say a word all the way into town, about Joe or anything. I imagine she figures I'd just rather not talk. She don't have any way of knowing what I know. And it's just as well. Because I didn't feel like telling her how I come to know it.

The jeep was bumping and bouncing and banging so much we couldn't of heard each other anyhow. There's chuckholes galore. The road's tore to hell after the storms, and the road crews are out working on it. Above the mountains there's lots of small, tight clouds cluttering up the sky, and the sun keeps going off and on, dodging behind first one and then the other. "Man, I'm drained to a frazzle," I say, but Viv doesn't hear. I lay my head down against the plexiglass window and just take it easy. The sun comes out bright as hell, like it was lit with more than light. I see that snarl of berry vine beside the road and it's like somehow it scrubs both my eyeballs clean of stuff that'd built up there without me knowing it, because I blink a couple times and look around and I'm seeing things clear as a bell. This kept happening, off and on. It'd be bright for a little bit, everything shining like chrome, waxy-looking, polished, then go dark as muddy water. Then bright again. It's the first time I've really been out since Joe bought it, and I can't help feeling that the world looks different. I tell myself that it looks so bright just because the light zooming on after that dark spell makes a diamond flash out of everything. But I ain't convinced. It still feels like that first dazzling swipe of berry vine scrubbed my eyes clear.

I just sit there in a kind of doze, looking out through the flicker of ditch willows zipping past along the road and enjoying the scenery. Maybe I was seeing things so clear because it was the first time in I don't know how many years I'd rode this stretch without having to do the driving. Maybe that's it. All I know is everything was shining like a new dime. There's rusty screen-topped cones of sawdust-burners vomiting sparks and blue smoke; widow's-lace fern waving around the mailboxes; busy glisten of little breezes blowing across the standing water . . . swoop of powerlines . . . spearmint bush so bright and new I smell them as we pass . . . squirrels hustling around . . . then more rusty burners. Leaves, bright, waxy green, scrubbed, sort of. Prismed light where the sun comes through the drops hanging off the leaves, shattered and pure and bright. . . .

I put my face closer to the little window so I could see more. There was the sky, the little clouds, then the treetops running into the steep sloped-off canyon down to the railroad embankment, then there's a wide drainage between the road and the track. This ditch is a mangle of scrubby little Himalaya vines; Himalaya blackberry got a pretty good flavor but loaded with seeds big enough to knock a tooth out. All the leaves had been whipped off the vines by that last big storm, and the vines look like a king-sized roll of steel wool. I bounce along, looking at them vines, thinking to myself if a fellow was big enough he'd just grab him a handful of that and scrub the world to a fare-thee-well, get shut of them clouds, *really* brighten things up. . . . This notion slid into a kind of open-eyed dream. I take a giant fistful of steel wool and go at it, working like a nigger. I can't stop somehow. I finish with the sky and go at the beach. Then the town, then the hills. I'm panting and sweating and scrubbing like a nigger! I step back and take a look: but instead of things getting brighter and clearer this time, it's just made them duller. Like it kind of faded the color out. I grab up the roll and tear into it again, and when I'm finished this time it's even more faded than before. So this time I really work it over. I scrub everything, the world and sky and my eyes and the sun and everything, and finally fall back, wore clean out. I take a look and it's bright all right, like a movie-show screen when the film breaks and you got nothing to look at up there but the bright white light. Everything else is gone. I throw away the steel wool; it's fine to brighten things up with once in a while, but too much of it, man, can rub *everything* away.)

In the Snag, Boney Stokes complains about the glare as he moves his chair closer to the window. Teddy finally gives Mrs. Carleson a call and she says sorry but she's too busy herself right then, but she'll send over her daughter. Big Newton watches Les Gibbons get drunker and fiercer but seriously doubts that the big liver-lipped monkey will ever get drunk or fierce enough. And the crowd lingering outside the funeral parlor swings suddenly around at someone's whisper to see a yellow jeep turn the corner of Nahamish and South Main, coming toward them, finally.

(So many folks had come to the funeral that we couldn't find a parking place closer than two blocks off. "Joe Ben would've popped his eyes out to see what a draw he was dead," I said to Viv. I pop-eyed a little myself; I knew he was the type guy always liked by everybody that knew him, but I didn't know this many even *knew* him. Walking back from the jeep, I saw that even the lawn on the family-entrance side of Lilienthal's was packed to the sidewalk with dark blue suits and black frocks. As I got closer I saw that the whole working force from WP was there, Floyd Evenwrite too—all standing and talking in respectful voices, and slipping off two or three at a time behind Lilienthal's big black '53 Caddy hearse where they could crack out their pocket stashes and have a nip out of sight of the women. Most of the women were standing up on the steps or just inside the door, touching their faces to little white hankies. The men nipped; the women dabbed. Everybody to their own kick, I figured.

They saw Viv and me come walking up toward them, and I heard the talk drone to a stop. The guys behind the Caddy quick stuck their bottle out of our sight. They all watched us walk past, working their faces, those faces you always see at a goddamned funeral. Little smiles, understanding smiles, and eyes like they borrowed them from cocker spaniels especially for the occasion. They watch and nod whenever I look their direction. Nobody says a thing. The crowd from around the other side of the building comes bustling to get a look, and a couple more women's heads poke out the door. Orland's car slides up to the side door, and Orland's wife helps Jan out. Jan's just as lumpy and owl-like as ever, for all the black net they'd hung over her. The crowd turns to watch her walk along so stooped for a second, but then turns right back to me and Viv. They aren't interested in Jan. Big a deal as a griefstruck woman is, she still isn't what they'd gone to the trouble of primping and preening and getting into their Easter Sunday costumes to come out and see. Jan's just the side attraction, the prelim. And they didn't come for that. A crowd comes to an event to see the main attraction, I thought to myself. And at a funeral the main attraction is somebody belly up. That ain't lumpy little Jan. And, much as I hate to steal your thunder, Joby, I'm afraid that you ain't the main attraction at this particular event, either.

Viv and me followed Orland and Jan and them into the dim-lit family room. Everybody else was there, sitting quiet in little padded folding chairs in front of a sort of gauzy curtain separating us from the main section. We could see them out there but they couldn't see in; they'd to be satisfied with what sniffs and sobs drifted out to them.

The heads of the family craned around at me and Viv as we sidled into our seats. I braced myself for the scalding looks I'd been expecting to get, but the heat wasn't there. I'd expected a verdict of guilty from every Stamper eye in the house, but got nothing except that same sad cocker-spaniel smile. I guess I was still a little rummy from the ride because this threw me pretty bad. I stared back at them, froze where I stood. . . . Good Christ, didn't they realize? Didn't they know I'd as well as killed him? I opened my mouth to demand at least one of them recognize this, but the only sound that came out was the moo of an electric organ someplace, then old lady Lilienthal singing. Viv took my hand and pulled me into my seat.

The organ mooed and bawled. Old lady Lilienthal tried to outdo it with "End of a Perfect Day," the same song she'd sung at my mom's funeral out at the house twenty years before, sung just as bad today, only slower. It took her hours. If she lasted another twenty years of funeral singing and kept getting slower, they would have to come up with some new embalming preservatives.

The organ played again. Somebody recited something from a book of poems. Lilienthal, who couldn't stay out of the show any more than his wife, read a list of names of folks who couldn't make it for one reason or another, and had sent flowers in their place. "Lily Gilchrest," he would singsong, "her spirit is with us today. Mr. and Mrs. Edward R. Sorenson . . . their spirit is with us today." La-da-dee-la-dee-la-da. It was a running battle built up over the years between him and his wife and that mooing organ, to see which one could drag out his part the longest. Then old man Toms got up and went to droning on. I thought about how funny it was that Joby should be drummed out this way . . . a guy who could cram more words into a minute than these three, going all at once, could get into a day.

I begin to get sleepy.

Brother Walker came out in his shirtsleeves, looking like a coach at half-time. He opened a Bible that bristled like a porcupine with place-markers and, using Joby's death like a man on a springboard, took a running jump at the stars. He lost me someplace during the dive.

Viv shook me awake. We were getting up out of the seats and filing through an opening in the curtain. The main room had already took its look and were waiting outside while we had our turn. I strolled past and looked in. By golly. You don't look so bad. The drowned ones I seen before always looked waterlogged. I guess you weren't in long enough to soak up much. Fact the matter is, you ugly little toad, you look a damn sight better than usual. They painted your face with some stuff that dulled the scars some, and you don't have your ordinary raw-meatball look. And a black tie. You'd be amazed. Oh yeah. Oh yeah. To see how godawful handsome they could make.

"Hank . . . Hank, please . . ."

Except. Damn, I wish they hadn't made you such a frigging sober-sides because it makes you look like.

"Please, the others are waitin'. . . . What are you doing?"

You need the *grin*, man. The goofy one. You taking it so serious. Swing with what you got. Here. Hold on, I'll just.

"Hank! Lord, man, you can't touch the—"

Orland grabbed my wrist and brought me out of it. "It was all that music and that crap," I told him. "Made me sleepy as a dog."

"Let's move on outside," Viv whispered. I followed her out.

My time with the tarp was justified; it had clouded over solid. I saw a little patter of rain hurrying up the street. It had been scheduled for the funeral but made it late; now it was hustling to be sure it didn't miss the burying. Men hunched their shoulders and women held the little flowery funeral programs over their hairdos and went to scurrying like chickens for shelter. It looked like it was going to open up all the time we were hustling to the jeep, but it never. It kept pittypatting during the funeral procession through the middle of town; just barely; holding back, like it was waiting. . . .)

Boney Stokes waits until the whole procession has passed. He wants to be sure the doctor is at the funeral grounds as well as Hank. It is a long walk from the Snag to the hospital for an old man—for a *sick* old man—and he doesn't want to chance being turned away from his goal, after enduring the journey, by some young fool doctor with orders otherwise. A *long* walk. Through rain, too, he noticed as he buttoned his long black raincoat to his skinny neck, through rain and cold and me with these weak lungs. . . . Oh, what a man of Christian intent will not endure for an old friend!

(At the graveside the rain got down to business and thinned the crowd down to only about a third what it was at the parlor. We bunched up close around the hole. They were burying Joby beside his old man, or beside all of his old man that had been brought back down from that shack where he'd disappeared to. Enough insult right there to make both of them plow the ground with turning. It was almost funny. If this judgment day Joe was always looking forward to ever comes round, I thought, and those two come up for air and find they been buried next to each other, then the fur is really gonna fly. Joe always wanted to be as far from his old man as possible, even got his face rearranged so he wouldn't look like Ben Stamper; he couldn't think of anything worse than growing up with what he called that handsome and hopeless face. I thought again about the way Lilienthal had fixed Joe's dead face—powdered over the scars, ironed out the grin—and I wanted to open that box and fix them for him. I wanted to so bad it made me clench up my fists till I could feel myself shake; it made me strain all over. Not to hold myself back from doing it, but because I knew I wasn't *going* to do it. I just stood there. I watched them straddle the grave rails, and lower the coffin, all the while clenching my fists and straining and wishing they'd get that mud thrown on that coffin and get it out of sight. And just stood there.

As soon as Joe was buried I took Viv's arm and started off. When we got to the jeep I heard somebody holler, "Hank! Hank boy!"

It was Floyd Evenwrite; he was yelling and waving out of the window of his big Pontiac to me. "You an' your woman jump in here with us. We got room to waste. You don't need to drive all that way back down to town in that leaky old jeep. Let Andy take it an' jump in here in a decent machine. . . ." Evenwrite gave me a big old toothy grin and waited. It was an open invitation to bury the hatchet, and everybody concerned damn well knew it. But I thought I saw what was almost a taunt behind that grin. Like he was grinning that, sure, just a week or so ago, Hank old boy, I was trying to sabotage your mill and stampede your whole summer's work down the river. But let's be buddies. . . . "What you say, boy . . . ?"

I looked at Viv, and at Andy standing near the crowd around Big Lou's car. They waited for me to decide; we all knew that Floyd and his bunch had a lot to do with putting that squeeze on us that helped to do in Joe. I tried to decide something, but all I could think was *I'm tired, I'm tired of being the villain.* . . .

"Be right with you, Floyd," I hollered back at him and grabbed Viv by the hand. "Okeydoke with you, Andy? Just leave it on Main someplace, the jeep." We scampered over to the door he held open for us. Nobody said anything during most of the ride. When we got down near town Evenwrite ask why I didn't drop by the Snag for a beer or so. I told him that I thought Viv was wanting to get on over to Joe's new house to be with Jan, and he said fine, we'd drop her by, but then what? I told him that I ought to go by the hospital and see how the old man was making out, but after that I'd think about it.

"Good. You do that. I'll drop Viv off and we can turn up Necanicum and take you right past the hospital. Then you think about it. Okay?"

I said okay. I tried to catch Viv's eye a time or two to see how she felt about my decision, but she kept to herself. And after we dropped her off I asked myself why should I care anyhow? I was glad to be in a good dry car. I was glad to be getting invitations for rides and beers. I was glad to have somebody stick out a hand to me.

We turned from South Main to Sillits Street toward Necanicum. I sank back in the deep cushion of the big car and listened to the wipers and the heater and Evenwrite make small talk with his family. I didn't care how Viv or Andy looked at me. I didn't care if there was a little taunt in Evenwrite's grin. I didn't even care what Joby would've thought about it.

Because as far as I was concerned the fight was finished, the hatchet buried . . . for good.)

The minute Hank was out of the car, Evenwrite's kids, kept in sedate behavior in the back seat for so long by the presence of two strange grown-ups and the solemnity of the occasion, begin to act up so that Floyd was forced to stop the car twice before he got home, to knock some ears down. He left his house in a fury, jumped back in the car, and screeched away from his yard toward the Snag, with his kids crying and his wife threatening and his bowels turning.

When he reached main he made two runs the length of the street, checking for Draeger's car, before he stopped; he by god wasn't about to go in there and have Draeger crow about the human heart to him! Not him! He was amazed that Hank could even consider dropping by, with "I told you so" on the tip of everybody's tongue. Amazed and, he found, a little disappointed: he'd expected more of Hank. And he felt that Hank had betrayed him some way or other, though he couldn't exactly say why. . . . And why *ain't* I satisfied how things worked out?

Indian Jenny pulls on her boots and begins her trek to the Snag. Sometimes direct action worked better than magic. Especially some night, in a bar. Be a lot of drunks there tonight. And who knows?

Simone opens the package just delivered by the young matchstick-chewer from Stokes's General. "No card from who?"

"No, no card or nothing'," he had told her. "Howie said be sure no card or nothin' . . . so's you couldn't send it back to somebody."

"Well you just take it right *back* to somebody—so pretty, though, how could he?—and you tell somebody I accept no gifts from strange men. . . . But *how* could he know to pick one so pretty and the right size, I bet?"

"His sister was with him to help, maybe?"

"Then you take it back to his sister."

"I can't do that," the boy said, moving to try to peek through the front of her housecoat. "I just deliver."

"Yes?"

"Yeah." He winked and shifted the matchstick to the opposite corner of his mouth and was gone before she could stop him. Simone hustled the gift into her bedroom before Mother Nielsen or her kids in the other half of the duplex heard and came snooping. She spread the frock on her bed and looked at. . . . So pretty. But no. She had promised. She could *not* disappoint the Virgin . . .

She had returned the dress to the box and started folding the tissue paper back over it when through her bedroom window she saw Indian Jenny passing, thick and dumpy and rubber-booted, in the dimming rain. Simone stared, lightly trailing her fingers along the rustling tissue. *That*—she grimaced at Jenny—is what I did not wish to become. *That* is the thing I did not wish to become. I made the confession, I swore on the Book, I promised the Sweet Mother of God to sin never again . . . but *that woman there* is what I do not wish to become.

She suddenly remembered her image in the mirror, and the pity in the eyes of the women who saw her on the street. Her eyes closed . . . I have had virtue. But it is almost that I have become through virtue what that heathen slut out there became through sin, a tramp, a shuffler in dumpy dresses. It is so now that to the women of the town I look like the town whore. Because of my appearance. Because I can't afford to *look* decent. Oh, *oh*, Sweet *Mother!* She pressed the tissue against her lips. Oh *give* me strength in my weakness . . .

The sin that she now felt from looking sinful, Simone realized as she sobbed into the tissue, was more painful than the sin she had once felt from sinning. "What has happened, Holy Mother, that I become so sinful?" she beseeched the wooden statue in her closet. "What has happened that I become so *weak?*"

But another thought was already growing like yeast in her mind: And you, Holy Mother, to let this happen . . . what has happened to you?

Fluorescent tubes fluttered and hissed. The air felt purified. The Amazon of a nurse had said, "Right this way, Mr. Stamper," as soon as Hank approached her desk, before he had even asked to see his father. She picked up a clipboard and led him out of the newer part of the hospital, down a corridor so low he found himself ducking involuntarily to avoid the overhead lights, through hallways so old he thought they might have been carved out of the bygone centuries by Indians and whitewashed in honor of the white man's coming. A section of the clinic that he had not seen before—wooden walls fossilized by endless scrubbings, linoleum floors worn bare by endless shufflings of white canvas shoes . . . and through open doors glimpses of old people propped like cloth dolls against brass bedsteads, hairless faces limp and wrinkled in the stony blue flickering of TV.

The nurse noticed his interest and paused, smiling into one of the larger rooms. "Each room's got one now. Used, of course, but still in excellent shape. The DAR ladies donated them." She adjusted a strap through the fabric of her uniform. "Gives the old folks something to look at, y'know, while they wait."

The picture in the room they were looking into had begun to flip; yet no one called for an adjustment. "While they wait for what?" Hank couldn't help wondering out loud. The nurse gave him a sharp look and started on down the corridor again toward the old man's room.

"We had to situate him where we had room," she felt compelled to explain, speaking sharply. "Even though he might not be classified geriatric. The new wing is always so crowded . . . babies and young mamas and the like. Besides, he's not exactly a spring chicken any more, now is he?"

The place stank of age, of all the accouterments of age, strong soap and wintergreen salve, alcohol and baby food, and, over everything, the keen reek of urine. Hank's nose wrinkled with distaste. But, he reasoned, when you come down to it, why shouldn't the old live in an old world and the bright new wing be reserved for babies and young mamas and the like?

"No . . . I guess he ain't exactly a spring chicken any more."

The nurse stopped at the very last door. "We did give him a private room, you see. Mr. Stokes is in there with him now." Her voice had dropped to a reedy whisper. "I know what you told us about nobody gettin' in to see him for a while, but I figured . . . well, my lands, they're such old friends I couldn't see the harm." She smiled quickly and opened the door, stepping in to announce, "Another visitor, Mr. Stamper."

The gaunt and white-maned head reared up out of the pillow with a bray of laughter. "By god now, I was beginning to think all my kin had give me up for dead. Find a chair, son. Sit. Wait. Here's old Boney. He's been here cheering me up, like a good soul."

"Afternoon, Hank. My condolences." The cold hand touched Hank's with a husking, parchment sound, then withdrew quickly to cover a practiced cough. Hank looked down at his father.

"How you makin' it, Papa?"

"'Middlin', Hank, middlin'." His brows lowered despondently over defeated eyes—"The doc says it'll be a piece before I can get back to loggin', maybe a long piece . . ."—then lifted quickly to reveal a flash of ornery green. "But he says I'll be playin' the violin again before the week's out. Oh yee haw, hee hee *haw!* Look out for me, Boney, they been shootin' me fulla dope an' I'm a caution."

"Henry." Boney spoke through his fingers, hiding the thin slot of mouth. "You had best take it easy now. . . ."

"Listen to him, son; don't you know he brings me a lot of pleasure comin' here? Here, sit down on the edge of the bed if you can't run down a chair. Nursie, don't I get but one chair? And what d'ya say you bring another scuttle of mud for my boy?"

"Coffee is provided for the patients, Mr. Stamper, not for the visitors."

"I'll *pay* for it, goddangit!" He winked at Hank. "I tell ya . . . when they fust brought me in here the other night you just would not *believe* all the crap and paraphernalia they wanted me to fill out. Seems as you *neglected* to, so I had to do it."

"That's not true!" the nurse hoped in horror; but there was no telling about that night staff. "I don't think it's true."

"Yessir, fill all kinds of the stuff out. Even was after my *finger-prints* by god till they seen I weren't equipped for it." The woman turned and huffed away down the corridor. Henry studied her departure with an expert's eye. "Hogs fightin' under a sheet . . . how'd I like to sink my long yellows in *that* an' let it drag me to my death?"

"If you was of an age," Boney added on, "to have long yellows." He wasn't giving a thing.

"Maybe you'd have to sink your gums into her, Boney. But I still got three my own teeth, if you'll notice"—he opened his mouth to display the proof—"an' two of 'em meet." This seemed to tire him momentarily and his high spirits waned while he lay for a few seconds with his eyes closed. When his head rolled on the pillow to look again at his somber visitor his good humor seemed strained. "You know, that damned woman, she's been waiting all the livelong day for this ol' nigger to give up the ghost an' get it over with so's she can make the bed. Now I believe she's peeved that I haven't."

"Maybe she's just worried," Boney observed solemnly. "She's had a lot of reason to be worried about you, old fellow."

Henry rallied to meet the challenge. "Reason the bull. I weren't even close, not even *close*, you goddam vulture. Listen at him, Hank, the old buzzard. Why I weren't even in *shoutin'* distance!"

Hank smiled weakly. Boney looked down at the floor with a slight shaking of his head. "My, my, my." It was his day, he felt, and he wasn't about to let his toll of doom be drowned out by a few tinkles of humor.

Henry didn't like that shake of the head. "You think no? I always said, didn't I, that I could outlog any man this side of the Cascades, with one arm tied behind my back? All right, now I get a chance to prove it. An' you by god wait an' see if I—" A sudden thought occured to him; he turned back to Hank. "Say, what come of that arm, anyhow? Because, y'know . . ." He timed a little pause before he announced, "I was kinda *attached* to it!"

His head fell back to the brass bars, mouth going wide in voiceless laughter. Hank knew the old man had probably been waiting for hours for the opportunity to make that announcement. He told Henry that he'd kept good track of the limb. "I had a notion you might want to keep it. I got it in the freezer with all the other meat."

"Well, you watch that Viv don't fry it up for supper," Henry warned. "For I was always mighty attached to that arm."

When Henry tired of his joke he fumbled for the buzzer button that dangled on a wire beside his head. "Where in hell that woman go to now? I ain't been able to get anything out of her all day, and I don't just mean coffee. Hank, I want you to bring me up on—here! damn it, ring this gizmo for me; she keep puttin' it on the wrong side where I can't get at it. On my wingless side. Hm. You be careful of that ol' wing, now. Damn. Where is that old cow? A man could die in this place and people wouldn't know it till the stink got bad. Listen, I want to know what's happenin' with the show an' if—Come on! don't just fiddle with it, buzz hell out of it. That's what it's here for. Boney, what's the matter'th you? Sittin' there like you lost your best friend . . . ?"

"It's only that I'm worried for you, Henry. Just exactly that."

"Balls. You're worryin' I'll outlive you is just exactly what. You been worryin' that ever since I can remember. Son, Jesus Christ ohmighty, give me that outfit!" Swinging it by the wire, he clanged the button loudly against the nightstand and called in a pained and angry voice, "Nurse! Nurse!" His eyes clenched with the effort. "Get me another shot o' that dope, and where the hell's that caw-fee!"

"Easy, Papa . . ."

"Yes, Henry . . ." Boney spread his web of fingers over the sheet covering Henry's knee. "You better take it a little easier."

"Stokes"—Henry's eyes, usually so wide that white could be seen all the way around pupils hot as Fourth of July flares, went narrow and cold—"git your fishy old mitt off'n my leg. Just git it off." He glared at Boney until the other's eyes dropped; he felt a surge of delight at finally voicing a feeling long unvoiced. He continued to look straight at Boney and went on, speaking with unusual softness, "You're just as bad as she is, Stokes; you know that. Except you been forty-five years at it. Hopin' I'll give up the ghost." He drew back the button-on-wire theateningly. "Now git it off, I tell you. Off!"

Boney withdrew his hand and held it at his chest, looking wronged. Henry dropped the button and began jerking about beneath the covers in a state of tense agitation.

"That's not true, old friend," Boney said in a hurt voice.

" 'S true. 'S true as the day is long, an' we both know it. Forty-five years, fifty years, sixty years. Nurse!"

Boney sighed and half turned in his chair, presenting a face pained by the injustice of the accusation. But there was something so false in his attitude of wronged friendship, something so vicious in the denying shake of his head, that Hank was certain that the whole act was a deliberate admission to all of Henry's charges. Fascinated, he moved back to the foot of the bed and stood there, half hidden by the yellowed bed curtain. The two old men had forgotten him in their confrontation of each other. Boney continued to shake his head sadly; Henry jerked about beneath the covers and glared sideways at the figure in the chair from time to time. After a minute of silence, he worked his mouth to express a feeling that had burned so long unworded that now it threatened to rage out of control.

"A good sixty years. Ever since . . . ever since . . . goddam you, Stokes, I can't even remember when it first started, it's been there so long!"

"Ah, Henry, Henry . . ." Boney chose to acknowledge the fire through his overdrawn denial of it. "Can you truthfully now recall me ever giving you anything but what I considered the soundest advice, the very soundest, in all our years? Can you?"

"Like which? Like the time you advised me and Ben and Aaron to bring Ma to go to Eugene for the *Welfare*, because we couldn't endure a season alone in those woods? Somebody that ain't used to it, you says, can't *endure* a season in these woods. You recall that advice? Well, we endured it fine, as I look back. . . ."

"You lost your mother that winter from your stubbornness," Boney reminded him.

"Lost her? She *died!* The woods didn't have beans to do with it. She just *got sick* and *laid down* and *died!*"

"It mightn't of happened in town."

"It'd of happened anywhere. She died that year cause she made up her mind that she was bound and *determined* to die."

"We all offered to help."

"I'll say you did. You helped us right out of that feed store."

"We all unselfishly offered the necessities of life—"

"And wanted what in payment? Our house an' property? A mortgage on the next ten years?"

"Henry, that's unfair; the organization made no such demands."

"Not wrote down any place, maybe, but they was demands made just the same. I never seen your old man—or that goddam organization neither one—get hurt from any of these unselfish offerings. You did all right with your offerings."

"Be that as it may, there's no one who can accuse us of havin' any-thing but the interests of the community at heart."

Before Henry could answer, the door opened and the nurse entered with a small paper cup of coffee. She set it on the bedstand, looked around at the silent men, and hurried back out without saying anything. Henry took up the cup and drank. He watched Boney through the rising steam. When he brought the cup from his lips, Hank saw that the rim bore mark of those two teeth out of three that met. Henry placed the cup back on the nightstand, never taking his eyes from Boney's bent head. With the sleeve of his white flannel robe he wiped his mouth. Boney continued to shake his head, clucking pityingly over his old companion's unbalanced state.

"Boney," Henry finally said in a flat voice, "you got any snoose on you?"

Boney's face brightened. "Surely, surely." He drew a can from the pocket of his coat. "Here, let me—"

"You give it here."

He blinked at Henry, then placed the can carefully on the sheet, unopened. Henry picked it up. He began turning it around and around in his pink hand as the thumb laboriously pushed at the lid; a fraction of an inch, turn, another fraction, another turn . . . Hank ached to take the can from his father, quickly screw the lid off, and end this thing, free both himself and his father from an obsession that seemed more and more senseless. But he somehow did not dare move from his hiding place beside the curtain. Not yet. Not until it was finished of its own accord.

The lid popped off. The coarse brown fuzz of tobacco boiled out over the sheet. Henry cursed, then, patiently, with Boney watching motionless, scooped the bulk of the spill back into the tin, replaced the lid, popped it tight between thumb and finger, tossed it into Boney's lap. . . .

"Much obliged."

Then swept the remainder into a small heap on the sheet, rolled this into a ball, and placed the wad between his lower lip and his gums. He concentrated a second as he maneuvered the charge into comfortable position, then flapped the grains from the sheet with a victorious flourish. The stained lips broke into a broad grin.

"Much obliged, old fellow, old friend . . . very much obliged."

Now it seemed it was Boney's turn to fidget. Henry's success with the snuff had shaken his complacency and placed the burden of the contest on his humped shoulders. "What do you plan on now, Henry," he wanted to know, trying to sound matter-of-fact, "now that things have changed?"

"Why, what do you mean, Boney? Just what I been doin', I imagine." The old daring confidence returned to Henry's eyes. "Plan to get back out there with the boys, I imagine, back out in the woods. Lettin' daylight in the swamp. Bullwhippin' the brush." He yawned and drew a long fingernail down the stubble of his neck. "Ah, I ain't foolin' myself. I ain't a pup any more. When you get into your seventies you got to think about slowin' up, lettin' the boys do the muley work while you rely on your knowhow and experience. Maybe even get me a chair out there. But, I don't know, when it comes right down to it—"

"Henry." Boney could stand it no longer. "You are a fool. Bullwhipping the brush . . . don't you see you're the one gettin' bullwhipped? You! Ever since . . . But I told you, all along I told you—"

"Ever since what, Boney?" Henry asked pleasantly.

"Since I told you that there is no mortal bein' capable of—of enduring all alone *this* country! We are in this together! Man . . . man has got to—"

"Ever since what, Boney?" Henry still wanted to know.

"What? Ever since I . . . What?"

Henry leaned forward intently. "Since Pa run off and I stuck? Since I survived that winter? Since I built up a business that you said nobody could?"

"I *never* had anything against men developing the land."

"But *one* man doin' it? One family? Heh? Heh? When you told us time an' again we *couldn't*. A 'community effort' is what you always said. God. I heard that pioneer-community-against-the-wilds shit so much the first years my belly was run over with it."

"It was necessary. It was mortal man's *only* hope against the untamed elements—"

"Sounds just like your old daddy talkin'."

"—that we strive together to survive together."

"I don't recollect as how I did much *strivin'* together, but I believe I did survive. Even gained a little bit on the side."

"Look what it's got you! Loneliness an' despair."

"Well, I don't know about that."

"Bedridden!" Boney stood from his chair, twisting his hands in his shirtfront. "An arm lost! Dying!"

"I don't know about that. It maybe winged, *nicked* me a little bit, but you got to expect that."

Boney started to say more but was stopped by a fit of rage and coughing. When the coughing stopped he took his coat from the back of the chair and stabbed his skeleton arms into the sleeves. "Out of his head with pain." He tried to dismiss Henry as he walked toward the door. The coughing had injured his throat so his voice squeaked comically. "That's all. Crazy with pain. And dope. He can't think reasonable." He wiped his mouth and stood fingering the smooth buttons of the coat.

"Leavin', Boney?" Henry inquired amiably.

"Burnin' up with fever, too, I'd bet." But he couldn't walk out the door. Not while out of the corner of his eye he could see that cursed imbecile grin, shellacked with tobacco, that face like the face of a heathen idol shining out against everything he knew to be holy and right, those eyes that had so long needled and irritated and made uncomfortable an existence that would have otherwise been a peaceful stretch of pleasant pessimism. He feared that if he walked out through that door that face might solidify itself in death; that way he would never escape it. . . .

"Well, I'll see you in the funny-papers, Boney Stokes, Bobby Stokes, sobby little Bobby Stokes . . . you remember that?"

That way not only would he be haunted by it for the rest of his days, but his whole past would be scooped out hollow, his whole life gutted. . . .

"An' listen, if you run across Hank or Joe Ben, tell 'em I said to get in here an' bring me up to date on where we stand."

That way, if he let Henry get the last laugh, his entire world would—"What? Stand? Joe Ben?"

Horrified, Hank watched the opening door stop, pull slowly closed. He saw the stiff, thoughtful pivot of Boney's turning, and his own realization mirrored there in Boney's yellowed eyes. "Henry . . . old man, don't you know?" No wonder Henry had seemed in such phenomenal good spirits; he hadn't been told. Of course, neither he nor Boney had mentioned it; it simply wasn't the sort of thing you talked about when visiting a man recovering from a serious—"Old boy?" But that *no one* had told him! "What I mean, Henry . . . hasn't the doctor or the nurse or someone?"

"What's got hold of you now, Boney?"

"Or about afterwards? What went on yesterday?"

"I *told* you nobody has been up to tell me anything."

And now saw a second realization settle like a soft light over Boney's whole face. Unconsciously, as Boney moved forward, Hank drifted farther back behind the curtain. Boney seated himself again, lighted up a large pipe, and began to speak in a pity-filled voice. He spoke quickly and confidently, without a hint of his usual cough. Through the tiers of blue smoke Hank watched the final scene of the drama; he had dropped out; he had become a spectator that just happened by for the last act, to sit in the very last row of a darkened balcony unseen and catch lines blown intermittent and disconnected through a drafty theater. He stared down on the two figures with unfocused eyes. He made no effort to concentrate. Without listening, he knew the lines by heart; without looking, he saw the action. A bit player with his part finished, waiting around to see the end, almost bored, almost dozing over familiar lines, until a repeated phrase told him it was drawing to that end.

"Hank did it because he didn't want . . . to risk anybody else hurt."

"I don't think so. . . ."

Bleakly running down as the lights dimmed.

"He did it because . . . he didn't want to risk anybody."

"I don't hardly think so, Henry."

As the curtain closed, as the echoes stood up to leave: He wouldn't of done it for any other reason—he didn't want to have anybody to have to take the risk just for—I guess not, old fellow, because there wasn't anybody but him left—He did it because—I guess not—because everybody left and he knows he can't run them logs down by himself—He did it because . . . he finally saw how it was . . . because . . . he finally saw that there wasn't any sense. Because of rust, of rot. Of push, of squeeze. Because there is really no strength beyond the strength of those around you. Because of weakness. Because of no grit, no grit anywhere at all and labor availeth not. Because all is vanity and vexation of the spirit. Because of that drum on the donkey forever breaking down. Of bruises from springbacks. Of sinus headaches and ingrown toenails. Of rain and the seas are still not full. Because of everything coming so thick and so fast for so long for so very long for finally too long. . . .

"Henry, Hank is nobody's fool . . . he knows better than."

Because strength is a joke, a fake.

"He's a smart boy, Henry, he sees how the land lays . . . it just is not a one-man world, never was . . . no mortal man can long endure . . ."

Because sometimes the only way to keep from losing everything is to give everything up. Because sometimes strength must for the sake of winning give in to—

"My, oh my," Boney said cheerfully, looking at a big pocket watch, "it's got late." He got up, stood up out of his chair again and finished up buttoning his coat. He coughed a little. He took the old man's hand up from the bed like picking up a rag and he shook it. "I got to be gettin' home, I guess, Henry," he says. "Long walk for a man our age, weather like it is"—and then dropped the hand back down. He shook his head. "I hated to be the bearer of the tidings about Joe Ben, Henry. I know how fond you all were of him. I'd as leave tore my tongue out as been the one to tell you. Oh . . . here. I'll leave this with you. Whyn't you have the nurse put you some out in a saucer so you can get to it easier? Well. Anthing you want me to bring when I come back? The *Saturday Evening Post?* I got a lot of back issues. Here. Let me sit this TV up on the chest-of-drawers where you can get you a straight bead on her. Might as well ruin the old eyes too, hadn't we?"

He flicked on the machine and turned to go before it warmed up. He stopped at that door again and looked back at the old man fingering at his nose. Boney'd clean forgot I was in the room. Both of them had.

"Chin up, old fellow," he said to Henry. "What do you bet we're still around chewin' the fat when the rest of these boys have cashed it in. Okay, don't let me hear about you giving that nurse a hard time, hey? So long. . . ."

And he walked out, strutting like a man with a good ten years of coughing and complaining left in him. I stepped out from where I'd been hid at the foot of the bed and started to say something to the old man, but with the way he looked I didn't figure it would do a whole lot of good. "Papa," I started, "you see what happened was—"

"Hm," he says. "Well anyway," he says, staring straight ahead at that TV, "anyway I still got . . . a good sense of smell for a nigger so old . . . an' a man can still lick it he keeps . . . but Hank he . . . but then I woulda thought . . . I suppose we . . . they got that cast on wrong . . ." And on like that, with his talk dipping into his thoughts now and again. He was looking kind of poleaxed. The dope getting to him. But not just that. His whole face is changing, getting calm and peaceful. The muscles under his cheekbones relaxing, letting the grin droop down; the lines between his eyes unraveling like old cotton string. The morphine's making him drowsy. . . . Then the eyes themselves went dull, like whoever was in there, like whatever was still left inside there, just went away through a door, leaving the empty body behind pumping air and blood and the empty face propped up there in the blue flicker of that television, like an old suit of threadbare skin somebody'd tossed onto a bed. . . .)

The lights flutter. The room drones as though the air is filled with big, drowsy flies. Muffled . . . muted . . . inurned between deep cotton-soft sheathings of morphine, the old man rolls his head and parts the sheath enough to look up a long spiraling of redwood columns supporting a high deep-green dome. A woodpecker hammers the air unseen; a jay screeches brightly across, pulling the eye around *splash* blue! "Wheeoo, lookit that!" to a splintering sight of the May Day sun trying to shine through the needles. "What a day! Man alive." *Pollen hangs in the windless still, solidifying the one yellow-bright beam from treetop to the ground* . . . "Haw! Look yonder . . ." *where a twirl of butterflies white and busy as stars flush from a patch of sheep sorrel at his tread, where no other white man's foot has ever trod before.* "Maybe no man's foot of no color ever before!" *He looks up one of the columns and spits on his hands.* "Okay, stan' clear. What d'ya think? I'm a bear got to hibernate? Let me have some bullyjacks. We got things to do. Cats to kill, eggs to hatch, trees to chop, an' ground to scratch . . . stan' clear, dammit!"

"Calm . . . calm does it, Mr. Stamper. We're calm and peaceful now."

"Who says I couldn't? Just you stand outa my way. Never you mind. Hum, man alive . . . Let me clear my ears a second." *And no other white man's ax has ever sounded.* "Oh. The springboard. Oh, the misery whip." *Then the sun is brushed momentarily aside by the gleaming green sweep of a thousand thousand rushing needles.* "Wham! Right down the old slot." *That was May, in the twenties, when redwoods still stood. Above, the dome is broken. The sun springs back, flooding light down over a stretch of ground unlighted for a thousand thousand years.* "Jees H. Christ, what time must it gettin' to be? Whoa. Just a minute now, what you think you're doin'?" *Scrappy, a little kitten, white and purply blue, just like a chicken gizzard, you know, useta scratch the bejesus outa—* "Ouch? Now what are you—"

"There we go now. It's all over. Calm and peaceful, now. It's done. Rest now. Calm and peaceful . . ."

Ray and Rod are setting up on the bandstand when Evenwrite arrives at the Snag. The taut tuning of amplified steel stretches out into the darkening street. Andy, sitting in the jeep, hears it and takes his harmonica from his pocket, beats it against his thigh to remove the lint and sunflower-seed shells, and blows softly into it; he has decided he'd as leave wait and ride back up with Hank and Viv as hitchhike.

Across the street he sees Hank hurrying toward the wet clatter of the Snag's neons and wonders forlornly how long he will have to wait. . . .

(By the time I come out of the hospital my belly was boiling around till I didn't know whether I could make it to the Snag for a shot or not. The only thing I wanted was about three fingers of Johnny Walker, something to put the lid on the boiling down there. That damn little hospital room had been worse than the jeep box. My diamond-bright day had got duller and duller, and the way I was feeling I didn't know whether the world was going to last anyway.

The Snag was mighty crowded for so early; most of the guys who hadn't gone to the cemetery had stopped off and they were pretty well oiled. They quieted a little when I first came in, but then they all came hustling over like they couldn't wait to shake the hand of the man who'd kept them out of a job for two months. Evenwrite bought me a whisky. The band got going and the old good-time honky-tonk sound started cranking up, like old times. And Indian Jenny dropped in and started buying drinks for the drunks. And Biggy Newton was there, looking tough. And Les Gibbons, slobbering and blubbering and staggering around. And, though it wasn't but Wednesday, the next day being Thanksgiving and a holiday made it just like good old Saturday night at the Snag the way it used to be, *except that it's not*, just like old times, *except that it's different*, with the guitars whanging and the beer flowing and the boys whooping and hollering and cussing one another and matching nickels and shuffling the shuffleboard . . . *except that it just isn't the same. I don't know how, but I know that it isn't. I know it's different. And so does everyone else.)*

In the droning hospital room, remember? On the community boat trip? On that Fourth of July celebration—The River Is Your Highway—some of the folks, they got sick account of not being used to water, so sick they thought sure they was gonna die, then finally got sicker and wished they would. *Motorboat races on the river; contestants joking back and forth*—"Ben, we can win this boogin' event with some leetle doin', what d'ya say?"—*and when it's over* "Them dern Stamper boys, ya see what they done? They put a big smithy bellows at the intake o' their carburetor an' forced air in . . . we gonna allow that?"

But that's July. This is May, May Day, let's see . . . *Another section of the green dome is ripped swishing away from the bluejay sky, crashing, falling across ghost fern and salal and witch hazel, and sun crashing after it.* "Git them hayburners up here an' hooked on goddammit before she mosses over an' rots o' age!"

At the Snag, shaved and shined and sharp as a razor, Ray begins to lift the crowd to his heights, and Rod along with them. The beat had picked up; the people been pouring in; and the copper pot in front of the mike stand filled with green and silver. *"Gray days, hurryin' by . . ."* Ray slapped the strings with a callused thumb, let his vision swim, and grinned out at the coast-to-coast TV hook-up; a year from now, his Trendex only a mildly impressive forty-one— next year he'd kick it over fifty. . . . *". . . when you're in love, my how they fly."*

The whole town was drunk with sunshine, optimism, and ringer whisky, delirious with good times. *"Never saw the sun, shinin' so bright; never saw things lookin' so right—"* Teddy looked through his long lashes—never saw as many people drinking as hard or laughing as much. You see one or two this way most of the time. Sometimes as high as thirty or forty, after a big salmon run or a big log-camp fight. But never before, only thing near it was at the peak of the recession scare. I don't understand. So much drinking. Even toasting Hank Stamper . . .

(My couple of whiskies didn't do me a bit of good. I tell the boys they got to excuse me but I can feel my little flu bug coming up outa his hidey-hole, preparing for another attack. I thanked them for the drinks and pulled my jacket on. When I left I waved to them all and told them to keep up the good work, that it was heartening for a man to see his fellows laboring so hard to get shut of the alcohol surplus, and they all laughed and told me to hurry back as soon as I could to give them a hand—that it was gonna be just like old times again. *But every one of us knows that it won't ever again be the same . . .*)

Unsheathed . . . wild . . . the first of May in the redwoods, out all day long till dark and the next day Sunday and no work but I hike back up just the same, alone, to see what it's like cut clean . . . *the morning sun walks across new ground, ground unlighted for a thousand thousand years, and finds dew necklaces strung by spiders across the sleek green throats of Darlingtonias.* Funny weed, them flycatchers. Lots of funny plants. Them Indians eat a outfit called a wapatoo, a tuber-like affair that grows under water in the sloughs, squaws wade around barefoot and grub them outen the mud with their toes. Touch-me-nots spring like traps when you touch them. Dwarf iris supposed to been planted by little people useta live in the woods. The pitch-ogres, remember them? awful boogers . . .

kids won't go out at night on account the pitch-ogres might mingle
with them and they'll stick to death. Death always right handy.
*On the beach, so close to the water that the waves sometimes touch
it, a grave is marked by a cedar cross and daffodils stunted by salt
air* . . . little Illabelle Sitkins one day sits out on the back step and
cracks open all the apricot seeds her ma'd throwed out whilst can-
ning apricots. July thirteenth, nineteen ought—hell, I don't know:
and she eats the pits because they taste like almonds you get for
Christmas and dies of the bellyache. I've tried 'em myself. July 15:
We had services at the Toms house for Illabelle, then all run foot-
races on the beach after the burying. Aug. 19: John kills a she-bear.
Sept. 4: Rained twenty-eight hours solid. Water under kitchen. Sept.
5: Rain and sleet and some snow. Big wind. Tree smashed up the
smokehouse. Sept. 6: got timbers to brace up smokehouse. Nov. 11:
Lord's Day the old lady very ill. Had doctor in he stayed all night.
Ben trapped some minks and got chewed up and the doctor patched
him up too.

Nov. 13: Dog ate some salmon washed up, pretty sick and broke
down in the hindquarters. Went into town and Stokes give me some
medicine for him. *Stokes, damn you, Hank did it because he seen
that* . . . Stayed to argue with him and help him hull wheat. . . .
*because he seen that maybe too many folks'd get hurt if.* . . .
Stokes said he wouldn't charge up the medicine but I ought to send
my mama to Eugene to Hospital. Hell with that.

Nov. 15: Went to Arnold Eggleston's place for road works meeting. John and me come on home but Ben stayed and danced and
got beat up by Sam Montgomery. Dog better when we get home.
Old lady too . . . But where's Hank?

"There goes a good old boy," Evenwrite proclaims when he sees
Hank's jeep pass.

"Stubborn, but straight," agrees Sitkins.

"A real squareshooter," the Real Estate Hotwire adds and drinks
to it.

From behind his bar Teddy pauses in his polishing to see what
will happen now that the guest of honor has taken his leave. That
the laughter and talk had been a bit strained while Hank was present was no surprise to Teddy; it didn't take an expert on barroom
psychology to understand that the merrymaking should have been
a little tense under the circumstances. But now that the circumstances
had removed himself, what would happen? How would they act?
Teddy watched. He could usually predict, almost to the joke, or the

curse, how his patrons would react after one of them had departed, but all day today their actions had been so anomalous, so out-of-the-ordinary, that he didn't even dare to guess. He watched, through a deep-sea cast of smoke . . .

As the band continued, finishing up a request, and Howie Evans twisted his chin sideways to pop a stiff vertebra. And Jenny buzzed heavily from table to table with her fistful of Indian compensation, buying drinks and dribbling change, from table to table like a rubber-booted bee. A usual Saturday night, Teddy thought; sporadic laughter, coughing, nose-blowing, cursing. Just like. *Except. What?*

(Andy was still in the jeep when I got there, tootling on his harmonica. Playing "Wabash Cannonball." "Damn!" I said. "Heave over. Damn. That damn harmonica. I thought it was Joe's little radio, and that—" I didn't finish and he stuck the thing back in his pocket. Then he said, "Hank? You ain't, by any chance, got any intentions . . . tomorrow—"

"Of runnin' them logs? Hell's fire, I ain't got any intentions of runnin' anything more than a fever tomorrow, Andy. What's wrong with you, anyhow? We ain't even got a quota to run!"

"Yeah we do," he said. "I made a count. That last log filled it."

"Hell," I said. "Didn't you hear what Bismarck said? That WP don't even *want* them no more, the way the river's comin' up. What the hell's wrong with you?"

"I just wanted to know," he mumbled and hushed up. I got the jeep started and headed out to pick up Viv. I was ready to call it a day. . . .)

"Gawd almighty damn." Les Gibbons lurched suddenly up from the booth when he noticed that Hank had left. Halfway up he became tangled about a chair leg and his lurch turned into an awkward struggle that reminded Big Newton of a man trying to wrench himself from a mudhole. ". . . a mighty *damn*," Les repeated when he was standing; he looked about the room with the blue bunting of his lips fluttering limply about his shouting. "I am one . . . fierce . . . *motherjumper!*"

Big tilted a bloodshot eye to check and didn't quite see it that way. "You don't look too fierce to me, Motherjumper."

Les was only piqued to more ferocity by the dissension; he squinted through the smoke at the laughing faces to try to see who'd dared doubt the first half of his title. "Fierce enough," he proclaimed, "to tear a new asshole in whatever nigger said *that!*"

There was more laughter, more jeering, but since no nigger was hurrying forward through the smoke to have his anatomy rearranged, Les sighed and elaborated. "Fierce enough that I jes' think I'll go over an' kick the hound outa that Hank Stamper over there!"

"Danged if I don't believe, Les, that you're about ten seconds late," Big said into his beer. "Hank just drove off."

"Then I'll foller him right to his hole and kick the hound outa him there!"

"Who'd tote you 'cross river to his house?" Big wanted to know. "Or would you expect him to come get you?"

Les squinted again but was still unable to locate his gadfly. "I won't need a totin'!" he shouted, as though the gadfly was all the way down at the depot end of the barroom instead of sitting in the chair right across from him. "I'd swim 'er, is what; I'd swim that river!"

"Bull, Gibbons," Howie Evans said; maybe Big could be patient, but some others were trying to hear the music and becoming more and more aggravated with this liver-lipped ape. "You'd drown ten foot from bank."

"Yeah, Les," another chimed in, "an' pollute the river for a month. Kill all the fish, probably most of the ducks. . . ."

"Yeah, Les, and we don't want you drownin' and killin' the game. You stay here in the warm and don't risk yourself."

Les wasn't to be pacified by their concern. "You think I can't swim that river?"

"Les." This time Big looked up, like a big lion raising its head off its forepaws. "I know you can't swim that river."

Les looked quickly about and saw who was speaking, thought for a moment about what Big had said, and decided not to appear immodest by arguing the point. "Yeah, well," he said, setting back into his place in the booth like a man deciding mud ain't so bad after all, "Hank Stamper ain't the only one able to swim a river, y'know."

"Maybe not, but he's the only one that happens to come to my mind just this minute."

"I don't know 'bout that," Les said petulantly.

"You hear what Grissom said the doc said who went out there?" Sitkins asked Big. "He said Hank got home that night an' found the boat missin' and swum across. I swear to golly, that's what they said."

"That night after those goons Floyd hired from Reedsport worked him over?"

"That's what they say."

"Jesus Christ," Howie Evans said. "You gotta give him credit for spunk even if he don't have a lot of sense. Hurt that bad, I woulda bet money when he left here he couldn't of *walked*, let 'lone swum a river."

"Maybe," Les said, "he weren't hurt so bad as ever'body thought."

"What are you talking about?" Big demanded.

"I don't know. Maybe he weren't hurt so bad as he acted. Maybe he just sulled to fool you."

"Are you kidding me, Les?" Big gripped his beer glass, feeling himself growing more angry at this blockhead than he'd thought possible. A little more and— "Listen, somebody better straighten you out before you say somethin' to him personally an' get your neck broke. Listen here: you talk about him *sulling* . . . ain't I spent three evenings right here in this bar entertaining you fellows by trying to make him do something along just that line? I worked him over about as terrible as a man can be worked over and still stand up—worse'n any little slappin' around—and, boy, I tell ya: if he ever sulled by god you could of fooled *me!*"

"Amen to that." One of the Sitkins brothers nodded knowingly. "Not Hank Stamper."

"Look here," Big continued, his voice trembling strangely. "You see where them teeth're missing? Hank slapped them out for me that Halloween night after he got up off the floor about the sixth time. If he was sullin' then, you sure coulda fooled these here teeth. I tell you what, Les; before you take on Hank, what do you say me an' you spar around some? To warm you up, sort of . . . ?"

"Ah, Big," Les said, "you know how I talk—"

"I *said* let's spar *around* some, godblessit!"

The band had stopped. Big had pushed back from the table and was rising in front of Les like a mountain. Les appeared to sink deeper into his mud.

"I *said*, let's get *up*, Gibbons! Get the fuck *up!*"

And the room, suddenly so quiet the deep drumming of the oil burning in the heater could be heard, felt that strange trembling fully. Waiting. Teddy swiveled softly from the laundry bag where he had just placed his dishtowel, moving carefully to keep from disturbing his specimens. Before him, the long room seemed stretched even longer by the silence, taut as a wire. But not the clenched anticipation that usually precedes a fight. Again, something different . . . what is it, this fear?

Across the turned heads Teddy saw Les Gibbons, the shabby form shrunk beneath the towering, outlandish bulk of Big Newton—a scene made even more ridiculous, even more comical, by Newton's monumental rage; *look* how furious he is with that pathetic Les! Big's face was blazing; his neck was corded with the bind of his shoulders; his chin quivered so that Teddy could easily see it, far away as he was. So much *fury* at such pathetic insignificance? It's a wonder someone doesn't break up laughing. Except—Teddy put down his polishing rag—*except it isn't rage. No!* Down the beautifully grained bartop, polished to an expensive luster by his years of face-watching, Teddy saw for one instant a common face—*Not rage or caution either*—a face he had never seen before in all his polishing years. As a collector of expressions, he thought he had seen and studied them all; it was his hobby, his *business*. For years of endless, outcast nights he had watched an endless sea of idiots tossed wave on wave across the beach of his bar . . . watched, and skillfully gauged every wink and grin, and carefully analyzed every fat drop of anxious sweat, every scared tremble of hand and frightened swallowing. My, yes, if anything, he knew expressions . . . but *never this face, never before this expression of . . . of—*

Then Rod slaps his guitar—"An-ee-time . . ."—shooting Ray a look to wake him up; ". . . *you're thinkin' of me* . . ." Ray joins in halfheartedly: "An-ee-time . . . *you're feelin' blue* . . ." And the taut wire of silence snaps, the tableau thaws. Big Newton thunders off to pee, his face once more bleak and surly. Les Gibbons laughs a blubbering laugh that sounds as though it had come up through purple clay. Mrs. Carleson's daughter begins rattling glasses in the sink. Evenwrite wanders out, looking either dazed or drunk. Jenny tugs on a drunk arm lackadaisically, her usual tenacity missing. Howie Evans contorts his unlovely back to relieve old kinks, looking for a woman. The Sitkins boys begin wordlessly razzing Les about his near-annihilation. Evenwrite starts his car and drives slowly east up Main with nine beers heavy and joyless in his belly. Old Henry shades his eyes against the May Day sun that shines through the broken green dome across a flowered meadow of months. January, nineteen-twenty-one, as I recollect, after the storm they still call the High Blow, Ben is farting around for one reason or the other down south of Florence near the mouth of the Siltcoos and he sees four whales left by the tides with the bar too low for them to swim back out to sea. And he—wait till I get that photograph—he gets a rowboat and rows out there and kills all four of them with an ax, so help me god! June bugs, hot and humming, hummmmmming. No. January? Oh yeah, Ben? Well, nobody'd *believe* he wasn't telling a whopper till me and John borrowed a camera from Stokes and—what in thunder did I *do* with that picture, anyhow? Around here someplace . . . I saw last . . . let's see . . . Nov. 17: Doctor out again to see the old lady. Says she looks mainly tired is all. Says dog is good as he'll get after salmon sickness, gimpy in the hindquarters but will be fine, will be able to trail just as good as—

Nov. 19: Dog died. Old Red? Brownie? No, Old Gray . . . from eating salmon, spine bowed the wrong direction and died.

Nov. 24: Thanksgiving—a different year?—old lady died. John and me build coffin out of Idaho pine. Doctor says he don't know why. Stokes says cannot endure. Hell with that. I say she just *Hank? Hank boy, oh Hank don't you know that the old lady just Hank boy you can't laid down and died boy? Hank boy if you the sun leaps springs back can't keep sun crashing on ground shadowed a thousand thousand* "Hank, goddammit, straighten up there!"

"Mr. Stamper! Lie back down! Doctor . . . Doctor, a hand, please!"

"And never by god give a boogin'!" *A pretty good world you keep the shadows off. Salmonberries: pale, translucent orange with a taste more delicate than the color.* "Listen to me now, Hank, son, I'm talkin' to ya!" *Butterflies busy as stars.* "Mr. Stamper . . . calm and easy now . . ." *The Walking Preacher, remember?* talkin' over Mama when she died, tell that he one time baptized a fella in sour mash; a real loud, shoutin' preacher sonofabitch you could hear carryin' on a good two miles, always hungry, always digging at his big nose, always talking about Christian Charity . . . *oh, those winters!* "Stokes, blast you, bringing out them cast-offs!" *Missionary barrels, packed by churches back East* always a big hullabaloo when the barrel came in on the boat, always the buttons cut off all the donated clothes, always teeth outen the combs . . . "Stokes by god I'll wear leaves an' comb my hair with fishbones afore I'll!" *The sun crashes into green shadows unlighted . . ."* "Before I'll give a goddam inch to your goddam!" *. . . springs back, cracking through the dome.* "Calm and peaceful, Mr. Stamper, there we go, now, there we go it'll just be a moment . . ." *Crashing once more out of blue behind the gathering rush . . .* ". . . hush, hush, hush."

"He's asleep. Thanks for the help." *The milky light flutters. The*

nurse draws deep, cotton-soft, gray curtains down over the first of
May. Andy drops Hank and Viv off at the house and drives the
jeep on up to the mill to row his skiff back across in the rain. Big
Newton tries to compose himself on the can by scratching letters
from the WASH YOUR HANDS BEFORE RETURNING TO WORK sign decaled
on the toilet door, changing the first line to WAS YOU HAD and adding a question mark after WORK. Ray finally wakes up enough from
the shock the silence has given him to step up the beat and the
volume. Jenny, growing suddenly weary of this game of maneuvering
drunks, thumps out the door, having thought of another game. Just
as Simone, resigned and irreligious in lascivious scarlet, whisks in
the same door and surrenders the sweet-cake naïveté in her heart
forever.

"Hey-hey, look who just flew in. How do, Simone; long time no
see."

"Boys . . ."

"An' goodness me, all feathered out like she's right off a magazine cover!"

"Thank you; I think it is nice. It is a gift. . . ."

"Howie. Say, Howie, Simone's here; Simone's back, Howie. . . ."

"Tut. Simone's back, everybody. Who will buy me a beer, a lot
of beer, please?"

"Teddy. A drink for zee little lady from Frawnce. . . . No, a
drink for everybody!"

Teddy turns from the face for the glasses draining on the towel
beside Mrs. Carleson's daughter—this expression. Now I know. Now I
see—his plump little body still tingling with the charge of that taut
instant. I thought this day, this sunshine, this well-being was selling
all this alcohol. I thought all my notions why people drink was all
wrong when this lovely day . . . but now I see. In the falling dark
his neons begin to stir. His hands come alive. Glasses tink together,
the till rings. . . . It just took some time to see what was happening. I thought I had collected all the dark situations; I thought I
knew them. I thought I knew all the expressions, I thought I had
seen all the fears . . . while the music and laughter glorious good
times blaze under his smoky ceiling . . . but never this face before;
never absolute, unspeakable, supreme terror!

*T*here occurs to me now one last anecdote, a bit long; skip it if you wish, it has nothing to do with the story. . . . I put it in because it seems to me somehow pertinent—if not to plot or parable, at least to purpose.

About a guy I met in the nuthouse, a Mr. Siggs, a nervous, quick-featured self-schooled hick who had spent all his fifty or so years except for Service time in the eastern Oregon town of his birth. A reader of encyclopedias, a memorizer of Milton, a writer of a column called "Words to Adjust By" in the Patients' Paper . . . a completely capable and sufficient person, yet this intense little self-styled scholar was perhaps the most uncomfortable man on the ward. Siggs was terribly paranoid in crowds, equally hung up in one-to-one situations, and seemed to enjoy no ease at all except by himself inside a book. And no one could have been more shocked than myself when he volunteered for the job as Ward Public Relations Director. "Masochism?" I asked him when I heard of his new position. "What do you mean?" He fidgeted, hedging away from my eyes, but I went on. "I mean this Public Relations job . . . why are you taking on this business of dealing with big groups of people when you're apparently so much more at ease alone?"

At this Mr. Siggs stopped fidgeting and looked at me; he had large, heavy-lidded eyes that could burn with sudden unblinking intensity. "Just before I came in here . . . I took a job, stock outrider. In a shack hid away outside Baker. A place a hundred miles from noplace. Nobody, nothing, far as I could see. Sweet, high country; beautiful . . . Not even a cedar tree. Took along complete set of Great Books. All the classics, ten dollars a month, book salesman took it out of my wages in Baker. Beautiful country. See a thousand miles any direction, like it was all mine. A million stars, a million sage blossoms—all mine. Yes, beautiful . . . Couldn't make it, though. Committed myself after a month and a half." His face softened and his blue stare dimmed again be-

neath his half-closed lids; he grinned at me; I could see
him forcing himself to try to relax. "Oh, you're right.
Yes, you are: I am a loner, a born one. And someday I
will make it—that shack, I mean. Yes. I will, you'll see.
But not like last time. Not to hide. No. Next time I try
it it will be first because I choose to, then because it is
where I am most comfortable. Only sensible plan; sure
of it. But . . . a fellow has to get so he can deal with
these Public Relations, before he can truly make it. Make
it like that . . . alone . . . in some shack. A man has
to know he had a choice before he can enjoy what he
chose. I know now. That a human has to make it with
other humans . . . before he can make it with himself."

I had a therapeutic addition to this: "And vice versa,
Mr. Siggs: he has to make it with himself before branch-
ing out."

He agreed, reluctantly, but he still agreed. Because at
that time we both considered this addition pretty psychologically profound and—in spite of its chicken-or-egg
overtones—the very last word in "Words to Adjust By"
at that time.

Recently, however, I found that there were even further additions. A few months ago I was sage-hen hunting
in the Ochoco Mountains—high, spare, lonely plains
country and certainly as far from noplace as any place I
know—and I ran into Mr. Siggs again, a healthier,
younger-looking Mr. Siggs, tanned, bearded, and calm as
a lizard on a sunny stone. After overcoming our mutual
surprise, we recalled our conversation after his acceptance
of the Public Relations job, and I asked how his plans
had worked out. Perfectly—after some successful therapy
he'd been discharged with honors over a year ago, had
his outriding job, his Great Books, his shack . . . loved
it. But didn't he still occasionally wonder if he were really
choosing his shack or still just hiding in it? Nope. Wasn't
he lonely? Nope. Well, wasn't he bored, then, with all
this sunshine and adjustment? He shook his head. "After
you get so you can make it with other people, and make
it with yourself, there's still work to be done; you still
have the main party to deal with . . ."

"The 'main party'?" I asked, right then starting to suspect that statement about his being discharged "with
honors." "What do you mean, Mr. Siggs? The 'main
party'? You mean deal with Nature? God?"

"Yes, it could be," he remarked, rolling on his rock to
warm his other side and closing his eyes against the sun.
"Nature or God. Or it could be Time. Or Death. Or just
the stars and the sage blossoms. Don't know yet. . . ."
He yawned, then raised his little head and fixed me once
more with that same intense look, a demented bright-blue
look galvanized by some drive beneath his leathery face
that sunshine—or therapy—could never adjust. . . . "I am
fifty-three," he said sharply. "Took fifty years, half a century, just to get to where I could deal with something
my own size. Don't expect me to work this other thing
out overnight. So long."

The eyes closed and he seemed to sleep, a skinny back-
country Buddha, on a hot rock miles from noplace. I
walked on, back toward camp, trying to decide if he was
saner or crazier than when I last saw him.

I decided he was.


Thanksgiving morn finds the town suffering under a drizzling
gray overcast and a driving black hangover, with a mouthful of yesterday's cigarettes, and thankful for nothing but the knowledge that
all such mornings pass. This morning Big Newton tries to purge
himself of the day before with soda and vinegar. Howie Evans uses
a spoonful of Sal Hepatica and a half-bottle of French toilet water,
genuine from Paris, which he steals from Simone and takes to his
wife as a peace offering. Jenny uses a page from Timothy. Les Gibbons tries cold water when, running down to the riverbank, he slips
while shouting to Andy rowing past; Andy heaves on downstream,
toward the mill, rowing obliviously past the man floundering and
cursing in the reedy shallows, as though he is rowing in his sleep.
Viv brushes at her teeth with salt. Ray sits muggle-headed on the
edge of the bed and tries to wash away his darker feelings with the
bright memory of his success last night and the glowing prospect of
his future. Simone tries to wash away similar feelings, using the
Blood of the Lamb. Evenwrite uses Vicks VapoRub and the words
from an old song of his father's.

*. . . When that line of smoky fire is drawn*
*Tell me which side are you on?*

. . . then gives up asking and falls asleep in the tub.

Jenny is more tenacious. The Bible page gone, she returns to her shack, tired but resolute. Ever since leaving the bar last night, she has been working doggedly at the old childhood ritual that was responsible for her early departure from the Snag. This is a kid's game with clam shells, recalled after all these years, a game the little girls of the tribe used to play to call up the image of the men the gods had ordained to be their mates. Across the foot of her dingy cot Jenny has arranged a white pillowcase as a background; once clean, the pillowcase now has a graying smudge in its center left by hours of casting and picking up shells. She stands above the pillowcase, bends slightly at her thick waist, moves her two clasped hands in a slow circle . . . then opens the hands, sprinkling a patter of opulent, surf-sanded shells onto the cloth. She studies them a moment, singing, "This bed is been manless too long too long, this bed is been manless too long . . ."—to the tune of "It Ain't Gonna Rain No More." She nods at what she sees and scoops the shells back into her hand to begin again: "Wah-kon-da-ah-gah hear my song . . . this bed is been manless too long too long . . ."

When Jenny was fifteen the trouble was that the bed hadn't been manless long enough; Jenny, you too young," her brothers had tried to tell her, "to go into business. . . . What *kind* of business this, anyway?"

"With Father. A trade. He voted for Roosevelt."

"He's a fool. Listen, why don't you come with us? Down the coast to the place Hoover built for us. Place better than this; good house, facilities inside and out . . . and we get paid for living on it down the coast there. So why don't you? . . . Mud anyway you look at it."

Jenny shook her head and turned a trim hip before the bright new house trailer that her brothers had bought for the move to the reservation; "I think I just stay if it's fine with all you." The dim aluminum image gave her a resolute nod of approval; then she lifted an orange skirt to display trim brown legs bare to the belly button. . . . "Father say the Indians come under the New Deal just the same as anybody. He say me and him got a trade if we decide we wan' to apply it. You like my legs?"

Her brothers gaped. "Jenny! My God! Put down your clothes! Father's a crazy fool. You come on down coast."

She hiked the skirt behind and turned, looking back over her shoulder at the brown spread of her mirrored ass. "He said if we stay right around here where they logging, we retire rich quick from our business. Mmm . . . how do you like orange, huh?"

Five years later her father demonstrated his crazy-foolishness by spending their savings on a new house made with sawed boards, split shingles, plastered in all the rooms . . . right next door to the Pringle mansion. That was his mistake; an Indian might have a business, he might even get by with a house with plaster rooms and shingles, but by god he oughta know better'n to put that house an' business right next door to a decent God-fearing Christian woman! especially if that woman is Pucker Pringle. The incensed citizenry burned the house before Jenny so much as spent one night under its new roof, then in a fit of righteousness drove the poor father to the hills. Jenny they allowed to remain, providing she come down in her aspirations as well as her prices, and move to a less observant neighborhood . . .

"It ain't so bad," she told her brothers when they came to re-possess her. "They give me this nice cabin out here. An' I ain't lonesome. I dance in the dance hall whenever I want to dance. That's why I stay, maybe." She neglected to mention the green-eyed young logger she had vowed to trap. "Also I get fifteen, twenty dollars a week . . . what the Government give you boys?"

She didn't mind the comedown, either in price or in property; with no one to divide with, she was actually making more take-home than before. Besides, she liked being back on the clamflats. She had never got used to the smell of that hotel room, or the sound of people you didn't know always walking past where you slept at night, waking you up and you laying there not knowing. "At least when you hear a footstep slop-slopping across the mud at midnight, in coldest night in January, you know somebody is come to see you."

The trouble was that with the passing of Januaries and the steady diet of clams, wapatoos, and choctaw beer, the brown ass grew broader and the footsteps became more and more infrequent. Financially, Jenny was quite comfortable: the land about her shack was abundant with cash as well as clams; literally hundreds of snuff cans containing fifteen or twenty dollars in bills enriched that mud. She had learned well the lesson of humility taught her father: Don't make a business look too successful—hide it. And, for a number of years, the frequency with which she was seen laboring away with shovel at all hours of the day and night prompted large tips of pity. So she didn't hurt for money. But, as the footsteps slackened, she came to miss the company. Enough to want to change things.

This time she made the trip. She found her brothers whittling myrtlewood bric-a-brac in an army barracks tent. They offered her a box to sit on. "The government hasn't got around to buildin' the houses now, with this war going on," they apologized. "But soon now . . ."

"Never mind. What tent's the old goatman put in? I got to talk to him. I need some magic."

The shaman took one look and advised her that it would take mighty magic to change things now, mighty big magic, bigger magic that he could lay his hands on. Okay, she would find it. In Coos Bay she bought a Thomas Mann novel and tried all the bus ride back to Wakonda to find out just where was this mountain full of magic this man was talking about. She gave up as she crossed the bridge into town, and tossed the book into the river. After that she brought her research material home from the lending library: it looked as though she might be in for a long haul with this magic thing, and a lot of books; and there was no sense buying any more than you had to when there were obviously so many going to be disappointments like the dud this phony German wrote.

There were for sure a lot of disappointments and duds, but she had plodded ahead with rubber-booted determination, working to alleviate her problem by attacking it at two levels: when she was home alone in her shack she plied an occult gleaned from haphazard thousands of books, a bastard brew of magic, unpredictable and nameless . . . when she was in the Snag she plied free glasses of Teddy's liquor on drunks, a bastard brew often as unpredictable and nameless as her magic, though it might be straight from a bottle marked Bourbon De Luxe. Over all, this second method had been far more successful than her spells and chants: on a good night with enough different drunks to work with, she could generally fill her manless bed at least briefly and, if the situation was right and she picked carefully, could sometimes even get a man still sober enough to be capable of filling more than just the bed.

Last night had been ideal for the administration of this method:

the men had started drinking early and were drunk enough when she arrived that there was little need for her to spend her money for drinks. Within an hour she had had two old friends at different tables ask her if she was still using that same sealskin blanket on her cot, and a fisherman barely forty years old remarked that maybe she needed help scraping the barnacles off that keel . . . an *ideal* situation!

But she had suddenly ceased her buying and her heavy-set flirting and collapsed in a chair by herself. Somewhere two men had been talking about Henry Stamper: seen 'im in the hospital an' that there old turtle looked like he was finally getting set to buy his piece of dirt. She had known this, of course—old man like that, a dead certainty he wasn't gonna live forever . . . but it wasn't until she heard someone else say it that the dead certainty became a fact. Henry Stamper was gonna be gone, pretty soon now; the last ragged remnant of her green-eyed logger was gonna be gone . . .

And, realizing this, she found she was no longer interested in bringing home one of these other men from the Snag. Not even the stout-looking fisherman. Dejected, she had slumped deeper into the chair, still holding the glass of liquor she'd purchased as bait for the fisherman. With a gulp she drank it herself. Need it. Got no man ahead of me, no one I can see ahead of me at all . . .

And just as she was about to order another glass, the old Indian seashell game came to her, the man-seeing ritual, coming from no whiteman's book or no white god's gospel but from her own childhood. She belched loudly, pushed herself to her feet, and thumped out, grim and gas-filled and indefatigable, across a score of manless years . . .

"Too long, too long, too long," she chants querulously. "Manless too damn long"—and makes another toss with the seashells. She sips absently from her glass of brackish liquid and studies the pattern on the pillowcase. The pattern is getting better every toss. At first, for a long time, there was nothing. Just scattered seashells. Then there was an eye, repeating itself in toss after toss. Then two eyes, then a nose! And now this *whole face* just like *this* for six or seven times in a row getting clearer all the time . . . !

She scoops up the shells and circles her hands slowly: ". . . too long, too long, too long, too long . . . this bed is been manless too long . . ."

In town the Real Estate Hotwire finally gets through to that nigger lawyer in Portland and finds that it is even worse than his sister feared . . . "Everything, sis, not just the insurance, he left her everything!" Even the theater, which he had expected was returning home to roost in his office for another six months. He shakes his head at his sister sitting across he desk from him. "She got the works. That snake must have lost his mind. Don't cry, Sissy-Britches, we'll fight it, of course. I told that nigger lawyer we weren't about to stand still for his kind of black—"

He stops abruptly, staring at the little wooden figure forming beneath his whittling knife . . . Blast! And that family from California threatening to move into his unrented four-room stucco out Nahamish . . . *that* would be a fine kettle of fish if they got away with it. And—hey, b' gorry!—those two letters asking about living upstairs in that room over his office . . . they sure never sent along any *photograph!* Blast and *double* blast! Won't they ever leave a man alone to make a mark in this ratrace? Must they always come slipping in to make trouble just when there's better times right round the bend? Blast the bunch of haunts . . . get away, get *away!* He flings the figure into the wastebasket after its shavings, giving up . . . whoever heard of a *colored* Johnny Redfeather, anyway?

Just as Simone disposes of her own haunting statue, putting it at the very back of the very highest shelf in the closet and stuffing her old wedding gown in front of it, feeling herself finally beyond the help of a virgin idol. . . . What good was such an idol to her now? Could a virgin be expected to understand safety jelly? or Listerine gargle? or the cold cyst that swelled like a frozen bubble beneath her skin, the cold, empty hollow left when you for now and evermore relinquished Virtue, and Contrition, and even Shame? Don't make me laugh, Mary-doll . . .

And as Ray finally stands up and walks away from the bed to the grimy sink in the corner of their room, giving up his attempt to brighten the morning with memory. He takes the cracked enamel basin and fills it with warm water. After putting the basin on the forbidden hot plate behind their trunk, he sits in the hardback chair and lights a cigarette, watching Rod rock and roll about the bed, snoring in three-four time. "Rodney, boy . . ." Ray whispers, "you never was *all* that bad with your beat, you know? For all my bugging you. You had your slow times and your fast times but you was usually in there pretty close. Me, man, I got a beat strict as a clock. And perfect pitch, you know? Oh, I ain't coming on, I'm just saying what I know. It's the straight stuff. I mean, I *know* it's there . . .

like last night, with everything swinging all the way, on top of it, tips, requests . . . *nothing* to stop me from going clear to the top, you know, man? I got Blue Skies, and a clear road, and not a thing in my way, *not! one! solitary! thing!* Rod man, to keep me from wailing clear to the top of the heap!"

He stops. The clock ticks. He daubs out the half-smoked cigarette in a chili-stained dish and stands up. He hears the water boiling briskly in the enameled pan. He walks across to the bed and pulls his guitar case from beneath the bureau and flips the snaps open. He takes out the instrument and places it on the floor beside the case . . . then for a moment just stands, looking down at the instrument's workmanship, at the pearl inlay, at the rhythmed flow of the cherrywood grain set off by the six parallels of gleaming steel . . . damned pretty, sorta like a good, organized run; freedom and style and order. He smiles at the guitar, then closes his eyes and steps onto it with both bare feet. The wires stretch, the cherrywood creaks. *Damned pretty, goddamned pretty . . .* He jumps into the air. *No reason, on a pretty piece like this, a man couldn't go all—*

There is a chonging crash. Rod rears up startled from his snores to see his roommate leaping up and down on the jagged ruin of his steel guitar. "Ray!" Rod swings his feet from beneath the blanket; Ray turns in his direction a face both harried and dreamily peaceful . . . "Ray, man, wait!" But before he can reach his friend, Ray has dashed across the room and plunged both fists to the wrists in the boiling water . . .

Lee is awakened by the scream, first excusing the sound: those two musicians across the hall, raising an awful row . . . but then a bang, then another scream, then running in the hall, shouting, doors opening . . . well, just one more nightmare to wake to.

He gets out of bed and dresses hurriedly, spurred to haste by the mysterious activity for the first time in three days. Except for meals, he has spent almost all of his time since leaving the house there in the hotel room, in his bed, reading, dozing, waking . . . sometimes awakened by the touch of slim, cool fingers tracing his skin, only to open his eyes and find that the room has become too hot again and the fingers are only rivulets of sweat . . . then rolling over to doze— and wait—some more.

And sometimes wondering, in his waiting stupor, whether those slim fingers, or the slim and ethereal girl who had applied them, had ever been more than a fantasy of temperature . . .

By the time he has dressed and headed down to the lobby, the manager and his teen-aged son have helped the musician corner his berserk roommate in the phone booth. Rod has pulled on Ray's trousers in the excitement, and they fit ridiculously tight about his thighs and waist. He is pleading in a gentle whisper at the booth. Standing on the stairs, Lee is able to look down into the booth and see the other man sitting with both knees jammed against the door, his head tipped sideways almost coquettishly as he fondly chides his two boiled hands lifted before him. Lee watches as a small crowd gathers. Occasionally Rod will look back over his shoulder and explain to one of the newcomers, "Ray's always been high-strung. Taut, like a G string. A sensitive musician is always high-strung. He had a lot of plans for the future, see, but it seems like he was just strung too tight and high to finish a gig, you see . . ."

The sheriff arrives with a tool box; they are getting ready to dismantle the booth door with screwdrivers and a claw hammer when Lee decides he has seen enough. Buttoning his coat, he continues on down the steps and out onto the sidewalk, stopping outside the hotel to look up and down the street and wonder now what? What are my plans for the future? Way-all, I concluded . . . one thing is certain: I'll have to be sure and know of a good convenient phone booth in case I also turn out to be strung too high to finish the gig.

Actually, this was in no way an accurate analysis of my mood . . . because I felt about as low-strung as a man can feel and still manage something as active as a slow stroll. I shuffled disconsolately down Main, as tranquil as the soft gray rain drifting about me, my hands hibernating in the deep, furry pockets of the jacket Joe Ben had given me that first day in the woods, and my head in an aimless fuzz. Three days of paperback mysteries in my aquarium of a hotel room had apparently mildewed all my motivation. I simply walked, neither going, nor fleeing, any place at all. And when I found that my wandering had brought me to Neawashea Street, near the hospital where my father was reported to be crumbling apart, I turned off, not really so much because I wanted to see the old man—though I had been damning myself for two days for putting off the visit—as because the hospital was the nearest dry place at the moment.

I was walking back along the same forbidding route that I had traversed in terror a few days before, but it seemed forbidding no longer, and I didn't feel the slightest fright. And when I felt none of the old muscle-knitting thrill at passing the cemetery, none of the apprehensive tingle as I approached the shack of the Mad Scandinavian Fisherman known to rush forth unexpectedly from his dank tarpaper lair and attack hapless pedestrians with a chinook salmon, I was struck with that feeling of inconsolable loss that the satiated big-game hunter must experience when he returns to camp, through the suddenly monotonous jungle, having slain whatever demon he feared the very most. My steely eyes, once alert and aglitter with the excitement of the hunt, had waxed muddy and dull behind fogged lenses that I made no attempt to clean. My sentinel ears no longer pricked outward to catch warning snap of the telltale twig, turning instead inward to the dull murmur of introspection. My sense of touch was disconnected by the cold. My taste buds atrophied. My keen nose, that had but a few days previous run silently ahead gleaning the shadows for the scent of danger, now only ran, not at all silently . . .

For the hunt was done, the danger past, the demon defeated . . . and what's left for a nose to keep keen for? "We must learn to accept the change," I tried to advise us. "We survived the slaughter of God and all his Heavenly Host quite handily; why, then, should we get so hung up over doing in the devil?"

But this advice served not at all to tighten my low string. Seemed to make it lower, if anything. There was nothing left. I was finished. Hardly caring, I realized at last that here was the thing Old Reliable had warned me to watch out for—the post-duel depression; my revenge against Brother Hank completed, what was left but the trip back East? A dreary journey at best, especially when made alone. How much less dreary, I couldn't help thinking, the trip would be, were one accompanied by a congenial travel companion—how much more *pleasant* . . .

So, for three days, since our night together, I had put off leaving and hid out in a three-dollar no-bath room, waiting and hoping that this companion would come seeking me. For three days and three nights. But I would wait no longer; my last three dollars were slept up, I badly needed a bath, and I think I had known all along that my hoping was hopeless; deep inside, I had known Viv would not come seeking me—I had seen to that—and I couldn't bring myself to go after her . . .

While I might be fearless and all that, what with the devil done in, I still hadn't reached the point of being able to go out to the devil's house for no other reason than to ask his wife to come away with me.

I shoved my hands deeper into my pockets as I approached the hospital, low-strung and wishing that I had either more courage to go with my fearlessness, or a good cowardly excuse for returning to the old house just one more time . . .

Viv washes off her toothbrush and returns it to the rack; and, holding her hair back with one hand, bends to the faucet to rinse her mouth out. She brushes with salt, to keep her teeth bright. She washes out the taste and straightens back up and faces her image in the medicine-cabinet mirror. She frowns: what *is* it? What she sees— or doesn't see—in the face makes her uncomfortable; it isn't age; the moist Oregon climate keeps the skin quite young, without cracking and lining. Skinny, but no, it isn't the lack of flesh, either; she has always liked her rather underfed look. So . . . something else . . . that she doesn't yet understand.

She tries to smile at the face. "Say, litle girl . . ." she whispers out loud, "how have you been?" But the expression that answers is as abstruse to her as to others who constantly try to plumb its mystery. What *is* it . . . ? She can brush with salt to keep the smile gleaming, but she is unable to reach behind the gleam . . .

"Foofawraw," she says and switches out the bathroom light. "That's the sort of thinking that leads a girl to drink." She closes the door behind her and goes downstairs to sit on the arm of Hank's chair and squeeze his hand tightly while the TV set booms "GO! GO! GO!"

"Be half time here in a minute," Hank says. "What about a egg sandwich or something?" (I was watching the Thanksgiving Day Classic when Viv came in . . . Missouri and Oklahoma, still nothing to nothing at the end of the second quarter with less than five minutes to play . . . )

"How about turkey-noodle soup instead, honey? I can open a can and heat it?"

"Fine. Anything, I don't care . . . just so's we can finish it during the half. And a beer if we got one."

"Not a sign," she said.

"Didn't you hang out the beer flag for Stokes?"

"Stokes doesn't deliver any more, remember? Up this far . . . ?"

"Okay, okay . . ."

(It was past noon and I'd laid in the sack till game time with a heat pad on my lower back, hadn't had any breakfast and was hungry. Viv got up and slipped off to the kitchen, barely making a sound in her tennis shoes. The house was damn quiet with just the two of us. Even with the TV turned way up, the house was too quiet for my liking. That lonely, *killing* quiet of nobody talking with anybody, of no kids squealing and giggling, no Joby coming on with some wild notion, no old Henry helling around . . . and the little times when Viv and I said something to each other, it seemed like it was quieter than ever. Because we were just talking, not with anybody at all. I hadn't really noticed the silence till then—I guess I'd been too busy with the funeral and what all to notice—and I hadn't really started to appreciate what a thorough goddam job the kid had made of it till I got the chance to notice this silence, and to wonder if Viv and me'd ever be able to talk with each other again. Yeah, you had to give the kid credit . . . )

Through the heavy glass door of the hospital I pushed, to a welcoming of warm air and the same old Amazon in white reading the same movie magazine. "You must *live* here," I remarked, trying to be friendly. "Days, nights, and Thanksgivings."

"Mr. Stamper?" she asked with a good deal of suspicion. She then leaned nervously toward me. "You . . . are you feeling *woozy*, Mr. Stamper?"

"It's woozy weather," I reminded her with some hesitation.

"I mean feelin' *bad?*" She rose from her magazine, eyeing me warily. "I mean I *know* you been under an enormous strain . . ."

"Your sympathy is very much appreciated," I told her, becoming more puzzled, "but I don't think I'm going to faint again, if that's what you're concerned about."

"Faint? Yes . . . maybe you can sit down while . . . I'll just whisk off an' fetch the doctor. You wait here, now, hear me . . . ?"

Before I could reply she had whisked off in a cloud of starch dust that hung in her wake like exhaust. I stared after her, perplexed by her sprinting departure. Certainly a change from our last encounter. What scared her? I wondered for a few moments, then concluded it was my new look. "The new presence of black disdain in my features . . . that's what." I curled my lip coldly. "Threw a bit of fright into the poor drudge is what, to come face to chilling face with the Total Absence of Fear . . ."

Then I bent to place a quarter in the cigarette machine and, in the mirror, caught sight of the visage that had sent her scurrying—a chiller all right: not quite so much a look of black disdain, I conceded, studying an unkempt, unshaven wastepaper basket of a face that peered back at me with red-rimmed and terror-filled eyes, as a look of bleak destruction. But a chiller, nevertheless.

I was a sight. Along with no bath there had been no mirror in my hotel room and I had not been witness to the decay. It had come with the insidious stealth of mildew; just as the wallpaper had become tracked overnight with the little delicate footprints of gray blight, my face had been marked by the passage of neglect. No wonder the Mad Scandinavian had chosen to cower behind his bolted door! After three days of cigarettes, private eyes, and mildew, mine was not exactly the face at which anyone—regardless of humor or nationality—would rush forth armed only with a fish.

The nurse returned with the bulky doctor in tow. Even this arch-fiend's filthy- and fat-minded good fellowship was intimidated by my appearance: he was unable to think of a single insinuation, he was so overcome.

"Good lord, boy, you look just awful!"

"Thank you. I cultivated the look especially for the visit. I didn't want my poor father to think I was ridiculing his present condition by showing up looking all bright-eyed and bushy-tailed."

"I don't believe you have to worry about what old Henry's thinking these days," the doctor said.

"Pretty bad?"

He nodded. "Far too bad to give a hang if anybody's bright-eyed and bushy-tailed or not. You should have come earlier; as it is now, you might be disappointed in his reaction to your—what'd you call it?—'cultivated look'?"

"Perhaps," I said, noticing that the good doctor was getting his old snide equilibrium back. "Shall we see?"

"Take it easy; you don't look capable of walking that far."

After a pulse check convinced him I was in no immediate danger, he allowed me to have a look at the shredded remnants of my illustrious sire. Not a very pleasant experience . . . The room smelled of urine; the air was warm and hothouse moist; the bed had side-guards. The old man's hardened grin had cracked in his baking nightmares, and a thin thread of red ran from his lips down his whiskered chin to his neck, like a lorgnette string attached to a wire-rimmed plaster smile. I stood looking down at him for as long as I was able—I've no idea if it was seconds or minutes—while the old fellow clacked and clattered against sleep with a bony tongue. One time he went so far as to open a matted eye to look at me and command, "Wag it an' shake it. Suck yer gut in an' git goddammit to affairs!" But ere I could comment, the eye closed, the tongue stopped, and the conversation was terminated.

I followed the doctor's broad backside down the corridor away from the old man's room, wishing that, just once, just this one time, my father had been more explicit about these affairs that I had been so long trying to git goddammit to . . .

On the pillowcase before her, Jenny sees a nebulous mouth forming; she has a quick sip from her glass, wipes her lips on the rough forearm of her sweater, scoops up the shells, and casts again, very hungry and very tired, but sensing the approach of something too big and too wonderful to risk missing in sleep . . . Teddy unlocks the door of the Snag and steps into air set like gelatin with stale smoke and flat beer and wild-cherry toilet disinfectant; it is early, much earlier than he usually opens, and his eyes are puffier than usual from his interrupted sleep, but, like Jenny, he anticipates the approach of something too big to sleep through.

Unlike Jenny, however, Teddy doesn't feel that he has had any part in bringing it about; he is only an observer, a spectator—content to just open up the arena and let other forces and bigger men cast the shells . . .

Jonathan Bailey Draeger wakes in his motel in Eugene, checks his watch, and reaches to the desk beside the bed for his notepad. He finds the appointment and reads it again to be sure: well . . . he isn't due at Evenwrite's to eat for three hours; one hour to get dressed, one to drive over . . . and one to put off the ordeal at the Evenwrite household . . .

Actually, he isn't feeling that much distaste for the prospect. Be a nice concluding episode. He lies back against the pillow, holding the notepad in one hand, and, smiling to himself, at the picture Evenwrite's name summons up, writes: "Status does not automatically generate aspirations to rise, just as food does not necessarily stimulate hunger . . . but a man seeing another in a position superior to his, eating food higher off the hog, so to speak . . . will go through heaven and hell to sup at the same table with the superior even if he has to provide the hog." And adds: "Or the turkey."

And Floyd Evenwrite, stepping from the tub, calls to his wife to ask how long it will be before their guest arrives. "Three hours," she calls back from the kitchen. "Time enough for you to get you some rest before he gets here . . . out all night, for goodness' sakes, what kind of 'business' could be so important to keep you out all *night*?"

He doesn't answer. He pulls on his trousers and shirt and carries his shoes into the living room. "Three hours," he says aloud, sitting down to wait. "Three by god hours. Time enough for Hank to stand up an' shake hisself . . ."

(Viv came back in with soup and sandwiches and we set up the TV trays to eat off of while we watched the bands and the twirlers parade around; we spoke about every five minutes, and then it was something like "She's good, that one in spangles . . ." "Yeah, she is, isn't she? Real good."

I was just *beginning* to appreciate what a thorough job the kid had done . . . )

In the doctor's office once again I took his offered cigarette, and this time sat down. I felt myself no longer vulnerable to the scurrilous comments and cattities.

"I warned you"—he grinned—"that you might be a little disappointed."

"Disappointed? With his little phrases of advice and endearment? Doctor, I'm overjoyed. I can recall periods when that statement would have seemed like an hour's chat."

"That's funny. You two never talked much? Old Henry always made out he was a great one for talking. Maybe, would you say, you just didn't care to hear what the old boy was talking about?"

"Whatever do you mean, Doctor? My daddy and I might never have *said* much, but we kept no secrets from each other."

He gave me his most knowing of smiles. "Not even you from him? The tiniest secret?"

"Nope."

He leaned back, creaking and wheezing in the swivel chair, and fixed his eyes on the past in rotund reverie. "Seems, though, that people were always keeping one thing or another from Henry Stamper," he recalled. "I'm sure you don't remember, Leland, but some years ago there was a story circulating around town"—he shot a quick look at me to make sure I did remember—"about Hank and his relationship with a—"

"Doctor, we aren't a nosy family," I instructed him. "Our relationships are not always posted on the family bulletin board . . ."

"Still—oh yes, I didn't mean to imply . . . But still, the point I was making is that the whole town was aware of this story—true or not—while old Henry seemed completely ignorant."

I felt myself becoming more and more irritated by the man, less, I think, by his insinuations than I was by his attack on my helpless father. "I'm sure you don't remember, Doctor," I said coldly, "that while old Henry quite often seemed completely ignorant, he nevertheless succeeded in besting all the rest of the sharpies in this town in some business deal, time after time after time."

"Oh, you misunderstand . . . I'm not disparaging your father's judgment . . ."

"I know you aren't, Doctor."

"I was merely—" He halted, flustered, finding me a little harder to intimidate than last time. He filled his cheeks to start again, but there was a knock on the door. The nurse opened it to advise him that Boney Stokes was here again.

"Tell him to stop in a moment, Miss Mahone. Fine old fellow, Leland; he's been here, faithful as a clock, ever since—Say . . . ! Boney, come on in a minute . . . you know young Leland Stamper?"

I started to stand to give the old skeleton my chair, but he put a hand on my shoulder and shook his head soulfully. "Don't get up, son. I'm going right on down to see your poor father. Terrible thing," he said in a voice dripping grief. "Terrible terrible terrible thing."

The hand held me in the chair as though I were a wedding guest; I muttered a hello, while fighting back the urge to cry out, "Unhand me, graybeard loon!" Stokes and the doctor spoke a moment about old Henry's deteriorating condition, and I tried once more to stand. "Wait, son." The hand tightened. "Mightn't you tell me how things are at the house, so I could pass it on, say just perchance Henry should come to for a bit? How is Viv? And Hank? My, you've no idea how heartsore I was hearing how the poor boy had lost his closest companion. 'A good friend gone,' my daddy used to say, 'is a shadow across the sun.' How's he taking it all?"

I told them I hadn't seen my brother since the day of the accident; they were both openly shocked and disappointed. "But you'll be seeing him today, won't you? Thanksgiving Day?"

I told them I saw no reason to trouble the poor boy, and that I was planning to leave on the bus to Eugene this afternoon.

"Going back East? So soon? My, my . . ."

I told the old man I was packed and ready. "My, my is right," the doctor echoed, and went on to ask, "And what do you imagine you'll do, Leland . . . now?"

I thought at once of the letters I had sent to Peters, because the skillful emphasis placed on the "Now" at the end of his question made me momentarily think—as I'm sure he hoped it would—that this gossip glutton knew more than he was saying; perhaps he had somehow captured the letters and was onto the whole plot from beginning to end! "What I *mean*"—the good doctor probed onward, sensing that he was near a nerve—"do you plan to return to college? Or teach, maybe? Or is there a woman . . . ?"

"I haven't exactly made plans," I answered lamely. They leaned down on me; I stalled for time with an old psychiatrist's trick. "Why do you ask, Doctor?"

"Why? Well, I'm interested, as I told you before . . . in all of my people. Back East to teaching, huh? I suppose is what it will be? English? Drama?"

"No, I'm not finished with—"

"Ah, then back to school?"

I shrugged, feeling more and more like a sophomore in the dean's office with his counselor. "Perhaps back to school. As I say, I haven't made any plans. The work here looks like it's finished . . ."

"Yes, looks like. So you say perhaps back to school?" They continued to pin me against the chair, one with his eyes, one with a hand like a pitchfork. "Why do you hesitate?"

"I don't know what I'll do for the money . . . it's too late to apply for a grant—"

"Say!" the doctor interrupted, snapping his fingers. "You know, don't you, that that old man in there is just as dead as if he was in the ground?"

"Amen, Lord." Boney nodded.

"You *realize* that, don't you?"

Taken aback by his gratuitously frank statement, I waited for him to continue, feeling less like a sophomore than like a suspect. When were they going to bring in the spotlights?

"Maybe your father won't be declared legally dead for a week, or two weeks, who can say? Maybe a month, because he's stubborn enough. But stubborn or not, Leland, Henry Stamper's a dead man, you can bet money on it."

"Wait a minute. Are you accusing me of something?"

"Accusing you?" He fairly beamed at the idea. "Of what?"

"Of having something to do with that accident up—"

"Good gosh, no." He laughed. "You hear that, Boney?" They both laughed. "Accusing you, that's something . . ." I tried a laugh myself, but it came out sounding like Boney's cough. "*All* I was saying, son"—he gave Boney a broad wink—"is that, if you're interested, you come in for about five thousand dollars when he is finally declared dead. Five grand."

"That's true, very true," Boney intoned. "I had not thought about that, but it's true."

"Why is it true? Is there a will?"

"No," Boney said. "A life-insurance policy."

"I happen to know about it, Leland, because I help Boney here—and myself, o' course; the doctor must have his 'cut,' as they say—by directing potential clients to his agency—"

"Daddy started it," Boney informed me proudly. "Nineteen-and-ten. Coastal Life and Accident."

"And some ten years ago Henry Stamper came in here for a physical, not particularly thinking about insurance, and I directed him—"

I held up my hand, feeling a little dizzy. "Wait just a moment. Are you asking me to believe that Henry Stamper has been making payments on a policy naming as beneficiary a person he hasn't seen in twelve years?"

"It's all very true, son . . ."

"And didn't *look* at a half-dozen times in the twelve years prior to that? A person to whom his last words were 'suck in yer gut'? Doctor, there is a limit to human credulity . . ."

"Say now, there's your reason," Boney exclaimed, shaking my shoulder slightly, "for going back to the house. You *must* get that policy, you see. To return to school."

His enthusiasm brought on a slow, dawning suspicion; "Just why" —I looked up the length of that stick arm—"is it I *need* a reason to go back to that house?"

"And when you see Hank"—the doctor overrode my question—"tell him we are all . . . *think*ing of him."

I turned from the stick figure to the lard man. "*Why* are you all thinking of him?"

"Lord, aren't we all old friends of the family, all of us? Say, I tell you what: My grandkid drove me here. He's sitting this very minute out in the sitting room. While I'm visiting Henry, the grandkid can drive you out in his automobile." They worked like a team. I was no longer a sophomore, or a wedding guest, but a suspect in the hands of two Kafkaesque interrogators skilled at keeping their victim from getting any idea what he was about. "How 'bout it?" Boney asked.

The doctor rose, blowing and wheezing, from his chair to answer for me. "Can't beat that kind of service, can you?" He circled the desk at me; I felt trapped by the pressure of his juggernaut advance.

"Wait a minute, now; what *is* it with you people?" I demanded, fighting my way to my fee. "What skin is it off your nose whether I see my brother again or not? What is it you are pushing?"

They were both genuinely innocent and astounded by my question. "As a doctor, I merely—"

"Say, I tell you what." Boney's hand snagged me once more. "When you see Hank you reckon you could tell him—and the wife —that our grocery truck's gonna be coming out that way again. Tell him we will be more than happy to start up delivery again now that the truck's making that loop. Tell him to signal what he needs on the flagpole just like always. Would you do that for me?"

I finally gave up seeking a reason for their grasping pressure; I just wanted out from under it. I would leave pressure to Hank; he was more accustomed to it. I told Stokes I would give Hank the message, then tried to move toward the door; his old white thorns of fingers hung on and the two of them followed me into the waiting room, reluctant to let me get away now that they had set me moving.

"Maybe," the doctor said, "say, Boney, maybe Hank'd like a turkey for the day. I'd bet money that with the excitement these last few days they didn't think to buy a turkey." He fished under his smock for his wallet. "Here, I'll just pay for a bird for Hank, how's that?"

"That's a very Christian gesture," Boney agreed solemnly. "Don't you thing it is, son? Thanksgiving dinner without a old roasted gobbler just ain't Thanksgiving dinner, is it?"

I told them I shared their feelings about Thanksgiving exactly and again tried to make a break for the glass door, but again that spiny hand detained me and, moreover, I saw that the pimply Adonis who had stolen the Hershey bar from the café blocked my way.

"This is the grandkid," Boney informed me. "Larkin. Larkin, this is Leland Stamper. You're going to give him a ride out to the Stamper house while I have my visit out with old Henry."

The grandkid scowled, snuffed, shrugged, and began zipping up his Jimmy Dean jacket, giving no indication that he remembered our previous meeting.

"Yes, now that I think about it"—the doctor still toyed with his

wallet—"I bet money there's a *lot* of people in town would chip in
to buy old Hank a Thanksgiving dinner . . ."

"We'll get a basket!" Boney exclaimed. I started to say that I
doubted that Hank was in such dire straits just *yet*, when I realized
that they weren't offering him the charity because he *needed* it—
"Cranberry preserves, too, son, yams, mincemeat . . . whatever else
he needs, you have him just phone me, won't you? We'll take care
of it."—but because *they* needed to offer it.

"Larkin, you just drop Mr. Stamper off and hurry right back for
me. We got things need attending to . . ."

But needed it for *what?* was the hanger. What and why? This
overblown offering wasn't like Les Gibbons' need to drag the champ
down off the throne. Because the champ was already down. So now
why all this need to bug him with their benevolence? And not just
these two clowns, but seemingly much of the rest of the town felt
the same need. "What is it," I asked the grandkid as I followed him
across the parking lot through the blowing rain, "that they want
from my brother, do you know? bestowing all this bounty on him.
What do they need?"

"Who knows?" he replied sullenly, opening the door to the same
hotrod that had kicked gravel in my face a few days before. "Who
cares?" he said as he slipped in behind the wheel; and, as I circled
the car to the other door I heard him wonder, "Or who gives a big
rosy rat's ass?"

Precisely, I thought, closing the door behind me; before I gave
these other weighty questions the attention they deserve I should ask
myself if I gave a big rosy rat's ass about the quaint and curious needs
of the quaint and curious little town of Wakonda-by-the-sea. None
whatsoever. Not *any* colored ass from *any* sized rat. Unless, of course,
by some chance, some obscure chance, some of the town's quaint
needs happened to correspond in some curious way with my own . . .

"Frig." The grandkid deftly snapped the car into gear and went
screeching across the puddled parking lot. "I oughta be home inna
whirlpool," he informed me, to keep the subject of candy bars from
coming up. " 'Stead of runnin' round gettin' *stiff*."

"Absolutely," I agreed.

"We had our last game of the season last night. With the Black
Tornadoes of North Bend. I got a knee racked up the third quarter."

"Is that why it was the last game?"

"No, I ain't but third string. That's why I oughta be home inna whirlpool, though . . ."

"Because you ain't but third string?"

"Naw, because I got my knee racked up. Say, does your brother know we was puttin' his pitcher on the blockin' dummies for a while?"

"I couldn't say," I told him, feigning interest in his sports activities while I tried to formulate some feelings about my own. "But I'll pass the information on to him when I get to the house . . . along with the free turkey and cranberries." It shouldn't be so complicated; I had my reasons for going out to the house: I was going out to try to get an insurance policy—I could tell Hank—and to try to acquire a traveling companion—I could tell Viv . . . Now; I should be able to come up with a story to tell myself . . .

"Damn right," the grandkid mused, "on the blockin' dummies an' the tackling dummy too. Hank Stamper's pitcher. Damn right! That was before the Skagit game. We was really choice before that game. We creamed Skagit. We was ahead thirty points in the third quarter, an' I got to play all the fourth quarter."

"Is that why you got in the game last night?"

"No," he said reluctantly, "I got in because we was twenty-six points behind is why. They creamed us, forty-four to fourteen, our only loss of the season since Eugene." Then he added, almost questioningly, "But North Bend *wasn't* that good! They'd of never even touched us if we'd been as choice as with Skagit!"

I didn't comment; I leaned back, planning ahead, thinking that there wasn't any reason why I couldn't give myself the same story that I gave Viv. Because I honestly *did* want her to come away East with me . . .

"No. They wasn't *that* tough," my driver went on to himself. "We was just off, that's all; I know that's all there is to the story . . ."

And, listening to him give himself his reasons while I gave myself mine, I began to suspect that there might be a whole lot more to it than either of us knew. . . .

The rain drizzles down. The sand-buggy bumps over the railroad tracks at the end of Main, turning up river. Draeger drives out of the motel yard, looking around for a restaurant where he can have a cup of coffee. Evenwrite sits beside his telephone, smelling of menthol, soap, and, ever so slightly, gasoline. Viv runs water over the empty soup dishes in the kitchen sink. Out the window, only inches above the river, two mergansers fly past wing to wing, flying frantically but barely moving . . . as though the current beneath them extended in a force field beyond its own surface, striking them head-on. Their struggle is strange, agonizing, and Viv feels her arms ache for them as she watches. She has always been possessed of great empathy for other creatures. Or possessed by it. "But say . . . I *know* about the ducks." Her reflection is there again. "How do you feel?"

Before the dim image in the kitchen window can be expected to respond, a car stops across the way at the landing. A figure steps out and walks toward the dock, cupping his hands to call . . .

(When I seen Viv come hightailing out of the kitchen, drying her hands on the apron, I knew what she'd seen before I heard him holler. "Somebody at the landing," she said, going past to the front-door hall. "I'll go and get him. You aren't dressed."

"Who is it?" I asked her. "Anybody we know?"

"I couldn't tell," she said. "He was all bundled up and it's raining hard." She was out of sight a second, climbing into the big oilskin poncho. "But it looked like Joe Ben's old mackinaw. I'll be right back, honey . . ."

She swung the big door booming shut behind her. I'm glad she said that about the mackinaw, I thought; I'm glad she gives me credit for having some eyes in my wooden head . . .)

Viv answered my call for a boat. I watched her hurry from the house down through the milling dogs, tugging a voluminous parka about her head in an effort to keep dry. When she swung the boat in alongside the landing where I waited I saw that she hadn't had much success.

"Your hair is sopping. I'm sorry to get you out in this."

"That's okay. I was needing to get out of the house anyway."

I stepped into the boat while she steadied it idling against a piling. "Our premature spring was short-lived," I said.

"They always are. Where have you been? We've been worried."

"At the hotel in town."

She gunned the motor and swung the bow banking into the current. I was grateful to her for not asking why I had spent the last three days in solitary. "How is Hank? Still under the weather? Is that why you are ferryman today?"

"Well, he isn't too bad. He's downstairs now, watching the game, but then he's never so sick but what he can't watch a football game. I just didn't think he was up to coming out in the wet. I don't mind."

"I'm glad you did. I've never been much of a swimmer." I saw her wince and tried to cover it over. "Especially with the water so high. You think it'll flood?"

She didn't answer. She angled the boat slightly when she reached midstream to allow for the current, and concentrated on the navigating. After a stretch of silence I told her that I had been in to see the old man.

"How is he? I haven't been able to get away . . . to see him."

"Not so good. Delirious. The doctor thinks it's just a matter of time."

"That's what I heard from Elizabeth Pringle. It's too bad."

"Yeah. It wasn't pretty seeing him that way."

"I guess not."

We concentrated again on the boatride. Viv fretted at her sopping hair, trying to tuck it into the poncho. "I was surprised to see you," she said. "I thought you had gone. Back East."

"I plan to. A new semester will be starting soon . . . I'd like to make it."

Without taking her eyes from the water ahead she nodded. "That sounds like a good idea. You should finish your schooling."

"Yeah . . ."

Then more riding; more silence . . . while our hearts screamed for us to stop and say something!

"Yeah . . . I'm looking forward to showing off my callused hands in various coffee houses in the Village. I've some friends who will be astonished to discover the word applies to the physical as well as the spiritual."

"What word is that?"

"The word 'callous.' "

"Oh, I see." She smiled.

I went on matter-of-factly. "Then too, a cross-country bus trip should be something in the middle of winter. I anticipate snowstorms, hailstorms, perhaps even to be trapped overnight by a blizzard of terrible magnitude. I can see it clearly: the bus motor idling away, precious fuel used to keep the heater going; a little old lady rationing out her sack of cookies and tuna-fish sandwiches; a Boy Scout leader keeping the morale high by leading us in camp songs. It could be quite a trip, Viv—"

"Lee . . ." she said without for an instant diverting her attention from the gray swirl of water in front of the boat, "I can't come with you."

"Why?" I couldn't help asking. "Why can't you come?"

"I just can't, Lee. There's nothing else to say."

And we rode on, with nothing else to say, it seemed, except

We reached the dock and I helped her secure the boat and a covering over the motor. We walked in silence, side by side, the dock, up the slick plank incline and across the yard to the Before she opened the door I touched her arm to speak again, she turned to me, shaking her head no before the words co start.

I sighed, surrendering speech, but held on to her arm. "Viv . . . ?" If this was the last of it, I wanted the last look of good-by. I wanted the reserve to be shed for that final glowing gaze of farewell that is traditionally awarded two souls that have touched, that is deserved by two people who have been so daring as to have truly shared, without reserve or fear, that rare, hope-filled moment we call love . . . I touched her dripping chin with my finger, lifting her face to mine, determined to have at least that last look. "Viv, I . . ."

But the hope was not there, only the reserve and fear. And one thing else, a darker, heavier shadow that was hidden beneath the dropping of her eyelids before I could classify it.

"Let's go in," she whispered, pushing open the big door.

(I kept worrying about what I was going to say to Lee when they got back. Since he'd left I'd been satisfied that it was done and we wouldn't have to say anything; I hadn't thought he'd come back; I hadn't even wanted to think about him. But now here he was again all of a sudden, and something was going to have to be said, and I didn't even have an inkling.

I kept watching the TV. The front door opened and he came in behind Viv. I was still sitting in the big chair. He came across toward me, but right then the teams came back out on the field and my problem was solved for a while anyhow: maybe something was going to have to be said all right, but there wasn't *nothing* so important it couldn't wait for the Thanksgiving Day Classic, Missouri and Oklahoma tied nothing to nothing at the start of the second half . . . !)

In the living room we found Hank seated watching a football game on television; with a quilt tucked about him, a glass of evil-looking liquid by his chair, and a large livestock thermometer dangling cigar-fashion from the corner of his mouth; he looked so much the archetypical invalid that I was amused and a little ashamed for him.

"How's it goin', bub?"—as he watched a rigmarole of pre-kickoff activities.

"As well as could be expected, for a being not accustomed to existing under water."

"How are things in town?"

"Dreary. I stopped in to see the old man."

"Yeah?"

"He's in a coma of some kind. Doctor Layton claims he's dying."

"Yeah. Viv talked to the doc on the phone last night and he told her the same thing. I don't know, though, I just don't know."

"The good doctor seemed very positive of his diagnostic skill."

"Yeah, well, you can't never tell about them things. He's a tough old coon."

"What's happening with Jan? I couldn't make that funeral . . ."

"Just as well. They'd put make-up all over him. It was kinda the last dirty trick Joby had pulled on him. Jan? She's took the kids to Florence to stay with her parents."

"I suppose that's best."

"I reckon. Now hang on; here comes the kick . . ."

Except to glance down once for his can of beer, his eyes never left the television. Like Viv, he kept his attention fastened away from me, as painfully aware as we were of the feelings our inane chatter sought to conceal. Neither did I seek his gaze. I was truly afraid to; behind the cloud of our spoken words our thoughts rustled like impatient lightning, charging the air of the old house with such intensity that it seemed that the only way to avoid detonating the whole room was by keeping the contact points insulated—should our eyes connect there was no predicting whether or not our wiring could support the voltage.

I crossed the room to the table, unbuttoning my coat. "I was just telling Viv that I plan to start back toward civilization right away." I picked a Golden Delicious apple from the bowl on the table and ate it as we talked. "To school."

"Is that right? You're aiming to leave us?"

"Winter term starts in a few weeks. And, since the word in town has it that the deal with Wakonda Pacific is off—"

"Yep." He stretched, yawning, rubbing his chest through the front of his woolen robe. "It's all she wrote. Today's the deadline. Everybody laid up one way or another . . . and I damn sure couldn't run them booms down by myself, even if I was in good runnin' condition."

"It seems a shame after we've worked so hard."

"That's the way she bounces. It won't kill us. We're covering ourselves. Floyd Evenwrite says this Draeger said they're going to get a sales agreement with the mills as a sorta fringe demand in the new contract."

"What about Wakonda Pacific? Couldn't they supply you with some help?"

"They could but they won't. I checked on that some days back. They're just like us; with the river coming up like it is, they just as leave not have all them booms on their hands. Keeps up out there like this, we're in for higher water than last week."

"Couldn't you lose the booms in a flood, all that work?"

He drank from the can and set it back beside his chair; "Well, what the dickens . . . it just seems like nobody wanted them goddam logs delivered."

"Except"—I started to say Joe Ben—"old Henry."

I hadn't meant it as a cut, but I saw him flinch, just as Viv had at the mention of swimming. He was silent a moment and when he spoke again there was the vaguest edge to his voice. "Then, by god, old Henry can just get his ass out of bed and deliver 'em," he said. And looked neither left nor right from the Gillette commercial.

"The reason I came out—"

"I was wonderin'—"

"—is about an insurance policy the doctor claimed exists."

"By gosh, that's right. I remember something about a policy. . . . Viv, chicken?" He called, though she still stood only a few feet behind his chair, toweling her hair. "You know anything about them life-insurance papers? Are they up in the desk?"

"No. I cleaned the desk of everything but papers to do with the business, remember? You said you couldn't find anything?"

"What did you do with the other stuff."

"I took it up to the attic."

"Oh Christ." He moved as though to stand. "The motherin' *attic!*"

"No, I'll get it." She tossed her hair back and turbaned the towel around it. "You'd never find it. And it's drafty up there."

"Okeedoke," Hank said and settled back in his chair. I saw Viv start up the stairs, her tennis shoes pit-patting a dim print, and I had sense enough to realize that this pit-pat was probably the final, fading knock of my last opportunity to be alone with her.

"Wait . . . " I dropped my apple core into Hank's abalone-shell ashtray " . . . I'll come with you."

At the end of the hall past the bathroom and the room used as an office, a ladder, made of two-by-fours nailed like horizontal bars across the window there, took us up through a hinged trapdoor into the peaked top of the house . . . a gloomy, dusty, musty room that ran from the front of the house to the back, like an elongated pyramid braced upright with crisscrossing diagonal beams. Viv slid up through the trapdoor behind me, quiet as a burglar. I helped her stand. She wiped her hands on her Levis. The trapdoor fell shut with a muffled thump. We were alone.

"I haven't been up here since I was five or six," I said, looking about me. "It's as delightful as ever. It would have been a nice little nook to repair to on some of these long rainy Sunday afternoons to sip tea and read Lovelace."

"Or Poe," she said. We were both whispering, the way one does in certain rooms. Viv stretched out a leg and rolled a mangy Teddy bear over with the point of her tennis shoe. "Or Pooh."

We laughed beneath our breaths and began to move carefully forward through the dim clutter. A small window at each end of the long room provided space and light enough to be a building site for spiders and a cemetery for flies; what light was left over strained through the little warped panes and sifted like soot from a chimney across an ominous array of boxes and chests and trunks, rough-hewn packing crates and ornate bureaus. A dozen or so orange crates were lined up on end, appearing to stand at brooding attention, like geometric ghosts. About this array of larger objects, like lesser spirits of gayer and freer form, were gathered incidentals like the Teddy bear Viv had rolled over . . . fifty years of paraphernalia, tricycles to tambourines, dressmaker's dummies to diaper pails, dolls, boots, books, Christmas ornaments . . . *you're wasting time*, and, over everything, dust and mouse manure by the bale.

"Of course," I whispered, "one would have to bring more than a book and a cup of tea: I think I might like a knife and a shotgun, and perhaps a radio so I could call in reinforcements in case I needed to put down a revolution."

"A radio by all means."

"By all means."

When this is all over, I told myself, you will hate yourself for wasting so much time . . . "Because some of these natives look restless and very revolutionary." I prodded a stuffed owl and it responded with a high-pitched squeak and produced from its feathers a little brown mouse which scampered off behind some Japanese lanterns. "See? Very restless." When you get yourself alone later you are going to call yourself all kinds of names for not taking advantage of this situation.

Viv had reached the window and was looking out through the webs. "It's too bad there isn't a room up here—I mean for living in . . . you can see so well. The garage across there, and the road and everything."

"It is a nice view."

I was standing right beside her, close enough to smell her damp hair—go ahead! try something! at least try something!—but my hands stayed in my pockets, safe and well-mannered. A wall of protocol and passivity rose between us—she would not breach it; I could not.

"That policy . . . where would you think we might find it?"

"Boy, in this mess," she said brightly, "finding anything is going to be a chore. Here; you start on this side and I'll start on the other and we'll work our way down to the other end. It's in a shoebox, I remember, but old Henry was always up here moving things around . . ."

Before I could think over a cozier way to hunt, she was off, rummaging through crates and crannies, and I was forced to follow suit. But you can still talk with her, idiot; go ahead and tell her how you feel.

"I hope . . . you didn't have anything else you were doing."

"Me?"—from the other side of the room. "Just breakfast dishes . . . why?"

"No reason. I didn't want to drag you away from something to help me beat about the attic."

"But I drug you away, Lee. You volunteered to come with me, remember?"

I didn't answer. My eyes had become accustomed enough to the gloom to see a path leading between the beams through the dust and debris to a corner with a pronounced diminishment of spiderwebs. I followed the path to an old rolltop desk somewhat less dusty than its surroundings. I opened the rolltop of the desk and finally found the shoebox I was seeking. Along with a museum of momentos so maudlin that I would have burst out laughing had not the laughter stuck in my throat like a fishbone.

I intended to joke about the find. I meant to call to Viv but I was voiceless, as in a dream, and I experienced again that bright billowing medley of excitement and trepidation and outrage and guilt that I had first felt that first time I placed my eye to a hole in the wall and spied breathlessly on a life not my own. For once again I spied. Except the life before me now stood bared so much more, so terribly much more, than had the lean white body that had come with snarls and grunts to mount my mother in the lamplight so long ago. . . .

Before me in the desk was a careful and terrible litter . . . of high-school dance programs pinned with flaky brown carnations, of certificates for letter awards, of dog collars, scarves, dollar bills with dates inked across the pressed faces—*Christmas 1933 John, Birthday 35 Granpa Stamper, Birthday 36 Granpa Stamper, Christmas 36 Granpa Stamper*—all tacked onto a shop-class breadboard with the woodburned inscription "Not by god Alone!" There was a feeble stamp collection and a shell collection, precious as diamonds in a jewelry-store necklace box . . . and a flag mounted on a suction cup, and a foxtail, and stacks of Christmas cards, an album of Glenn Miller 78s, a cigarette smoked to the fading lipstick stain, a beer can, a locket, a shot glass, a dog tag, a service cap, and pictures, pictures, pictures . . .

The pictures were as typically American as the suction-cupped flag. There were sets of snapshots in their little yellow envelopes; and studio portraits in glass frames; and family reunion shots swarming with devilish youngsters making faces between the legs of pompous grown-ups; and the five-dollars-for-a-dozen pictures signed and exchanged your senior year in high school and generally thrown away the year after. I picked up one of these from its place on the shelf; across her white cashmere a sultry sixteen-year-old had penned: "To Hank the Hunk; a gorgeous Hunk of male I hope to let clean out my car pocket once again. Doree."

Another hoped he might "see fit to be a little more friendly in the future with certain interested parties." Still another advised him that any such interest "wouldn't get him nowhere so don't go getting any ideas."

I had seen enough; I tossed away the bundle . . . *high school pictures!* I would have never believed my brother to be so banal. I picked up the boxful of policies, planning to sort through them in the better light downstairs, and was just turning to announce my find when I noticed, sitting behind a large maroon photo album, one of those cheap pasteboard frames holding a photograph of Viv seated beside a small bespectacled boy. The child, about five or six—one of the up-and-coming younger Stampers, I surmised—glowered solemnly in the direction of the photographer's telltale shadow that fell across the grass before him. Viv was seated with her skirt spread about her, hair swirling, laughing open-mouthed at some remark made by the clever shutterbug intending to pierce the hard looks of the youngster.

The photograph itself was of very bad quality; obviously blown up from a small and very bad snapshot, it was practically a masterpiece of the hazy focus and the direct lighting . . . yet, for all its faults I understood why it had been chosen for enlargement and framing. That the photograph did not resemble the Viv that one saw every day wiping back a delinquent lock of hair as she hummed over a skillet of frying sausage, or sweeping dried mud into a dustpan or hanging wet clothes over the stove in the living room or rummaging about the attic in dirt and tennis shoes . . . this was not important; the picture's singular charm lay in the accidental entrapment of the girl one sensed waiting *behind* that skillet of sausage or that pan of dust. The laughter, the blowing hair, the tilt of the head showed her caught in an attitude that perhaps for that one instant fulfilled completely all that her slight smile perpetually suggested. I decided I must have that picture. Didn't I deserve at least a bit of a snapshot to show the boys back home? The photograph was rubber-banded to a small bundle of other papers for which I had no use, but if I could detach the picture and slip it inside my shirt no one would ever be the wiser. I set about trying to slip the rubber band off but it was sticky with age and I only succeeded in binding the picture more tightly to the bundle. *Don't, picture, please* . . . I brought the packet to my mouth to try to bite the sticky bands; my hands were shaking and I was nervous beyond all proportion to my theft. *Don't be this way. Please. You can be mine please. You can come with me please* . . .

"I can't, Lee."

Until she answered I had not been aware that I was talking out loud.

"I just can't, Lee. Don't, oh, Lee, don't . . ."

I had not even known I was crying. The photo flowed before my eyes, as the girl swept across toward me, through dust and cobwebs. "Why not, Viv?" I asked stupidly. She had almost reached me. "Why can't you just flick everything here and—"

"Hey . . ." A hoarse word stopped us. ". . . ain't you two found that outfit yet?"

He was speaking from the trapdoor; his bodiless head could have been mistaken for another piece of the clutter.

"You clucks oughta get some more *light* up here, for chrissakes. It's like a grave. Find anything . . . ?"

"I think I have it here," I called to him, trying to control my voice. "A lot of policies to check through. We're almost finished."

"Okay. Say, listen, bub: I'm gonna go slip into some clothes and run you back across. The air'll do me good. You be ready to move when I get my clothes on."

The head disappeared. The trapdoor thumped shut. She was in my arms. "Oh, Lee, *that's* why. *He's* why. I can't leave him like he is now . . ."

"Viv, he's just putting you on with this sick bit; he isn't sick . . ."

"I know that."

"And he knows, too. He knows about us, couldn't you tell just now? This sick bit, he's just doing it to keep you."

"I know that, Lee . . . but that's *why* I say I—"

"Viv, Viv, baby, listen . . . he's no more sick than I am. If he and I were off out of your sight someplace he would probably beat the daylights out of me."

"But don't you see what that means? How that means he *feels?*"

"Viv, baby, listen; you love *me!* If I ever knew anything I know that."

"Yes! Yes, I know! But I love him *too,* Lee . . ."

"Not as much as you—!"

"Yes! As much! Oh, I don't know . . ."

Desperately, I grasped her shoulders. "Even if that's so, that you love him as much, I need you more than he does. Even if you love us equally, it's all the more reason; can't you see I *need* you to keep—"

"Need! Need, is that *all!*" she wailed against my chest, her voice muffled by the heavy wool and her near hysteria. "Viv," I started to say again, but she pushed back to seek my eyes. Beneath us we could hear Hank returning, heavy-heeled. "Let's make it," he called from below the trap. "Hear me Lee? Viv?"

At the sound, her look of conflict and anguish suddenly changed, and her eyes dropped, as though borne to the ground by the weight of an awful shadow, that same shade I had seen across her face at the front door but hadn't recognized. Because, I would have never believed it possible to find that shadow on Viv. But, now, it was unmistakably nothing more mysterious than plain old shame. I had not recognized it earlier because it was not shame for herself or her guilt, or for me in mine, but shame for the man so weakened by his illness that he was unable to let his wife disappear momentarily from his observation into the attic, so stricken with fever that nothing would do but take me across the river himself to keep her from being alone with me that little time more . . .

"Say, Viv, can I borrow this family album for a while? To show off my heritage back at school?"

And being responsible for some of this weakness, she was trapped by it. It would be her memento of the thing we almost had, just as that photograph hidden inside that album was mine. I could think of nothing to say. She walked from me, away from the trapdoor toward the window—"You better go, Lee; he's waiting, "—moving slow, weighted. That a shame focused on another should burden one as terribly as the personal variety was practically inconceivable to me. The poor kid is just too compassionate, I told myself . . .

And yet, as I climbed down the ladder into the hallway, where Hank waited gnawing on a hangnail, I felt that I too was encumbered by a shadow as unnatural as it was unwieldy.

"Let's go, bub," he said impatiently. "I'll pull on my boots downstairs."

"A bit ago you were too sick to bend at the joints."

"Yeah, well maybe a little of that nice fresh-washed air out yonder is what I been lackin'. Is that okay with you? You ready to make it?"

"Fine with me. I've got everything I came for . . ."

"That's good," he said and started down the stairs. I followed, thinking, *Unnatural, and unwieldy, and a hundred times heavier than any of the score of personal varieties that I have so often carried. Hank, my shame for you, believe it or not, is as great as that I hold for myself. Maybe greater. And, brother, that's going some . . .*

From the attic window through cobwebs, Viv watches as they walk to the boat and get in. The boat starts, noiseless at this distance, and begins to creep across the river like a little red water beetle. "I don't know any more, Lee, what I want," she says, like a small child. And becomes aware of her image once more, vaguely reflected in the dirty attic window: what does it mean, all this concern about our images?

It means this is the only way we ever see ourselves; looking out, at others, reflected through cobwebs from an attic window . . .

(I ferried the kid back across; we were pretty casual about it. I said I didn't blame him for wanting to shake the Oregon mud off his shoes and go back to hit the books. He said he was sorry to take me away from my ball game. We were getting along all right; standing pat seemed the best way to handle things . . .)

"It'll be nice to get back to some drier country . . . even if it is colder."

"Sure. A fella gets tired of this friggin' drizzle all the time."

As the expanse of water lengthened between myself and the slim blond girl alone in the echoing wooden house, I began searching frantically for some last hope, some last unplayed trump that would win me this hand; I no longer cared about beating my brother, I cared about winning the game. And there is a difference . . .

"By the way, the doctor and Boney Stokes told me to ask how you were feeling . . ."

(I'd had some things to say to him, on this boat trip across, but what the hell, I figured, don't go picking at scabs . . .)

"I'm probably gonna survive."

"They'll be happy to hear that."

"I'll bet they will."

When the bow touched dock I was desperate to the point of bursting; I felt I must do something or die! In another minute I would be gone from her for good, and she from me . . . for good! So do anything! Kick, scream, throw a tantrum for her to see and so she'll know that—

"Look who's pulling up in the jeep. It's Andy, big as life. Hey, Andy boy, how's it hangin'?"

I barely noticed as Hank waved to Andy climbing from the jeep. I had seen something far bigger . . .

"What's up, Andy, man? You look draggled."

Something far better . . . across the river, at the top of the old house, in the little attic window, like a candle lifted as a signal to me, at last . . .

"Hank," Andy approaches them, panting, "I just come from the mill. Somebody set it on fire last night."

"The mill! Is it burned?"

"No, not real bad; rain kept it down pretty much so's it hadn't burnt more than the green chain an' some stuff. I put it the rest of the way out . . ."

"But for chrissakes the *mill*? Why? How do you know somebody lit it?"

" 'Cause there was this stuck to the glass on the front office." Andy unfolds a smudged circular sticker and holds it to Hank. "This: a black cat, grinning . . ."

"The old Wobbly sign? Who in god's green world . . . with a *Wobbly* sign?"

"It seems you have enemies, brother," I said. He turned to look at me suspiciously, wondering if I'd had anything to do with the mill; it amused me a little, knowing that he was suspicious of my past when sabotage was already cooking in the future. "Still, it also seems you have some very devoted friends. For instance, Boney Stokes was most insistent that I pass on his regards."

"That old spook," he said and spat (besides, I figured, to myself, there's no sense me and the kid getting into it), "someday I'm gonna trip that old bastard and bring him down like a stack of dominoes . . ."

"Oh, you misjudge him . . ." I glanced again across at the house. "Mr. Stokes is full of appreciation for you"—she was still framed in that dark square of window—"and determined to *prove* his good faith to you."

"Stokes? How's that?" He looked at me, puzzled. (I figured, There no sense in saying any more when everything we could say we both already knew . . .)

"Well, he asked me to advise you—" *She's still watching. Still at the window. He doesn't know!* "—advise you that, due to another change in his *delivery route* . . . he will be coming up the river this far and is willing to give you the benefit of his services once more." "Yeah? Stokes? Is that right, now?" (I figured, There's no sense doing anything when everything's already been done . . .) "Yes, that is right; and he furthermore asked me to say that he was *indeed* sorry— wait; what was it?" *Go ahead! It's the only way. You know that it is!* ". . . sorry for any inconvenience he might have caused you during your, let's see, *weakened* condition, Mr. Stokes put it, I think. Is that right? Have you had a weakened condition, Brother Hank?" "You might say so, yeah . . ." (I had figured, I'll just go on and drop the kid off in town and leave things where they are, just stand pat . . .)

"Also, the good *doctor* told me to tell you that he was buying you a turkey—" "A turkey?" "Yes, a turkey," I went blithely on, acting as though I were completely unmindful of the line of anger tightening about Hank's lips like a bowstring—*Go on! you have to go on it's the only way!*—as though I were completely unaware of the disbelief and shock in Andy's eyes. "Yes, the good doctor said that he was paying for you a nice big gobbler for Thankgiving, compliments of the hospital." "A turkey? Wait a minute . . ." "A free turkey, brother; it almost seems that you should get in a sick and weakened condition more often, doesn't it?" "Wait a minute; what's this all about, goddammit?" (I had figured, Yeah, there's no reason dragging up the ashes, he's finished with what he set out to do and there's nothing I can do back, so what the hell . . . let it stand pat.) "And then Mr. Stokes said—let me recall—that 'Thanksgiving dinner without the traditional gobbler just ain't Thanksgiving,' and that he considered the doctor a true Christian in Heart and Deed for helping you in your time of need." "My time of need, he said that?" "That's what he said. Boney Stokes. The good doctor said something different." "What did the good doctor say?" "He said Hank Stamper *deserves* a free turkey for all he's done for us." "Doctor Layton said that? Goddam you, Lee, if you're—" "That's what he said." "But I didn't do anything to deserve—" "Now, now, brother . . . in a moment you'll be saying you didn't deserve to have your mill burned." "Didn't really burn, I tol' you, Leland, I got to it—" "Okay, Andy . . ." "—they jus' *tried* to burn it, but the rain—" "Okay, Andy." (Yeah, that's what I had figured . . . that it was all done and over. But the kid had a different notion.) "Yes, you have a lot of friends, Hank." "Yeah." "A lot of people *interested.*" "Yeah. Wait; let's see if I get it right; Boney *Stokes* . . . is coming *here* to push a turkey off on *me*?" "I don't think Mr. Stokes is looking on this as a business transaction. Or the doctor either. I think it is more a consideration, don't you, Andy?—a show of gratitude for Hank's cooperation." "My *cooperation*?" "Yes, about the contract and all . . ." "What in the hell do they think I want with charity or gratitude . . . or a goddam turkey *either* for that matter?" "Oh, and there are other incidentals, too . . . that the citizens are going to donate. I think a whole basket. Mr. Stokes mentioned yams, cranberry preserves, mincemeat—" "Hold it." "—pumpkin pie, dressing —" "Hold it now, I said—

"—for just one goddam minute . . ." Hank stood up in the boat, his hand held slightly before him as if to hold off an attack of air. "Now just you tell me, bub: what are you driving at? just let's have it straight, once." (Yeah, I had figured everything had been done . . .) "I mean I didn't order any goddam mincemeat or yams. Are you shitting me? Or what the hell are you driving at!" "You must not understand, Hank; I know you didn't order. Mr. Stokes isn't selling this to you . . . he's giving you the groceries. Or donating might be the better word. He said that anything else you might need, just hang out the flag for it. Simply hang out the flag. Can you handle that? In your weakened condition?" "Hold it . . ." (But I was wrong. He was still pushing. There was something left after all.) "Say, Hank—" "Hold it, bub . . ." *Don't stop now; you can't stop now.* "How is your condition, by the way?" "Hold it, bub, don't push it too far . . ." (He don't even act like he knows what I'm signifying; can he be that dense?) "Push what, Hank?" "Just don't is all." "How far is too far, Hank?" "Okay, bub—"

He stopped speaking and looked at me. I stood up; the boat, only tied at the stern, rocked and bucked beneath us. Andy looked back and forth from each of us. Hank stepped over the center seat. This was it; here comes the bomb. We stood facing each other with the boat bobbing and the rain bristling between us, and I waited . . .

(He just stands there grinning at me. I feel that old mounting howl swirl in my stomach and arms, tightening my fists . . . and he just *stands there* grinning . . . what's with him? What's he got going *now* for the chrissakes?)

And, waiting, I noticed for the first time that Hank was a good two inches shorter than myself. The revelation in no way excited me. How interesting, I kept thinking, as I waited for the bomb to drop; how peculiar. "You were going to tell me, Hank," I asked again, "that one has to push . . ." He started to clench his jaw. "Maybe instead I oughta just come right out an'—"

"Over there!" Andy shouts and points. From across the river comes a moist, cracking explosion, like wet lightning followed by a rumbling of heavy earth. The three figures start, turning to the crash in time to see a great section of the bank pitch out from the foundation and slide crashing onto the boathouse. For a second the earth floats on the little structure, then the boathouse rolls over, the way an ice cube rolls with sugar piled on it. (I stopped, watching the bank shredded two-by-fours and frayed rope and snapped cables. It gapes bright and dry and deep as a shell crater, ragged at the edges with shredded two-by-fours and frayed rope and snapped cables. It gapes this way a moment, from the bank below the barn. Then the earth, heavy with water, drops to fill the hole, carrying part of the barn down with it. Dust muddies the rain. Animal hides and gunny sacks swirl away, gathering foam. Broken red planks thrust floating upright for a moment, then flatten out to float away. Some of them veer into the foundation around the house, actually shoring it up against the current as though the barn has sacrificed itself for the house. The cow lumbers bellowing from the ruin, up toward the orchard. Another small slide heaves down about the half-submerged barn, clattering and scraping; then it is still.

None of the three have moved during the half-minute. Now Lee steps out of the boat up onto the dock with Andy, and Hank follows. (I stopped then, with my mouth hung open. It wasn't the cave-in that really made me spin my wheels. The cave-in just distracted me for a second; it was something else, something I seen at the house that really pulled me up short. And the kid seen it, too, way before I did . . .) On the dock, I saw that Hank had noticed my concerned glance at the attic window . . . (Viv was up there, up there still in the attic! And the kid'd known all along she was watching. *That's* why he was pushing . . .) "You knew, didn't you?" Hank turned toward me with a slow, restricted control that made me think of the Tin Woodman of Oz straining against the rust in his joints. "You knew she'd see if I fisted you . . . ain't that right?"

"That's right," I told him, watching him closely and for some reason still waiting; because, though he was onto my reasons and my plan, he still didn't sound like he'd dismissed earlier intentions. "Now everybody knows," I said and waited . . .

(Then it all come over me; I mean for the first time *really come over me*, just how nigger slick he's got it all balanced out. He's got it near perfect. He's built it like the hanging nooses we useta build as kids, that can't get any way but tighter; he's built it to where I can't advance any direction but what I'm bound to lose ground. He's arranged it so's I'm stuck in a place where it's damned if I do and damned if I don't, whipped if I fight and whipped if I don't . . . *That's* now nice he's got it balanced.)

. . . waited, watching him weigh the situation carefully. Andy rocked from boot to boot in mute confusion, like a big perplexed bear, while I waited and Hank thought it over . . .

(And seeing that, I think to myself, bub, right here is where your genius outfoxes you; because you've got it arranged better than you know. "Bub, we've tore up too much of each other to stop now." Because you got it worked out so well that it doesn't matter to me any more that she's watching. "We've messed in the nest now, bub, messed in it good," I tell him. Because he'd got the balance heavier on one side than he knew, the noose tighter than he realized. "Because there's too much salt, bub, rubbed in, to stop now just because she's—")

I started to ask Hank what he meant when an abrupt, almost involuntary twist of his neck stopped me. His chin was being tugged to the right, toward the house. He would pause, look at Andy, at me, then the neck would twist again, further right . . . then back at me, at that black-cat sticker Andy held, then right again as though he were being jerked by an invisible rein leading across the river up to that attic window. The rein pulled taut. He faced the house for a moment, looking at that slim glow in the dark window, then the rein snapped in two and his head swung back, facing me . . .

("Yeah, there's too much rubbed in to leave now," I told the kid. Because he'd finally made standing pat tougher than advancing, and losing ground easier than standing pat . . .)

"So get your best hold," Hank said and drew a deep breath, grinning at me. ("Because we've messed in it," I said, and let him have it, for all I was worth, right on the side of the head.)

The blow surprised me no more than had the discovery of my advantage in height: How interesting, I thought, as I saw stars sparked from my cheekbone. (The kid took the punch. He just stood there and took it. I guess I knew he would, with her watching, because that's another part of the way he's got it so worked out . . .) How interesting, I thought—Lee spins backward, tripping, slamming into the side of the garage; Andy bobs and weaves along the dock; Hank moves forward; Viv watches the tiny figures, her fists at her throat— how very interesting and peculiar, I found myself thinking, as bells rang in my ears and birds sang round my head just exactly the way it is described in the pulps . . . (He went down at the second punch and I figured that was that, he's let her see all she needs to see . . .) Viv throws open the window, shouting through cobwebs and rain, "Hank! Don't!" as Lee slides down the mossy boards of the garage wall. "Hank!" Hank steps backward, crouching, throwing back the hood of his parka like a catcher tossing off his mask. (I heard Viv hollering something at me from that attic window, but I was past the

point of being hollered at.) Lee lifts his head, groaning . . . Nor was
I really surprised by his second blow, which started as a mere white
speck in the distance, then swelled suddenly before me into a great
knobby hammer of fist that splashed Fourth-of-July crimson in all
directions. (I popped him again, bloodying up his nose . . . that
oughta do it, I figured.) "Hank! Stop! Stop it!" Viv's voice stretches
across the water, as Hank hunches, waiting for Lee to push himself
groggily from the wall. (But, by god, he got back up again. I busted
him another one.) Lee pushes himself upright, frowning, annoyed by
the numbed and useless hinges of his jaw. Only one side of the jaw
seems to function. His mouth opens at a slanting angle. Hank waits
until the weaving stops and the mouth closes "Hank, no! Please,
honey, no!" (I hit him again, harder) takes deliberate fastidious aim
and fits another fist over Lee's nose and lips, carefully missing the
glasses . . . Nor was I much more than slightly surprised to discover
myself still standing when the crimson splash cleared. It all seemed
natural, somehow, at the time . . .

(The kid just kept sticking his face out. Fall down and stay, I kept
saying under my breath, fall down and stay or get up and fight or I'm
gonna beat you silly, or, or I'm gonna beat you to death.) "Hank!"
Lee snaps back bouncing again from the wall, and begins sneezing.
"Hank!" He sneezes violently, three times, creating a thin red mist
between them while Hank waits, crouching, cocking his arm again.
(. . . you just stand there keep letting her watch me pop you goddam
you I'm gonna beat you clean to death!) . . . But I must confess
that I was thunderstruck to find, that, after I had blinked the tears
and terror away, I was striking back! IMBECILE! DON'T . . .
"Lee! Hank! No . . . !" Lee's hand jumps, springing forward, seemingly of its own accord, like a small animal into the air after a passing
insect; the coat's weight throws it off its aim so the blow is short,
glancing off Hank's chin and thumping against his Adam's apple
IMBECILE! WHAT ARE YOU DOING? FOR GOD'S SAKE
DON'T FIGHT BACK! (Then I think the kid got the idea, that if
he didn't do something I was going to pound him to death. Because
he finally went to hitting back. Maybe he sensed it, that I'm going
to kill him. But now it's too late. I figured, You waited too long and
now I'm going to kill you.) My thunderstruck astonishment, however, compared to that of my back-reeling, eye-popping, air-sucking
brother, became mere wonder; Hank dropped to one knee, making a
noise like a man swallowing his tongue, and his face was a study of

stupefaction: What's *this?* he marveled; Who can *this* be belaboring me about the chops? (I know I'm gonna kill you, I figured.) Who can *this* cat be, standing there in little Leland's coat and pants, pasting me in the puss? (Because there just ain't any reason any more *not* to kill you.) After my initial pride and astonishment receded, I cursed myself for losing control. Why did you have to go and hit back, imbecile? WATCH OUT! Now he's down and you've got to let him get up and knock you down once more; do you think Viv is going to come rushing to the victor? Now; taunt him again but this time be cool. "Do I—" My voice quavered pathetically with a mixture of grim and giddy panic as I goaded him once more. "Do I now go to my neutral corner?"

From his kneeling position of disgrace Hank half smiled at my attempt at humor, not his usual hidden grin of mock shyness, but an icy, cruel, reptilian smirk that turned my wet hair brittle and my saliva to slush. WATCH OUT! a voice warned, and Hank said "You better be reh—reh—" I tried to take heart from the fact that he was having a worse time speaking than myself; I had clearly landed a telling blow to the larynx. "—you better be by god ready to go a sight farther than that," he went on, and the voice in my skull shrieked WATCH OUT WATCH OUT NOW WATCH OUT! "Because I'm gonna *kill* you goddam you . . ."

When I saw Hank come up off his knees and advance toward me behind his frozen lizard's smile—RUN! BEFORE IT'S TOO LATE!—I knew that my blow to the larynx had been a good deal more infuriating than telling. It had stunned nothing but his reason; there was a look now of trapped, futile rage. That one blow was the straw that snapped the animal's mind! I told myself. NOW YOU'VE DONE IT, NOW HE'S GOING TO MURDER YOU. RUN! RUN FOR YOUR MISERABLE LIFE!

(I can't see any reason not to kill you, don't you see. You've outfoxed yourself making it too tight . . .)

RUN! the voice kept screaming, RUN! But the river swirled at my back and the voice said nothing about swimming. And for once, I wasn't *able* to run for my miserable life. I could not back up at all. In spite of the hysterical demands for retreat, I could only move forward. Thus, while the voice screeched IMBECILE! IDIOT!, while my ears rang and Andy shuffled wordlessly, and Viv's calling came again over the water, my brother and I finally, totally *wholeheartedly* embraced for our first and last and oh so long overdue dance of Hate and Hurt and Love. Finally, we quit fooling around and fought, as Andy kept time with his foot. It kept reminding me of a dance. Clinging to each other in a paroxysm of overripe passion we spun the fight fantastic, reeled to the melodious fiddle-cry of rain through the firs, and the accelerating tempo of feet on the drumhead dock, and the high whirling skirl of adrenalin that always accompanies this dance . . . jointly trampling my surprise, Andy's shock, and Hank's astonishment underfoot in the action. (I have to kill you now. It's what you've been begging for so long . . .) And, for never having danced together before, we came on passing fair if I say so myself . . .

Viv watches in horror as the two of them, with Andy shuffling so close he appears to be refereeing, crash together through the rain. She has stopped calling. "Don't," she whispers. "Please don't . . ."

(I have to go ahead and kill you because you pushed too much . . . ) After one overcomes his natural aversion and hesitation and takes the first steps, enters into the spirit, so to speak, of this particular form of primitive gavotte, he finds it is not nearly so unpleasant as his apprehensions had given him to believe. Not at all. Certainly it can be a bit more difficult than fox-trotting at the Waldorf or mamboing at the Copa, but then it can also be, in the final analysis, a good deal less painful. For although a clout on the side of the head can set up a ringing sting that makes the ear burn like the fires of hell for the duration of the dance, who has not suffered more violent attacks on that same organ in the calm and cozy two-step? The clout will cease its ringing and the ear its burning, but who hasn't suffered a few well-placed words breathed softly cheek-to-cheek over the strains of a hotel orchestra? words with the power to ring on for months and years, and not just burn the ear but char one whole side of the brain as well? In this fistic dance a glaring misstep may leave you open for a quick, heavy, sickening punch in the stomach—I managed twice to lace the dock with my Golden Delicious—but this gut-rolling sickness is a sickness you know will pass, a pain you can endure by reminding yourself Hang on; it *has* to be over in a moment—whereas I have made missteps in far more placid dances, and have suffered lighter slower lower punches that still sicken with a pain that compounds itself by reminding you that it may never go away.

(Yes; he'd pushed more than he'd need of. But. To where he knows I can't but kill him. But. Kept rubbing things in like one red

flag after another in front of a bull until— But *why,* if it's just for
Viv?)

We reeled and shuffled from the dock up onto the gravelly bank;
we rocked and rolled down the bank through a litter of roadside garbage. Always with Andy right beside us, cheering neither one nor the
other of us. Always with Viv's voice trickling out of a gray distance,
pleading with Hank to stop. Always with that other voice screaming
from a much closer gray—IMBECILE—and demanding the same
thing of me: STOP FIGHTING! RUN FOR YOUR LIFE! HE'LL
KILL YOU!

(Like everlastingly pestering a man who has a gun until the man—
But *why* does he keep on?)

YOU KNOW YOU CAN'T BEAT HIM. IF YOU KEEP
FIGHTING HE'LL KILL YOU. LIE DOWN! STOP!

(Like prodding a bear with a stick until— But if he knows that already, then why is he—?)

HE'LL KILL YOU, Old Reliable kept screeching, LIE DOWN!
But something had happened. In a fist fight there is a point, after a
cheek has been split or a nose broken with a sound in your skull like a
light bulb being popped in mud, when you realize that you have already survived the worst. DON'T GET BACK UP! the voice from the
shadows insisted as I struggled to free myself from a deep green net
of berry vines where I had been thrown by a booming, eye-closing
right. JUST LIE HERE. IF YOU GET UP HE'LL KILL YOU!

And the voice, for the first time in a long, long reign over my
psyche, met with opposition. "No," said a stranger in my head. "Not
so."

YES. IT IS SO. LIE STILL. IF YOU GET UP HE'LL KILL
YOU.

"Not so," the voice dissented again, calmly. "No, he can't kill you.
He's already done his damnedest. You've survived his worst."

DON'T LISTEN! RUN FOR YOUR LIFE! HE'LL BEAT
YOU UNCONSCIOUS, THEN STRANGLE YOU WHERE
YOU LIE. FOR GOD'S SAKE DON'T GET UP!

"Listen to me. He won't kill you. If he wanted you dead he could
have gutted you with that peavey pole leaning aganst the garage
there. Or he could have cut your throat with that whittling knife he
carries. Or just could have stomped your head in with those boots
when you were looking for your tooth over there in the gravel pile.
He's not *trying* to kill you."

"OH?" the first voice stopped its shrilling and demanded with a sly arrogance. "THEN *WHAT* . . . ARE WE FLAILING AROUND TO GET UP OUT OF THIS BERRY VINE FOR? TO STAGGER BACK OUT IN THE GRAVEL AND LOSE ANOTHER TOOTH? IF . . . HE *ISN'T* BENT ON HOMI-CIDE, WHAT LOGICAL REASON HAVE WE FOR TRYING TO RISE TO DEFEND OURSELVES?"

I ceased my thorny struggle for a second, perplexed by this new tack. Yes, now that you mention it, why? I pondered the question as the world of my left eye rapidly shrank to a blue-lined slit. Why indeed? Then Hank, mistaking my hesitation for surrender, stepped over to extend a hand of aid. I took it and he dragged me from the vines . . .

(Because if he knows already that I can, could have killed him—might have killed him . . . would have! would have just as sure as sin if he had kept on just standing there letting me beat him up in front of Viv . . . just like he would have drowned under that car at the beach on Halloween if it had been left up to him . . . but this time he didn't just stand, to my everlasting surprise the kid had fought back, even after she'd seen all she needed . . .)

"Well?" Hank asked. "You had it?"

I was grateful for the opportunity. "I think so."

"Good goddam deal . . . because I'm shot clean to hell. Let's wash up." (This time he had fought with nobody to pull him out from under what he knew was maybe death when he crawled in under it . . . nobody to pull him out but himself.)

We walked back to the landing and squatted there, tossing water into our faces. I rose to get the album with Viv's photo from the boat, then returned. Andy silently offered a handkerchief and we silently accepted, taking turns. There was no more shouting, either from across the river or inside the head; no more stomping, no more voices . . . it was quiet.

(And when I saw this I gave up my notion of homicide. I had already cooled down a good deal, for one thing—because I got to realizing that whether Lee knew it or not, him prodding me into a hassle was for much more than just Viv's benefit . . . and for an-other thing, it just ain't so light a chore doing a man in—I don't care how hot you are under the collar—if that man himself decides to do something against it.

We finished up washing and walked up to stand in the garage.

The kid was looking pretty stunned by all the action he'd been in, so was old Andy, and me too, I imagine; none of us thought Leland had that much gumption to him. "Well, you can take the jeep on in if you want," I told him. "I'll stay an' talk a little with Andy, I believe, about this mill fire business . . ."

"But how'll you get it back from town?" Lee asked me and said, "I can hitchhike . . . I've done it before. If you want to keep it here."

"Naw." I patted the jeep on the hood; it was still hot. "Go on and use her," I told him. "I'll send . . . somebody in in a little bit, with Andy, to bring her back."

Lee didn't say anything to that; he was looking pretty solemn up at that window. But some way I felt like kidding a bit.

"The only thing I ask, is you take care of her. She's mighty finicky sometimes."

"What?" he said; it tickled me to fruster him that way; it always had. "What are you—"

"The jeep. I'm asking, will you take care of her?"

He looked at the dock. "Best that I can . . ."

"She may need gas." I took out my wallet. "I can give you some cash—?"

"No. I'll be all right. With my wages and policy."

"You're sure? You'll say so if you need some more money? You'll get word back?"

"I promise."

"Andy, man, what do you say me and you ride over t' the house and get me some of Lee's blood outa my hair and talk about grinning black cats and the like, hey? . . . over a bottle of Johnny Walker, what say? Okeedoke, then, bub; so long and maybe we'll see you around sometime."

And we left him there, starting the jeep, and walked back down to the boat. I was feeling all right, maybe not in God's pocket because it ain't so easy a thing losing a wife, but more all right about myself than I had in a good spell . . .)

In the attic, Viv reaches out to pull the window closed. In just the short time it has been open the rain has swollen the edges enough to make shutting it difficult. By the time she has it wedged shut again the jeep has pulled away down the road and Hank and Andy are returning in the boat. Hank seems cheerful when she greets him downstairs; she doesn't mention the fight; she can't tell if he knows she was watching or not. He is talking to Andy at a great rate about a fire at the mill.

"Was it bad?" she asks Andy.

Hank grins at her and answers for Andy. "Just enough, chicken, just bad enough. Tell you what I'm thinking about doing; I'm thinking—since I already missed my game, nothing else to do, can't dance, too wet to plow—that me, and Andy here might take us a little tug-boat ride."

"Hank!" She really doesn't need to ask. "Are you going to try to drive the booms down river to Wakonda Pacific?" She knew the moment she saw him. "Oh, Hank, by yourself?"

"Pee on that Oh-Hank-by-yourself business. Don't you think Andy's gonna be in there helpin'?"

"But it'll take one of you to pilot. Hon, you can't control all those logs by yourself."

She watches Hank waggle a loosened tooth with his forefinger, speaking around it. "A man's always surprised just how much he can do by himself. Anyhow, what I want you to do . . . is Lee took the jeep in, see, so you ride in with Andy and bring it back out. Go look Lee up at the hotel and—"

"Lee?" She tries to catch his eye, but he's busy fingering his tooth.

"That's right—and tell him I sent you to—"

"But Lee?"

"You want to go or not? Huh? Okay, then. Andy, while you're gone I'll gather up a good supply of chains and peavey poles and get me some eggs . . . and I'll put us up a big Thermos of coffee, too, because I expect we'll need something hot—can you get a boat offn Mama Olson? She's liable not to care about getting out on Thanksgiving to rent one, especially when she hears what it's about . . ."

"Yeah, I'll get a boat . . ."

"Good man. Can you pilot one?"

"I'll get it up here. I'll have it up here the way the tide's comin' in now in about an hour."

"Good man. Now . . ." Hank slaps his belly; Viv starts at the flat, sudden sound. "We better get to moving around, I reckon."

"Hank." She reaches to touch his arm. "I'll stay and cook you up some breakfast if you—"

"No, you go on. I can burn me some eggs. Here—" He takes out his wallet and removes all the bills; he divides them between Andy and Viv. "This is for Mama Olson, and this . . . is in case the jeep needs money. So let's get in gear—Listen: what's *that* now?"

The four measured notes of a musical auto horn reach them faintly. Andy goes to the window. "It's that delivery truck from Stokes' General," he says. "Lee said they was coming past, remember? You want me to go up the flagpole and signal or something?"

"I'd like to signal him with a good salt load, the old spook. No, wait, Andy; wait . . . a . . . minute. I think I'll—Listen, you two head on out; I'll handle the signals." He grins, striding into the kitchen. "Where's that arm of the old man's, chicken?"

"In the deep freeze where you put it. Why?"

"I may fry it up to go with my breakfast. Now you two get gone and leave me to business. I got things to do, eggs to hatch, wood to chop, and ground to scratch. I'll see you in about an hour, Andy. Good-by, Viv, chicken. I'll see you when I see you. Now move, for Pete's sake! I got to run everything in this boogerin' two-bit show?"

In her shack on the mudflats Indian Jenny casts her shells more and more slowly; any time now, baby, any time. In his bed Big Newton belches tremendously, and sleeps. Evenwrite waits by his phone, hoping Draeger had been as right about this one prediction as all the others. In the foyer Viv is once more climbing into the big rain poncho when Hank comes down from upstairs with Lee's leather-elbowed jacket. "Looks like the kid forgot his coat. You better take it to him: he ain't gonna look very spiffy runnin' around New York City in that old mackinaw of Joby's. And bundle up good, it's commencing to blow to beat the band out there."

After pulling galoshes on over her tennis shoes she rolls the jacket into a small bundle and tucks it up inside her rain poncho. She stands then with her hand on the knob, feeling the door tremble with the force of the whipping rain. Andy is waiting silently beside her in his great brown coat. She stands, holding the door for a moment, waiting for Hank to say something else. "Hank—?" she starts. "Get gone, slowpoke," she hears him call from the kitchen, amused-sounding, over the hiss of frying sausages. She pushes the door and goes on out; she had wanted to talk with him but the tone of bitter amusement, though slight, is still clear enough to render looking at him unnecessary. Even without turning, she can see the look perfectly.

Across the river the mountains and naked rock of the railway embankment loom in blurred relief, appearing almost flat, two-dimensional like a photograph, and scratched slantwise by the rain as if the photo had been scoured diagonally with a stiff wire brush. The effect seems extremely strange to her, though she can't at first decide why. Then she realizes it is because the scratches run from the upper right-hand corner of the picture down to the lower left, instead of from left to right as the rains usually fall. The wind is blowing from the east. The East Wind. The slides far up river, the constant grumble of the skies, and the vicious rains have wakened the old East Wind from his hermit's lair high up in the pass.

Viv lifts the hood of her poncho against this ranting wind and hurries behind Andy down to the boat. Before she gets in the boat she tries to zip the front of her garment up to her throat to keep her hair dry, but the zipper snarls in her long tresses. She snatches at the snagged hair for a second with chilled fingers, then gives up and climbs into the boat, leaving the front of her blouse bared to the wind and her hair getting wet again in the rain . . . He's seen me before, she thinks wryly, with my hair a little straggly . . .

In the Snag, Lee has already purchased his bus ticket. He is sipping a beer and checking through the policies in the shoebox while he waits for the bus. There are a lot of extra policies; he'll have to leave all those that do not concern him with Teddy. He finds the one naming him as beneficiary and shoves it inside the photo album and feels there the picture he appropriated up in that attic. Forgot all about it. And the little scuffle couldn't have helped it much . . .

The album, though it had been in the boat during the fracas, had still been splattered with mud and blood, but the photo was still in as good condition as ever, which wasn't saying a whole lot; the only thing the scuffling had done was succeed where I had failed in separating the photograph from the papers. I started to drop these papers in the shoebox with all the other stuff I was planning to leave with Teddy, when the handwriting on one of the envelopes caught my eye. *For an instant he is lost from time, the past and present crisscrossing through his mind like bright swords dueling in the dawn fog.* They were letters from my mother, dating from our first years in New York up to the time of her death. *The letters tremble, rustling; the picture in his other hand slides away unnoticed to the floor.* In the dim barroom light it was almost impossible for me to make out much more than the barest of details. *He sinks over the first letter, forming the words "Dearest Hank:" with his lips as he brings the faint rustle of scented print close to his eyes . . . Damn him, he has no right, no he has no right.* I was able to make out however various requests for money, anecdotes, sentimentalities . . . but even more infuriating than these things was the discovery of that *that* perfume? little booklet of my high school poems *White Lilac?* that I remember she claimed she had no right lost in an Automat on Forty-second Street years before. The poems I had written and hand-printed meticulously *the scent falls, white lilac* for her birthday, now, here *from the trembling page, her perfume* it turns up, a few thousand miles *like crumbling petals* from dear old Forty-second *shaken from a faded lilac* . . . and in the mail of my brother! *He has no right she has no right with my poems!*

As I scanned the letters I went quietly mad. *Because he has no right* it became increasingly apparent that she had *never been mine* my dearest Hank I have no way of telling you *in all those years together she had still been his* how much I missed your hands your lips *and they had no right it can't be* can we ever see each other again *but each word, each scent* without my *bringing back so cruel* Sweetheart the snow here turns black and *actual movement of her hand* the people here are even colder and blacker but *as it lifted her hair to touch the bottle of perfume* I do so wish that we might have *beneath her pearled earlobe* of course Lee does much better in school *scented dark pendulum of her hair* still, we may not have to wait as long as *he has no right to my twelve years* darling until *he had his twelve years he has no right to mine* we can find that place alone in the sky *please to write more* until, by the time the door opened, with all my love, *Myra* and Viv was there, crying, nondescript in her big poncho *PS Lee needs tuition and the doctor writes that the payments on the policies have lapsed again; could you?* By the time the poor girl arrived *the insurance too?* I was almost beside myself with rage. *They had no right to do this!*

And by the time Viv had stopped crying long enough to tell me he was taking the run down the river, "Just he and Andy. And he'll drown out there . . . and I hope he does!" I was already feeling that the years had used me badly. When she finished choking out her news I felt as though I were being raped by time itself. *Again! Just like he did before when he let her go!* I tried to explain, but I fear it was largely gibberish. *Again he will let her go and steal her forever from me!* I could only try to tell her, "When we fought, Viv, he asked if I'd had enough. But hadn't I taken his best punch? Hadn't I! Hadn't I!" I demanded shouting at her, lashing out in a fury of denial and affirmation, but she didn't understand. "Viv, don't you see, if I let him do this I'll just lose all over again. I didn't have enough. I can never have had enough as long as he makes me say that! I can never have you as long as I let him make the heroic runs down the river. Don't you—? Oh, Viv . . ." I gripped her hand; I could see she had no idea what I was talking about; I could see I would never be able to explain it. "But listen . . . for a while there, do you see? out on the bank? I was fighting for my life. I know it. Not running for my life as I've always done before. But fighting for it. Not merely to keep it, or to have it, but *for* it . . . fighting to get it, to *win* it?" I slapped the table. She was saying something but I didn't hear. "No! by god I don't care what he thinks *I haven't* had enough. And the pompous prick, he doesn't have any goddamned right— Where is he, anyway, still at the house? Well, where's Andy with the boat? I'm not going to let him, not again. Not this time! Here, take all this stuff. I've got to catch a boat."

She was saying something but I didn't hear, I ran, leaving her behind, toward my brother . . . leaving her and blindly hoping she might see that I was making it possible to perhaps someday have her. Her or someone. Later. For the dance between my brother and me was not finished. It was just intermission, just a bloody break with both partners supine and saturated . . . but not finished. Maybe never. Each of us had sensed that, on the bank, that when the partner is equal there exists no end, no winning, no losing, and no stopping . . . There is only the intermission while the orchestra takes five for smokes. Were I to have pounded Hank unconscious— I use the subjunctive because I had lost too much blood and smoked too many cigarettes for the possibility to be other than hypothetical —I still would have proved nothing but his unconsciousness. Not his defeat. I know it now, and I think I even knew it then. Just as he must have known when I struck back that my defeat was now beyond the reach of his weapons. The peavey pole I had worried about could only snatch out my innards; the cork boots could only tear my neurons to bits with my Golden Delicious; even by threat, even if he had held his twelve-bladed whittler knife at my throat while forcing me to sign a paper swearing everlasting allegiance to John Birch, the Ku Klux Klan, and the Daughters of the American Revolution combined, he would have defeated me no more than I would have defeated him by following him right into the sanctuary of the polling booth and forcing him at gunpoint to vote the straight Socialist ticket.

For there is always a sanctuary more, a door that can never be forced, whatever the force, a last inviolable stronghold that can never be taken, whatever the attack; your vote can be taken, your name, your innards, even your life, but that last stronghold can only be surrendered. And to surrender it for any reason other than love is to surrender love. Hank had always known this without knowing it, and by making him doubt it briefly I made it possible for both of us to discover it. I knew it now. And I knew that to win my love, my life, I would have to win back for myself the right to this last stronghold.

Which meant winning back the strength I had bartered away years before for a watered-down love.

Which meant winning back the pride I had exchanged for pity.

Which meant not letting that bastard make that goddam run against the river without me, not again, not this time; even if we both drowned, I did not intend to spend another dozen years in his shadow, no matter how big it loomed!

Viv sits at the table, staring after Lee, her hands resting on the album. It is beginning to dawn on her that she has never really understood, not just since Lee came to Oregon, but since she came.

The phone beside Floyd Evenwrite rings. He jumps, jerking it from its cradle. As he listens his face becomes redder and redder and just who the motherlovin' hell does he think he is, damn him anyway, calling a man on Thanksgiving Day with news like that . . . ! "Clara! That was Hank Stamper! The sonofabitch is gonna try to run them logs down to WP; what do you think of that kinda chickenshit business? I told that Draeger you couldn't trust them hardnoses . . ." Who the hell does he think, calling a man just sweet as you please to tell him he was about to have the rug jerked out from under him . . . well we'll by god just see about that! "Get me my boots. An' listen, Tommy, you get in here an' listen . . . I got to get out an' see if I can do something an' I want you to make these calls while I'm gone. To Sorenson, Gibbons, Evans, Newton, Sitkins, Arnsen, Toms, Nielsen . . . hell, you know . . . an' if that Draeger calls, tell him he can find me out at the Stamper house!"

Lee sees the tug pushing through the heavy rain and swings the jeep to the side of the road. "Andy! Over here, it's Lee!" We'll see who's had enough and who hasn't . . .

Jenny finishes her bottle and lets it drop to the floor. She picks up the shells. "Any time, now, honeybunch, any old time . . ."

Viv gathers all the papers together that Lee left with her, tamping them neat and even and returning them to the shoebox. Then she sees the picture on the floor . . .

Hank, grinning broadly, labors over one of the laundry trays beside the deep freeze on the back porch; steam clouds the cold air . . . (Soon as Viv was gone to meet the kid I get me that wing of the old man's out of the freezer. It's froze dry and light and the color of wet driftwood. And brittle as ice. When I try bending the little finger of it, it snaps off clean as a whistle. So I take it to the laundry tray and run tapwater over the rest of the fingers to thaw them limber. Cold water, too, at first, just like they say you're supposed to treat frostbite. Then I got to laughing about that and figured What the hell, meat's meat . . . and gave it the hot . . .)

Steadying himself on the slippery foredeck, Lee watches Andy jockey their tug in as close to the destroyed boathouse as possible, tooting its little air horn. "There he is up yonder," Andy says, pointing to the second-story window; "and just *look* what he's hanging out. Golly, golly . . . I mean just *look!*"

Shading his eyes against the blowing rain, Lee leans out to look; "The devil," he says, grinning up at the arm. But if he thinks I've had enough . . . !

As Viv looks at the photograph she absent-mindedly works at the zipper of her poncho, trying to free her hair. That hair. All the zippers of her life, it seems, have been snarled with that hair. That darn hair. Snarled in a zipper when the weather was cold or sweated to her brow and throat when the weather was warm. As a child her uncle had allowed her neither to cut it short nor to put it up. "Your mother did enough of that sort of thing for the both of you," was the way he looked at it, "and while you stay with me you'll let it hang like God and nature aimed it to hang." And spent her summer days hoeing irrigation trenches through the heat-weaving Colorado melon fields, with her hair prickling her neck and sticking to her face and hanging the way it was aimed to hang. Her nights she spent trying to keep it from hanging in the zipper of her sleeping bag where she lay near a flashlight and a four-ten single-shot guarding against the bands of young thieves that her uncle claimed were waiting to pillage his fields at night.

In a country where melons grow wild along every waterhole, her uncle believed every poor soul in his jail to be secretly guilty of stealing his watermelons. The only marauders Viv had ever had a chance to rout were the jackrabbits and the prairie dogs, but the long wide-awake vigils gave her time to dream anyway, and to plan. She, and the stars and the big flatland moon had worked to build her a life from the dark, a life complete to the very flowers she would plant in her yard, detailed to the names of the four children she would have. What were those names? The first, a boy of course, was to be named after her husband, but he was to be called by his middle name, Nelson, after her dead father. The second . . . ? Was it a girl? Yes, a girl . . . but the name? Not after her mother. No. It was the same name as the doll her father had given her. Starting with N, also. What was it? Not Nellie . . . Not Norma . . . It seems it was an Indian name . . .

She shakes her head and has a sip of Lee's beer, giving up trying to remember. That had been so long. And that dream that a little girl had helped the moon and the stars forge so painstakingly from the dry, crisp Colorado nights wasn't built to stand up against weather like this. The dream had been like the sandpaintings of the Hopis, permanent only in the dry. In this kind of weather the colors ran, the edges softened, and the dream which had once shone so sharp and precise in the future now remained only as an ambiguous lump to mock the little girl who had dreamed it so long ago.

She jerks again at the zipper, smiling: "But I do remember this part real clear: that the man I marry is going to have to agree to me cutting my hair short. That was one of the first things, the hair, I remember . . ."

Suddenly she feels that she wants to cry, but that she has been robbed of her tears somewhere along the way. She hunches down inside the poncho, like a snail . . .

"I remember . . . I promised me—her—that I would never marry a man who made me keep my hair long. I—she trusted me to keep that promise. She trusted me to get my hair cut short . . ." A skinny child looks up from the task of picking cockleburs out of her hair and watches Viv with curious eyes; after a moment she speaks. "You were going to have a boy and a girl and two more boys. Nelson, Neatha, Clark, and William after little Willy, the rope doll?"

"That's right. You're right . . ."

The little girl reaches a slim hand to touch Viv's cheek. "And a piano. We were going to get him to buy us a piano, don't you remember? And teach the kids to sing? Kids and a piano, and teach them all the songs Mama and Daddy sang, who studied at Juilliard . . . remember, Vivvy?"

She moves nearer, looking up into Viv's face.

"And a canary. Two canaries, we would call them Bill and Coo. Real German rollers that could sing as good as the ones in the United Motor Parts and Radio Repair . . . Weren't we going to have two canaries?"

Viv looks past the child to the present, down at the photograph in her hand. She examines the face in the picture: the eyes direct and powerful, the hands folded, the shadow, the little boy standing there so serious in glasses . . . back to the girl's face, and the smile that laughs at her through the hair, the tossed swoop of hair out over her left shoulder like a glossy black wing fixed in time . . .

"And most of all, Vivvy, that Someone, remember? He was to be Someone who wanted the real us, me, who wanted—truly—what I am—was. Yes. Not a Someone who just wanted what they needed me to be . . ."

She turns the picture over and brings it closer to her face: Rubber-stamped on the back was the studio name, "MODERN'S . . . Eugene, Oregon," and the date, "Sept. 1945." She hears Hank now for the first time, trying to tell her, and Lee, finally hears them, and sees for herself how they had all been cheated . . .

"I love them, I do. I truly can love. I have that . . ."

But this minute, for this woman, this dead image, she feels a hatred that sings in her ears like steam. This woman has been like a dark fire, a cold fire, that melted them all almost beyond recognition. Burned them until they barely knew themselves or each other.

"But I won't let her use me any longer. I love them but I cannot give myself for them. Not my whole self. I have no right to do that."

She slips the picture inside the shoebox and picks up the bus ticket Lee has left lying on the table.

The rain drives against the earth; the river swells, glutted and still hungry. Hank leaps from the yard over the berry vine, one foot striking the bank, one on the overturned boathouse, and on into the back of the tug; he is surprised to see Lee, but his hand covers his smile . . . "Can you swim, bub? You may have to do a little swimming, you know . . ."

Jenny casts her shells.

Evenwrite charges about the bank among the gathering loggers, outraged and righteous and sweating in his underwear. "Just where does this big-ass Stamper think he gets off?"—and still smelling of gasoline.

"Just you?"

"Just me . . ."

Teddy watches Draeger hurry from his car toward the Snag's front door. *There are bigger forces, Mr. Draeger. I don't know what they are but they got ours whipped sometimes. I don't know what they are but I know they aren't making me a dime.*

And Draeger, walking past the gently throbbing glow of the juke-box, the shuffleboard, through the partitioned gloom of empty booths—*I want to know what happened, and why*—finally finds the slim blond girl. By herself. With a beer glass. Her pale hands resting on a large maroon album. Waiting to tell him:

"You must go through a winter to get some notion . . ."

Viv closes the large book. For some time now she has been turning the pages in silence as Draeger watches, entranced by the flow of faces. "So," she says, smiling. Draeger starts, his head coming up. "I *still* don't understand what happened," he says after a moment.

"Maybe that's because it's still happening," Viv says. She gathers the strewn papers and photos into a neat pile on the table, laying that picture of the dark-haired woman and boy on top. "Anyway . . . I think I hear my bus now. So. It's been nice running through the family history with you, Mr. Draeger, but now—as soon as I . . ."

Viv borrows a knife from Teddy and frees her snagged hair in time to board the bus. Just she and the driver and a gum-chewing child. "I'm going to Corvallis to visit my grandmother and grandfather and their horses," the child informs Viv. "Where are you going?"

"Who knows?" Viv answers. "I'm just going."

"Just you?"

"Just me."

Draeger sits his term at that table. The juke bubbles. The whistle buoy moans in the bay. Cables ravel. Johnny Redfeather sings "Swanee." The tug heaves against its load.

The booms begin to move, groaning, behind the chugging wake of the tug; Hank and Lee hurry to secure the couplings between the great carpets of logs. "Keep on the bounce," is Hank's advice, "or they'll go to rollin' under you. It maybe don't look it, but it's safest to keep on the bounce."

The bus hisses through the swirling rain; Viv takes a Kleenex from her pocket to wipe the fog from the window to get a look at the two tiny figures leaping foolishly from log to log. She rubs and rubs, but the mist just doesn't seem to clear.

"They're nincompoops!" Gibbons proclaims. "They cain't make it in this water . . ."

On the boat Andy repeats over and over to himself, in spite of Hank's admission of worry before going out onto the booms, "*Nothin'* to sweat, nothin' to sweat . . ."

Evenwrite calls a group into the garage near the landing. "We got some things to work out, boys . . . in case they do make it."

Big Newton, still belching, begins doing push-ups on the living-room rug.

The arm, dangling in front of the dogs, twists and slowly untwists in the billowing rain.

Jenny steps back from the face before her, dropping her eyes.

"Jenny . . . is that your name, Jenny?"

"Yeah. Not really. People just allus call me Jenny."

"And your real name?"

"Leahnoomish. Means Brown Fern."

"Lee-ah-noo-mish . . . Brown Fern. That is very pretty."

"Yeah. Look here. You think I have a pretty legs?"

"Very pretty. And the skirt also. Very very pretty . . . little Brown Fern."

"Haw," Jenny says triumphantly, lifting the mud-hemmed garment on off over her head.